SPARK OF LIFE

SPARK OF LIFE

by

GINNA MORAN

ISBN 978-1-942073-26-0 (soft cover)

Cover design by Silver Starlight Designs
Cover images copyright Depositphotos
Fonts: Ostrich Sans, Adobe Garamond Pro, Love Moon, and Linna

For Inquiries Contact:
Sunny Palms Press
9663 Santa Monica Blvd Suite 1158
Beverly Hills, CA 90210, USA
www.sunnypalmspress.com
www.GinnaMoran.com

Table of Contents

DIVING UNDER

WELCOME ABOARD THE OCEAN JEWEL

CRISP SEA AIR BLOWS STRANDS of my blond hair across my face, veiling the view of the Ocean Jewel, the luxury yacht I'll be calling home for the next week. The three decked, two hundred and fifty-seven foot monster of a boat waits at the end of a long dock in the middle of Azure Waters' harbor with dozens of other boats around it, none of which are comparable in size or extravagance. I'm the last one on the dock, standing in the dead center as the deep, blue-green ocean surrounds me only feet away.

From twenty feet ahead, my best friend, Giselle Nash, waves a hand over her head, trying to grab my attention. When I don't move, she drops her bag in front of a man in a dark blue blazer and khakis—one of the crew members—and jogs my way without glancing at the dock beneath her. I tense, imagining her tripping on the wooden beams and falling into the sea, but she makes it to me without a problem.

She stops a foot away, placing her hands on my shoulders, and stares at me with her amber eyes. "You can't change your mind, Ava. We're already here, and if you turn around now, you'll regret it. Look at that thing." She points to the yacht. "We're not traveling to sea in a rowboat."

She's right. Yet I still can't suppress the fear that freezes me in place. You'd think that after all this time I wouldn't be so afraid of the ocean. It's been nearly eight years since the accident that swept my older sister away and left me almost drowned. I'll never forget the silent look of terror on Bailey's face as the ocean current broke us apart moments before she disappeared under.

"So, are you coming or not?" Giselle asks, shaking my shoulders, forcing me to draw my attention away from the yacht.

I open my mouth to say, "not" but instead, I say, "Yeah, just give me a minute."

With a deep sigh, my best friend spins on her heels. Her bronze hair flies behind her, and she skips down the dock and back to where our group of friends waits for what's supposed to be the best adventure of the year, thanks to Sapphire King's eighteenth birthday, an obnoxiously large trust fund from her grandma, and as a gift to all of us for graduation.

When the others climb the ramp to enter the deck, I finally find the nerve to start walking. My bag hangs heavy in my fingers, but before I make it halfway to the yacht, a boy my age, wearing the same blue blazer and khakis as the other crew members, jogs to my side to take it from me.

He meets my eyes with a smile that manages to ease my fear of the ocean enough to where my legs no longer tremble. I really needed this incredibly hot distraction. Scruff covers his handsome face, his skin bronzed with a deep tan gorgeous enough that someone like me, who doesn't get much sun, would pay a lot for.

"First time out to sea, huh?" he asks, amusement lining his eyes.

"That obvious? I haven't even been in the water since I was a kid," I say.

I expect him to ask why and get ready to tell him the same story everyone in Azure Waters already knows. But he doesn't say anything. Instead, the boy offers his free arm to me, and I take it, hooking my hand around the sinewy muscles of his forearm.

"I wasn't even going to come, but my best friend basically threatened me—mostly with a good time," I add to fill the silence.

His smile widens as he glances at me in the side of his vision. "I can promise she's right. The Ocean Jewel speaks true to her name. I even have fun, and I'm on the job."

As we reach the ramp that'll take us onto the Ocean Jewel, I slow down. Everyone has boarded, and no one waits for me. They're probably already heading to their staterooms or exploring the upper decks. Apparently, the sundeck contains a hot tub and pool, according to Sapphire.

This is my last chance to turn away and run when none of my friends are looking. I wouldn't even have to explain myself for a few days, and by then, they'll all have moved on.

As I start to turn away, the boy blocks my path. "Why don't you board before you make the decision to bail? We won't leave port for another twenty minutes or so. You can change your mind if you hate it. And if it makes you feel any better, I'm an excellent ocean swimmer and diver. We've never had a single person fall overboard, either."

"And I'm supposed to trust you? I don't even know your name." Crossing my arms over my chest, I hold myself, imagining being in the middle of the ocean with no signs of land. The thought unsettles me.

He holds out his hand, but I don't take it right away. "Carter Stevens, deckhand, steward, activities coordinator, cook—basically, I'm at your service..." His voice trails off, his eyes smiling though his mouth remains firm.

I meet his blue-green eyes that match the ocean around us and reluctantly shake his hand. "Ava Adair."

He cracks a smile, holding my fingers long enough to make

me uncomfortable. Instead of releasing me, he pulls me forward onto the short ramp, the sudden movement causing it to shake under our feet. Using my free hand, I grip the single guardrail and shoot him a death glare that only makes him smile wider as he pulls me the short distance onto the yacht.

Without giving me a chance to glance at the calm ocean beneath us, he guides me up a set of stairs, and we cross the main deck and head into what he calls the saloon. The lavish room shines with metal, glass, and light wood, all gleaming to perfection. Two short, white leather sectionals face an eighty-inch television stationed in an entertainment center that also serves as a room divider to another sitting area with a few tables and chairs. The magnificence of the room is breathtaking. I almost feel like I'm in a swanky penthouse hotel room. Almost.

Instead of guiding me all the way around the main deck, he directs me to a small elevator past the sitting room and hits the call button. The door opens, and we step on and ride it to the upper deck where our staterooms are located.

Voices hum through another lounge area surrounded by a panoramic view of the harbor and the ocean that disappears into the blue horizon. Giselle waves her arms when she spots us, flicking her eyes to Carter before pursing her lips at me in a look that says I must've found the hottest crew member on the boat. I'd be lying if I didn't agree.

"I already picked out our room." She takes my hand and pulls me toward a short hallway where voices echo from within the opened doors of the staterooms. There are five rooms altogether, and another suite toward the bow of the yacht where Sapphire's parents will be staying since they're the ones chaperoning our vacation.

Carter follows behind us, still holding my bag, and I grin at Matty and Logan, who each sit on the end of a twin bed next to each other in one room, and then to Sapphire, who talks to

Daisy and Chloe in her own room with a queen bed and a view of the ocean through the porthole. I poke my head into two more staterooms, both with queen beds, which Giselle and I could've taken since Giselle is Sapphire's cousin, but we agreed to share a room because there was no way I was sleeping on the ocean in a room alone.

Our stateroom is the last door in the hall, and two beds, identical to the ones in the room where Matty and Logan are staying, sit against each wall of the white and blue room. A long window allows sunlight to shine across the white-carpeted floor, and along another wall is a flat screen TV and built-in drawers. It's simple yet chic, and my fear of coming aboard disappears the moment I perch on the edge of the comfy bed.

Carter sets my bag on the other bed and flashes another smile. I don't think I've ever had someone smile so much at me besides Giselle. It sends my heart beating faster, and not because I'm about to embark on a luxurious vacation on a yacht.

He places his hand on the doorframe. "This is your last chance to get off," he says.

Giselle swings her gaze to mine. "You're not going anywhere."

I lean back on the bed. "You're right. I'm not."

Carter hovers for a second longer. "Enjoy your stay aboard the Ocean Jewel, Ava."

Giselle smirks at me as she waves goodbye to Carter. Covering my face with my hands, I release a long sigh. This is less terrifying than I expected, and I'm glad I decided to come.

Giselle flops next to me, the bed small for two bodies. "He's cute. This is going to be a blast."

I grin. "Should we go explore the rest of the boat?"

"I bet we could get your hottie helper to show us around."

"That's exactly what I had in mind."

Without missing a beat, Giselle pulls me from the bed and

we fly into the hallway. Voices hum from the other staterooms, and I grin at Giselle when I see Carter talking to a man outside the elevator.

The man looks over at us and smiles. "Welcome. It's a pleasure to have you aboard the Ocean Jewel. How do you like it?"

I politely turn my gaze from Carter to the man. "It's lovely, thanks. We were actually going to just ask Carter to give us a tour."

Carter offers a warm smile from next to the man, sending my heart racing.

Before he can respond, the man says, "I'd be happy to show you two and the rest of your friends around. I'm Hank, by the way."

I force my mouth to remain smiling though I want nothing more than to frown. "That would be great, thank you."

Giselle sighs next to me but just shrugs when I look at her.

"Perfect, I'll be waiting in the saloon for when you're ready. We'll leave port shortly thereafter." Hank nods once to Carter before heading to the stairs instead of the elevator.

"You two have fun," Carter says, still grinning at me. "You'll get a better tour with the first mate, anyway. But I'd be happy to take you out on the water when we anchor after lunch."

Giselle grins. "Definitely!"

I shrug, disappointment creeping into me. The last thing I'll do is go out into the water, no matter how cute Carter is or how much he smiles. *Oh well.*

Voices sound from behind us as the others leave their rooms, and Giselle hooks her arm through mine. "Come on, Aves. Let's get the stupid tour over with."

I glance up to Carter. "I guess I'll see you around."

The dining terrace overlooks the sprawling ocean on the stern of the yacht opposite to where our staterooms are located. It's enclosed with floor to ceiling windows, which pop open to allow in the salty sea air. The sturdy wood table with seating for twelve sits on top a navy blue and gray rug that matches the curtains that could be pulled down, like anyone ever does that with such a startling, vast view.

A buffet table displays hot trays filled with all sorts of food from the chef on board. Warm dinner rolls steam from a basket, and the scent of garlic wafts through the air. My mouth waters as I follow Giselle. She grabs a white and blue ceramic plate from the stack near the start of the buffet. The others trail around us, and we all greet Ruby and Carlton King, Sapphire's parents and Giselle's aunt and uncle.

A familiar face pops up from his position behind a small bar where he scoops ice into glasses. Carter greets me with a dazzling smile, his ocean eyes quickly trailing from my face to the rest of me, taking in my strapless swimsuit cover. I won't be riding jet skis with the others, but my fear of the ocean won't stop me from hanging at the pool on the sundeck.

After a woman in her mid-twenties fills my plate with seared salmon on baby spinach, a side of garlic pasta, and one of the rolls, I set my plate down and head to the bar.

"What can I get you, miss?" Carter asks, taking on a more formal approach with Sapphire's parents behind me.

"Lemonade," I say, resting my elbows on the shiny counter. "And it's Ava."

As Carter stands in front of me, glass in hand, all I can think about is how good he looks in his dark blue polo since he's no longer wearing the blazer. He rubs a lemon wedge on the rim of the glass before dipping it onto a small tray of sugar. "Okay, *Ava*," he says as he sets the glass in front of me. "Anything else?"

"A Coke for Giselle."

He tips a glass of ice against the soda fountain and then hands it to me. "Enjoy your meal."

I try to think of something more to say, but Matty pushes up next to me, forcing my conversation to end with Carter. As much as I want him to ignore my friend, I don't want him getting in trouble on my behalf. We'll be on this yacht for a week, so I'm sure there will be plenty more chances.

I smile once more at Carter before turning my back and heading to where Giselle sits across from Sapphire on the opposite side of the table from her parents. I set the glasses down and take a seat next to my best friend.

"The bartender is checking you out," Sapphire says, leaning over her plate of salmon. "God, he's hot."

A warm blush blossoms up my neck. "His name is Carter."

Her eyes widen. "That was fast."

"What was?" Matty says, plopping down next to Sapphire before giving her a kiss on the cheek.

I shake my head, letting my hair veil in front of my face. "Nothing."

"The bartender," Sapphire says, causing me to blush even more.

"Oh, shit. Sorry, Ava. I totally messed that up, huh?" Matty wags his eyebrows before tearing into his roll. With his mouth full, he says, "I can go back and put in a good word."

"Oh, my God, you guys!" Giselle exclaims, throwing her hands up. "Shut up about it. Ava's got it under control."

Whatever *it* is, Giselle's right. I can handle it. I pick up my roll and chuck it at Matty, who catches it and takes a bite. "What she said."

Logan, Daisy, and Chloe join the rest of us, and I lose myself in my thoughts as Logan and Matty talk about the jet skis and share stories from last summer—stories I've heard a dozen times since I was the only one who stayed out of the water. My friends, while sometimes clueless, never make fun of me about my fear, but it also leaves me out of a lot of plans since we live in a beach community. They probably all took bets on whether or not I'd actually come.

"So, you're sure you'll be okay if we all go out riding?" Giselle asks. Even if I wasn't okay, I wouldn't say so. The way to guarantee people don't bother you about your weird quirks is to make sure it doesn't interrupt their own lives.

"Yeah, totally cool with it. Look at this place. I'm sure I can find some sort of entertainment." Leaning back in my chair, I gaze around the dining terrace, trying not to stare at Carter as he helps his coworker clean up the empty food trays.

Giselle bounces in her seat. "Perfect. You'll tell me if you're not okay, right?"

I exaggerate a long exhale. "Yes, Mom. Don't worry about me."

She hugs me before joining the others. They leave the table to head to the jet ski garage. Carter glances at me once, before following behind them, probably to help. I'd follow, but I want nowhere near the swimming platform that leads directly into the water.

Instead, I head to the elevator and ride it up to the sundeck and find a few padded lounge chairs surrounding a pristine, rectangular swimming pool with swimmer jets and a round spa on a raised platform. I scoop a towel from the cabinet under a covered lounge area and head to the lounge chair closest to the railing to get a better view of my friends. Carter helps them launch the jet skis into the ocean, and my heart sinks into my stomach when Giselle and Chloe take off at an unsettling speed. *They're wearing life jackets. They're excellent swimmers. It'll be okay.*

As much as I want to turn away, I can't. As Carter helps the rest of my friends onto the other two jet skis, I find that I'm gripping my knees for dear life. Laughter and playful screams echo through the salty air. The jet skis fly over the water, leaving glittering bubble trails in their wakes.

Giselle navigates the jet ski in figure eights before turning in a circle and jetting off again with Matty and Sapphire hot on her trail. I'm so afraid that if I look away from them for even a second, the ocean will swallow them whole like my sister.

A shadow falls over my shoulder, but still, I don't turn away. "I can take you for a ride if you want when they're finished." Carter's voice causes me to jump, and I spin around and bump into his chest.

Ignoring his offer, I say, "Shouldn't you be down there watching them?"

His brows furrow when he catches the fear cross my face. "I asked Keith to take over. They're fi—" He snaps his mouth closed for a second before adding, "Ouch."

Spinning back to the railing, horror sweeps over me. I spot Giselle and Chloe bobbing in the water a few feet from their jet ski. Logan and Daisy are closest, but neither of them does anything except laugh.

"Oh, God. Come on, Giselle. Get back on," I whisper under my breath.

It must've not been low enough, because Carter makes a point to say, "They're fine, Ava. If they were in danger, Keith would get them."

"But how do you know they're not?" I watch Giselle struggle to climb back on with Chloe in the water next to her. I imagine a hundred horrible things that could possibly happen before Keith could even have the boat in the water. We're not in some lake. This is the same ocean that took my sister.

My hands grip the guardrail so hard my arms shake. Carter reaches out and touches my shoulder. "Hey, whoa. It's okay. Look." He points at Giselle as she helps Chloe back on the jet ski, proving my fear to be unwarranted.

Blinking away embarrassing tears, I pull myself from the guardrail, watching Giselle speed away again. I'm so mortified I can't even meet Carter's eyes. His silence speaks volumes, and all I can think about is getting away from him. Coming on this trip was a terrible idea.

"Excuse me," I say, nudging past Carter before he can block my way. "I need to lie down."

"Ava, wait up," he says from behind me as I stride toward the elevator.

I don't wait, though. Instead of getting on the elevator that could trap me and force me to explain myself to a boy I've just met, I fly down the stairs and head to my room, locking the door behind me.

I should've stayed home. If only I could magically transport myself to dry land.

DIVING UNDER

AFTER PULLING MYSELF TOGETHER, I force myself to leave my room to join the others. They regroup on the sundeck after showering off the saltwater. The sun sets on the horizon, casting an orange glow over everything. The water no longer looks blue-green but murky gray, and I shiver, imagining what hides in its depths.

Giselle sprawls out on a lounge chair, soaking up the last rays of sunlight, the air cool around us, causing goosebumps to prickle across my arms. Sapphire and Matty are nowhere in sight, probably sneaking around in Sapphire's room. Logan and Daisy come from the elevator holding plates of food, and behind them, Chloe chats with Carter as he helps her with an extra plate, which I assume is for Giselle.

"Oh, hey Ava. I'd have brought you a plate had I known you were up here," Daisy says, setting her food on a small table near her lounge chair. "We decided to eat up here to get the best view of the sunset."

"It's okay. I'll go ahead and grab something myself," I say as Carter starts to open his mouth, like he's going to offer to get something for me.

Strolling past him, he hesitates for a moment to make sure everyone else is happy, and then he rushes up behind me and puts his hand on my shoulder to slow me down. When I spin to face him, he crosses his arms though a smile plays on his lips.

It stops me from snapping at him. Instead, I say, "I apologize for earlier. I'm a little on edge being here. You don't need to worry or check on me, though. I'm fine."

He nods even though he clearly doesn't believe me with how intently he stares into my eyes. I don't know how to convince him otherwise. It's been so long since someone has looked at me this way, with eyes of curious pity, and it crawls under my skin. No one truly understands what I go through among my friends. I doubt Carter would either. He loves the ocean enough to work on a yacht.

"Really, I am," I add for good measure.

His eyes, now the same murky gray of the ocean in the sunset's golden light, don't waver until I force myself to look away. Turning toward the elevator, I glance once over my shoulder to watch both Giselle and Chloe peering at me. Neither comes to my rescue. They learned long ago that nothing can save me from myself.

Carter presses the call button for me when I don't move. Imagining being in such a confined space with him does nothing for my anxiety. The scent of the salty ocean and sunscreen clings to him, a constant reminder of the sea, but I can't help sucking in a breath. He stands close enough for me to feel the heat radiating from his bronze skin.

Just as the silence of the short trip to the dining terrace starts to unnerve me, the door to the elevator slides open, and I take in the view of the sitting area near the staterooms. I stride off the elevator, readying to dash away to save myself from the boy who leaves me confused and anxious.

"Ava," he says, nearly whispering.

It's enough to freeze me in place. The sound of my name on his lips sends my heart racing in a good way, like his voice alone can strip my fears away from me. His tone is neither sympathetic nor curious, and when I shift to look at him, a smile plays on his lips. Who knew a boy could smile so much.

I can't help myself and smile back. "You probably think I'm ridiculous."

"No, I think you're intriguing is all, but that's not what I was going to say." He actually looks nervous, rubbing the back of his neck, his arm muscles flexing with the gesture. It's enough to make me nervous, too.

"What is it then?" I ask when he doesn't continue right away.

He breathes a small sigh from his lips. "I know this is your vacation, and you and your friends are here for a good time, but I was wondering if maybe later tonight you'd hang out with me."

"You make it sound like hanging out with you won't be fun. Is this a line you use on every girl who catches your attention on one of these trips?" I don't know why I ask, but it did cross my mind.

"I—what? No." Just when I think he's going to abandon me due to my lack of tact, he shifts on his feet and stares at the floor.

Reaching out, I brush my fingers on his forearm. Giselle would probably laugh so hard at how embarrassingly awkward I am when I'm trying to figure out what to say to a cute boy. She says I have a problem with pushing them away before they even have a chance with me. Maybe I do.

"So, do you want to?" he asks again.

I consider saying no, because after everything, Carter seems so different from me and a week on this boat could end up feeling extremely long if things turn weird. On the other hand, it could also fly by and leave me hurt because the reality of my life will come crashing back to me. *It's summer. You deserve a little fun.*

"I'd like that," I finally agree.

He grins. "Cool."

Carter strolls next to me, and we walk toward the dining terrace where another buffet awaits on hot trays. Ruby and Carlton sit in the same seats at the table, enjoying a quiet candlelit dinner, and I wave, heading to the unmanned buffet table. Before I can reach to fill my plate myself, Carter takes his place on the other side and serves me a plate of crab legs, mashed potatoes, and mixed veggies.

If Ruby and Carlton weren't talking softly behind me, I'd insist on serving myself. If I did that now, Ruby would chide me for not letting Carter do his job and to enjoy being taken care of, as though I'm incapable of doing things for myself. It's one of those things Sapphire has complained about for years—especially after the disaster last year where she tried to bake Matty a birthday cake and discovered she didn't even know how to turn on her oven. Luckily for her, baking is one of my favorite pastimes.

"Will you grab a few water bottles and a can of Coke to take up?" I ask, taking my plate from Carter before he carries it for me. I can see in his eyes that he would carry everything in an instant and not only because he thinks it's his job.

With his hands full, he leads the way back to the sundeck with me, walking so close that my arm brushes against his every so often. We're met with grins and crinkly eyes from my friends, and Giselle hops up and steals the Coke from Carter's hand that I had him bring especially for her.

Before my friends can make a scene, Carter whispers, "I'll come find you tonight." He offers me a warm smile and strides away, looking back twice.

As I find my place on an empty lounge chair next to Giselle, placing my plate of food on the table between us, I turn my gaze up to meet my friends. They'll never let me hear the end of this if I don't say something now. I'm the only one out of the four of us girls who hasn't had a serious boyfriend—though I have been on a few terrible dates.

"Did I just hear what I think I did?" Chloe asks as Carter disappears down the stairs.

I hope he's out of earshot. "You did."

"Oh, my God. It's a miracle," Daisy says, laughing. "Ava has a date."

I blush, thankful for the darkening sky so no one can see. "It's not a date. We're just hanging out."

"It's definitely a date," Logan says, chiming in.

Giselle reaches over and smacks his arm. "You're going to make her nervous. Can't we all just celebrate that Ava came along and now she's going on a date with a really hot guy?"

I cover my face in my hands, shaking my head. "You guys. Stop. It's not a big deal."

"Hey, it is," Logan says. "I lost fifty bucks the moment you stepped on board and another twenty when you stayed." How did I even know they'd be placing bets? It doesn't bother me, though. Matty and Logan bet on everything.

It's Daisy's turn to smack his other arm. "Seriously?"

"It's fine," I say, interjecting. "Matty deserves the seventy bucks for having faith in me."

"Harsh, Ava-babe. I have plenty of faith in you. I'm willing to bet Carter will kiss you by the end of the night."

"Not helping your case, Lo," Giselle says, throwing a cloth napkin at him.

"I'll take that bet," Matty calls out, trailing next to Sapphire as they stand near the elevator.

I sink lower into the lounge chair. Thank God Carter is probably on another deck out of earshot, because I'd probably die from embarrassment, especially because I kind of want Logan to win that bet, despite his quips.

Sapphire holds up a green glass bottle in one hand and an

opaque white bottle in the other, drawing everyone's attention away from me.

"The wardens have retreated to their suite for the night. Who wants to join us for some festivities in the saloon?" she asks.

I sigh a relieved breath, knowing that all conversations about Carter are now completely off everyone's minds. Giselle pulls me to my feet, and we trail behind the others. They take the elevator while Giselle follows me to the stairs.

She stops halfway down and turns to me. "You're having fun, right?"

"Starting to," I say, nudging her to keep moving.

Grinning over her shoulder, she laughs as she says, "It'll keep getting better. I'm sure Logan will win that bet."

"You think?"

"Totally."

Carter hovers just outside of the saloon on the pathway that circles the perimeter of the yacht. The nearly full moon casts white light over him, sending streaks of silver-blue through his honey brown, sun-kissed hair.

Gulping the rest of my flute of champagne, I push to my feet and shuffle across the vast space ignoring my friends as they shout overly friendly greetings at Carter from their places at the table where they play card games while finishing off the alcohol Sapphire got her hands on.

Without his uniform, Carter looks even better, his sinewy muscles on display without the sleeves of his polo. His light blue tank top and dark board shorts bring out the blue color of his eyes. When I close the distance between us, he offers me the hoodie he clutches in his hand.

The scent of the sea and sunscreen clings to the worn fabric as I slide it over my head. A cool breeze blows my pale hair over my shoulder, and I stop myself from drawing my eyes to the black ocean around us. Only the sprinkle of lights in the distance reminds me that we're not hovering in some empty void where my deepest fears linger in waiting.

He guides me toward the back of the yacht where a barred railing surrounds the open deck where we get a clear view of the bubbling tracks left behind the yacht as we head north in the night. Built-in seats line one side, while a table with an umbrella sits in the center of the space. Without the light pollution of the sprawling city, the stars blaze brightly overhead like millions of shiny pearls sewn into endless black silk.

He motions me to the table, lit with dim, flameless candles. A silver tray of miniature desserts rests on top, and I turn to Carter with wide eyes. It's easy to ignore the fear of the vast expanse of dark, churning water behind me when he pulls the chair out for me to sit down.

"I know this might not be as fun as—"

I press my finger to his lips. "It's perfect, Carter. If you haven't noticed, I'm the outsider in my group of friends. They're used to me bailing on them."

"Why is that?" he asks.

Shrugging, I say, "We have different interests is all. Kinda like me and you." There. I said it. I had to get the words off my mind and put them in the open so Carter doesn't think he's going to magically change me and give me the courage to do things I'm afraid of. Just because he convinced me to come aboard, doesn't mean I'll be hopping on the back of a jet ski or going for an open ocean swim any time soon.

He smiles at me like I've said the silliest thing. "You say that like you know me."

"You love the ocean. I don't."

He leans closer to me, close enough to where I catch the coconut scent of his damp hair, fresh from a shower. "That's where you're wrong. I love the land more."

Frowning, I tilt my head to meet his gaze to see if he's joking with me. When he doesn't smile, I say, "You're not joking."

"No."

"But you work on a yacht."

"It pays well, and I have a place to live."

Wind gusts around us, the yacht rising and falling over a swell big enough to make my stomach drop. I grip the sides of the chair, fear pulsing through me, making me lose my train of thought. Carter's intense gaze studies me for a moment before he reaches out his hand and laces his fingers through mine.

My knees tremble, but I suck in a deep breath of the briny air. "So, you don't have a place near Azure Waters?"

"Only when we dock there."

Before I realize it, my lip pouts out and disappointment washes over me. What's the point of getting to know Carter when the moment we return home, he'll return back to sea, and I'll go back to staying far from any large bodies of water?

"Oh." It's all I can say to hide my disappointment.

He smiles, despite my reaction. "I'm not gone as often as it would seem. We charter a lot of weekend getaways and day long excursions up and down the coast, but anything more than a week or two only happens two or three times a year. Plus, I have most nights off."

Hmm. Maybe this could work after all. *Aren't you getting a little ahead of yourself?*

"That's a pretty adventurous life, Carter. You probably think I'm so boring. I mostly split my time between home and Giselle's and Sapphire's houses. I do volunteer at the Surf and Swim Museum downtown two weekends of the month."

He smirks. "Sounds fun."

"Liar. Just so you know, there's not a lot to do that doesn't involve the ocean in our town."

Instead of disagreeing with me, he only nods. "You know, I'm a great swim instructor."

Here we go. I knew it wouldn't be long before I'd have to explain why I am the way I am. I was hoping it could wait until I knew Carter liked me for sure. It's easier to play off when someone already likes me. But now, he'll probably find some way to let me down.

"I know how to swim," I respond to him after a moment.

"I can protect you from all the ocean animals, too."

I roll my eyes. I can't help it. "It's not that either."

"Something happened to you." It's not a question. My silence is enough of an answer. Carter doesn't pry though. He doesn't ask me to bare my soul to see if there's anything he can do to save me from my fears. The usual words of encouragement I get from people never come. Instead, he says, "I'm sorry."

I open my mouth to tell him not to be sorry, but a loud voice cuts through the quiet air as Matty, Sapphire, and Giselle stumble in our direction. Sapphire laughs when Matty kisses her, and Giselle jogs forward, nearly tripping on her flip flops.

I jump from my chair to grab her, my worst fears playing out in my mind as they stroll next to the guardrail. Carter is on his feet in a flash, pulling Sapphire to sit at the table next to Giselle, but Matty brushes him off.

"Ava-babe!" he yells, even though I'm standing only two feet away. "How's your date? You guys kiss yet?"

I cringe, heat rushing up my neck. Matty reaches out and grabs my hand, pulling me toward him in one of his infamous drunken bear hugs. He squeezes me, rocking back and forth, causing me to laugh. When he pulls away, he grins, wagging his eyebrows. His sloppy movements make me nervous. All I want him to do is to sit down with the others.

The yacht rises and lowers on another swell, causing me to

freeze and scream. Warm hands grip my waist, stopping me from stumbling, and I exhale a breath of relief when I meet Carter's gaze.

"Hey, Aves. Come here! Look into the water," Matty says.

"Don't be a jerk, Matty," Giselle snaps from her place at the table.

When I turn to glance at Matty, my heart nearly explodes from my chest. He stands on the first rung of the guardrail, his arms spread out wide like the wings of a bird. He rocks as another swell lifts and drops us against the dark ocean. My stomach rolls but not from seasickness. I'm terrified Matty will slip and fall into the ocean.

"Matty, get over here before you fall over," I say, inching closer to him and pulling away from Carter.

He laughs for a split second and starts spinning his arms, twirling them like windmills, and he yells out. Without thinking, I rush forward, stretching out my arms to grab the back of his shirt. A million horrible images flash through my mind.

"Matty!" I scream, the world slowing with the swell of another wave.

While spinning to face me, Matty starts to say, "Hey, cool it. I was only mes—" But before he can finish his words, his outstretched arm clocks me in my back.

The force is enough to send me reeling forward toward the guardrail. The world kicks into motion, too fast for me to do anything. The barrier hits my stomach, and I flip over, staring at the dark ocean below. My friends' screams reverberate through my bones. I don't even have time to scream myself or take a breath as my head splits through the water. I dive under, the ocean swallowing me in a merciless swell.

This is it. I always knew the ocean would kill me.

I'm about to die.

LOST

I NEVER THOUGHT THE OCEAN was peaceful. But in this moment, as my body twists and turns in the swells of the night water, all I can think about is how quiet and comforting the dark sea is. Though my throat burns, I kick my legs, hoping to break through the surface. The pain of going without oxygen only squeezes my heart a little. It's because I've given up. I'm lost at sea, crashing among the black waters. Maybe I'll see my sister soon.

No longer able to hold my breath, my mouth automatically opens, and I gasp for air that isn't there. Salty water fills my throat and as much as I fight to swim to the surface, it's like it's no longer there.

Then I feel nothing.

My body numbs, my consciousness fading in and out. With a quick jolt, I swim apart from my own body, floating on the underwater current, watching my body get lost in the sea. Regret rushes through me. I should've never gotten on the yacht. I should've stayed home and lived my life in utter safe boringness. This is all Carter's fault. I'm dead because I liked the way a boy smiled. I'm so stupid.

A flash of light, like an orange spark beneath the water, draws my attention to it. But the image is impossible. Fire and water don't mix. The ocean is an indestructible force to be reckoned with. But alas, the spark remains, a burst of light in the darkness, and it pulls me to it.

I swim forward in my ethereal form, unaffected by the current or the darkness. The spark leads the way. Swimming faster, I glide through the murky depths until the spark is inches away from my fingers, its heat pulsing into my hands unlike anything I've ever experienced. It's mesmerizing and perfect—and in this moment, I know it's mine.

My fingers caress the spark. It sinks into the palm of my hand, the orange glow traveling through my arm and over my shoulder, lighting me in a soft glow as it consumes me. I gasp, not water but air. The spark lights my lungs and splits to travel from my head to my toes. And then the dark ocean lights up like someone flicked on the sun. It shines above me, lighting my way to the surface.

"Ava, please. You can do it. Follow the light." The familiar voice calms my nerves. I do exactly what it says, hoping to find something brilliant and eternal as I kick up to the blinding blue light shimmering above me.

When I break the surface, the light clicks off, leaving my vision hazy and my thoughts cloudy. The now freezing water sends my teeth chattering, but as quick as I feel the rush of ice, it's dulled by the heat of something—another body much hotter than my own. Hands grip under my arms, forcing my head to stay above the water, and I spit and cough up what tastes like gallons of the sea.

"Ava, you're okay. You're alive. Just keep breathing. Stay with me." Carter's voice rings in my ears, and I realize I'm no longer alone in the dark waters.

"I—I died," I whisper, my throat burning, another round of coughs seizing my chest. "But now I'm alive."

He laughs, holding me tighter. Another swell lifts us higher in the water before lowering down again. "You're very much alive," Carter confirms. "But I have to tell you something."

Before the words can escape his mouth, a bright light shines over us, coming from an inflatable motorized boat. I blink, shock and relief coursing through me as crew members from the Ocean Jewel come to pluck us from the sea.

"Ava," Carter says again. The sound of my name coming from him sends a million butterflies racing from my stomach to my chest. "Ava, listen."

But I can't focus. My head swims, exhaustion taking its toll on me.

"Ava, please. Look at me," Carter says.

Forcing my eyes to open, I peer into Carter's deep, green-blue eyes lit by the flashlight from one of the crew members as their boat cuts through the water. Something looks different about him, but I can't put my finger on it.

Then I see them. Along each of his forearms are short, thick ridges that look similar to small fins. As quickly as I see them, they disappear, and Carter wraps his arms around me.

"I'm truly sorry for this," he whispers into my hair.

But I can't wrap my mind around what he's saying.

"I didn't have a choice," he continues. "I couldn't let you die."

Shaking my head, I try to understand his words, but all I can think about is the bright light from the boat, the faint memory of another light—a spark—tickling the back of my mind. But the spark is gone, and now I'm so tired. I don't want to think any longer.

"Ava?" Carter says again. "Ava, please. Listen to me."

But I can't.

Listening to the sound of Carter breathing, I succumb to my exhaustion. The last thing I see before I close my eyes are Carter's eyes, but for once they're not smiling at me.

Carter sits on the cot across from me as the onboard medic examines me. The last thing I remember is opening my eyes to a team of people rushing to pull me from the inflatable motorboat to take me to the lower deck to what I heard someone call the sickbay, which is a small room with a few medical supplies near the crew's cabins.

Ruby hovers in the doorway, anxiously wringing her hands together. She watches as the medic, who I recall someone call Sasha, checks my vitals, shines a light in my eyes, and asks a series of questions about where I am, how old I am, the date, and if anything hurts.

"I'm fine," I manage to say. "Can I please just go back to my room?"

"You're very lucky, Ms. Adair," Sasha says. "Your temperature is slightly lower than it should be, but I think with some rest and some warm liquids, you should feel fine in a few hours."

"So, we don't have to cut the trip short?" I ask. Out of everything I've been through, the thing I was most worried about was having to go to a hospital, cutting Sapphire's eighteenth birthday/graduation vacation short.

Sasha shrugs. "That's up to Mrs. King."

Ruby frowns from the door. "Are you sure you feel all right, Avie?" Very few people still call me by my childhood name, Ruby being one of them. I've been friends with Giselle and Sapphire since our diaper days because all our moms went to college together. "Your health is more important than this vacation. Maybe I should call your mom—"

I raise my hand out. "No! You'll freak her out for nothing. I'm not hurt or anything. She doesn't need to know. Please, Ruby. You remember how she was after—" The words stick in my throat. I can't even say them. Our town's small, and the whole place mourned after Bailey was swept out to sea. They even kept the search up long after it would have been possible to find her alive.

Ruby solemnly nods. "I suppose you're right. I want you to come back here and check in with Sasha in the morning, okay?" Turning to Carter for the first time through this whole ordeal, she says, "You were very brave for jumping in to save Ava, young man. You don't know how grateful we are, and after speaking to my husband and Captain Briggs, we'd like to reward you."

Carter rubs his hands over his knees. "I don't need a reward, ma'am. I'm just thankful I was there to help."

"As are we, and that's why the captain agreed to grant you time off for the remainder of the trip, and we're providing you with a bonus," Ruby says, smiling.

Carter doesn't smile like I expect him to. He shakes his head, his wet hair sticking to his cheeks. It takes a long moment for him to bring his gaze from the floor to meet Ruby's eyes. "That's very generous, ma'am—"

"Ruby. Call me Ruby."

"Ruby," he says, like the name feels funny on his tongue. "But I can't take you up on the offer. It's not fair for the others who'd have to pick up my slack."

Sasha scoffs. "Carter, we'll survive. Captain Briggs wouldn't have agreed if he didn't think we could handle it. I'm sure the others will agree with me."

"Then it's settled," Ruby says. "And tomorrow, we'll see you at breakfast."

With that, Ruby draws her attention to me, and I slide off the cot and follow her out to head to the stairs that'll take us up since the elevator doesn't come down to the lower deck. She wraps an arm around my shoulders, hugging me to her, and I breathe in her floral scent.

"I like that boy," Ruby says instead of asking me how I'm feeling for the millionth time.

She watches my face, and I can't resist smiling. "Me too."

As we ascend into a small hallway that leads to the saloon, I'm greeted by all my friends, Carlton, and a few crew members. Giselle is the first one to her feet, flying across the vast space. She throws her arms around me, yanking me from Ruby, and starts bawling her eyes out into my already salty hair.

"You scared the hell out of me, Aves," she whispers.

Matty shuffles up next to her. "Next time you can push me in instead, okay? I'm at your service the rest of vacation. You need something, I'll get it."

"It was an accident," I say. Matty had no idea I was going to try to save him from his fake stumble. It's the last thing I remember apart from opening my eyes, soaking wet, before being taken to the lower deck for medical attention. Everything else is a blank, like my mind pushed everything away to save me.

"I was an idiot," he says.

I smirk. "We already knew that."

After enduring hugs from the rest of my friends, I mention how tired I am, forcing them to let me retreat back to my stateroom. I take my time in the hot shower, sending away the chill that still clings to my bones.

Giselle joins me a bit later, chattering about all the craziness of the day and how happy Sapphire is that I refused to end the trip. We put on a cheesy, romantic comedy, and within ten minutes, Giselle is fast asleep, breathing deeply from her bed.

My gaze flicks to the almost full moon shining soft light through the window. The mesmerizing glow lights my skin in a pearlescent radiance, like someone painted a makeup highlighter over my skin. It tingles, warmth breaking through the coolness in my bones, and I find myself shifting off my bed to stare out the window.

Unlike earlier, the ocean radiates in a light blue color, the dark waters glittering like being lit from within. It ignites a memory of a spark in the water and how I followed the sun to the surface though the night was pitch-black.

And I remember Carter and his ocean eyes. How safe I felt with him. I remember...

A soft knock sounds on the door, pushing my faint memory away. Padding across the carpet, I make my way to the wooden door and crack it open to find Carter standing on the other side. He holds his finger to my lips to stop me from talking and pulls me from my cabin and into the small hall that leads to the sitting area.

We don't stop there, though.

Grabbing a throw blanket off the back of one of the leather sectionals, he wraps it around my bare shoulders. I'm only wearing a tank top and pajama shorts because I didn't bring anything warmer.

We take the elevator up to the sundeck, and he guides me to the farthest lounge chair, one that has a clear view of the glowing sea. It matches his sad eyes as he gazes at me for a long moment without saying anything.

Reaching out, I run my fingers along his cheek. I can't stop myself. Something about Carter in this moment captivates me. Maybe it was my fall into the ocean, or the memory of him saving me, wrapping his arms around me—something tonight brought me closer to the boy I just met this morning, and I can't put my finger on it. The thought excites and scares me.

"You look awfully sad for being my hero," I say, leaning closer to him.

His hand cups over mine and presses it firmly to his cheek, like he needs to feel the weight of my fingers against him. "I'm not a hero, Ava."

"You saved my life," I whisper, my smile melting into a frown. His gloomy gaze cuts into me, stirring the grief that has always lingered in my soul.

"Do you remember anything?" He ignores my statement, his voice deepening with his question.

I miss the easy smile he had for me all day, now long gone. He nearly leaves me speechless, and I find myself pulling away from him. I can't explain it, but the longer he holds my gaze, the more painful memories surface. I'm no longer remembering the fall into the ocean or the warmth of his skin and the relief of being pulled from the water. I remember all the other stuff—the fear and pain of losing my breath, of getting lost on the current. The pitch-darkness that made me feel trapped in a void.

"I died," I whisper, shivering against the memory. "I know it. But you—you saved me."

"Yes," he confirms. "But do you remember how?"

Closing my eyes, I try to recall everything again—the shifting color of the ocean, the fire underwater, the voice whispering to me. But none of it makes sense. Those are probably not even memories at all but hallucinations.

Taking a deep breath, I say, "This is going to sound crazy, but I touched an underwater flame. The spark..." My voice trails off, my head swimming with thoughts of the ocean. I wobble on the chair, my eyes training on the glowing ocean. "Everything looks weird, Carter. Something's wrong with me. Maybe you should take me back to Sasha."

Instead of helping me to my feet, he cups my face, looking deep into my eyes. He leans in, pressing his lips against mine, kissing me ever so softly. My heart pounds against my ribcage as I taste the salt on his lips, and then through my closed eyelids, I see the spark. The flame underwater.

Memories rush back to me, more clear than ever, and I envision my body floating before me, a large figure—an animal—circling me. It's unlike anything I've ever seen, with a glittering tail and muscular torso, two finned arms, a ridge across a muscular back like a dorsal fin. And beautiful—the creature radiates with life—and then I watch as it wraps my lifeless body in its arms.

The memory shifts, and I no longer watch from the outside, but from a different perspective. It takes me a moment, but I realize this new memory isn't mine. It's about me, though. I stare at my hair floating around my face, my eyes wide and afraid and empty. My mouth hangs slightly open and one last bubble erupts from my lips. Fear courses through me as the last of my breath travels upward, leaving me at the mercy of the sea.

A moment later, my perspective changes again, and now I stare through hazy waters at a blurry image of someone familiar—Carter. Deep in my heart, I know it's him. I can finally see past the spark glowing from where his heart would be. The light travels up his throat and to his lips, and he pulls me closer and kisses me like he kisses me now. Somehow, the memory comes to life, playing like a movie in my mind, blending and merging with the present.

I gasp as the spark engulfs me, setting me aglow, and I pull away from Carter, pushing the memory of us—one I'm not even sure is real—from my mind. When I snap my eyes open, my hand flies to my lips, electricity tingling from them, an energy sparked from Carter's kiss.

His sad eyes lock on me again. "Ava, I'm so sorry."

Why he's apologizing for kissing me, I do not know. The weight of the world hangs between us, Carter holding the majority of it on his muscular, bronzed shoulders. A thousand thoughts swirl through his eyes as he holds my gaze.

"I'm so sorry," he repeats again, bringing his hand up to brush the stray blond hairs from my face.

"Stop apologizing for saving me." My voice barely comes out a whisper. "Everything is fine. I'm fine."

"Ava, what did you see when I kissed you just now?"

My mouth suddenly dries. Saying the words out loud

would make me sound insane. The boy who sits before me now isn't the same boy who saved me in the water as much as I want to deny it.

"You're a merman." The moment the words escape my mouth, they become utterly real—there's no denying the truth to them. "And you breathed life back into me—the spark, it still lingers in my heart. I can feel it with every beat." It matches the same rhythm as Carter's, because now, when I look at his chest, I can see the spark within him, too.

Silence falls between us—the silence confirming every last one of my words. The world shifts as shadows edge my vision. I fall back, lying on the lounge chair, trying my best to pull myself together—to think things through. The brilliant moon hangs in the sky, calming my nerves, and then I feel Carter's warm fingers twine with mine.

"I'm like you now," I whisper. "That's why you're apologizing. You didn't save me. You changed me."

But I still have my legs. I still feel like me.

"You'll transform under the full moon," he whispers, answering my silent question.

Panic trembles through me, imagining what's about to happen to me, how I'm now cursed to enter the one place I fear the most. The place that stole my sister from me—that killed me.

"But it's not forever, right?" The thought is the only thing that keeps me from breaking. Carter sits before me, legs and all. He's not confined to the ocean. He still has a life.

He tugs a chain hiding beneath his shirt with a silver ring encrusted with an unfamiliar turquoise stone. I realize he's wearing one on his hand, too. "This is an enchanted stone infused with the ocean."

I catch the swirling water within the tiny stone. "It's beautiful."

"It allows me to transform at will...except for the full moon."

"What happens otherwise? Will I be trapped in the ocean? Oh, God. My parents—I can't put them through this. You have to fix me." My voice cracks, the words flying from my mouth. Tears pour from my eyes, blurring my vision. "I can't be like you, Carter. Please, fix this."

Sobs heave in my chest when he doesn't say anything. He can't fix this. It's already too late. But why even let the crew members find us? Why put me through the torture of knowing my hours are limited before I must succumb to the ocean?

Strong arms wrap around me. "I can't stop the transformation, but I'm not going to force you into a life you clearly don't want, Ava."

"How?" Pulling away, I meet his sad eyes.

He unclasps his necklace and pulls the ring from it. "With this. It was intended for the one I choose for a mate, but I want you to have it."

My eyes widen. "I barely know you."

"I'm not asking you to be my mate. I'm offering you a chance to continue to live your life the best you can. This is all my fault."

But it's not his fault at all. It's mine. I'm lucky to even be alive. "Carter..." My eyes draw to the ocean. "Are you sure you want to give that to me? I'm thankful to even be alive. It's just—why?"

He uncurls my fingers for me and slips the cool ring into my palm. "I couldn't let you die," is all he says. "I've never met someone who loves the land more than I do. I couldn't just let the ocean have you."

"But it does have me."

He shakes his head. "No, Ava. You now have the ocean."

4

PULL OF THE MOON

I SNEAK BACK INTO MY stateroom minutes after the sun rises. If I didn't have to worry about meeting the others for breakfast, I'd have stayed with Carter even longer. A few hours of talking wasn't nearly enough time to take in what's going to become of my life. And come sundown, when the full moon rises into the sky, I'll transform into a mermaid. I barely even believe it.

Born in the ocean, Carter has spent his entire life traveling from land to sea with his parents who had also chosen a life on land. Every merperson has the choice to decide, but it's rare for them to choose land over their beloved waters with the danger of discovery. And somewhere far beneath the waves hide several colonies of merpeople, all under the protection of King Attilonious, though Carter says I'll probably never meet him.

So many questions still swim through my mind. But first things first, I have to survive the day and figure out how to get away with leaving after dark when the moon rises. If someone discovers we're missing, there's no coming back aboard. There's no going home at all.

I flop back on my bed, turning to face Giselle as she remains asleep. Her bronzy brown hair hangs around her pillow like she neatly arranged it before falling asleep. I'd give anything to wake her up and confide in her, tell her what's going to happen to me—even ask her to join me too, but that's impossible.

According to Carter, since I'm human-born, I can't turn a human. As for Carter, I was his one and only chance. He still can't really explain why he did it, why he chose to save me, but it is what it is, and there's no going back.

The thing that concerns me the most above anything is that one day, Carter could decide I'm too much to deal with, and I'll be left alone and confused and incapable of dealing with this curse on my own. What if it turns out we don't actually like each other? What if he resents wasting his one chance to transform someone on me? What if I start despising him?

Pushing all the what-if questions away, I close my eyes, trying my best to sleep for the short period of time I'll have until breakfast is served. Carter's image dances on the inside of my eyelids, and I watch as the spark in his heart thrums to the sound of my own heartbeat. The change in my vision, seeing light where there is nothing but dark, is a side effect of the transformation. I'll never have to fear the black waters under the moon again, because now, they'll always be light.

Just as I doze off to sleep, the bed shifts under me. "Ava? Aves, wake up." Raising my arm, I smack Giselle away when she starts to shake my shoulders.

I groan. "Leave me alone."

"Not after last night."

Oh, jeez. I hope she's not serious, because I'll never get away tonight if she is. "So, I can't sleep in because of it?"

She laughs. "Exactly, now get up. I want to swim before breakfast."

After the five minutes it takes to slip into our bathing suits, I stroll next to Giselle, and we head up to the sundeck together. Bright sunshine bathes my skin in its warm rays. Giselle pulls me to a stop, and I notice a figure on the last lounge chair, the one I shared with Carter last night.

With a towel shading his eyes, Carter sleeps sprawled out

with his hands hooked behind his head. He must've come back here after he took me to my room, probably because he mentioned he shares a cabin with three other people.

Giselle grins, holding a finger to her lips, and then tiptoes to the edge of the pool. She motions for me to follow her lead, and we stand on the other side of the shallow, rectangular pool, facing Carter. I know exactly what she wants to do.

Without warning, she grabs my hand and pulls me forward with her, and we splash into the water, shooting up a small wave which lands right on top of Carter. He bolts upright, the towel falling onto the wet deck. When he sees us in the pool in front of him, he smiles. It's the first one since he revealed what he had done to me last night. It's bright enough to leave me weak in the knees.

"You're swimming," he says, trailing his eyes from my half damp hair to my halter bikini top before meeting my gaze.

"More like wading," Giselle quips. The water barely goes above our torsos.

Pools have never scared me. In fact, I swim all the time at home in my own pool. It's the deep, ever moving water that scares me—even lakes. Anything deep enough to lose myself in.

I lick my bottom lip as he continues to stare at me. "So, are you going to just watch us or are you coming in?"

He leans back on the lounge, and Giselle laughs, splashing him with water. A moment later, he tugs his tank top over his head, showing off his ripped stomach in all its golden goodness, and it's my turn to take in the drool-worthy view. Giselle nudges my shoulder with hers, having the same thought as I am. *Wow.*

Carter sits on the edge of the pool and swings his legs into the water before slipping under. I half expect his legs to turn into a tail the moment he gets wet, but after a lot of explaining, it turns out that would only happen without his sea stone, and it would be triggered regardless of touching the water or not.

He sinks lower into the pool, the water rising to his neck, and then he swims in my direction faster than I expect. Without warning, he grips my waist and lifts me into the air before dunking me under water completely. When I break the surface, I laugh, half squealing, and swim away before he can toss me again.

Giselle jumps on his back, pushing him under, but he straightens up to his full height, tossing her in my direction. We all laugh, the heaviness of unspoken words and worries no longer weighing us down.

Giselle joins me on the edge of the pool, water dripping from her dark bronze hair, and she touches my knee. We watch Carter swim a small lap. "So, will there be a second date with the bronzed god?"

I wish I could tell her that there will be one at least once a month, but instead I say, "Tonight. I really like him, Gi."

"I can tell." She trains her gaze to Carter as he swims toward us but doesn't surface before he heads back to the opposite side of the pool. "He likes you, too."

I smirk. "If only we wouldn't be interrupted again, maybe Logan could finally win a bet." I don't tell her that he already did win, that Carter kissed me last night, but it wasn't exactly the kind of kiss I was expecting. It was his way to help me remember. I try not to put too much meaning behind it because everything is just so out of control and confusing.

She bounces next to me. "Oh, I know! I'll sleep in Matty and Logan's room, since neither of them has slept in there. You know Logan went straight to Daisy's and Matty slept in Sapphire's last night?"

Of course they did. Why wouldn't they? Ruby and Carlton haven't checked on any of us because we're all almost adults, and this is Sapphire's trip. They came along to be with each other in the romantic owner's suite. They haven't even been on the sundeck because they have their own hot tub and balcony. Giselle's plan is pretty perfect.

I hug her. "You sure you don't mind?"

"No way. It's not often I see you all smiles for a boy."

When Carter stops swimming, I hop from the edge of the pool and cross the water to him to tell him that I have it all figured out. His cheeks darken, and I almost think he's blushing when I explain how Giselle is letting us have the room for the night, despite the fact that we won't be anywhere near it.

"It might just work," he finally says, twining his fingers through mine underwater.

I suck in my bottom lip. "It has to. I'm really counting on it."

The fiery hue of the setting sun warms the entire saloon, making the white leather couches golden. Sapphire rests her head on the arm of the couch with her legs sprawled over Matty. Chloe and Giselle play a game of cards while blasting music through the surround sound. Logan and Daisy sit together in a recliner, staring at the screen of Daisy's laptop.

Across the room from everyone, I sit with Carter in the window seat, constantly glancing between my friends and my future, as the sun threatens to disappear, bringing night. Up until now, we haven't had a moment to talk about what happens next—and honestly, I'm absolutely terrified.

Carter leans in close, brushing his lips against my ear. "We're going to wait as long as possible after sundown to hit the water. I can resist the transformation for a few hours, which makes it a lot easier to slip away unnoticed, but you won't be able to. Not yet. You'll also start to feel what I can only describe as an uncomfortable pull at any moment. Don't let it scare you. Your transformation will take a bit since it's your first."

My heartbeat pounds in my head. "Is it going to hurt?" The idea of suddenly growing scales and having my legs fuse together just seems so unpleasant.

"It'll be an adjustment for you. But pain? No, I don't think so." Thinking is far from being certain. His words do nothing to settle my nerves.

I feel like I'm going to vomit at any second. It's like the time I waited in line with Giselle to ride the new Death Spiral rollercoaster at Sailor's Bay Amusement Park. All I could think the whole time in line was how terrifying the first drop would feel, sending my stomach into my throat and then crashing it to my feet—the thought alone was enough to make me almost back out, but by the time I realized I didn't want to ride, I was already harnessed in, and it was too late.

Now feels like the anticipation of that first drop. Like then, I can't back out now either.

"I'm going to be sick," I say, wringing my hands together in my lap. "I can't do this. Maybe I'll just lock myself in the bathroom."

He gently pinches my chin. "That's the pull of the moon you're experiencing. Resistance will make you feel like you're dying until you do. You're a mermaid now. Without the sea, you won't survive the night."

Tears threaten to spill on my cheeks, my heart heavy in my chest. "Please," I whisper. "There has to be a way."

The muscles in my legs spasm, and it takes everything in me not to cry out and draw attention to us. The last thing I need is for someone to think I'm sick and send me to Sasha for an exam.

Carter rises to his feet, pulling me up from the window seat. His brows furrow, lowering over his blue-green eyes. My legs shake, but with the help of his arm around my waist, I stroll next to him, resting my head on his shoulder.

Giselle catches my gaze, her eyes crinkling in the corners for a second, before I offer her my best smile. I wink at her for good measure, just hoping she doesn't come to our stateroom to check on us. She already moved whatever she needed into the boy's room after lunch. She blows me a kiss, and Logan yells out that he's going to finally win a bet. The nausea rolling through me is enough to stop me from being embarrassed.

Carter guides me onto the elevator, and we head to my room first where I grab the waterproof bag he'd given me and lock the door so no one can barge in to find it empty. When we make it out on the empty sundeck, the crisp ocean air pushes my sickness away as I stare at the darkening purple sky.

Gripping the guardrail, I peer over the vast ocean. Fear trickles down my spine, and I imagine the unsettling fall last night. This one is a much taller drop, but it's the best place at this time of day since I can't stop the transformation like Carter. If he were alone, he'd wait until much later when his cabin mates were asleep to slip away. Now, most of the staff should be cleaning up or eating in the galley. Sapphire's parents have already retreated to their cabin at the front of the boat, and all my friends are hanging out in the saloon.

A tingling sensation crawls down my back along my spine, shooting cramps into my legs. Bending over, clutching my knees, I know it won't be much longer. The wind whistles around me, blowing my blond hair from my face. But still, I can't find the courage to straighten my back—to face the water and the moon as it feels like it's pulling my insides out.

The boat rocks on a small swell, and I groan, holding myself. The yacht glides over the current at a much slower pace than last night, and as long as I jump far enough, I won't have to worry about getting hurt.

The purple sky fades to dark blue. I can feel the pull of the ocean deep in my bones, the moon shining in the sky. If I don't jump soon, I'll surely die.

"Get ready to jump, Ava," Carter says, circling the small deck once for signs of anyone strolling the pathway that winds around the lower deck. It's dark enough now that it'll be harder to spot us. And I'm counting on the fact that everyone is busy and Carter knows the crews' habits from working on the yacht for a while. This isn't the first time he's been on the Ocean Jewel during a full moon. He promised it'll all work out as long as my friends stay away.

Swallowing my fear, I shimmy out of my dress and fold it neatly into the waterproof bag. My toes tingle like I've sat with my legs curled under me for too long. It's more annoying than painful, but the newfound sickness swirling in my stomach threatens to send me reeling.

When I glance up, Carter stands a foot away, his shirt and board shorts dangling in his hands in front of his naked body. Blush blossoms up my face as he takes the bag from me and shoves them in, and I look everywhere else but at him.

If the call of the ocean doesn't kill me, my racing heart just might.

"You can undress. I promise I won't look," he says.

Keeping my head up, I shift my eyes to stare at him. "What? I'm not getting naked here."

"You might rip your bikini."

"I have more."

He doesn't argue, though I do loosen the ties on my bottoms. I really, really love this bikini, but I don't know Carter well, and I didn't imagine the first time I'd be getting naked in front of a boy I liked would be because I'm about to sprout a tail. What is wrong with my life?

Another wave of cramps rushes through me, and I suck in a deep breath while gripping the guardrail. I'm afraid if it happens again, I'll fall instead of jump and end up a bruised and half broken mess splattered across the sea.

"Come on. It's time to go," he says, taking the lead. Climbing up a rung, he swings his leg over the guardrail. He helps me over, his muscled arms rippling, and I try my best not to look at the view of him as I find my footing. He smirks at my obvious averting eyes but doesn't say anything.

"What if I don't jump far enough?"

"I'll make sure you do."

"What if someone sees us?"

"They won't."

"What if—"

He reaches out and takes my hand, silencing the millions of what-if questions clouding my thoughts. "The moment we hit the water, we're going to dive, okay?"

I nod without answering.

"Are you ready?"

I inhale a shuddering breath. "No."

"Ava, look at me," he says, his voice deep and smooth and calm enough to quiet my screaming fear. When I meet his blue-green eyes, he says, "I won't let go of you until you're ready. If you want me to hold your hand until morning, I will."

Oh, God. I have to jump. The moon pulls at my very essence, forcing me to inch my bare feet forward toward the ledge.

Closing my eyes, I squeeze Carter's hand, imagining I'm a million other places than standing at the edge of the sundeck ready to plummet into the churning ocean. "Okay, count to three. Let's get this over with."

"Remember, jump out and then when we hit the water, dive."

Another shaky breath releases from my mouth. "Okay."

Carter shifts the waterproof bag on his shoulder before saying, "One. Two. Three."

Bending my knees at the same moment Carter does, we propel out and away from the yacht. The sea air whooshes around me, and my stomach rises into my throat. As my feet touch the water, ice swallows me, sinking into my bones. The last thing I see before my head goes under is the bright, round moon taunting me from the sky.

Then all I see is the glowing water.

JUST BREATHE

CARTER YANKS ME DEEPER INTO the ocean, not giving me the chance to even think. He swims with a grace I'll never manage to have, his body shimmering and morphing into a form more fitted for the sea. Through hazy eyes, I watch the spark in his chest pulse through him, binding his legs together until a shimmering, teal tail appears, matching the color of his eyes. The scales gleam as if they're made of gemstones. My fingers reach down without my mind's consent and brush along their smooth and slippery texture, like a fishtail but with the strength and toughness of the skin of a dolphin.

My vision shadows the longer we're underwater, my lungs threatening to burst from the lack of oxygen. Fear laces around my heart, squeezing me in its icy grip when I realize I'm far too deep in the water to ever make it back to the surface for another gasp of air. I kick my legs, still unchanged, and I know I'll die if the transformation doesn't happen soon. I'll be the only mermaid ever to drown.

Thrashing, I struggle to break the grip Carter has on me. As I pull away, he only holds me tighter, his handsome face too blurry to tell what expression he's giving me.

My heart hammers against my ribs, threatening to explode from my chest. Something is wrong. Nothing is happening. No more tingling sensation, no cramps, nothing. And no air to breathe. What if Carter was wrong, and he didn't use his one chance to transform me into a mermaid?

Just when I'm about to lose myself to the panic consuming me, Carter releases my hand to only cup my face between his palms. His face lingers so close to mine that his eyes shine clearly in the strangely glowing water.

"Just breathe, Ava. You must breathe." He mouths through the water, though his voice doesn't reach me.

Everything tells me not to breathe. Because if I breathe in, water will fill my lungs and I'll drown.

"Breathe," he mouths again.

At this point, my lungs are about to explode, and I automatically open my mouth, sucking in a gallon of ocean water. But unlike when I drowned, the water doesn't burn. It's a relief. The ocean fills me with life, and my lungs—gills—pull precious oxygen from the water allowing me to breathe among the fish.

Closing my eyes, I allow the water into my mouth and out the gills that have formed on my neck just under my ears, following my jaw line. Dull cramps seize the muscles in my legs, traveling from my toes to my thighs. Heat expands from my heart and circulates through my veins, pushing the chill of the ocean away.

I turn my gaze away to stare down as the shimmer from my own spark crawls along my body. The strings of my bikini dance in the sea, and while swallowing my embarrassment, I tug them until my bottoms float away. Carter doesn't take his eyes off my face. His eyes sparkle like two jewels, holding me in their precious gaze.

Another series of cramps rush through me, forcing me to arch my back. Scales burst from my skin, a cerulean blue with a metallic sheen, and I wish I had a mirror to check myself out. The muscles on my arms spasm and smooth, bone-like ridges press against the skin of my forearms. Even my fingers change slightly. My nails grow sharp and thin webbing connects my fingers together up to my knuckles.

"That's it, Ava. You're almost done." Carter's smooth voice echoes in my mind, sending my heart racing. His hand moves from my shoulder to my fingers, and he clasps his fingers around mine, swimming back a foot to take in the full view of my transformation.

The expanse of my caudal fin is wider than Carter's, glittering like jewels are encrusted in every blue scale. A small ridge protrudes from where my tail meets my torso, wrapping around my waist like a belt, and when I reach behind me, I feel a firm yet versatile small dorsal fin. The rest of my once human skin takes on a shimmer like a pearl, my pectoral fins on my arms nearly unnoticeable.

My blond hair flows in the water, twirling and swirling with the current, and I wish I had something to tie it out of the way with. A smile creeps along my face, my fear of the ocean, the transformation, the end of my old life, drifting away in the water.

Floating in the current, all I can do is watch Carter smile at me. A soft glow pulsates from where his heart is in his chest, and without having to look, I know mine mirrors his. Something flashes in his turquoise jeweled eyes—an emotion I can't decipher—but it's just for me. He drinks in my appearance, and I find myself leaning closer.

With a flick of his tail, he closes the distance between us, slides his arms over my shoulders and around my neck. Tiny bubbles escape his nose, oxygen still clinging to us through the water, and he studies my lips like they're the most fascinating thing he's ever seen.

"You're beautiful, Ava." His voice wraps around my mind, drawing me closer.

His lips brush softly against mine, just enough to tease me, test me—to see if I'll kiss him back. It's the complete opposite of the kiss we shared when he brought back my memories. This one's different. The images that flicker through my mind aren't my own. They're his.

An image of me in my mermaid state—my sparkling blue, metallic-like tail, my pearlescent skin, my cerulean eyes clearer than the brightest sky on a sunny day—settles in my head as I see what Carter sees. I kiss him more deeply, slipping my tongue into his mouth, clinging to him like the current will sweep me away. His fingers tangle in my flowing hair, and we hover in the middle of the glowing ocean for a long moment.

"Whoa," I say, realizing that my own voice falls flat as it projects telepathically to Carter.

The intensity of his gaze sinks deep in my soul. He blinks a few times, his face relaxing, and then he jerks his head before motioning me to swim.

In this moment, I realize that the swimming skills Carter possesses don't come from him simply being a merman. When I flick my tail, I shoot sideways, dragging Carter with me as I cut through the water like a drunken fish.

Embarrassment washes over me, and I try to compose myself. If I can't manage to swim in my new form, we won't get very far. Carter laughs out bubbles, wrapping his hands around my waist and gently tips me forward so I'm parallel with the surface looming overhead. A school of silver fish with black spotted tails swims over us, dancing with the water. It isn't until this moment that I take in the vastness of the ocean.

Beneath us, kelp stretches toward us like giant green ropes reaching for the surface. A menagerie of fish dart through the kelp forest like the tall plants cage them in. Yellowtails, some almost half my size, swim with powerful fins.

A shadow crosses over us, sending fear into me, as a boat floats on the surface above us. Carter glances up but doesn't give it more than a single thought. In the dark water, no one can see us from the surface.

As the thoughts of fishing equipment and radar whirl through my mind, Carter presses his fingers into the skin between my bikini-covered chest over my heart. "No human device can detect us. The light you see, our life force, protects us. It causes interference. It also disguises us from above. No one can see us as we are when we're underwater. It's surfacing that's dangerous."

He doesn't lessen the pressure of his fingers, my heartbeat drumming against his palm. His other hand settles on my lower back, rubbing gently across the short dorsal fin that runs from the top of my tail to the string of my bikini top.

Ever so gently, he guides the motion of my body like the ripples of a wave, showing me how to control my swim without stroking my arms out like I usually would in a crawl stroke, the most comfortable swim stroke for me.

After a few minutes, he nods his head, smiling at me. The motion feels more natural the more I do it. His hands release me, the heat of his touch still lingering on my skin. I jet forward, cutting through the water of the current that pushes me along.

Carter never leaves my side, holding my pinkie finger with his. We swim with our arms at our sides, propelled by the strength of our glittering tails. He guides me deeper into the kelp forest, and we navigate our way through like Carter has swum these waters a million times. I wouldn't doubt that he has.

Fish dart away, clearing a path, and I catch sight of a bat ray swimming like an expansive butterfly along the bottom of the ocean floor. Tugging Carter toward it, we descend until I can nearly brush my fingers along its back. The only time I've been so close to a creature of this beauty was at the local aquarium, which doesn't compare to the greatness hidden beneath the place I've feared most.

As we weave in and out of the kelp, my every movement matches Carter's. I thought I was aware of his body before, but it doesn't compare to this moment. Every glance he sneaks at me, every smile, every squeeze of my fingers. My attraction to him consumes my thoughts. I just hope he doesn't hear the thoughts I want to keep privately to myself.

When we reach a clearing in the water, I slow down. He circles me, creating a small whirlpool that twirls my hair in front of my face. I peek at him through my hair, letting myself float up a few feet toward the moonlit surface. The exertion of keeping his pace wears me down, but I don't want him to notice. I have the sudden need to prove that I can live in this new underwater world he's shared with me.

But even my hair can't hide my fatigue when a current catches me, pulling me away from Carter. He doesn't allow it to take me though, just like he promised. Instead, he motions for me to hold onto his broad, muscular shoulders. With my stomach pressed against his back, his short dorsal fin slightly digging into my skin, he takes off, pulling me along to more shallow waters. His skin radiates with warmth, and it's like energy pulsates between us, charged by the closeness of our bodies as we move as one through the water. He swims so fast, I can't even catch sight of our surroundings and any sense of direction is lost to me.

With a flick of his tail, we ascend, shooting up to the surface. A jolt of surprise leaves me breathless when we break through. Cold air wraps around me, the ocean air blowing against my wet hair. We bob through the waves, Carter sweeping his tail in the water to keep us in control.

I rest my chin on the crook of his neck, and he shivers when I release a breath of air near his ear. My body instinctually adjusts from breathing water to air, the action effortless. Ahead of us, lights sparkle from an island in the close distance. The moon casts a brilliant light over the ocean, creating a silvery trail to the waves crashing against the shore.

Boats pepper the harbor in the distance, sleepily floating on the water. Jetting rocks sprout from the waves ahead of us, and Carter swims in their direction. The muscles in his arms tighten as he uses only his upper body to pull himself from the water to perch on the edge of the rocks with his tail smacking the waves. Reaching down, he grips me under my arms and lifts me next like I weigh nothing at all.

My tail rests across his lap, my caudal fin lightly tapping the black surface of the rock. He removes the bag that was strapped to his side and sets it beside us. Through the clear plastic, I spot my bikini bottoms, relieved he thought to grab them, though now our clothes lie in a damp heap.

He absently trails his fingers along the side of my tail. We sit quietly, watching the waves crash into the shore from a far enough distance away that no one will spot us. I never thought I could be so at peace in the water that stole my sister away, but as long as I suppress the memory, I can see the ocean as a bright new world.

"For someone who was terrified of the ocean, you're doing surprisingly well," Carter says, his voice cutting through the air. Hearing the words out loud makes me miss the sound of his voice in my head.

"You're as surprised as I am. I never thought I'd ever go back in the water, let alone explore its depths."

"Why is that?" I knew the question would come up eventually. I was hoping I could avoid it, but what's the point? I share a new bond with a boy I never imagined I would. The ocean and this unbelievable secret binds me to him—at least for now. It's all so new.

Taking a deep breath of salty air, I hang my head to veil

my face with my hair. "When I was a kid, my sister and I were playing in the waves late in the day. We got caught in a riptide, and she drowned. The ocean swept her away. It was a miracle that a neighbor managed to even save me."

He doesn't respond with words of sympathy or apologies like I expect. All he says is, "And now the ocean finally got another girl it wanted." The tone of his voice surprises me, like he's angry. Yet, his gentle touch says something else completely.

"You hate that I'm here now." It's not a question but a statement. I was angry and scared and confused until the moment I took my first breath of the ocean. But sitting here with Carter takes all those negative emotions away. It'll be strange come dawn when I'll return back to my normal life like none of this ever happened. A secret that'll weigh on me with every interaction with my friends, every step I take—even every time I suck in a breath of air.

"I hate that you never had the choice—I hate that I'm selfishly enjoying your presence, how I got so lucky to have such a beautiful, smart, caring girl with me now, sharing my world. I hate that I don't regret anything." Without meeting my gaze, he brushes his hand through his copper streaked hair, lit with a silvery glow from the moon.

I reach out and take both his hands in mine. The gesture relaxes his shoulders, and he brings my cool fingers up to his mouth and blows on them. Even though the air chills me, it doesn't bother me.

"I'm not going to lie. Everything about this terrified me. I'm still terrified. You wasted your one chance at transforming someone on me. You gave me, a girl you've known for so little time, the ring that was intended for your mate so I could return to my life back in Azure Waters." The words rush so quickly from my mouth, I feel like I'm bearing my soul. "And I don't even know what will happen when I get back." Tears threaten to fall onto my cheeks, but I blink them away.

"I didn't waste anything on you, Ava," he whispers, staring up at the stars.

He says it now, but what about in a few months? A year? Things can change in a split second. What if I realize I don't even really, truly like him? I can't imagine the thought, but what if my crush is temporary like the one I had for Chase Gibbons my freshman year of high school? It lasted all of two months, and then suddenly, I didn't like him anymore.

"The sea air might be getting to your head," I say, because it sure feels like it's making me crazy.

Instead of frowning like I expect, he tilts his head back and laughs. "It clears my mind if anything. You make me think past the day that's ahead of us."

I don't respond. How can I tell him the only thoughts of our future end badly in my mind?

He wraps his arms around me. "Please, don't look so sad."

Leaning over, I rest my head against his shoulder. His arms slide around me, pulling me close, and I listen to the sound of his heartbeat that thrums in perfect sync with my own. I can't think about my future when I don't even know how I'll slip back into my life as a human.

"It's just—I can't envision my future, Carter."

"Then just be with me in the now."

I nod. "Okay. I can do that. Why don't you show me more of your world?"

He smiles, giving me the look that I know is only for me. "You mean *our* world."

Our world. It has a nice ring to it.

Shifting me off his lap, he adjusts the bag across his side and jumps back into the water. I dive in after him, wrapping my arms around his shoulders. In one quick motion, he takes off, diving us back into the ocean's glowing depths.

6

SPARK OF LIFE

IT'S NOT UNTIL ALMOST DAWN that we make our way back to the yacht, now docked in a harbor in a cove off Catalina Island. It's one of the first stops on the way up the coast to San Francisco, which happens to be where Carter has spent most of his life. I had no clue we'd be stopping, but I guess Ruby and Carlton wanted to surprise Sapphire as a birthday treat.

The moon will set any moment, the sky lightening with the rise of the sun. Sneaking back on the boat will be the ultimate test. There's no way I—the girl who's terrified of the ocean— could ever explain an early morning swim in the sea. According to Carter, Captain Briggs is probably already up with a few other crew members, but all their work will keep them inside and out of sight for now.

"We'll enter on the swim platform," Carter says, his voice echoing through my mind. A seal darts by us as we float just feet below the yacht.

"What if I can't transform back?" It wasn't until this moment that the thought crossed my mind.

"You will, I promise."

A second later, Carter closes his eyes, still holding my hands, and the spark of his life force flows from all over his body to enter his heart, making the spot on his chest glow brighter than ever. The intensity of his jewel-like eyes fades and his scales vanish, retreating back beneath his tanned skin. When his transformation is complete, he treads under the water in front of me, blowing out small air bubbles as he now relies on his lungs to breathe in the oxygen he needs to live on land.

But he doesn't surface. He remains at my side, completely naked, waiting for me to transition back to my human self.

Closing my eyes, I try to will my body to transform but nothing happens. I can no longer hear Carter's voice in my mind either. I motion for him to rise to the surface, but all he does is shake his head.

Come on, body. Don't be stubborn. As soon as the words enter my mind, a jolt of ice shoots up my legs and cramps grip my stomach, traveling down my tail to my caudal fin. My body convulses, the transformation taking hold, splitting my tail down the middle. I bend down, jerking away from Carter and hug myself. Another round of cramps travels to my arms, and then I'm forced to arch my back, a glimmer of pain seizing my spine. It's much worse turning back to human, my skin freezing in the cold water and my legs aching.

And then my lungs burn as my gills disappear.

I thrash, suddenly terrified that I can't breathe. Carter hooks his arm around my waist, yanking me toward the surface. As we break through the water to air, I cough, choking and spitting out the now disgusting saltwater. Carter rubs my back, patting me gently, and I rid my lungs of the sea to take a gasping breath.

I shudder, feeling weak. All the swimming of the night now hits me hard. I bob back underwater, this time holding my breath. Carter doesn't let me stay under long, the strength of his arms wrapping around me.

It takes me a moment to orient myself when I realize that like Carter, I'm naked from my torso down, and I'm pressed against his hips as he holds onto me and the swim platform.

Before I have a chance to blush, Carter tugs the other half

of my bikini from the bag on his other side and hands it to me, keeping his eyes on my face. Awkwardly shifting away while his hand remains firmly on my waist to keep my head above the water, I tie my bottoms in place.

"Okay," I say when I'm ready.

He pushes me onto the swim platform with one arm, and I roll onto my back and stare at the pink sky of early dawn. Goosebumps prickle over my skin, my chest heaving. I catch my breath, getting used to the feeling of solid wood beneath me. With a small splash, Carter pulls himself next to me, tugging his clothes from his bag to get dressed.

I groan, sitting up on my elbows. I ache everywhere like I've hit the gym with my mom's personal trainer. I only went with her once, and my legs burned for a week. This is worse though. Much worse. I'm not even sure I can get back to my feet to make it to my stateroom.

Carter stretches his arms over his head before reaching for his toes. Water drips from his hair into his eyes, and then he shakes his head, spraying me with saltwater. My gaze lingers on how the rising sun shines golden on his skin. His eyes smile when they meet mine, though his lips press into a thin line.

He holds out his hand for me to take, but instead of letting him help me up, I fall back to stare at the sky. "I can't. My body's on fire, which means you lied to me, you know."

A dimple flashes through the scruff on his cheeks. "You asked if the transformation hurt. I find it uncomfortable, so technically I didn't lie from my experience."

Sighing, I wiggle my toes in front of me to make sure they still work. "You're just going to have to leave me here. I really don't think I can get up."

"I guess I'll have to carry you then." He laughs, grinning, and he bends over to scoop me into his arms.

I playfully slap his chest. "Carter, put me down."

Instead of setting me on my feet, he moves to put me on the row of seats lining the guardrail on the deck and off the swimming platform. He slips me my dress from the waterproof bag. I slide it over my head, the damp material clinging to me, and I run my fingers over the skirt to try to press the wrinkles from it.

I catch my reflection in the shiny metal trim along the wall of the yacht. My wet hair hangs limply and the pearlescent sheen of my skin is nowhere in sight. I just look like I've been thrown in the ocean. The only reminder of the night is the faint glow in my chest, the one only Carter and I can see.

Voices echo from above us as the crew starts to set up breakfast on the dining terrace. If we don't hurry, we'll get caught out here in the same clothes we wore last night, soaking wet, with a lot of lying to do.

Carter holds out his hand to me. "Come on."

With shaking legs, I manage to push to my feet. He half carries me into the empty saloon. We quietly cross the room. Each step gets easier the more I remind myself that I've been walking since I was eleven months old, according to my mom.

Carter calls for the elevator, and another two voices echo from upstairs. It's Giselle and Sapphire. They mention my name. When the elevator door opens, we don't get on. Carter pushes me toward the stairs and nudges me up, stopping just for a second to make sure no one spots us climbing to the sundeck.

Thankfully, it's empty. Carter runs to the cabinets near the closest lounge chair and grabs two towels. He strips off his shirt and wraps the towel around his shoulders. Following his lead, I tug my dress from last night over my head and wrap the dry towel around my cold body.

The elevator slides open and Giselle and Sapphire stand in front of us in their bikinis. Sapphire raises her eyebrows while Giselle blinks a few times, confusion crossing her face.

"I was just at our room trying to wake your ass up, but the door was locked," Giselle says, glancing from me to Carter.

I frown, squeezing my eyes shut. "Crap. I must've accidentally locked it."

Carter touches my shoulder. "Hey, don't worry. I can get the spare key." His fingers brush over my shoulder as he abandons me to the curious gazes of my friends. I'm tempted to run after him, but my legs still ache, and I might trip and fall flat on my face.

"So," Giselle says, a smile lighting her entire face.

Heat claws up my neck. "So."

"You look tired."

I lean against the cabinet of towels. "Been up for a while."

Sapphire snickers from next to Giselle. If I could throw myself over the guardrail and back into the ocean, I would. My friends won't give up unless I give them something to talk about. It's sort of a tradition. We've all definitely kissed and told—but only to each other. And out of everyone, I haven't had much to tell.

"Spill, Ava," Giselle says, pulling me away from the elevator and the stairs.

"It's not a big deal." It's a huge deal, though. And one I can never share as much as I want to. Giselle would flip if she knew my secret. She'd beg me to figure out a way to turn her into a mermaid. She'd beg Carter for a friend. She still has the pretend mermaid fin she got for her birthday a few years ago locked away in her pool shed.

As tempting as it would be to have my best friend going through the same thing I am, Carter would never go for it. Plus, Giselle would have to drown, and Carter said there was no guarantee. A lie will have to do.

Giselle hits a button to start the jets in the hot tub and cranks the heat up a bit. I slip on the small step, nearly falling in. My legs still tremble from the transformation. Knocking her knee into mine, Giselle meets my gaze with another brilliant smile. Her warm skin glows in the early morning light. As the jets kick on and the water warms, I sink lower until I'm covered to my neck. After swimming all night, it's a strange relief to just sit in the hot tub and relax.

"If you think we had sex, think again," I finally say. Because honestly, that's the first thing I would think if I knew Giselle spent the night with a boy. And it's definitely what happens when Sapphire and Matty share her cabin, though they've been together since sophomore year and friends since he moved to Azure Waters in the sixth grade.

"Hey, I wasn't thinking that," Giselle says. *Sure thing, BFF.*

"But we did kiss...and I saw him naked." I cover my face with my hands as I say the words. Because they're true. I technically did see Carter in all his muscular goodness, but I didn't exactly see all of him, though he clearly doesn't care whether or not I do.

"Oh, my God," Sapphire squeals. "I bet he's so damn sexy."

My cheeks heat so much that it feels like I'm getting a sunburn. "You have no idea."

"Oh, but I think I do," Giselle says.

Her eyes flick away from me and toward the elevator where Carter stands, holding a tray of breakfast foods. He's still in his board shorts without a shirt. A smile plays on his lips as he sets the food down on a nearby table. There's no way he didn't just hear our conversation.

The three of us girls start laughing—not only from embarrassment but because of how funny the situation is. My heart flutters, and I imagine what a night alone in a room with Carter would be like instead of under the sea. It's enough to send me under the bubbling water to pull myself together. If only I could still breathe.

The water rocks me when another body enters the hot tub and slides next to me. Carter's hand nudges my head up until I break the surface. His dazzling eyes smile at me, and I sigh, releasing the breath I was holding.

"You heard it all, didn't you?" I ask, darting my gaze to my friends as they hold back laughter.

Before he can respond, Giselle splashes water at us. "Look, Carter. Just so you know. If you want to hang out with Ava, you have to know that I'm her BFF, and we talk. Actually, all of us talk, and you're new, so we're going to talk about you."

"Only good stuff," I say quietly, nearly dying of embarrassment. Jumping into the ocean is looking better than ever, though fear still lingers in the back of my mind. I'm probably the only mermaid with an unhealthy fear of the sea.

"Especially the good stuff," Sapphire says.

I skim my hand across the water, splashing her in the face. Her laughter echoes through the air followed by Giselle's. Carter laughs as well, but I think he's only doing it to be nice. I, on the other hand, sink lower into the water. Carter slides his arm over my shoulders, and I tilt my head toward his chest.

"And another thing," Giselle says.

Oh, great. There's always more with her.

"If I start to hear anything bad, you better watch out. I know people."

I groan. "She doesn't know people."

"Oh, you know I know people, Aves," she says, her voice staying serious though she's really joking.

"Got it," Carter says.

"Good."

Sapphire giggles across from us. "Now that everything's settled, are you joining us for a day of adventures?"

Her mention of plans leaves a sinking feeling in my stomach. Today of all days had to be the one where we're not going to relax on the yacht. We just had to dock at an island where I'll be forced to do stuff. All I want to do is crawl into bed and sleep. Thank God it's summer or I'd die if the next full moon fell on a day I had to wake up early. *But you start college in the fall.* I guess night classes are out.

"Whatever Ava wants to do," Carter says, drawing my attention back to my friends' conversation. "I'm pretty sure all ocean activities are out, right?" He eyes me.

"Just because Ava doesn't go in the ocean, doesn't mean you can't," Sapphire says.

I shrug. "She's right."

His eyes turn serious. "I live most of my time on the ocean, but hanging with you is something I haven't had much time to do."

The hot tub is about to turn into a mess of melted girls as we all swoon at his words. Sapphire audibly sighs, and I lock my fingers with Carter's under the water.

"Okay, you're definitely not invited to go snorkeling with us," Giselle says. "Ava, he's all yours."

Even though my heart pounds and butterflies swarm in my stomach, all I can do is laugh. I never imagined meeting someone who can fit so easily with my friends, especially one who happens to be a really hot merman.

"I expect him to show you a good time, too," Giselle adds.

As I look at Carter, I know he will.

BREATHLESS

AFTER RETURNING TO MY STATEROOM and sleeping for a few hours, I shower and get ready. My light blue sundress with a sweetheart neckline clings in all the right places. My hair, now clean and free of chlorine and saltwater, sits in a ballerina bun on top of my head. My cheeks and lips are the perfect pink from my lip and cheek stain, but I don't wear much more makeup.

Stepping into my sandals, I stare at myself in the full length mirror on the back of the door. I expect to look as different as I feel, but I look like I always have.

A knock sounds on the door, and I step forward and swing it open to find Carter standing on the other side. He smiles, his shaven face revealing his sexy dimples. The scent of coconut shampoo, sunscreen, and the ever present hint of the salty ocean wafts from him, sending my heart fluttering. Just his presence alone stirs something deep within me, almost like the pull the ocean had on me, but this pull is different—it embodies everything good in me and drags it to the surface.

Carter sucks in a small breath, drinking me in with his blue-green eyes. It's enough to send heat from my heart to my feet. I never knew how much a look could speak to me, but after last night, I can almost see my own reflection in his mind, and I love what I do to him. It makes today a lot less daunting, because in this moment, I don't doubt Carter wants to spend time with me and not only because he transformed me into a mermaid on a whim. How long that that look will last? God, I hope forever.

I twirl once, allowing the airy fabric to twist around my thighs before settling when I stop. He rubs his lips together, his eyes trailing to my mouth. I force myself to smile even though I'm suddenly feeling awkward, unsure if I should kiss him, if he's waiting for me to make the first move.

"You look beautiful," he finally says. He hovers in the hallway outside my room.

"Thank you. I wasn't sure what to wear. I didn't really pack for hiking or anything." On the island, there's not much to do outside of water activities except hiking, biking, shopping, and dining.

"You're perfect the way you are," he says, nudging a basket at his feet. I didn't notice it until now. "Come on. Keith's waiting to take us to the dock."

I should be more afraid than I feel about having to ride in the inflatable boat to the dock that leads to land, but I'm not. I suppose being a mermaid has its benefits.

As he takes my hand, I pull him closer. "Do you think I should tell my friends that my fear of the ocean isn't what it used to be?"

His forehead crinkles for a split second. Pulling my hand up, he rubs his finger across the sea stone in the ring on my ring finger. "This stops you from a forced change, but it doesn't stop the transformation all together. Once it starts, you can't just stop it either."

"Oh."

"I'm not saying stay out of the ocean, but you have to be careful. You've only transformed once..." His voice trails off.

"And I wasn't exactly that great at it," I finish for him.

He reaches up and brushes his fingers along my cheek.

"You did perfect, but something as little as a thought could trigger you to change. It's better to just stay out of the water for now unless you're going in to transform. The ocean will be more alluring than ever, and you might actually never want to return to shore."

I frown, tilting my head to the side. "Doubt it but okay. I don't want to risk messing things up."

It's almost a blessing that I've spent my life away from the water. It won't be anything new to my friends. I couldn't imagine surviving this trip if I did love the ocean and did all the things my friends like to do. I've hated myself for fearing the ocean, and now it's finally saving me from more than my morbid thoughts.

I can't help being sad, though. I've missed so much over the years.

"It won't be like this forever, Aves."

I smile at the nickname Giselle sometimes calls me. "You hope."

He chuckles. "I know so. Now, come on. We only have a few hours to enjoy the land."

Then I remember what he told me the first day I met him, and how he prefers the land over the sea. It's why he's here and not at some hidden merpeople oasis.

I just wonder if I'll still feel the same about land as he does. What if one day I don't? Pushing the thought away, I lace my fingers through Carter's. I can't think about all the stuff that doesn't concern me in this moment. Right now, I'm here with Carter, and he's who I want to be with regardless of the land or sea.

Palm trees stretch toward the bright blue sky, decorated with puffs of white clouds. The sea breeze lifts the stray blond hairs on my neck, pulling them from my bun. I tilt my head toward the sky, absorbing the golden sunlight.

On the blanket next to me, Carter leans back on his elbows, his bare chest too irresistible not to touch. I'm starting to think that apart from his work uniform that he won't have to wear for the rest of the trip for being a hero—*my* hero—that all Carter owns are board shorts. I can't complain about the lack of shirts though. My friends were right. He's incredibly sexy.

We sit alone on the long stretch of pebbly beach. Being early summer, the water is still quite cold to swim in without a wetsuit, and the waves where we are aren't worth surfing if you could call them waves at all. Two kayakers took off from a spot just down the way, but apart from them, we've been alone, unless you count the fishermen in their boats in the distance. Most of the tourists hang out on the beach near the marina where the sand is powdery soft.

"Favorite color?" I ask, running my toes over the smooth rocks at my feet.

He rubs his chin for a moment. "Green."

"Mine's gray."

"Gray?"

I nod. "I know. Did I mention I'm boring?"

He laughs. "Far from it. Favorite food?" We've been shooting questions back and forth for a few hours now, like we're trying to catch up with everything else that has tied us together with a pretty, knotted bow.

"Mexican. Cheese enchiladas in a red sauce to be more specific. Maybe tacos. Yours is seafood, isn't it?" Apparently, I'll start to really enjoy sushi. Giselle will be ecstatic that I might eventually go with her to Sushi Days, but even then, there's a huge difference between nibbling on a California roll that barely counts as sushi and taking a bite straight from a still moving fish. Yuck. Nope, I'd rather starve.

"You'd think, since I eat a whole lot of it but no. It's any type of dessert. I could eat it for every meal no matter what it is. I might even trade my tail for some if given the option."

Laughing, I playfully smack his arm. "Well, it's a good thing I bake."

"Don't mess with me."

I laugh. "I'm not. You get permission from the chef, and I'll make dessert tonight."

His eyes light up, causing me to laugh. It's the same look all my friends give me when I tell them I've been busy in the kitchen. I was the one who ended up baking the triple fudge brownie batter cake for Matty's birthday to save Sapphire after her failed attempt at using an oven.

"I'm holding you to it," he says, brushing his fingers along my arm.

Leaning in, he rests his head against mine. We sit together, our bodies touching, as small waves lap at the pebbly shore. With anyone else, the sudden quiet would force me to make small talk, but with Carter, I can just sit and enjoy our peaceful surroundings without a single word.

I draw my gaze to the stretch of clear water before us. The crystalline sky meets the turquoise water in the horizon in a gradient of mesmerizing blues. In the distance, a pod of dolphins swim just offshore, a few jumping and diving, splitting the far off waves as they play in the water that whispers for me to step in.

A strange feeling washes over me. I watch another dolphin propel from the sea, barely splashing as it dives back under. Jealousy sneaks through my mind, causing me to shrug away from Carter to push to my feet. All I want to do is get a closer look at the creatures that I now share the sea with. In this moment, being on land doesn't feel right like it used to.

Before Carter has a chance to react, I stride to the lapping waves, allowing them to wash over my bare feet. My mind screams to back away, warning me of the dangers of the ocean, but my heart—the spark of my mermaid essence—begs me to stroll in a little farther.

"Ava, what are you doing?" Carter asks from behind me.

I point my finger at the dolphins. "Aren't they beaut—" As the words escape my lips, a tingling sensation crawls from my heart and down my torso to my legs. Cramps grip at my toes, sending me stumbling to the pebbly shore. A small wave laps over my legs, soaking my dress.

Terror washes over me as I realize what's happening.

"Carter!" My voice echoes through the air. "It's happening! I can't stop."

My back arches, cramps seizing my spine. Fear shoots through me, the struggle between wanting to dive into the ocean and the more dominant part of me not wanting anything to do with it, threatening to tear me apart.

I'm not even in a foot of water, but it doesn't make a difference. My body craves to transform, *needs* to transform. Resisting only makes me nauseated. The problem with transforming among the lapping waves is that if I sprout my tail in this spot, I won't be able to drag myself into the water. My arms already feel weak from last night's swim.

Cerulean scales sprout from my skin, sending tears into my eyes. Each scale glitters with a metallic sheen in the sunlight like they have a mirrored surface. I blink a few dozen times, wishing them away. But wishing doesn't work. There won't be a miracle to stop me from changing now.

My breathing quickens, full blown panic consuming me. The ridges of my pectoral fins emerge on my forearms, and my now sharp nails scratch lines into the pebbles. In just a few moments, I'll be a mermaid for anyone to stumble upon.

This can't be happening. Why is this happening? Carter had warned of the risk, but I didn't think it was that big of a possibility. I didn't think I'd end up in this form again for another month.

Carter sweeps one of his arms under my transforming legs while cradling my back in his other. He charges into the ocean, the cool, salty water muting the silent screams echoing through my mind. Relief courses through me, my body reacting to the ocean the deeper Carter takes me. He doesn't stop holding me until he's waist deep, and then he lets me go only to tug me by my arms, forcing me under.

My blurry vision clears, my sight adjusting to the water. Carter tugs my dress over my head in a quick motion, stopping my dorsal fin from ripping the fabric. I try to shimmy out of my bikini bottoms, but another series of cramps rush through me. The side strap starts to rip, and Carter helps me take them off as quickly as he did my dress before shoving them in our bag. I have no time for embarrassment, because a second later, my legs fuse together, a numbness rushing over them, and then I flick my tail, diving deeper and away from Carter in his human form.

My mouth fills with water, and I breathe my first breath of the ocean, the burning in my lungs dissipating. My heart hangs heavy behind my ribcage, my mind clouding with terror just thinking about how close I was to becoming a mermaid on land. It was easy to treat last night's transformation as a dream, more of an inconvenience. Now that I triggered it in broad daylight, on a beach that could've been full of people, I realize how awful this whole situation really is. How quickly my normal life is slipping from my fingers to be dragged out to sea by the unforgiving waves of the ocean that just refuses to let me go, even all these years later after taking my sister when it was unable to steal me away, too.

I spin around in the clear water with no idea of what to do next. I'm too afraid to break through the surface, but Carter isn't here with me. What if he's waiting for me to transform back? I don't think I have enough energy to do so in this moment. But if I don't, someone could see me. It'd end badly.

Swimming in a quick circle, I assess my surroundings. The water is shallow enough that if I stretch upright, my tail will sweep the sandy bottom. I'm unnervingly close to the shore. Someone snorkeling could swim up on me and then I'd have no idea what to do. Stop them and beg them to keep my secret? Maybe they wouldn't see me at all. Carter wasn't specific. He said we were safe in the ocean, but what if a person was in the ocean, too?

"Ava, calm down. There's no one around, and if they were, they can't see us. We're safe." Carter's voice rings in my mind. He swims up next to me in his merman form, taking me into his arms.

"But I can't change back," I say, panic lining the thoughts I project to him. Pushing a bubble through my lips to calm myself down, I peer around us again like I'll suddenly spot a bunch of people. But the ocean only holds aquatic life.

Bright green sea grass drifts back and forth with the waves like it's blowing in a breeze. Starfish cling to the rocky bottom while small fish jet around. Sunlight dances across the rippling water overhead close enough that if Carter flicked his tail, we could feel the fresh air on our skin.

"Then why don't we go for a swim? I could tell how much you wanted to see the dolphins," he says, lacing his fingers with mine to pull me deeper into the surf.

It takes me a moment to orient myself with the water, flipping my tail to propel myself alongside Carter as he speeds off faster than any fish I've ever seen. He navigates the bottom of the shallows, staying deep enough and forcing us to move fast enough past the boats that fish the kelp paddies.

When we reach the end of the kelp forest, Carter slows,

spiraling around me. His tail slips against mine as he swims below me, barely an inch away. His fingers cling to my waist, guiding me to spin with him through the water. My blond hair floats around us, half pulled from my bun, veiling the view of the underwater world.

Grazing his lips against mine, he kisses me softly, half-smiling against my mouth. It's playful, teasing me, testing me for a reaction. An image of my sparkling eyes appears in my head as Carter's mind collides with mine. It's a side effect of his kiss, of who we are, and it makes me want to kiss him more deeply, to know him on a level no one could ever experience.

He grins at my reaction, and I hold him closely. The ridge across my waist rubs against his, sending tingles through me. Carter picks up speed, swimming without looking where we're going, and I can't stop thinking about the feeling of his stomach against mine.

He pulls away, a strange look crossing his face. Something holds him back from letting his emotions take control, and without words, I can see that I'm driving him a little crazy in a good way. The intensity of his gaze burns through me, and he tugs me along even faster. With him, I don't even have to really swim. I just float along with him, saving my energy.

A high-pitched, melodious sound unlike anything I've ever heard cuts through the water, drawing my attention away from Carter's pouty lips. I can't see where the noise is coming from, and I don't ask Carter what it is. I'm afraid that if I speak, this surreal moment will end.

He concentrates on weaving in out of a school of bright orange fish sparkling in the water like a sunset when they catch the light from above that beams rays around us. On the sand not far below, leopard sharks glide over the bottom, hunting for their next meal. There's at least a dozen, all on the smaller side, and Carter dips us down and swims right over them so I can study the beautiful pattern of spots on their backs. They don't bother us, just swimming along like we're not even there.

"We have no predators in the sea," he explains, his voice cutting through my mind, clearing the daze that holds me in a rainbow bubble. Reaching down, he runs his fingers gently above the animal without touching it. He flips to swim under me, facing upward to look at me. Holding out his hand, he presses two fingers gently against my chest, over my heart. "Our essence protects us."

I didn't even think about the possibility of being hunted by greater predators—everything too mesmerizing to even put those thoughts in my mind. The only fear I have is the silhouette of a boat crossing overhead. It's strange for me to fear what's above the water and not below for once.

Carter wraps his arms around my waist and propels us far from the shallows into the open water of the blue sea. I cling onto him, pressing against him so no water cuts between us. His heartbeat races against my chest, and I bury my face in his neck as the underwater world blurs around us.

Another high-pitched sound pulses through the water. It's like a bell ringing, bouncing through the current, playing an underwater melody just for me. It isn't until I see the dolphins that I realize it's the pod that creates the magical sound. I'm hearing them with new ears, because they sound nothing like the squeaks and shrill calls I've heard a dozen times on TV.

Carter slows, trailing along next to the pod with over two dozen dolphins as they coast along the surface above us. A female dolphin and her pup dive down and swim alongside us. Another one, a much larger male, chatters from our other side, and I reach out and run my hand along its smooth, gray side. Breaking away from Carter, I keep pace with the dolphin, its tinkering calls bouncing around me in a harmonious song.

A smile crosses my face, and I dance through the water, the

pod surrounding me, nudging me toward the surface. As the water warms slightly, and I can see the sun overhead, the large male nudges my side, pushing me up. If he continues his playful gesture, I'll be forced to break the surface.

"Ava!" Carter calls. "Dive. There's a boat up ahead."

But I'm trapped. The dolphins swim and bump against me, trapping me within their formation. A few ascend the short distance to the surface and pop out, flying through the air. It's enough to draw the attention of any nearby boaters.

"They think this is a game," I call through my mind.

Two dolphins flank each of my sides, their flippers slapping against me. They swim close enough that their smooth bodies graze mine, forcing me to keep their pace as they prepare to launch from the water.

Closing my eyes, I cover my face with my hands. I flick my tail, trying to gently push the dolphins away. It's a matter of seconds before my face will break the surface. The boaters are about to get the show of their lives. And with everyone having cameras, I'll be captured on film for the world to see.

I bet Carter will regret saving me now.

A moment before the dolphins can push me up, forcing me to jump out of the water, something grips my caudal fin, yanking me away from the pod. They launch up and out of the water without me and then dive back under, continuing their peek-a-boo show. Pain sears through me, the sheer force enough to make me scream underwater. Carter drags me down deep enough that it'd be impossible to catch sight of us even if they'd just assume we are some sort of fish. Our bodies blend well enough with our surroundings that it'd be hard to see us at all though.

My tears mix with the water, and I curl my tail up to stroke my fingers along the base where Carter grabbed me to pull me free from the pod. It hurts to move, like I've dislocated whatever new bones lie under my scales.

Carter treads next to me, gently fanning his tail back and forth. He lowers himself so I don't have to move much while he inspects my tail. His warm fingers brush along my scales, a tingling sensation coursing through me. The pain eases some under his fingers, but it's not because of anything he's done.

His shadowed teal eyes meet mine as a series of cramps rushes through me. The sudden pain radiating through my tail is no longer caused by being jerked down but because I'm transforming again. The shock of the pain must've set me off.

"Carter!" My words shout from my mind.

We're at least two-hundred feet below the surface, and there's nothing I can do as my human form threatens to take control, leaving me breathless.

HEAD ABOVE WATER

WITH LIGHTNING SPEED, CARTER SCOOPS me into his arms and zooms toward the surface. Without air in my lungs, the pressure change doesn't affect me like it would've had I breathed in air to dive. Carter pushes me to the surface, my transformation back into my human form completing when I break through to air. Ocean water sprays from my nose and mouth as my lungs jump into action.

Kicking my legs, I tread water, my head bobbing up and down. Pain radiates in my ankle, and I push past it. If I want to continue to breathe in the salty air, I don't have a choice. I blink through my blurry vision until my eyes clear and search the area for the boat Carter had mentioned, but it's already en route toward the island miles away.

My muscles ache, exhaustion hitting me hard like it did after my transformation this morning. It'd be easy to reach the shore within minutes if I still had a tail, but now, I can hardly manage to keep my head above water.

The chill of the water makes me shiver. "Carter? Carter, no one's around," I say, waving my arms under the water. I'm not even sure he can hear me, but I know it's the reason he didn't surface with me. Had the boat been here, I could've claimed to have been swept away or something.

He surfaces next to me an instant later.

"I'm too tired to swim. I'll never make it." My voice is

barely audible over the roar of the sea.

"Try to transform back. The distance might be too far for me to swim you back in my human form, and it's not safe for me to coast the surface." He cups my face in his hands. "You can do this."

Closing my eyes, I wait for the cramps to seize my muscles but nothing happens. No tingling sensation. Nothing but the ache in my ankle to remind me that in this form, I'm no match for the ocean.

"I can't concentrate. My ankle hurts pretty badly," I say. "It's what triggered the transformation back."

His brows lower over his blue-green eyes. He bobs under, sending a small wave over me. I can't see him clearly, but his warm fingers touch my ankle. It makes me highly aware that I'm not exactly dressed.

A second later, he pops up next to me. "It's bruised, but I don't think it's broken. You're still moving it well. You'll probably heal within an hour or so—one of the benefits of being a mermaid."

"Think we should wait it out and see if I can transform in a bit?" An hour is an awfully long time to tread in place, though I know Carter would help me.

His jaw twitches. "We might be missed."

"Then they'll have to miss us, because I can't swim or transform." Annoyance washes through me. "This whole situation is ridiculous. I probably deserve to be found out here floating half-naked."

Carter doesn't smile like I expect him to. "Don't blame yourself. I should've been more careful. If I hadn't grabbed you the way I did—"

"Those dolphins would have forced me out of the water. This isn't your fault," I say, interrupting him.

He brushes his wet hair from his face. "But I—"

I interrupt his words with a kiss, his tense muscles relaxing when I slide my arms around his neck. Slowly pulling away, I say, "Stop. Blame isn't going to help me get back to the shore."

"You're right. But I will. I have an idea." He tugs the strap of our bag over his shoulder and pulls out my half ripped bikini bottoms before handing them to me. I guess I won't be trying to transform back into a mermaid after all.

After a few embarrassing failed attempts, I manage to slide my legs through my bottoms. Carter smirks when I huff out a breath and meet his eyes. Slapping my hand against the water, I splash him in the face, and he sinks under the surface before circling me a few times. His tail brushes my torso, and I can't stop the excitement forcing my annoyance and fear away.

He stops in front of me and bobs his head back up from the water. I suck in a small breath at his sudden closeness, and he reaches out and pushes wet hair from my face. "You have to stop looking at me like that."

"Like what?" I know well enough what he's talking about. I can't hide the desire to kiss him, to trail my fingers along his muscular shoulders, the desire to stay near him.

"Like you don't want me to take you back to the shore."

"Maybe I don't."

He sinks back under and swims around me again before popping up. "Ava," he says, the sound of my name sending my heart racing. "Be careful what you suggest. You have friends—you have family—all waiting for you on land."

It's enough to force my lingering thoughts away. I could never just give them all up for the sea. They'd be devastated if I disappeared without warning. I couldn't put my parents through that. Not again.

"You're right," I say, even though a part of me wants him to be wrong. "I guess we should try to get back." Back to the secrets, to the pretending. "You said you had an idea?"

"I'm going to need you to hold your breath for a bit, okay? It's not safe to swim the surface with you, but I can take you under. It'll be slow going, but unless you transform back, I don't know of a better way."

I pout my lip. "I'm sorry for being so much trouble, Carter."

Water splashes between us as he stares intently into my eyes like he can peer into my very essence. Wrapping my arms around him, I run my fingers along the short dorsal fin that travels his spine. He shudders, leaning forward to kiss me. I catch a glimpse of what I look like in his eyes, our kiss letting me peek into his head.

When he pulls away, he says, "You're worth the trouble, you know. Like I said before, I don't regret anything."

I smile. "How did I get so lucky?"

"Lucky? I—"

"You saved my life. Given me so much more than I ever thought possible." I trace my finger along his jaw. "I don't know how I'll ever repay you."

"You don't owe me anything," he says.

I kiss him again, imagining what it would be like to trail my hands along his ripped body. I must've projected my own thoughts through our kiss, because he releases a low moan into my lips. He eases away and dips back under the cool water. With the heat of him near me constantly, I'm no longer even cold.

He surfaces again, turning his back toward me, and motions for me to slide my hands around his neck. My chest presses against his broad shoulders, and I breathe heavily in his ear as nerves tighten my chest.

"Ready, Ava?" he asks lowly, his voice sounding as breathless as I feel.

"As ready as I'll ever be."

"Okay, take a deep breath and hold on."

Sucking a long breath into my lungs, I tighten my hold on Carter, wrapping my legs around his waist while pressing my cheek into his shoulder blade. In a quick motion, he dives under, taking me with him.

My ears pop the deeper we descend, but I can't see anything with my normal sight. Carter swims too quickly, the world zooming by as we head toward the shore. To calm my racing heart, I count the seconds ticking by the longer I hold my breath. My lungs burn by the time I count to fifty-eight, just under a minute. Squeezing his shoulder, I alert him that I need air, and he ascends to the surface, and I release him and break through the water. He never surfaces and tugs me back under the moment I suck more air into my lungs.

We continue on in this stop and go motion for what feels like eternity. My head swims with dizziness from having to hold my breath with only moments to refill my lungs. Just when I feel my hold loosen on Carter, he slows down and pushes me back to the surface.

My chest heaves, and I gasp a few burning, salty breaths. Carter circles around me a few more times but doesn't pull me back under to my relief. The shore lingers in front of me but still quite a bit of distance away. A few boats leisurely float in the distant harbor, but luckily, we have a clear path to the shore from here.

After a few minutes, Carter bursts to the surface next to me. He spits out ocean water before inhaling a long breath. Rubbing a hand over his face, he clears the water from his eyes before smiling at me like this is the most fun he's had in a while.

"And you thought you were trouble," he says, treading the water next to me. "It's not every day I get to have a beautiful girl cling to my back."

Heat crawls up my neck to blossom in my cheeks. I can't think of a response, so I don't say anything at all. His smile widens as he closes the distance. Wrapping his arms around me, he stops me from bobbing under. His soft board shorts graze my thigh, his legs brushing against mine.

Without saying another word, he swims forward, pulling me with him toward the shore. The waves push us along, and I nearly fall over when my feet touch solid ground. Carter takes most of my weight, and I limp toward the pebbly beach right where we left our blanket and basket. I pull Carter to the ground, resting my back on the smooth rocks, and he lies next to me, catching his breath.

"Please, tell me it's not always going to be like this. I don't think I can handle being so out of control all the time. I thought this ring was supposed to help." I wave my hand over my half ripped bottoms and bruised ankle.

Carter leans up on his elbows. "It does, believe me. If you weren't wearing it, you'd never change back. Your body's adjusting, Ava. It'll take a while to figure it all out."

I sigh. "I don't have time, though. You saw how fast I ran into the ocean. What if that would've happened while we were on the yacht?"

"Then we'd figure it out."

Sitting up, he leans over me. He blocks the sun from my view as he grazes his lips against mine, kissing all my worries away. I react to his touch, my back arching up to him, and he slides his warm fingers around my bare lower back before pulling me into his lap. My fingers trace up his firm chest, it rising and falling under my hands. He moans when I wrap my legs around his waist and kiss him more deeply, imagining what it would be like for him to explore my body with his gentle touch.

He breaks away from me, a smile on his lips. The adrenaline from our near disastrous swim runs hot through me, and I realize that I projected my desires into his mind.

But I don't care. I hope it drives him crazy. I want nothing more than to tempt him back into the ocean where we can find privacy from the world.

"Ava," he whispers. "Ava look at me."

I slowly open my eyes to meet his intense, startling gaze. His ocean eyes travel from my mouth down to my heaving chest to my ripped bikini bottoms. His desire mirrors my own but something holds him back.

"Ava, your thoughts." He shakes his head. "As much as I want to carry you back to the water, I can't."

"Why not?" The question surprises even me. It's like the ocean hypnotizes me, trying to trick me to return. If Carter wasn't in better control than me, I'm sure I'd remain a mermaid forever.

He inhales another deep breath. "I might regret this later, but you belong on land. You belong with your friends and your family."

"And you?" I ask.

"Right now, I belong where you are."

His words hang in the air. My attraction to him is crazy intense, but it makes me wonder if this is all because of the spark we share.

Would I still like him as much if I were still human? Would he like me? Does it even matter? I don't even know what's going to happen after this dreamy vacation is over, and I have to return to my normal life back in Azure Waters.

"What about when we return home?"

He pulls me closer. "If you're worried about what happens to us, don't. We'll make this work, okay?"

A sliver of doubt creeps into my mind, but I push it away. I can't think about what happens next when I'm still trying to figure out what's happening now.

All I know is that if I survived today in the water, I can survive anything.

I'm going to be okay.

DREAM ABOUT THE LAND

"OH, MY GOD, AVS! WHAT the hell happened?" Giselle jogs in our direction from her spot on the dock while everyone waits for our ride back to the Ocean Jewel.

I'm a mess. My half wet hair hangs limply around my shoulders, my ballerina bun nonexistent since I first hit the water. My damp sundress clings to me around my thighs, and she'd have a million more questions if she saw the rip on the side of my bikini bottoms. My slight limp doesn't help any. My ankle feels a lot better than it did, but it's still annoying to put too much weight on it.

I lean into Carter. "You know me. I'm accident prone."

Her eyes widen. "You fell in the ocean *again*? Seriously, maybe you shouldn't even be standing on the dock. Are you okay?"

Pouting my lip slightly, I try to appear frazzled even though I'm calmer than I've ever been. "Yeah, I'm okay now. My sandal got caught when we were walking down the beach, and then with my stupid luck, I got knocked over by a wave. I thought I was far enough away, but the ocean just snuck up on me." I turn to glance at Carter who holds a straight face through my flat-out lies. "I warned Carter I don't do well with water. He believes me now."

He smirks. "Hey, I've always believed you."

Giselle tugs me away, hooking her arm through mine.

"Don't you know you don't have to impress that boy? He's madly in-like with you."

My shoulders shake from my laugh. "In-like, Gi?"

"Duh. I read it in *Teen Romance Weekly*. It's like this instant attraction you have for someone. I could tell from the moment he brought your bag into our room—total in-like." Giselle smiles over her shoulder. "Right, Carter?"

"Right, Giselle," Carter says, clearly unfazed by Giselle talking about him like he's not listening from two feet behind us. He's more amused than anything.

"See, Aves. Now no more falling into the ocean. Saving your ass is going to get boring." She laughs at her own joke, which makes me laugh. If I had actually fallen in the water, she'd have a point.

"You always have the best advice," I remark, a hint of sarcasm in my voice.

It only makes her smile wider. "I know."

When the inflatable motorboat arrives to pick us up, Matty, Sapphire, Logan, and Daisy ride to the yacht first before it turns around to get the rest of us. An ounce of fear prickles in my mind as ocean water sprays across my face. Carter wraps his arms around me, squeezing my arm slightly. I have no idea if sea mist could trigger my transformation, but I'm deathly afraid of finding out.

"Relax. Don't think about it," Carter whispers.

I bury my face into his damp shirt without responding.

My fears prove to be unwarranted. We reach the hydraulic platform, and a crew member, who Carter greets as Brooks, helps me onto the yacht. Everyone heads back to the main deck to our staterooms. Carter heads to the lower deck to grab a few things while I head to my own room to shower and change into dry clothes.

Carter sits on the edge of my bed when I stroll into my

room after my shower, a towel wrapped around my undergarments. His eyes trail up my body before he smiles the smile he saves just for me. A dimple peeks on his cheek, and he motions me to sit next to him.

The way he watches me excites me so much that I can't stop myself as I unwrap my towel and head to my built-in dresser to grab a pair of pajama bottoms and tank top. Even though Carter has glimpsed me naked, being alone in the room and in clothes that aren't meant for swimming seems to change something between us. I'm not standing here because I'm about to transform. I'm standing here because I want him to see me as more than the girl he has given his spark of life to. I want him to see me as who I've been all my life without the allure and magic of the sea.

I pull my tank top over my head and meet his gaze. He sits utterly still on the bed, his hands gripping his knees. His chest rises and falls with every breath, and it's easy to forget all the complicated emotions swirling through me—my fears of revealing our secret, the fear of what happens next, the confusion of what to expect from my future—none of that seems to matter.

Getting caught up in the moment, I cross the small distance until I'm standing in front of him, sliding my arms around him. Pushing him back, I lie on top of him, pressing against him.

He leans up and kisses me. As his tongue caresses mine, a tiny shock erupts through me, traveling from my lips and down my neck to stop at my heart. Even while we're both dry in this room, in our human forms, he still reminds me of the ocean. The slight saltiness to his kisses, how he smells of the crisp air, how his muscles remind me of all the times he guided me through the water...

"Ava," he whispers. "We should stop."

His voice brings me back from our private underwater

world. I sigh, rolling off him, and snuggle next to him, my heart still racing.

"Your thoughts are making it difficult to remember why I chose land over the sea in the first place. They might trigger your transformation."

I twist my lips into a half-smile. "I can't help myself."

"Then let me help you."

He bends down, pressing his lips to mine. A million images flash through my mind—his memories. He shows me what I looked like the moment he saw me, staring into the distance with scrunched brows, my bag dangling from my fingertips. The image transforms to the first night on the dining terrace, me laughing with Giselle and Sapphire, and then to the image of me watching my friends on jet skis on the sundeck. The final memory he projects of me is when we sat on the lower deck moments before I fell. How I smiled and walked beside him, wearing his sweatshirt. How I closed my eyes when I ate a cookie. All of the memories are of me standing on my own two legs.

As I envision the moments of me in my human form, it reminds me of the me before all this happened. I remember all the times Giselle and I danced in her bedroom, how I'd spend my mornings running the paths along the beach without ever looking at the water. I'm even reminded of my favorite pair of jeans—all the little things I enjoy that I can't enjoy in the water.

The memories travel from my mind to Carter's, and he kisses me harder, deeper, until the only thing left on my mind is him as he is right now. The way his leg rests between mine, the way the fabric of his shirt pulls tight against his chest, though I can still see his heart glowing with every beat. How his dry hair falls over, longer on top than on the sides. The way his warm breath tickles my bottom lip when he hovers an inch away, pressing his forehead against mine. It's something I can't feel in the water. All that he is on land is completely different than who he is in the sea, but it's him all the same.

I pull away breathlessly and stare into his oceanic eyes, sparkling brightly against his deeply tanned skin that holds the warmth of the sun. It takes everything in me to not lose myself in their depths. I trail my gaze to his lips instead but then turn it to our hands, afraid I'll lose myself in his kisses next. His presence is all consuming in my small room.

"I think I understand now," I whisper. "I think I figured out how the transformation works for me." It's caused by a battle of wills between my heart and my mind, and I must disconnect them. I must sever the two and realign them. The land is where I need to be. It's where I need to stay. The ocean already stole so much from me. I refuse to allow it to take my future, too.

He smiles, pushing my hair behind my ear. "Want to test it out?"

I think about it for a moment. "No, not right now. I think I've had enough of the water for today. I just want to dream about the land."

With those words, he kisses me again, showing me everything he loves about the human world through his eyes.

Sunlight trickles through the window, warming my skin even more than Carter does. My hand rests on his chest, my stomach and chest cuddling against his side. I've been awake for a while, just lying here on the bed that should be too small for the both of us, but we somehow make it work.

I tried to sleep more, but my mind wouldn't let me. All I could think about was how unreal this feels, like at any second I'll awake from a strange dream. I've been through a lot the last few days, and it's hard to think about anything else. It gives me a major case of anxiety comparable to what I used to feel just looking at the ocean, but my anxiety now falls onto the fact that

I'm afraid I rely too heavily on Carter. He just makes it so easy to like him and trust him. But my anxiety doesn't stop me from wanting to stay by his side. It doesn't stop me from believing in his words, about how we'll somehow make it work. At least, until it doesn't.

You liked him before you were a mermaid. It'll be fine. I push the thoughts away because I'm not so sure. And that's what really bothers me most. How can I be certain about anything when we're bound by this secret? Should I even care? The old me might've. The old me would think I was crazy for feeling like I don't want to be without him. I can't say that what I feel is love, because even that thought is definitely insane, but what I feel is more like a deep-seated need. Our heartbeats share the same rhythm for a reason. But Carter doesn't talk about that. He skips around anything that involves him saving my life.

Shifting, I look at the ceiling instead of Carter. The aches in my bones no longer bother me, and my ankle feels as good as new, no signs of bruising from when Carter ripped me free from the pod of dolphins.

Carter moves when I sit up. He stretches his arms over his head, arching his back, and my eyes linger at the tightening of his muscular stomach as his shirt lifts up on his torso. Reaching out my hand, I run my fingers along the curve of his sharp hips and up his side. He sucks in a breath under my touch, and I slide into his arms, my messy hair veiling our faces, and he kisses me softly.

A knock sounds on the door, drawing my attention away from him. Giselle calls my name through the wood. I groan, getting to my feet, and cross the room. I crack the door open, meeting Giselle's overly ecstatic grin. She presses her face into the opening to peer past me at Carter rubbing the sleep from his face.

"You have to get ready, stat. While you two were busy

sleeping, we docked in the bay, and we have until tonight to see the city." Giselle pushes the door open and saunters past me into the room.

Carter lifts the curtain to reveal the Golden Gate Bridge hazed in the distance. I almost wish it wasn't there, because it means our vacation is halfway over and in just a few days, I'll have to figure out how to deal with my new life at home.

"So no ocean activities?" I ask.

She grins. "Nope. Just shopping, dining, and exploring."

I turn my eyes to Carter. "You don't have to come if it doesn't sound like fun." Unlike Matty and Logan, Carter has a pass from being subjected to the hours we're bound to spend checking out every store we pass.

"And miss showing you around?" The faint memories of San Francisco trickle through my mind, hints from Carter's life growing up.

A warm apartment, decorated in blues and whites, in a square complex with a pool in the center near the water springs to my mind. The flash of a green sign hanging from a restaurant in an old machine shop with an amazing view of the water comes next. People walking along a string of shops in a packed downtown area, sprawling hills of eclectic houses, the same bridge I stare at through the window, but glowing against the dark night—all the memories he's shared through our kisses are enough to make it feel like I've known him all his life.

"You grew up here?" Giselle asks. "That's so cool. You definitely can't bail on us then. Don't worry, Matty and Logan don't get a pass so you won't be forced to hold our shopping bags alone."

Carter's eyes dart to mine for a second, and I laugh, nudging Giselle to the door. If he can survive a day with my friends on land, I'm pretty sure things just might work out between us.

Giselle laughs when I close the door on her so she doesn't

scare Carter off. He leans back on his elbows, a smile playing on his lips.

I relax my shoulders and puff a breath of air out of my lungs. "There's still time to change your mind."

He pulls me forward, and I sink into his lap. "Nope. I've showed you my world, Ava. You can't keep me from yours."

I kiss him. "If you can handle it, it'll be your world too, you know."

His eyes darken with something I can't decipher, but as quickly as it came, it disappears. "I'd like that. More than you'll ever understand."

After spending the morning shopping in Union Square, we head to Fisherman's Wharf by cable car for lunch. As Carter put it, it's the most touristy thing we could do to see San Francisco.

"Why didn't I pick a university here?" Sapphire says.

We stand in front of a giant, dull-yellow sign with a crab in the center introducing Fisherman's Wharf of San Francisco. The circular sign is shaped like an old boat steering wheel, matching the nautical décor of the lively, crowded wharf.

Matty kisses her cheek. "Because you're going to UCLA with me." As an heir to her grandmother's beauty and fashion empire fortune, Sapphire can do whatever she wants. If she changes her mind about moving into the penthouse apartment in downtown LA that she already signed a lease for with Matty, she could easily do so.

She giggles. "Oh, yeah."

He laughs, tugging her away from us. Chloe, Daisy, and Logan trail behind them, but I don't move. Giselle spins around, taking in the view, before smiling at me. In the corner of my eye, I watch Carter watch me.

"Are you two going to college?" Carter asks, drawing my attention away from my best friend.

"Yup. UCSD," Giselle says for me. "We're going house hunting when we get back. I want a place on the beach like I have now, but away from my parents. I know it'll take Ava some convincing. She already told me we better be somewhere she can no longer hear the ocean."

I suck in my bottom lip. "Actually, I think I might be okay with that idea now."

She tilts her head to the side like I've said the strangest thing in the world—which it probably is coming from me. I haven't thought much about college in the fall, but I'm really thankful we decided to stay close to home—my mom guilted me into throwing away all the brochures for the schools in the dead center of the country away from all bodies of water because she wanted me to stay near home.

Giselle turns and pokes her finger into my chest. "Who are you and what have you done with my best friend?"

I laugh, flicking her hand away. "You're going to argue now that I agreed to move on the beach with you?"

She smiles. "You're right. You better not change your mind, though."

I don't even think that's possible. "I won't."

Hooking her arm through mine, she drags me in the direction where our friends wait for us. Carter strolls silently behind us, and I wish I could hear what's on his mind. After a moment, he slides up next to me and laces his fingers through mine. He squeezes my fingers, his eyes unusually serious, and if Giselle wasn't pulling me along, I'd stop to turn to him.

All through lunch, the others laugh and talk, making it a competition to tell the most embarrassing stories about each other. I recount a story about Giselle and I stumbling upon Matty hiding naked under Sapphire's bed because they thought we were her parents coming home early from one of their fundraising galas.

Matty rubs his reddening face. "What about you, dude?" he asks. "I can't be the only one caught naked somewhere."

"Somewhere?" Sapphire says. "Did you forget the time you and Logan thought it'd be funny to streak through the middle of my beach party last year? Remember how you left your clothes too close to the water and ended up having to leave in a towel."

Carter laughs. "That's happened to you, too?" While I doubt Carter would streak through a party, he's probably lost his clothes a few times over the years during his transformation.

The two boys bump fists across the table, and I lean back and enjoy how nice everything is in this moment. Carter fits in so well with my friends; I almost can't imagine him ever being born in the water.

After everyone finishes lunch, we split up to wander Fisherman's Wharf separately. Carter holds my hand, guiding me to a pier where dozens of tourists watch a ton of sea lions bask in the sunshine while some swim through the rippling water.

The melodic sounds of the sea lions hum in my ears like they're singing a song just for me, definitely different from the cacophonous noise I'm used to when I've encountered the animals in a time before we shared an underwater world.

A sea lion circles the water under the pier below us and jumps up, opening its mouth in what I can only describe as a smile. Carter tugs me back instinctively like this playful creature will somehow share our secret.

Carter waves his hand, and the sea lion swims away and slides back onto its wooden dock with the rest of his colony.

"He was just being friendly," I say, smirking. A few more of the sea lions dive into the water.

"Exactly," Carter says. "So were the dolphins."

I roll my eyes. "I'm not going to jump off the pier to join them."

"Until you start feeling the pull."

"I told you I think I get how it works for me," I argue. "Want me to prove it?"

He shakes his head, his brown hair flying around with the motion. Sliding his hands around my waist, he pulls me from the guardrail of the pier. We stroll a few feet through the crowd, maneuvering around people taking pictures. An idea suddenly strikes me, and I pull my cell phone from my bag and hold it up to take one of me and Carter. Giselle and Daisy have been taking the most pictures, but if I only remember to take one, I want it to be of me and Carter.

Leaning down, he brushes his lips against mine, drawing my attention away from my phone. The sea lions chatter from next to us, trying their best to entice me to join them in the sea. It's enough to make me hide my face in Carter's shirt to block out the rest of the world for a second.

"Carter?" a feminine voice says from behind me.

Carter visibly stiffens under my touch and holds my chin to stop me from peering around when I jerk my head up. The sudden reaction sends fear trickling to my heart. My hands shake, dropping to my sides so Carter doesn't feel them. His stare jets from mine to the woman I can't see standing behind me.

"Who is it?" I whisper.

Pressing his lips to my ear, he says, "Why don't you go find Giselle? I'll meet you back at the yacht later, okay? And please, stay away from the water for now."

He kisses my forehead before pulling away, leaving me standing on the pier in confusion. I touch my fingers to the warm spot where he kissed my forehead. Spinning around, I search the crowd for Carter, but all I glimpse is his back as he strolls away with his arm around the shoulders of a woman.

Before anger and rejection can sneak up on me, the woman

glances over her shoulder, her blue-green eyes sparkling in the sunlight. She's absolutely gorgeous with her smooth, tanned skin, waves of dark hair the same color as Carter's, and a perfectly white smile. The resemblance is uncanny.

Carter's mom waves her fingers at me from over her shoulder, and I can't help sighing a breath of relief that he abandoned me on the spot. Because for some reason, I'm terrified to meet his mom. I don't know if it's because she's a mermaid or because she's the mom of the boy who used his one chance to transform someone into a mermaid on me. Or maybe, because meeting her makes things between us completely real.

10

MERPEOPLE TRADITIONS

CARTER BOARDS THE OCEAN JEWEL minutes after Ruby announced we're going to cruise the bay during sunset. I almost thought he wouldn't make it and was about to leave to wait for him on the dock.

When he enters the saloon, I gaze up from the unread book resting on my lap. Sitting with my legs curled under me, I've been hanging out alone for over an hour as the others chill on the sundeck. None of them complained about my absence, and I'm pretty sure Giselle knew I was worried about something though she never asked more after I told her Carter met up with his mom.

He slides onto the couch next to me, sinking against me. His head rests on my shoulder without saying anything for a long moment.

"Did you have a nice time with your mom?" I ask when I don't think he's going to say anything at all.

"I'm sorry for ditching you like that, but I—" His words cut off as he thinks about what to say.

"Your mom doesn't know about me. I get it," I say.

He shakes his head. "Yes and no."

"What is that supposed to mean?"

"I told her that I was seeing you." He rubs his hands over his knees.

"But not about..." I wave my hand over me to show what I

can't risk saying out loud in case someone is listening.

"She'll find out soon enough," he says quietly.

I frown. "We're leaving later tonight. Are you going back out? Staying?" The thought of having to make the trip back down the coast to Azure Waters alone scares me.

"We'll be okay if they leave without us. I can catch us up."

I swallow. "Us? You mean..." Oh, God. If he means what I think he means, I'm pretty sure I'm going to pass out from nerves.

He turns to me, taking my hands in his. "If I could get us out of it, I would, but it has to do with merpeople tradition, and she saw us. But it'll be okay, Ava. They're going to love you."

Whoa. Holy crap. Merpeople tradition? I want to ask him more about it, but I can't stop thinking that this is next level relationship stuff. *He turned you into a mermaid. Now that's next level stuff.*

"And if they don't?"

A smile dances in his eyes. "They will. I have to warn you, though. What I did was kind of a big deal."

Obviously. "You think?" My voice rises higher than I expect it to. "You can't just call them and tell them? God, Carter. What if I can't even—" I wave my hand over my legs again to silently finish my sentence.

He grins, leaning closer, his breath tickling my ear. "What happened to the girl who wanted to prove to me she could?"

Damn him. My heart drops into my stomach. "She ran away."

He laughs while pulling me to my feet. "I guess I'll have to chase after her, huh?" He slides his arm over my shoulders, guiding me toward the elevator. "Now, come on. You need to pack a bag. Dinner is at nine."

★★★

We sneak away from the others when they settle down for a movie marathon after dinner. No one noticed that all I did was push food around my plate, because I'm pretty sure if I eat anything now, I'll throw up from nervousness.

The swim deck is empty when we reach it, only a small wall light illuminating the area before us. The yacht moves slowly through the water of the bay before heading back out to sea. By morning, we'll be on the way home with plans to anchor for the day for water activities tomorrow as we travel along the coast.

Rubbing my bare arms, I gaze down at my now least favorite torn bikini. I hope it doesn't take all night to catch up. Carter swears it won't. He swears he's taken this trip several times, and Captain Briggs never strays from his itinerary.

"You should undress here," Carter says, handing me the waterproof bag with a towel and our clothes.

Sighing, I don't argue. He unties his board shorts and tugs them off before handing them to me to put in the bag. I don't even realize I'm staring right at his night shadowed body until he strolls closer to take the bag from my hands so I can slide my bottoms off.

I stand in front of him, half naked, but his eyes never leave mine. I toss him my bottoms to put in the bag and then move to stand next to him on the swimming platform. He secures the bag across his chest before taking my hand. It's a lot easier to jump from here than the sundeck, and it's dark enough that even if someone were to be staring at the ocean from above, they wouldn't see us.

"Ready?" Carter asks.

I'm not. But I don't tell him. Instead, I nod my head and jump with him into the glowing water.

My mind races as I hold my breath, orienting myself. Carter tugs me deeper and away from the yacht. He's already transformed by the time my lungs burn, needing to breathe. But I haven't changed yet.

You can do this, Ava. As the thought comes to me, I remember how good it feels to glide through the water, to explore the ocean's depth, how easy and uncomplicated the sea is compared to my human life. How mesmerizing Carter is swimming alongside me. How perfect things are.

Cramps seize my toes, traveling up my legs to my thighs. I arch my body, the muscles in my back tightening as my dorsal fin rises from my spine. My skin tingles, and scales grow over my legs in a beautiful, glimmering cerulean blue. I inhale a deep breath of the ocean, letting it fill my lungs and push out through my gills.

"That was much faster," Carter says, his voice swirling through my mind. "I knew you could do it."

His fingers link through mine, and he pulls me to swim forward, not giving me a moment to peer around the glowing water as my eyes adjust to the salty ocean. Navigating the water I'm unfamiliar with, Carter dives us deeper. I match his pace, staying right by his side. I'm not sure I'll ever be familiar with the ocean like Carter is. It makes me wonder how much he's seen and explored. I wonder what it would be like to keep swimming and never stop.

As we pass over seaweed, I trail my free hand over it, feeling the slimy plant against my fingers. Fish dart away from us, and we rush through the water too fast to even take much in. We reach the shallows, and Carter slows. It's as close as we can get to the shore in our merpeople forms without having to worry about stumbling upon someone.

"Think you can transform here and swim the rest of the way with me?" Carter asks, projecting his voice into my mind.

I nod even though I won't be sure until the process already starts. I hover below the surface, closing my eyes, imagining what it would be like to walk on the land, to dance with Giselle in my bedroom, to feel the air on my skin...

Nothing happens.

Not because I can't, but because I don't want it to. If I don't transform, I won't have to meet Carter's parents. Staying in the sea, exploring its vastness, is a lot more appealing at the moment.

"Ava?" Carter questions.

I turn to meet his gaze without answering.

"Please, try. For me."

Closing my eyes again, I wait for the muscle spasms to travel through my body. It takes longer than I expect, because even though my head wants to return to the land, my heart is still having trouble. Being a mermaid is the most amazing feeling, and I don't want to give it up so soon. I feel like I just changed minutes ago.

When my legs split apart, I kick to the surface and spit out the ocean water before sucking in a deep breath of cold air. Carter bobs up next to me, splashing me with a small wave. He slides his hand around my waist and pulls me with him, swimming with one arm. I can swim just fine without the help, but I like the feeling of our bodies next to each other in the water.

Up ahead, city lights glow brightly across the land. The moon sparkles its silver beams over the rippling water, like a dancing pathway that leads to the sandy shore. Carter tugs me through the waves, and we emerge on the beach. As much as I want to fall down and lie in the sand, I don't because I don't want to show up at Carter's parents' door covered in sand.

Carter shakes his wet hair, pelting me with cold water. Removing our bag from across his chest, he pulls out the towel and wraps it around my shoulders as I shiver. Goosebumps prickle over my skin. He rubs his strong hands down my arms, pushing the cold away.

His warm breath tickles my skin when he kisses my bare shoulder while sliding the towel down my back, stopping at my waist. His hands fall away, and he takes the towel to dry off. A moment later, he hands me the teal sundress I had picked out to wear. Keeping my back to him, I pull the strings on my bikini top and let it fall to the sand before pulling my dress over my head. Carter helps me tie the halter strings, his body close enough that I can feel his body heat.

I slide on my bikini bottoms under my dress before shaking the sand from my top to put it back in the bag. When I turn around, Carter's already dressed. He rubs the towel over his hair, letting it stick up in every direction.

He grins, tossing the towel back to me, and I wring out my hair the best I can before running the brush I brought through it. I wish I had a mirror to apply some makeup, but if I'm going to end up back in the water in a few hours, it'd be pointless.

My wet hair drapes down my back, clinging to my still-damp skin, but this is as good as it's going to get. Carter looks me up and down for a second, his eyes intently staring at me, his approval lingering in his dazzling smile.

When we reach a cement walking path, I slide into my flip flops while Carter remains barefooted. It takes less than twenty minutes to walk to his parents' apartment, the one I saw in his memories.

The three story building is just a few blocks away from the ocean. Green lawns and flowerbeds decorate the outside of the small complex. The U-shaped layout surrounds a swimming pool, every door facing the courtyard of the property.

A man smokes a cigarette on a small balcony across the way. He raises his hand to Carter and waves.

"Hello, Mr. Mooney. How's it going?" he asks the old man as we meander around the pool in his direction.

"Good, boy. You haven't visited in a while. Your mom says

you're working on a boat? Fishing?"

Carter shakes his head. "No, sir. Luxury cruises."

The man stomps out his cigarette, laughing. "Whatever pays the bills." He doesn't ask about me, and all I do is smile and say goodbye when he returns to his apartment.

Slowing down, Carter grips my hand in his. He guides me to the ground level apartment below the man. Light shines through the opened window, and I catch sight of Carter's mom dancing around a small dining room table while she sets down silverware.

His Adam's apple bobs in his throat as he swallows, and I'm starting to think he's as nervous as I am.

"What if they don't like me?" I whisper, running my hand along his lower back to half hug him, and so he can stop me if my body decides to turn and run.

"They will," he whispers back.

"Then why are you nervous?"

"Because I've never introduced anyone to them. Merpeople are different. I'm worried they'll scare you away."

I laugh. "Not like I'm going far."

Carter's mom lifts her gaze to the window when she hears our voices. I puff air through my lips, forcing my mouth to smile through my anxiety. Carter doesn't let go of me, and I watch the woman dance across the room to whatever music she's imagining.

"Mateo, they're here," Carter's mom says, calling over her shoulder.

She opens the door for us and lets us inside. A man more chiseled than Carter strolls from a hallway. His skin is darker than Carter's, and his eyes match the deep brown, almost black of his hair color. He strides across the room, standing next to his wife. I freeze under their curious gazes.

"Mom, Dad, this is Ava Adair. Ava, meet my parents,

Mateo and Starla."

I don't even have time to brace myself before Mateo's strong arms pull me in for a hug. He rocks us back and forth, nearly knocking me over. I laugh against the man's broad chest, surprised by such an unexpected greeting.

The moment he releases me, Starla embraces me much more gently and says how good it is to meet me into my hair. She smells of tropical fruit—a blend of mango, coconut, and pineapple—and also the subtle scent of the ocean that clings to Carter.

"Mom, please," Carter says. "You're smothering her."

Starla laughs, but it sounds more like a giggle—a chiming of bells even. It's the kind of unforgettable laugh that makes you automatically smile.

"It's fine, Carter. I'll take a hug any day," I say, thinking how much better this is than I expected. I thought for sure they'd stare at me with suspicious eyes while thinking how I'm a terrible choice for their son.

"See," Starla says, pulling me with her into the quaint living room.

Large sea shells decorate a few shelves, and watercolor paintings fill most of the walls. It's like they've done their best to embody the ocean in their décor without having to be in the water. They chose the land long ago after Carter was born.

"I still can't believe you were passing through and weren't going to stop in to say hello," Mateo says. "Already forgetting your poor parents."

"Dad," Carter says, heaving a long sigh. "I didn't expect to even leave the yacht. Plans changed, though." Carter's gaze flicks to mine. *Yeah, they do.*

"Do you work on the Ocean Jewel, Ava?" Starla asks, walking to the kitchen to check whatever she's cooking in the oven. I expect her to pull out some sort of seafood, but instead she pulls out a glass dish of lasagna.

"No, just a passenger." My heart hammers against my rib-cage. Starla's eyebrows lower for a split second. I wonder if I should've just lied. "I live in Azure Waters with my parents, but I'm moving out with my best friend before college in the fall."

"Oh, you plan to attend college?" Mateo asks it like it's a silly question.

Carter slides up behind me and rests his arms around my neck, nudging me toward the round dining room table. "I've considered going myself."

"So, you two are pretty serious?" Starla sets the casserole dish in the middle of the table before dancing her way back to the fridge to pull out a bowl of salad.

The question hangs in the air, neither of us knowing how to respond. Carter and I look at each other, waiting for the other to answer. While Carter's parents aren't suspicious, it does feel like they're interrogating me. I almost want to excuse myself to the bathroom just to escape their curiosity.

"Mom," Carter says, "Can't you give us a moment to sit down before the interrogation?"

She giggles again. "Sorry, sweetheart. It's just we have so little time with you and Ava."

"And there will be plenty of time to get to know her," Carter says, pulling out my chair for me. "Maybe we can visit later in the summer and stay longer than a few hours."

"We'd love that, son," Mateo says, joining us.

Starla sits down, and Mateo dishes out the lasagna before passing the salad bowl around. Carter's parents keep the conversation light, talking about the good business at their shop at Fisherman's Wharf, where Starla caught Carter and me kissing in front of the sea lions.

Everything feels so normal, and no one mentions anything merpeople related, and that's probably because by the time we arrived, both of our hair was dry. Carter mentions that I'm still too new to be recognized by other mermaids, and apparently only I can see the spark in his chest that holds his essence.

An hour passes, and I help Starla carry the dishes to the sink when we're all through eating. I remain on edge, listening to Carter recount how we met on the dock as I contemplated whether or not I could gather the courage to get on the yacht.

"Obviously, she got on," Carter says, smiling at me.

Both his parents stare at me with the strangest expressions.

"You're afraid of the ocean?" Mateo finally says after a moment. It must be an absurd notion for a merman to wrap his mind around. The irony still makes me shake my head in disbelief. "But Carter loves the ocean."

"When I boarded the yacht, yes," I say, shifting uncomfortably under his gaze.

"Dad, please."

Yes, please. I wish his dad would change the subject. I know any minute Carter's going to have to tell them about my transformation. But now, I'm nearly shaking in my seat. They'll either be relieved or upset. Maybe even both. The anticipation's killing me.

Starla's heavy gaze remains on me, like she can somehow see into my head and figure me out. I brush my hair behind my ear and glance at Carter, begging him to end this so we can go. I rest my hand on his on top of the table, twining our fingers together.

His mom audibly gasps as she stares at us with wide eyes. The reaction to me holding her son's hand is loud enough to startle me. I pull my hand away and rest it under the table in my lap.

"Ava, your hand," his mom says.

I pull it up to stare at it, thinking something's wrong, but I don't see anything out of the ordinary.

"The ring."

Oh.

"You gave her your ring, Carter?" I expect his mom to yell, but instead she waves her hands in front of her face as tears rim her beautiful aqua eyes.

"It's not what you—"

"Oh, Ava. I'm so happy you've accepted my son's proposal," Mateo says, reaching across the table. He takes my hand in his and inspects the sea stone glittering in the light.

Proposal? What? *The ring was intended for his mate…*

"Um, I—"

"There's so much planning to do," Starla says, interrupting me. "Summer is the perfect time for the transformation ceremony."

Darkness edges my vision.

"Mom," Carter says.

"And it'll give you just enough time to say goodbye to your family," Starla continues, ignoring her son.

My throat tightens. "What? I'm not leaving my family."

"But—"

"Mom!" Carter yells, his voice echoing through the room. "Stop! You need to listen."

The world spins as dizziness washes over me. This wasn't anything like I expected. Whatever this ceremony she's talking about—saying goodbye to my family—it's not happening.

Falling over, I crash onto the floor, the need to escape washing over me. But instead of triggering the mermaid transformation, I pass out.

The last thing I see in the darkness is the spark in Carter's chest but even that goes out.

LIFE ON LAND

VOICES CUT THROUGH THE DARKNESS, but I don't open my eyes. I will the voices to disappear so I can stay in this quiet, peaceful world with nothing to worry about.

A cloth rests on my head, and I'm lying on something soft. A couch? Strong fingers hold onto mine, and Carter's sunscreen and ocean scent wafts over me, calming my nerves.

"I promised Ava she could go back home." Carter's voice is barely audible over the sound of my heartbeat. "I'm not going to take her away from her family because of some stupid tradition. She didn't agree to any of this."

His words resonate through me. I didn't even think about other merpeople or their traditions. Carter told me about the colonies, but they still feel almost mythical to me, like Carter and I are the only merpeople in the sea. It's felt like that since the full moon, even with Mateo and Starla. I can't wrap my mind around the alternative to a life on land, one I'll fight to keep.

"Oh, son. You should've called us sooner." It's Mateo. He sounds more sorrowful than disappointed, the pity for his son, for me, clear in his voice.

"What difference would it have made? I stole away Ava's choice to decide. I'm not going to steal her decision of what happens to her future as well. I'm letting her make the choice if she wants to be with me, and I doubt she'd know for sure after a few days." Carter sounds just as sad, putting his thoughts out loud. It reminds me of the moment he told me what he did to save my life, like because he made that decision for me, it's my job to decide everything else, including what happens between us.

"For your sake, I hope so, son," Mateo says.

"I'm ready to accept whatever happens, even if it doesn't happen how I imagine," Carter says.

It breaks me apart and puts me together at once, knowing that Carter really does want to be with me. I know he likes me. I can feel it deep in my bones, but the fact that he's unsure of where I stand and thinking things could change leaves an ache in my heart that beats in sync with his, for him, and because of him. The last thing I want is to hurt him and make him regret his actions, though I'm kind of sure he does. It makes this all so much harder.

If I didn't think they'd stop discussing what happens to me, I'd sit up and throw my arms around Carter, telling him not to worry about my choice, because I do want to be with him. I want him to be included in my future. This isn't only about me.

Mateo sighs. "I think you really need to think things through. You can't just hope for the best."

Carter's thumb rubs over the side of my hand. "I'm not hoping, and I can handle this. We have things under control."

"But Carter, she's a liability," his mom says, cutting in. "She needs to be in the sea. She needs to be with our people until she adjusts. You can't just put the sea stone on her finger and expect her to master the transformation without really knowing what she's capable of. What happens if she loses control in the car? Or in the middle of a mall? She said she's going to college. Could you imagine what would happen if she changed in the middle of a lecture hall in front of hundreds of people? We've survived so long by remaining a secret. As her mate, it's your job to protect her. This isn't a game. It's her life."

With a heavy heart, I slowly open my eyes.

"I *am* protecting her. It's more than just the transformation and keeping our secret. It's about protecting her heart too, and you don't feel her like I do. I can't devastate her like that. You two should know this."

His parents fall silent. Carter bows his head, and a tear trickles from his closed eyes onto my cheek. Reaching up, I run my finger under his eye. He inhales a deep breath before opening his eyes to meet my gaze. The sorrow sweeping across his face is enough to bring tears to my eyes. It's how he looked after he had given me his spark after I drowned.

"Carter," I whisper. "Please, don't be sad."

"But I've ruined your life," he says, his voice cracking.

"How could you have ruined a life I wouldn't have had?"

Though I try my best to comfort Carter, holding his hand, letting him know he didn't ruin my life, his mom's words rest heavy on my soul. I can't imagine having to leave my life in Azure Waters behind to remain in the ocean. All the hope I had for my future drifts through my fingers like the powdery sands of the beach outside my house, sweeping away on the same waves that stole my sister. And now, my parents will have to live the rest of their lives knowing that the ocean stole me, too.

"See, son," Mateo says. "She understands. Ava's a reasonable person. She wouldn't want to put our people at risk."

I frown at his words. "Of course not, but you can't expect me to never see my family again, especially if I can live on land."

"But Ava—"

I hold my hand up, cutting Mateo off. Turning to Carter, I lean up and whisper, "Can we leave?" His parents will probably hate me for being rude, but I can't process everything with them sitting in front of me. I'm afraid if we stay any longer, they might not let me leave at all. And then what?

His jaw tightens, but he doesn't tell me no. Instead, he helps me get to my feet. Turning to his parents, he offers them a sad smile.

Starla closes her eyes while shaking her head. "Please, Carter. What you're doing...it's not right."

"It's right for Ava—and me." He leans over and kisses his mom on the cheek. "Please, respect our choice to live how we want."

He pulls me toward the door with him without looking back. Peering once over my shoulder, I watch Mateo take Starla into his arms. Neither follows us to try to stop us, but it's clear that to protect my heart, Carter broke both his parents'.

We walk in silence back to the beach we emerged from, Carter holding me like if he lets me go, I might float away on the wind. It's safe to say that dinner was a disaster, and I'm pretty sure we won't be visiting again anytime soon.

When we reach the beach, Carter pulls me into a hug in front of the water. He buries his face in the nook of my neck, breathing in and out a few long breaths. We just hold each other, listening to the waves crash on the shore under the soft moonlight.

"I'm sorry about tonight, Ava," he whispers into my hair. "I thought my parents would understand. They haven't lived in the ocean all my life. I thought they'd respect our decision not to as well."

"I don't blame them for worrying. They don't even know me and were right about my lack of control." I hate admitting it, but the thought had crossed my mind. What would happen if I triggered the transformation in the middle of a college classroom? It'd take at least thirty minutes or longer to get to the beach, if I could even get there at all.

"You're getting better. We'll keep practicing. We'll swim every day so you never have a chance to miss it. We'll figure this out," he says.

His words are encouraging enough that the worry gripping my heart releases so I can take a deep breath without my chest tightening from the anxiety threatening to sink me to the bottom of the sea. He put a lot of thought into this. He's known the risk, yet he thinks I'm worth it. For that, I'm grateful.

Standing on my tiptoes, I kiss him, cupping his face in my hands. He embraces me, his hands sliding around my waist to my back where his fingers brush through the tips of my hair. His tongue slips in my mouth, caressing against mine, and I suck on his bottom lip.

"I'm so glad it was you who chose me as your mate," I whisper breathlessly against his lips, his words about protecting my heart flashing through my mind. The memory is vivid enough in my mind that I project it to him.

He grazes his lips against mine again, lifting me off my feet only to set me down in the soft sand. My fingers run down his sides until I find the hem of his shirt to pull it off his head. My dress hikes up around my waist, and he trails his fingers over my thighs and along the waistband of my bikini bottoms, sending tingles through me.

He pulls away, gazing into my eyes before he tugs my dress over my head. The moonlight bathes my skin in a soft glow, and he licks his lips, drinking in the sight of my body for what feels like the first time—a time where it wasn't out of necessity but because I want him to see me. His warm chest presses against me when he lies on top of me, resting his arms in the sand while I rub my fingers across his shoulders.

"You're so amazing," he whispers through kisses.

Ocean water sprays across us, sending a chill over my warm

skin. I hug Carter tighter, remembering how hot he looks in the water, how his muscles flex when he swims, how his eyes sparkle like the sun on the sea.

Tingles flourish from my toes to my torso, but Carter isn't responsible for the electrifying sensation now coursing through me. The sensation overtakes my desire like I've jumped from the hot tub into the cool pool, clearing my thoughts enough to realize what's happening.

I could scream if I wasn't so worried about someone hearing us. Just when I thought I had a handle on my transformation, here my body goes, ruining another next-level moment between me and Carter, a moment that I want so badly.

I quiver through the ache that runs deep in my bones as Carter rests on top of me. He freezes mid kiss and snaps his eyes open to look at me. To my horror, my pectoral fins jut from my forearms, and glittering scales emerge from my skin.

I don't even have time to tug my bikini bottoms off before they rip away. My legs fuse together faster than ever, leaving me on the sand in my mermaid form where anyone with a flashlight could see. My lungs burn with every gasp of briny air I inhale into my lungs. Oxygen isn't what I need in this moment. I need water to finish my transformation. I need the ocean before I drown on dry land.

I open and close my mouth, trying to push words through my lips. Carter's already to his feet, panic lining his eyes. It's enough to send a wave of fear over me.

"Hold on, Ava," Carter says, scooping me up into his arms. If he wasn't here, I'd probably die in the sand, because there's no way I'm strong enough to pull myself the twenty feet it would take to even touch the water.

He jogs the short distance to the waves and runs into them with me in his arms. Water splashes our faces, and he sinks deeper into the cresting waves. My tail flops against the surface, setting me off. My body takes control, and I fight away from him, forcing him to let me go so I can dive under. I submerge into the water, inhaling a deep breath of the sea. My chest relaxes in relief as I adjust to the transformation. The speed in which I transformed into a mermaid ignites a hopelessness within me I haven't felt before. How on earth can I go home now? What will I do?

My tail smacks the shallow bottom of the shore, and I bob my head out of the water. Carter is back on the beach collecting our clothes before undressing and entering the waves. He doesn't even have to search for me. He just swims in my direction in his human form.

"That was close," he whispers, handing me my bikini top.

It *was* close. Unsettlingly close. How could I ruin such a perfect moment?

Carter helps tie my bikini top around my neck and back after a few failed attempts on my part. My hands won't stop shaking, adrenaline still coursing through me. Taking my hand, he pulls me farther into the sea. It's not until my tail no longer smacks the ground that he dives down to transform into a merman.

"I'm sorry, Carter," I say, projecting my voice into his mind while sliding my hands around his taut shoulders. "I really suck at this."

"You don't have to apologize. It's okay. It was probably for the best anyway." A smirk crosses his face, tiny bubbles clinging to his cheeks.

But I feel like I do have to apologize. I wanted Carter so badly but just thinking about him reminds me of what we are. It was enough to make my body want to be in the water with him instead of the land where my mind really, really wanted to be. The disconnection between my heart and mind is more prominent than ever, and it feels like they're at war within me.

"I shouldn't have rushed things like that. Your emotions are connected to your transformation, and you clearly enjoy me in both my forms," he continues. He grins, sending heat crawling up my chest to my neck and cheeks.

"You have no idea." Covering my face with my hands, I try to calm my racing heart.

"I think I do."

He doesn't let me hide my face for long, because a moment later, he's tugging my hands away to kiss me again. I cling to him while he flicks his tail, shooting us deeper into the water.

Even after everything that happened at his parents' home and after learning what was supposed to be my fate, I can't bring myself to even think about those things. In this moment, it's just me and Carter and the ocean that has quickly become our own private world.

But thoughts of the land sneak up. No matter how much I enjoy this, I can't lose myself to the sea forever. I have a life to return to. I have family.

And now, I have Carter. Because he chooses the land, too.

No one can take that from us.

The moon hangs high in the sky when we catch up to the yacht, heading south on the Pacific, following the California coastline. At the speed Carter swims, we could probably make it home by the afternoon, leaving the yacht behind in our wake if we wanted to.

The yacht glides over the water, a bubbly trail cutting through the surface behind it. Even at the slow speed it's traveling, there's no way I'm going to be able to catch up to it to climb back on board in my human form. All the other times we've snuck back on have been when it was anchored.

"I don't think I can make it back on the swimming platform after transforming," I say, my voice traveling into Carter's mind.

He presses his lips together and thinks, "If you transform now, I can push you up."

Tugging the strap of our bag over his head, I remove it before sliding it across my chest. There's no way I'm going to end up naked on the swimming platform alone if someone spots us. Luckily, only part of the crew is awake and most likely in the cockpit where we won't even appear on their radar.

"Whenever you're ready, Ava," Carter says, wrapping his arm around my waist to pull me along to stay with the yacht.

The moment I close my eyes, the transformation rushes over me in a wave of dull pain and shock as I start to feel the cold water in my human form. Carter was right about my transformation speeding up. What took minutes before took less than a minute now. If only I could get a handle on changing back and forth effortlessly. It'd make my life easier. My house is on a private beach. It'd take seconds to rush to the ocean to transform, and if I could change back immediately, it'd be fine. The water isn't crystalline, so people wouldn't even see me in the waves. Maybe I'll just not leave my house for the next three months unless I get better control. And if I move in with Giselle on the beach, it could be just as manageable. I'll make it work. I have to.

Carter breaks the surface with me so I can clear the water from my lungs. His pearlescent bronzed skin shines in the soft moonlight. He turns his attention from me to the yacht, studying it in his intense gaze.

"Get ready to hold your breath," he says, cutting through the water, closing the distance between us and the swimming platform.

I inhale a quick breath of salty ocean air before Carter pulls me under. My eyes blur in the saltwater, and the usual glow of the water seems darker as my human eyes try to orient to the direction we're heading, my sense of direction lost on the current.

Before I have a chance to prepare myself, Carter launches me out of the water, and I spin through the air, hitting my hip hard on the platform. The sandpaper-like lining scrapes against my naked skin, sending pain through me. I slam into the wall of the small garage that holds the jet skis, the majority of my pain now radiating from my back. Gasping a few sharp breaths, I slap my hand over my mouth to stop from crying out.

My chest heaves, and I push through the pain. I don't have time to sit here and cry like I want to. I need to grab my dress from the bag before I'm discovered. The last thing I want is to be added to the list of embarrassing naked-in-weird-situations stories my friends just love to share.

A small wave of water splashes over my legs. Carter pulls himself onto the deck without using the ladder. I can't even wrap my mind around how fit he is. I, on the other hand, need to seriously work on my strength and stamina in the water. Ocean swimming is a lot harder than wading in a pool.

Carter groans, stretching his arms over his head. His eyes meet mine, and he scrambles toward me. He silently brushes his fingers outside the scrape on my thigh. Nudging his hand away, I stop him from trying to get a look at my naked back. I just want to get dressed and hide in my stateroom the rest of the night.

With a shaking hand, I pull my sandy, half wet dress from the bag and shimmy it on over my aching body. I hand the bag over to Carter, and he slides on his shorts, leaning his back against the garage door next to me. He tilts his head back and stares up at the clear sky with an expression I can't decipher. Now that we're out of the water and away from his parents in San Francisco, I'm sure everything he's doing is starting to really sink in.

"Ava?" The loud whisper cuts through the air over the sound of the waves. "Ava, are you there?"

My eyes widen, and I grip Carter's hand. He rolls over to gently lie on top of me and rests on one arm. He kisses me, blocking the both of us as a figure emerges from the pathway that surrounds the deck.

"Oh! Whoa!" Giselle says, her voice cutting through the air.

Carter presses his lips together to hide his smile and pulls away from me. His bare chest gleams with the water that drips from the both of us. We're still sopping wet, and Giselle's surprise is obvious. We have a lot of lying to do, and even if I told the truth I doubt she'd believe me.

"Hey," I say, baring my teeth in an awkward smile. "You found us."

"What're you doing out here?" she asks, glancing between us.

"What does it look like?" Heat crawls up my neck.

"You're wet. You cannot tell me you fell into the ocean again." She places her hands on her hips.

I laugh. "Of course not."

"We came from the pool," Carter says. *Please, don't say you were just at the pool, Gi.*

She opens her mouth to respond, but I cut her off by adding, "And got distracted on our stroll. The room was feeling small."

Narrowing her eyes, she tries to decide whether or not she believes us. It's not like there is a better explanation, so she doesn't argue.

After a moment of awkward silence, she says, "You should really make sure not to accidentally lock your door. I knocked forever like an idiot before getting the spare key to open it only to see you weren't there. I was starting to get worried since I hadn't seen you since dinner. I don't want to sound lame, but I want to hang out with my BFF, too."

I pout my bottom lip. "Sorry, Gi. You were all watching a movie, and we just felt like going for a swim."

"Well, do you want to go again?" She glances between me and Carter, including him in her suggested plans.

I think about the fact that I'm only wearing half a bathing suit under my dress, but the look on my best friend's face says that I can't back out of it. This is our vacation after all. Carter was never a part of our plans. She's not the jealous type, but in our group of friends, it's an unspoken rule that we always include everyone in all our plans. I've been the third wheel the last time Giselle had a boyfriend, and we've all been third wheels to both Sapphire and Matty or Daisy and Logan, but it's not uncomfortable like most think. We're all friends. It's just how it is.

Giselle taps her foot, waiting for my answer. I'm taking too long. A million different responses flit through my mind, nothing sounding like a good reason not to. And I'll definitely never hear the end of it from any of my friends if I suddenly pull away from them for Carter.

"Sure," Carter says, answering for me because I'm clearly incapable of responding under pressure. If he wasn't so sweet, totally understanding the situation without me having to spell it out, I'd pummel him for putting me in this awkward position. Of course, if I did, it would draw suspicion from Giselle.

"Um, actually," I say, clearing my throat. I shift my legs, fiddling with the hem of my dress.

Giselle tilts her head to the side. "What?"

Carter's brows furrow, a silent question crossing his face. Flicking my gaze down to my hands, I tug on my dress. My predicament dawns on him a moment later, and he has the nerve to laugh.

I flush, elbowing him in the side, but I still don't respond to Giselle. Carter might think it's funny, but I'm pretty mortified that I can't just explain how sprouting a tail caused my bottoms to rip right off me.

Giselle fake glares while pointing her finger at us. "I don't like this. I'm supposed to be included on inside jokes." She smiles as she says it.

"You have to swear not to say anything to Sapphire. Matty wouldn't let me live this down," I say.

Her smile widens. "Okay, spill. What is going on?"

With a sigh, I grip my knees. "I seem to have misplaced my bikini bottoms."

Her mouth drops open as she laughs, tilting her head toward the clear sky. If it was anyone else, I'd be even more embarrassed about what my words could possibly imply, but I'm sure my friends probably already assume that I've slept with Carter, considering we haven't even left each other's sides for more than a few hours. There won't be a question about it now, and maybe if it actually happened, I wouldn't feel this way.

"This is so hilarious, Aves. I'll help you find them," she says.

Carter clears his throat. "No point. They're gone."

"What?" Giselle is eating this up. I almost believe it, my sudden transformation happening while I was about to give myself to Carter a distant memory. This is how it should've ended anyway. *Stupid surprise transformation ruining my already bad night.* I just hope she doesn't ask for the details.

"Yeah, it's fine," I say. "I'll go grab another bikini."

"Oh, my God. You guys!" She cracks up, clapping her hands. "How do you expect me to keep something so funny a secret?"

I laugh. "Gi, come on!"

She waves her hands in front of her face. "Okay, okay. Only because I can't be the only one without a hilarious, awkward naked story."

Carter helps me to my feet, sneaking the waterproof bag behind his back so Giselle doesn't question it. I move ahead and stroll next to Giselle. A flicker of guilt squeezes my heart, knowing that our friendship is never going to be the same again, because I can't share with her my deepest secret. And she'll never have any idea. Not to mention how close she came to catching us emerge from the ocean. A life on land, remaining as I was before the transformation, is looking more impossible than ever.

How can my life just slip through my fingers like this?

I'm afraid I'm already too far gone from my human self to make it out of this unscathed.

12

BELONG TO THE WATER

I TRAIL NEXT TO GISELLE, following the others off the yacht and onto the long dock of the Santa Barbara Harbor. The picturesque view of the cream-colored sands and blue ocean was enough to draw me from the yacht instead of following through with my plan to hide in my stateroom all day.

"You sure I can't convince you to surf? Chloe's an excellent instructor, way better than Matty. I was able to pop up on the board after only a few hours. And I was twelve." Giselle swings her arms at her sides, knocking her hand into mine.

"Hey, I'm a master," Matty says. "I could have you riding the waves in an hour."

I roll my eyes at Matty. I doubt he has anything on Chloe. Her brother is sponsored by a major surf company, and she's been surfing since before I was afraid of the water. "Are you seriously asking me this, Giselle?"

"Yeah, I am. Because look—" She waves her hand to me and then to the ocean of the harbor surrounding us. "You're not sweating or shaking or crying when all I'd have to do is swing my arm to knock you in. I think this trip might be wearing you down."

That's one way to put it. The fear I felt before isn't even a faint memory. It feels surreal to think I was ever afraid to begin with. She's right, I'm not panicking like I would've last week. I don't even think I could pretend.

I sigh. "Maybe it is, but there's no way I'm willingly getting into the ocean."

"Then why don't you build sandcastles and watch us for a bit? You might change your mind."

I turn to glance at Carter over my shoulder, who talks to Chloe and Logan about surfing. It's all any of them have been talking about like they don't do it often enough at home. I guess being at a new beach is exciting. The swells are supposed to be pretty decent too, but I wouldn't know anything about that.

Carter catches my eyes and smiles but continues with his story, leaving me struggling for an excuse.

"Okay, I'll watch for a bit, but then you can't complain about my dread of the ocean."

Giselle claps her hands. "Yay! Did you guys hear that? Aves is gonna watch us."

"And you can take pictures," Sapphire says, waving her phone. "I don't have enough to show off."

"Well, if you're going to watch, then Carter can surf, too. There's nothing this dude can't do on the water," Logan says, slapping Carter's shoulder.

He blinks a few times, studying me for a moment like he's trying to come up with an excuse against going in the water to stay with me. He can't think of one, and I'm not going to seem like a needy girlfriend, but damn. Watching my friends in the water is one thing. Watching Carter? The temptation is real. Oh so drool-worthy real.

"I don't know," Carter says.

"You deserve a little fun. You saved Ava-babe from drowning at sea because of Matty's dumbass. How often do you get a vacation with awesome people like us, anyway?" Logan shakes Carter by the shoulders.

"It's fine, Carter," I say. "He's right. You should have fun."

"Yeah, my mom would be sad if you don't enjoy what she arranged for you," Sapphire says.

Carter smiles though his eyes don't. He looks even more uncomfortable than I felt last night standing outside his parents' apartment. He chose the land to be around humans. He enjoys everything about our lives, but I don't think he's been this immersed in our world. Working on the Ocean Jewel allows him to socialize with passengers and other crew members, but according to him, he's never made the effort to connect and form relationships with anyone. It was a means to living on land.

And here I am, taking it away because I can't be trusted not to blow our secret. I can see the nervousness in his eyes, though I can tell he wants to join in the fun with my friends. I wish I could, too. After staying out of it for so long, I can finally enjoy the water with them—but my state of uncertainty leaves me out once again. This blows.

"It's set," Giselle says. "You two aren't ditching us."

"I guess not," I say quietly.

Carter falls in step next to me, sliding his arm around my waist. "Don't stop thinking about the land," he whispers.

But it's already too late. Because my heart belongs to the water.

So far, so good. I've managed to find the perfect place under a palm tree away from any beachgoers. Luckily, it's a brisk day—not quite summer warm—so most of the people on the beach are wearing wetsuits as they surf the equally cool water.

I sit back in the chair I rented from the same surf shop the others picked up their boards and dig my feet into the sun-warmed sand. With my earbuds firmly in place, I can't hear the lull of the waves over my music. I almost forgot what it was like to relax and do nothing but lose myself in my favorite songs.

From this distance, I can't really see the faces of my friends.

They float on the water, straddling their boards, waiting for the swells good enough to surf. I refuse to glance at Carter at all. I bet he looks so hot on the water all glistening and wet and... *Stop it!*

Shaking my head, I send my blond hair sweeping across my face, so I'm not tempted to draw my gaze to my incredibly hot merman in disguise. When Sapphire sees the few photos I took, she's probably going to be disappointed because I didn't even look at the screen as I took them. At least she'll have the posed ones on the beach.

A shadow falls over me, and I remove my headphones.

"Don't look so bored," Giselle says, plopping down on the sand next to me.

I shrug. "I'm not."

"You look like you're going to die of boredom. You should see your face." She wrings out her wet hair before flicking me with the seawater.

I quickly swipe it off my bare arm like it burns. "Sorry, I'm just thinking."

"About Carter?"

"He looks amazing out there," I say without answering her question specifically—Carter's only part of what's on my mind.

"It's like he's part fish but without the gross scales," Giselle says with a laugh.

My mouth drops open for a second before I catch myself gaping. There's nothing gross about his glittering scales. Or his fins. There's nothing gross about him at all. Of course, she doesn't know that.

"Jeez, you look like I've offended you," Giselle adds after a moment.

I force myself to smile. "What? Oh, no. Sorry. I was thinking about something else."

She laughs. "Obviously."

"Sorry."

She flicks more water at me from her hair. "Well, this is enough of you sitting here looking bored. Why don't you come closer to the water? Put your feet in."

"Not happening," I say.

"Come on. You've fallen in and lived to tell the tale. I've never pressured you before because I knew how afraid you were. You'd pale at just the mention of the ocean, but something's changed. You can't tell me it hasn't. I want my BFF to have as much fun as I am," she says.

So, she has noticed something different in my behavior. Before, there was no possible way I could get over my phobia or anxiety. Some days, I'd even be physically ill over them, especially right after Bailey died. My parents forced me to see a therapist until I refused to go. I just readjusted my life and kept living. But now? It's like my transformation reset everything in me. I'm still Ava, but I'm a new version of myself. Ava 2.0.

"I *am* having fun," I say. "Right here on shore." Apart from my new fear of sudden mermaid transformation, I don't want my friends or parents looking too much into things, not that they can guess that mermaid magic cured me. It's just easier to stick to my old habits the best I can. I won't be under their scrutiny forever. I just have to survive these next few months. Carter's certain that time and practice is the key, and I'm depending on it.

"O-o-okay, Aves. I think you should try sometime, though. Carter looks miserable out there with you here on the beach. It can't always be about you."

Her words sting but not because Carter's out there and I'm not. It's because, in a way, they're true. Everything in my and Carter's relationship so far has been about me and what I want. I'd give anything to run into the water, to swim to him. Play human. Be normal—at least, as normal as I could be now. But it's just not possible. I couldn't imagine what the consequences would be for me if someone were to ever find out. Horrifying, probably.

"Ouch, Gi." I clutch my knees.

"You know I'm not saying it to be mean, but I see how you and Carter are around each other. You're getting serious pretty fast, and I don't want you to get hurt."

"We're fine. He understands."

"For now."

It takes everything in me not to snap at her and tell her she has no clue what she's talking about. I have no idea where this conversation's coming from. I didn't think she was jealous about all the time Carter and I spent together, but maybe she is. And she might have good intentions, but she doesn't know any-thing. The thought is enough to stir sadness within me. It's a reminder that she never will.

Pushing to my feet, I stand and turn away from Giselle. She struck a painful nerve within me, and I'm afraid I'll say or do something I'll regret, all because I can't tell her the truth. "Thanks for the advice, Gi. I'm going for a walk alone if you don't mind."

"Aves, wait," she calls.

But I don't look back. I can't. I need to get away before she realizes this isn't even about Carter or what she thinks about our relationship but has everything to do with our friendship with each other and how I'm grieving the loss I know is inevitable.

I rush through the sand to the bicycle path. My flip flops slap against the concrete as I run from the truth I'm going to have to eventually face. And it sucks. This was supposed to be the best summer ever. *Calm down. You'll figure it out. It's not over.*

Tears stream down my face, my breathing heavy, but I don't stop. I keep running until the pathway ends, and I enter a secluded area with only a hill behind me with a road that overlooks the ocean. From here, unless someone comes down the beach, no one can see me.

Standing at the edge of the surf, I allow the waves to crash into my legs. I tug my sundress over my head and wrap it around my phone before I toss them both behind me far enough that the waves won't wash them away. And then, I jog forward, allowing the water to splash over me.

I swim farther and farther from shore until my feet no longer hit the sandy bottom. Closing my eyes, I let the ocean carry me along, dragging me away from the land. Here, among the waves, I can think. My head is free from all the worry that comes with living on the land.

After a few minutes, I tug off my bikini bottoms and wind them around my wrist so they don't float away. It's the first time I'm in the water without Carter. I need to prove to myself that I can do this on my own. I need to prove to myself that no matter what happens, I'll be okay. That I can do this.

Peering around the blue waters once more, I take a deep breath and dive, kicking my legs to propel myself under. Bubbles erupt from my mouth, and I exhale the air from my lungs. I sink lower into the ocean with nothing but my thoughts to hold onto.

And then the cramps rush over me, sending my back arching and tightening the muscles in my legs. I don't open my eyes until the pain stops, and I inhale the cool ocean water.

I did it. I transformed alone without having something trigger it. It feels better than I ever imagined, so freeing, so perfect, knowing that I'm in control for once. Flipping my tail, I surge forward, dipping down to the ocean floor to trail my fingers over the sea grass. Silver fish swim around me, darting away as I spin in a circle, swirling the sand up around me.

I follow the ocean floor as it descends. The light filtering from the surface fades the farther I swim. I only stop when my heart stops racing. Smiling, I peer around and take in the vastness of the blue water so full of life. I twirl my arms at my side, resting ten feet above the sandy bottom. A squad of squids dances through the current at a leisurely pace nearby, bobbing sideways. Swimming through them with deadly precision is a handful of hammerhead sharks as they stalk their prey. Their majestic beauty and grace tempts me to move forward, but I only get close enough to watch the start of the feeding frenzy.

A huge silhouette crosses overhead, blocking the pale light above. Fear sneaks into my heart as I watch the boat drop a net into the water, scooping up a school of unlucky fish.

I flick my tail, propelling up another ten feet, but I don't do anything. The fish push against the net, fighting the inevitable. It reminds me of an old mermaid movie I saw when I was a child, where the mermaid ripped the net, saving whatever trapped animals. I consider doing it myself, since my nails are sharp enough to impale a fish, but the shadow of the boat freezes me in place.

"Ava!" Carter's voice echoes through my mind, drawing my attention away from the boat. It passes over my head completely while retrieving the net.

Before I have a chance to see him, I flick my tail and jet away, swimming from him instead of toward him. I can't bear to face him. He'll hug and kiss me, tell me everything will be okay, that everything will work out, but I don't want to hear any of that. I want to hear how as much as I love my family and friends, I can never have the life I once had. I can't even share my secrets with Giselle. The tear in my heart is far too great to be mended with comforting words and affection.

How will I face my best friend after all this? She wanted to save my heart, but who will save hers? Who will protect her from the hurt I'm surely going to cause her? Cause everyone in my life, maybe even Carter. None of this was supposed to happen. My plan was to go to college, get a job, travel the world, not find myself immersed in a world I have no business really being a part of.

I swim as fast as I possibly can. Maybe I'll make my way to Hawaii where I can live offshore in the warm, tropical waters. Maybe I'll figure out how to get to Australia. I imagine being anywhere other than here where my human life waits for me to screw up.

Gliding faster in the water, I navigate through the ocean life, nearly missing kissing the tail of an enormous gray whale as it swims with its pod.

As I dodge past another, something strong hooks around my waist, startling me. I automatically dive deeper into the ocean. Carter swims above me, holding me against him, but he doesn't force me to slow down or stop. Instead, he lets me lead as I swim into the vast blue. His chin rests on my shoulder, his warm, taut chest pressing against my back, and I enjoy the feeling of him with me.

We swim together without a word until my body begs me to slow down and rest. And even then, Carter propels us forward with the strength of his magnificent tail.

"Carter," I say, my voice barely a whisper in my own head. "What are we doing?"

"Swimming."

His answer makes me laugh. I shift in his arms, and he loosens his hold on me enough that I can twist to face him, pressing my chest against his. His spark glows in the same blinking rhythm as mine, and I swear I can see pulses of energy connecting us.

Resting my face in the crook of his neck, I close my eyes, relaxing against him. It isn't until we're miles and miles from shore that he slows down to finally stop swimming to search my face. We stare at one another, his hair floating around in the current and mine veiling the space between us. He's not doing any of the things I imagined him doing. All he does is wait for me to make the next move.

"How did you find me?" I finally ask when the intensity of his gaze threatens to unveil all the thoughts I hold in my soul.

He presses two fingers to the glowing spot in my chest. "I followed you."

"I didn't know you could do that."

"You can do it, too."

He doesn't ask the questions clearly written on his face. His lips tilt downward, probably matching my own expression, and his eyebrows hang low on his forehead. I wish he'd smile. His smile can change my world. It did.

"Oh." It's all I can say. It'd be a lot easier spilling my guts to him if he'd just ask the questions on his mind, if he would pry. "I don't know how to do it."

"All it takes is you wanting to find me, Ava. If you want me, you'll find me. You might not feel it like I do, but we're connected."

His words burrow inside me. He found me because he wanted me. This isn't about doing the right thing or trying to make it up to me. As much as I tell him I'm glad to be alive, he still blames himself for bestowing me with this priceless gift.

"Giselle thinks that I'm being selfish," I finally say. "She thinks everything between us revolves around me. And she's right."

He raises his eyebrows, shaking his head while he laughs, surprising me. "Ava, Giselle doesn't know what she's talking about."

"That's what I thought, but it really got to me. She'll never know. I lost the person I told everything to. It's just—" I close my eyes for a second. "This is really hard."

He lifts his hand to my face, caressing my cheek with his fingers. "That's why you ran."

I nod. "I want so badly to slip back into my old life like none of this ever happened. If I could just shut off my heart and turn my back on the ocean, I could make it work. I know I could. But then I—I'd be miserable. It'd be so much easier if I could tell my family."

His lips disappear as he presses them in a thin line, his expression matching the thoughts he projects to me. "Ava..."

I avert my eyes away from him. "I know, Carter. I can't. I won't. It's just—maybe I'm better off not going back."

"You really think so?"

I shrug. "Maybe."

"Okay then. We won't go back."

I guess I shouldn't expect him to fight for my old normalcy. If I could cry underwater, I would. The idea of never returning to land, while sounding like a good idea in my head, doesn't sit right in my heart. All I can think about is how much my family and friends would miss me—how much I'd miss them, too.

"No," I finally say.

He leans closer, forcing me to look into his alluring eyes. "Ava, what is it you want?"

"That's the problem. I don't even know anymore. But this isn't just about me, Carter. You said it yourself. It's about us. Your feelings matter to me, too."

He smiles before he kisses me. It isn't until now that I've said those words out loud. Since the night he asked me to meet him out on the deck, before I fell overboard, I knew I had liked Carter. I liked his confidence, how he made me feel like I wasn't crazy because of my fear of the ocean. I wanted to get to know him—I knew he was someone I would think was amazing—and I do. Then after the fall, the transformation, all I thought about was how I was going to manage this, because Carter shouldn't be bound to me by his guilt for saving my life. But this isn't about him or me. It's about us together and what works to make us both happy.

"I'd like to go back," he finally says. "I love living on land. The beds are much more comfortable and the food is better. If you think it's too hard to be with your family. If that's what this is all about, we can move anywhere, Ava. It doesn't have to be your family or the sea. We have a choice."

Choices. It hasn't felt like I had many until now. "I don't want to say goodbye to my family forever. I want to stay with them for a while before we figure things out."

He nods. "We'll make this work."

It wasn't until now—until I actually settled on a plan that felt good in my heart—that I believed things could work. I could have the land in my mind and the sea in my heart.

13

ONE HEART IN TWO BODIES

PACKING MY STUFF IS A lot harder than I expected it to be. The last day has flown by, and by sunset, we'll be anchoring back in the harbor of Azure Waters. Carter lies on the bed behind me as I lay my clothes across the other bed. He hasn't left my side since we returned to the yacht in Santa Barbara. Even when Giselle and I fell all over each other with apologies, Carter quietly observed us like he was lending me his strength.

"I can't believe I'm actually going home. I wasn't sure I was ever going to make it," I say, folding my sundresses to fit in my small bag. "How am I going to sleep knowing you're not nearby?" The reality of my situation sinks in the more I think about it. Carter won't be by my side all day and night when I leave this yacht. Vacation is over. I thought returning to the Ocean Jewel the morning after my transformation was hard. This seems impossible.

He smiles with sad eyes, and it hurts my heart. "I'll be around so much you won't even have a chance to miss me."

But that's not entirely true. Carter works on the Ocean Jewel. They leave again tomorrow afternoon for a short trip to Orange County. I'll be stuck at home, forced to gaze out my door at the sea. That is, if I can even make it through the whole day without triggering a transformation. *You've made it until now. You have to stay in control. It's the only way.*

"I already miss you," I complain. It sounds completely

cheesy, but it's true. The anticipation of returning weighs heavy on me.

He pushes off the bed and stands behind me. Brushing my hair from my neck, he kisses just below my ear. I give up folding my clothes and just start shoving the rest of my belongings into the bag so I can give him my full attention.

His hands slide down my shoulders and collarbone until he rests them on my chest over my heart, just feeling each beat against his fingers, thrumming in sync with his, beating for him, because of him. Standing utterly still, I relish the scent of his skin, the sunscreen and ocean fragrance that radiates from him. His chest presses into my back, and his presence consumes my attention until I can't think about anything but him. About my attraction to him, my need to be with him.

Turning my head, he meets me for a kiss without moving his hands from my heart. A flash of myself appears in my mind as he shows me a glimpse of how he sees me. How much I consume his thoughts, too.

Ever so gently, he hooks his fingers to the fabric of my dress, tugging my straps from my shoulders. I catch his eyes flicking to my reflection in the door mirror, and his breathing quickens seeing me in my bra. He's seen me in a bikini nearly this whole trip, but this feels different. It's more intimate. We're alone in my stateroom without the allure of the sea or my out-of-control emotions trying to replace one feeling with another. This is all him and me and us wanting to be together before reality threatens to change everything.

My dress slips to my feet, and his lips trail down my neck to my shoulder, sending chills over my body as it reacts to his touch. The brush of his fingers drives me crazy, and I spin in his arms to face him and kiss him fervently, almost frantically, like his kisses alone can somehow guarantee we'll both be okay, that even if everything changes around us, we'll remain the same.

Pushing him back, we fall together on the bed with me on top of him. My hair veils our faces, and I suck his bottom lip between mine. He moans, rolling me over and trails his gaze across my bare skin. I tug his shirt off and run my fingers along the sharp curve of his hips along his muscular stomach and then up to his neck to pull him down.

His hands travel down my sides, sending my heart racing. I can't see his spark, but I know his heart matches mine beat for beat like we are one heart in two bodies. I never thought to ask, but in this moment, that's exactly what it feels like.

Carter explores every inch of me with his hands, from the curve of my hips to my stomach, trailing them up until they run through my hair. He holds himself over me, his eyes meeting mine, searching for something within them.

His sudden hesitation speaks volumes, and I suck my bottom lip between my teeth, knowing what he's looking for. He's trying to see how my body reacts to him—whether or not I'll be able to maintain my human form. It's a thought I pushed into the dark recesses of my mind. I'm not ruining this moment again. I want nothing to do with the ocean and everything to do with him. It's all I can think about. How much I want him in this form, on this bed, in the air and not the sea.

I kiss him, sending him an image of us in this very second, showing him exactly where my mind is—in the here and now.

"Ava, are you sure you want to?" he asks quietly.

Leaning over, I grab a small box from my suitcase that Giselle had left for me on the night of my first transformation when she thought I wanted to spend the night with Carter to be alone with him. It still has the note on it saying that Matty had over-prepared with a winking smiley.

"I do more than anything," I say, placing the box in his hands.

He smiles as he whispers, "You're the best thing to ever

happen to me."

I answer him with another long, desperate kiss, showing him exactly how much he means to me to.

Carter stands with me outside of my house, staring up at the grand, newly remodeled Victorian-styled home my grandfather bought in the eighties. The sea green paint stands brightly against the white trim. Palm trees line the circular driveway while hydrangeas bloom in giant, pink bouquets under the windows.

The ever-present hum of the ocean echoes through the air of the beachfront property, though I haven't been on the beach behind my house in eight years, not since Bailey was lost to the waves. That's about to change, though I have no idea how I'll explain my sudden change of heart to my parents. They've spent thousands of dollars on therapy over the years to try to help me with my fear, but when I turned fifteen, I refused to visit Dr. Hari again. I didn't need to be fixed or changed. I didn't need the reminder that I was the only person in all of Azure Waters who couldn't even look at the water outside my own bedroom window, which now faces the street since my parents allowed me to switch with the guest room when I was twelve.

My legs tremble the longer we stand in my front yard. "This is home for me." Carter doesn't leave again until tomorrow so I invited him back to my house because it felt weird just leaving him behind on the Ocean Jewel. "Are you sure you want to come in? You can say no."

"It's only fair for me to meet your parents after the fiasco with mine," he answers, smiling. "It can't be any worse than that, right?"

"Right," I say, "and you won't have to worry about an interrogation. My dad will be leaving for the hospital at any second, and my mom will soon lock herself in her office like every night."

My dad's an emergency surgeon at the Betty Green hospital in Sunset Terrace, a town over from Azure Waters. If he hasn't been called in already, he'll be leaving for his once a week overnight soon. As for my mom, she splits her time as chief editor for the Azure Waters Gazette or planning one of the dozens of fundraisers alongside Ruby and Giselle's mom, Anaya. Over the last ten years, they've raised millions for different organizations.

After a minute, we still remain just outside my house. The moment we decide to enter, everything will change. I'm not sure if I'm ready. I'm not sure if I can handle returning to my old life. Returning to the me before Carter.

I gaze up at the purple clouds scattering across the darkening sky. The scent of the ocean wafts through the air, blowing long tresses of my hair behind me. Streetlamps illuminate a deep orange glow across my quiet street, the lamps dark enough that I can still see the stars speckled across the night through the breaks in the clouds.

Inhaling deeply, I lock my fingers with Carter's and pull him toward the red brick steps that lead to the double doors with window cutouts that sparkle with the light on within my house. I open the door, swinging it wide to peer into my spacious living room. The floor gleams under the lights of the fan. Unlike Carter's parents' apartment of blues and white, my house is warm with tans and dark woods. The only things that pop with color are the framed abstract sea and sunset paintings my mom bought from a local artist.

"Mom? Dad? I'm home," I call out as I tug Carter along into my living room. We pass the stiff tan couches that border an empty coffee table, facing a wall entertainment center.

To the right is a formal dining room with a long, sturdy

table with seating for ten. The brass chandelier dangles in the dark though the light from the living room gleams off the metal.

My parents sit at the small dining table in the kitchen with the curtain drawn open to show off the side deck and pool that sits on the side of the house. Cups of coffee rest on the table in front of them, and they share a piece of the chocolate cake I had baked and put in the freezer the night before the yacht trip.

"Oh, Ava. You've brought a friend home," Mom says, putting down her fork.

"I've never seen you before. Did you wash aboard the Ocean Jewel? I didn't think Ava would take me serious about the whole plenty of fish in the sea spiel."

"Dad, seriously?" If only he knew. "Carter works on the yacht." *He saved me from the ocean, turned me into a mermaid, and we'll be leaving Azure Waters soon to make it easier to hide my new life from you,* I imagine saying.

Instead, Carter steps forward and holds out his hand. "It's nice to meet you Dr. Adair, Mrs. Adair."

"It's a pleasure, Carter. Please, call me Beatrice," my mom says, shaking his hand next. "Are you two hungry? We have some leftover Chinese food or cake."

"We ate already," I say.

"But cake sounds great," Carter adds, grinning at me. He sets my bag down at his feet when my mom motions for us to sit down. Neither of them questions why I brought him home, which is a relief to me. They've treated me like an adult even before I turned eighteen. It helps that I'm not a troublemaker...or at least I've never been caught doing something I shouldn't have.

I don't sit down when my dad pats the back of the chair next to him. I shift my weight between my feet. "Is it okay if we take it on the back patio?"

My mom tilts her head to the side, not because she's confused about why I don't want to eat in the kitchen, but because I haven't been on the back patio in forever. She's going to realize how different I am soon enough.

"Uh, yeah. Sure, sweetheart." She shoots a quizzical look at my dad, who smiles widely at Carter.

My dad rises to his feet. "You feeling okay, Avie? You hate the beach." He says it in a way that wouldn't embarrass me if Carter didn't already know about my previous fear of the ocean.

"I feel great, Dad. A week on the water has given me a new perspective on things." I close the distance, giving my dad a hug. I didn't realize how much I missed my parents until now.

My dad hugs me tightly, pulling away only to grin. "Really?"

"Yeah," I say.

I stand awkwardly through a minute of silent smiling, like they're speaking through their gazes. My parents excuse themselves, but before my dad leaves, he tells Carter to come back anytime. It's probably the best introduction I could've asked for. I'm sure they'll save all their questions for later when Carter isn't here.

Taking both our plates, Carter follows behind me as I cut through the game room to the decorative glass doors that'll take us to our fenced in patio that faces the ocean. The white caps shine under the moon on the water, and Carter stares into the dark distance.

"I haven't stepped foot on this patio since I was a kid," I say, hugging myself, staring at our small patio table and chairs, the original palm frond pattered cushions now replaced by simple green ones.

He doesn't ask why. He doesn't need to. I'm sure my face says it all. Even when we're not kissing, Carter seems to know what I'm thinking. I wear my feelings splattered across my face with him instead of the unbreakable mask I'm hidden behind with everyone else.

I set my plate on the table instead of taking a bite. Carter holds his while he stands next to me, scooping a piece into his mouth. I grin, watching him close his eyes to savor the sweet flavor.

"Like it? It's my grams' recipe. She's the one who taught me how to bake and comes to stay with us during the winter to get away from the cold of the East Coast."

Carter bobs his head. "So good."

He devours the piece in a matter of minutes. I love how something so simple can make him so happy. After setting his plate next to mine, he takes my hands in his and then leans down to press his sweet lips to mine. Sliding my hands around his neck, I hold onto him for a moment, resting my cheek against his chest. His heartbeat drums in my ear, seeming to beat just for me, reminding me of our afternoon together.

My cheeks warm at the memory, and I can't stop from kissing him, reminding him exactly how much I don't want him to go. Tomorrow he'll be on the ocean for a night in the OC, and I'll be here, dreaming about a life after I can leave. A life where I don't have to worry about the consequences that come with my lack of stability. The dangers I'm putting every-one in just by being here. Dangers I know Carter wants to keep me from.

"You really are going to make it hard for me to leave," he whispers into my lips.

I flick my tongue across his bottom lip once before smiling. "Is it working?"

He moans, kissing me instead of responding. I break away and twine my fingers with his, tugging him toward the back gate that leads to the beach. I leave my flip flops in the sand, and we trail away from my house. The crisp night air blows my dress around my thighs, and I release his hand to dance around him with a smile on my face. I twirl in front of him, wiggling my fingers for him to follow me toward the water. It's all I could think about since the moment I got home. My last transformation in Santa Barbara feels so long ago, and I can't wait to just give in to my heart's need to be with the sea.

My dress clings to my legs in the breeze, and I pull the fabric up and over my head, stripping into my bikini far enough away from my neighborhood that without a flashlight, I won't be seen. Without saying a word, Carter removes his shirt and jogs to catch up to me as I saunter into the waves.

His strong arms embrace me, tugging me deeper into the surf. It doesn't take long for him to hook his fingers along the sides of my bikini bottoms to pull me to him, pressing his hips against mine. Under the soft moonlight, in the crashing waves, I allow him to undress me before our transformation.

Carter picks me up, carrying me deeper. The cold water flows around and lifts us off our feet with every wave. Sea spray splashes our faces, specks of water drops sparkling on his cheeks and hair. His eyes shine like jewels, glowing like the sun penetrating through the blue-green waters of the ocean, shining from within.

The cramps don't even bother me as the ocean calls me into its depths. I break away, surging under before Carter. Inhaling a breath of sea water, I dive away from him, spinning through the bubbling current. It doesn't take more than seconds for Carter to swim up next to me. He slips his hands around my waist until his chest presses into my back and guides us through the surf until we reach some black rocks not far from the shore.

We break the surface together, and Carter helps me slide out of the water. The waves collide on the rocks, splashing over our glittering tails and pearlescent skin. From this spot, I have a view of my beachfront community, and it reminds me of how separated I am from it now.

Leaning over, Carter kisses me sweetly. "I can see why you love it here." He gazes in the direction of my house, the splatter of lights from the mansions lighting the shore like man-made stars.

"It doesn't feel the same as it did when I left," I say, puckering my bottom lip.

He runs the pad of his thumb over my lips before cupping my chin in his hand, forcing me to turn toward him instead of the shore. "Maybe that's a good thing."

He's right. It doesn't feel the same because I'm not the same. It helps ease the sadness clinging to my heart. "Maybe it is. Either way, I don't want to think about it anymore."

Carter propels from the rocks and back into the water. Popping back up, he holds his arms out to catch me. "Then come on. Let me help you forget."

14

LIFE GOES ON

SUNLIGHT TRICKLES THROUGH MY CURTAIN, warming my face. I stir in Carter's arms, feeling the heat of his body as he curls against me under my blankets. His breath tickles my shoulders, and he releases a soft sigh before brushing his lips across my skin.

After our swim last night, it was easy enough to sneak Carter into my room since my mom never left her office. My parents have been pretty relaxed the last year and even lifted my curfew after graduation a few weeks ago. They'd never admit it, but I'm pretty sure they're just as excited as I am—was—about me moving in with Giselle closer to the university.

Dad wants me to be able to enjoy college because he never really got to, since he struggled financially all through it and at one point slept on a couch of a friend's before he met Mom. The deal is that I have to actually go to classes and get good grades. I also have to keep volunteering when the time allows, all of which I never minded until now.

"I wish you didn't have to leave," I mumble, rolling over to face him. His arms circle around me, and I rest my forehead on his muscular chest.

"I know what you mean, but working is now more important than ever," he whispers. "Living on land costs money, and you probably don't want me to live on the *Ocean Jewel* forever, right?"

I definitely don't. "Of course not."

"And while I have a pretty good savings already, I need to be ready to take care of—" He snaps his mouth shut, probably noticing the fear suddenly sweeping over me at his words. It's that tiny bit of doubt in his voice that makes me question what we're doing. What I'm doing.

Despite what his parents insinuated, I'm not his responsibility. All of this shouldn't be on him, and the last thing I want is for him to feel that way.

"Carter..." My voice trails off. We shouldn't have to be discussing something like this yet in our relationship. It's as crazy as his parents thinking he proposed to me and I said yes because I was wearing his ring. "I hope you don't think that I expect you to take care of me, because I don't."

"I know you don't, Ava," he says, brushing his lips against my forehead. "It was just a thought."

"Okay, but to be clear, I'm capable of helping out. This isn't all on you," I say. "I'm not your respons—"

He cuts off my words with a kiss, purposely interrupting me. "You have enough to worry about. I don't want you worrying about something I was just thinking about," he says against my lips. "Let's just enjoy the morning before I have to leave, okay?"

Pulling back, I gaze into his eyes. "Fine, but only because I like you rudely interrupting me like that." I smile despite the sinking feeling settling in my stomach.

He kisses me again, combing his fingers through my blond hair. We stay in bed for a few more minutes before Carter slides to his feet and shrugs his T-shirt on. If I don't take my eyes off him, it's easy to forget I'll be without him for the first time since we met what feels like forever ago.

He holds out his hands to me, smiling the smile he saves just for me, and helps me out of bed even though I'd rather just bury myself in my covers for the rest of the day. Carter watches me get ready like I'm the most fascinating person in the world. I change into shorts and a shirt, and he can't resist trailing his fingers over my bare neck when I pull my blond hair up into a ponytail.

Reluctantly leaving him upstairs, I rush down the steps to see where my mom is. A sticky note hangs from the fridge, reminding me about dress shopping later today for the King's Scholarship Foundation Gala that I'm to attend on Friday night. At the bottom of the note, she tells me to invite Carter as my date.

I guess life really didn't stop even when I grew a tail. I had completely forgotten about the gala. We usually don't shop so late, but with finals, graduation, and vacation, I never made time. It didn't help that Giselle and I didn't want to go. The galas are always so stuffy and dreadful, totally not our thing.

"Carter, we're alone," I call up the stairs. "You can come down."

His soft footsteps sound on the stairs, and when he enters the kitchen, I hold out a plate of muffins my mom left out. He takes one, peels off the wrapper, and consumes it in a few bites. His eyes crinkle in the corners as he grins at me before wiping the crumbs off his chin with a paper towel.

Dangling the sticky note from my fingers, I hold it in front of Carter's face until he takes it and reads it.

"You busy on Friday? I know it's last minute, and you probably have to work..."

"I—"

"They're really boring anyway," I say, interrupting him before he can finish.

"Then we'll be bored together, because we return to port Friday afternoon and don't leave again until Saturday," he says.

A smile creeps over my face. "You have to wear a tux."

"I look good in a tux."

I grin, because he looks good in anything. "Then it's a date."

"I like the sound of that."

Thirty minutes later, I pull my silver BMW into the parking lot of the harbor to drop Carter off. He lingers in the passenger's seat, not wanting to get out as much as I want him to stay. But he can't. He still has his own life like I have mine.

"It's just until tomorrow night," he says quietly, staring out the window at the docks filled with all types of boats, from fishing boats to yachts like the Ocean Jewel. He plans to sneak away to swim to me when everyone's sleeping.

"I know," I say, squeezing his hand.

He chuckles. "I was reminding myself." With a strong hug and a soft kiss, he pulls away and opens the door. "Call me if you need me, Ava. I'll figure out a way back if I have to."

I nod. "I'll try to think of a good reason."

He smiles, flashing his dimples, and then exits, closing the door gently. He looks over his shoulder a dozen times, making his way down the dock until he disappears in the maze of boats.

I consider staying here to watch the Ocean Jewel leave, but it won't be for another hour or so. Like the universe knows how pathetic I'm being, my cell phone rings from my center console. It's the first time it's rung in over a week, since I've been with everyone who calls me.

Giselle's smiling face pops up on my screen, and I answer it after the third ring. "Hey, what's up?"

"You better not bail on me today. You know how crazy my aunt is about these things," she responds. "She's shocked we waited this long. I threatened to wear my prom dress."

I laugh. "Want me to pick you up now? I just dropped Carter off at the harbor so I'm close." Hanging out with Giselle sounds a million times better than moping in the parking lot as my merman heads off to sea without me.

Giselle puffs air through the phone. "Totally. Come save me so I don't have to go with my mom. She mentioned something about matching colors, and I do *not* want to end up in another salmon pink dress. If we beat her, I can already have something picked out."

I cringe at the thought of her last fundraiser's dress. "Oh, God. I hope my mom hasn't talked to yours."

"She's already here, Aves," Giselle says, giggling.

"Okay, I'll save you soon. Meet me on the corner of Surf and Sunset. If they see me, we might get stuck riding together with them."

"I'm running out the door now."

It takes less than ten minutes to reach Giselle's street. She waves her arms over her head on the corner of the street exactly where I told her to meet me. Fake panic crosses her face, like she's signaling me to rescue her from a school of hungry piranhas.

I hit the button to open my window and yell, "Get in!"

Hopping in, she buckles her seatbelt, releasing a loud laugh. She smacks her hands on the dashboard, bouncing in her seat. I fly around the corner and head onto Ocean Boulevard. Her bronze hair blows in the wind coming in through the window, and salty air wafts around us.

"You're a lifesaver, Aves," she says. "I for sure thought I was going to drown in pink satin."

"I'm glad you called when you did. I was about to sit in my car with a pouty face until Carter left."

I expect her to roll her eyes or remark about how ridiculous I'm being, but instead, she says, "I'm sorry he had to go. If only our vacation never ended. You two could've been married by next week, and I'd have made the best maid of honor."

"Whoa, Gi. There will be no weddings anytime soon."

"You sure about that?" she says, pointing at my left hand. "That ring on your finger says otherwise." She's clearly joking, but I can't stop the dozens of explanations flying through my mind.

A deep blush blossoms across my cheeks. This is the first time she's noticed it since Carter gave it to me and probably only because I'm the one gripping the steering wheel.

"It's not what you think," I say.

"I'm not thinking anything...except that my BFF is wearing a ring that she would never pick out in a million years."

I playfully slap her arm. "If you must know, this is just a token from vacation. It doesn't mean anything other than I thought it was pretty, and Carter wanted to impress me."

She hums as she sighs. "That boy is perfect. Too perfect, Aves. Just be careful."

"I thought you were all for it?"

"I *am* but he better not mess up our house hunting plans. My mom scheduled an appointment with a realtor to check out what's for lease in La Tortuga Point. It's the perfect place between here and school."

I can't control the frown crossing my face. Luckily, my dark sunglasses hide my expression, and Giselle is too busy trying to get a better glimpse at the sea stone.

"It's pretty there," I say, navigating downtown Azure Waters in the direction of the dress boutique our moms had made appointments at.

"I know. I'm super excited you're actually on board for a beachfront place. My mom said they're almost done with some new condos. They'll be ready by the end of the month, and they still have vacancies."

I pull to the curb in front of Tatiana's Bridal and Gowns. "I figured we'd wait until right before school to move."

"Why? We started off the summer with a bang, might as

well keep it up. And think about it. Carter can stay whenever he's in town. I'll allow it if he promises to clean up after himself and not leave dirty towels all over the bathroom." She tilts her head against the seat, smiling at her own would-be-awesome plan if it didn't mean that I'd have to eventually hurt her by moving out.

"That sounds amazing, but—"

She holds up her hand. "But nothing, Ava. Our parents are on board. It's set."

I force myself to smile at her though my heart sinks into my stomach. The old Ava would be bouncing in her seat, excited and ready to pack up her bags and leave home. Part of me is still really excited but guilt holds me back. Maybe this is a sign. Maybe this means I can maintain my normal life after all. I just wish Carter was here so I could get his opinion.

Giselle pushes her door open and hops out, waiting for me on the sidewalk. When I join her, she nearly drags me into the boutique. She hums her version of the wedding march the second we pass a few mannequins in wedding gowns, and I snort a laugh. My mermaid transformation might have rushed things between me and Carter, but I'm pretty sure he'd agree there won't be a wedding in the near future. I want to at least make it to college first.

Tatiana, the owner and a friend of my mom's, greets us with a smile halfway toward the back of the store where the dressing area is. I keep my eyes trained on the prom dresses and formal gowns, far, far away from anything in the color white so Giselle will quit joking about it.

"I hope you don't mind if we're here early," Giselle says to Tatiana, greeting her with a hug. "But we had to get here to try on dresses before our moms add in their two cents."

"I take it you don't want complementary gowns this time?" Tatiana asks, laughing.

"Definitely not," Giselle says.

"I think I can arrange that. I have a few new pieces I think will look stunning on the both of you already picked out."

Tatiana leads the way to the back of the store where several private dressing areas take up the back wall. Upholstered chairs line the walls and surround a platform outside of the rooms for bridal gown viewing. Mirrors hang on every available wall including inside the changing rooms with curtains to give us privacy from the other shoppers.

Tatiana already has several dresses waiting for us on rolling racks. She pushes the rack intended for our moms against the wall and focuses on the one meant for us. Giselle quickly looks through, eyeing each dress before pulling out a floor-length, midnight blue gown with pearlescent black beads sewn in an intricate swirling pattern along the sheer top fabric. The deep V-cut guarantees she'll be taping her boobs in place, but none of that matters to her. She's picking something unlike anything her mom would ever wear.

"That's super sexy," I say. "Try it on."

She takes it behind the dressing partition while I run my fingers along the flouncy fabric of a deep red number. We spend over an hour and a half twirling and spinning, trying on and taking off before trying on again, several different styles. If we don't pick something soon, our moms will show up to give the final approval.

"Why don't you try this one on? I think it's a better fit for you than the others, Ava," Tatiana says. "It'll match your pretty eyes." She holds up the dress I've been purposely avoiding. A cerulean, mermaid-cut silhouette dress made of the lightest fabric I've ever felt sparkles in the light. Tiny pearls swirl along the rounded, strapless neckline, trailing down the front and around the skirt of the gown.

Surprise keeps me frozen in place. If she'd have suggested

this dress a few weeks ago, I'd have never even given it a second thought before trying it on, but it's like I'd be tempting fate if I do.

"Oh, yes! Try on that one, Aves. You'll rock the mermaid look. Imagine how Carter will drool. It's perfect and will accentuate all the right places." Giselle holds up her dark gray gown to keep the hem from dragging on the floor.

"I don't know," I say.

"Well, I do. Try it on."

With a sigh, I dangle the hanger from my finger and head behind my own partition. It only takes a moment for me to strip off my clothes and shimmy my way into the gown. It's a tiny bit long, but with heels, it won't graze the ground.

I step into the viewing area and spin around once before meeting Giselle's gaze. Her smile lights up her entire face, forcing her eyes to squint. She claps her hands, in true Giselle excitement, and rushes to snap a picture with her phone.

"Don't even bother trying on any more. That dress is yours. It's so gorgeous." She rushes closer and waves her hand over the dress without touching it. Grabbing my hand, she says, "And look! Your ring even matches it." Before I have a chance to stop her, she slides the ring off my finger to hold the sea stone against the fabric.

My mouth falls open, fear seizing my heart. I stare at the one thing keeping me out of my mermaid form in the hand of my best friend. Snatching it back, I slide it on my finger, praying I don't start the transformation in the middle of the dress shop.

Without hesitating, I rush to get out of the dress, leaving it crumpled on the floor and throw on my shorts and shirt. I'm not sticking around here to find out. This is different than all the times I triggered it before, and luckily, I don't just suddenly change. If that were to happen, I'd probably die since I wouldn't be able to complete my transformation without a breath of the sea. *Oh, God. Please, let me make it.*

"What's wrong, Aves?" Giselle asks as I fly from the partition.

"I have to go! I'm sorry, Gi. Take my stuff and my car, and please cover for me. Tell my mom I want the gown." I run toward the front door without stopping.

Giselle stays on my heels before reaching out to grab my shoulder. "Ava, wait!"

I tug from her. "I'll explain later. Please, just do what I asked and don't follow me. You have to trust me, okay?"

Without looking back, I dash through the door, running barefooted toward the end of the block where a set of stairs leads to the beach below. *Please, don't let me transform. Please, let me be okay. It was ten seconds.*

My feet sink into the sand, and I run as fast as I can down the beach and toward the water. A few beachgoers lie in the sun, and a few surfers wait for a good swell, so I keep running toward the cliffs where the beach remains empty. The rocks are too sharp and slippery and the tide will rise too high.

Cramps travel up my legs before I even reach the water. The transformation is definitely happening, and there's nothing I can do to stop it. I bolt into the ocean near the rocks, swimming through the tightening muscles on my back. I barely manage to remove my shorts before scales sprout on my legs. It's already too late for my T-shirt. The tight fit pulls against my dorsal fin and rips through on the sharpness along the lower back. At least my bra was tough enough to survive.

Inhaling a deep breath of ocean water, I dive deeper, traveling along the bottom, scraping my stomach against the rocks. I swim past the waves until the ground drops out from under me, and I can descend away from the surface.

If anyone saw me dive in and not come up, it might cause

some serious trouble. At least I didn't recognize anyone, so while they might put the effort in to find a missing person, my name wouldn't be attached to it. It's the only thing that stops me from erupting into full blown panic.

I just hope I can figure out what to tell Giselle about my sudden fleeing. While fear nudges at me, the rest of me feels complete relief. This could've ended horribly. I never in a million years dreamed that someone—especially Giselle—would remove the ring from my finger and leave me vulnerable. I'm just thankful I had the chance to get to the water. I don't know what I'd have done if my mom decided she wanted to go to one of the department stores more inland.

And now, here I am, clutching my wet clothes against my chest as I drift along the current in my mermaid form without Carter nearby. *Why did this have to happen now when he is already somewhere on the sea so far away...*

His face pops into my mind, and a need unlike anything I've ever felt consumes me. I want nothing more than to find him. It's all I can think about. The thought is so powerful I can't even manage to transform back into my human form.

I close my eyes and concentrate but nothing happens. A sudden tingling sensation crosses my chest, tugging at my heart. If I don't follow it, my heart might escape my ribcage and leave me behind. Instead of trying to force myself to change back into a human to find Giselle to try to fix things, I dart away from the shore and let my heart lead the way.

15

ON LAND OR IN THE SEA

THE OCEAN JEWEL FLOATS AHEAD off the coast in what I can only guess is Orange County. I'm not even sure how to find my way back home except for going south, and even then, it'll be hard to find my town among the dozens of beach communities along the way.

I circle the water below the yacht, weaving in and out of the sunbeams cutting through from above. I can't break the surface in fear of being seen, so the only thing I can do is wait for night to come and pray Carter walks the deck so I can call out to him.

At least he's here. I know it. I can feel him as he caters to the guests aboard.

After a few minutes, I swim around the yacht a few times. The wait is torture. I'm already too far from home to turn back, but I'm not risking going to shore either. I don't know these beaches. A random girl rising from the waves will surely attract attention if someone sees me.

I stare up at the bottom of the yacht, watching as whomever the guests are launch the jet skis from the hydraulic platform. Leaving behind a glittering trail of bubbles in their wake, the jet skis take off away from the Ocean Jewel. I follow along behind them out of boredom. Anxiety crosses my mind—not because I'm afraid of the riders but because I'm worried about their safety as one of the jet skis cuts through the water in a drunken-like pattern.

The jet ski flies along the top, bouncing across the surface before spinning and tipping over. A man flies from the craft, splashing into the water, though his lifejacket prevents me from seeing his face. He treads the water, kicking his legs to swim back to his jet ski. As I watch him, he struggles to climb back on. Every time he tries, it pushes the jet ski farther and farther away. He's quite a ways away from the Ocean Jewel, and after a few minutes, he gives up.

His muted voice sounds through the water as he calls for help. I glance around at the few fish darting away, afraid of the commotion he's creating. And he's sure making a lot of it. If I couldn't see under the surface myself, I'd think hungry sharks in the mood for something obnoxious were heading in his direction. But then I notice something strange floating through the water. Clear, orb-like jellyfish drift on the current. They float right near the surface, and in the clear water, he'd be able to see at least the one that floats two feet away from him.

He swims away from the jet ski in the direction of the yacht. He's too slow to get away from the jellyfish, and one brushes against his leg. His yells penetrate through the water to me, and I can't stop myself from swimming closer. If I get too close, he might think I'm some ocean monster, but I'm pretty sure his focus remains on the pain caused by the sting of the pesky jellyfish.

Getting as close as I can, I flick my tail, sending a current toward the jellyfish, shooing them away from the man. I fan my tail a few more times until he's free from the small school.

Another jet ski glides across the water, stopping near the man. A familiar figure jumps into the sea, helping the man up onto the craft here to help him. My heart nearly explodes in relief when I see Carter duck under the water to swim toward the abandoned jet ski to retrieve it.

I propel up to him, swimming just beneath him, and he freezes next to the jet ski before sinking under a foot to peer around. The surprise on his face is priceless, and he unexpectedly inhales a gulp of ocean water. In his human form, it causes him to choke, and he kicks back to the surface.

Staying on the side away from the yacht, I pop my head from the water where he treads. His eyes widen when he sees me, but he doesn't yell at me to dive back under. He only reaches out and rubs his fingers under my chin before he pulls himself onto the jet ski.

He peers down at me with sad eyes. "Ava, what are you doing here?"

"Giselle took my ring right off my finger in a moment of excitement while we were dress shopping," I blurt.

The horror that crosses his face mirrors what mine surely looked like at the time. "You transfor—"

"I made it to the water in time," I say, cutting him off. Holding up my hand, I show him the ring he gave me back on my finger. "But she knows something was wrong. I was so upset by the whole incident that I couldn't force myself to change back and somehow, I ended up here."

"Because you really wanted to find me."

A tear trickles on my cheek, mixing with the saltwater on my face. Carter glances around, turning his gaze to the Ocean Jewel.

"I don't know how to get home," I say, drawing his attention back to me. "What do I do?"

"Give me a few minutes. I'm going to take the next group on the water, and I want you to follow me. There are some caves along the cliffs where you can wait for me until tonight, okay? I don't want to risk leaving you out here in case you trigger the transformation back."

Without waiting for me to respond, he propels forward on

the jet ski toward the Ocean Jewel, and I sink underwater to wait.

Ten minutes later, I watch all three jet skis take off together, cutting through the water. The glittering trail they leave behind guides me down the shore. One of the jet skis breaks off from the other two, navigating in a wide circle. Carter dives in the water, pretending to lose control. He smiles at me, pointing his hand behind him, and then he kicks to the surface and climbs on his jet ski before taking off with the others behind him.

My heart aches with every passing second, the trail of bubbles left in Carter's wake now popped along the surface. I wish he could come with me now, but it'd be impossible for him to escape without drawing attention to himself or causing people to panic, thinking he fell overboard. He'd never be able to show his face again, which means that I probably wouldn't be able to either, not if I can't handle this on my own. Obviously after today, I know I can't. I don't want to even if I could.

With one more longing look in the direction Carter left, I swim toward the cliffs. Waves pulverize the scattered rocks leading up to them, and even with my underwater vision, I can barely see past the stirred up sand and bubbles.

It's like a maze navigating the shallow water, and my tail skims the rough surfaces of the rocks as I fight the current to make my way to the caves only the brave would ever attempt to explore. It'd be humanly impossible to make it to them by sea without getting injured. No boat could fit through the spaces between the rocks, the waves threatening to send even me back deeper into the sea. To safely get to them, a person would have to rappel down the cliff and still fight off the angry, rising tide that protects them.

Remaining in my mermaid form, I pull myself from the water and drag my tail into the narrow cave. Water splashes me, knocking me deeper within. Darkness sends a chill to my bones though it fades as my eyes adjust to the dark waters.

Another wave crashes against me, flipping me backward, and I fall into a glowing pool of water that laps gently around me, rising and falling with the waves. It's the size of a small swimming pool and just deep enough that I can float upright without breaking the surface or hitting my tail against the bottom.

Sparkling jewel-like rocks form the walls, the gems flickering in imaginary light. It takes me a moment to realize that their power source isn't coming from within them, but they're catching the light emanating from the spark in my chest. Their soft glow quiets the stress and anxiety in my heart, and after a few minutes, I drift in and out of sleep, wrapped in the safety of this beautiful place with only a sliver of dread tickling my mind about what's to come and how my life might soon be changed forever once again.

"Ava?" Carter's voice enters my mind, tugging me from sleep.

Snapping my eyes open, I peer around the jewel-encrusted pool, trying to orient myself to my surroundings. Without seeing the sun, time escaped me, sending fear rushing through me again. I should be used to the constant state of panic, but being with Carter has been such a relief.

"Ava, I'm here." He slides into the pool, stirring up the sand along the bottom.

I close the distance between us and embrace him. A mixture of emotions courses through me—from excitement and joy to trepidation and uncertainty, but most of all just sweet relief. I pepper him with kisses, so glad that he's here. Laughing underwater, he pushes bubbles from his mouth, a smile lighting his entire face. He brushes his fingers through my floating hair, brushing it from my face before meeting my lips with his for a long, passionate kiss.

When he pulls away, he studies my eyes, a seriousness now narrowing his lips and lowering his brows on his forehead. "You okay?" His soft voice trickles through my mind like a whisper.

Pouting, I say, "I don't even know if I am or not. What time is it anyway? I'm sure my mom's put out a search party by now."

He glides his hands down my sides, hooking them around my hips to keep me floating in front of him. "It's almost nine."

It's been hours. So long so that I don't even know what kind of excuse I can make up. If Giselle took my car for me, it'd be less to explain to my parents, but I have no idea what to even say to her. I don't know what I would do in her situation, but I hope that she trusted me enough to hold off before going to the police or something.

I groan. "We need to go."

"Okay." He pulls me closer. "But I want you to be prepared. If your family has already put out a search party, we're not going to be able to stay. It'll draw too much attention and unwanted questions."

If my heart wasn't anchored in my chest, I think it'd slide out of me and splatter on the sandy floor. I squeeze my eyes closed, tears burning but never falling because they blend with the sea. I was afraid this might happen, but the fact that Carter says the words to me makes it worse. It was always a what-if possibility, but it's turning into a what-must-happen situation.

Carter pulls me close, resting his chin on my shoulder, pressing against me. He rubs soothing circles on my back, but it does nothing to ease the pain of knowing I might have to say goodbye to my friends and family forever.

"Carter." I hide in his neck. A million thoughts rush through my head as I try to think of something—anything— that I can use as an excuse to explain my disappearance to make anything bad that might've happened go away. Nothing sounds believable, though. Maybe I can just not say anything at all. Fake amnesia.

He kisses my temple. "Please, Ava. Don't panic just yet. Everything might be okay. We might not have anything to worry about. I just need you to be prepared in case."

"Okay." The words barely sound in my mind. I'm not even sure if I projected them to Carter.

Hugging me to him, he guides me to the edge of the glowing pool. The water churns with his sudden movement as he propels himself onto the slippery floor first and then helps me up, pulling me along through the darkness until we reach the cave entrance that drops back into the ocean.

He exits first, jumping into the shallows with enough precision not to hurt himself like he's done this dozens of times. I sit on the ledge, my tail smacking the water. It takes him opening his arms for me to fall into before I launch from the cave and back into the sea.

Even with the glowing night water, it's hard to see a few feet in front of us because of the white foam and sand. Rocks skim against my tail as Carter swims us back to the open water, me locked under him in his arms so tightly that it's like I'm just carried on the waves.

The ocean floor steepens, Carter diving us deeper in the open water a good distance from shore. His grip loosens, and he lets me go but only so I can move to ride on his broad back. Without looking around, I press my cheek between his shoulder blades, just feeling his body against mine as we jet through the current.

After what feels like no time at all, Carter slows down. He swims us into shallow water near the same rocks I recognize to be the ones not far from my neighborhood. We break the surface, and I peer around. The beach is empty this time of night, and I sigh a breath of relief when I don't see anything out of the ordinary at my house. If my parents thought I'd gone missing, there'd have been dozens of people around like after Bailey disappeared. The whole community would be on alert.

"Can you transform?" Carter asks softly, his breath blowing against my hair. He holds me to him so I don't drift away.

I close my eyes, imagining the land, but after a few minutes, nothing happens. No cramps or tightening muscles. Only thoughts of dread and despair.

"I can't," I finally say after a long moment.

"Try harder." Carter dips under the water before popping up to spit water away from me. His legs slide against my tail as he waits for me to follow his lead. The fear and anxiety of leaving the water proves to be too much, because even after another ten minutes of trying, I just can't get myself to return to my human form.

"Carter, I don't think I'm going to have to explain myself. I can't change. Something's wrong with me." I brush my wet hair from my face before bobbing under.

He pulls me back to the surface. "What do you want to do? We can wait it out, or we can head back to the Ocean Jewel, and I can quit tomorrow. We'll head up to San Francisco to see if my parents will help, but you know what they'll say."

I cover my face with my hands. "I just want to change b—"

Carter's words, the idea of going back to San Francisco to prove his parents right, is enough to trigger the transformation. Muscle spasms seize my legs, and tingles rush through my body. Carter holds my hand as I thrash underwater, the pain of the transformation burning through me like fire while the icy water licks over my skin. It takes a lot longer than usual, but after another minute, I spit out water, clearing my lungs.

"It's a lot harder to come back when it's the lack of the sea stone that sets you off," Carter says, forcing me to swim next to him even though I just want to sink back under the waves.

I don't respond. I can't. Exhaustion takes hold of me, and the only reason I manage to make it to the shore at all is because Carter carries me. We lie together on the sand without moving, the waves crashing over our bodies. Carter turns his head to look at me and offers a small smile, not the one he usually saves for me. Under this one lies pity and sorrow. Things I don't want or need right now. I don't call him out on it, though. This is bad enough as it is.

After another minute of rest, he helps me unwind my clothes from my arm. They leave a deep indent in my skin, but there was no way I was going to lose them and end up naked somewhere. When I'm dressed in my ripped shirt and sandy shorts, Carter pulls his own board shorts and shirt from the bag across his chest.

"I'm not leaving until we make sure everything's okay," he says, dusting the sand from my arms. "And if it's not, we'll stay around long enough for you to pack a few things."

I swallow, a lump in my throat making it hard to even speak. "Okay."

Carter leads the way up the beach to my house. The back porch light shines over our patio, but I don't see any other lights on. Sneaking around to the front, I peer into the window near the door, but I can't see anything in the darkness.

I head to the side stairs that lead to the balcony of the guest apartment over the garage and pull the key from the combination locked box on the wall. Cool air drifts out as Carter follows me inside. I enter the hallway and pad my way across the carpet to my parents' bedroom. It's empty.

"It's not unlike my parents to have drinks at the vodka bar near the marina with their friends on my dad's night off," I say, hoping I'm right and they're not searching the area for me.

Carter follows me downstairs where I find the sticky note

on the fridge from my mom saying she left money on the counter so Giselle and I could have a nice dinner somewhere and that she really loved the dress I picked out.

I puff a breath of air through my lips. "Everything's fine with my parents. Giselle covered for me."

His brows scrunch together. "But what about Giselle? She's going to expect an explanation, Ava. You can't tell her."

I crumble the sticky note in my hand. "I know that!" I can't stop the anger from entering my voice. "Give me some credit. I know how important our secret is."

He blinks a few times, probably because I've never directed my anger at him before. It's just the day's events have my emotions all over the place. I was expecting the worst possible outcome, and Carter reminding me doesn't help the situation.

"I'm sorry. I just know how close you are," he says softly.

Relaxing my shoulders, I turn to face him. "And it kills me not telling her, but it is what it is. I get it, Carter. Don't ever doubt me."

"I don't." He leans over and brushes his lips against my forehead.

As I gaze into his eyes, I can see that even though he says he doesn't doubt me, a part of him still does. It's enough to make me step away and turn my back on him. It's hard for me to meet his eyes and face this reality. Not because I'm hurt by his lack of faith, but because I might doubt myself as well. It would be so much easier to tell Giselle, to trust her with my secret. I have a million reasons to do so. She'd never betray me. We have the kind of relationship that could survive something even as absurd as this. But it's the secrets that might be our undoing.

After a minute of silence, I turn back to him and say, "I'm going to call Giselle and then hop in the shower. Want me to walk you back to the beach? I can handle my best friend without you."

The concern that crosses his face disappears with a small shake of his head. "You don't look so sure."

I force myself to smile. "I am, promise."

He doesn't question me or argue though the doubt still lingers in his eyes. This is his way of letting me figure this out on my own, letting me make my own mistakes. I can't blame him for not putting up a fight. I wouldn't if I were him. But even so, his trust in me emanates from him stronger than the spark of doubt, and it's enough to calm my nerves, to make me feel like I won't screw this up. That everything will be okay no matter what happens in the end.

I slide my hands around his neck, standing on my tiptoes to kiss him. He relaxes under my touch, kissing me back like our kiss is all that he needs from me, like it's more important than where we find ourselves in the world, whether it's on land or deep within the sea.

When he pulls away, he grins, flashing his dimples in the smile he saves just for me. "You know, my life has gotten so much more exciting with you in it."

"It's safe to say I feel the same," I say with a laugh.

I stroll next to him to my back door, and we step onto the patio together. The moon shines above us, casting soft light on the water, and my heart aches a tiny bit as he kisses me once more.

"I'll come back tomorrow night, okay?" he says as he pulls away.

All I can do is nod. Gazing after him, I watch him undress and head into the ocean. He looks back once to wave, and then his tail cuts through the water as he dives, leaving me alone, damp, and cold on the beach.

Hugging myself, I turn and head back inside to face what's to come.

I hope I can figure it out to save everything Carter's

worked hard for to stay on land. I hope I can figure things out to save me as well. I don't want to be responsible for forcing us into the sea.

16

DEVASTATING SECRET

THE HEADLIGHTS OF MY BMW illuminate my front door. Giselle pulls my car into my driveway, keeping the car running. I dash down the steps and climb into the passenger's seat, a whirlwind of emotions leaving my hands shaking in my lap.

She doesn't say anything, driving my car back onto the street and in the direction of her house. The tension between us is suffocating, nearly unbearable, because I know what's on her mind, but she's waiting for me to say something first. If only I could find the words to make this better.

I inhale a slow breath through my nose. "Gi, I—"

"You don't know how damn worried I was about you!" she yells, smacking her hands on the steering wheel, jerking the car in the lane. "What the hell happened?"

My words stay locked in my throat as her anger sizzles between us. This is worse than the time I ditched her during a party last summer when someone suggested they move things to the beach. I can feel her emotions ten times more than I can feel my own with the way she directs her worry, fear, and fury at me.

Instead of answering, I stare out the window. Nothing I could come up with excuses my erratic behavior and sudden disappearance today. The only plausible thing I can think of is the truth, and there's no way I can let Carter down like that. I know there would be consequences if someone were to find out, and they're bad enough that Carter won't even tell me besides the fact that we'd have to disappear.

Giselle's anger fizzles out the longer I don't say anything. "Aves? Are you okay? Did something bad happen?"

I still don't respond, because whatever I say won't be able to answer her questions.

She reaches out and grabs my hand. "Please, say something."

I blink away tears. "I'm okay, Gi. I just—I can't answer your questions. You have to trust me that everything is fine. I rushed out today because—because—" I take a deep breath. "I can't explain."

Giselle side-glances me in her vision before pulling over to park next to the curb. She cuts off the engine and shifts in her seat to look at me. Her amber eyes, dark in the orange glow of the streetlight above us, study me. I focus on the shadow cutting across her face instead of her eyes, because I'm afraid she'll somehow read the truth in my mind if I let her see the emotions lingering on my soul through my eyes.

"If you're in trouble, I want to help you," she finally says. "Does this have to do with—" She snaps her mouth shut before saying Carter's name. I know it's him she's thinking about.

I shake my head. "Carter's not even here, Gi. And you can't tell him either, okay?"

Her twisted lips and furrowed brows tell me she's going to reach out to him the moment she can. Carrying the kind of worry she has for me is enough to make her confide in someone close to me, and at this time, it happens to be Carter.

"I'm serious, Giselle. Please, just trust me when I say I'm fine."

"If our places were switched, would you trust me? Wouldn't you do everything you could to make sure I was okay?"

She's right. I would. "But I *am* okay. I swear, if I wasn't I'd tell you. I just—I can't tell you or anyone what happened."

"Why not, Ava?"

I sigh. "Because if I do, it'll ruin my life."

She's quiet for a moment, processing my words. Then she surprises me by saying, "Please, tell me you didn't murder someone or something."

I laugh. I can't help it. "Do you honestly think I would murder someone?"

She frowns. "This isn't funny. What am I supposed to think if whatever you can't tell me is capable of ruining your life?"

"Just trust me. It's nothing illegal."

"I do trust you, but it's not going to stop me from being hurt and angry with you because I want you to trust me as well. I'm your BFF. That's best friends *forever*, you know." She brushes her hair behind her ears with her fingers.

My heart aches with every passing beat knowing how this one devastating secret is enough to tear my friendship apart. But what would be worse? Damaging my friendship with Giselle or losing it altogether?

"Gi, please. You have to understand."

"I can't, Ava. I'm trying, but I can't."

I sigh, tears of frustration splashing onto my cheeks. "Okay, here's the deal. Something happened to me on vacation. It does involve Carter, but he's not the bad guy. This secret I'm keeping—it's his, too. If anyone were to find out, we'd have to run—disappear—and I'd never see you again. So, I'm sorry if you're hurt and angry. But I don't want to give up my life to make you feel better. I'm willing to piss you off so I don't lose my BFF, because I want it to be *forever* more than anything."

Her mouth falls open, and she sobs hysterically, crying into her hands. It sets me off, and together we bawl our eyes out on the side of the road overlooking the dark ocean. She sniffles, wrapping her arms around me, and I embrace my best friend like I'll lose her if I let her go.

"A-Ava," she says, hiccupping. "I-I'm so scared f-for y-you."

I nod my head, tears blurring my eyes. "Don't be. I'm not in danger. I—I just have to keep this secret."

Taking a deep breath, Giselle composes herself enough to wipe the tears from her face with the back of her hands. "Okay," she finally says. "But if you do decide to tell anyone, I better be the first to know."

"Deal."

We hug each other for a long while, just sitting in the car with the soft sound of the radio to drown out our sniffles. It isn't until the dashboard clock blinks midnight that Giselle starts the car again and pulls from the curb.

"Want to spend the night?" I ask as we head onto Surf Way. "We didn't get much time on vacation."

The corners of her glassy, red eyes crinkle as she smiles. "I'd like that. I'm really missing my BFF."

"Well, don't. 'Cause I'm right here."

For now... I push the thoughts away. I can't bear to even think them.

★★★

"Ava-babe, you decided to come!" Logan yells from his spot next to Daisy on the sand.

I kick sand up, strolling next to Giselle. We head down the beach toward the massive fire pit glowing on the shore. Sapphire and Chloe sit next to each other while Matty stands, holding a wire hanger with a marshmallow stuck to it into the flames.

"Gi, how did you convince her?" Sapphire asks, smiling.

"She didn't have to," I say. "I'm here by my own freewill and desire to hang out with my friends. Besides, half of us aren't going to be here for much longer."

Chloe groans. "Don't remind me. I'm going to be the third wheel with these two." She points at Logan and Daisy who both laugh.

"We won't be far," Giselle says, plopping on the sand next to Sapphire.

I take the empty spot next to Chloe with my back to the ocean. While staring at the fire, I can almost pretend I'm not on the beach. I really wanted to bail on Giselle, but I still feel really bad about our confrontation last night. She hasn't asked me more about what I'm hiding, but I know it's constantly on her mind.

"LA's not that far either," Sapphire chimes in. "We'll have a spare bedroom so you all can visit anytime."

"Which we will," Daisy says.

"Definitely," Logan adds.

As my friends talk about what's ahead in our futures, I can't help thinking about what's next for me. I was accepted into the same school as Giselle—we have plans to live together—but it's starting to feel impossible. I know it'll only last a short while, but even so, how will I explain staying out all night every full moon? Or why I come home soaking wet when I'm supposed to be terrified of the ocean?

"Ava-babe?" Matty's voice cuts through my train of thought. He snaps his fingers in front of my face. "Aves, hello?"

I jerk my head up. "Huh?"

"Jeez, zone much?" Sapphire asks, laughing.

"Sorry, I was just thinking. What's up?"

"I asked about Carter. When's he coming back? We're supposed to make plans to go surfing," Matty says.

"Oh, tomorrow. He'll be going to the gala with me," I say.

Giselle listens quietly while watching me, but she doesn't say anything. I know she probably thinks badly of Carter now. Why wouldn't she? I wish I could say something to make sure she really knows that none of this is his fault. He saved me.

"Cool, we can all ride together. The limo picks us up for a little pre-gala partying. You know how those things are," he says.

I smirk. The obligatory pre-party is the only way any of us has ever made it through one of these boring fundraisers people pay a fortune to attend to sit around and make small talk with people they gossip about behind their backs. I've been gossiped about along with the rest of my friends for one thing or another.

Last year it was because Chloe's brother gave up his full scholarship to Stanford for a surf sponsorship. The year before that, it was because Logan was arrested for trespassing. This year will surely involve either people speculating how quickly Sapphire will blow through her trust fund, how Daisy's taking a gap year and probably won't even go to college, or even me, because I'm bringing a boy none of the elite in our community has ever met. They'll probably talk about all three. I'll have to smile my brightest for the photo that'll appear in the Azure Waters Gazette.

"Matty, it's your year to be the center of attention," Sapphire says. "I already told a dozen people you pushed Ava off the yacht."

Heat blooms in my cheeks. "You didn't!"

She laughs with a shrug.

Giselle rolls her eyes. "She didn't, Aves."

"Should we take bets?" Logan asks.

I toss a marshmallow at him. "You always lose."

My friends laugh, retelling their version of how I flipped over the guardrail, and how Carter flew off the yacht moments after me. Now that we're all still alive and sitting in the sand, the horrors of that night are just one of the adventures we've all shared. That night feels like a blur to me as well. I only remember Carter apologizing and the spark. Everything else came from Carter's memory.

When the topic shifts to what dresses us girls are wearing, I hop to my feet and stroll around to face the waves. Giselle shows Sapphire pictures of our gowns, and I wonder which one Giselle ended up picking out. She never once mentions my erratic behavior.

As I stare at the ocean, a glimmer of light within the water catches my attention. It cuts through the waves, like a small beacon of light, luring me to follow it down the shore away from my friends.

"Ava? What's up?" Giselle calls from behind me.

I'm already strolling away through the sand. "I'll be right back," I call before I start to jog.

"You're not going to jump in the ocean are you?" Matty calls out.

I shake my head, whipping my blond hair back and forth. "I'm going to the bathroom if you're that interested."

Thankfully, no one gets up to follow me. The public restrooms are visible behind the empty lifeguard tower, so my friends can watch me walk, but probably only Giselle stares at me. No one else has reason to be suspicious. Though going to the bathroom is the least thing for her to be suspicious about.

I round the corner of the bathroom where the women's restroom is, but I don't go inside. I keep jogging down the beach, using the building to block my friends' view of me. Turning my gaze back to the ocean, I study the light moving closer to the beach, and then I see him.

Carter emerges from the waves, his dark silhouette contrasting with the whitecaps shining under the moon. He pauses to slide on his swim trunks and then jogs through the sand to me. Smiling, I close the distance, wrapping my arms around his wet body not even caring that water soaks through my shirt. He promised he'd come to me tonight, but I thought it'd be much later and where I could swim with him amid the waves.

"I expected you later," I say, pushing his wet hair from his forehead. "I'm not alone."

He licks the saltwater from his lips. "I couldn't wait. I've been anxious all day."

"I told you I'd handle it, and I did..." My words trail off.

"But?"

I exhale a long breath. "Giselle kinda thinks we're involved in something awful. She asked me if I murdered someone."

He laughs, having the same reaction I did to her question. "She's gonna hate me."

"She'll get over it. All that matters is that she won't ask any more questions."

"Good," he says, kissing me again.

His lips taste of the ocean and something sweeter, like he's just eaten dessert, and I sink into him, letting him pick me up off the ground a few inches. Even after how I left Carter last night, it's so easy to forget that he might've doubted me. And now, he won't ever doubt me again.

"Ava?" Giselle's voice rings out over the sounds of the surf and our beating hearts.

I cringe, pulling away from Carter. "You have to go!" I whisper-hiss, pushing him back.

"One more kiss," he says, tugging my arm. He pulls me to the back of the building, facing the water. Cupping my face, he kisses me deeply, teasing me with his tongue, until I consider following him back to the ocean.

"Ava? Where are you?" It only takes Giselle's voice to call me back to the land before something happens that I'll regret.

Carter kisses my cheek once more before he charges toward the water and dives under. Turning away, I stroll around the building and watch as Giselle comes out from looking in the women's bathroom for me.

When she sees me, she tilts her head to the side in question. "Why are you wet?"

I brush my fingers over my damp shirt where I was pressed against Carter's dripping chest. The thought sends a shiver through me. Rubbing my hands over my arms, I play it off like I'm cold and not thinking about my hot merman boyfriend.

"The stupid hand dryer is broken again," I say, stepping up next to her.

"But why were you over there?" She points to the back of the building.

"The water fountain." The lie comes so easily that I almost believe it. But for some reason, doubt crosses her face though she doesn't admit it.

"We're all heading back to Sapphire's to use the spa. Wanna come?"

I consider it for a moment, but the thought of Carter sits in the back of my mind. "I have to decorate a few cakes for the gala. My mom's paying me. Want to come help me instead?" I only ask because I know baking is the last thing she likes to do.

She frowns. "It can't wait?"

"I can get up early," I say.

She shakes her head. "No, it's okay. I don't want you to crash halfway through the gala. I can't survive it without you."

We kick our way back to the others through the sand. Daisy helps Logan put out the fire while the others pick up the blankets and trash.

"I can drop you off if you want," I say, glancing at the ocean every so often.

"Sapphire can drive me," she says, hugging me. "I'll come

by tomorrow before our hair appointment with lunch to make up for not helping you with the cakes."

I laugh. "Thanks."

The others groan when Giselle tells them I'm bailing on them, but only Matty offers to help decorate the cakes I already finished this afternoon while Giselle was having lunch with her mom and grandma who came in from out of town.

"You can't eat them, though," I say, teasingly, knowing well enough that Matty doesn't actually intend to decorate any-thing.

"Damn, you're on your own then, Ava-babe," he says, climbing into the front seat of Sapphire's Tesla.

I climb behind the wheel of my car and start it up, but I don't leave. I wait for my friends to turn the corner before I shut off the engine and climb out.

After dropping my clothes in the sand under the lifeguard tower, I rush into the ocean before diving under.

Carter greets me with a smile, and we swim away from the shore.

17

IRREPARABLE DAMAGE

BRIGHT SUNSHINE WARMS MY SKIN as I lean against my silver BMW, eyeing the docks anxiously for signs of Carter. I only have tonight and tomorrow morning with him on land, and I want to enjoy every second of it.

The black bag of his tuxedo hangs on the back window of my car from where I picked it up from the rental place only an hour ago. He had picked one out in Laguna and had it sized and rush delivered to the local mall near my house just in time.

When Carter enters the parking lot, he's all smiles, striding to me. He stops in front of me, bringing his hand to my cheek and gazes into my eyes for a moment. He's never seen me wear this much makeup ever, but Giselle insisted on fake lashes and glittery eyeliner to match the shimmery pearls of my gown.

"I almost didn't recognize you," he says, running his fingers behind my ear to graze them over the curls of my low bun.

"It's a bit much, huh?"

He shakes his head. "You're still just as beautiful."

After a moment of admiring me, he kisses me softly before pulling away to stick his duffle bag behind my seat. He then opens the door for me, and I get behind the wheel and start the engine as he gets in the front seat beside me. Locking our fingers together, I drive from the harbor with one hand, glancing at Carter in my peripheral vision every so often.

Fifteen minutes later, I pull into my driveway, parking in

front of the door instead of the garage. My mom greets Carter with a warm smile when we enter the house. She's already ready, wearing a floor-length, capped sleeved gown in a deep burgundy color that brings out the dark streaks of gold in her hair.

"I'm so happy you could make it, Carter," she says, offering him a hug instead of a handshake. "Ava told you that you could stay in the guest apartment, right?"

He nods, beaming a smile. "Yes, thank you for the offer, Beatrice."

"My pleasure. Now, if you two will excuse me, I have to find Ava's father so we can head out. Ruby wants to go over her speech once more before the gala starts." She turns to look at me. "Don't be late, Avie."

I sigh. "Can't promise that, Mom. Matty rented the limo. He's in charge."

She shakes her head. "I'll see you two later."

I guide Carter up to my room where Giselle sits at my vanity table taking pictures of herself in the mirror. Her bronze hair cascades in soft curls down her bare back. The backless, navy blue gown has a deep V neckline and small cutouts that run up the sides, starting at her hips, showing off tiny slivers of her smooth skin.

"Our date has arrived," she exclaims, grinning, but something in her eyes makes my steps falter.

"How did I get so lucky to have two of the prettiest girls of Azure Waters on my arms tonight?" he asks.

Giselle's eyes soften. She's a sucker for a compliment. "We're sure to be at the center of the gossip."

"Totally," I say. "Can you imagine Mrs. Goldberg's face?" Mrs. Goldberg sits on the scholarship board along with our moms. She once tried to ban people under the age of eighteen from attending the gala a few years ago, but it didn't stand well considering that the rest of the board members had children.

"She's going to be huffing about how inappropriate we're being at such a prestigious event," Giselle says, rolling her eyes.

"Do I have time to back out?" Carter asks with a teasing smile.

"No way. We might just send you in alone."

Carter laughs, adjusting his tuxedo bag on his arm.

"Let me show you to the guest apartment so you can get ready," I say, pulling him away.

"Yeah, you can't see Ava again until after she's completely ready, so go downstairs when you're done," Giselle calls as I guide Carter from my room even though he knows the way.

After I get Carter settled in the small suite over the garage, I head back to my room to change into my gown, the one I've dreaded wearing since it nearly ruined everything. *That was you, not the dress.*

Giselle helps me zip up the side and hooks a pearl necklace my mom let me borrow around my neck. Matching pearl earrings shine from my ears, the perfect addition to my dress. I touch up my makeup, add a few jeweled bobby pins to my curled bun, and grab my clutch off my dresser before turning to Giselle.

"We're so hot," she says. "Like, I just want to stare at us in the mirror the rest of the night. Everyone will be looking at us. Who knows, maybe I'll actually meet someone tonight."

Nerves tighten my stomach at the thought of being under the microscope. "I just hope I don't fall on my face in these shoes," I say, lifting my dress to show my ivory strappy heels.

"Well, if you do, I promise to fall, too. You can do the same for me."

I smile and hug my best friend. "We'll take Carter down with us. Might as well make it a dramatic performance if it were to happen."

She giggles while pulling away to grab her own purse. "Speaking of Carter, everything okay with you two?"

"Yeah, it's great. Promise."

She nods. "Okay, let's go find him. I can't wait to see his reaction to you."

We head downstairs where we find Carter hovering by the back door, gazing out the window at the ocean. As he turns, my heart flutters at the sight of him in his slim-fit, dark gray tuxedo with a matching bowtie. His dark hair is styled back out of his face, and he's shaved, his dimples in clear view when he smiles his perfect smile as his gaze lingers over me.

"Wow," he says breathlessly. "Ava, you're—you look just like..." His voice trails off.

"So hot, right?" Giselle says, laughing.

"Beautiful, stunning, breathtaking," he says, leaning down to kiss me softly.

"Okay! Enough with the gushy stuff. We need pics. The limo will be here any minute." Giselle grabs my arm to pull me away from Carter.

Carter takes a gazillion photos of us on the back patio with the ocean as our backdrop. I manage to get her to take a few of me and Carter before we all squeeze together for Carter to get one of the three of us.

Giselle, now swept up with the excitement of the night, doesn't look at Carter with suspicious eyes anymore. She's all smiles and twirls, acting like she did while we were on vacation. It's such a relief considering how uncomfortable we all felt knowing that there is basically a whale-sized secret hanging out next to me.

Ten minutes later, the doorbell rings, and we rush out to join the others who yell and catcall from the limo. Logan helps me in, and I slide in on the opposite side of him, leaving room for Carter, who climbs in last. Giselle sits on the other side of

Carter and forces Daisy to take another picture.

When the limo takes off, Sapphire pulls out a few glasses from the drink compartment, and Matty helps her pour champagne into the flutes to pass around. It's prom night all over again, except I actually have a date who can't stop looking over at me.

Carter clinks his flute with mine, taking a small sip. Giselle downs hers in two gulps and holds out her glass for Sapphire to refill. Matty laughs at Giselle, holding his glass up before gulping it down just as quickly.

"You might want to finish that," Logan says, tipping his glass toward Carter. "Because these things suck. If my mom wasn't on the board, I'd have bailed and left Daisy to fend for herself."

Daisy glares. "I guess you don't want to have fun at *my* after party."

Logan laughs. "You know I'm just playing, babe."

The two of them kiss, and I turn away to gaze out the tinted windows as we wind up the coastal highway toward the Grand Le Mer hotel, which sits atop a cliff overlooking the water. I finish my champagne, and Sapphire fills up my glass again before I have a chance to decline since Carter still babies his drink. I wonder if it's because alcohol and merpeople don't mix. I can't exactly ask him, but he only smirks when I clink my glass with Giselle's as she downs her third.

If she continues at this pace, Carter will be dragging her into the ballroom, and we'll be forced into our dramatic falling on the floor entrance. Her cheeks flush even through her makeup, and she giggles, reaching across Carter's lap to grab my hand.

"You're my BFF, Avie," she says, using my childhood nickname that my mom uses. "And Carter, you're my BFF now because she's my BFF." Uh-oh. At least she's being a sweet drunk. That I can handle.

The others laugh, grinning at her need to be affectionate.

"I love you too, Gi," I say, squeezing her hand.

"You know you guys can tell me anything, right?" she continues. *Shit.*

Carter stiffens next to me, but I force my smile to remain. "Yes, Giselle. I know we can."

"Okay, because I hate secrets."

"Giselle," I say.

"No, Ava. I've been thinking about it a lot lately," she says, waving her empty glass through the air.

Silence falls around the limo as the others realize Giselle's getting serious. My heart pounds in my chest, though she doesn't know my secret to tell, only that I have one big enough to change my life.

"Giselle, please. Just stop," I say.

She sighs. "Fine, but only because I don't want you to run away with Carter."

I close my eyes to compose myself. When I open them, the others stare at me with expressions of surprise and curiosity. Carter just stares at his hands, folded in his lap. Things get awkward quickly, and we can't arrive at our destination fast enough.

Sapphire leans forward. "What the hell is she talking about? You two planning on eloping or something?"

I place my right hand over my left to hide my ring even though it's not an engagement ring in the sense they'd think. I can't exactly explain that it stops me from growing a tail. Like that'd go over well.

"Because that'd be crazy," Chloe says, speaking up for the first time from her corner of the limo.

"You two just met," Matty says.

"I think it'd be romantic," Daisy says, smiling. "I know you all think love at first sight is cheesy, but I think it's possible.

Right, babe?" she asks Logan.

He shrugs. "Sure, babe."

I cover my face with my hands. "Okay, you all need to stop. You're embarrassing me. Carter and I are *not* getting married. And if we were, you'd all be invited."

"Then why would you run away?"

"Honestly?" I ask. "If I told you I'd have to kill you."

Everyone except for Giselle busts up laughing. As quickly as they were prying for answers, they drop the subject. Carter twines his fingers through mine, relaxing the best he can, and then he gulps the rest of his champagne. The limo pulls to a stop outside of the Grand Le Mer. A glittery blue carpet lines the entrance while a few photographers gather on the walkway to snap pictures of anyone they find newsworthy. There are always a few celebrities at the events held by the Kings, mostly the faces of their beauty brands.

Sapphire pours everyone one more glass, finishing off the third bottle of champagne, and we all clink our glasses together. I try to catch Giselle's gaze, but she refuses to look at me as she gulps down the last sip of her champagne.

Heat blossoms up my shoulders and neck, the alcohol settling through me, making me feel lightheaded. The chauffeur opens the door, and Giselle hops out without a word. Sapphire shrugs at me before exiting with Matty, followed by Logan, Daisy, and Chloe.

I turn to Carter. "I'm sorry. I'll fix this."

He scrunches his brows. "I'm not so sure you can. Suspicion makes people take a closer look. We can't have that. It's not safe."

"Will you please let me try?"

He nods as he steps out of the limo before me to help me out. "Yeah, of course, Ava. I just don't want you to get your hopes up. Secrets tear people apart."

That's what I'm afraid of.

An array of art pieces—from paintings to sculptures—decorates the ballroom, surrounding the perimeter. The sea of people, all adorned in their finest attire, moves and shifts through the ballroom like a wave of luxury and power. Azure Waters' finest gleam with glittering jewels and an air of wealth thick enough to suffocate me in.

Carter gazes around the room. Some spectators laugh and clink champagne flutes while others glare through the room looking for someone to talk about. A few eyes fall on me, following my every move. I weave through the crowd in search of my mom to make my mandatory round of greetings to all her friends. Once that's over, we'll be free to do whatever we want.

"Ava, dear, don't you look stunning," Mrs. Tenant says. Bright purple orchids cascade out of a cylindrical vase in the center of the table she sits at. "Your mother said you'd be here tonight."

"Thank you, Mrs. Tenant. I love the color of your dress," I say. Pulling Carter closer, I add, "This is my date Carter Stevens. Mrs. Tenant's husband is on the board of directors at the Betty Green Hospital where my dad works."

Carter kisses the back of the old lady's hand in the perfect gentleman fashion. "It's lovely to meet you, ma'am."

She chuckles. "What a charming young man you have, Ava." Turning to Carter, she says, "I'm afraid I don't know any of your family, dear. Are you new in town?"

"He's from San Francisco," I answer for him. I dart my eyes in search for an escape before she starts questioning his entire existence. "His parents own a business up there."

"How interesting."

I spot my mom across the room. "Oh, I hate to have to excuse ourselves, but I must check in with my mom. It was nice seeing you again, Mrs. Tenant."

Before she can respond, I drag Carter away through the crowd. Giselle stands at her mom's side, looking bored. An older man talks to her, waving his arms around as he tells her something he obviously thinks is fascinating but clearly she doesn't. She doesn't even try to pretend, yawning, wobbling slightly on her heels.

"Are you going to speak for me all night, Ava?" Carter asks, pulling me to slow down for a minute before we can approach my mom. His words surprise me even though he smiles while he says them.

"Only when it's someone nosey and gossipy like Mrs. Tenant," I say. "She has to know everything about everyone. It's better not to give her too much to go on."

He raises his eyebrows but doesn't question me.

When we reach my mom, she smiles at me and then kisses my cheek. "The dress looks gorgeous."

"It's a shame you didn't stay around to give us your opinion on our gowns," Anaya, Giselle's mom, says from next to her daughter.

"I think you did a fabulous job without us," I say instead of trying to explain my absence. "I love the bead work," I add, twirling my finger over the delicate beads sewn into the skirt.

"Thank you, darling." Her gaze turns to Carter. "This must be the boy who saved your life."

My mouth drops open, and I flick my gaze to Giselle.

"It wasn't me, I swear," she says. The heat in her voice she had in the limo is barely a whisper of warmth now that she's had a minute to cool off. Even after everything, she doesn't want to hurt me. Even after I hurt her by not telling her what's going on. I suck. This sucks. Everything just sucks.

Fear flashes in my mom's eyes before it quickly disappears. "It's okay, Avie. Ruby told us when I asked about Carter. I'm just thankful for what he's done. I don't know what I'd have done if I..." Her voice trails off as she loses herself in her memory.

"It was nothing," Carter says casually, like him jumping overboard is not a big deal when we both know it was a huge, life changing, world imploding deal. One I was lucky to sort of survive.

"It was everything," I whisper.

Carter wraps his hands around my waist from behind and then leans down to brush his lips against my cheek.

Anaya's gaze flickers between us for a moment. "It's a shame you don't have a brother for my daughter."

"Mom!" Giselle exclaims. "I can find my own boyfriend, thank you very much."

Carter laughs. "I have a few cousins, though I haven't seen them since I was a kid."

"I can't imagine why," Giselle says with a fake smile, clearly thinking that Carter is the worst person in the world, though she has no idea.

Ignoring her words, I tilt my head to the side, thinking about his family outside of his parents for the first time. They must not have been part of his life because he didn't include anyone else in his memories when he shared his life with me.

Silence falls between us, and a moment later, Giselle excuses herself, leaving me and Carter shifting awkwardly in front of my mom and Anaya.

Anaya places her hands on her hips. "Don't let her get to you, Ava. She's been moody the last few days. It's hard when your friends start splitting their time with boys. Don't you remember how it was, Bea? We almost didn't talk for three months when I met Griffin."

My mom bobs her head but doesn't smile. "She's right."

But she's not. This has nothing to do with spending time

with Carter and everything to do with the secret that threatens to tear me from my human life.

Instead of agreeing, I say, "I should go talk to her." I turn to Carter. "Why don't you find Logan and Matty?"

Without waiting for a response, I cut through the crowd. People part away from each other as I rush through them only nodding when they say hello. When I don't find Giselle in the bathroom, I head out of the ballroom to the only place that could provide the privacy she wants.

Pushing open the glass door to the empty balcony, I step out. The ocean breeze clings to my skin, blowing up from the sea below. Giselle rests her elbows on the stone partition on the balcony. The air is chilly enough and the night dark enough, that it stops anyone from wanting to stay out here long. All the fun's happening inside, anyway. Even the front entrance is clos-er for the old lady smokers who sit out most of the event, gos-siping between each other about how scandalous some people are.

"Giselle," I call.

She doesn't turn around.

"Please, we need to talk."

Bowing her head, she rests her chin on her arms without looking at me. "Why? So you can make me feel like crap."

My brows scrunch together. "No, Gi. That's the last thing I want."

"Then why don't you just go find Carter. Apparently he's the only one worthy of your secret."

Anger and sadness wash through me. "I told you already. It's not only my secret."

"It doesn't matter. I don't care anymore!"

"You don't mean that. It's the alcohol talking," I say, clos-ing the distance between us.

"I thought I was okay, Aves. I thought I could handle you

not telling me whatever it is you're so afraid to, but I can't. Best friends don't make each other miserable like this. I just—I think it's better that you do your thing until you figure it out."

Tears spring from my eyes, sending a glittering haze across my vision. Hurt sweeps through my mind, and I consider telling her my secret this very second. Life would be more bearable to share it with someone I've been close to all my life. But I can't. I can't do anything to stop her from basically breaking up with me as my best friend.

"Giselle..."

"No, Ava."

Pain pounds against my ribcage, my heart shattering into a million pieces. The one person I used to always rely on, the person who saw me through the worst moments of my life, the person who I never thought I'd ever live without can't even look at me. She shifts away, putting distance between us, and sobs, her cries catching and disappearing on the wind.

This is what it felt like when I realized Bailey wasn't coming back. But this feels even worse. It wasn't the ocean who stole my best friend this time. It was me. It was who I've become. The damage is irreparable between us, and as much as I want to, need to, there's nothing I can think of to fix it.

Neither of us moves from the balcony, like the moment one of us leaves, it will truly be the death of our friendship. Despair settles through me, and I shift my gaze away from Giselle crying to stare off into the dark night. I drag my feet to the cement partition, resting my elbows on it not far from her. I can't go back inside like this. I'm sure my makeup's already a mess.

"You know what hurts me the most, Aves?" she asks after a minute of silence. The fact that she's even talking to me at all sends my heart racing.

I don't have it in me to list all the things that have hurt her.

I feel bad enough that my new existence, the stupid secret, the ocean, all of it has turned me into someone I'm not used to having to be. Someone who would rather hurt my best friend than give up the life I have here in Azure Waters. But this isn't all about me either. I'm saving Giselle the hurt. She'd blame herself when she realized I wasn't lying about disappearing. I can't put her through that guilt no matter how easy it would be to just say the words and fix this.

Finally, I ask, "What, Gi?"

"That even after all this—after knowing how you're ruining our friendship—you just accept it like I'm not worth fighting for. I don't give a damn if you've done something unthinkable. Yeah, it would be super disturbing if you loved a boy who turns out to be a murderer, but I'd still love you. That's what friends do. That's why this hurts me so much. You've chosen a boy you've just met over me."

I close my eyes. "I didn't choose him. You have to believe me. I chose you, Giselle. It's why I'm here right now."

"You're here because you're afraid I'll make a scene."

I release an angry breath between my lips, closing the space between us. "Are you kidding me? You have no idea! I didn't mean I chose you because I'm standing on this balcony. I meant I chose you over everything. The only reason I'm standing in front of you is because I chose you."

Her brows knit together in confusion, but I don't know how else to explain it without revealing anything else. "Ava…"

"Let me finish," I snap, inhaling a deep breath of sea air, letting it sink to my core. The dull roar of the waves hums from below us, and I imagine what it would've been like just leaving with Carter in San Francisco so I didn't have to face Giselle's hurt eyes right now.

"Ava—your arm." As she says the words, a series of cramps rush through me, buckling my knees.

I stare at my arm in horror. My pectoral fins jut up from the skin of my forearms. I heave forward, spinning around for somewhere to run, but the only exit off the balcony leads back inside the hotel far from the front door.

Panic laces every quick breath I take, and I try to will the transformation to stop. I'm trapped high above the ocean with nowhere to run, about to reveal everything to Giselle. It's like my body purposely went against my mind to save me the trouble of holding onto a secret that leaves the two of us broken and devastated.

I lean against the partition, pain threatening to send me sprawling to the ground from my weakening knees. I won't be able to stand much longer, let alone get to the ocean if I don't act quickly. It doesn't help that I'm about to change into a mermaid in front of my best friend at the worst possible moment without warning. *This can't be happening!*

"Ava!" Giselle yells, her eyes widening. "What's wrong with you? What's happening? Oh, my God."

My heart tears apart at the sheer fear lining her words. "Gi, please don't freak out. I have to go, but I can't go back in there."

Confusion replaces the anger she held for me moments ago. "What? I don't understand."

"I can't explain now. But this is what I've been hiding." I cry out, another spasm shooting up my back, forcing me to bow forward. I turn away, blocking her view of the short fins on my arms, my now webbed fingers, and the gills burning for the sea on my neck.

"Ava..." Her voice trails off. She's stunned speechless.

My pearlescent skin shimmers in the soft lighting. "You have to promise not to tell anyone. No one can know. If my mom asks, I got sick, okay? And please, go find Carter."

I heave myself over the partition, feeling the tingling sensation of my scales sprouting over my legs. The ledge is barely wide enough to stop me from falling, but I'm afraid to jump just yet.

Giselle grabs my shoulders. "Ava, please. Don't do this. Don't jump. We can work through this."

I arch my back, my dorsal fin now pressing against the fabric of my dress, threatening to break through.

"You have to trust me. I'm begging you. Don't tell anyone."

She only nods, tears smearing her mascara. "Okay."

"Ava!" Carter's voice echoes through the night.

But it's too late. I have no choice. I have to let go.

PROMISES

CARTER WRAPS HIS ARMS AROUND Giselle, pulling her away from me. Both their eyes widen as I complete the transformation and dive from the balcony. I free fall into the glowing sea, inhaling a deep breath of saltwater to stop the burning in my chest.

I don't stay underwater long. Popping up to the surface, I float on the churning sea. Giselle screams once, and Carter covers her mouth with his hand to stop her from drawing attention from anyone who might be nearby. His attention shifts from her to me in the water. A strange expression crosses his face, but he doesn't look at me for long, not with Giselle freaking out in his arms.

He bends down, whispering something to her I can't hear from here, and then they run from the balcony together. Whatever he said was enough to get her to cooperate, but I wish he'd have just dived after me instead. Because now, I don't even know what to do.

My beautiful gown clings to me, half ripped and completely ruined by the water. My once perfect makeup is probably now a streaky mess. Swirling amid the waves, I unzip the side of my gown before I'm dragged anymore through the rough waters and slammed into the rocks that line the cliffs. If it weren't for the balcony extending over the water, I'd probably have died, turning into a splattered mess across the surf.

Once I shimmy from my gown, I roll it up and hold it to me. Part of me wants to let it wash away with the waves, but another part of me wants to cling onto the last part of my human life.

With one more glance at the empty balcony, I swim away, heading out to sea. From here, I can find my way back to my house. It rests only a few miles down the shore. I don't know what I'm going to do—Giselle saw me. She watched in horror as I changed before her eyes. It'd be different if it was some random person who didn't know me, a person who people would laugh at for claiming to have seen something so ridiculous. But with Giselle, there's no way to talk myself out of this. I jumped off a balcony into the brewing sea.

How can we even leave now? What will happen to Giselle? The fear is enough to propel me faster through the water. I dart through the shallows, speeding along the shoreline as fast as I possibly can.

When I reach the rocks near my house, I slow down. I swim through the waves, getting close to the shore, because if I'm too far out, I'll never be able to swim with the gown, and I refuse to let it go.

Bobbing in the surf, I close my eyes and concentrate. My tail slaps against the sandy shore, and I drift back and forth in the current. Fear holds me back from changing immediately, but the thought of not being able to explain to Giselle is enough to push me forward. I have no idea what Carter's told her, but it should be me who fixes this mess. Not him. *There's nothing to fix, Ava. It's over.*

As the thought rolls through my mind, I spot two figures emerge from my house. They stand on the patio, watching the waves, and I duck under a few times to wash the tears from my face. Carter's spark glows in the center of his chest, unfazed by his tuxedo. I assume Giselle stands behind him, but the shadows of my deck hide her from view.

My muscles tighten, the transformation grabbing hold of me. This is the easiest it's ever been to change back, because the only place I want to be is with them on land, far away from the ocean. It's what ruined my friendship and now is about to ruin my life all over again like when it stole my sister from me.

The waves push me forward until my feet find the soft sand below. I drag my gown with me, using it to cover my naked body. Carter rushes through the sand, yanking off his tuxedo jacket. Waves crash against his legs when he closes the distance, wrapping the jacket around my shoulders.

I don't make it far before my knees give out, and I fall to the sand, lying on my gown. Carter doesn't give me a chance to lie with my cheek pressed into the beach for long. He scoops me into his arms, uncaring that my sandy, wet body is about to destroy his tux.

He doesn't say anything, quietly carrying me to the back patio. Giselle stares at me with startled eyes, but she doesn't say anything either. I don't even know what she could say. All of this is probably incredibly hard for her to wrap her mind around.

Carter sets me on one of the patio chairs, looking my body up and down. "Are you hurt?"

I shake my head. "No, I missed the rocks."

He releases a long breath, pulling me against him to embrace me in a long hug. His warm breath tickles the nape of my neck, hot in comparison to the chilly night. Goosebumps prickle over my arms, and I shiver.

He turns to Giselle. "Can you grab a few towels?"

Without hesitating, she dashes inside and returns with a stack of towels. Carter takes my destroyed gown from my fingers and lays it across the patio table. Giselle absently runs her hand across the torn fabric, grazing her fingers along the pearls—half of which are missing.

My eyes turn to Carter's hard gaze. He wraps the dry towel around me before stripping from his own wet clothes. Giselle blushes and turns to look away until Carter wraps the towel around his waist. He gathers up our clothes and folds another towel around them, and Giselle offers to take them.

After a long moment, tears escape from my eyes again. "I'm so sorry," I say, my voice barely audible over the roaring white-caps behind us. I don't say it to either Carter or Giselle specifically, because I owe them both an apology. "I didn't mean for this to happen."

Carter helps me to my feet. "It could've been a lot worse."

"I'm sorry, too, Ava. I never imagined that this—" She waves her hand at the world in general. "This wasn't what I was expecting."

I can't stop the laughter bubbling from my throat, coming out almost like a sob. "At least you know we're not murderers."

"You're a mermaid," she says, like it's finally sinking in. "I don't understand. How?"

I glance at Carter. He only shrugs in response. It's already too late to try to make up another story when she saw me.

"When Matty knocked me off the boat..." My voice trails off. How do I tell my best friend that I drowned? "Carter saved me."

"He couldn't save you without turning you into—into a— a mermaid?" Her voice rises through the air, and she shoots a glance at Carter like he's given me some incurable disease.

Carter's shoulders slump. "I would've loved to have done that, Giselle. But in my human form, swimming that distance to get to her—the ocean already took her under. I tried, but it just wasn't possible. I was already too late by the time I transformed."

Her mouth opens and closes. "I don't think I understand.

Are you saying...?"

"Giselle, I drowned," I finally say.

Tears burst from her eyes like I'm actually still dead. She rushes forward, wrapping her arms around my shoulders. Shaking, she cries into my wet hair, and I rub my cold hand along her back until she calms down.

"I wasn't even supposed to allow her to return to the Ocean Jewel. I defied tradition and broke a few mer-laws. The only thing protecting us was that no one knew our secret. But now you do."

She huffs. "I swear on my life I'm not going to tell anyone."

"The same way you promised Ava you wouldn't tell everyone we had a secret in the first place?" Carter asks. I can almost see a flash of fire in his eyes as he directs his sudden anger at my best friend.

She cringes. "You're right. That was messed up of me, but I was worried."

"You should've trusted Ava."

I pull myself together and cut between them. "Just stop it. It's happened, she knows, and there's nothing we can do to change it."

"So, what now?" Giselle asks the question I'm not ready to face, because I already know the answer to it.

"Ava and I have to leave," Carter says.

"Why? I swear I won't tell. You can trust me. For real," Giselle says.

I see her point. "I agree with Gi. Now that she knows our secret, she won't be begging for answers. If anything, she can help. She can cover for me."

Carter rubs his neck. "Ava, it's not about Giselle knowing. It's you."

My heart slides into my stomach. "Because I'm the one

who transformed?"

He nods. "You're too unpredictable. This is a small town where everyone knows you. It isn't safe. Bringing you home was a mistake. It's too risky to stay."

"But where will you go?" Giselle asks.

He shrugs. "I don't know. Living on land is expensive. It's not like I can continue to work on the Ocean Jewel. I'll be accused of hurting Ava if she disappears."

The thought sends fear up my spine. "Carter, I can't just disappear. You *promised*. You promised I could keep my ties to my family."

"You don't think they'll search for you if you run away?"

I place my hands on my hips. "I'm eighteen. I can legally do what I want, and there's nothing they can do. I'm not going to just dive into the water and disappear forever. When I get better control, I can come back."

"And how exactly are you going to explain your absence?" he argues.

I cover my face in my hands. "Who cares? They'll just be happy I'm back."

"She makes a good point," Giselle says.

He shoots a glare at Giselle. "This is between me and Ava."

She throws her hands up. "I'm only trying to help. I can't lose my BFF."

I press my hands to Carter's chest, feeling his heartbeat thrum against my palms. "Why don't we just pack a few things and stay somewhere else tonight? It'll give us a chance to think and figure things out."

"My parents own an apartment in the city," Giselle says. "We can go there."

Carter's jaw twitches as he clenches his teeth. "Giselle, it might be better if you stay here. Make sure no one saw anything." His voice is a lot softer now.

She wrings her hands together. "No way."

"Giselle," I say softly. This isn't just my life we're talking about. It's Carter's, too.

"Don't *Giselle* me. I know what he's thinking." She waves her hand at Carter. "The moment you two are away from me, you'll be gone."

I flick my gaze to Carter, but he doesn't disagree with her.

I puff air through my lips. "Okay, you can come, Gi. But I do have to leave. You know this, right?"

"And I'm staying with you until then. Got it?"

I wrap my arms around my best friend. "Got it. I promise I won't leave without telling you goodbye."

She swipes the back of her hand over her cheek. "I wish you didn't have to say goodbye at all."

A PLAN

DARKNESS SURROUNDS ME WHEN I open my eyes. Giselle sleeps on the bed next to me, but Carter is gone from the chaise lounge. Giselle refused to leave my side, so she won the spot next to me on the bed. I guess Carter didn't want to leave my side either because instead of taking the couch bed, he curled up on the lounge.

Sitting up on my elbows, I peer through the darkened bedroom. Through the opened curtain, I can see the lights of the building next to us but no sign of the moon in the light-polluted sky. An orange streak of light cuts across the wood floors, lighting my way as I head to the door.

Carter's soft voice trickles down the hallway, and I tiptoe across the warm floor runner to eavesdrop. Peeking around the corner of the hallway, I find him perched on a barstool with his phone glued to his ear. His shoulders slump forward, and he leans his elbows on the granite counter, facing the open kitchen.

My fingers curl on the corner of the wall as I steady myself so he doesn't notice I'm here. I should feel guilty about creeping up on him, but he obviously didn't want me to hear his conversation or else he would've done it while I was awake.

"Dad, please," he says softly into the phone. "Mom can't be reasoned with. I called you because I need your guidance. Ava slipped up. I need to know what to do."

I hold my breath, willing for his dad's voice to echo

through the line, but all I can hear is Carter's own breathing while he listens.

"No, you don't have to worry about the human. It was a stranger. No one will ever believe such a story."

I cover my mouth as Carter lies to his dad. For whatever reason, he doesn't want his family to know that it was my best friend who saw me. He's protecting Giselle. For that, I owe him.

"There has to be something else we can do. She won't go for it," he says.

Tears line my eyes at his desperation. He's never sounded so defeated before. It breaks my heart that this all stems to me and what I want and don't want.

"No, Dad. I'm not going to make her." He listens into the phone a moment. "That's not true. I'm taking her side because I love her, and I think what she wants is what's best for her. You out of everyone should understand. You chose the land over the sea. We chose it, too."

I slide my back down the wall to sit on the floor. He just admitted he loved me to his dad before he's even admitted it to me. I've known all along that Carter cares for me. We have a bond that I can't even explain, connected through our hearts. This whole time I believed he went along with what I wanted because he felt bad for putting me through this. Another part of me thought it was because he loved the land as much as I do. I don't know why it's so hard to think that maybe he truly does love me. Could I love him, too? If I didn't, I'd fight a lot harder to maintain my old life. I would have to be dragged away kicking and screaming. But in this moment, all I can think about is what this is doing to Carter and how much I want him to be happy as well.

"I don't know why I bothered calling you. You might've chosen the land, but you still think like you live in the sea.

Goodbye, Dad." After hanging up the phone, he rests his head on his folded arms.

I push off the floor and cross the room. He turns to look at me before I can sneak up on him, like he knew I was already here. I hug him, wrapping my arms around his shoulders. He takes my hands in his and presses them to his cheek, closing his eyes like all he wants is to feel me near him.

"Your parents don't want to help us," I say, my voice cracking.

"I asked if we could live there for a while until we got things situated, but my mom said no. She's too wrapped up in the mer traditions. My dad stands by her decision. He said if I loved you, I'd do the right thing, but they have no idea what that even is."

"You love me," I say the words quietly, because I'm afraid he might've just said them to his dad to prove a point.

He turns his gaze to mine. "More than I could've ever imagined." He brings his fingers to my chest, where my spark glows. "It's what happens when a merman gives his life to someone—he gives his heart, too. Have you ever noticed ours beat in an identical rhythm?"

"Oh," I whisper. No wonder there's a ceremony involved in the transformation. "But what if I never drowned?"

"Ava, are you questioning whether or not what I feel is real?" he asks, a smile playing on his lips.

"I'm just thinking about where we'd be if I didn't."

He brings my hands to his lips and kisses my knuckles. "We'd have a lot more dates away from the water."

I laugh but don't say anything.

"You want the real reason I saved you? It wasn't only because I didn't want you to die. I gave you my life because I felt like we could have something together. I saw a future with you, living on the land with the girl who loved it as much as I did.

And then when you went overboard, I saw it all being ripped away from me. I've never met anyone like you, Ava. That's why I did what I did. I had hoped that one day you could love me back."

"And if I didn't?"

"It was a risk I was willing to take. I don't blame you if you can't ever love me, especially after all this."

I lean over and kiss him sweetly, brushing my lips lightly against his. "Don't be ridiculous," I say before I kiss him again. "I wouldn't be standing here with you right now if I didn't feel something for you, Carter. You know, I think a lot about my life and my future but never once was it without you in it."

We sit together on the barstool for a long while, me cradled in his lap, my head resting on the crook of his neck. The world feels so simple when we can sit and just be together. No ocean, no worry, just the sound of our hearts beating.

When the sky lightens through the window, reality sets back in. Carter wants to leave, and as much as it hurts me, I know I must go...at least for now.

"Carter, I think I know what I'm going to do about my parents," I say, drumming my fingers against his chest. "But it involves me going home. Just for a few hours. I can't leave without saying goodbye."

"A clean break is better."

"Not for me. I had plans this summer. I was supposed to move in with Giselle. We were going to start college in the fall, and my parents were going to pay for it. I'm going to ask them to give me the money for the rent instead so I can travel until school. And then when school comes around, I'm going to tell them I'm postponing and taking a gap year instead. Hopefully we'll have jobs by then, because taking a gap year wasn't on the agenda, and I doubt they'll just give us money without me be-ing in school." It's the perfect plan to get away from here without having to worry about money for now, but also to make sure my parents know I'm alive and safe. That I'm just living my life, which is exactly what I'll be doing. Just not in the way I imagined.

"And what about Giselle?"

"What about me?" Giselle asks, yawning in the hallway.

"I need you to stay in Azure Waters. At least until the fall," I say. She opens her mouth to argue, but I raise my hand. "Please, Gi. I'd feel a lot better about leaving if I knew you would be around. Plus, you're the only one I can visit if everyone else thinks I'm traveling the country."

"Or I could just go with you."

Carter shakes his head. "You can't exactly go everywhere we do."

She sighs. "If only I could sprout a tail."

"Are you willing to risk your life for the chance? It's not always successful. Plus, you'd be stuck with whoever transforms you like Ava's stuck with me." Carter says it like he'd be willing to find Giselle a mate to do it.

She frowns. "No thanks. I have commitment issues."

It's enough to gain a laugh from Carter, which lightens the depressing mood. I slide from his lap and hug my best friend. She sniffles into my hair, and I let my tears fall onto the T-shirt she borrowed from me.

"This summer's going to suck without you, Aves," she says into my hair. "I'm going to kill Matty for this, you know. He's the reason you're in this mess."

I laugh. Even after everything, I can't be mad at Matty. It was an accident. A really, stupid, terrible accident. And if Carter really thinks we'd be together regardless, it's easy to think we just took a shortcut and bypassed all the awkward stuff.

"It's not so bad. I got over my fear of the ocean," I say. "And when I can go in it without worrying about transforming,

I'll take you up on your surf lessons with Chloe."

She squeezes me once more. "You better."

Making plans with Giselle makes my leaving feel less final. It helps me hold onto hope that one day I'll be able to come home, and Carter and I can have a normal life together, acting as humans.

I'll do anything to make that happen. If it means I have to say goodbye to my life for now, then so be it.

Both of my parents sit in the kitchen, sharing a piece of leftover cake from the gala. The simple act they always do together will change when I leave. This will be the last cake they'll share that I've baked for who knows how long. At least they look like they're enjoying it.

Carter and Giselle took my car to the harbor to give Carter a chance to put in his resignation and give them Giselle's address so they can mail him his last check. I needed them to be gone so I could do this alone. I need to share one more moment with my parents that I can hold onto for a while.

"Oh, Avie. You're home," Dad says, setting his fork on his plate with a clank.

"You must be feeling much better," Mom says, a smile on her lips. "You know, you didn't have to lie to leave. I would've understood. I know how boring those events can be, and I'm the one who helps throw them."

I cover my face with my hand. "I'm sorry about that."

She pats the seat next to her. "It's okay, Ava. Carter seems like a really nice boy."

Oh, great. And now she's going to think I'm crazy with what I'm about to ask next.

I swallow the lump in my throat. "I'm glad you say that."

The rest of my words fly out of my mouth as I tell my parents about my desire to travel, and to travel immediately. I give them a thousand excuses of why I need to go. I even guilt them, telling them that I've never traveled much outside of Azure Waters. When I'm through, they both sit there with surprised expressions.

"Ava, why didn't you ever tell us this was how you felt?" Mom asks.

I shrug. "I didn't know that it was how I felt until our trip up to San Francisco. I just don't want to sit around until school starts. I want to do something, you know."

"Well," Dad says. "You are eighteen. We technically can't stop you from going. But I do have some concerns about you taking off with Carter. We don't really know him all that well."

"You want to do a background check or something?" The hint of annoyance in my voice sends my dad's eyebrows peaking on his forehead. "I like him a lot, and this whole thing is my idea. If you don't want me to go with Carter, then I'll go on my own. I just thought knowing that I was with someone would make you feel better."

My mom raises her hands. "Whoa, Ava. We didn't say no. But what kind of parents would we be if we didn't worry?"

I take a breath. "I get it. I'm sorry. It's just I like Carter, and you two should as well. He jumped off a yacht to save my life, he's been respectful toward me, and I introduced you to him the moment I got back from vacation. You need to trust that I know how to pick a boyfriend."

"You have to promise to check in all the time, okay?" Dad says.

My heart flutters with excitement. "Promise."

"Then okay. We hope you have a great time," Mom says.

"You don't know how much this means to me. Thank you!" I jump from the table and hug both of my parents. "Carter's going to be so excited. We're going to leave tonight."

"Tonight?"

Uh oh. "Yeah, there's—" I rack my brain for something, anything, to tell them before I finally say, "There's a music festival up north. I don't want to miss it. We saw flyers when we were exploring San Francisco. Giselle wants to come as well if that makes you feel any better." Giselle's going to hate me for dragging her into this, especially when she can't really go.

My parents are quiet for a long while, looking at each other. My attention draws to the window that overlooks the pool, but something beyond the wrought iron fence catches my attention. A familiar woman stands along the waves from my narrow view of the beach.

It can't be.

"Wow, that sounds like it's going to be a great time. I guess we better transfer you some money now, huh?" Mom asks.

I turn my gaze back to my parents. "You two are the best! Seriously, the best."

I hug them again and head out of the kitchen. Instead of going to my bedroom, I race to the game room. Through the glass doors, I gaze at Carter's mom standing in the surf in a two-piece bikini and a sarong. A bag hangs from her arm, and I'm pretty sure she didn't drive down here. But how did she find me?

She glances in my direction, smiling at me from her spot on the beach. Everything in me tells me to turn around and run. To find Carter and to escape. But instead, I open the door and step out onto the patio.

"Starla? What are you doing here?" I ask.

She motions me to walk closer, but I hesitate. "Please, Ava. Just hear me out. We need to talk."

UNREASONABLE HOPE

HUGGING MYSELF, I STROLL DOWN the beach next to Starla, staying just out of the water. All I can think about is her turning against me and dragging me away against my will. If she's dead set against me living on the land, I wouldn't put it past her.

"You're afraid of me," she says after a long moment where neither of us talks.

I flick my gaze behind me, my house growing smaller the farther away we go. "Can you blame me?"

"I know it might not feel like it, and Carter seems to believe we don't, but my husband and I do have your best interest at heart. Neither of us can imagine what you're going through—what Carter did, well, he shouldn't have done such a thing to you."

"You mean save my life?"

She reaches out and grabs my hand, pulling me to a stop. "No, of course I wouldn't wish you dead. But Carter should've taken you to the sea immediately instead of giving you unreasonable hope like he has. It was cruel."

I can't imagine what I'd have thought had he taken me to sea as a mermaid instead of allowing us to be rescued. I'd have probably flipped out and held it against him despite that he saved my life. I know I would have.

My nose crinkles. "I think your idea of cruel differs from

mine. What would've been cruel is if I'd never gotten a chance to say goodbye to my family. Stealing away my right to decide what to do with my future would be cruel. Forcing a human into the ocean is cruel, Starla."

"You're not human anymore. We follow different rules. This—" She waves her hand around the land. "Living on land comes with responsibility. You might have legs, but that doesn't mean you're still the girl you were before the transformation. She died. She's not you." Starla squeezes my fingers more tightly, forcing me to face the ocean. "You can't continue this half life as you are. You need to learn our ways."

"I *am* learning. Maybe if you didn't turn your back on your son and allow us to stay with you, I could learn more."

"That is our home as much as this is yours. We can't risk your instability." Sadness hangs in her words. "If we could, I'd gladly take you in. You're my family now."

Dating her son does not qualify as family. If anything, I'm a burden. "We're not family. My family would never turn their backs on me no matter what. I bet if I went home right now and told them I was a mermaid, they'd still accept me."

Her eyes widen. "You cannot talk like that, Ava. Not to anyone. You understand? Not only for your safety, but for your family's sake. Hasn't Carter told you anything? Just like humans have laws, so do merpeople. Our king is a kind and understanding man to a point, but when it comes to the sake of his people, he will not hesitate to snuff out the risk. You're so fortunate your accident occurred in front of a stranger. That's forgivable. But for someone who knows you, they'd face a morbid fate."

I blink, surprise washing over me. Giselle saw me transform. If anyone were to ever find out, something terrible would happen to her. I couldn't live with myself if my mistake would hurt her in any way. Just the thought leaves me sick to my stomach.

"Your kind is as cruel as the ocean that stole my sister," I say, yanking my arm from her.

"Our kind," she corrects.

Crossing my arms over my chest, I stare at her, wind tossing my hair behind me. "Either way, you don't have to worry. Carter and I are leaving Azure Waters tonight. No one will have to worry about any mistakes I make."

"You should reconsider, Ava."

"Is that why you're here?"

She nods. "I want you to come with me. I'll take you somewhere safe where you can adjust."

"But Carter prefers the land as much as I do. How could I do that to him?"

Something changes in her expression—her eyes softening as she smiles for the first time since she showed up on my beach. "You care for my son."

I frown. She says it like she's surprised. Like I'm somehow incapable of giving Carter the love he gives me. The bond might be one-sided, but when you know someone on an entire new level, it's different. Carter has opened up to me so much so that I feel like I've known him forever. I've lived his life through the memories he's shared. My attraction for him goes soul deep.

"I do, and I know we'll both be happier on land. You know as well as I do that if I went with you to wherever it is you think I need to be, Carter will follow me." My gaze shifts to the waves, and I try to imagine some underwater colony of merpeople. It's hard to even imagine. The vast ocean makes it easy to believe it's just me and Carter.

"Of course he'll follow you. He should be the one taking you in the first place. You shouldn't have to stress about whether or not you can maintain your human form. You should be able to enjoy our world. You say you love the land, but I bet you could love the sea. The Pacific colony is breathtaking.

You'd be near the palace."

I can't imagine the world she speaks of. Underwater cities, palaces—it all sounds like a fairytale. *You're a mermaid, Ava. It is a fairytale.*

"I—I'm sorry, Starla. It all sounds fascinating, but I'm not going to just go with you without talking to Carter. We already have a plan and a means to do it. He'll be here any minute for me. Maybe if our plan fails, then I'll consider it. But until then, no." I turn my back on her. She's wasted enough of my precious time trying to convince me to do something I'm against. All I want to do is run back to my house and hug my parents.

"Ava, please," she calls. "Don't make this mistake."

I dash back to my house, the sand kicking up with every step. How can the choice that makes me the happiest be a mistake? Now more than ever I want to prove his parents wrong. I want to show them I can do this. It's enough of an incentive that maybe I won't accidentally ever change again. Like Carter said, we'll swim enough that my mind will never yearn for the sea. Without having to worry about my parents and friends all the time, it'll make things possible.

When I return home, I rest my back against the glass doors, my hands trembling at my sides just imagining how much Carter's parents will be disappointed in us. They probably think I'm the worst. I've always gotten along with people's parents, but I've also never been in a situation like this where I've downright disagreed with their wishes.

It takes everything in me to move away from the door. I don't have much time. I have to pack and get things ready to go. How do I even decide what to take and what to leave?

I head upstairs to my room and take a long moment to look around. I haven't even unpacked my bag from vacation yet. Dumping out its contents into my dirty laundry basket, I shuffle to my dresser and stare at the heaps of bikinis that lie in a mess in my top drawer along with my undergarments. I have at least a dozen pieces to choose from. Instead of deciding, I scoop them all up and tuck them in the bag. I ignore my jeans and head to my closet to slide all of my sundresses off their hangers. I'm not too worried about the colder weather just yet. I can always buy more clothes later. Right now, all that matters is choosing stuff that can survive an accidental transformation. *You won't. You'll stay in control...* But if I don't, I need to be prepared.

After I pack a few necessities and change into a bikini and sundress, I sit on the edge of my bed and stare at my corkboard full of pictures. I pick out a few of my favorites and stuff them into a Ziploc bag that had held some of my beauty products to stop them from spilling.

Even with a few items missing, the room still feels like mine. It gives me the hope I need to carry to know I'll be able to come back someday. I'll always have a home here in Azure Waters no matter what happens elsewhere.

A knock sounds on my door, and I pad across my room to open it. Carter hovers in the hallway, a smile on his face when he sees me.

"I came in through the guest apartment. I'm going to assume everything went okay with your parents?" he asks, glancing at my packed belongings.

"Surprisingly well. They were a little unsure when I told them we were leaving tonight, but I told them we wanted to go to some festival in San Francisco," I whisper in case my parents are around to listen.

He frowns. "I hope they're not expecting pictures because San Francisco is the last place we'll be. My parents would never let us hear the end of it."

I shift nervously when he brings up his family. "I don't think distance will stop them. Your mom showed up on the beach. She was trying to convince me to leave with her."

His aqua eyes darken for a moment. "Of course she did. She just won't let this go."

"Maybe we should head to the East Coast," I say. "It'd take her a lot longer to interrupt our lives."

He twists his lips to the side. "I don't know if you're ready for that kind of trip, Ava."

He's right. I couldn't possibly journey to the East Coast by car. What would happen if I transformed in the middle of the desert? That'd be a disaster. And a plane? That'd be worse. It'd cause hysteria, which could be deadly in the air.

"I liked Santa Barbara," I say. "We could just slowly make our way to every beach city."

"That sounds like a good plan to me." He leans down and kisses me. "We'll plan as we go. Who knows, maybe we can even go to Hawaii."

Thinking about all the places we'll go and explore makes leaving my family seem more like a vacation than anything. It sounds a lot more exciting than staying in Azure Waters anyway. And Hawaii? I've only ever seen the islands in pictures. My parents have gone, but the idea of flying over the vast ocean and staying somewhere surrounded by the sea was never something I wanted to do since Bailey.

"I'd like that," I say, smiling.

"So, do you think you're ready to go then?"

I kiss him. "Yeah, I think so."

"Good, because I'm ready to start this new life with you."

The sun sets on the horizon, casting its fiery glow over the sandy shores of Azure Waters. I can't believe this is my last sunset in front of the home where I spent my entire life—the life I can never get back.

As I stare out at the vast ocean, a sense of relief washes over me. Carter laces his fingers through mine, standing next to me, and I rest my head on his shoulder. In just a few minutes, we'll be getting in my car and driving up the coast. And then tomorrow, who knows where. It'll be far enough from here that we won't have to risk being known.

The back door opens, and Giselle steps out. She wraps an arm over her chest, holding her other arm and glances between me and Carter. I know she's upset I have to go, but she's being optimistic for my sake.

Her lip quivers as she smiles. "Everything's set, Aves. My mom arranged a hotel in Santa Barbara for the night and one in San Francisco for the weekend."

"You know I owe you," I say, hugging my friend.

She blinks away tears. "I know you'd do the same for me. Plus, a night in a hotel in Santa Barbara? Amazing. I just wish I could go up to San Francisco."

I purse my lips. "You have to stay far away from there."

She bobs her head. "I know. I expect that I'll get sick and have to go home tomorrow afternoon."

Though Carter protested against her leaving Azure Waters, he understood why I did it. I had to make sure my parents didn't put up too much of a protest. I kind of didn't want to have to sleep in the ocean if they didn't agree to pay for my "road trip."

Carter turns to Giselle. "And remember, if a stranger ever asks you about us, you don't know us. Understand?"

Her eyes line with fear for a second. "Definitely. I think I'll give up talking to strangers all together for a while."

I close my eyes, tears threatening to spill on my cheeks. Starla's words about the merpeople laws and how it doesn't end well for people who discover the truth sit heavy in my chest. I wish there was a way to turn back time, but I'm just going to have to trust that Giselle will be safe. She's smart. I have faith she can keep us all out of harm's way by protecting our secret.

"Good," Carter says. "Then we should probably head out."

With one last look around, I silently say goodbye to the shores that were supposed to be my home.

21

MERMAID LIFE

SAYING GOODBYE TO MY BEST friend turns out to be a million times harder than saying goodbye to my parents. It doesn't help that Giselle knows what I'm going through and what I'm giving up. She also fears that she'll never see me again.

We sit on the small couch of her beachfront hotel room with a view of the darkened Pacific Ocean though the blinds to her patio are tightly closed. It's like Giselle doesn't want to even glance at the sea we'll soon be diving into. Until I can get better control over my transformation, we'll be swimming nightly in hopes that it'll keep me human during the day. Getting in a routine will help, Carter thinks. I just hope so.

"I'm going to miss you so much, Aves. You know the others are going to freak when they find out you left without saying goodbye." She rubs her hands over her face.

"Tell them it was spontaneous, and I promise to call all of them in a couple of days, okay?"

She bobs her head. "Okay."

My eyes water with hot tears. "And I will come back to visit."

She sniffles, a tear splashing on her cheek. "You better."

"I'll call you whenever I have a chance. We can video chat," I say.

She beams a smile through her tears. "That reminds me." Pulling her cell phone from her pocket, she pops the case off. "I want you to have this. It's waterproof up to fifty feet. I expect a ton of awesome pictures."

I laugh. "I'm pretty sure that might be against the king's rules."

"The king?" Her eyes widen.

"Crazy, right? I wish I could tell you more, Gi. But just knowing about us puts you at risk." I take the phone case and pop it onto my cell.

She crinkles her nose. "Well, I don't care about those stupid rules that keep us apart."

Carter clears his throat. "Obviously we don't either, so don't worry. We'll send lots of pictures. Just not of us."

She bounces on the couch. "And to think I thought you were bad news."

Giselle gives Carter a quick hug before turning back to me. She flings her arms around me, rocking us back and forth. Her dark hair glows almost red in the soft lighting of the lamp, and her amber eyes remind me of the land unlike Carter's blue eyes that look just like the ocean.

Carter pulls me to my feet, encompassing me in his arms for a moment. "Ready?"

I nod. "I guess so."

Giselle jumps to her feet and gives me one more hug. "Stay safe. Call me if you need anything at all. If your parents ask if I've heard from you, I'll always say yes."

I smile. "Thanks, Gi."

"Best friends forever, remember?"

"And always."

Carter takes my hand, and we stroll to the back door. He slides the glass open and cool sea air wraps around us. A shiver trails down my back as I inhale the damp, salty air. It sinks deep into my soul, and excitement courses through me the closer we get to the waves.

In the darkness away from the hotel, Carter helps me take off my dress before he strips down and puts our clothes in our bag with my cell phone so I don't lose it on the bottom of the sea. In the morning, we'll come back for my car and the rest of our stuff.

Lacing my fingers with Carter's, I pull him with me into the water, allowing the waves to crash around us for a few minutes. My hands circle his neck, and I lean up to kiss him for a long while, tasting the salt on his lips. I want to cherish this moment forever. This is where my mermaid life will truly begin. Instead of falling into the waves like so many times before, I'll be diving in willingly. I'm ready to accept that I'm now a mermaid posing as a human. This is who I am.

Carter tilts his head back, smiling at me with the soft moonlight illuminating his face. He dives in before me, dipping under the water. I spin once more, taking in the dark beach, and then I dive in after him.

Cramps seize my legs as the transformation takes hold of me. I arch my back, floating along the current, feeling the dull ache from my fins popping up from my back and arms. The tingles consume my legs, and I flip my tail, propelling me deeper into the sea.

Carter greets me with a kiss the second after I inhale a deep breath of water. He circles around me, creating a small whirlpool, and I let it catch me, sending me into his arms. Through the glowing water, his eyes shine like two beautiful gemstones. It reminds me how much I now love the sea.

"What is it, Ava?" Carter asks, his voice traveling into my mind. "You okay?"

I smile before I kiss him, bubbles still clinging to both our faces. "It's almost easy to forget the land when we're together out here."

He cups my face. "I know what you mean."

Taking my hand, he launches us forward through the deep water. The sea grass looks magical this time of night with the way my eyes adjust to the darkness. It never ceases to amaze me how active and alive it all is while the world above sleeps quietly, unaware of what truly lies beneath the waves.

Schools of red, silver, and black spotted fish dart around us, and a few bat rays glide across the bottom of the sand. Tall kelp forests reach for the night sky, shifting and moving on the currents, and I tug away from Carter and weave in and out of the green ropes. He chases after me, always right on my tail, and every so often, he swims right above me, reaching out to hold me by my waist.

I flip over and swim with my back facing the ocean floor so I can wrap my fingers around Carter's shoulders, allowing him to pull me along. My back arches when he dives deeper, me still holding onto him. My hair floats in my face, creating a veil between us. He only stops when we're deep enough that the glow of the moon barely shines above us. My body adjusts to the cooler water and heat crawls over my skin.

He touches his fingers to my chin, guiding my head to peer up, and a white shark, longer than Carter is, swims with such precision and grace. I can't help but admire the beauty of the beast people fear.

"She's magnificent," I say, watching the shark push through the current to wherever she's heading. "You sure she won't bother us?"

He shakes his head. "You have to be more careful of the playful animals like the sea lions and dolphins. Some whales, too. They think they're guppies when their tails could knock us all the way to Hawaii."

I grin, remembering my terrifying swim with the dolphins who just wanted me to have as much fun as they were having.

"I'd like to go there someday," I say, my voice echoing

through my mind. "Grand Cayman, Tahiti, Jamaica, too. I want to see the ocean from different shores."

He smirks. "One day I'd love to take you. We'll practice your long distance swimming. You'll have to be brave enough to try the fish, too. Can't exactly order a pizza down here."

I grimace, and Carter laughs. I'd stick to the land for the food alone. I haven't tried his version of sushi yet, and I'm not exactly interested in doing so. I can't help it that I think all the fish are so cute as they bolt around me. I feel like I'm visiting an underwater aquarium and not an all-you-can eat seafood buffet.

"It's not bad, I promise," he says, smiling. "It's no dessert, but I'm sure I can find something you like."

Ugh. "I'm not ready," I say. "Can we start with a sushi restaurant on land?"

He kisses me. "You're the only mermaid in the world who was afraid of the ocean and displeased by the meal options."

"I guess that means we can never leave the land," I say, smiling.

"And we won't."

He swims around me once, smiling, but then suddenly his smile fades. A strange shadow casts over us, and my heart nearly stops when I see the silhouette of another mermaid swimming above us.

And then I see another and another.

Carter's eyes widen as he charges toward me, sliding his arms around my waist and flies through the water faster than I've ever seen. His heartbeat races against my back. I half swim and he half drags me in the direction we came.

"What's wrong?" I cry, my voice echoing loudly through my mind.

"You don't hear them? They're calling us," Carter says, worry in his voice.

But I don't hear anything but my own panic screaming in

my ears. Whoever is calling us has Carter fleeing through the ocean. I can't help but think we might be in trouble—or danger.

"Ava, listen to me," Carter says in my mind. "I need you to transform when we hit the kelp paddies. I'm going to propel you as far as I can through the waves, and then I need you to run, okay?"

What? From who? Doesn't running make us look like criminals if we're in trouble? I'm not even sure I could transform back as quickly as he wants me to. What happens if I can't? Fear grips at me, twisting knots in my stomach.

"What about you?" I ask, panic in my thoughts.

"I'll be right behind you, okay?"

"Okay." My voice barely whispers in my mind. I'm not so sure I even thought it.

The ocean blurs around us. Carter swims along the ocean floor, weaving in and out of any animals that get in our way. I blink through my blurry eyes, concentrating on keeping myself together when fear threatens to tear me apart. This was supposed to be our first night of freedom. The first night of our adventure learning how to find balance between life on land and the sea.

And now, I can hear the voices. They sneak through the water, slinking into my mind like invaders.

"Don't make this hard on yourself," a masculine voice says, louder than my own thoughts. I hate it. I despise the sound more than anything. Carter's voice is the only one I've ever heard in my head, and I want to push this stranger's voice from my mind.

"We're not going to hurt you, Ava," a feminine voice says, knowing my name.

"Be reasonable, Carter," another feminine voice says, one so familiar it sends a shiver down my spine. It's Carter's mom.

She's come looking for us, and this time she has others with her.

Carter ignores the voices like I do and swims as fast as he can, practically dragging me like a rag doll. Every time I flick my tail, all it does is slow us down. So instead, I relax. The sea brightens the closer we get to shore, the moon's light shining through, making the tiny bubbles sparkle through the water.

"Get ready," Carter says into my mind. "The kelp forest is up ahead. You'll have only a minute."

Closing my eyes, I prepare for the transformation by clearing my mind. If I fail, the other merpeople will catch us. They won't allow me to return to land. I know it. As much as I thought I could accept my life as a mermaid, knowing they're going to try to steal my ability to live on land makes me want to enter the beach and never look at the ocean again. I can't let them catch me. I can't let that happen. I won't.

"Do it now, Ava!" Carter shouts in my mind.

I squeeze my eyes shut, willing my human form to take over to help me leave the water. My stomach tightens, and nerves rush over me when nothing happens. My own inability to consistently change will prove Starla right. If I fail, it'll be my own fault. And I'll end up dragging Carter into the deep with me. *Come on! Transform!*

The thought of failing Carter kicks my body into action and cramps pulse over me. My hair flies behind me as Carter propels us through the current, and then the comfortable water turns icy. He picks up speed without the weight of my tail slowing us down and ascends toward the surface so I can take a breath of air to clear my lungs of the ocean water.

My head breaks the surface, and Carter throws me as far as he can toward the shore. Flying through the air, I get a head start over Carter. The whitecaps swell up to catch me, and I hold my breath, landing in a cresting wave that pushes me forward to the shore.

I kick my legs, swimming as fast as I can through the night-rough waters. It feels like every time I get ahead, a wave gets pulled back to the sea, dragging me with it. Exhaustion slows me down but determination keeps my head above water.

"Hurry, Ava!" Carter calls from behind me. "Head toward the hotel. They won't follow if it'll draw attention."

Another wave knocks me forward into water shallow enough that I can kick against the sand to push me forward. Saltwater stings my eyes, and my hair clumps to my cheeks. Seawater sprays my face as I fight through the waves, but the shore's so close that I'll be on land with the next wave.

A figure pops up next to me, startling me, and I scream out. When I see it's Carter, I take a heaving breath. He tugs me faster through the surf until we crash onto the shore together. I barely have time to find my footing before he jerks me forward.

I fall to my knees, tripping over my weak legs. Voices sound out over the waves, no longer in my head, and I turn to glimpse behind us to see a man only feet away. He launches forward, landing close enough to me to grab onto my ankle. I wail, thrashing to get out of his grip.

Carter yanks me by my wrists, sending pain through my arms, but it's enough to get the man to let go of me.

As I turn to show my relief to Carter, a woman charges him, knocking him right off his feet with a strength that seems impossible for her petite frame. He tumbles through the sand in front of me, landing on his stomach. I stand frozen, watching as she presses his face into the sand. If my heart wasn't threatening to escape me, I'd blush at the sight of these naked strangers. I'm sure it'd be an eyeful for anyone to see.

"Ava, run!" he yells, thrusting the woman off him and back into the surf.

But I never get the chance.

Strong hands wrap around my shoulders, pulling me toward the waves. I scream as loud as I can, the heat of a naked body pressing into my back. If we attract attention, they might leave. But my scream only goes so far. A swell engulfs me, hitting me in the face. I choke and spit on saltwater as the man shoves my face underwater. Twisting in his slippery arms, I elbow him in the ribs, taking the moment to jet forward, but then another hand grabs me by the wrist.

"Mom, don't!" Carter yells. "Please, don't do this."

I flick my gaze to Carter standing helplessly on the shore. Another wave drags me farther away from him, away from the life we were trying to manage together. With me in the grip of his mom, no one bothers him or tries to force him to come after me. Hopelessness settles on my soul.

From behind him, my eyes dart to Giselle's hotel room, the one I was hoping to reach, and the blinds shift as she peers at us from within her room. As much as I want to call out for my best friend to get help, I can't. All I can do is watch her watch me with horror in her eyes.

Seeing her gives me the strength to keep fighting, to do anything I possibly can to get away. Swinging my arm out, I smack Starla in the shoulder. Her nails dig deeper into the skin of my wrist, and someone else grabs me from behind, holding me in place.

"Just let me go," I cry, thrashing. But it's no use. I'm outnumbered.

"Ava, calm down before you hurt yourself. I'm not your enemy," Starla says. "I'm saving you."

But she's not. She's destroying me, destroying my world. Digging her fingers into my palms, she pries at my hand. My knuckles crack, and I'm pretty sure she's willing to break my hand to force my fingers to open. The pain in my hand is enough that she doesn't have to. My fingers relent, automatically spreading open, and she slides the sea stone ring off my finger.

Everyone lets go of me, putting distance between us as I spin, screaming. They're already too far away for me to try to steal my ring back.

"No!" Carter yells, rushing closer to me.

But there's no point. It's too late. I've lost the one thing that offered me a second chance at living my human life. Without the ring, I'll be anchored to the ocean by my mermaid form. In a matter of minutes, my entire human world slips through my fingers like the sand slips through the waves to sink to the bottom of the ocean.

Covering my face, I sob into my hands, grief stealing my breath away from me.

A soft hand touches my shoulder. "You're going to be okay, Ava. You'll be happy, I promise," Starla says like she could possibly make this better with soft words after she basically broke me into pieces.

But I don't think I'll ever be happy again. Not unless I can have a piece of the human world.

My grief turns into pain, spasms pulsing through me because of the forced transformation. I groan, sinking deeper and deeper into the waves, my mermaid form pushing me into the sea against my will with nothing I can do to stop it.

Starla tries to touch me again, encouraging me to submit to the sea to take a breath. "Stop resisting. It's just making it worse. Let me help you."

"I hate you!" I scream.

Starla blocks my view of the others with her, including Carter. They're purposely keeping us apart. "I'm doing the right thing, Ava. One day, you'll understand," she says calmly, standing strong in her convictions.

"How is destroying my life the right thing?" I ask, my chest burning. The moment I go under completely, I'm afraid I'll never see the shore again.

"Ava, please," she pleads.

"Just get away! Don't touch me!"

I flail away from her, flicking my tail to propel me forward. She might've forced me to transform, but I refuse to let her control me. I'll stay on the shore near home. I'll stay anywhere that she isn't.

I don't get far before the merman flanks my side. His long brown hair floats around his face as he looks at me with pitiful dark eyes, like he feels sorry for what he's done. But his sympathy won't return my ring to me. It won't let me have a life on land. All it does is make me hate him, too.

When the merman relaxes, thinking I'll willingly go with him, I dive down and circle back toward shore, fleeing from him. I don't care if I don't have my ring. I'll figure out how to change. I'll will myself to do it. I can't just go away with these merpeople. I can't just give up.

I swim right into Carter's chest. His arms circle around me, and he buries his face into the nook of my neck.

"I'm so sorry, Ava," he whispers into my mind. "You can't go back."

My lip quivers as I stare into his ocean blue eyes. "My family. I can't leave them. They'll freak out."

He squeezes me tighter. "Please, forgive me. I swear we'll figure it all out, okay?"

"But—"

"Please, Aves. The more you fight, the more trapped you'll be. I have no influence where we're going. You have to try to be strong. We'll get through this."

But I'm not so sure. Even though I'm breathing in the water, I feel like I'm drowning. I'm drowning in all of the lost possibilities. I can't even force myself to feel an ounce of hope. The sea took my life like it took my sister's. The ocean won.

"I don't know if I can," I whisper in his mind.

"Please try."

I sink against him, feeling his heartbeat against mine. It takes everything in me not to break down and sink to the depths of the ocean—to disappear. I don't even bother to swim. Carter cradles me in his arms as he's forced to follow his mom by the other merman.

After a while, the water shifts around us, a magical light cutting through the darkness of my closed lids. I don't look around though. I can't. If I open my eyes, this becomes real. And I can't have that.

"Welcome home, son," a masculine voice says, cutting through my mind though it's directed at Carter. A soft hand touches my shoulder, but I still refuse to look. "Welcome to Pearlestria, Ava," Mateo says to me. "Welcome to your new home."

I slowly lift my head and glare through my blurry eyes. "This is not my home. You dragged me away from my home. This—" I wave my hand at the water around me. "This is my prison within the sea."

 EPILOGUE

ROUGH WATERS

THE CLEAR OCEAN WATER SPARKLES outside the look-out from my underwater room made from a mixture of stone and strange, colorful glass. The walls shine with a pearlescent glow like I'm inside a person-sized seashell.

The small city beyond, Pearlestria, bustles with the life I never could imagine. The merpeople colony, which surrounds a massive underwater castle made from the same magical stone that gives my room its pretty sheen, is protected by some unexplainable shield that prevents humans from ever discovering us.

The last few days have been pure torture. I can't go anywhere without being escorted, so I don't leave the small house—if that's what you can even call it. The enclosed space could fit in the guest apartment above my garage back home. *Home...*

Not a second passes that I don't think about the world above me, the world just out of my reach. The world I can't be a part of because I broke the laws. I transformed in front of a human, and because of that, regardless if it was a mistake or not, has given Starla reason to steal my ring away. She claims it wasn't her decision, but King Attilonious', yet it doesn't stop me from placing blame on her. It's her fault I'm here. She could've left well enough alone. And for that, I won't even talk to her. I hate that she's decided to stay in Pearlestria with me at all, leaving her husband on the land.

Pulling myself away from the window, I sink down to the soft sand on the floor. The room is mostly bare apart from a small bed made of sea grass, a few empty shells I've piled in the corner, and a pesky little butterfly fish that has made its home in the reef along the wall under my lookout.

I lie flat on the ground, kicking up sand as I lift and drop my caudal fin. The ceiling above me sparkles with pretty blue and yellow rocks in a pattern that looks like the sun in the sky. If only I could break the surface, but it's not allowed yet. I'm not trustworthy enough.

"I've brought you something to eat," Starla says, swimming into my small room. She holds a netted bag with what looks like oysters above my head.

I turn my eyes away before shifting onto my side. I don't respond, and she settles down next to me and cracks open the shell with her sharp nail. Pieces of the innards float in my direction as she slurps down the meat. I flick my hand, waving the pieces away. I want to yell at her to get out, to stop ruining my sanctuary with things I refuse to eat.

"Come on, Ava. You should at least try them. I know this is hard, but your stubbornness is just making things harder. You can't be comfortable so hungry. It's been days." She touches my arm, and I pull away.

Luckily for me, as a mermaid I don't have to eat like I did as a human. I could go a few weeks without eating if I wanted to, though she's right about being uncomfortable from hunger.

"If you don't want to eat, let me take you somewhere. How can you learn to love Pearlestria if you've made this house into your prison? There are so many merpeople who'd love to meet you. It's not very often to have a human-born among us." Her voice drifts softly through my mind.

But I still refuse to talk to her. If I ignore her long enough, she'll give up. And if I were going to talk to her, I'd tell her to leave me alone and go enjoy the life she chose for herself on land—the place I'd give anything to be.

"They want to celebrate your life," she continues. "Remember the ceremony I told you about? The one to welcome you? I'd like to start planning it. It's important for Carter too, you know? He has the only mate in the ocean who refuses to make it official. Do you know how sad you're making him by acting like it's the end of the world?" Her voice grows angry in my head.

It takes me biting my tongue to stop myself from retorting.

"You're being so selfish and—"

"Mom," Carter says from the archway that leads to the just as boring living area. "Leave Ava alone, please. You're not helping her any. Why don't you go visit Dad so I can have some privacy with her. You've been smothering us both."

"But—"

"You know we can't run away. Please, just give us some space."

Starla flips her beautiful pink tail, propelling away from me. She hugs her son once before disappearing without another word. My eyes linger on the archway, expecting her to change her mind and come back.

But she doesn't.

Carter swims forward and settles down next to me, sliding his arms around me until I'm nestled against him, my tail resting across his. I press my cheek to his chest, trying to remember the scent of what he smelled like as a human—like sunscreen and the sea—but I smell nothing at all.

"I'm sorry about my mom, Ava. I know she can be overbearing," he says, brushing the floating strands of hair from my face.

"She accused me of destroying your happiness because I'm depressed," I say.

His lips turn downward. "You know that's not true. I'm unhappy because of what they did to us."

"She thinks I'm embarrassing you."

"Are not. You never could. The only one embarrassing me is her."

He brushes his fingers along my quivering lip before he kisses me. His soft lips taste of something familiar, something sweet, and I pull away and tilt my head to look at him. He grins as I study him, like he's hiding some exciting secret from me.

"You taste like home," I say.

He sucks in his bottom lip. "I surfaced."

I close my eyes, horribly grief-stricken that he got to feel the sun on his skin without me. Unlike me, Carter doesn't get to sit in a room and do nothing all day. He must help out in the colony doing whatever it is he does.

He frowns, rushing to tug the bag off his shoulder. "Wait, wait. I brought you some things."

The sadness gripping my heart slides away at his words. "You can do that?"

He nods. "I had to wait for the chance, but I finally got it today."

He unlocks his waterproof bag, and I realize all the contents within it are in plastic Ziplocs. He holds out a baggie of cut fruit and another with a lettuce wrap. I don't even care that the saltwater messes up the flavor of the apple slices. I didn't realize how hungry I was until I chewed and swallowed.

"I can't believe you brought these," I say, my voice projecting to Carter while I continue to shove the pieces of fruit into my mouth without slowing down.

"I couldn't let you starve, Ava."

I smirk. "You know I would've eventually eaten."

"That's what my mom said, but what kind of boyfriend would I be if I didn't try to make you as happy as I possibly could?" He pulls out another Ziploc from the bag. "I also picked up the pictures you took from home."

My heart soars when I see the stack of pictures within the Ziploc. In a separate baggie is a postcard in familiar handwriting. *Giselle…*

"You saw her?" I almost don't believe it.

"She found our bag with your phone on the beach by the room and has been pretending to be you to your parents. She'll keep the charade up as long as she can."

"So, there's still hope?" I ask. I almost don't believe it. "I can go home?"

"I'm going to do everything I can, but you're going to have to do some things as well."

My brows scrunch together. "Like what?"

"You're going to have to pretend you've come to terms with your mermaid life."

"Is that all? I think I can handle faking it."

"We'll get out of here, Ava. I promise."

I hug him again. I haven't been so hopeful since I left home. Carter hugs me for a long moment before I finally bring my gaze to the postcard from Giselle. It's a picture of the harbor of Azure Waters with the Ocean Jewel among the boats.

Ava,

The sea seems so cruel now that it's taken you. Be strong and fight the current. The waters might be rough now, but they're no match for the girl who survived the waves twice. I love you, Aves. I know we'll see each other again soon. I'll head to sea if I have to. I'll figure out a way. Be safe and don't get into any trouble. I'd like you back with your legs one day, because no one would believe me that

Tugging the postcard from its protective bag, I let the water erase the ink of my best friend's words. I can't risk anyone seeing this and hunting Giselle down to destroy another part of my life. But her words sit heavy in my heart. She has faith that I'll return to her.

I slide my fingers through Carter's. "Thank you. For everything."

He kisses me on the lips, sending a dozen memories and thoughts into my mind—of Azure Waters, of Giselle, of me strolling along the beach. He imagines kissing me on the sand, running his fingers along my human legs, the thought so vivid I can almost feel the heat of the sun on my skin. And he imagines a future that had felt lost to me.

But not all is lost.

The ocean can't imprison me forever. I won't let it.

TREADING
WATER

HOME, SWEET HOME

SUNLIGHT TRICKLES THROUGH THE DEEP blue ocean, sparkling off the cerulean scales of my tail. I bask in the middle of the sea grass beds in the only place I can go to escape the watchful eyes of the inhabitants of Pearlestria.

It must be midday on the surface with the way the sun haloes up above in a white blanket of glowing light. It's the only time of day that I can pretend to be home on land in Azure Waters with the warmth of the sun on my skin, the crisp sea breeze in my hair, the soft sand between the toes I severely miss. But instead of the dry air, I have the swirling current of the ocean, the diluted light that can't even warm the water at this depth, and my tail that slaps the sandy floor in annoyance.

It's been forty days since I was dragged away from my human life and forced to accept a much less glamorous one under the sea. Without my family or friends, the time spent here feels like eternity. My only reprieve is when my boyfriend, Carter, sneaks me something from the shore. He tries his best to keep me connected to the human world, but I'm afraid the world will pass me by before I ever have the chance to escape the place that's supposed to be a haven but feels much more like a prison.

I flop from my back to my stomach, kicking up sand with my tail. It drifts through the water in a haze. Running my finger through the sand, I trace circles that wash away before they're complete. A school of mackerels casts a shadow over me, swimming through the water like a silver cloud. Dolphins circle the fish, wrangling them in the water to feast upon. This is as entertaining as it gets here within this underwater city's rock walls.

In this magical place, merpeople can live their lives without human interference, protected by whatever magic sets off the sparks within our chests. At the moment, I'm the only human-born mermaid in Pearlestria, but I've heard rumors of there being others at the different colonies throughout all the oceans of the world. I'd like to travel to them one day, if I'm ever forgiven for accidentally flashing my fins to a human—my best friend to be exact. No one knows it was someone I know. She'd be murdered for the sake of protecting our kind, though I highly doubt our kind needs any protecting most of the time.

"Ava, there you are," a feminine voice rings through my mind. It still unsettles me that anyone can just push their voice into my head any time they please, but it's especially unnerving to hear Starla, the mermaid responsible for my capture. "I thought you might've—"

I flick my tail, sending another sand cloud into the air. "Might've what? Swam away?" Running away isn't possible without legs. "You know I've come to terms with this arrangement." I force myself to smile, but I'm pretty sure I'm just baring my teeth. I wouldn't know. I never knew I could actually almost forget what I look like without a mirror.

"I was going to say found some friends. You know there are plenty of mermaids your age here. It'd be good for you." *Yeah. No, thanks.* As it turns out, I have very little in common with the merpeople of Pearlestria for the simple fact that the majority have never been to the surface.

"I'm fine, Starla. I've never been much of a people— merpeople?" I fumble over my words. "I'm not much for socializing." *Says the girl who has a close group of friends on land who think you've run away to travel the world with a boy you just met.* Thinking about my friends makes me miss them more than ever. Giselle, my best friend, promised she was pretending to be me to everyone, but I'm not sure how long that can even go on—I'm sure Sapphire, Chloe, and Daisy will realize it soon enough when she can't produce the photos they want. Matty and Logan are probably taking bets on whether or not I'll ditch them all eventually.

"Ava? Did you hear me?" Starla asks. Of course I heard her but my mind wandered to the place I want to be, and I shut off the sound of her voice in my head.

"What? I'm sorry."

"I think you've been here long enough. I'd like to start planning the coupling ceremony for my son."

Oh, that. Before I was transformed into a mermaid, Carter worked on the yacht I had vacationed on with my friends. In a freak accident, I fell overboard and drowned. Carter gave his one opportunity to transform someone into a mermaid to me, giving me his spark along with the bond that came with it.

"Why? Shouldn't that be up to Carter and me?" The coupling ceremony is some weird tradition that's supposed to involve the transformation for a human, but since he did things a bit out of order, it'd be a ceremony to make our coupling official—which is basically marriage in the mer world. A marriage I'm not even close to being ready for. Carter understands. He's lived on the land. Merpeople traditions mean nothing to him, but for Starla, his mom, they mean a whole lot.

Her brows scrunch. "This is important, Ava. How will you ever fit in if you don't at least try to pretend you care about our traditions?"

"I don't care about fitting in. I care about getting the control I need to stay on land so I don't have to live here. I don't even see how that's possible if I can't have my sea stone ring back. How am I supposed to practice?" I flop back, flicking my tail hard enough that she has to swim to stay next to me. The sudden current widens her eyes, but she doesn't project to me the thoughts clearly written on her face for me to decipher. She just flicks her tail harder to stay close enough. Always too close for comfort.

If it weren't for Starla, who stole the sea stone ring right off my finger, forcing me into a permanent mermaid form, I'd probably have gotten the hang of not transforming at random. Carter and I had managed to convince my parents that traveling before college would be good for me. We were going to find somewhere I wouldn't have to worry about being seen by someone I know. We had everything worked out and the means to do so. But Starla wouldn't hear it. All she cares about is turning me into the perfect mermaid bride despite her own self living among humans most of the time.

"It's not about practicing, Ava. It's about knowing who you are and where you belong. You have to be anchored to the ocean before you can live on the land as my husband and I do. Being born a human makes things a little harder. Your feelings are all over the place. Your heart and mind have to be in agreement at all times. It's something that will happen eventually. Give it a few years."

Years? I don't have that kind of time. I have a human family waiting for me to come home before I leave for college in the fall.

"Whatever you say, Starla." I swim from the sand to meet her eyes dead on. "My heart and mind are in perfect agreement. Neither wants to be trapped behind these walls. For one, I feel like I'm in a tank. And two, how can I be grounded to the ocean if I can't even enjoy a good swim?"

"You want more freedom," she says, confirming what I've wanted all along.

"Is that so hard to believe? I can't even swim without strangers watching me, some even stalking my every move. You tell me to make friends, but no one even attempts to talk to me here. They treat me like an outsider. Like I'm here for their amusement." What makes it even worse is I can't hear the whispers. I can assume they talk about me telepathically. It's easy enough to cut people out of our mental conversations. "You want to plan the coupling ceremony, but for what? No one would come."

She twists her lips to the side, sending her voice into my mind. "Everyone would come, including King Attilonious, since this is his home colony. And to be fair, you don't look approachable with the scowl you constantly wear—" She twirls her finger at my chest. "And the bikini top is a constant reminder of your difference. If you're really uncomfortable with your body, I could fashion you something that doesn't make you stand out in a crowd."

Heat rises into my cheeks. Carter always found it funny I wore half my bikini, but he never bothered me about it. While some mermaids here choose not to cover up, some still do for fashion, I guess—like Starla. She wears a grass woven, strapless bra, and while it doesn't look out of place, it looks uncomfortable. My bikini top is like a baby blanket. I'd feel lost without it.

"Thanks, but no. I'm fine." I hate that I'm having this conversation at all. "And don't you think it'd be kind of weird to invite the king...or anyone else for that matter? Can't it be a private ceremony?"

For this being the king's home colony, I've never actually seen the merman. He feels more like the king in a fairytale and not the actual ruler of the seas that contain me. It's his laws and traditions that put me here. I'm not so sure I could even force a smile.

"I'm starting to think you don't want to be with my son at

all," she says, her nose crinkling.

I roll my eyes. "Can you stop?" I don't have to prove anything to her. "If planning the stupid ceremony is so important to you, then do it, but I'm not going to pretend like I want this now. I'm only eighteen."

"Which is the perfect age."

I rub my hands across my face. For living on land most of the time, she really doesn't understand what I'm going through. "You're impossible. I don't even know why you're pushing for this. I know how much I bother you. Why would you even want to claim me as your family?"

Her forehead furrows with a frown. "Ava, you *are* my family. You're my daughter now, and I care about you immensely. If I didn't, I wouldn't have fought so hard to make sure you'd survive in this world. I wouldn't be here checking to make sure you're okay. I wouldn't worry about you fitting in."

Ugh. How can I even respond to that? She infuriates me one second and then makes me feel guilty the next. Sorrow washes over me as I think about my own mom on land. Isn't this something she should be included in? I never imagined going through any of my big life stages without my parents. *It's only a coupling as merpeople. It's not marriage in the human sense. You'll manage. Do what makes life easier.*

I close my eyes for a moment. "I'll try harder, okay?"

She smiles. "And I promise to allow you to have more freedom. But it has to be supervised by either me or Carter. I can't allow you to leave the colony on your own."

It's better than nothing, I suppose. I won't be asking Starla anytime soon, but Carter will be thrilled to be able to take me out of here.

Pulling me against her, Starla hugs me, petting my floating hair down to my back. She leans away with a smile before hooking her arm through mine. For the first time in over a month, I don't want to strangle her with kelp. I never would, but I have imagined doing so a dozen times.

"Thanks. You don't know how happy this makes me." Officially coupling with Carter isn't the worst thing in the world. Our bond is deep-seated and irrevocable anyway. We share a life, a heart—everything—split between our two bodies.

She guides me along. "Good. Your happiness is important to me, too."

★★★

I lounge on a kelp-wound rock in the corner of our small living room. The pearlescent walls shimmer through the bubbly current that drifts in from the cutouts in our walls. A few bright orange and white clown fish dart through the colorful coral lined perimeter that makes the space feel less empty. Without the need of furniture or the luxuries that come from the human world, there's not much I can do to make this home-like. I took advantage of having everything at my fingertips as a human so adjusting to a simple life hasn't been pleasant. It's been downright maddening sometimes, especially knowing the human world above us goes on without me.

"Ava," Carter calls into my mind before I see him drift through the archway. "I'm back."

I swim through the water and tackle him before he even has the chance to clear the entryway. We spin together, flying to the sandy yard in front of our underwater house. He lands on his back with me on his chest, and I lean down and shower him with kisses.

"You must've had a good day," he says into my mind, sliding his arms around me, pulling me closer to kiss me deeply, sending chills over my skin. His happiness drifts over me, extinguishing the despair I cling to in the lonely moments when he's gone.

I'd never admit it to Carter, but I feel utterly pathetic my life has resorted to me constantly waiting on him to return. He's basically my sole form of entertainment, and it's something I never want to get used to. The ocean stripped me of my identity, of my ability to do things for me. My sole existence shouldn't be for a boy no matter if I'm in love with him.

But if I told Carter, he'd hold onto the guilt I think he's finally let go of about transforming me. Just because I'm miserable doesn't mean he has to be. It was my devastating mistake that put us in this position.

"It was the same as usual, but I've missed you," I say, smiling against his lips. I don't have to fake it with Carter. My smile comes easy enough the moment I see his jewel-like eyes holding me in their intensity. "I thought you might've decided to stay on land."

His smile fades, a darkness flourishing in him like a sudden storm on the horizon, a reminder he can see past my smile into my mind. He knows this life isn't for me—for either of us. "Never without you."

"I'm teasing." Mostly.

Flicking his tail, he propels us from the sandy floor and carries me with him back inside our home. He swims with me in his arms through the quaint living area to the bedroom before setting me on a bed of woven kelp. The sand is soft enough beneath us that we don't need much more, and I'd be comfortable in Carter's arms regardless.

The vibration created by his moans against my lips ignites shivers through me. His fingers trail down my sides until they graze the backside of my tail. Pulling me closer, he presses against me, sending me images from his day, including images I've waited over a week to see.

He finally made it to the surface to check on my family, and through his eyes, I take in the scenery in front of my house, a remodeled Victorian, with my mom sweeping the sand off the patio. After that, another image floats into my mind of Giselle's smiling face as she uses my phone to snap a photo of Carter.

A bout of envy sneaks into my heart at the sight—I would give anything to hang out with my best friend. It sucks that Carter gets to and I don't.

He eases away to peer into my eyes. "You're upset," he says after a moment.

I shift my gaze away. "I'm sorry. It just doesn't seem fair I'm always down here. That I have to accept a fate under the water and you can still go to the shore."

His eyebrows knit together. "I'll stop if you want me to. I don't have to go."

"No, I'd never ask that of you. I just miss home is all." This is the reason I try to hide my feelings the best I can. Carter, while he loves the land, would give it up in a heartbeat. He was born in the water after all. This isn't new to him. But if he did stop going to the surface, I'd have no one to watch over my family, and Giselle would have a harder time keeping my disappearance into the sea a secret.

Reaching around, Carter pulls his waterproof bag from the floor beside us. "I brought you some things."

My sadness melts into excitement. This is one of the better things about him returning to shore. I still haven't gotten used to a mermaid diet, and I'll spend days without eating, because I can't get up the nerve to tear into the freshest form of sushi. Carter did manage to get me to try some seaweed, which was basically like chewing on a slimy salt rope with a hint of lettuce. I couldn't exactly survive on the stuff.

Rummaging through the bag, he pulls out a variety of fruits and vegetables in a few separate plastic pouches. The water is cool enough to keep them for a couple days so I don't have to gorge myself. In another, I find some deli meats and cheese without bread or crackers since those turn to mush the moment they hit the water. As long as I eat them quick enough, everything just tastes a little like the ocean.

He hands me another bag with a broken chocolate bar, and I grin, shaking it in my hands. I never knew I could miss so many things until I no longer had them. The final baggie he gives me contains a few photos of Giselle standing in front of a white wood condo on the shore of a beach. On the back of one of the pictures, she wrote, *Home, Sweet Home. Three bedrooms, two baths, walk-in closets, beach front. Our home for college.*

My eyes widen as I look at Carter. "Carter, you didn't give her hope I'd be home for college did you?"

He laces his fingers through mine. "She holds her own hope, Ava. She said even if you couldn't live there, she wanted you to have a place to stay for when we can return."

If I could cry freely without the water interference, tears would be running down my cheeks. Giselle and I had plans—we were going to rent a house while going to college at UCSD. It was supposed to be the time of our lives. And now, she's still moving forward with the plans without me. The last thing I want is for her to be alone, holding out for something that most likely won't happen anytime soon, if ever.

"You have to tell her the odds are slim," I say.

He shakes his head. "I'm not going to burst her plans when we don't even know that. Maybe we'll get out of here sooner than you think. I've—"

"Carter, Ava? I'm home." The sound of Starla's voice cuts through our minds. At least she can't hear anything unless we direct our thoughts to her. It's a lot of fun having our own conversations in front of her without her even knowing what's on our minds.

Starla stops in the archway to our room. When she sees us lying together on the small bed, she smiles. "I see you've told Carter already."

What? I think for a moment. Oh, crap. The coupling ceremony.

Carter shifts his gaze to mine, keeping a straight face. He sends his thoughts only to me. "Told me what?"

I bare my lower teeth in an awkward smile. "I might've agreed to the coupling ceremony."

He blinks in surprise before a smile crosses his face. "You what?"

"Yeah," I think to him. "Looks like this is going to be official."

MEET THE FAMILY

STARLA GRINS AT THE SMILE on her son's face. It's the same one he saves just for me, the one where he's all dimples and squinty eyes—all the happiness in the world lighting his face. It's the one that makes my heart race, makes me forget that the world still spins outside the two of us.

But now, the smile feels different.

Carter laces his fingers through mine, lightly squeezing my hand. "I'm assuming you've agreed to plan the ceremony?" Carter asks his mom.

"It's my job as your mother. Your father will be thrilled—the rest of the family, too," she says. "Everyone's been dying to meet you, Ava."

I shift my eyes to my glittering scales. I knew Carter had other family down here, but I have yet to meet anyone personally. I haven't wanted to for the simple fact I don't want to learn to like it in Pearlestria like Starla hopes. Not to mention how awkward it is.

"Then why haven't they come by?" It's a simple enough question. Starla's always pushing me to socialize, but no one has ever dropped by. That is, unless this little prison of mine doesn't accept visitors.

Her smile falters. "You're not exactly approachable, Ava."

"Mom!" Carter snaps.

Oh, great. Another fight. It's all too often Carter gets into it with his mom over me. It mostly ends with him sending her away.

I touch his hand. "Carter, it's okay. She's right." I only say it to diffuse the situation. Carter is fiercely protective of me, and I sort of feel bad watching as Starla's eyes widen, looking like two giant saucers the same color as the ocean around us—the same color as Carter's eyes.

"She's far from right, Ava," he thinks only to me.

"Please," I whisper in his mind. "Not tonight."

He frowns in defeat, but he doesn't argue. Instead, he says, "Ava's doing the best she can. If it would make you feel better, I'll take her to meet some of the family."

Starla's smile returns. "What a wonderful idea! You two should go out this evening instead of staying home like always."

I can't stop the frown from pulling my lips down. "I don't know..."

"What if I allow Carter to take you for a swim after? Would you do it then? You really don't want to show up to your coupling ceremony and know no one." She's bribing me. Not because she wants me to make friends but because of the coupling ceremony. Everything constantly revolves around the mer-traditions and ways. I should know this by now.

"Outside of the walls?" I ask. She did promise earlier. I just didn't think she'd allow Carter to be the first one to take me.

She nods. "And I trust you not to do anything stupid or dangerous."

I roll my eyes. "I really had my heart set on breaching in front of some tour boats."

Carter laughs while pulling me from our bed. "She'll be on her best behavior." As we swim past Starla, Carter stops to kiss her cheek. "Don't wait up for us."

When we exit the house, I can't stop the fear from slowing me down. Meeting people has never been hard for me before, and the old me would've never stayed home so much, but this is different. Who knows what the other mers think about me. Starla already made it clear I don't fit in.

It takes Carter a moment to realize he's the only reason I'm moving. I float behind him like a balloon tied to his wrist. He swims in a circle around me, causing me to spin in a small whirlpool. The fast movement makes me laugh until he catches me in his arms. The gesture is something he does when he's unsure what to do with himself...or me for that matter.

"You're nervous." He doesn't have to ask. My fingers tremble against his chest.

"They're going to think I'm weird," I say.

"Why do you say that?"

"Because I'm wearing a bikini top." I still can't get over Starla's remark from earlier about standing out.

"Well, you know I won't complain if you take it off," he says with a grin.

My cheeks flush, and I slap my palms against the hard muscles of his chest. "You're so not helping."

He wraps me in his arms. "I just want you to do what makes you comfortable. No one will say anything about your top. They all know you're human-born. If anything, they probably wish they had something like it. Why do you think some mermaids create tops? The human world is fascinating."

"Your mom said—"

"My mom says a lot of things, Aves. You know this. Don't let her get to you."

I sigh, blowing out a small bubble. "She already has."

Sadness crinkles his eyes in the corners, but he doesn't say anything. Instead, he flicks his tail, propelling us toward the center of the colony where it's busy with life. Watching the merpeople feels as scary as it was to watch the ocean after my sister, Bailey, was swept away years ago. I can't put my finger on why it's so scary to immerse myself in the world I'm clearly now a part of, but it might have to do with the fact that I didn't choose to be here.

When we reach the main stretch of houses, I say, "You should probably let me swim or they might think you're forcing me to socialize against my will."

The seriousness in his eyes fades as he half smiles. "I like holding you in my arms. Plus, I'm afraid you might swim away if I don't."

I laugh, tilting my head forward until my blond hair floats between us like a veil. "Okay, you might be right, but you can hold my hand."

Reluctantly, he releases me to only twine his fingers through mine. We don't swim long before Carter slows in front of a house twice the size of ours that looks to have been carved out of a huge, glittering boulder. The entrance sits halfway up the dome shape through what looks like a porthole on a ship.

Carter stops just before entering. "My grandma lives here. But I have to warn you, so does my—"

"Carter, my boy!" A deep, familiar voice reverberates through my head, and I recognize the merman before I even see him. "You finally brought Ava."

Anger snakes through my mind when a merman with long, dark hair pops his head through the hole. It's one of the merpeople who helped Starla drag me away from the shore. And I can't help the hate I feel for him. I wish Carter had brought me anywhere but here.

Carter side glances me. "Easy, Ava. He was acting under my mom's authority when she asked for help. Uncle Tobias isn't a bad man," he says only to me. He turns his gaze to the merman. "I figured it was time Ava met our family. My mom tell you about the coupling ceremony yet?"

The merman, Tobias, grins. "She spent all afternoon here

talking about it."

Carter pulls me up toward the entrance to the dome house. Tobias pops back in, giving us room to enter. My mouth falls agape at the sight before me. Decorative stones line the walls and ceiling in a kaleidoscope of colors, swirling in an intricate pattern that looks like a sunset on the water. Faint light trickles in through the circular cutout in the middle of the ceiling. Large rocks create partitions throughout the home, so that even though it's divided into rooms, each one has a view of the magnificent walls. The sandy floor appears pink from the reflection of the deep red stones, which resemble rubies. Who knows? Maybe that's what they are.

Large flat rocks, covered in the softest looking sea grass, form a circle in the living area so when you perch on them, you have to face one another. The room is filled with all sorts of interesting things. A gigantic anchor rests near a partition, and next to it is a metal chest with a few vases sitting on top. The steering wheel to a ship hangs out in front of one of the window cutouts, making it so no one can exit that way, and on the floor, half stuck into the sand are various different glass plates. It's like they've scavenged shipwrecks to decorate the place.

I run my fingers over the jeweled wall. "You have an interesting collection," I say to anyone willing to listen.

"Thank you, Ava," Tobias says. "Humans are such interesting creatures. The pieces always give me something to talk about when we have visitors."

I blink a few times at his comment but don't respond. He doesn't consider me human. As far as he's concerned, I'm a mermaid—which is hard to forget with my tail.

"Carter? Is that Ava with you?" A mermaid rises from behind the partition behind the anchor. Her golden brown hair, streaked with blue, is tied in a long braid that stops halfway down her tail. Her blue eyes, the same as Carter's, crinkle in the corners. Though her skin is relatively smooth, I can tell she's probably older than Starla with the way she carries herself in such wise confidence. A woman who has probably seen all that the ocean has to offer.

"Yes, Grandmer," Carter says, tugging me along with him. "Ava was finally feeling up to visiting."

The mermaid swims closer and pulls me away from Carter, wrapping her slender arms around me. I'm so surprised by the gesture that I don't hug her back. Instead, I force myself to smile when she releases me.

"Well, I'm delighted to meet you, Ava. Are you two hungry?" she asks, swimming back. "Tobias was about to bring in some dinner."

My stomach lurches at the thought. "No, thank you. Carter might be hungry, though."

He kisses my cheek. "Starved."

"Starla mentioned your difficulty transitioning your diet, Ava," Grandmer says.

Great. I'm about to get another speech about how I need to get over my food aversion, because this is the mermaid life.

"She's making progress," Carter says, interjecting.

"I hate it all," I say, shrugging. "Don't get me wrong. I like some fish but not raw. Even if I did like raw fish, humans prepare it differently. I'd rather starve than eat something that's trying to swim away from me."

Grandmer laughs like I've said the funniest thing. "I appreciate your honesty, dear." She motions for me to join Carter on one of the sea grass beds.

Carter wraps his arms around me, pulling me against his chest so I'm sitting on his lap. The one thing I've come to notice is how affectionate merpeople are. And it doesn't bother anyone. Public displays of affection are so common that people notice if a couple isn't at least holding hands.

"Thanks for not thinking I'm being ridiculous. It's just been really hard on me. I can't do any of the things I loved down here." I don't know why it's so easy to open up to Carter's grandmother, but she just seems to understand.

"What did you like to do?" she asks.

Tobias leans back with his hands behind his head, just listening without interrupting.

"I like to bake," I say. "Can't exactly do that here. My best friend isn't here either. We'd always hang out."

Tobias waves his hand at Carter. "Carter's right there."

"Carter's my boyfriend," I say.

Tobias raises his eyebrows. "But you've coupled."

This gets a laugh from Carter. "Uncle Tobias, relationships work differently on land."

"Is it not normal that I don't call you my best friend?" I think only to Carter.

"It's fine, Ava," he says to me. He turns back to his uncle. "While Ava might be my best friend and mate, it doesn't mean I have to be her best friend."

"But that friendship is over," he says. "You're not a human and those relationships don't matter anymore."

I stare at Carter's uncle, speechless, for what feels like an excruciatingly long moment. How can he even say that? Do merpeople give up their relationships if they choose the land over the sea? Obviously not. If they did, Carter wouldn't be here.

To stop myself from giving him a piece of my mind, I tug away from Carter and swim up toward the exit. This was a bad idea coming here. I should've just forced Carter to let me keep to myself. This merman doesn't even care that he helped Starla rip me from my life. He thinks everything is all good.

Well, it's not.

"I'm sorry. It was nice meeting you, but I have to go."

Without waiting for a response, I dart from the house to the channel of sand running between the houses. A few mers stare in my direction, but I don't meet their gazes.

Instead, I swim. I swim as fast as I can toward my favorite place near the boundary wall of Pearlestria. I don't even wait for Carter. I just swim up toward the surface until I can dart over the wall.

And then I'm in the open sea.

OUTSIDER

NEARLY FLYING THROUGH THE WATER, I ascend closer to the surface. I have no idea where I am or where I'm going. All I know is I won't feel better unless there's at least a dozen miles between me and Pearlestria. I obviously can't make my way to land, and I'm sure if someone were to find out I rose to the surface, I'd be in trouble because I have no idea what lies above the magical underwater city.

So I remain thirty feet below, just high enough to catch a glimpse of the white moon rising above. The sea glows with its magical light, allowing me to see through the pitch darkness. I doubt any humans would see me if I surfaced now, but I'm already worried I won't ever get my sea stone ring back.

A bale of sea turtles, caught on a current, drifts over me. I startle at the sheer size of them. I had no idea how big the creatures were, and they're at least half my size. I swerve in and out of the turtles, taking in how graceful they look as they move together. After following them for a few good minutes, I dip back down deeper.

A massive coral reef extends the bottom of the ocean the shallower the water becomes. From my place, it glows in vibrant colors, and all sorts of animals move around the fascinating reef. A few black tip reef sharks swim toward the surface, not straying far from where I catch them feeding on a school of gray fish. One of the sharks propels in my direction, swimming right toward me, but it darts around me at the last second to head back toward the reef.

I float in the water, hovering with the mild current. My hands circle at my sides, and my blond hair drifts around me. A spiky, striped fish swims near my head, tangling with my hair. I shake my head as it tries to yank free, but it ends up getting stuck worse.

After a minute of it pulling and tangling my hair, I finally wrap my hands around it to stop it from trying to rip free.

"Need help?" Carter slips up next to me, smirking as he watches me struggle to free the fish.

I shake my head not only to respond to him, but to spread my hair through the water. "I'm fine."

"You don't look fine."

I slide my fingers through the hair around the fish. "I don't need help, okay?"

I sink lower until my tail smacks against the sand. Carter continues to smile at me, flashing his dimples. Just watching him watch me struggle infuriates me. I don't want his help, but he doesn't have to mock me. I'm plenty capable of managing things on my own.

After another minute of tug of war with the pesky fish, I throw my hands out and give up. The fish swims in circles around my head, tightening its hold. Crossing my arms, I fall back to the sand, lying on my hair, shortening it enough that the fish can't pull it far. Carter silently swims closer before easing onto the sand above my head.

In one quick motion, he jabs the fish with his sharp nails, killing it right in front of my face. He unwraps my hair from the poor dead fish and then proceeds to peel the skin away and takes a bite right from it.

I cringe at his unexpected actions. "What are you doing?" My voice rises in my mind. His actions shouldn't bother me.

This is how things are for us now, and eating the freshest fish is part of the merpeople diets, but it's like he's purposefully reminding me.

"What does it look like?"

"You killed it."

"I had to. I couldn't get it otherwise unless I cut your hair. Plus, it's not like I'm wasting it." Carter uses his nail to cut off a square of meat. He holds it in front of my face. "Want to try it?"

I squirm away, knocking his hand from my face. "You know I don't."

I can't take my eyes off him as he carves away at the weird fish, popping small bites into his mouth. It's ten times better than how Starla eats, just biting the fish—most of the time while it's still moving—but the thought still grosses me out.

"That's fine. More for me." He continues to eat right over my head.

I sit up, but I don't swim away from him. My tail thuds against the ocean floor, and I continue to watch him pick apart his catch—well, technically my catch. When Carter finishes, he feeds the rest of the dead fish to one of the black tip reef sharks that eats it directly from his hand like a dog getting scraps at the dinner table. The shark circles us, expecting more, but Carter waves his hand, shooing it away.

Carter turns his gaze from the shark to me. He props his body on his arms, resting his palms against the sand. His blue eyes sparkle in the glowing ocean, and he doesn't say anything as he watches me.

I know he's waiting for me to say something first. He always does when I'm in one of my moods. And it drives me crazy how calm he is when all I want to do is yell and scream my frustration.

"Are you not going to ask me why I ran out of your

grandma's?" I ask after a moment. I'd rather him drag the information out of me. It's easier to voice my thoughts that way.

"Nope. I know you well enough to know why, Ava," he says.

I sink my fingers into the soft sand. "It's just—I can't get used to the social norms and customs. And it makes me feel awful. Am I hurting you, Carter? Does it bother you that I only consider Giselle my best friend? People are going to think I'm the crappiest mate in the world. Maybe—" I sigh. "Am I really the *one*? Your *one*. You deserve better than—" The words are more difficult to form than I expect. I pull my hands from the sand and wave them in front of me. "You deserve better than me."

He doesn't say anything for a long while. "You're having doubts about the ceremony."

"It's just—your mom was pestering me. She made me feel like I was a huge disappointment to you. And I think I am."

The face he gives me, pouty lips and pinched brows—a look of complete despair—nearly causes my undoing. He wears the hurt of my words for me to see and take in unlike his usually stoic expression when I complain about how tough things are. It's enough to tighten my chest, squeezing at my heart that beats in sync with his.

"Ava." The sound of my name coming from him into my mind sits heavy on my very being. "You mean everything to me. *Everything.* I don't give a damn what my mom thinks or what anyone else thinks. But I do care what you think, and hearing you say that I deserve better than you kills me. There is absolutely no one better in the world than you are for me."

"I'm sorry," I whisper into his mind. "I feel like I'm failing all of this—because I want to fail."

"And that's okay. We're not staying here forever."

"It feels like it."

"I swear to you, Ava. I'll figure out how to get you back to shore, even if it means I have to give you my ring to do so." He holds the chain that carries his sea stone ring in front of my face.

"That would mean..."

"It's the worst case scenario."

I bury my face against his chest. I couldn't imagine returning to land to only leave Carter behind in the sea. He doesn't have to tell me he'd do it now if he thought we could get away with it—if he knew I could manage on my own without him. But I'm not even confident in myself to push for such a thing. Not to mention how awful the idea of returning to land without Carter makes me feel, like I'd be leaving half my heart in the ocean. It'd be enough to tear me apart. It'd probably make it impossible to get my heart and mind to agree, not when Carter would be bound to the sea.

"I can't leave you," I finally say. "I don't think I could even if I wanted to."

He holds me tighter. "I don't want you to leave me, but if that's what it takes to fix things. I'll do anything for you, I'd—"

"I said I'm not leaving you," I say, cutting him off.

Bringing his lips to mine, he sends a dozen images flashing into my head. Along with his thoughts of me comes a wave of emotion. Emotion that swirls and mingles with my own. Feelings I've known were inside him all along, but it's different when he projects them directly to me. He's never done it before, and the sheer warmth of our bond as mates pushes away the cold lingering in my once human bones despite having already adjusted to the freezing waters.

"Whoa." My voice barely sounds like a whisper in my own mind. "That was—" I can't even come up with words to describe what that was or how that felt for me.

"I'm sorry. I didn't mean to do that," he whispers. "I already know your own feelings are enough for you to handle."

"You can feel me?"

"Sometimes"

"I'm sorry."

He laughs in the water, pushing tiny bubbles from his lips that float up toward the surface. "Don't apologize. It's mostly the good stuff...well, except today."

Twining my fingers with his, I hold his hands, bringing them up to my mouth so I can kiss his knuckles. I can just imagine the feelings I sent into him, especially at his grandma's house. No wonder he always knows what to say to me in moments like those.

"Is there anything I can do to stop that?" I ask.

He shrugs. "Maybe try not to let my mom put doubt in your mind about me again."

I purse my lips. "That's impossible."

Frowning, he says, "Then things are going to have to change."

"What do you mean?"

He pulls me off the ground with him. "Come on. Let's head back. You'll see."

If an argument could heat the water, our living room would be boiling right about now. I hunker in the corner of the room as Starla and Carter have a mind shouting match with each other. To me, it's mostly random words thrown in here and there because they're directing their heated thoughts at each other, leaving me mostly out of it, but they're both so angry that some things slip through.

"This is *my* house, and I want you out!" Carter's voice trickles through my mind.

My eyes bulge, hearing the words. I didn't know this place belonged to Carter. I had assumed it was Starla and Mateo's, and that we were just staying here for the time being.

"You're being unreasonable!" Starla flings out her arms.

"Unreasonable? You're jeopardizing my life with my mate!" Carter's eyes flicker to mine before he reins his voice in so I can't hear the next words directed at his mom.

She whips her head to look at me, but Carter swims between us, blocking her view. His towering form is like the perfect protective wall, sparing me from whatever she was about to aim at me.

All these weeks, I knew Carter had been on the outs with his mom. I just assumed we didn't have a choice. She told me she was the one who was supposed to help me adjust. It's why she left her home on the land with Mateo.

"Ava," Starla says to me even though I can't see her past Carter. "Please, you have to say something. He listens to you. I know I might've said things that hurt you, but it wasn't my intention. I'm just trying to help. How can you fit in if you don't know that you're acting like an outsider?"

I frown. "That's because I am an outsider. I agreed to the coupling ceremony to make you happy. Isn't that enough?"

Carter turns to peer at me from over his shoulder. He heard what I tried to send only to Starla, but she left me flustered and I usually always include Carter in my thoughts. His fuming expression melts to one of concern, but just as quickly as it came, it disappears. "Is that true, Aves?"

I don't respond. I can't. Because it is the truth. At least it was when I agreed to it with Starla. At the time, I didn't know how happy it'd make Carter. He never made it seem like a big deal that I didn't want to participate in what I thought was a silly tradition. But now, I can tell it was a façade. Carter is a merman after all. He might've adapted to the land, but he still follows the rules of the sea.

Pushing from the floor, I swim the few feet to Carter and

wrap my arms around his taut shoulders, resting my chin on the crook of his neck. He relaxes under my touch, running his hands down my back until he tightens his grip around my waist.

"Ava?" he asks just to me because I still don't answer.

"It's true," I finally say. "But it doesn't matter. I see how happy the idea makes you."

I expect him to smile, but he doesn't. He blinks a few times, like he's trying to process my words. The two of us just float together in silence for a long while. Starla doesn't speak either, or if she does, I can't hear her. The anger they shared has fizzled out, and I swear the water cools around me.

Lowering his shoulders, he turns his gaze back to his mom. "Do you think you could stay with Grandmer?"

She silently nods and swims toward the exit.

"Hey, Mom," Carter says before she can leave.

"Yes, son?"

"Can you let everyone you've already told know that the coupling ceremony is off?"

Her face falls in disbelief, but if she says something, it's not directed at me. She darts from our house without another look, leaving me alone with Carter. My heart thuds in my chest as his words sink in. He just called off the coupling ceremony, which I know is a huge deal. I doubt any merperson has ever done such a thing.

I thought I didn't want to go through with it, but now that I don't have to, I can't stop myself from feeling awful. A part of me already accepted the silly ceremony, and while my relationship with Carter is brand new, I can't even imagine being with anyone else.

Would it be possible to change my mind one day? I'm young. I never even thought I'd get into a serious relationship until after college. I had questioned if I was good enough for

Carter but never the opposite. Carter is perfect for me. His spark lies in my chest. How could I ever be with someone else if it's his heart that beats in sync with mine? If it's his thoughts and memories that I carry in my mind? If it's his life that allowed me to live? I couldn't...could I?

"You know, you lied to me about the coupling ceremony. You said it didn't matter. You said it wasn't a big deal to you," I say, looking into his aqua eyes, trying to figure out what he's thinking before he even says it to me. I wish he'd push his emotions into me again, but even his face remains expressionless though our hearts beat faster than usual and not in a good way.

"It isn't, Ava," he says.

Pulling away from him, I cross my arms. "You're lying again. I saw the look on your face when your mom told you I had agreed. You were so happy."

His eyes soften. "Of course I was happy. The girl of my dreams wanted to officially be mine in the eyes of the merpeople and the ocean."

Confusion settles over me. "So why did you tell your mom to call it off? If it makes you that happy..."

"Because how can I really be happy if I know you only agreed to the coupling ceremony to please my mom? Seriously, Ava. What kind of guy would that make me?" He swims back, putting distance between us. "What were you even thinking?" Hurt lines his words, and I feel even worse.

"I—" What am I even supposed to say? I'd give anything to call Giselle to ask her what I should do.

Had I known any of this—how I'd make him happy just to accidentally devastate him, I'd have never relented to Starla's annoying persistence. But I'm also irritated that Carter wasn't honest. Sure, he says none of this is a big deal, but it clearly is or we wouldn't even be discussing it.

"I'm sorry." It's the only thing I can say. "I just thought

going through with the ceremony would make things easier on everyone."

He nods his head once without smiling. "I get it, but that's not what it's about."

"I know, I—"

He cuts me off with a kiss. Locking his hands around my back, he pulls me closer until our bodies are touching completely. His smooth skin radiates warmth through me, and I moan when he slips his tongue in my mouth, gliding it over mine.

"Ava," he says, still kissing me, his voice wrapping around my mind. "If we go through the ceremony, it's going to be because we want to be together for the rest of our lives. It's going to be because you have absolutely no doubt in your mind, and because you want to do it for us—not just me."

He swims back with me clinging to him, guiding me to our bedroom. Gently lowering me to the sandy floor, he lies on top of me with his hands pressed into the kelp bed on both sides of my head.

Slowly pulling away, I lean all the way back to gaze at him. "Not *if* we go through with it. I do want to go through with it, Carter. I don't envision my future without you. But, I want to be excited about it. Right now, I'm not."

He hugs me, sinking me deeper into the sand. "I promise to change that, Ava. Things are going to change around here."

His certainty should be enough for me not to question it, but I can't stop myself. I purse my lips in a half smile. "Really? How?"

"Well, for starters, my mom's not going to interfere in our relationship anymore." Just hearing that Carter's going to stop Starla from trying to get us to do things her way is enough to make me lock my fingers around Carter's neck to kiss him sweetly.

A thought lingers in my mind though, Starla's own words

digging into my soul. Without her, I won't learn what I'm supposed to learn to get out of here to resume my life on shore. "But who'll teach me the mermaid ways? Isn't it against the rules for you to do it?"

"I have an idea, and we'll worry about that later. Right now, I just want to be with you, if that's okay?"

It's more than okay. Smiling, I gaze into his eyes, focusing on intentionally sending all the intensely good emotions rushing through me to him.

His eyes widen, and he leans in to kiss me, but I raise my hand up, pressing it to the spark in his chest to stop him for a second. I might've agreed to the coupling ceremony to get Starla off my back, but I also had agreed to it because I'm in love with Carter—words I've yet to say to him not because I haven't wanted to, but because our love resonates enough that we've never felt the need to do so. But I feel the need in this moment. I've never felt it so desperately.

"I'm in love with you, you know?" I ask.

And I thought agreeing to the coupling ceremony made him happy. The smile he gives me is brighter than the sun reflecting off the crystal clear ocean. His joy and pleasure nearly smother me in all the goodness that he is. They're enough to push away anything negative that was lingering in me.

He kisses me deeply, his skin hot against mine. We lay together, our hearts beating against each other, and I shiver, excitement rushing over my skin. Carter's fingers explore my body, slowly making their way around my back to untie my bikini top. It floats away as he trails kisses down my neck to my collarbone.

His love washes over me, drawing me in. I lose myself in his kisses and desire. I lose myself to him completely.

4

NEWFOUND FREEDOM

CARTER BRUSHES HIS LIPS AGAINST my bare shoulder, holding me from behind. Tingles rush down my tail like a small jolt of electricity courses through me. I moan, turning over, and stretch my arms up before embracing him. Memories from last night linger in my mind, but only the good stuff. The memories that make my heart race and my mouth smile.

"God, you're beautiful," he says, resting his forehead against mine. An image of me lying on the sand under him flashes through my mind when he kisses me. "I could stay here all day if you'd let me."

I grin, sucking in my bottom lip. "You know I would."

Leaning closer, he kisses me again. "Then it's settled."

I laugh, tilting my head back as his lips tickle my jaw and trail to my neck. His fingers grip my waist, pulling closer until my chest presses against his.

"Carter? Ava?" The sound of his mom's voice echoing through my mind forces me to frown. Of course she'd show up now despite everything that happened between us. "Can I come in?"

Carter's jaw twitches as he stiffens. "Give us a minute."

Reluctantly sitting up, Carter peers around the room before he finds my bikini top stuck to the coral under the cutout that's supposed to be a window. He helps me tie it around my neck and back before twining his fingers through mine. I'm tempted to tell him to face her alone, but we're stronger together when it comes to her persistence. She's probably going to try to change his mind about the coupling ceremony.

When we enter the living room, Starla floats outside the archway in our front yard. She holds one arm over her chest, slowly rubbing it up and down her other arm. Her blue eyes line with sadness, and I can't help feeling a tiny bit bad about the tension between us.

"What is it, Mom?" Carter asks without greeting her.

"I thought long and hard about things last night, and I think it's best if I go home for a while. You were right about a lot of things. I'm sorry to have caused either of you pain. I realize that you already have hard feelings toward me, and I had hoped that we could work past them, but staying here isn't helping any. I don't want you to grow to hate me more than you do."

"I don't hate you, Mom," Carter says.

She glances at me, but I don't say anything. I don't do it to be mean, but I just can't find it in me to coddle her with fake feelings after everything she put me through. Not to mention how jealous I am that she can just choose to leave and go back to live her life on land like she wasn't the reason I lost my chance to do so.

"Thanks for being here all these weeks, but you're right. It's best if you return to Dad. I know he has to miss you. I think it'd be better if someone less invested in me were to help Ava adjust as well. She doesn't need your motherly pressure right now." Carter squeezes my fingers.

She frowns. "So, the ceremony is still off?"

He nods. "For now."

"You know the king will be unhappy," she says. "He's been overly generous allowing Ava to take her time, you know."

"And I can deal with that if he has something to say,"

Carter says.

All hail King Attilonious for claiming to be a kind and fair king when it's his rules that have stolen my life. It's his rules that would be the death of my best friend if anyone were to find out she knows of our kind. It's his stupid rules that want to force me into a ceremony for the sake of fitting in. I couldn't care less about the king's happiness when he has no regard for my own. He shouldn't have anything to do with my relationship to Carter in the first place. I'd never say that to his face, though. If he's anything like I imagine him to be, I'd probably force myself to stay in control of my disdain toward him so he doesn't assure I never see the human world again.

"If there's no changing your mind..." She rubs her hands together.

"There's not."

"Then I guess you know where to find me."

Carter hugs his mom for a long moment, and I can see an exchange of words I can't hear through their gazes when they pull away. Starla reaches out and takes my hand in hers instead of hugging me. I'm glad she doesn't try to because I'm pretty sure I wouldn't allow her the opportunity.

She smiles with sadness in her eyes. "I hope you can find it in your heart to forgive me someday, Ava. This was never how I imagined things would be between us, and I hope they'll change eventually."

"It is what it is," I say. I don't respond about the forgiveness. Petty? Totally. I don't care.

"Please, take care of my son."

I nod. "You know I will."

Starla lets me go and swims away, looking back only once as she reaches the end of the row of houses that lead to the main channel of Pearlestria.

Turning my eyes to Carter, I study him for a moment to

decipher his serious expression. I'm sure it can't be easy for him to have this kind of strain on his relationship with his mom. It stressed me out more than a dozen times over the weeks.

"What now?" I ask when he doesn't move from my side.

"I have an idea," he says.

"Okay..."

He pulls me from the house. "Come on. It's going to be fun."

I cling to Carter's back, the world zooming by us at a speed I haven't felt since we had arrived at the merpeople colony. He propels us through the water, swimming away from Pearlestria and the walls that have been my prison. The bright sun shines fifty feet above us, but I swear I can feel its warmth on my skin as the rays sparkle through the clear blue water around us.

"Where are we going?" I ask, my hair flowing behind me from the speed of his swim.

"It's a surprise," he responds, turning his head to peek at me while I rest my chin on his shoulder. He didn't even wait a few minutes after Starla left to return to San Francisco before taking advantage of our newfound freedom away from his mom's ever-present need to control us.

He ascends toward the surface the shallower the water becomes. Through the rippling waves, I see the azure sky reflecting above us, making everything even bluer than it already is. A smile crosses my face, excitement and relief washing through me at the realization of what we're about to do.

"Are you serious?" I ask, nearly trembling in anticipation against Carter.

"Get ready."

Seconds later, I spit out water and suck in a deep breath of fresh ocean air. Saltwater drips down my face, and I blink as my eyes adjust to the surface light that blinds me for a moment. It's been so long since I've seen or felt the world from above, it's hard looking around. I close my eyes, absorbing the sudden heat of the sun and the feeling of the breeze against my skin. I had almost forgotten how good it feels to be out of the water. My hair sticks to my already drying cheeks, and I push it behind my shoulders.

I float on my back, trying to get out of the water as much as possible. Carter slides his hands under my back and lifts me higher, flicking his tail so we're treading water. The air circles around me, caressing me in a feather light touch that I want to cling onto forever.

Reaching my arms over my head, I stretch out, arching my back. Carter spins me around, sending my hair splaying out in surprising soft tendrils on the wind, and I laugh. Hearing the sound of my voice makes me laugh harder. Who knew such a simple thing could make my heart feel ten times fuller and lighter.

Carter lowers me down, flicking his fin to keep us at the surface. "I've missed your laugh so much, Ava."

I shower him with kisses all while laughing again. "It feels so amazing to use my voice."

He cups my chin in his hand, brushing his lips against mine for a long while. Kissing him above water is a thousand times better. All my senses feel so much more intense—the sound of his breathing in air, the scent of dry saltwater on his skin with a faint hint of sunscreen, the weight of his body heavier without the buoyancy of the water—everything about him so familiar of our time on land.

"Want to see your house?" he asks after a moment.

I press my lips together, tasting the saltwater more now that I'm not submerged underwater. "I don't know."

While the thought of swimming close to shore to see my house with my own eyes is what I've dreamed about for weeks, the idea depresses me. How can I be so close but unable to transform into my human form to walk the beach? It might be better to just stay right here in the middle of the vast ocean with the sun on my skin and happiness in my heart.

"It's just not the same," I finally add.

"I know it's not, but I want to do something for you—something I haven't been able to manage since your ring was taken." He smiles as he says it, flashing his dimples. The smoothness of his voice wraps around me like a comforting embrace, and I'd probably agree to just about anything he says at this point.

I slowly nod. "What is it?"

He lowers me back into the water. "You'll have to wait and see."

Taking his hand, I swim next to him in the direction I assume is toward Azure Waters. We cut through a school of yellowtails, some of the larger fish bumping against me, and I graze my fingers over their silvery backs. The shallower the water gets, the more we swim under the shadows of the boats off shore.

Fear tickles the back of my mind as we weave in and out of a couple of fishing lines. I slow down when I catch sight of a leopard shark struggling to free itself from the hook of one of the nearby boats. It struggles to swim forward with the line dragging it backward in a tug of war for freedom. Carter glances at me in the water in silent question, and I point to the shark.

He lets go of my hand, and I swim away from him, careful not to catch myself on the other few dozen lines hanging off the medium sized vessel. In one quick motion, I slice my nail across the line hooking the shark and cut it free.

Before I have a chance to do anything, the shark speeds away. Carter propels forward, snatching me around the waist from above me. We fly through the water as one, my arms outstretched in front of me, quickly catching up to the shark.

Carter dives down, weaving us through a kelp forest, after the fleeing shark.

Carter releases me, bolting ahead to carefully hold the shark. I expect it to put up a fight and thrash, but it just rests in Carter's arms as he slowly turns it over onto its back. It reminds me of a puppy with how it lets Carter stroke its belly, nothing like the scary white sharks you see trying to devour unsuspecting humans in the movies. This one isn't even half my size.

"I need you to unhook the line," Carter says, sending the thought into my mind.

Nodding, I swim closer, peering closely at the metal circle hook sticking from the side of the shark's mouth. The shark's tough skin makes it difficult to slide the hook free, and I frown, afraid of causing damage.

"Use your nails," Carter says after a minute.

My nails are tough, but not tough enough to cut through the metal, so instead, I make a tiny cut near the hook and slide it free. The shark isn't fazed by the tiny incision, and the moment Carter rights it and loosens his hold, it swims off toward the sandy bottom.

He takes the hook from me and hangs it from his necklace instead of dropping it into the current.

Looking around once more, he laces his fingers through mine and pulls me through the kelp forest and back to where the boats block out the sun on the surface. This time, he guides me away from them and toward the shallows that lead to the shore.

"You can't tell anyone about the shark, okay?" he says into my mind, swimming next to me. "It's against the king's law to meddle with human affairs, especially in what he considers their territory. He considers all the coastlines to be part of the human world, so we're only ever to observe. Fisherman would notice if we started cutting all their lines."

"Is there a list of laws or something?" I ask. I feel like I should attend some sort of mermaid school for this information.

"That'd make it easier, wouldn't it? The king, while mighty, also is forgiving. It's why he's ruled all the oceans for over a hundred and fifty years without an uprising."

"What? You never told me we live longer," I say.

He shrugs. "That's if we plan to live in the sea. We age at a human rate on the land. My parents plan to return to the sea at the end of their human lives."

"We can do that?"

"If that's what you want."

Maybe by then, it wouldn't be so hard to let go. It's a strange thought to even consider.

He smiles, watching me process the information. "We have a long time to consider it, Ava. Our whole human lives."

He's right. I need to focus on the present and not the future.

The water grows warm the closer we get to shore, and I search around the familiar shoreline. Carter slows down when we near some huge black rocks—rocks I never thought I could be so happy to see—and he stops in the water, staying just below the surface.

"If I ask you to wait here, would you?" He pulls my hand to his lips and kisses my knuckles.

"Where are you going?"

"It's a surprise."

I narrow my eyes while smiling. "I guess I can."

Carter kisses my cheek before he takes off, disappearing into the surf. Sinking to the bottom, I relax on the sand, curling my tail to my chest. There's no way I'm going to break the surface now without Carter, especially not this close to home.

A few fish swim by, but the water remains pretty empty

around me. Waiting here is excruciating. I propel myself from the floor after what feels like forever and swim a few anxious circles like I'm stuck in a tank.

Come on, Carter. Whatever he's doing is taking longer than I expected it to, and I'm starting to wonder if he's ever going to come back. I descend a few feet and tilt my head up to gaze at the surface only a few feet above me.

That's when I see them. Two people share a surfboard, fighting against the bubbling waves about thirty feet away. All I see are four legs as one person straddles the board and the other kicks behind it. The surprise of seeing them sends me swimming backward and deeper into the water. We're pretty far from shore, too far to catch the swells that the surfers of Azure Waters love.

Just when I'm about to bolt, the surfer straddling the board swings its leg over to sit sideways before jumping off the board to dip under. From this distance, I can tell it's a brunette girl with perfectly tan skin but not much more than that.

She spins in the water once, like she's searching for something, and then stops when she faces me. She shouldn't be able to see me as I am, but I still worry. Maybe I'll scare her away. Instead of trying to get away, the girl lifts her hand and waves in my direction. The only thing I can think to do is flee.

DOUBLE LIFE

CARTER WAS CRAZY FOR BRINGING me near the shore while it's still daylight. Not only is he risking my safety, he's risking the safety of the poor humans. Unlike him, I can't just transform into a human to wait.

And I'm pretty sure the surfer saw me—the real me. If someone from Pearlestria followed us, they would probably drown the person. The only reason I got away with accidentally flashing my fin to Giselle before was because Carter told his parents it was a stranger, and it was already after the fact. Now, it's easy enough to get rid of my spectator. The ocean is a dangerous place. Drowning happens. I could never go through with it, though.

"Ava?" Carter's voice drifts into my mind. "Where are you? Come back to the rocks."

"I can't. Someone saw me. This was a terrible idea."

"Just come back. It's safe."

Reluctantly, I swim back toward where the surfer girl had spotted me. Carter waits for me underwater. His glittering teal tail sparkles in the light penetrating through the sea. The spark in his chest glows brightly, drawing me in, and there's no sign of the surfers.

Meeting me halfway, he hooks his arm around my waist. He studies me with his brows knitted together like my thoughts project from my eyes for him to see. My bottom lip quivers, fear still gripping me in a hold that makes me want to flee. Bringing his hand to my face, he brushes his index finger over my lips. Then, he hugs me.

His lips brush my ear as he holds me. "Ava, it's okay. You're safe. A stranger didn't spot you." His voice is utterly certain in my mind.

"The surfer waved."

"What else would you expect from Giselle? She can see you as you are, you know, because she knows of our secret."

His words swirl through my mind, sending my heart racing. My eyes widen when he nods his head, and I stare at him in disbelief. I can't believe he just told me the surfer I spotted was my best friend. I was too scared to recognize her—Carter for that matter.

"Are you crazy?" I ask. "You're jeopardizing my best friend." All I can think about is how someone might find out that Giselle knows our secret. I could never forgive myself if she got hurt or worse. I'd probably end up the same because there's no way I'd ever allow that to happen.

Carter's smirking face melts into a frown. I guess this wasn't the reaction he was expecting from me. It's obvious he had hoped to make my day, to make me feel better after all these weeks, and I'm grateful he tried, but at the same time I'm upset.

"I've taken precautions. I swam the area to make sure it was safe. Please, trust me when I say it's safe. I'd never do anything to put Giselle in danger." He tries to take my hands, but I cross my arms over my chest instead.

"But this *does* put her in danger. I worry enough as it is about you visiting her on land. I'd rather just go home and hope for the day I can return to land with my legs. I'd rather wait years to see her safely than risk everything." The words kill me to say. I feel physically sick as they leave my mind. Because I want so badly to see her, to hear her voice, to talk to her about everything. But I can't.

I turn away from Carter. "Can you tell her I'm sorry, but I can't see her?"

Carter grabs my shoulder, spinning me around in the water. "No. You tell her yourself, Ava."

"What?"

"I said tell her yourself," he repeats. "Because I know you'll regret it if you don't. I know you're trying to do the right thing by her, but I can't stand to see and feel you so sad all the time. Giselle is willing to take the risk. If she wants to visit with you, then let her. It's not only yourself you're hurting."

"Carter..."

His forehead wrinkles as he stands his ground. "Ava, please. I'm trying my best to do right by you. I don't ever push you, and I always let you have the final say. But this—" He waves his hand behind him. "I'm making you do. So, you can either go tell your best friend you don't want to see her, or we can both leave together right now and leave her waiting."

Anger sneaks up on me, and I narrow my eyes. Heat crawls up my neck, my hands shaking as I curl them into fists. I can't abandon Giselle while she waits on the rocks so far from shore. She could get hurt paddling back to the beach. Carter knows this.

"You can't be serious," I say. He has to be bluffing. I don't understand why he's doing this. If something happened to Giselle, I'd blame him. I'm not sure I could ever forgive him, either. The fact that Carter is definitely aware of that makes this even worse. His confidence is the only thing that makes me swim past him in Giselle's direction. He's betting on our relationship that everything will be fine—and I know how important I am to him. It still pisses me off, though. I've never been this angry at him before.

I spin to face him, sensing him right behind me. Pressing my hands to his chest, I stop him in his tracks. "Uh-uh. You stay here and keep watch."

He clenches his teeth, his jaw twitching in his annoyance. "Ava it's—"

"I *said* stay here." With my words, I flip in the water and flick my tail to swim back to the rocks where Giselle waits for me.

The surf near the rocks is empty, and bubbles drift through the water as waves crash against the rocks. I peer at the surface for a moment before I ascend and spit out water to take a breath. Giselle grins as she perches on the back side of the biggest rock, the spot where no one can see her from the shore. Her surfboard sits next to her, and she offers out her hand to me.

I don't take it.

She frowns. "You look mad as hell."

She knows me all too well. We've grown up together. Giselle can read me as good as, if not better than, Carter, just like I can read her. Concern crosses her face, and I know she knows why I'm pissed without me even having to say anything.

"Of course I'm pissed off!" My voice sounds out through the air louder than I expect it to. "How could you even agree to this?"

She glares at me. "It was *my* idea. I told Carter if he could ever get you to the surface that I'd better be the first to know. It's my fault you're down there in the first place. I can't just forget about how my insecurity sent you to mermaid Hell."

I can't help the smile that lights up my face. "That's a bit dramatic. It's not even hot there."

"But you live in a rock!"

I laugh. "Carter told you that?"

She reaches out her hand again. This time I take it while

flicking my tail to propel myself onto the rock next to her. My cerulean blue tail shimmers in the sunlight, my caudal fin smacking against the waves that hit the rock, splashing cool water onto me, keeping me damp.

Giselle stares at me with wide eyes. It's hard to stay mad at her. I can't even tell her that I don't want to see her while I'm without legs. All my arguments fall away as my best friend reaches up her hand and holds it above my tail.

"Can I touch it?" she asks. "You don't even know how mesmerizing you look. Remember how I used to pretend to be a mermaid in the pool with that slip-on tail? God, this is so cool—" She runs her fingers across the side of my tail before I have a chance to agree. "And so flippin' insane. Ugh. I hate it and love it at once. It's so beautiful, but it keeps you away."

I sigh. "Right?"

She touches one of my pectoral fins on my arm. "This is kind of freaky, though."

I spread my fingers in front of her face, showing off the short webbing that ends before my knuckles. "This is, too."

"Whoa!"

I snort at her amazement. "You don't even know how much I've missed you—missed talking with you. I have nothing in common with the merpeople, and it's as exciting as dirt. I basically lie around all day and stare at the fish."

"That's gotta change. I'm going to look for more waterproof stuff to have Carter give you." She taps her fingers against my tail, like she still can't believe it's real. "I wish I could give you your phone."

"Even if you didn't have to use it to keep in contact with my parents for me, it'd just die. Can't exactly charge it." Being underwater is like living how I imagine a caveman would live. But we don't even have fire.

"I'll figure something out," she says. "Oh, and speaking of

phones...I brought yours." She moves her board off a small pouch hooked to the tether of her surfboard. She pulls the lock up the string and uses her fingers to widen the opening before digging out my phone still in the waterproof case she had given me.

My heart smacks against my ribcage at suddenly being able to be connected to the world I was ripped from. I never knew withdrawals were possible when it came to disconnecting from technology, but they're very real, and I still have trouble not being able to just turn my phone on and have access to all my friends all the time. And now, I can finally call my parents.

I open my favorites in my contact list and hit my mom's name. Giselle quietly listens as the ring echoes over the ocean air.

"Ava, what a nice surprise. You usually just text." my mom says. "How's Seattle?"

I side glance Giselle. "Found some free time, and Washington is beautiful." I have nothing else to really say because I've never actually been to the state.

"I could tell from the pictures you sent. The postcard's stuck to the fridge with the others." My mom's voice triggers sadness to wash through me. She thinks I'm having the summer of my life, and there's no way I can ever tell her I'm absolutely miserable most days.

"I'll keep sending them."

"Send more of yourself, too," she says.

I blink tears away. "Will do."

"Great!" There's a short pause. "Hey, Avie. I hate to do this, but can I call you back later? I'm in the car about to leave to meet Ruby and Anaya for a late lunch."

My lip trembles as I say, "Okay, sounds good, Mom. If I don't answer, I'll call you back when I can."

"Love you, Avie."

"Tell Dad I love him, too."

I smother a sob with my hand when the line cuts off. Giselle slides her arms around me and hugs me against her as I try to get myself under control. That was a lot harder than I had expected it to be. I'd give anything to see my mom right now—to hug her, to smell her floral fragrance. But I don't even know when or if that'll ever happen again.

"Ava," Carter's voice echoes into my mind. I blink, almost forgetting he was in the ocean still. "Is everything okay?"

"It's fine," I think back to him.

Turning my attention to my best friend, I smile at her through my tears. "Seattle, huh?"

"I pay people online to take cell phone pictures so I can send them to your parents. The same goes for postcards. They mail blank ones to me with my address stickered on so I can peel it off and write in your parents names and forge quick notes. The location stamps make it look legit." She grins as my mouth falls open. "People will do anything for cash."

"It's really scary how easy it is for you to fake my existence on land," I say.

"It's shocking how many people live double lives, Ava. I found a message board with so many ideas. Since I'm an expert at your writing, your parents have never even second guessed it. The only problem is the pictures of you they ask you to send." She holds up the camera. "Speaking of pictures. I should take a few of you."

I raise my brows. "Like this? No way."

"Just your head. I'll pay someone to photoshop you onto a different background," she says.

I tilt my head back and look at the sky. "I don't even know what to say. You're way too good at this."

She laughs and points my phone at me. "Just look happy, okay?"

I force myself to smile.

"I *said* look happy."

I practically bare my teeth.

She snaps a few photos. "Good enough, I guess."

A wave crashes over both our legs, and Carter pops his head above water. He glances between the two of us, like he's interrupting a private moment, but then he turns his gaze to me.

Panic seizes my chest. "What's wrong?"

He wraps his fingers around the base of my tail, stopping himself from getting taken back under by the tide. "Nothing, we're fine, but we need to head back home. We'll be missed."

I frown at Giselle. "I hate that I have to leave."

"We'll meet again, okay? I don't care if you think it's dangerous. I'll rent a boat or something. We'll make this work." She squeezes my hand. "Promise me you'll see me again."

The words stick in my throat, but I nod my head.

Wrapping my arms around Giselle, I hug my best friend one more time before I jump back into the waves. I don't resurface. I can't find the will to say goodbye. I'd rather just end things with a hug and a promise.

"Go ahead and start swimming home, Ava," Carter thinks to me. "I'm going to make sure Giselle makes it back to shore, and then I'll catch up."

I don't move. "I'm fine waiting."

He reaches out and brushes my floating hair away from my face. "I'm going to transform."

"And you don't want me to see," I say, finishing his thought.

"This is hard enough on you as it is. I can see it in your eyes." His voice is soft in my mind, like he's afraid that his words could break me.

He's right, though. I'm jealous enough as it is that he can

do something I can't. Just knowing that he's about to take on the form I so desperately miss depresses me. I can almost close my eyes and imagine what it would be like to kick my legs instead of flick my tail.

I suck in my bottom lip and drop my gaze to the sand a few feet below me. "You don't have to always protect me, you know. I'm not made of glass."

"I'd protect you even if you were made of steel," he says in my mind, kissing my cheek. "I'll be quick."

He waits for me to pull away and swim. I propel through the water, diving deeper, and head back toward the open ocean. When I'm just far enough away, I stop and turn around, straining to see Carter in the water.

With a heavy heart, I stare as his body transforms before my eyes, his scales disappearing into bronze skin before it splits apart, and he kicks his legs to reach the surface. He's breathtaking in his human form, everything I remember him to be from our time on land. It's enough to force me to look away.

I do the only thing I can.

I swim.

6

KING ATTILONIOUS

CARTER'S STRONG HANDS WRAP AROUND my waist when I'm already a few miles away from shore and past the few fishing boats. He spins me around with him like we're rolling in the water, and then he flicks his tail, pushing us faster as one. I'll never get over the feeling of swimming with Carter pressed against me, feeling the heat of his skin as he propels us faster than I could ever dream. I still swim on the slower side, but I can't blame myself for that. It's not like I've had the chance to build my speed and stamina while hiding away in a merperson colony.

Stretching my arms in front of me, I pretend to fly underwater like Superman. Carter's lips brush my shoulder, sending tingles through me. It's hard to still be mad at him for the ultimatum he'd given me regarding Giselle, but just because it worked out, and I've cooled off, doesn't mean I'm going to easily forget.

Carter bends forward, and together we dive through clear blue waters for another few miles. He doesn't say anything to me as we swim, and it reminds me of all the times we spent enjoying just each other's presences while navigating the ocean.

A pod of sperm whales dive down to our level. Their giant, round heads cut through the water, creating a current strong enough to catch us in. Carter weaves around one of the young whales, and I slide my hands across the top of its smooth back.

Carter dives deeper when we reach the front of the pod, and they follow along behind us for a few dozen feet, creating turbulence that rocks me against Carter, but he never loses his grip on me. His laughter echoes in my mind as one of the larger whales opens its mouth next to us, displaying a row of big teeth as if its smiling.

Bending forward, Carter descends down, but the whales stay together and ascend back to the surface.

In moments like these, I wish I had an underwater camera. Ocean photography could totally be my new hobby, but I wouldn't really be able to show anyone. Instead, I have to just imprint it in my mind and hope I never forget. Unable to share this new world with the people I love most takes its toll on me.

"You sure we have to go back? I forgot how good it was to swim with you," I say, sending my thought to Carter.

He shifts his hands, flipping me around so my back faces the sea floor, and our chests press together. He grins at me, his eyes full with hints of desire—the same look he gives me when he comes home after being gone all day.

I brush my lips against his throat. His Adam's apple bobs as he holds me tighter. Bringing my hands to his neck, I run my fingers up to his head and into his hair. He meets his lips with mine, sending me an image from what feels like forever ago—one from my vacation up the coast to San Francisco on the Ocean Jewel yacht with my friends. It was the long swim from the San Francisco Bay to the yacht hours away.

It was when I had almost given myself to him right on the sand before my transformation was triggered. It was also when I met his parents, but neither of them stay in my mind for long. All I can think about is swimming forever like this in Carter's arms.

The water suddenly shifts, warming around us, and I force my eyes to open. Below us lies the colony of Pearlestria. It looks even more foreboding than ever even though it shimmers and glitters with colorful rocks and merperson-made houses with pearlescent walls—the reason for the colony's name.

The sky blazes orange far overhead, casting an eerie glow around us as the sun sets on the surface. I haven't spent much time outside my little rock house later in the day, and I can't even remember if I've ever really seen a sun set from down here. It's just as amazing as from on land, but more intense and vibrant, the water rippling in warm colors with the current overhead.

Fish pepper the water above us, like black spots among the fiery surface. They swim around, some in large schools and others all alone. The sea life above makes it hard for me to go back to what awaits me below on the sea floor.

"I promise to take you out again as soon as I can, Ava," Carter says, navigating us down and into the center of Pearlestria.

At least a dozen merpeople swim the sandy channel, making their ways back to their homes as the night falls upon us. The looming castle of King Attilonious shines like polished gold in the dimming light, and I wonder what it looks like on the inside, behind the gleaming walls.

I expect Carter to let me go so I can swim myself next to him, but he doesn't. Resting my chin on his shoulder, I take in the view of the small colony with a few dozen houses all made from the same shimmery rock material. With a clear view of the castle, I notice a few merpeople exit from different cutouts, before I catch sight of a merman with flowing salt and pepper locks adorned with a silver crown on top his head, muscles twice the size of Carter's—bulging arms, ripped abs, a sturdy chest—and a sparkling golden tail that glints like tiny diamonds are embedded in his scales. He holds a golden staff in his hand, leaning on it, and I swear he's watching me watch him. He's far enough away that I can't tell what his eye color is, but he's obviously smiling. And then, he raises his hand and waves.

Lifting my hand from Carter's neck, I hold it up and wave back.

The king smiles wider before offering me a bow from his place above on his balcony.

"Carter," I say in his mind. "The king."

Carter lifts his head to follow my gaze. I practically stare upward along the shimmery wall outside the castle where the king watches me. Slowing down, Carter arches his back so we're vertical in the water. I ease myself away from Carter and bow when he does. The king nods his head before he winks. Then, a moment later, he turns around and disappears into his castle.

I turn my wide eyes to Carter. A million thoughts circle through my head, but I can't form a single sentence. I've met royalty before—my mom was declared a countess for all her fundraising by a prince of Malta—but I never dreamed of meeting a merman king—my king. The man responsible for me being here. And I suddenly feel no hatred toward him. I'm actually a little star-struck.

My cheeks burn in embarrassment. "I can't believe he waved at me."

"He complimented me on my choice in a mate," Carter says.

My eyes nearly bug out of their sockets. "He talked to you?"

"I'm just as surprised as you are," Carter says, hooking his hand around my waist to pull me along in the direction of our home. As we swim, he nods to a few people in greeting, and I offer a small smile when they direct their words to address me.

It feels like everyone's staring at us. I'm sure they've already heard about Carter cancelling the coupling ceremony and kicking Starla out. This is a small colony despite having the king here. Just over a hundred merpeople live within these walls, which Carter says is half the size of most of the other colonies.

I tug on Carter's hand, pulling us faster. "Can we hurry? I feel like I'm under a microscope."

"It's because we are. People are already talking."

I knew it. They're probably judging me, because there's no way Starla would've told everyone it was Carter who called off the coupling ceremony. She probably blamed it on me to save herself from embarrassment.

"Ugh!"

"No one will be brave enough to confront us, though. We don't owe them an explanation, either," he says, squeezing my fingers.

A few bright blue fish swim around us from one of the reefs outside our little house at the end of the sandy channel. It's on the outskirts of Pearlestria, which makes it easier to hide away from the curious eyes of the others.

"That's easy for you to say." My voice echoes through my mind. "You're not the girl breaking the heart of her mate for denying him such a tradition."

He tilts his head back, laughing not only in my mind, but in the water, causing a few tiny bubbles to escape his mouth. He pulls me to him. "Do I look heartbroken, Ava?"

I shrug. "No, but people will assume."

He shakes his head, his short hair floating in the water. "If they're talking about anyone, it's me. Everyone knows I had taken the unconventional route. They feel badly for you. It's why no one is intruding on your space, forcing you to adjust and enter society before you're ready. If anything, I'm the merman who stole the human girl's choice."

I relax in his embrace. "I'd have chosen this."

"Would you have really, though?" he asks, his aqua eyes boring into mine.

I think about his question for a moment. Who would choose death over a second chance, even if it is in a new body, in a new home, in a new life? I'm pretty sure had Carter taken me away the moment I had fallen off the boat, I'd still have fallen in love with him. I'm thankful he didn't do what would've been the right thing according to his mom, because losing my family and putting my parents through the loss of another child to the ocean would've hurt me for the rest of my life.

"Yes," I say.

The suspicious look he gives me speaks volumes. He obviously doesn't believe that I'd have chosen to be a mermaid if the circumstances were different and it wasn't an option between life and death and only a decision between one life or another. "But you had to think about it."

I gently pinch his chin between my index finger and thumb. "Not about whether I'd choose to be a mermaid. I was thinking about everything after."

"Oh." I'm sure he's thought about it a dozen times as well. "I don't regret taking you back to your friends. I'd do it exactly the same all over again—except I would've fought harder to stop my mom from stealing your ring."

As much as he can replay that terrible day in our minds, I don't think there was anything he could've done to change my fate. If it wasn't that night, it would've been one of the many after. We were outnumbered, and it would've been impossible to hide on land forever—not with the rise of the full moon that forces us back to the sea once a month.

I smirk, kissing him. "I know you would. But let's not dwell on the what-ifs. They just make things worse. Trust me."

"That sounds like something I'd say, Aves." He wiggles his nose against mine as he pushes us through the archway that leads into our living room.

I kiss his nose. "Don't let this get to your head, but you

might just say some really smart things to me, even if I pretend to ignore them half the time."

We don't even make it to the bedroom before Carter lies on top of me on the floor. His elbows dig into the sand on each side of my head, and he presses his weight against me, keeping me anchored.

Bending down, he kisses me deeply, desperately—the kind of kiss that would've left me breathless on land. Tingles blossom from my stomach and zing down my tail. I smack it against the sand, kicking up a small cloud, and he sucks my bottom lip between his, grazing his teeth over it in such a way that makes me shiver.

He cups the back of my head with his hands, combing his fingers into my blond hair. My fingers explore the curves of his shoulders as I work my way over his solid chest to his muscular stomach. I slide my finger along his skin right along the ridge of his tail, and he reacts with a moan reverberating through the water from deep in his throat. I don't hear it, but I feel it vibrate against my lips.

"I could stay with you here forever as long as we can stay like this," he says, flashing an image of me beneath him into my mind.

His words send my heart fluttering. Spending eternity in Carter's arms in our own private world helps keep the sadness away. How can I be sad when he says stuff that makes me swoon?

"You make me happy, you know? Even when I'm sad and homesick, just you holding me and whispering in my mind, sends the grief away. I love you, Carter. I love you so much that I look forward to my future with you. You might not feel it, and I'm sorry if it comes across like I don't want this sometimes, but you do make things good for me."

He smiles the smile he saves just for me. "I thought I

might've messed things up this afternoon."

I kind of wish he didn't bring it up. I stiffen in his arms. "What you did..."

"Can you forgive me for my lapse in judgment?" he asks instead of arguing.

"You make it incredibly hard to stay mad at you."

Smiling again, he leans forward and brushes his lips against my temple. "Good."

I let the conversation drop for the sole fact that I don't want to think about it. I loved seeing Giselle today. I loved talking to my mom. I loved that Carter forced me to go against my decision and made me do something I didn't want to for the first time since we came here. Maybe it's what I need to adjust. A little more pushiness and less coddling. I won't tell him that, though. I like being coddled—and cuddled and loved like I'm the most important mermaid in the world.

"Carter?" A voice sounds through both our minds from outside our house. I recognize it as belonging to his grandma.

Carter doesn't get off me. Instead, he thinks, "Come in," projecting his voice to her.

Grandmer swims into our living room, her hair neatly braided as it floats behind her. She eyes us on the floor but doesn't look anything other than happy when she greets her grandson with a smile.

"This doesn't look like two mers who just called off the coupling ceremony," she says, raising her eyebrows.

I blush. "That was Carter." I don't know why I say it, but I feel like he should take the blame. He was the one who called it off even if I agreed for the wrong reasons.

Carter crinkles his nose at me in a fake glare. "It was a mutual agreement for now."

"Your mom is extremely disappointed, you know," she says. "But I understand. She couldn't believe how you stood your ground. I thought I'd never hear the end of it last night." Grandmer flicks her gaze to the ceiling. "No wonder you asked her to leave."

Carter's smile melts into a serious expression. "You have no idea, Grandmer."

Her lips pull up in the corner. "I think I do. And that's why I'm here. I'd like to take over as Ava's teacher if you'd allow it. You won't have to worry 'bout me pressuring you into the ceremony either."

Carter turns his gaze to mine. "How do you feel about it, Aves?"

I shrug. "I guess that would be okay."

"Then it's settled." She turns her attention to Carter. "Why don't you get us some dinner, and we can get started tonight."

I frown. "Tonight?"

She plops in the sand next to me. "Actually, now."

I lean my head back on the sand as Carter pulls away from me. It seems so sudden, and I had planned on spending all night in the soft sand with Carter, but his grandma doesn't look like someone I can argue with.

Instead of complaining, I remember it could be much worse with Starla. "Okay," I say to Carter's grandma after a moment. "Where do we start?"

GIFTED

GRANDMER STUDIES ME AS I pick through one of the bags of fruit I had hidden from Starla under one of the few decorative rocks in my room. She'd have thrown a fit had she known Carter brought me food from the surface. Grandmer, on the other hand, couldn't care less. She even takes an apple slice from me when I offer the bag out to her.

Carter sits a few feet away, picking apart a bright red snapper. I try not to watch him carve his sharp nail through the fish, but I can't help it. After a few minutes, he steals one of my small bags of lettuce and wraps a leaf around a small piece of meat.

"I want you to try this, Ava," he says.

"No thanks," I say.

Grandmer watches us quietly. A smirk pulls the corner of her lips up, amused by us. Her deep blue tail matches the blue streaking her golden brown hair. Wound around her chest are a few pieces of long seaweed strung through a bead-like rock that gives it shape. I expect her to tell me to stop being stubborn and to try the damn fish, but she doesn't. Instead, she takes the piece from Carter and pops it into her mouth.

"Carter, offering Ava a fish you killed and cut in front of her, especially after she's already stated she can't stomach the idea of eating something she was swimming with a minute ago, isn't going to make her want to try it even if you disguise it in lettuce." Smart mermaid. I can already tell I might actually enjoy spending time with her. She might've chosen the ocean, but she told me she spent years on the land with her husband before he passed away, which is why she returned to the water.

"Yeah, Carter. You know how cute I think our fishy friends are," I say, grinning. "If I could talk to them, I would."

He covers his forehead with his hand for a moment. "So, if I bring something back you haven't seen and disguise it in something you like, will you try it for me?"

I play with my floating hair for a moment. "Only if it's something I can pick up at a human grocery store. And it has to be tiny."

"Really?"

I shrug. "Only because of the trouble you'd have to go through for me."

He smirks before swimming closer to kiss my cheek. Wrapping my hands around his muscular bicep, I stop him from swimming away. I lean up and kiss his lips for a long moment to show my appreciation. I'm not exactly looking forward to whatever he brings back, but if he does this, I have to at least humor him.

"I'll be right back. Will you be okay with Ava, Grandmer?" he asks.

I wrinkle my nose, because part of him still thinks I might be a little bit difficult. Maybe for Starla or some poor merperson who doesn't understand my human ideals and culture.

"I'll be better than fine, dear. You picked a lovely mate, and I've been dying to get to know her since the moment she arrived." Grandmer reaches over and pats my hand. Her smooth skin contrasts the age and wisdom in her eyes. I could only hope to look as good as she does when I'm a grandmother.

"You have?" I ask, watching Carter swim through the archway, leaving us alone. "I thought Starla might've ruined my image for everyone."

"I know it doesn't feel like it, Ava, but Carter's mom does care about you. She hated she had to be the bad guy in all this. Your situation with Carter is rare—non-existent. Most merpeople wouldn't know how to deal with it in the first place. The king himself has never had to deal with a human turned mermaid who was given the mermaid life on a whim. Most merpeople choose mates within their colonies, or if they do choose to live on land, they spend years with a human to make sure they're the one. We can only choose once, you know. That's why the coupling ceremony is quite the affair. It would not only have been where you'd vow your life to Carter, but it would've been the moment you had given up your human life as well. In most situations, the gift of his life wouldn't have worked because of your initial lack of bond. But clearly, you're special. You two—" She pauses, gathering her thoughts. "You basically eloped with my grandson, and no one was invited."

I don't respond to her comment about being special. I don't even want to think of the loss of my life had Carter's spark not worked to transform me. "Kind of like a drunk couple in Vegas?"

She snorts. I wasn't sure she'd get the reference, but Grandmer seems to know the human world well. "Exactly. Except there are no annulments under the sea."

"It's a good thing I love Carter then. At least we had one date before I took the plunge," I say.

Grandmer's smile widens at my words. "A lot of folks 'round here have been concerned about your feelings for my grandson, but I've always known not to doubt Carter's choice."

"Maybe you could spread the word," I say. "I grew up in a small town—well, not as small as this—but I know how people talk."

"Don't you worry about anyone else but you and my

grandson. Everything will fall into place how it should be. I think without Starla interfering and pressuring you, you might actually start enjoying yourself. Who knows, maybe you'll figure out what you like to do here. Mermaids are gifted with certain affinities. I think yours might have to do with the ocean animals."

"Starla never mentioned that," I say. Well, she technically didn't mention much besides the coupling ceremony and whether or not I'd eat something she brought me.

"I'm sure she'd have gotten around to it," Grandmer says.

"What's yours? What about mermen?"

"Like Starla, I'm a healer. I'm gifted with the ability to help those hurt or injured. I was a nurse on land," she says. "Very few mermen have affinities. King Attilonious is gifted with the power of ocean magic. It's he who now creates the sea stone that allows us to change. He's the only one who doesn't need it to transform. He's also the most powerful mer in existence. It's why he's king. He controls the sea."

I nod my head even though I never questioned that the king wasn't powerful. He'd have to be in his position. Just the sight of him screams power. It's Carter that I wonder about.

"My grandson was gifted with the speed and strength of a warrior, just like his dad. They're the protectors of our colonies—the ones who the king will look to first," she says. "Well, not Carter just yet. He has many years to go."

I always knew Carter was a fast swimmer, but I always thought it was because he's been doing it all his life. I guess that means I'll never be as fast as him.

"No wonder I always feel safe with him," I say with a smile.

Silence falls between us for a few minutes. Grandmer continues to explain how merpeople tend to spend their time doing the things they enjoy, which also serves to better the colony. There are mers who hunt, those who keep humans from discovering our secrets, healers like herself, caretakers, and even merpeople who do their best to care for all the creatures of the ocean.

Carter's voice drifts into my mind after what has felt like a long, informative evening with Grandmer.

"Close your eyes," he says into my mind. "And no peeking."

I shift my gaze to Grandmer, who has taken it upon herself to braid my hair as she speaks of all the endless possibilities of being a mermaid. She nods with a smile before I close my eyes. Carter swims into our living room, creating his own current that sets me adrift. He gently takes my hand, stopping me in place. I can't see him through my closed eyes, but I can feel him hovering in front of me.

"Now, open your mouth."

I cringe at his words. "Do I have to?"

"Yes. I spent the last two hours hunting and preparing this dinner for you, so open your mouth." His voice is teasing in my mind and not annoyed like most people would be after jumping through hoops to make something only to be greeted with complaints.

I slowly open my mouth and brace myself for the worst. My only saving grace would be the fact that the salt of the sea masks the fishiness of everything, blocking my sense of smell completely and dulling my taste buds.

Carter chuckles, his voice echoing through my mind. He takes an excruciatingly long time to stick whatever it is he brought me into my mouth.

"Seriously, you better hurry or I'm just going to spit it out," I say, sending the thought only to him. The anticipation doesn't send my heart racing in a good way.

And I'm sure he feels it, because a second later, his fingers brush against my lips as he holds something to my mouth.

"Take a bite," he says, waiting for me to decide how much I'm willing to try.

Skimming my teeth against another lettuce wrapped piece of fish, I take the tiniest bite possible, not even sure I got a piece of its meat with the lettuce. I open my eyes when I move the piece of lettuce over my tongue, not really tasting it with the saltwater.

Carter holds up the lettuce square again, and I notice the deep red color of the piece of fish within it. He brings it to my lips, his eyes narrowing as he smiles, and I lean forward and take a bigger bite. It's surprisingly mild and meaty, and not as gross as I expected it to be.

Carter unrolls the lettuce from the fish. "Raw tuna actually tastes better with seaweed. You can find it at most sushi restaurants."

It's probably why I *think* I like it. I eat tuna pretty regularly. I just never really wanted to eat it raw. "It wasn't so bad. I still wish we could cook it. I miss warm food." What I would give for a plate of steamy enchiladas with their melted cheese goodness. I'd probably be happy with a piece of toast fresh from the toaster at this point.

Grandmer pats Carter's shoulder. "I think you have things under control. Your parents would be proud, Carter."

He smirks, staring at me take another small bite. I really want to hate it and hold a grudge against the undersea eating habits, but Carter looks so cute with how he grins, his shoulders straight, his chest nearly puffing with pride. He'd probably give himself a high five if I wouldn't laugh at him for doing it. Who knows? He still might.

"People will now think I'm the spoiled mermaid," I say. "How do you even deal with me? I'm not even sure I'd deal with myself."

He wraps his arms around my shoulders, stealing a bite of

the piece of tuna from my fingers. "I'd be bored if you made things easy." Turning to his grandma, he says, "Let me see you home, Grandmer. It's getting late."

Grandmer smacks her deep blue tail against the sandy floor to propel herself up. I swim closer and give the old mermaid a hug, happiness settling into my soul for one of the very few times since I came here. She's so easygoing and understanding that I wish it was her who had taken me under her fin from the beginning. It'd have eased the tension with Starla, and I might've actually grown to like my future mother-in-law. Now, I'm not sure I ever will. I'll be cordial for Carter's sake, but I won't seek anything more from her.

Carter kisses my cheek. Holding his arm out to his grandma to take, he guides her from our house and into the glowing night waters shimmering with the magic created from our sparks. Their forms blur the farther they swim until they disappear, leaving only a swirl of sparkling sand in their wakes.

It's so strange not having a fight with Starla before heading to bed. Tonight actually felt normal—something I could get used to if I had to. *You do have to...*

Turning my back on the door, I peer around the room at my simple house. It's weird to think of it as mine and Carter's. I almost wish I could figure out what else to do with it. Like Giselle said earlier today, I live in a damn rock.

Sighing, I finish off the few pieces of tuna Carter spent all evening preparing for me and continue to think about my best friend, missing her just as much now as I did yesterday before I got to see her again—if not more. Giselle would be so proud that I ate the tuna and would exclaim how she couldn't wait to take me to Sushi Days, her favorite sushi restaurant in Azure Waters.

I can't help thinking that maybe this life would've been better suited for my best friend. Not only does she love the ocean—she does basically every water sport—she also loves raw fish. She'd probably be brave enough to eat it mermaid style. I imagine bottling up Giselle's essence to hold with me. I'll get through this. I know I will.

"Ms. Ava?" An unfamiliar voice sounds through my head, calling my name. I spin in my living room, almost disoriented by the foreign thought that doesn't belong to anyone I've begrudgingly met so far in the colony.

It takes me a moment to see the figure floating a few feet from the front cutout. "Yes, come in," I say, projecting my thought to the unfamiliar merman. I'd never invite a stranger into my house in Azure Waters, but it feels weird hearing this man in my mind and not being able to confront him. I've never been one to talk on the phone with anyone other than my parents or my friends, so it feels just as awkward as that but worse.

A merman with short black hair and a thick black beard pokes his head into the archway of the living room, gripping the frame in his hand without swimming completely in. His dark eyes look like two black onyx stones in his face, and two fish hooks hang from his ears.

"I'm sorry to bother you so late. Is your mate home?" he asks.

I shake my head. "No, Carter swam his grandma home. Is there something you need?"

He swims a foot into the room through the archway. Even without seeing him extend to his full height, I can tell he's a good few inches taller than Carter, nearly hitting his head on the roof. He sweeps his deep indigo tail across the sand, creating ripples through the room that force me to flick my own tail to stay in place.

"I'm here with a message from King Attilonious. It's only respectful to wait for your mate to arrive before I deliver it." Peering around our small room once, he then shifts his gaze to me. His eyes flick over my bikini top for a split second in curiosity, but it's not in a creepy or mocking way. Just taking notice that I'm wearing something out of the ordinary compared to the rest of the mermaids in the colony.

I wave toward one of the kelp wrapped rocks. "He'll be home shortly. Have a seat if you'd like."

The merman glides through the water before lowering himself on the rock, splaying his tail out in front of him. He leans back on his palms, making me feel all sorts of awkward with his silence. It's the first time I've had a strange guest in my house, and I'm freaking out just a bit since he claims to have a message from the king.

Fear trickles in my mind. "I hope everything's okay," I finally say after a long moment.

The merman sits up straighter, nodding his head wildly. "Oh, yes. Sorry if I made you think otherwise."

I find a place near him on the sandy floor and curl my tail to my chest. "You'll have to excuse me. I'm not exactly sure of the mer etiquette. I'd usually offer a guest a drink, but—" I shrug instead of finishing my sentence.

The merman smiles. "This is perfect. Thank you. Most mers don't even invite me in to sit."

"Oh," I say. I hope I didn't break some rule by letting a strange merman into my home. I doubt it, though. Everyone is treated equally here. "I'd hate to be forced to wait outside." *Like it's much different from inside here.*

His smile widens. "You're a lot nicer than I expected."

My lips turn downward in a frown. "Thanks, I guess." I knew people were probably thinking the worst of me, especially since the whole colony probably believes it was my complete decision not to go through with the coupling ceremony, not to mention I hide in my house all day.

He waves his hand. "I'm sorry. I didn't mean to make you

upset."

Things are getting awkward really quickly. I knew I'd fail at having a normal conversation with a merperson, especially one who I'm nearly certain has never even been on land. "No, it's okay. I was just caught off guard." I know people are curious about me considering the circumstances, but to actually have to sit here and think about how someone didn't think I was nice is torture.

I wish I could bury myself in the sand until Carter gets home, because the more I sit here, the more uncomfortable things get. The merman's eyes train on me, studying me a lot harder than any normal human on land would do in these cir-cumstances. I regret wanting to be polite. But now I can't even ask him to wait outside in fear of him changing his mind about my nicety and then spreading the word about how everyone was right. I'm Ms. Unapproachable.

"Carter, where are you?" I project my question to the sea.

I'm so flustered that the merman picks up the thought in-tended for Carter. My feelings must be splashed across my face, because he moves from the rock in front of me and takes my hand between his.

"My apologies again, Ms. Ava. I really didn't mean any-thing by it," he says, twisting his mouth into a frown.

Instead of accepting and since it couldn't possibly get any more uncomfortable, I ask, "So people assume I'm mean?" I have to know what people think of me and if it's as bad as I im-agine. Carter doesn't tell me anything except not to worry about what others think. But how can I not? I've cared about what others thought all my life.

"Forget I said anything." The merman's thoughts come through my mind laced with something that sounds like worry.

"No, please. I'm not upset. I just want to know."

Releasing my hand, he backs up and blows a small bubble

through his lips. "It's not that I didn't expect you to be nice. I expected you to act differently. Everyone knows how Starla dragged you from the shore and that you hate this life."

"I don't hate—"

"It's been a long time, Tide." Carter's thoughts interrupt what I was going to say.

Of course people think I hate the mermaid life—I do—did. I mean, I have mixed feelings. I like having a tail...sometimes. I do miss my legs though, miss all the little things about the land that I didn't even know I would miss. But the last thing I want is for people to think I hate their way of life. Because I don't. I just hate it for me. There's a huge differ-ence.

"I imagine you're not here to just say hello," Carter adds, pulling me from my own thoughts.

The merman, Tide, swims the distance to Carter and gives him a half hug before they tap their tails together in a gesture I haven't ever seen before. I equate it to a fist bump on land, like the ones my friends Matty and Logan give each other.

"You know it's the king's order not to come here without an invitation," he says. What? The king ordered people to stay away unless invited? While I'm sort of thankful for the lack of interruption from strangers, I'm also annoyed that no one told me people were commanded by the king to stay away.

I tilt my head to the side. "Why's that?" This whole time I thought they were staying away for their own reasons—mostly because Starla said so—but I had no idea it was an actual order. I feel a little bit better about things with the knowledge that people aren't just avoiding me at all costs.

Tide turns to me. "In ordinary circumstances the whole colony would stop by to meet the newest resident, but he didn't think overwhelming you was a good idea. Our king is very kind and empathetic. I'm sure you'll be as fond of him as everyone here. Which brings me to why I'm here uninvited."

"The message from the king," I say, anxious to hear it.

Tide turns his gaze to Carter. "King Attilonious requests that you bring Ms. Ava to the castle at first light."

My chest clenches. I never dreamed of meeting the king, and now he's requesting my presence. But why? It's been weeks since I've been here. He's had plenty of time to summon me. I'm excited and scared all at once.

"Thanks for the message, Tide," Carter says, patting his old friend on the back.

With a quick nod, Tide leaves without another word to me, though I think he and Carter share a few private words I don't hear.

Carter crosses the room to where I slide to the sand, piling it over my caudal fin with my fingers. He settles next to me, trailing his hand along my tail, brushing off the sand I've nervously buried myself in.

Sliding his arm under me, he lifts me onto his lap. "This is a great honor, Ava. King Attilonious doesn't just invite anyone over."

"I'm going to make a fool of myself," I say, resting my head on his warm chest while listening to the rhythmic sound of his heart beating. It sounds as if it does so only for me.

Carter runs his hand over my braided hair. "I highly doubt that's possible."

"Your friend expected me to be mean or something," I say. "What if the king's already formed an opinion of me? He already knows I disagree with his stupid laws."

"The king complimented me, remember? I highly doubt he thinks so little of you if he went out of his way to say such nice things. As for Tide, he's terribly sorry and embarrassed for upsetting you. He was more nervous meeting you than he let on. He's never met a human-born before." Carter rests his chin on my head. "Don't let any of it bother you."

That's easy for him to say. He's merely the talk of the town by association.

"Think we can get out of it?" I ask. "I think I'm feeling sick."

He holds me tighter. "We'll be fine."

But he doesn't sound as certain as he should be. It's enough to leave me feeling afraid. "I hope so."

After a minute of silence, he uses his tail to propel us from the sand and toward the entrance to the bedroom. "How about I distract you for a while? Take your mind off things." He nuzzles his face into the crook of my neck, and I tilt my head back.

"I'd like that," I say.

Unfortunately, even Carter's kisses can't calm the unease settling through me. I don't think anything can.

If only I could flee.

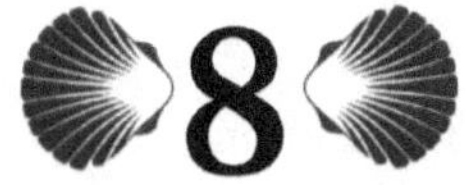

TREADING WATER

I SLEEP WITH MY TAIL curled to my chest like always since it's one of the few circumstances where I can sort of pretend that I still have legs. Carter kisses me awake, pressing his body weight against me from behind. His hands brush my tail where my hips would be if I had legs, and he runs his hands over the ridge that separates my tail from my stomach.

It's not even light out, and I wish that the king would've invited us later in the day. Whether I'm in the sea or on the land, I'll never be a morning person. Carter does make waking up a bit easier because I'd rather have him wake me up instead of an alarm any day. I just can't figure out how his body knows when he needs to be up. It might be instinctual like he has an internal alarm, something I definitely don't have.

Flipping in his arms, I press my chest to his to feel his heart beat against mine. The glow of our sparks lights the water around us, and I'm tempted to close my eyes to fall back asleep. I'm dreading heading to the castle. I'd rather bite a chunk out of a swimming fish.

Carter grins into my lips. I must've sent him that thought in my tired state. He leans his forehead against mine, his closeness blurring my view of him in the rippling water. After a moment, he pulls away and stretches out, nearly touching the opposing walls at the same time, one with his caudal fin and the other with his fingertips. I don't let go of him, though. I cling to his side as he swims from the floor and circles the room a few times.

Sliding his hands under my arms, he practically peels me away, laughing the entire time he does. I sink to the floor, crossing my arms over my chest all while pouting my lip. It makes him laugh harder in my mind. I only glare at his amusement.

He scoops me up for another kiss, and I comb my fingers through his dark hair, sliding my tongue into his mouth, sending a dozen images of all the fun we could have if we skipped our summons to the castle.

The images tempt him enough that he sets me down, rubbing his eyes for a moment, trying to clear his thoughts without saying anything to me. I reach out and try to touch his tail, but he swims circles around me a few times, making me spin in the center of the room. I can't stop the smile that crosses my face. I know how hard it is for him to resist me, especially since he only swims circles like this to keep himself in control.

Closing the distance, he swims up to me and nudges me back into the far wall until my body rests against the pearlescent rock. "It'd be terribly rude to not show this morning."

"I'm okay with rude." I cup his face in my hands and hold him in place.

"Ava..." His voice fades in my mind. I know he wants to give into me, and it bothers him that he can't.

I rub my nose against his. "It's fine, Carter. I'll survive."

He smiles but sadness furrows his brows. "I'll be with you the whole time."

"I know."

He touches my chin, kissing me gently, sending a wave of love over me. Within the love lies an ounce of desire that he suppresses to keep himself together.

I send him a few images of all the things I'd rather be doing, including staying here with him for the rest of the day, making him smile.

"Don't think I'm not saving those thoughts for later," he says.

I respond by sucking my bottom lip between my teeth. If I were on land, I'd take the time to get ready, to dress up, prepare, but there's not much for me to do. I pick the knot out of the end of my braid and unravel the work Grandmer did on my hair last night as my only form of getting ready. I'd rather have my hair to veil my face since I've grown so used to hiding behind it.

"Ready?" he asks, brushing my hair behind my ear.

All I do is nod and take his hand. He pulls me through the house like a half deflated balloon being tugged around by a string. When we reach the door, Carter glances at me before hooking his hand around my waist only to flip me onto his back.

I tighten my hold around his shoulders when he jets off, speeding through the sandy channel that sits between the houses. He navigates the colony with ease, weaving in and out of the few fish that dart around.

A few merpeople peek their heads from their homes as we pass—some even waving to Carter. I force myself to smile at anyone who shows me any interest. I don't want to be known as the mean girl who hates the merpeople way of life. That's a terrible reputation to have. I don't want to be pitied either.

It doesn't take long to reach the looming castle, which is nothing like the castles I've seen pictures of on land. Morning light gleams off the pearl-like stones giving it an almost ethereal, magical feel. Decorative stones embedded throughout the walls create a pattern that looks like the sea around us. Two tall rock towers sit on each side of a rounded center that raises a few stories tall. Underwater, it's hard to judge just how massive the castle is. There are dozens of cutouts, leading to different parts of the palace, but Carter swims directly through the arched entrance in the center. Unlike the castles on land, this one is unprotected and open. Only one merman guards the place, but he looks half asleep, leaning against the wall by the entrance. I doubt the king even needs his protection. According to Grandmer, he's the most powerful in all the sea.

Carter flips me off his back, and we enter a cavernous room that looks like the inside of a diamond encrusted, blue walled cave. The deep midnight color mimics the night sky and diamond-like stones sparkle like stars. In the center on the high ceiling is a circular cutout and from this angle, it looks like a sparkling blue moon as the sky lightens way above us on the surface.

Along the far wall lies a huge coral reef with all sorts of rainbow fish dancing through colorful sea plants, some I've never seen before. A few human artifacts decorate the vast room, from the broken bow of a small vessel to a gold-plated treasure chest; all of the things that seem to be lost to the sea end up among the merpeople.

Trailing my eyes over every detail of the place, I shift my gaze up the wall to a small balcony two stories up. King Attilonious grips the banister while peering down at me. When our eyes meet, I smile before bending forward to bow just like yesterday. The king's salt and pepper hair floats around his head, and he offers me a huge smile, one that speeds up my already racing heart.

"Welcome to my home," the king says, thrusting his arm out over the cavernous room. "I'm so pleased to officially meet the newest mermaid in my kingdom."

He motions for us to join him, and Carter laces his fingers through mine and ascends until we swim in front of the king.

"Your majesty," Carter says with another bow. "Thank you for having us."

I tilt my chin down, finding it hard to meet King Attilonious' eyes. "It's an honor to meet you, my king. Thank you for accepting me into your kingdom." I've rehearsed what I was going to say a dozen times, using my knowledge of movies to reference how I should greet him. But all the rehearsing over night didn't prepare me for how ridiculous I feel in this moment.

King Attilonious might tower before me. He might wear a jewel encrusted crown on his head and carry an air of regality. But he still doesn't truly feel like *my* king. None of this life feels like mine, though. I should be used to it.

"It was not me who has accepted you into my kingdom, Ava." His words dance in my mind, his eyes holding me in their curious gaze.

Reaching out, he takes my hand and brings it to his chest. He presses my palm over his heart, startling me, and I feel it thrum under my fingers. I hold utterly still, his strong hand covering mine, forcing me to feel the smooth muscles of his broad chest. I'd like nothing more than to pull away, but I just gaze at him until a subtle glow arises from under my fingers, revealing the king's own spark. It disappears as quickly as I saw it, and I blink, unsure if it was even there to begin with. I shouldn't have been able to see it. The intensity of this moment might be making me go a little crazy.

"It was the ocean that accepted you, Ava, but I'm happy it did. You're such a lovely girl. No wonder Carter had impulsively given you his life." The king doesn't say it in a way that'd make me feel bad for being alive, though I hope he thinks I'm more than a pretty face.

"Thank you, my king. I couldn't have asked for a better merman to love me," I say.

"And do you love Carter?"

I'm taken aback by his question. Too many people underestimate my feelings for Carter. Yes, in the beginning, all I felt was a strong attraction to him, but it's grown into something much more in a short period of time.

"Yes." The answer is simple enough to say, but I feel like King Attilonious is expecting more.

It's easy to say you love someone—it's proving it to the world that is harder for me. Carter feels my love—he knows it's there. But the colony? All they see is the once human girl, who barely leaves her house, refuses to participate in the coupling ceremony, and the mermaid who fails at most mermaid things.

The king studies me for a long moment before turning to Carter. He slides his arm over his shoulder and pulls him away in a conversation I can't hear. The two of them swim away from the balcony, descending toward the entrance, and I remain in my spot.

With curious eyes, I gaze at the king escorting Carter to a cutout that leads to some other part of the castle. A mermaid greets the two mermen, and Carter shifts his gaze to me. The mermaid bows to the king and Carter before motioning Carter to follow her, leaving me desperately wanting to follow him or swim right through the cutout in the ceiling to make my escape.

"The king wants to speak with you alone, Ava. I'll be waiting in the dining hall." Carter's voice drifts through my mind as he leaves me alone.

Panic seizes my chest. "Why?"

"I don't know, but it's okay. You have no reason to fear King Attilonious."

King Attilonious' massive figure appears before me, blocking my view of the cutout Carter left through. He hovers in front of me, his tail glittering in the faint morning light shining on him from above like a spotlight. His caudal fin expands out three times the size of mine, thick and powerful, yet breathtaking as it waves to keep him floating before me.

My eyes trail up the king's ripped stomach to his boxy jaw and sharp nose. For the first time, I notice his deep sapphire eyes that look like the fading night sky. His silver crown sparkles on his head, decked with precious jewels that I didn't think could be found in the water unless the crown was retrieved from a shipwreck. I wouldn't put it past him. Even so, it's perfect for him.

"You're nervous," the king says, sending his powerful voice into my mind.

I clench my shaking hands. "I'm sorry, my king."

"Don't apologize, Ava. You're allowed to feel and process things in your own way. The transformation opens you up to the mermaid way of life—it's ingrained in your very essence to feel things more intensely than you did as a human." King Attilonious waves his hand to get me to swim next to him, and his fingers brush against my lower back, guiding me along.

We head through the cutout in the balcony and into another great room, but this one contains a throne grand enough for the king. Decorated in thousands of pearls, the high-back throne looks like it was made from the shell of a giant clam, though the seat is made from a smooth black stone. It sits atop a flat rock that looks like a platform. Behind it, the water glitters as thousands of pinprick holes pierce the rock that curves up into a dome, allowing in sunlight from the surface as the sun rises.

In here, the floors are made of smooth, deep brown stones, the first time I've been inside a place without sand for the floor. A curtain of seaweed hangs over another cutout to the right, and I realize it leads to his private living quarters. He pulls the curtain aside, motioning me to enter a living room with what looks like a pool filled with black sand from somewhere that isn't Pearlestria. A big rock, wrapped in woven seaweed, sits against the far wall. Above it, hooked to the wall, is a sheet of metal etched with a wave pattern. I spin around the grand room, glittering with stones like the rest of the palace, and then tilt my head up to look through a series of small holes that make the place feel open because I can see the surface. The silhouette of a boat crosses overhead, and a trickle of fear seeps into me.

"Your palace is breathtaking," I say, swimming forward to run my fingers over the black sand pool.

"Thank you. It's stood here for as long as anyone can remember." He settles down on the edge of the sand pool. "How do you like Pearlestria?" he asks, his sapphire blue eyes watching me sit down across from him.

I'm not sure whether or not I should lie. My mind says yes, lie, lie, lie, but my heart tells me I had better be honest. "It's not bad." It's sort of the truth. It's not awful, but it's not enjoyable either.

"You're unhappy," he says for me.

"Not always."

"What makes you happy here?" This seems more like an interrogation than anything. I guess it's better than the king assuming things or hearing it from someone else.

"Carter." *Blah.* The answer sounds so lame as I say it. I hate that the only happiness I find in this endless ocean world revolves around another person. My mom would tell me I had better work on finding happiness within myself like all the characters in the novels she reads—the ones who find their own happily ever after.

But in this moment, I don't even know how to do that. My happiness lies in the world I was dragged from. It lives and breathes with my friends, with my old human life, with being able to do things I can't do down here.

I can't exactly tell the king all that. Well, I could, but there's no way I would.

"Yet you won't agree to the coupling ceremony with him.

Why's that?" I wish he'd say something more than ask questions, and I definitely wish he wouldn't ask what's on basically all the merworld's mind.

"It's complicated." I didn't want to get into it with Starla, and I definitely don't want to get into it with King Attilonious.

He rubs his chin, annoyance clearly written on his face. "You're going to have to give me more to work with than that."

Can I get away with denying the king answers to his questions? I have no idea. I'm not sure I'm willing to risk it.

"I care deeply for my merpeople, Ava," he continues without letting me attempt to respond. "I have all of your best interests in my heart, and I want nothing more as a king than to make sure my kingdom lives happily and safely. Unfortunately for you, those two things don't seem to coincide. I'm well aware of yours and Carter's decision to live on land, but due to the strange circumstances you've found yourself in, that isn't possible at the moment. And I'm sorry I have to hold firm in my decision. With saying that, I need a better answer to why you're unwilling to couple with the merman who clearly would do anything for you, one you claim to love." His serious expression sends me curling my tail to my chest.

I don't push my floating hair from my face, letting his words sink in. Would he even understand my argument? Would he understand Carter's? Does any of it even matter in his eyes? He's about his kingdom as a whole. We're the first to do things differently around here. Maybe that's a bad thing.

I grip my tail tighter. "I don't only claim to love Carter, your majesty. I do love him, and I want to couple with him—just not now. Carter doesn't want to go through with the ceremony if my heart's not in it. He wants to do it when the idea makes me happy. And in all honesty, I'd only be doing it for him and your kingdom's ways. I could not happily go through with it until I'm happy in my own scales."

He leans his elbows on the rocks beside him, stretching his tail so far forward it rests on top of mine. "Ava, you've been given a tremendous gift most humans will never understand. Turning your back on our ways will always leave you feeling unsatisfied in your new body. I hate that it has to come to this, but as your king, I'm commanding you to agree to the coupling ceremony with your mate, and you will not tell Carter about this. You will tell him you're ready to accept who you are and your position as his mate."

My brows furrow. Everyone has always gone on and on about what a fair and kind king King Attilonious is, but he wouldn't command me to do this if that were true. "What? Why are you doing this?"

His chest heaves, pushing water from his gills. "Because it has to be done. I can see how much you resist the mer way, and I don't think you'll ever be happy in your skin unless you do. That makes you a risk to my kingdom."

"But I can't lie to Carter," I say. "He's my mate."

"Then you better come to terms quickly so you don't have to lie to him."

I dig my fingers into the sand, turmoil threatening to leave me broken. I can't even respond to the king.

He takes my silence as agreement. "I'm doing this for your own safety, Ava. The call of the land seems to have pushed the call of the sea from your mind. Until they're balanced, you'll never be able to live the life you want."

If I could cry, I would. "But I—"

"This is final. The ceremony will fall on the next full moon. It's time for you to accept your true place in my kingdom and under my rule."

Any respect I had for King Attilonious disappears with his serious expression. I can't stand to be under his gaze a moment longer, so I flick my tail, knocking his tail off mine and bolt toward the closest window cutout. But even if I could swim as fast as Carter, it doesn't compare to how quickly the king swims up and blocks my way, forcing me to stay in the room with him. He waves his hand, knocking me back, his lips twisted as he loses his composure.

Fear and anger threaten to consume me, stealing away everything good I desperately cling to so I don't lash out and make things worse for me. Without Carter here to protect me, to guarantee my safety, I'm not so sure I'd actually make it from this room if I were to act out on my frustrations. But I might if the king won't let me leave.

I turn away, covering my face with my hands. "Why won't you allow me to leave? I need to process this. It's not like I'm going to leave the colony. I have nowhere to go."

"Because you're upset, and it's in my best interest that no one sees you like this." He reaches out and latches his strong fingers to my elbow. "Now, sit back down. We're not through yet."

He doesn't really give me the choice as he pushes me to the black sand pool. Taking my place across from him, I sit silently, thinking about how the full moon is only days away—it's the time where every mermaid must leave the land to rejoin the sea. Starla will be over the moon excited, thinking I've come to my senses.

And now, I'm just going to have to suck it up and remember it's not the end of the world. I've grown to love Carter, but it's just hard to swallow that I've lost control of my life. That's my biggest problem. Being a mermaid, I don't have the privilege to live how I see fit. Carter swears it's only for now, but how can I trust that? Giselle can't pretend to be me forever.

"You know, Ava, I'm not as bad as you probably think right now," he says, filling the silence.

"You don't know what I'm thinking," I snap, turning

sideways and pulling my tail to my chest so I can rest my chin on it. It stops him from resting his tail on top of mine, from dominating the space I need to calm down. It's one thing to force me to comply with his wishes, but to also force me to lie to Carter about all this—if Carter were to find out—I don't even know.

He leans back like he's sure I won't try to bolt again. And he's right. "I understand Carter has managed to maintain your human life on land—something no other human-turned-mer has ever accomplished and I—" He pauses, gauging my reaction without finishing his thought.

Great. Just great. He's going to force me to cut ties to my family, and I won't stand for it. Heat travels from my chest to my hands, and I shake my fingers out, causing the black sand to swirl from the pool in a whirlpool and into the air without touching it. A strange feeling washes over me, the water seeming to move around me in a comforting blanket despite the natural current, like I caused it to move more than it should've with my motion. One look at King Attilonious' intense gaze sends the reassuring feelings fleeting, drifting away from me, leaving a chill in my bones.

He still doesn't continue but just watches me and the sand, making me completely uncomfortable in his gaze. Something lingers in his eyes—curiosity? Intrigue? Surprise? I'm not sure. But he doesn't speak or do anything except watch the swirling sand between us.

I force myself to fill the silence with more important matters. Creating tiny whirlpools is nothing exciting or important. "So, you're going to make me give up my human life now?" The question burns within me, my voice resonating from my mind and to the king in a sharp wave.

He jerks his attention from the sand, surprised by my tone, and smacks his tail once to push the sand in the water away.

"It's what I should do."

My chest tightens with his words. I consider calling out to Carter, begging him to find me, to take me away from here, but we have nowhere to go. And if Carter sees me like this, he might do something that would make things terrible for the both of us. I wouldn't put it past the king to take his ring as well.

"But I think doing so will only hinder your ability to adjust to the sea. You still have a lot to learn, but you can't with the constant desire to return to the world above," he adds, his hard voice softening in my mind.

Hope rises in front of me so close that I can imagine grasping it. Going through with the coupling ceremony might be worth it if the king doesn't rip me away from my family forever. "So, what are you saying?" I ask.

"That I'm going to proceed with caution. You do understand the consequences that happen if humans discover our kind, right?" he asks. "For the sake of your family—your entire town—I cannot allow you to return to live your life as you had planned. You cannot go home because it would put everything at risk—"

"That's basically forcing me to sever my ties then," I say, cutting him off. I was stupid for even trying to hold onto an ounce of hope. I'm sure the king is capable of wiping Azure Waters off the map. If that were to happen, if anything were to happen to my home, I don't think I'd survive.

He raises his hand. "Let me speak!"

I cringe under the wave of heat that comes with his words. But once again, he reels in his anger quickly. I don't like his unpredictability. One second he's calm, nice even, but the next it feels like he'll strike me with the staff he rests next to him—all for the sake of his precious kingdom. I bet no one has ever questioned his authority like I have. But I can't stay silent. It's not right.

He draws a pattern in the sand with his finger, drawing out the silence longer than necessary before he says, "Because this has never happened, I'm going to allow you to return to land once a month for a few hours. You may not see your family, though. I know there are other ways of communication, and one of those must suffice. If it turns out to be too difficult, or they start to question too much, then I'll insist that you cut your ties."

I frown. I can't help it. "I can't ever see them? Like forever? Then what's the point?"

His brows furrow with a glower. He rubs his chin, thinking about what he has just said. "I'll allow you one visit a year under my supervision."

"You? How would I explain that?"

"You should be grateful, Ava. Would you prefer to not go at all?"

I shake my head, forcing my grief away the best I can even though I don't feel right about the situation. I don't know what I was expecting. I should appreciate the compromise. I should be satisfied to be alive. But now having to live my life by the rules King Attilonious creates on a whim? It's awful.

I'll never get to live how I wanted now. I had planned to eventually go home after everything was under control. I wanted to go to college with Giselle. That future is as lost to me as my human identity. My future feels non-existent.

Swallowing the lump in my throat, I direct my thoughts back to the king. "I appreciate your thoughtfulness, my king. I didn't mean for my concern to come off as ungrateful. You've been nothing but kind to me when you don't have to be." It's half a lie. He doesn't feel kind to me. He feels like he's pretending to be nice only to talk badly about me behind my back. But at this time, all I can think about is faking my way through this so I can leave and be alone. I'll agree to anything if it gets me out of this room.

King Attilonious smiles, showing off his slightly pointy yet straight teeth. "Every merperson is important to this kingdom, whether they choose to live on the land or not. I know you didn't choose this life, but I'd like for you to choose to accept it. You have the potential for great things but also terrible things if you don't learn our ways."

"I already have accepted things."

He leans over and takes my hand. The gesture feels too personal for my liking, but I can't tell if it's customary to intrude on someone's personal space. I'm still lost to everything. Unfortunately, he's right about all I need to learn. "Now that all this is settled, I'd like to make a formal announcement about the coupling ceremony. Once that takes place, I'll grant you your first adventure back to shore. Is that acceptable?"

I nod, thinking about how Carter will be so angry if he ever finds out I'm not going through with this by my own freewill. It's just as bad as agreeing to it to please his mother—this time, it's for the king. Someone neither of us can deny.

"Yes, your majesty," I say.

He grins. "I'll put the ceremony into my court's hands. It'll be a royal affair. It's been a long time since we've had such a celebration."

Starla's going to have a fit when she finds out, but I'm secretly satisfied it won't be in her hands. I just hope I can get through this without losing my mind.

"Sounds wonderful," I say, though my heart's truly not in it. "I guess I should tell Carter."

King Attilonious propels up from his spot, pulling me with him. "Don't look so defeated, Ava. You should be excited you're going to make your mate the happiest merman alive."

I know he should be right—I should be happy—but it just

feels so wrong. I feel like I'm treading water, trying to stay afloat, trying to get through this, but eventually I'll get tired and sink to the ocean's depths.

I can't think about that though. I can only hope that instead of sinking, I'll learn to swim in this strange new world.

OFFICIALLY COUPLING

CARTER CUPS MY FACE IN his hands, smiling through another kiss. His joy is contagious, and it's easy to forget how just an hour ago, I was breaking inside as all my freedom to make my own decisions was ripped away by the king who has taken great interest in my life as a mermaid.

I haven't even had time to process things and just go where the current takes me.

"What changed your mind, Ava?" Carter asks through another eager kiss.

King Attilonious watches with a stern expression from behind Carter, daring me to go against his command. Guilt nudges into my mind at Carter's question, but I force it away like all of the other nagging feelings threatening to be the cause of my undoing.

I suck in my bottom lip, soaking in his palpable excitement like a sponge. "I promised I would when I found my happiness here, and I *am* happy. I love you, Carter. I can't think of anything else that would make this life even better."

He frowns for a second when my voice hitches in his mind, but I kiss him again so he can't see the worry that flickers on my face.

His doubt fizzles out when he leans away, and I've pulled myself together to act genuinely thrilled. "We're going to have an amazing life, you know. I promise."

I believe him with every fiber of my being. It's the one thing that keeps me from turning around and swimming away. The ceremony might be happening sooner than I'd like, but it's also the key to my first approved trip to the shore, one I probably wouldn't get otherwise.

"I know. The king has everything planned out." I wish I could take back the words, but it's already too late.

He holds his lips against mine without pulling away, blocking anyone from seeing the look of concern flitting across his face. To the several onlookers, including the king, we merely look like two merpeople in love, showing our affection for the world to see.

"Ava..." The sound of my name coming from his thoughts nearly ruins everything.

"It's okay, Carter. Really. It's not exactly what I had in mind, but it's better than the alternative."

"Which is?"

"We'll talk about it later. I'm fine, though. I couldn't be happier to be here with you."

Slowly detaching myself from him, I beam my brightest smile. Carter blinks a few times, hiding his oncoming emotions with a smirk. He knows me all too well to accept that everything is fine, but he won't question it. Not here in front of the king.

Carter turns his attention to King Attilonious. "Thank you, your majesty. I haven't seen Ava this happy since—" He doesn't finish his sentence. No one needs to be reminded that my happiness comes from the land.

I twine my fingers through Carter's, tugging him close enough to wrap my arms around his shoulders. "I've never been so happy."

Carter bows to the king, but I don't. It doesn't seem to bother King Attilonious either. He just peers at me with a small, approving smile. One that tells me I've done a great job and that he's satisfied with my acting. If only I could be as convincing to myself.

The more I think about the situation, the less it becomes about the coupling ceremony and more about how the king basically threatened me into doing what he wanted. It's nothing short of unsettling how my fate lies in his hands, in his rules, in a merman who could very well destroy me if the mood occurred.

A familiar black-haired merman swims into the room, drawing my attention away from the king. Tide stops in front of his majesty and takes a deep bow. They have a silent conversation for a quick moment.

King Attilonious turns his attention back to me. "Ava, if you'd please follow Tide, he'll show you to your changing quarters where Luna will help prepare you for the coupling ceremony announcement."

I consider arguing, telling the king I'm fine how I am, because all I want to do is leave and hide in my house, but my desires fall flat with a pointed look from my ruler.

My eyes dart to Carter's for a split second, but he doesn't say anything. He doesn't know what's going on in my mind, because for what feels like the first time since I've come to Pearlestria, I've built a wall around my heart and mind to protect the both of us.

Nodding my head, I bare my teeth in what I hope is an acceptable smile. Things are happening too fast, and I have no idea what the king means by preparing me. It's not like I can do my makeup underwater.

I reluctantly let go of Carter to follow behind the merman. Tide doesn't say anything, swimming in front of me from the king's quarters. He's probably afraid he might say something to upset me like last night. At this point, I'm pretty sure anything anyone says might get under my skin.

We swim through a narrow tunnel that leads to a small room with a human mirror attached to a wall. In front of the mirror rests a smooth, white rock meant to be a seat. A shelf cut into the wall holds all sorts of colorful stones, bright coral pieces, and pretty shells. A young mermaid, no older than me, with black hair and a golden tail, sits in the sand with a dozen pieces of long, bright green sea grass strewn across her lap.

Tide stops in the middle of the room, and she brings her eyes to his and smiles before offering me one just as bright. With a slight nod, the merman leaves us. Wringing my hands together, I float nervously in the middle of the room, taking everything in.

"You must be Ava. I'm Luna. The king told me you'd need some help getting ready for your first real public appearance." The mermaid motions for me to swim closer.

I can't take my eyes from the mirror. The only time I've ever seen myself as a mermaid is through Carter's eyes, and to see my reflection now is mesmerizing. I feel like me, but I look like a stranger. I don't remember my hair looking this light while wet or my face being completely blemish free. Even though the sea has been hard on me mentally, it's at least made me look good while feeling bad inside.

"If he says so, then I guess I do." I perch on the rock next to her, finally answering her.

"You seem nervous," she says, weaving a few pieces of grass together without looking at me. Moving from her place on the floor, she rests on her bended tail in a kneeling position behind me. She loops the sea grass around my chest before cutting off the excessive length with her nail. "But there's no need to be."

"Why do you say that?" I shift my tail so it doesn't knock into the mirror in front of us.

"You're trembling." Her fingers move so fast, my eyes can

barely keep up with them as she braids a few pieces of grass to-gether. Without asking, she hooks her fingers on the clasp of my bikini top and snaps it open.

I brace it against my chest. "Hey! What are you doing?"

She twists her lips to the side. "You can't wear that for your big announcement."

"But—"

"I'm going to make you something much prettier, unless you'd prefer to go without. It's your choice. Either way, the human top has to go. The king was clear about that." Luna un-ties my top strap, leaving me holding my hands over my chest. I don't think I'll ever get used to how nonchalant merpeople are about their bodies. I know I shouldn't care, but swimming top-less in front of a bunch of strangers is fitting for one of my nightmares. I'd die of uncomfortable embarrassment.

"I'm not going topless," I say.

"I like to dress up, too," she says, motioning to her own sea grass top with shells woven through it.

All I do is nod instead of tell her it's more than a fashion choice, but I doubt she'd understand. Instead, I force myself to pull my bikini top away so she can measure a few more strands of the sea grass.

While she works on my new mermaid-approved top, I gaze at my reflection more in the mirror. My long blond hair floats around my head, appearing aqua in the soft light coming in through the cutout in the wall next to the mirror. My eyes, the same color as my cerulean tail, look wider, more anxious than I remember. My skin shimmers with a pearlescent glow, like someone dabbed my skin with a makeup highlighter, and it's smooth and hairless apart from my eyebrows and head.

Luna holds out a thick strip of woven sea grass, wrapping it around my back before criss-crossing it over my chest to tie the loose strands around my neck. She shifts on her tail, leaning toward the shelf on the wall, and grabs a few seashells and stones.

She carefully uses her nails to string small loops through the woven grass before tying a few dozen blue stones into my top. It sparkles in the light, matching perfectly with my tail. She takes a braided strand of sea grass and ties it at the bottom part of my new top, using another few pieces of grass to tie it to the woven band. It creates a triangular cutout on the center of my chest where my spark glows brightly from my heart. Only Carter can see it, and I'm pretty sure she chose this style just for him. Scooping a few seashells from the shelf, she picks out a scallop shell. She pokes a hole in it with her nail and ties it to a strand of grass before attaching it to the band of woven grass so it dangles in the cutout.

Surprisingly, the top is more beautiful than I could've imagined. It's nothing like the one Starla wore. Hers was made from wrapped seaweed and didn't have any of the decorations. This is the type of top I'd expect to find on a mermaid. I'm kind of excited to show it off. I bet Giselle would love it.

Trailing my fingers over the halter strap, I grin at myself in the mirror. "This is amazing, Luna. Thank you."

She grins. "You're welcome. If you'd like, I can make you a few more. I love having a variety."

I nod. "I'd love that."

She rests her hands on my shoulders, hovering behind me, and studies me for a moment before running her fingers through my hair. Taking a few pieces of bright purple coral, she braids it into my hair, creating a crown along my hairline. She leaves the rest of it loose, but it's pulled back enough to keep it out of my face.

I can't even believe my reflection. It's like Luna waved a wand, turning me into a fairytale mermaid, the kind you find on pretty trinkets in one of the many souvenir shops of Azure

Waters.

Luna claps her hands when she's finished. "Beautiful! All the mermen will be jealous of your mate for having found you."

I smirk. "They should be grateful. I tend to cause a lot of trouble."

She laughs, her eyes nearly closing as bubbles release from her mouth. "You're so funny, Ava. I bet Carter doesn't think you're trouble at all. You know, I've seen you both in passing, and I couldn't believe how in love you both look yet you refused to officially couple. So many mermaids would've loved to have been chosen by that boy."

I never thought of the possibility of Carter choosing someone else as a mate. I had always known he'd given up his one chance to transform a human on me, but I didn't realize it also meant he'd never get to choose even a mermaid. If I had denied his love, he'd have lived a lonely life. It's why humans aren't transformed on a whim.

I push the thought away. I can't stand the thought of Carter being lonely.

"Can you not choose your own mates?" I ask.

She shrugs. "It's more common for a merman to pursue a mermaid."

Kind of like the human world, though my girl friends are bolder than most. Sapphire, Giselle's cousin, had asked her boyfriend Matty out first. She loves telling the story of how awkward and shy he was the first time they hung out.

God, I miss my friends.

"I guess Carter did ask me out first." I'll never forget that day since it was the day I drowned, but it was more than that now. It was our one and only date with me as a human before the sea changed things forever.

"So, you knew him before he transformed you?" she asks. "I bet it came as such a surprise."

No one's really asked me how it all happened. I had assumed Starla had told everyone I was a klutz who fell overboard of the yacht Carter worked on during our first date and drowned moments before he could save me.

I think about that day more, remembering how nervous Carter was when he asked me out, and how I teased him because he had made it sound like hanging out with him wouldn't be as fun as hanging out with my friends. I remember how he gave me his hoodie to wear, like he knew I didn't pack for the cool night, and how he had prepared a tray of desserts, which I now know is his favorite food.

I don't remember Carter jumping off the boat after I fell overboard or drowning, but I do carry his memory of the events with me. The only memory I know is truly my own after falling under is the spark in the water, his life essence, and how it called to me. How it chose me.

"He worked on the yacht I was vacationing on and thought my fear of the ocean was interesting," I say. It feels so normal having such an odd conversation. I didn't realize how much I craved a friendship outside of Carter here. Luna seems nice enough.

"Oh, my Ocean. Afraid of the sea?" She giggles into my mind. "I couldn't imagine."

It wasn't so funny before my first transformation, but now, it does seem kind of ridiculous. I had good reason for my fear. I don't mention it to Luna, though. The thought of Bailey still flourishes a deep ache in my heart—because I was the lucky one.

Silence falls between us after a moment. Right on cue, Tide pops through the hole that leads to the tunnel that'll take us back to the grand room. Luna quickly runs her fingers through the loose hair cascading from my braided crown once more before hooking her arm through mine to pull me toward the hole.

Tide lets us enter first and follows behind as we leave the dressing chamber. When I exit the tunnel and swim into the grand room, King Attilonious and Carter wait near the old ship bow. A warm blush moves up my chest to flourish on my neck, and I meet Carter's gaze. Loving emotions cross his face. He smiles the smile he saves for me, dimples flashing and a strong intensity to his gaze that makes me feel incredibly beautiful.

Carter doesn't even give me a moment to swim closer before he closes the distance between us and wraps his arms around my waist to spin me around. With the adoration and desire he holds for me in his eyes, I can almost forget I didn't actually agree to the coupling ceremony. I can believe that maybe King Attilonious was right—Starla, too. Making my life official with Carter is the best thing to do...except, with it, I feel like I'm losing a part of myself I've been clinging desperately to. The human side of me that thought this was crazy for someone my age.

"You look absolutely stunning, Ava," he whispers into my mind, brushing his lips against mine. "I can't wait to show you off to the colony."

King Attilonious' shadow casts over us as he swims closer. Carter pulls away but doesn't take his hand off my waist. The king tilts his head slightly, gazing at me for a moment, but not in a creepy way. It's more like he's appreciating a piece of artwork.

"Like a shining pearl in the night-darkened ocean," he says after a moment. "You really do belong to the sea."

Except I don't. I might look the part of a mermaid, but my humanity begs to break free.

I don't have a chance to dwell on it, because the king motions us to follow him to the wide balcony that overlooks the colony. He unhooks his golden staff from the wall and swims to face his merpeople. Carter twines his fingers through mine and practically drags me to the king's side.

The sea of smiling faces greets us, and dozens of voices echo into my mind at once. The sudden cacophony of chattering voices causes me to swim back. Everything has been so silent until now. It's like I'm hearing the world for the first time, and it's scary and loud and all-consuming. The rush comes so quickly, I can't even distinguish one person from another.

The only thing stopping me from clutching my ears is that Carter's voice echoes the loudest in my mind, drawing my attention away from the merpeople in the crowd all here to see me.

"Shut them off, Ava. You don't have to listen to them," Carter says, raising his voice loud enough for me to hear. "Just listen to me."

I close my eyes, concentrating on isolating his voice and how warm and loving it feels compared to the intruding strangers all begging for my attention.

"That's it, Aves." Carter's words turn into soft humming to the melody of a song I recognize. It's enough to calm my heartbeat and get me to focus on what's happening.

The voices dissipate, and my mind no longer feels crowded as the king raises his staff into the air. The light from the surface sparkles in the giant diamond at the top of it, sending rainbow colors through the water. He then holds his hand toward me and Carter, and Carter swims us to the spot at the king's side.

"Today is a spectacular day, merpeople of Pearlestria. I'm here to announce the official coupling ceremony of Carter, son of Mateo and Starla, to Ava, the newest mermaid of our very own Pearlestria colony, which will be held here at the palace during the full moon. It is officially a royal affair as the sea has given Ava the greatest gift of all—a home among us. We shall celebrate her new life as mermaid as well as another love that'll last all eternity."

The king lowers his staff, smacking it on the stone, sending a cloud of bubbles toward the surface. Carter bows, and I follow suit, and then all the merpeople below also bow before their king. A moment later, loud cheers burst in my mind, nearly scaring me out of my skin. I bend forward, clutching my temples, my head feeling as if it'll explode.

A million emotions rush through me. Fear, surprise, love, anger, sadness, hope—it's too much to handle as I realize how real this is—how I'm giving myself not only to Carter forever, but also to the sea. This is something I should do with my family. They should be the ones excited and cheering, but they'll never be a part of my life like this ever again. I'll always be a voice over the line, a million miles away.

Panic seizes me, the voices pushing away even my own thoughts. My head swims with the foreign thoughts about me. Some mers congratulate me and send their approval while other's stand in disbelief because of the sudden unhappiness they see cross my face. I try the best I can to push them all away, but it's hopeless. Carter's voice can't even reach me.

Shadows darken my vision, and I flick my tail to escape. Propelling back into the palace wall instead of through the cutout, I hit my head and back hard on the rock, shooting pain through me. The last thing I see is the pretty ocean blue color of Carter's eyes before darkness consumes my very being.

❧ 10 ☙

FATE AS A MERMAID

"AVA, GIRL. CAN YOU HEAR me?" The familiar feminine voice echoes through my mind, breaking the barrier I put up to protect myself from the intruding voices that tried to rip my mind apart. "Ava?"

Light flickers in my vision against my fluttering eyelids. The tiny bit of light shoots agonizing pain through my skull, radiating from a spot on the back of my head. I haven't felt this bad since the time I drank too much champagne for Giselle's eighteenth birthday months ago.

"Do you have any aspirin?" I ask without opening my eyes completely. I'm not sure I even projected the question to Grandmer.

A cool hand settles on my forehead, half covering my eyes to shade them from the light. The gentle touch helps ease some of the pain. "There's no aspirin down here unfortunately."

I squeeze my eyes shut, trying to remember what happened. All I can remember is the horrible disharmony of too many voices in my mind. And the king.

"Where am I?" I stretch my arms up, my fingers knocking into a warm, solid body.

"Oh, God. You don't think she's forgotten who she is?" Carter's concern enters my mind, and a smile creeps across my face.

I lock my fingers around his waist. "I know who I am,

Carter."

Soft lips brush against mine. "I was worried you might've forgotten you were a mermaid."

I flick my tail, squinting into the hazy water. "The tail would never let me forget." I shimmy against the sand until Carter pulls me onto his lap. "What happened anyway? Where did you come from, Grandmer?"

"You hit your head at your coupling ceremony announcement," she says, wrapping her cool fingers around my right hand.

Oh, that. I was hoping that might've been a dream...or nightmare. The whole day's events rush back to me in a hot wave. How the king took away my ability to make decisions in regards to my relationship, how he's forced me to lie to Carter so he thinks it's all my idea, how the king took a normal future with my family away and tossed it to the unforgiving sea. How he broke me to shape me into who he wants me to be under his so-called kind and generous rule.

"You do remember you agreed to make things official, right?" If Carter didn't sound so worried, I would consider lying to him once again and telling him I had no idea what he was talking about. But, I can't do that to him. Not now. I already hurt him once before. The king wouldn't be happy either. I just wish it really was all a dream.

"How could I forget?" I try to sound happy about it, but it comes out more like a whine.

It's enough to make Carter frown. "What's wrong, Ava?"

"My head is killing me." I know that's not the answer he wants to hear, but it's the best I have to offer. Hopefully he'll buy it, since I can't hide the sinking feeling that sends my heart into my stomach. I can never tell Carter that his king isn't exactly who everyone portrayed him to be.

"Are you sure everything else is okay?" He helps me sit up

by lifting me from under my arms. I sprawl my tail over his, relaxing in his comforting embrace.

My only response to his question is to lean my head back and rest it on his shoulder while closing my eyes again. Avoidance is my best bet.

Grandmer's figure shadows the light filtering in through the cutout of our home. I didn't even realize I was here until this second. The old mermaid uses her fingers to pry open one of my eyes completely, sending a shooting pain to my brain.

"Ava, did you hear Carter?" she asks, sending her voice into my mind.

I blink my eyes open to get her to stop trying to look into my closed eyelids. "What?"

Carter and his grandma look at each other, concern crossing both their faces. I don't speak up though. All I want to do is close my eyes and feel Carter's body against mine, holding me together when the ocean tugs at my very essence, threatening to rip me apart.

Guilt nudges at me for making them worry, but I'm afraid that if I try to lie now, I'll break down into a confusing mess. I need to be strong if I want to hold onto even a small semblance of my human life.

"Ava?" Grandmer asks again.

I scrunch my face, knowing neither will leave me alone if I keep avoiding answering their questions. "I'm fine. It's just a headache."

"I'm not so sure, dear. You seem disoriented. I'd like to take you back to the palace for another opinion," she says.

My eyes widen. "No! Please, no."

Thrashing away from Carter, I swim across the room. I slide to the sandy floor against the wall, flicking my tail out when Carter tries to get near me. He flies back a few feet at the sudden current too strong to have been created with just my tail, especially with his powerful swim.

It's like what happened with the swirling sand of the king's pool.

"I'm fine," I say, pushing the thought from my mind. Carter looks too concerned with my attitude to think anything about it to me either. And Grandmer remains utterly silent. I can't even look at her.

"Ava," Carter says, swimming a foot closer. "Are you sure?"

I nod without saying anything. I refuse to go back to the castle. I refuse to be in the presence of the king. And I know Carter would take me back to the palace because he's worried about me. But I can't even fake being normal when the ocean feels wrong. I feel wrong and out of control. If I wasn't bound to the sea, I'd probably trigger a transformation.

And I hate everything about this now. The king stole from me the one person I talk to by commanding me to lie to Carter. He didn't tell me what would happen if I told Carter, but I'm sure it'd have something to do with cutting me off from my family, and I can't risk it. I'd rather push Carter away even with how much it hurts me, physically makes me ill, than see him freaking out over me.

I cover my face with my hands so I don't have to look at him. All I want is to get away from here to clear my mind—to think things through.

"Ava, you're scaring me." Carter's worried voice nearly breaks my heart.

"You can't make me go back to the palace. I just—I need to swim. If I swim, things will be better." I direct my thoughts only to Carter, peeking at his expression through my eyelashes. My reaction is enough to stop him from dragging me to him by my caudal fin. I can refuse to tell him all I want, but I know he's going to want to know why I won't go. And I'll have to lie again.

If I thought I could get away with it—if my world wasn't on the line—I'd dart back to the castle and give King Attilonious a piece of my wrath. I've never hated someone so much in this moment, not even Starla. I think even Carter can feel my heat in the suddenly swirling water from an odd current that snakes around the room, circling me, moving my hair out of my face when all I want to do is hide behind it.

Carter turns to his grandma. "I think I need some alone time with Ava, Grandmer. Can you come back later to check on her?"

Grandmer frowns but doesn't argue. "She could be really hurt, Carter."

He shakes his head. "I know Ava, and this is something else."

They have another silent conversation before Grandmer turns her sad gaze to me. She swims forward, touches the end of my caudal fin, and then swims through the window cutout instead of heading through the house to the front door.

Carter cautiously swims closer, waiting for me to lash out at him again, but I don't move. He eases to the floor next to me and wraps his arms around my shoulders. I still don't react. I can't let him see me break again. He doesn't need to share my stress. This is supposed to be the happiest time of his life, and I refuse to ruin it because of the king's demands. It wouldn't have been so bad if he didn't turn the situation into something devastating. I know I could've gotten over the fact that I'm being rushed into the coupling ceremony. I'm merely mad I don't have a choice in the matter, and I have to lie to Carter. What really threatens to damage my very essence is that my human life is in jeopardy.

"Still want to swim?" Carter asks after a moment instead of asking me what's wrong again for the millionth time. He's never one to pry or ask questions. For the first time, I'm thankful for that.

Nodding, I slide my hands over his shoulders and around his neck until I'm riding on his back like the dozens of times before. Carter reaches up his hand to caress my cheek once before he takes off, swimming through the window cutout. He circles the house around back and bolts toward the colony wall a few hundred feet in the distance.

His speed pushes my hair out of my face, and I let the current wash away all the thoughts on my mind. When it's just me and Carter swimming in the vast ocean, everything else doesn't seem to matter. I can almost lose myself to the sea.

A pod of dolphins swims near the surface, drawing my attention to the fading light of the sky above. They jump out of the water as they swim, peacefully and happily enjoying the freedom they find among the rippling ocean. I wish I could bottle up their enjoyment to hold onto it for later.

Carter swims upward, just below the dolphins, and two of them dive down to greet us. A smile crosses my face when one swims right next to me, close enough to touch. It nudges Carter as it swims, and I reach out and glide my hand over its smooth skin.

Diving down a moment later, Carter takes us away from the pod before they start to play games. I grin into Carter's shoulder blade, wishing I could go back to when we first met. I wouldn't take so much for granted.

A familiar landscape appears in front of us, and Carter slows down. He navigates the bottom of the ocean through a kelp forest, and I know that if I head south-east, I'd end up on the beach in front of my Victorian mansion in Azure Waters.

"I thought bringing you somewhere familiar might make you feel better," Carter says, coming to a stop.

He grabs me and flips me over his shoulders to hold me in his arms. Hovering an inch away, he gazes into my eyes, trying his best to see what's going on in my mind. But I've closed it off from him.

"Thank you," I say, spinning around to watch a seal dart past us toward the shallows. Carter watches me expectantly, waiting for me to say more. "This helps a lot."

"Do I have to swim you through all the oceans of the world, or will you tell me what has gotten into you? As of right now, I'm fearing the worst." He reaches out and cups my face in his hand. "The only thing I can think about is how you met with King Attilonious alone and came out with a whole new attitude. Did he hurt you, Ava?"

I blink a few times. "No. He just wasn't what I expected." The king didn't physically hurt me. If Carter thinks he did, I'm afraid of what he'd do. I'm sure he'd be hurt or worse if he tried to go after the king.

"And what was that?"

"Nice," I say simply.

"But he's hosting our coupling ceremony—you seemed so happy..." His thoughts cut off as he thinks to himself.

I wish he wouldn't push this, because with him I'm a terrible liar. He'll see right through me if he doesn't already. I just want the next few days to fly by so I can get the ceremony over with, accept my status in Pearlestria, and have my first visit out of the sea.

I force myself to smile. "And for that I'm grateful. It's just that he's decided my fate as a mermaid." The king never mentioned that I couldn't divulge to Carter what he's decided about my life on land. I just hope Carter doesn't put the two things together.

His blue-green eyes darken as the silhouette of a boat crosses over our heads. "I don't understand. He gives everyone a choice."

"He has limited mine." Instead of telling him every detail, I kiss him and send the memory of my conversation with the king to him, leaving out his demands about the coupling ceremony. I'm not risking Carter finding out that. He'd never agree to go through with it, and I'll be left in pieces because all I want is to return to shore.

After the memory ends, Carter pulls away with a frown on his face. "I'm so sorry, Ava. I had no idea he'd do that."

"There's no way I can keep up this charade. My parents will become suspicious. What if they hire someone to look into my life and find out that I'm lying? What if they dig too deep and discover what I am? They'll be killed. King Attilonious would probably murder them himself." I close my eyes for a second to push the thought away. "It's over, Carter. My human life as Ava Adair is officially over. I have to cut ties."

He shifts his eyes to gaze around the kelp forest like he might find the answer in its tangled depths. "Don't give up so easily, Aves. We can manage a year. I know it."

It's not just the year—it's forever. "I need to see Giselle," I finally say after a moment. In a time where my world feels like it's sinking under, Giselle has always been the person I turned to, even as kids. She stuck by my side through everything that happened with my sister. She's protected me all this time, always by my side without pushing me. And now, I need her more than anyone in the world. She'll help me figure this out. It involves her life, too.

"Wait here. I'll see what I can do." He kisses me once before bolting away, leaving me alone in the kelp forest where it feels like I'll soon lose my human life—I'll soon lose a part of me.

The water is nearly completely dark before I sense Carter again. The sun has long since set, leaving me in the glowing depths of the lively kelp bed. A few boats have crossed overhead, but most have gone back to shore until an hour or two before dawn when the fish will surely bite. Unfortunately for them, I've been extremely bored. For every fish they snagged on the line, I've unhooked it, letting it swim free. It's kept boats from lingering long. They probably assume one of the playful seals have stolen their catch.

"Ava, can you swim near the harbor?" Carter's voice enters my mind though I don't see him anywhere.

Just as I start to follow his voice, it suddenly disappears. Emptiness settles through me at his absence, and despair crosses my mind thinking about how horrible the ocean would be if he never returned to me. While we're officially not coupled in the eyes of the king, I know in this moment that it doesn't matter. I'm as attached to him as he is to me, and our souls are already coupled. The thought ignites the pull of his spark, drawing me to him through the water even though I know he isn't a merman now.

It's enough to know that I'd go crazy alone in these waters. How he'd go crazy if he ever resorted to giving me his ring, something he'd do if the king decided to never release me from the ocean's depths. It's in this moment that I know I would never go through with it. I'd never abandon Carter to the sea for a life on land with everything I love. I'll remain in hopeless despair forever to save him from that kind of fate.

Weaving through the busy kelp forest, I avoid a few large bat rays and a leopard shark as I stick near the bottom of the ocean floor, following the sand as it inclines toward the shore.

As the purpling sky fades to black above, I flick my tail and propel myself toward the surface to get a better view. I can't swim all the way here without at least sneaking a glimpse of the shore. Peeking only my eyes above the water, I peer around the open air, cool with the ocean breeze. Light flickers from the mansions lining the shore, and it only takes a second to find my beautiful renovated Victorian that had once belonged to my grandfather.

A figure moves on the other side of the doors that leads to the beach. Like I've been granted a miracle, I gaze at my mom stepping outside. She crosses her arms over her chest, glancing at the dark waves of the night. She wouldn't be able to see me from here, and I can barely see her, but I'd know her anywhere.

I'd give anything to transform into my human self so I could swim to shore and throw my arms around her and explain the mess I got myself into. I'd apologize for ever leading her to believe I was fine, and I'd tell her the truth about being a mermaid. I imagine she'd understand it isn't safe for her to continue seeing me, but she'd accept I have a new life. That as long as I'm away, everyone would be safe.

But those dreams could never happen. She can never know. She'll have to spend the rest of her life wondering where she went wrong to push me so far away that I only see her once a year—if that would even be possible.

Shaking the grief from my head, I dip back underwater and head north toward the harbor, following the pull from my spark, guiding my way. It takes me twice as long as it would with Carter, and when I get there, I don't see him at all. I remain off shore, quite a ways away from where dozens of boats and huge vessels remain at the docks for the night. I float underwater, bobbing around the current, and wait for what feels like forever until I decide to break the surface.

Spitting out water, I inhale a deep breath of salty air, letting it settle into my soul to remember later when I'm hidden in the protected depths of Pearlestria. The lighthouse near the cove shines its bright light over a long trail of rocks that disappear into the ocean. It's where I had gone to transform when Giselle had taken off my ring before she knew what I was. For only being a mermaid for a short period of time while I was trying to keep my human life, I have a lot of memories I'd do anything to relive again.

A dull light from a small motorized boat shines across the water, startling me. I dip under, afraid that the night fisherman might've spotted me in the water. The last thing I need is to have them start the rumor of the mermaid of Azure Waters. I can just imagine the king locking me away somewhere in his palace for the rest of my long mermaid life.

The boat crosses right over my head, sending a trail of bubbles behind it. The dull light from the boat shines into the water and blinks a few times. I shift my eyes, looking around. That's not something a normal fisherman would do, but I have no idea if I should risk breaking the surface.

"Carter?" I ask, sensing him nearby. His voice remains silent still.

Then the light flashes again.

Instead of popping up next to the boat, I swim a dozen feet away and ascend to the surface without spitting out water to gasp for breath. The light turns from the water and shines in my eyes as the boater directs it at me.

"Ava!" Giselle calls. "It's us!"

I flick my tail, sending my head and chest out of the water completely. I clear my lungs to suck in a breath and use my arms to swim me toward the boat. Carter cuts off the flashlight he's holding and sits down on the cracked leather seat next to Giselle, who has taken the driver's position behind the wheel.

"You stole Logan's boat?" I ask, pulling myself onto the side to dangle my arms near her legs. The boat rocks a few times, but it's not going anywhere.

"Borrowed," she corrects. "It did take a lot of convincing. He wanted to come."

Of course he did. Logan loves adventures, even if it was just a boat ride after dark. "How'd you convince him otherwise?"

She reaches down and dangles a paper bag from her fingertips. "Tacos." She hands the bag to Carter so he can open it. "Your boyfriend said you could use some comfort food, and I know they're one of your favorites and easier to eat than enchiladas. I brought you a cupcake for dessert, too."

Tears burst from my eyes. The hot saltiness of them startles me, and I hiccup. It's been so long since the ocean hasn't automatically washed them away before they had a chance to brand warm streaks down my cheeks.

Covering my mouth with my hand, I muffle another sob. Giselle stares at me with wide, watery eyes, watching me break down. Carter leans over and squeezes my shoulder. I wish he'd just jump in to hug me.

But he doesn't have to. Giselle pulls off her sundress and flips herself over the side of the boat, splashing me. She treads in the water next to me, hugging me to her. The flick of my tail keeps us both above water, and I cry into her shoulder as she rubs her hand up my short dorsal fin.

She cries right along with me even though I haven't even told her anything. Just knowing how upset I am is enough to set her off, and I can't help the ridiculous laugh that bubbles from my throat.

"Why are you crying?" I ask, choking back a half-laugh, half-sob.

She swipes a hand across her cheeks. "Because it hurts me to see you like this. Carter mentioned that things have changed. He didn't tell me what, though."

I suck in a deep breath, refusing to let go of Giselle. "It has. I'm so sorry, Giselle. I'm not going to be able to ever come home to live as a human. The king has forbidden it."

She covers her hand with her mouth. "But college!" Her dreams of us sharing a house together while attending UCSD get lost in the current around us.

"I can't go."

"And what about your parents?"

"The king says I can call once a month and visit once a year."

"What the hell? That's totally not going to work," she says.

I throw my arms into the air, and Giselle dunks under before popping back up. I grip her arm to keep her above water. "That's what I said."

She turns her attention to Carter. "There has to be something you can do."

He turns his gaze to the star-speckled sky. "I wish there was."

"I'll figure something out, Aves. I swear. I won't let those stupid rules ruin our life together. We're going to be best friends forever. No stupid ocean or king is going to ruin this. This isn't over, okay?"

I nod my head, wishing I could gather the hope she clings on to. But in this moment, all feels lost to the black waters.

11

THE KING'S DAUGHTER

"WHOA, AVES. HERE, TAKE MY last taco," Giselle says, handing me the carne asada taco she cradles on her lap.

I take it from her despite the embarrassment burning my cheeks. I've eaten both mine and Carter's tacos, and now half of Giselle's. But I can't help it. I'm starving, and tacos really are my favorite. Tasting the spicy salsa and hearty meat is like heaven. Not a single bite has the salty taste of the ocean, and I wish there were a dozen more to eat.

I consume the taco in four bites. "God, I love you both. And these tacos. The world doesn't seem so bad as long as I know that there will be more of this in my future."

Giselle laughs. "If you can sneak away tomorrow, I'll bring Chinese."

My mouth waters at the thought, and I shift my gaze to Carter. "You have to make that happen."

He smiles softly, but then shakes his head. "Tomorrow's not good."

Giselle huffs. "Why not?"

"Tell her, Ava," Carter says.

"Huh?" And then I remember the coupling ceremony and its obligations. "Oh, that."

He frowns. "Yes, that." I'd be upset for wanting to ditch our ceremony for Chinese food, too.

Giselle throws her hands up. "Tell me already!"

For Carter's sake, I beam my brightest smile at my best friend. If I say it any other way, Carter will doubt that I agreed by my own freewill. He'll piece it together.

"Well, Carter and I are coupling on the upcoming full moon, and we'll be spending the next few days getting ready," I say.

She raises an eyebrow. "What does that even mean and should I be excited?"

"It's like the equivalent to getting married on land," I say quietly.

"What! You're getting married? But you're only eighteen. And what about me? What mermaid is going to be your maid of honor?" Giselle rocks the boat, reaching down to me and shakes my shoulders. "This is crazy and—" Her words cut off when I hold her gaze for a long moment, begging for her to reel it in. "Congratulations! How so freaking exciting! You guys are totally meant for each other."

Carter flashes his sexy dimples, meeting my gaze. My fake smile turns genuine as Giselle's confusion and doubt shift to joy, even if she doesn't mean it. She has the same feelings I do. She doesn't have to tell me to know.

Keeping her back to Carter, she narrows her eyes at me in a way that says she wishes she could talk to me alone. "I swear! If this is legit in the ocean, you better not skip out on an actual marriage on land."

I laugh. "That's not happening any time soon."

Carter's head tilts to the side, thinking about what I've just said. We've never talked about a formal human marriage ever. It's the last thing on my mind, but I guess he assumed we'd make it official across both the sea and land.

"I want to wait until I have my legs full time," I add. Because it's true. But maybe when I'm like twenty-five.

"That makes perfect sense," Giselle says before Carter can

say anything. "You'll have to make sure your one day in Azure Waters is during the summer. It's the best time of year here for a wedding, you know."

I smirk while shaking my head. "Why don't we get through this whole thing first before making those kinds of plans?"

She rolls her eyes. "You're right. Because one thing's for sure, I'm not waiting a year to see you. Carter better tell me where you're going to be when you get to call, and I'll figure out how to get to you. I don't care where."

I smile. "You know I owe you my life, right?"

She hugs me. "You don't owe me anything."

Tilting my head back, I dip my dry hair under the cool water. It muffles the sound of Carter's voice as he says something to Giselle, but I can't hear him over the sudden pounding in my head.

And then I hear it.

"Ava? Carter?" The masculine voice wraps me in familiar anguish, but only because I know where Mateo is, Starla will soon follow.

Panic seizes my chest. "Carter, your dad is calling us. We have to go!"

Giselle shifts in her seat. "Oh, crap."

Carter tugs his T-shirt over his head. "Ava, go find him. Keep him occupied. I'll be there as soon as I get Giselle back to the harbor." He starts the small engine of the boat, and it hums to life.

I meet my best friend's startled gaze. "Thanks for everything, Gi. I'll see you again as soon as I can. Please, be safe."

She hugs me once more before the boat takes off, leaving me in the bubbling water. Bobbing underwater, I spin around and peer through the glowing ocean, afraid that I'll spot Mateo watching me descend from the surface. But he's not there.

Diving deeper, I dart along the shore and away from the

harbor back toward the familiar beach in front of my house.

"Ava? Carter?" Mateo's voice swirls through my mind again.

I swim as fast as I can. "Over here," I say, sending my voice to Carter's dad.

It doesn't take long for the muscular merman to find me among the kelp forest, holding onto the strands of the green plant in my hands. The sudden shift of water pushes me back, and I drift a few feet on the current created by Mateo.

I haven't seen Carter's father since my first night in Pearlestria when he kissed his wife goodbye so he could return to take care of their business on land. His bronze skin, darker than Carter's, glimmers a faint gold in the water instead of the pearl shimmer both mine and Carter's contains, and his almost black, shoulder length hair floats around his head. When he draws his gaze to mine, I see my own reflection in his dark irises, like I'm looking into two black pools.

Without a word, he wraps me into a strong hug, rocking me back and forth in the water. It's the same way he greeted me on land before he discovered that Carter had given me his spark to transform me into a mermaid. Pulling away, he kisses both my cheeks and gives me a smile that reminds me of the one I fell in love with on his son.

"My beautiful daughter," he says, giving me the once over like he hasn't seen me in my mermaid form before. "What are you doing so far from Pearlestria and so close to your home? And where's my son?"

A million lies tumble through my mind, but none of them sound good enough to believe.

"To celebrate, Dad," Carter says, his voice wrapping me in comfort. "You know how much Ava loves the waters of her home. She made me the happiest merman today, so I thought I'd make her even happier tonight." He lies so easily that I almost believe the words he says.

Carter swims up behind me and hooks his fingers on my hips before leaning in to kiss my cheek. Mateo looks between us with a smile that takes up half his face. I didn't even know someone could smile so big.

Mateo closes the distance and flings his arms around the both of us, squishing me in a merman sandwich. "I wish I had been here for the announcement. Couldn't get away from the shop until closing though."

"It wasn't that great," I mutter, bringing my hand to the back of my head even though it doesn't hurt any longer. My mermaid blood heals me faster than if I were human.

Carter squeezes my hand when Mateo frowns like I've said the rudest thing in the world. "Don't mind Ava, Dad. She's a little embarrassed about knocking herself out cold in front of the entire colony."

A wave of heat flourishes up my neck and in my cheeks. I hadn't even thought about that. All this time I was worried about what the king said and how it affected my life that I didn't even think about how merpeople must be talking about how I injured myself during a royal announcement. God, can't I ever catch a break?

Mateo reaches out and squeezes my shoulder. "I'm sure it's fine, Ava. When everyone comes to celebrate your big day, they won't even remember that stuff."

I can only hope so.

"Thanks, Mateo," I say, puffing out my bottom lip, thinking the words to him.

"Call me Dad, Ava. You're my daughter now. I've been waiting forever for one, you know. Did Mom ever tell you I had hoped Carter was a girl?" He laughs, looking at his son.

"You don't have to call him Dad," Carter says to me. "I know it's kind of weird."

"Well, I'm glad you didn't get your wish, *Dad*," I say, the words feeling incredibly wrong coming from my mind. My dad is probably overlooking his patients at the hospital right now. "Because then I'd have never met Carter."

"You're right, Ava-girl." Mateo holds out his hand. "How about we head back? Your mom's waiting on us. She's completely thrilled."

I swallow back the anger I still hold toward Starla. "Sure."

Without even letting me prepare myself, Mateo yanks me forward, taking off, speeding in the water even faster than Carter.

Carter laces his fingers through my free hand and balances me out so I'm not strung along like a rag doll. I don't even bother flicking my tail as the two mermen swim me along through the vast ocean. In this moment, things don't feel so bad. As the surroundings rush by, I feel like I'm flying on the current.

If the protective walls of Pearlestria didn't sneak up so quickly, I could imagine being free. But the moment we enter the walls, it's like a door closes on my underwater prison cell.

This time of night, the colony is empty as merpeople hang out inside their houses. The palace glows with a strange white light, like the king has somehow managed to install electricity underwater, but I'm sure it's just another magical thing I'll never understand.

If it weren't for my mermaid vision, the colony would appear pitch black. Strange sea creatures swim through the sand channels this time of night, exploring without getting shooed away by the merpeople.

Carter points out the freakiest looking shark I've ever seen. Its long, pointed nose makes it look like Pinocchio when he tells too many lies, and its weird mouth looks like it escapes its head as it gobbles up a nearby fish. It's the type of creature I'd love to take a photo of to show to Giselle. Something she'll never get to see in person.

"That's a goblin shark," Carter says into my mind. "Some of the mers call it the nosey night guard."

Carter always uses the human words for all the sea creatures like he doesn't want to forget that part of him. The language of the merpeople is different, mostly told in images through thoughts, but my brain translates it for me. Everyone's distinct thoughts come through in a particular voice, but Carter says most sound identical to what they would sound like if they were using their vocal chords.

"It's so ugly it's cute," I say, watching the shark swim by.

Mateo laughs, bubbles erupting in the water. The faint sound of his voice drifts to my ears, though the water muffles it. It's one of the only times that I've heard a sound that wasn't the ocean, except for the times I've made Carter laugh out loud, and it feels weird.

Carter smirks at me. "My dad has trouble adjusting back to the ocean. He rarely comes here."

Mateo shrugs, now laughing into my mind. "I'm sure Ava understands, son."

More than anyone.

When we reach our small house, Starla waits for us on our front sands with her arms crossed. I frown, wondering why she hasn't gone inside, but then I remember that it isn't her house, and it's probably just as rude to barge in here as it is on land— or maybe she doesn't because she's used to the land.

She greets Carter with a huge smile but doesn't bring her eyes to mine. They share a silent conversation, and Carter bobs his head before he glances at me in his peripheral vision.

I'm getting pretty annoyed that so many people have been having private conversations with Carter lately. I have a feeling Starla is required to be here for the coupling ceremony, but she knows we're still mad at her. It hasn't been long since she left.

I turn to go inside, but Carter reaches out and grabs my hand. "Is it all right if my parents stay the night with us? It's kind of crowded at Grandmer's."

I twist my lips to the side. "Of course they can stay. They're your parents, Carter. What kind of person do you think I am?"

He narrows his eyes for a minute. "I think you're the most amazing person in the universe. I was asking because this is our house. The decision is for both of us to make."

Instead of arguing, I wave my arm toward the door, smiling. If I fake it long enough, I'll start to believe myself. Maybe that's what the king was hoping. "Why don't you two stay with us tonight," I say way sweeter than I normally think. "We're so happy you could join us."

Mateo hugs my shoulders, nudging me inside and peers around our bare living room. After seeing the palace, I think about all the things I could do to make it feel more like a home. Maybe Carter can find a shipwreck to salvage something cool from, or even ask Giselle to go shopping.

"I see you got rid of your bikini top," Starla says, directing her attention to me. "You look even lovelier."

I glance down at my grass woven top. Giselle thought it was the most amazing piece of clothing and asked me to bring her one. "Thanks, Starla. One of the king's servants made it for me. Luna was her name."

Starla's eyes widen. "Princess Luna is not a servant."

I close my eyes for a quick second. Neither Luna nor the king mentioned she was his daughter and the princess of all merpeople. Thank God I didn't say something crazy in front of her. Things could've ended badly. How embarrassing.

"Oh, I didn't know," I say.

"Of course you didn't. I wasn't here to tell you."

Oh, great. Not this. I'm too exhausted to deal with her. So instead of telling her off like I want to, I say, "Make yourselves at home. But if you don't mind, I'm going to get some rest. It's been a long day."

Carter slides his arms around my neck. "I'm going to let Grandmer know you're okay and visit with my dad for a bit if that's okay."

I nod. "Have fun."

Starla and Mateo watch me swim to the room. I don't lie down on my kelp woven blanket in the sand though. I don't think I could sleep even if I tried.

Gazing out the cutout window, I decide to swim through it and around the house to the long stretch of sand that will take me to the spot I go to when I want to get away. It's the first time I've gone at night, but I can't think of a better thing to do to clear my head.

But unfortunately, when I arrive at my little underwater grass meadow, someone is already there, sprawled out in the grass bed.

"Ava?" a feminine voice asks. "Is that you?"

I swim forward and face the girl I just found out was actually the king's daughter. I never expected her to be outside of the palace alone, especially at night. But I guess this isn't the human world, and she has nothing to be afraid of.

"Oh, hi Luna," I say. "I didn't expect anyone to be out here. I come to this place to think."

She smiles, patting the grass next to her. "Me, too. The king has been anxious all afternoon since your coupling ceremony announcement."

"You mean your father." I only say it because I want her to confirm that she's actually the princess.

She brushes her black hair from her face. "You know."

"I wish you would've said something, princess. I wouldn't

have complained so much," I say.

"Don't start with those annoying titles. My name is Luna. Plus, I didn't think you complained much. It was nice being around someone not from around here. I've always dreamed of going to land."

My mouth drops open. "You've never been? Why not?"

"The king doesn't think it's a good idea. Unfortunately, what he says goes for me."

I frown. "Same."

"Sorry about that. I overheard him consulting with one of his advisors. I couldn't imagine not being able to see my father all the time. He might be difficult sometimes, but I love him." Luna stretches out her tail in front of her.

I don't respond. There's no way I'm saying anything she could report back to the king. The last thing I need is to have someone telling him my every move. It'd probably be best if I just made an excuse to leave, because I shouldn't even be here, but it's been so long since I've had any socialization in the colony besides Carter and his family.

After a long moment of contemplation, I say, "I understand. Even people on land have problems with their families." Though, I don't. Not with my parents. When you lose someone close to you, like how we lost Bailey, things change.

"Will you tell me more about it?" she asks.

"The land?"

She nods.

"Yeah, I'd like that."

Instead of worrying about what I say about my feelings toward the king, I take the opportunity to reminisce about everything I love about my home—about the land. It's the first time someone has really asked. Most of the merpeople, including Carter, think reminding me is only going to make my adjustment harder.

I tell Luna about the things I loved to do, like baking and hanging out with my friends. I tell her about my favorite music and try to explain TV to her. She listens with wide eyes as I describe everything the best I can.

"This is so amazing. No wonder you didn't want to leave," she says.

"I'm going back as soon as I can," I say. "Your father promised me one trip a month."

She sits up, smiling. "Think I could come?"

I frown. The last thing I want to do is bring along the king's daughter on my one chance to enjoy the land, but something about her excitement gets to me. I feel bad. It's easy to put myself in her position, and I wonder which of us is worse off—me, because I had the chance to grow up and experience the human world, to enjoy it, rely on it, find solace in it, but also had it all stolen away from me. Or is Luna worse off, not ever getting to experience it at all? It's hard to decide. She can't miss it like I do, but she can always have that nagging what-if wonder.

"Um, I thought your dad doesn't let you," I say.

She shrugs. "I have access to his collection of sea stone rings. He'd never have to know."

Hearing her talk about the rings sends excitement through me. What if she could sneak one to me? I could run away with Carter, and this time, no one would be able to stop us. I'd figure out how to get away and never come back. I could convince my parents to move away from Azure Waters.

I think about it for a long moment. It all sounds so easy, but it also sounds too good to be true. This could all be a test. "I don't know, Luna."

"You don't trust me because I'm the king's daughter," she says, reading my mind though I don't share those thoughts with her.

I shrug. "Not completely, but don't you think the king would come down on me instead of you if we were caught? I have a lot at stake."

She digs her fingers into the sand. "We won't get caught. Please, Ava. Just once. Maybe just to the beach. It's something I can't do alone. No one ever goes to the surface around here."

Except Carter. I don't say it though. "I'll have to talk to Carter."

She flings her arms around me. "Thank you! I never even hoped of getting to experience land, and now I might get to. You won't regret it."

Her excitement rubs off on me, pushing away the nagging doubt of what happens if this plan fails. But how can I not even consider it an option, a way out? If I can convince her to get me a ring in exchange for taking her to the shore, I could figure my way out of all of this. It's the first time in weeks that I have a fighting chance to make my future the way I want it. Because as of now, the king is forcing me to remain in the sea. Monthly visits ashore isn't enough. He didn't guarantee my permanent return to land, but getting a ring back might do just that. This has been what we've been waiting for.

With Luna, I might actually get my freedom back, and she doesn't even have a clue.

Maybe she'd want to join me.

If the king wants to steal my happiness away, maybe I can take his and show him just how it feels. Maybe it's all I need to get my life back.

12

ACCIDENTAL LOVE STORY

IT'S NOT UNTIL LIGHT BREAKS through the surface that I realize I've been lying back in the sea grass with Luna all night, and Carter hasn't checked on me once. I sit up on my elbows and peer around the quiet waters. The colony will be arising soon.

Luna braids another few pieces of sea grass together before tying it around my wrist. We each wear a dozen, all adorned with the tiny shells we've dug from the sand. After talking to Luna for hours, I've realized a few things about the king's daughter. For one, we have more in common than I realized. She's desperate for a life she controls, one of her making. And two, she's starved for a friend. As starved as I am for someone to talk to apart from Carter. Someone who won't give me every-thing I want. Someone who'll tell me when I'm acting insane.

"So, will you come with me?" Luna asks, twirling her hands in the air, pointing to the surface. She's asked me to surface with her to watch the night sky turn to day. It's as close as she's made it to the human world, breaking through to take a peek at the ocean from a different perspective.

"I don't know. Carter will probably be looking for me soon." I haven't seen a sunrise above the water in weeks, but I feel like this is something I have to talk to Carter about. Only he's taken me to the surface. I'm not sure if I'm forbidden from doing so—not by him but the king. There have been unspoken rules set upon me. Like leaving the colony alone.

"So," she says. "If he wants to find you, he will. You don't need to ask his permission. He's your mate not your ruler."

She's right. I've never felt like he controlled me or what he says goes, but he might question my judgment. So many things could go wrong following the princess to the surface. What if King Attilonious discovers us? I'd seriously be testing my luck.

"I know, but your dad—"

She rolls her eyes in a very Giselle fashion, making me miss my best friend already. "It isn't forbidden. Look around, there are no boats. I've done this a million times."

"Okay," I say, only because I love the idea of breaking the surface. To feel air fill my lungs instead of water is as close to transforming into a human as I can get. "But just for a few minutes."

Taking my hand, Luna pulls me from the spot next to her and nearly drags me up to the surface. I glance below at the sleepy colony, still absent of life as the merpeople remain in their rock houses. From here, it looks like I'm gazing down at some magical place meant for storybooks. It doesn't feel real. It feels like it's all just a dream I'll wake up from when I gasp for breath.

We swim side-by-side, holding hands to keep pace with each other. Luna's golden tail shines like tiny mirrors encrust each scale, and her hair cascades behind us like a black waterfall. She beams a smile bright enough to outshine the rising sun, and I wonder if I could ever look so happy.

"Get ready," Luna says as we near the rippling surface.

"For what?" I ask.

She spins to swim facing me while taking both my hands in hers. It isn't until we're mere feet away from the air that I realize we're not going to stop to cautiously break through. We're go-ing to breach.

Luna flicks her tail, launching us out of the water and into the cool morning air. We both spit out water, flipping in the air to dive back under in a graceful arc. When we pop back up, Luna spits water in my face all while laughing. Her black hair hangs in her eyes before she tosses it back, creating a wave on the top of her head.

I suck in a deep breath and tilt my head back to stare up at the clear sky. Soft yellow light sets my golden hair ablaze as the sun peeks up from the horizon in the east. The wide ocean surrounds us with no sign of land or boats or even birds to let me know that humans might be nearby. Here, treading water above Pearlestria, it's like we're alone in the world. I never thought I'd be hanging out with a mermaid princess, but here I am, living my childhood dream before the day the ocean took my sister.

"Isn't this amazing?" she asks. She laughs, her voice musical over the hush of the swells that lift us closer to the sky before dropping us back down. "Sweet Blue Ocean, my voice. I forgot I sound like this. I've never broken the surface with someone to talk to before."

"It's pretty. I didn't even think you could talk, especially in my human language." I giggle, watching her float on top of the water, smacking her tail on the surface.

She splashes water in my face. "How do you think we've been communicating telepathically? Plenty of merpeople can speak many languages of the human world, especially those who want to explore the shores. It's easy to learn things from each other. My mom was fascinated with the land and showed me as a merbabe. Hasn't your mate showed you? I've seen you kiss."

"Oh," is all I can say. I haven't heard anything about Luna's mom before, who would be the queen, but I don't want to ruin the mood by asking now. I let the thought drop.

"Yeah." It gets another musical laugh from her, and I think about what she says for a minute about the way merpeople learn, the thought making perfect sense. It's how Carter showed me his entire life in a day. He shows me stuff all the time. I guess I never really put things together.

Mirroring Luna, I lie back and stare up at the crystalline sky. We're surrounded in a world of blue—one that seems less complicated than it did last night. "I'm glad I came," I say, changing the subject. I don't want to think about the merpeople while the salty air dries tendrils of hair around my face.

"Me too. I wasn't sure if you would."

"Why?" The one thing that really pushed me into coming to the surface was I didn't really want to go back home.

She slightly turns her head to glance at me. "Most mermaids don't like to leave their mates. It's one of the reasons I haven't chosen one, though the king occasionally brings someone he thinks is worthy enough for me to meet."

"Maybe your mate awaits for you on land," I say instead of responding to her comment about not wanting to be away from my mate, since she's clearly curious and surprised by my actions. I also don't want to admit that I'm not like most mermaids. My only thoughts of Carter over the last few hours have been how he'll probably freak out when he realizes I'm not asleep in our room.

Luna splashes her tail. "Then I'll probably be lonely forever."

I grimace at the thought. Relationships are obviously the most important thing within the colonies. It makes me sad to think that Luna might never get to meet someone she likes if she's not given the opportunity to widen her search. Maybe the king fears she'll fight to remain on land. How would that look if a mermaid princess chose to give up the sea?

"That's what friends are for," I say, splashing her with my tail.

A smile lights her face before it flickers away. "But you'll leave me one day, too. Carter has already chosen the land, and so have you."

Which is true and will happen hopefully sooner if she gives me a ring. Because at this point, the king will only approve once a month visits. He might never approve more than that. Not with me, at least.

I don't tell her what I'm thinking, though. "You don't have other friends?" I ask.

She shrugs. "No one important."

I thought my life was bad. I couldn't imagine being in her place. "No wonder you want to come to land with me."

She's quiet for a long moment. "You know, we don't have to wait until my father gives you permission to leave after your ceremony. He has the whole ocean to watch over. It takes the focus off me."

If she had suggested it last night, I wouldn't have considered it at all. I'd have shot her down and swam away. But now, after spending all night getting to know her, I realize she doesn't approve of the king's rules. She isn't trying to test me or set me up. Like me, she wants to break free of her limitations, to make her own decisions. She wants the life I'm desperate to get back.

But fear of the unknown has kept her back.

Going on land alone has never been an option. She doesn't know the human ways. She's been sheltered into the perfect mermaid princess.

"Carter would never agree to take us now. He won't put his own ability to go on land at risk. It's too important in maintaining my human life as much as possible," I say. I don't want him to risk it either, but I can't imagine going alone. *What are you talking about? Yes, you could.*

"Does he have to come? We can sneak away late tonight. No one will ever know." It's like she can read my mind.

The sinking feeling in my stomach says not to agree. It's

too risky. But, what do I have to lose now that my human world is already slipping through my fingers the way the waves steal the sand from the shore. I've lost my legs. Now, I have the chance to get them back. It's not the same as running away, but it gives me the option if I wanted to.

I open my mouth to tell her it's a bad idea, but instead say, "That's true. It might just work."

We smile at each other as our plan sinks in. It's really happening.

Another swell lifts us higher into the air, but instead of falling back down, hands grip my waist, holding me above the water. A wave splashes over Luna, causing her to laugh, and I flip backward to dive under only to meet Carter's curious gaze.

I knew he'd discover I was missing sooner or later. I'm surprised it wasn't sooner.

I flick my tail to propel us to the surface where Luna remains. "Apparently Carter started to miss me," I say.

Carter slides his hands over my shoulders. "I figured I should get you before my parents realized you stayed out all night when you claimed to be too tired to visit with them."

I cringe. "You knew?"

He chuckles and kisses my cheek. "I saw you leave."

Luna raises her eyebrows. "Okay, you two are the strangest mers in the ocean. First you wait forever to couple, and then it doesn't bother you to be apart. Maybe I need to hang out closer to shore to see if I can save a human of my own."

The thought bothers me more than it should. It's different than finding a human and giving them the choice to immerse in this world. While I might've eventually chosen this life to be with Carter, I wouldn't have done so on a whim. I'd have done things a lot differently. Carter knows this.

A flicker of sadness darkens his eyes. "It wasn't that simple. I got extremely lucky. She might not have fallen in love with me," Carter says.

Luna raises her brows. "How could she not?"

A rosy blush blooms across Carter's tan face, but he doesn't say anything.

"Right?" I ask. "There was never a doubt in my mind I wouldn't love the boy who changed my world. We were both lucky." I hope my words make him feel better. Every time he sees me unhappy, I know he blames himself. And even though I'm miserable at times, I'm thankful he saved me, a girl he had only known a short time.

He spins me around to kiss my lips. "You changed mine, too."

Luna releases a long sigh as she smiles at us. It's enough to make me laugh and pull away from Carter. Giselle would probably make a face and tell us to get a room if she were here. That's how different merpeople and humans are. Luna has probably spent her whole life thinking about finding her mate—Carter, too. But me? No. Dating was the last thing on my mind. I never imagined my life would turn into an accidental love story.

And I refuse to believe that's what my life will always be about.

Carter turns his gaze to the princess. "Well, Luna. Thank you for keeping Ava company through the night."

"I had fun," she says to me.

She dips under the water, and I follow suit to grab her hand to stop her from leaving.

"Hey, want to have breakfast with us? We have some plans to make, remember?"

She grins, releasing a breath of bubbles. "I'd love to."

I haven't looked forward to something as much as I do in this moment. And for once, my plans don't revolve around Carter. If only I didn't feel bad about it.

"Say it again, Ava," Starla says, swimming around my room.

I pop the last piece of the seaweed wrapped tuna Carter spent nearly an hour fishing and preparing for me into my mouth. Luna smirks at me from the spot near my window where a butterfly fish floats over her shoulder, hiding in her black tresses.

"I hereby promise to share the very essence of my being with the merman who—" The words fade from my thought. The coupling ceremony is a lot of memorizing, and I usually use note cards for this kind of thing.

"Promised his life to me to live as part of the great sea," Luna says only to me.

I repeat what she says so Starla can hear. "I promise to cherish the gift of life with love, loyalty, respect, and thankfulness," I add, remembering what I'm promising to Carter. I kind of hate that none of these are my own words.

Leaning back, I thump my tail against the sand. Luna grins at me while Starla glares. She places her hands on her hips and would probably wag her finger at me if she thought she could get away with scolding me like a child.

"You need to try harder and say it like you mean it," Starla says.

I roll my eyes. I can't help it. "Well, I don't mean them when I have to say it to you."

Luna gasps in my mind, hiding her smiling face with her hands. She slinks toward the window cutout, preparing to exit if things grow even more uncomfortable.

"Are you going to hold everything against me forever?" Starla asks, sinking into the sand. "I thought you might've changed your mind since you agreed to go through with this."

It's no different than when I did it to get her off my back. I don't say it, though.

I direct my attention to only her to tell her that of course I'm going to hold a grudge against her forever—that she doesn't deserve anything less for stealing the ring Carter gave me right off my finger. For pressuring me and belittling me and making me feel like my emotions don't matter.

But Carter swims into the room, cutting off my thought. He wears a ridiculous sea grass bow around his neck, looking like the sea version of a shirtless male dancer my mom and her friends laughed over when they went to Vegas last year.

"What're you wearing?" I ask only to Carter. "Please, tell me you're planning to give me a private dance later."

I've never seen him turn so red in the face. Ever. Nothing usually fazes him, but I guess he thinks the bow-tie is as stupid as I think it is with his bare chest and aqua tail.

He rips the bow-tie off and tosses it at me. It drifts through the water on the current created by his tail, and I snatch it from the water and twirl it between my fingers, smiling at him as he composes himself.

"I knew that thing was a horrible idea," he says only to me. "But my dad—"

"Oh, my God. It's part of the coupling ceremony, isn't it?" I slap my palms on my tail and laugh through the water, bubbles escaping my mouth. "How on earth am I expected to hold a straight face?"

He rubs the back of his neck. "I could wear it until it stops being funny."

"Only if it comes with a dance."

He grins, swimming toward me to wrap his arms around me. "I think I can work something out."

Luna and Starla watch us without a word as we share our private conversation. They probably thought the bow-tie was cute. After a moment, Starla excuses herself to talk to Mateo in the living room.

"I take it you hate the coupling bow," Luna says with a smile.

Carter steals it from me and tears it in two. "You'd understand if you ever lived on land."

"Maybe I could come up with something different," I say. "Does it have to be a bow-tie? What about a necklace or a cord?"

Luna claps her hands. "I could help! Would you mind if Ava came to the palace with me? I planned to create something for her as well."

Carter leans back on his elbows. "Even if I did have a problem, which I don't, Ava could go if she wanted to."

While I don't want to go to the palace, I know I must agree because in a few short hours, Luna will be stealing two sea stones that'll allow us to return to shore in human form. All through the afternoon, we've been discussing ways to get away without people noticing. And going to the castle to work on my coupling ceremony top seemed like the best excuse—one no one could deny me.

"That'd be great, Luna," I say like it's the first time I've heard the suggestion.

"Then it's settled." She pushes off the floor to take my hand. "Let's go."

With a quick kiss to Carter, I let Luna drag me through the window cutout so we don't have to face Carter's parents, since Starla might ask to join us. Instead, we dart through the colony, all smiles, thinking about the open air, the crashing waves of the shore, and the beautiful legs that'll soon take me home.

13

BREAKING THE SURFACE

"GOOD EVENING, YOUR MAJESTY," I say.

Luna guides me from what she likes to call her workroom and into the grand hall of the palace. She spends a lot of time in her little space creating different tops, because she always dreamed of going to the land.

"What a nice surprise, Ava. I hope you're feeling better after yesterday," the king says, swimming closer. He acts like he didn't just threaten to ruin my life yesterday, but it's not like I can give him the attitude he deserves.

My cheeks warm, fighting between embarrassment and anger. "Much better." The less I say the better.

"Ava and I were just working on some pieces for her big day," Luna says, cutting in. "So, if you don't mind, there are some things we need to collect if that's okay, Dad. I thought some sea glass jewelry would look amazing." Luna holds up a grass woven bag, which contains everything we need to go to land.

He grins without looking at its contents. "I don't mind at all. Will Carter be escorting you two?"

Luna nods for me. "He's just finishing up some family obligations and will meet us soon."

She lies so easily that I almost think Carter will show up at any moment to guide us over the walls and into the vast, darkening sea. In reality, he has no idea we're even leaving. If he did, we'd definitely not be heading toward shore.

"Then have fun, you two." The king responds like any normal dad would, and I'm kind of taken aback that he doesn't insist on seeing Carter first. All he does is smile once more before turning and swimming away to his living quarters, leaving Luna and me in the grand room.

Luna watches the archway to her father's living quarters for a moment before she motions for me to follow her. Heading toward a small tunnel below the balcony, she waves me forward and then enters first with me right on her tail. We enter a windowless room with a shocking amount of glittering jewels scattered about. Different jewelry pieces, including several crowns and tiaras rest on small shelf cutouts. My eyes immediately fall on a gold box, like a small treasure chest, but it isn't locked. The lid is open and within it are hundreds of silver rings just like the one Carter had given me.

"It's rare for someone to request one, but they're always here to show people they can make a choice," Luna says.

"I'm surprised the king allows anyone to leave at all," I say.

"He does because all merpeople eventually return to the ocean. Living among humans also brings knowledge to the seas. He has his own reasons, but those are the two I know for sure." Luna scoops up two rings and hands one to me.

"Have you ever transformed before?" I ask as I slide the ring on my finger.

She shakes her head. "I'm nervous. I don't even know how it works."

I tilt my head to the side wondering if I should stop her from putting the ring on. I let her do it anyway. "I think I can help you. We'll wait until we're swimming distance to the shore though before I explain. The last thing I want is for you to accidentally try and do it right here. I once transformed when I was way below the surface, and I could've drowned."

She slides the ring off her finger and sticks it into the bag across her chest. "That sounds awful."

I shrug. "It was but not the worst thing to happen to me." Actually drowning is probably number one followed by my sister getting swept away to sea.

Luna peers around once more. "This was, wasn't it?"

I shake my head. "This is just the low point of a swell. You're about to make things a million times better. I just don't know how I'll ever repay you."

She smirks. "You don't owe me anything. This is enough for me." She sounds like Giselle. I wonder how she would react if I introduced her to my best friend. Giselle would die of excitement if she knew she met a mermaid princess. *Too dangerous, Aves.*

I twist the sea stone ring on my finger. This one feels differently than the one Carter gave me—this one is simply the key to transforming into a human and not the ring that held a promise of eternity.

"I think we have everything we need," Luna says. "Ready?"

I smile. "More ready than ever."

Luna holds my hand as we swim through the glowing water. She's not nearly as fast as Carter, and I'm able to keep up with her pretty easily. We don't talk much, racing through the current, swerving around schools of fish, the occasional shark, a jellyfish bloom, and even a squad of squids.

The more I swim toward home, the more familiar the sea is to navigate. When we reach the familiar kelp forest, I slow down. In a few short minutes, we'll be on the shore of Azure Waters, and I'll have my legs.

"We need to get as close to the shore as possible," I think to Luna. "It's dark, so the beach should be empty near my house."

"I can't believe I get to see where you lived as a human," she says, spinning excitedly in the water, tangling her arm in kelp.

With a quick slice of my nail, I cut her free. "If you like it enough, maybe we can come back and actually explore a little. But we'd need to prepare more. People wear actual clothes."

She bobs her head. "I can't wait!"

Taking her hand, I pull us forward, weaving our way along the bottom of the kelp forest. Only one boat floats along the surface, and I let it be instead of cutting the hook from the empty line that floats through the current.

The water lightens as we enter the shallows that will lead to the beach. The almost full moon hangs in the sky, casting a luminous glow on the rippling surface. With a wave of my hand, I motion for Luna to wait for me while I ascend to the surface. Slowly popping my head out, I peer around the black sea. Whitecaps crest in the close distance, lighting the shore just for us, welcoming me home.

A few lights glow from the beach mansions, but the sand looks abandoned from here. I dive back under and wave for Luna to follow behind me, and I head close enough to graze my tail along the sandy floor when I float upright.

"Go ahead and put the ring on. All you have to do is want to go to the land with all your heart. Your body will do the rest. Don't be afraid when you feel the pain. It happens pretty fast," I say, cringing when she frowns. "It's only like mild cramps. Don't worry."

I close my eyes when she closes hers. I imagine what it was like the first time I changed back to my human form. How Carter held my hand, talking me through it. How my body felt like a thousand pinpricks were tickling my skin. How it felt to kick my legs.

The familiar cramps start from my caudal fin, trailing up

my tail to my stomach. My muscles seize, causing me to bend forward and grip my tail as my slippery scales smooth to human skin.

"Whoa, Ava," Luna says in my mind.

I don't open my eyes until the temperature of the water changes. I stare through the blurry water, Luna in front of me still in her mermaid form. If she's thinking anything, I can no longer hear it, and if I don't break the surface soon, I'll drown because my new lungs beg me to release the saltwater to take in air.

Fear doesn't even have a chance to take hold. Luna arches her back and then bends forward, transforming right before my eyes. The shimmer of her golden skin fades into a deep tan. I watch in awe as her gold tail smoothes and browns right before it splits apart and transforms into two human legs.

Her eyes snap open a moment later, fear lining her deep blue eyes, and she reaches out to me. Together, we head toward the surface and expel the ocean from our lungs.

Luna struggles in the water. She tries to kick her legs, but they're unfamiliar to her like the first time I got my tail. Carter had to teach me how to use it. Slinging one arm around her, I kick toward the shore for the both of us.

Luna watches how my arm cuts through the water and how I use all my limbs to help us along unlike how we usually swim with our tails. After a moment, she doggie paddles with both her hands until a cresting wave propels us toward the shore.

My knees hit the sand, and another wave washes over us. Luna coughs and spits next to me, not used to relying on air, and I push her forward into the sand. I drag her by her wrists until we're both out of the crashing waves, and then I fall over next to her and laugh, staring at the glittering night sky.

"I did it!" Luna yells out, her sweet voice echoing through the air. She sounds child-like with the excitement, and it makes me smile even more.

I fling my hand out and cover her mouth. "Shhh! People live like twenty feet behind us." I didn't exactly pick the most secluded place to return to shore, but I don't care. About a half a mile away lies my house.

"Who cares? We have *legs*." She lifts her foot into the air and runs her fingers over her knee, admiring herself.

"Yeah, but we're half *naked*. Where's your bag? It's not normal to find girls half naked in the water. It'll be bad enough if they see us wearing sea plants."

Luna pulls the sea grass woven bag from across her chest and pulls out the two skirts we spent all afternoon weaving together. They're only about seven inches long, but we didn't have a lot of time to make something more appropriate.

It doesn't matter though. I don't plan on bumping into anyone.

Luna hands me the grass skirt, and I tie it around my hips. It's just long enough that I'm covered, but if I bend over, my butt would show for the whole empty beach to see. It takes me a moment to compose myself, and when I do, I find the energy to stand. Surprisingly, my legs don't wobble. Even though I've been without them for weeks, I still haven't forgotten how to use them. The almost eighteen years of walking has helped.

Luna claps her hands like I've just performed the most amazing trick. I laugh, brushing back my wet hair. Kneeling next to her, I help her with her own skirt. Her black hair clings to her damp skin, and we're covered in sand, but that doesn't stop us from enjoying every minute we have of breathing in the cool ocean air.

The goosebumps don't even bother me. I enjoy the chill that causes me to shiver.

"I'm going to need some help," Luna says, holding out her arms to me.

I grab her hands and pull her to her feet, but she stumbles and falls back to the sand in a fit of laughter. I sit down next to her, tapping her new legs. They're longer than mine and so smooth and unblemished. Brand new.

"So, you have to make sure to bend your knees. Take it slow." I get back to my feet and help her up again.

This time, she just stands in place like a wobbling newborn giraffe. Her legs shake, supporting her weight, but she doesn't fall over.

"This is amazing, Ava. Thank you." She hugs me as she holds onto me.

"I should be thanking you, Luna. You don't even know how much this means to me. If Carter weren't back in the water, I'd suggest we stay and never go back." I shift her weight against me and take a small step forward.

"I wish. I just want to see everything!" She studies how I move my feet through the sand and takes her first step without stumbling.

I continue to shuffle, one step at a time, slowly showing her how to use her new legs. After twenty minutes, Luna manages to take a step without leaning all her weight on me. She'll be walking in no time, adapting easily to her new form.

Gaining more confidence, Luna lets go of me and stumbles a few feet forward without falling. She holds her arms out wide for balance and glances over her shoulder at me with a brilliant smile on her face.

"Did you see that?" she asks.

"You walked!" I clap my hands. "Soon you'll be running."

She takes a few more steps before she falls to her knees. "I'll walk the entire beach if I have to. I'll get these legs working."

I move forward and help her back to her feet. "Maybe in the other direction. That's my house." Raising my hand, I point at the beautiful sea green Victorian mansion looming a few houses away. No lights glow within, and I guess tonight must be a Friday night, because it's one of the few days my parents go out.

"It looks empty," Luna says, gazing to where I'm pointing.

"My parents go out sometimes."

"We should check it out."

I turn to stare into Luna's smiling face. My mind screams that her suggestion is a terrible idea, that I could get caught and will have to explain how I made it back from Washington so soon and without Carter.

But it's my home, and I miss it. My heart wants nothing more than to take a quick peek.

I don't say anything for a minute. I've already made the decision, but I can't find the will to force my legs to do the moving. So Luna does it for me. She grabs my hand and yanks me along, making me fall over as she tries to walk too fast on her wobbling knees.

When we're standing mere feet from my back patio, I stop in place and peer around at my neighbors. Mr. Johnson's bedroom light is on, but the rest of his house is dark. And like my parents, the Franks are out enjoying their Friday.

"Wait here," I say to Luna. "I'm going to go around front and let myself in. I'll open the door for you."

She grins as I motion her to sit on the patio chair. She kicks her legs up on the table and stares at her toes while I walk through the side gate that'll take me to the stairs leading up to the guest apartment.

I punch in the code to the key box and let myself into the guest apartment. Only the nightlight in the hallway illuminates the place. I stop in front of my bedroom, peering in, seeing it exactly how I left it, though all the clothes I left behind on the floor have been put away.

I jog down the stairs and head to the game room to open

the back door for Luna. Reaching out my hand, I pull her from the chair and help her climb the small step into my house. The more she walks, the steadier she gets on her feet.

Using a towel from the storage bench, I dust the sand off her as to not leave behind traces that we were ever here. She peers around my dark house with a smile on her face and shuffles toward the wall of pictures my mom has had hanging in this room since I was a child.

"You have a sister," Luna says, pointing to a picture of me and Bailey on the beach right outside this house.

"She died," I say. I'd love to just simply answer yes, but then Luna would have more questions for me.

A frown crosses her face. "I'm sorry."

I shrug. "It was a long time ago."

Sliding my hands over her shoulders, I guide her to my favorite place in the house—the kitchen. Her eyes widen, and we step into the wood and marble room with gleaming stainless steel kitchen appliances.

She perches on a barstool, running her fingers over everything she can at the bar that looks out the window near our pool. I immediately head to the fridge and open the door. There's no way I'm going to let her go back to Pearlestria without trying human food.

On the top shelf in a plastic container is a half eaten cheesecake. I frown as I stare at it, but what was I to expect? My parents love dessert and their baker is supposedly traveling the coast. I just wish it didn't feel like they were cheating on me with the Azure Waters Cake Boutique.

Luna watches me pout into the fridge, and I force myself to grin as I pull out the cheesecake. Taking out two paper plates and two plastic forks from the bottom cupboard of to-go stuff, I serve us two small pieces of the cheesecake using a butter knife. I rinse it off and stick it in the dishwasher with the rest of the dirty dishes.

I hold out Luna's fork. "Try this. Carter tells me that he'd give up his tail completely if it meant he could eat dessert for all of eternity."

She doesn't hesitate before she sticks the fork in her mouth, much braver than me when it comes to trying new foods. She'd probably taste anything I gave her. Closing her eyes, she moans, savoring the piece of cheesecake.

"Mmm," she says, shoveling the rest of the small piece in her mouth, barely chewing it. "I could get used to this. Way better than fish."

"Right?" I eat my piece of cheesecake just as quickly.

When we're done, I bury the evidence deep in the trash before I guide Luna through the house. I turn on and off the TV, blast the radio for a minute, and then I grab the house phone from its receiver.

"I'm going to call my friend real quick. Then we can go," I say.

She pouts but doesn't argue. "It's weird that you can't just send her your thoughts."

"Telepathy only works when we're mermaids. In human form, we use telephones, which is pretty close. I just dial a number, and she'll pick up and talk to me without actually being here." I dial Giselle's number, one of the only ones I have memorized, and wait for her to answer.

"Hello," she says after the third ring.

"Hey, Gi," I say. "I don't have a lot of time, but I just wanted to call you and say hi."

"Oh, my God! You're *home!* Does this mean—"

"Yes and no. I'll tell you later, okay? I wanted to see if you wanted to meet again. I need to borrow some *things.*"

"You're not alone." She picks up on my need to keep things simple.

"No."

"What about tomorrow? I can leave a bag on the rocks for you."

I open my mouth to say yes, but a door slams, causing me to drop the phone to the wooden floor. It clatters away, leaving me no choice to forget about it. I can't risk getting caught. Instead, I grab Luna's hand and spin to look in the direction of loud footsteps.

14

BAD IDEA

"AVA! PRINCESS! WHAT THE HELL are you two think-ing?" Carter's angry voice echoes through the hallway leading to the game room.

Luna steps in front of me like she can somehow lessen the blow of being discovered. Neither of us answers as we meet his narrowed gaze. He's completely naked, dripping saltwater on the wooden floor, and I just stare at him in all his humanness. He came straight from the sea, following the spark that guaran-tees we can always find each other no matter the form we take.

"Well?" he asks, placing his hands on his hips. I wish he'd at least try to cover up in front of Luna, but he's so mad that he doesn't even care. I'd die if my parents came home this second to discover the three of us in the house.

Luna clears her throat. "This was all my idea."

I slide past her to face my mate. It wasn't Luna's entire idea. I did agree to come here. "Please, let's talk about this out-side. I have to clean up before my parents get home." It might also give Carter a minute to cool off.

He finally realizes he's dripping sandy water on the floor while giving us both a show, though Luna keeps her eyes trained on Carter's face and not the rest of his muscular body. Pushing him toward the back door, I gently press my fingers into his shoulders hoping my touch will calm him down. He's never been this angry at me, and I hate it more than I thought I would. I don't think he should be angry at all. He should be happy I had the chance to transform into my human body.

I scoop up the towel I used to dry Luna off with and hand it to him so he can cover up. I steal another towel from the cupboard and do my best to clean up the floor while Carter and Luna wait for me on the sand a few yards from my back patio. I flick off the light, lock the back door, and jog toward the others.

"They won't miss the towels," I say, wringing the one I used to clean the floor between my hands. "We have dozens."

Carter turns to face the ocean without responding. I half expect him to grab my hand to pull me back into the waves with him, but he doesn't. He just stares at the almost full moon reflecting on the black waters.

"I'm sorry, okay?" I say, his silence screaming at me louder than his voice ever could. "I didn't think you'd freak out so much. We're just having fun. Luna wanted to see the land, and she has access to sea stones, so we figured why not? No one will know."

His spins around. "You think this is a game? You *stole* from the king and went against his wishes. You put the princess in jeopardy. This is serious, Ava. Why would you risk our futures for a trip to shore?"

"What future? The king stole *my* future!" I don't mean to scream. My loud voice is bound to wake the entire neighborhood. "I knew you wouldn't understand. This is why I didn't tell you. You're so concerned about yourself and your access to the land that I'm pretty sure it wouldn't even matter to you if I never transformed into a human again."

Carter jerks back like I slapped him.

Luna steps a few feet away, and I wish she didn't stand there and listen as I basically stoop as low as I possibly can because I'm so upset that Carter doesn't understand me at all. I've been dying to come to land, to get my legs back. Instead of humoring me and letting me enjoy this moment, he's made me feel like a criminal—like I'll be the reason we don't have a future.

I can't bring my eyes to Carter. He stands in front of me, his shock and hurt flooding through me in waves. I know I'm not being fair by putting words in his mouth, but nothing is fair in my life.

We all stand in silence for a long while. Luna shifts on her feet, probably wishing to head back to the ocean. Carter doesn't do anything but stare at me like I'm some stranger standing before him. Maybe I am. Now that I have legs and remember everything I've been deprived of, I can't help thinking that going along with things like a good little mermaid is the wrong way to go. I should fight harder for what I want. If the king thinks he can push me around, he will. *But he can push you around...*

I swallow the lump in my throat. "Say something, Carter."

He kicks at the sand. "I don't know even know how to respond, Ava. How can you even think that? If it makes you feel that badly about me returning to land, then I won't." He tugs his ring off his finger and tosses it onto the sand, throwing the one thing that keeps him in his human form to the ground.

My eyes widen, and I jerk down to swipe it from the sand before the surf carries it away. I grip the ring in my hand, watching Carter slowly back away from me. I can't believe he did that.

"Carter, take it back," I say.

He shakes his head. "No. I want you to understand, Ava. I don't care about the land or the sea. I don't give a damn where we end up. All I care about is you. I chose you."

With those words, he dives into the ocean, leaving me and Luna on the sand. I step forward into the water to go after him, but I'm not so sure I can face him after all this. All I want to do is run back to my house and crawl into my bed. I want to pretend like I didn't just shatter the heart of the boy who'd die for me.

Instead of doing either, I fall to my knees in the sand and sob. Salty tears blend with the ocean water splashing my face. Even though I'm sucking in huge gulps of air, I still can't breathe.

Tonight was supposed to be the best night ever. It was supposed to be fun as I showed Luna what my world was like before turning into a mermaid. But now, my human life doesn't seem so important anymore. Legs mean nothing if I can't run into the arms of the boy I love.

I sniffle, wiping my cheeks with the backs of my hands. "I'm sorry you had to see that. I ruined everything."

Luna kneels next to me, sliding her arm around my shoulders. "He'll forgive you, Ava."

I press my lips together, staring at the dark sea. "He shouldn't."

"Why? We made a mistake."

"Because I still don't feel like it was a mistake, Luna. And I want to come back again." I shift my gaze to watch her reaction.

She smirks. "So do I. I don't even want to leave."

I don't want to either. But I have to. Because my heart hurts too much to even think about leaving things as they are when I know I need to suck it up and make things right with Carter. I'm supposed to spend the rest of my life with him. The coupling ceremony is in two days. Unless I don't show up. *How can you even think that? Don't lash out at Carter for something the king did.*

"But we have to," I say, pushing myself from the sand.

Luna stands next to me. "I know."

We peer around us once more. Luna removes the sea stone ring from her finger and drops it into her grass woven bag. I slide Carter's ring onto my finger on top of mine for safe keeping, though his is too big. As much as I know I should have Luna return my ring to the king, I can't find the nerve to give it back to her. I want to have the option to return to land if I ever need it.

Luna holds out her hand for me to take, and we walk into the waves together. I help her swim far enough away from shore, and we transform back into our mermaid forms without a problem. It's easier to control than I remember, and Luna doesn't have a choice since she's not wearing her ring.

A soft light glows in the distance like a beacon calling my name. I know it's Carter without even having to see him up close. He might be angry, but he wouldn't abandon me to find my own way back. Just knowing he still cares enough to watch out for me makes me feel a tiny bit better. Luna was right about him forgiving me for tonight, but I can't help wondering if he could forgive me for my unofficial plans to return in the future. At what point will he stop forgiving me?

I hope I never find out.

Without saying a word, Luna and I swim in Carter's direction. He doesn't greet me with a smile, but he doesn't pull away when I twine my fingers through his. As long as we're swimming, I can forget about all my troubling feelings. I can pretend the world doesn't keep spinning and time doesn't keep ticking. I can pretend I didn't hurt the boy I'm about to vow my life to.

But pretending won't change things. Only I can do that.

After dropping off Luna with a promise to meet with her tomorrow, I follow Carter back to our house where I hear half a dozen unique voices echo through my head as Mateo and Starla visit with their friends much too late for me to deal with. All I want to do is sink into bed and hope that sleep can erase at least some of the hurt in Carter's eyes.

By the frown puckering his bottom lip, I can see he had the

same idea as me. But it'd be rude to ask the others to leave. It's part of merpeople customs for guests to treat the home like it's their own. It's why I didn't know our house didn't belong to Starla.

Before Carter can swim through the door, I pull him to a stop. His shoulders sag, and I take both his hands in mine, studying his face for the first time since the beach. His blue-green eyes shadow with a sadness comparable to the day Starla stole my ring right off my finger, condemning me to the ocean, and I hate that this time the sadness isn't for me but because of me.

I pull both rings from my finger and hold them out to him. "I want you to hold my new ring for safe keeping. This way you'll know when I choose to go back to shore."

He rubs his hand over the back of his neck. "You're going to let me hold the ring even though you know I don't want you going back? How do you know I'll give it back to you?"

I puff a bubble through my lips. "Because I trust you, Carter. And I don't want to have to lie to you about it any-more." I already have a heavy heart from the lie I'll probably take to my grave.

He puts the rings on the chain around his neck and swims closer until our noses almost touch, but he doesn't kiss me. Instead, he rests his forehead against mine. "I wish you didn't lie to me in the first place. I know you were desperate and the op-portunity arose with Princess Luna, but what if the king was using her to set you up? What if this was all a big test and you failed?"

As quickly as the fear arises, it fades, because I don't think the king would do that—or Luna for that matter. Why go through the trouble to test me when the king already holds my world in his hands? And as for Luna, she wanted it more than I did. I could see it in her eyes. She wasn't lying to me.

"She doesn't like to be called princess, and I know it wasn't a test. Luna doesn't agree with her father." A million other reasons storm through my mind, but I don't share them with Carter.

"I hope you're right," he says.

"I *am*. Trust me."

Carter closes the inch of distance between us and kisses me like our lips can erase everything that has happened tonight. He holds me against him, our hearts beating against each other in perfect sync. Sliding his hands down my sides, he explores the curve of my hips before scooping me into his arms, holding me from the backside of my tail.

"I do trust you, Ava," Carter says, projecting his voice into my mind. "I'm just worried. The king could change his mind about anything at any moment if you give him a reason to."

"I'm aware of that. He made it crystal clear," I say.

"He threatened you." He doesn't have to ask. He already knows. I'm not great at hiding the emotions that cross my face.

"He's the king. He's looking out for his kingdom." It's all I can say to stop myself from pouring my heart out to Carter about everything.

"And I'm your mate. I'm looking out for you."

"Then you understand. I'm looking out for you too, Carter." Cupping his face in my hands, I peer into his eyes, hoping he sees the truth in my words. "I know I'm selfish, and I can be a pain most days, but I just want you to know that I want you to be happy, too. I want to keep you safe and protect your heart. I am really sorry for how things unfolded on the shore. I said those awful things because I was hurting."

"I'm sorry, too. Sorry because you were partially right. I don't want to lose my access to the land. I hate that I feel this way; it's why I gave you my ring. Because you were right, and I shouldn't think like that." His eyebrows knit together as he speaks the words in my mind. "But you do matter to me. I would care if you could never transform again. I'd risk stealing a ring myself, and if that didn't work, I'd give you mine."

I hold the two rings around his neck between my fingers. "But now you don't have to. Luna won't tell, you know. She's keeping hers, too."

A smirk crosses his face. "So you're willing to take the risk to go to land?"

"The king has already stolen my chance to choose everything in my life. I'm only stealing back the one choice that was supposed to be mine to begin with," I say. "And admit it, even though you were mad at me, you loved every second we were together on the shore."

He sucks in his bottom lip. "So, so much."

"Then let's go back. Just me and you. No one will miss us."

He hesitates. "This is a bad idea."

I kiss him, sharing with him a memory of me with legs he won't be able to resist. "But a good one, too."

He shudders before breaking away to swim in circles around me a few times. "Ava." His voice sounds barely above a whisper in my mind. "You make it incredibly hard to say no."

"You're saying no?" It wasn't exactly the answer I had expected. My bottom lip pouts, but there's not much I can say or do.

He swims around me a few more times before stopping for another kiss where he projects the same image I shared with him back to me, like he can't get it off his mind. "I said you make it hard to say no, not that I was saying no."

I pull his bottom lip between my teeth. "Really?"

Without answering, he hooks his arms around my waist, and we take off into the dark ocean.

15

BACK TO REALITY

THE EARLY MORNING SUN WARMS my skin. I stir in Carter's arms, water lapping over our legs. We lie together on the secluded beach of an uninhabited island somewhere in the Pacific Ocean. It was the only place he agreed to come with me far from humans.

When I shift to sit up, Carter moans before pulling me back down next to him. Sand clings to his tan skin, his chest rising and falling as he breathes in the crisp sea air. The roar of the waves hums in my ears, and I can't stop myself from curling against him.

The night couldn't have been more perfect—exactly how I imagine it's supposed to be—just me and him, enjoying both the land and ocean with no one to worry about. Another wave crashes the shore, rolling over us, and it's enough to pull Carter back to reality. The one I've wanted to avoid—the one where I have no control.

Carter's blue-green eyes shine bright in the sun. I had almost forgotten how pretty they were in the light. He tucks my sandy hair behind my ear before kissing my jaw only to work his way to my lips. He smiles against my mouth, inhaling a deep breath of the sea-perfumed air around us.

"I don't want to go back," he says after a moment. "It could take them a while to find us if we stay right here."

I close my eyes, just imagining what it'd be like to make

this beautifully desolate island our home, but it's no different than the sea. My family and friends aren't here. It's probably the type of life the king would expect us to have, far from human civilization.

"Not with the full moon tomorrow," I say. We can only stay out of the ocean for so long before it forces us back. And with the full moon comes our coupling ceremony. I couldn't run to shore to escape it even if I wanted to.

"And our ceremony," Carter adds, thinking the same thought as me except he says it almost dreamily.

"Yeah, that." The words come out flat.

He takes my hands in his. "Why do I get the feeling you're less than thrilled about it? I thought this was what you wanted."

"It's you I want. The ceremony—" I snap my mouth shut. "I'm nervous is all." Better than saying the king made the decision for me.

"I am, too." He tilts his head to the brilliant blue sky. His words make me feel slightly better. "But we'll be together. I'll make sure it's everything you hoped for."

Except I haven't hoped for anything. All I hope is to get through it without puking from nerves or making a fool of myself. At this point, I just want it to be over with so I don't have the expectation hanging over my head. And it sucks that I feel this way.

"I need to be honest with you, Carter," I say.

I don't know if it's because we're cuddling on a beach in our human bodies or if it's the fact that the king is far away and can't intimidate me here—either way, I can't stop thinking about how I'm lying to Carter. It makes it even harder to swallow the idea of the coupling ceremony if we start our new lives together with me being dishonest. The king was crazy to think I could never tell Carter. I have to. Even if it risks losing the hope of remaining in contact with my family, however far-fetched that is under the king's new rules for me.

He sits up straighter, digging his bare feet into the sand. "You don't want to go through with the ceremony." Rubbing his hands over his face, he groans while shaking his head, like he knew it was coming, though it's not what I'm about to say.

"It's not that, Carter." I suck in a deep, shaky breath to help me get through this. "It's just—well—" Why can't I spit the words out? *Because you don't want to hurt him.*

Continuing with the lie will hurt more if he ever found out.

"Ava," Carter says, "you can tell me anything."

Doesn't make it any easier. "The coupling ceremony wasn't my idea," I finally say. "King Attilonious didn't give me a choice. He thinks by not agreeing to officially couple with you that I'm turning my back on the sea. He thinks the only way to accept who I am is if I accept my position as your mate. But Carter, please, you can't tell him. He told me I couldn't let you know." Telling the truth has never felt so good and awful all at once.

His expression morphs to anger, and he shoves his hands into the sand. "Damn him. He had no right. And to demand that you lie to me?"

I'd love nothing more than to watch Carter swim home and stand up to the king, but that can only end badly. I wrap my arms around his tense shoulders. "This doesn't change anything, Carter. We're going through with the ceremony."

"But you don't want to," he says.

I rest my cheek on his shoulder. "I didn't say that. I said the king didn't give me a choice. Tomorrow, we're making this official in the sea, and then we can focus on the rest of our lives, okay?"

"I don't know, Ava." He shifts in the sand to reach up and run his fingers down my cheek as he looks into my eyes.

"What don't you know? I thought you wanted to do this?"

"When I knew you were in it for us, without a single doubt in your mind."

It is the only reason I'm doing it—for us. To help us while we're under the king's fin. Leaning forward, I brush my lips against his, hoping he can sense I'm not saying my next words only to make him feel better. "This is for us, Carter. Don't you see? Everything I agree to do is for us. I love you, and even if it's not how I imagined things turning out, it doesn't mean I don't like how they're going. I realize that now more than ever. So, will you go back with me and make things official? Or should I prepare to be stood up?"

He's quiet for a long moment. "I'd never stand you up, Aves. But after tomorrow, I'm not going to sit back and hope for the best. I'm getting us out of Pearlestria and away from the king."

"How?"

He shrugs. "I'll figure it out."

We sneak in through the window cutout like I would if I were coming in late at home in Azure Waters. It's silly, but the last thing we need is to be bombarded with questions while his parents are here, living in our house for a few days like they own the place.

Carter stores my new ring in the metal chest where we keep all my other human possessions—at least the ones he managed to bring me from the shore—before we settle onto our blanket in the sand. I smack my tail against the ground a few times, still adjusting to the lack of legs I had quickly grown used to having.

Carter rests on his side, leaning on his elbow, tracing circles on my stomach, occasionally pinching the ridge that separates my skin from the scales of my tail between his thumb and index finger.

Even though he doesn't send his thoughts to me, I can see he has a lot on his mind. I hate that he knows I'm only doing the ceremony willingly to make things easier. He says he'll get us away from here, but I know it doesn't mean escaping to land. We're in Pearlestria for a reason. The king wants to keep an eye on me.

We don't have a moment to discuss it though, because Mateo's voice rings through our minds, asking if we're awake yet.

Neither of us answers right away. We lie quietly next to each other like if we don't move, Carter's dad will just go away.

"Son? You have a visitor," Mateo says, hovering in the archway. Carter's father's dark hair flows around him like a curtain, and he smiles at us as he pushes it from his face. "It's King Attilonious and Princess Luna"

I stiffen in Carter's arms. The last merperson in the ocean I want to see is now in our house. A million fearful thoughts rush through my mind. What if he found out I took Luna to the shore? Or that I told Carter the truth? So much could be so wrong.

Carter side glances me, but his face remains expressionless. He pushes from the sandy floor, tugging me along with him by my waist. He knows I won't move unless he makes me. I'd rather hide in here until he finds out what the king's visit is about. It must be important if he didn't send a messenger to summon us.

"Oh, God. He knows. You were right." I direct the thought only to Carter as we slide past Mateo.

"Calm down, Ava. Our ceremony is tomorrow. It could be nothing," he answers.

I grip his fingers. "It could be the end."

"Ava!" Luna swims across the room when she sees us and thrusts her arms around me in a hug comparable to one Giselle would give me. Who knew a friendship could blossom so quickly, but things are much more intense in the sea than they are on land. "I can't wait to show you the finished pieces for tomorrow."

I stand still in her arms a moment. She projects her voice to everyone in the room. A moment later, I realize I'm frozen solid, and I bring my hands up to hug the mermaid back. "I'm so excited!" I send my own voice to everyone. "I don't even know how to thank you."

She brings her gaze to mine, directing a thought to only me. "You already have. Everything's fine. Relax before my dad thinks something is wrong."

I release a bubble through my lips and turn to the king with a bow. "Welcome to our home, my king."

Carter bows as well. "It is an honor, your majesty." The thought is as relaxed as he is, and I wish I could learn to compose myself at all times.

"If I'd known Ava's company would bring my daughter such happiness, I'd have summoned you both sooner," King Attilonious says. Except I might not have enjoyed her company if I were forced so quickly into things in Pearlestria. I don't mention it, though.

Carter bows to Luna. "Princess Luna has made quite the impression on my mate as well, your majesty. A friend apart from me was exactly what Ava needed. You know how the human world works. Relationships with friends can run as deep as family."

"Is that true?" Luna asks only me.

I nod my head. "I love my friends dearly. Just as fiercely as I love Carter. You know, Luna. You remind me of my best friend on land. I'd love it if you could meet her. I think you'd get along."

"You want me to meet your human friend? Oh, Ocean. I'd

love that. I think I understand what Carter meant about differ-ent relationships. I can already feel a bond to you." She smiles shyly.

"Same," I say. And I mean it. There's something that draws me to Luna, and I trust her.

"Ava? Did you hear King Attilonious? He asked if it would be all right if you and Luna spent the day together so the rest of us can get things prepared for tomorrow. She can help you with everything you'll need to do." Carter asks, breaking my attention away from Luna.

With heated cheeks, I turn my attention to the king. "I'd love that, my king. But are you sure I'm not needed?"

Luna grabs my hand. "Why would you be? It's Carter's job to prepare everything, not yours."

Hmm. Well, that's different. I thought everything would fall to me, like most things fall on the bride in the human world. All I know is I have to memorize the vows I don't really want to say. I always imagined writing my own. Maybe I can still say some of my own things.

Starla places her hands on her hips, drawing attention to herself for the first time. If she'd have stayed against the wall, I could have pretended she didn't exist. "Things are different here, Ava. Carter chose you, so it's our responsibility to plan the ceremony. All you need to do is show up. I've even agreed to stand with you."

My brows furrow. "What?"

Carter swims up behind me, twining his fingers with mine. "It's like the maid of honor position. She'll make sure things run smoothly and help you if you forget."

My frown deepens as disdain crosses my face. "Can't your dad or grandma stand up with me?"

Carter keeps his face straight as the others watch us have our obviously private conversation. The king leans on his golden scepter with an expression I can't read—like he's waiting for me to just accept whatever everyone says.

"No, Ava. My dad is standing up for me. Grandmer won't get in my mom's way. It'd be rude," he says.

I shift my gaze across the room until I meet Starla's confident eyes. She's daring me to have an outburst in front of the king.

But what she doesn't know is that I don't give a damn about what the king thinks of me at this point. "I don't want her to stand up with me, Carter."

Carter's jaw tenses as he clenches his teeth. "I know, but what am I supposed to do?"

I pull away from him and stand to face Starla. "I'm sorry, Starla. No one consulted me about you standing up with me. If I had known, I wouldn't have asked Luna."

Luna's surprised expression nearly gives my lie away. It's the only thing I could think to do to make it look like I'm not still holding onto my eternal grudge against my future mother-in-law. I can't help it. I know she means well, but she could've left us alone. I refuse to have her by my side.

"Oh," Starla says. "I didn't think that you—"

"That I what?" I ask.

She shakes her head. "Never mind. What an honor to have the princess stand up with you."

If she agrees. Luna still looks like she's in utter shock. After a minute, a smile finally crosses her face as she brings her eyes to mine. "It's my honor to do it. I never thought I'd get the opportunity."

If Carter wasn't still holding my hand, I'd sink to the floor in relief. He smirks at me, flashing his dimples at my quick thinking, probably relieved he doesn't have to stress about me being miserable at our coupling ceremony.

"What a wonderful ceremony this will be," King

Attilonious says. "It'll be one remembered for ages."

All because I'm the girl who was transformed on a whim.

"We can only hope," Carter says with a small smile. He turns to me and kisses me softly on the lips. "You have fun with Luna, okay? You know what to do if you need me."

Luna swims up next to me, and I take her hand when she offers it out. Instead of heading out the front cutout, I pull her toward my bedroom first. I need to make a stop, because there's no way I'm wasting another opportunity if the king will be busy.

Luna has the same idea as me, because she jiggles a small woven bag in front of me. "We'll have until dusk."

I grin. That's so much time. Closing my eyes, I send a private thought to Carter. "We're going back to shore."

"Ava," Carter says. I expect him to rush into the room to stop us. I expect him to argue with me. But he doesn't do either. All he says is, "Be careful."

I smile though he can't see me. "I will. Promise." Turning to Luna, I ask, "Ready?"

She swims through the window cutout and waits for me on the other side. "More ready than ever."

16

MERMAID OUT OF WATER

"WAIT HERE," I TELL LUNA as we reach the rocks where I hope Giselle left a bag of clothes for me.

Luna remains near the sandy floor while I peek my head above the churning water. A gray bag rests on the rocks exactly where Giselle sat the first time I saw her after I was allowed to leave the colony. I swim closer and use my tail to propel me up and out of the ocean.

Opening the bag, I smile at the four different bikinis and three sundresses. She thought I might want options, and I'm glad for her thoughtfulness. I won't have to figure out how to get Luna something to wear. The dresses might be on the shorter side, but we're about the same size otherwise.

I pull two of the bikinis out of the bag before closing it up so the water doesn't soak the rest of the stuff. Dipping back underwater, I wave the bikinis at Luna, who stares at me with wide eyes.

"Carter brought these here late last night," I say to answer her silent question. There's no way I'd let Luna know that a human knows our secret. We might have a budding friendship, but when it comes to life or death for Giselle, I'd do anything to protect her.

Luna rocks back and forth in the water, taking the black bikini from me. "I told you he'd forgive you."

I nod. "He's not happy about it, but he understands."

She doesn't think about it much longer because the shore calls to us.

Swimming closer to land, we bob in the waves just deep enough that our tails touch the bottom. The transformation takes hold of me immediately, and the cramps last merely seconds before I'm kicking to the surface. It's the fastest I've ever transformed, and I can't help but think that maybe Starla had been right about how living in the ocean would help me gain better control. I'd never admit that to her, though.

It takes Luna a few minutes but not nearly as long as it took me to transform in the beginning. She's lived in the ocean her whole life and has dreamed about the land. I doubt she'll be out of control like me. I'm almost jealous of how easy it is for her.

She spits out a mouthful of water and smiles at me, kicking her legs to stay afloat. I stop her from sinking under, and we trade our sea grass tops for the swimsuits. I help Luna swim toward the shore, staying near the rocks where the closest beachgoer is far enough away not to notice us emerge from the water.

When we tumble through the waves and into the sand, Luna laughs loudly. Her voice echoes through the air in a musical sound fit for a siren. She flips on her back, chest heaving, and stares at the sun shining overhead. I fall next to her, not caring that the sand sticks to every inch of me.

"I can get used to this," she says, digging her feet into the sand to kick it into the air. It rains down on us in a soft shower.

"Right?" I sit up and pull her up with me.

I manage to help her to her feet without as much trouble as last night. She wobbles for a moment, but then steadies herself. We trudge through the sand together to the public beach in the opposite direction of my house. After a quick rinse off in the outside shower, we let the cool breeze dry our skin before I pull the dresses from the bag.

It's not until then that I realize there's a phone in the bottom of the bag along with a couple of twenties. Giselle is totally the best person in existence. I'd give anything to have her in both my worlds as long as it didn't mean she had to give up everything, too.

"What's that?" Luna asks, pointing to the stuff in my hand.

"The cell phone is so I can call my best friend. The money is if we need to buy anything," I say.

"Like what?"

"Food, clothes, transportation—you have to pay for everything on land," I say.

Her eyes widen. "Really?"

"Yeah."

"That's so weird."

I shrug. "It's probably why not many merpeople venture on land."

"It's not going to stop me, though."

I smile. "Good. It shouldn't."

I send Giselle a text message instead of calling her so I can secretly explain I'm bringing a new friend with me. Giselle offers to pick us up where we are, and I immediately agree. I'm not worried about the consequences. I just want to spend some much needed time with my BFF on land.

Ten minutes later, I guide Luna to the parking lot where Giselle pulls up in her dark blue convertible Mustang. She rarely has the top up because she usually sticks her surf board on the backseat, but she left it at home today. Idling the car, she hops out to throw her arms around me. She bounces in my arms, laughing, and it takes her a long moment to pull away.

"I've missed you *so* much!" She shakes me by my shoulders.

I blink my tears away. It hasn't been more than two days since I've seen her, but it feels like forever since I was stuck in the water last time. "I've missed you, too." I hug her once more before turning toward Luna. "Giselle, I want you to meet Luna. She's a friend of Carter's. Carter's visiting with his family, so I invited Luna to come hang out here for the day."

Giselle offers Luna a wide smile before hugging her like she would any of our friends. "I'm so glad you could come. How do you girls feel about grabbing some lunch and then checking out our—my—new house?"

Luna looks to me to respond. Everything is so new and exciting to her that she doesn't even question why Giselle isn't suspicious of my story.

"That would be great! Are you okay with that, Luna?"

She furiously nods her head with a huge smile. "Yeah, totally."

"Perfect," Giselle says, heading back to the car. "Then let's go."

I had expected Luna to hesitate before getting in the car, but she didn't. She didn't even need help with the seatbelt. She caught on by watching me, mimicking my every move. No one would ever know she's never really been into the human world before. I'm super proud of her ability to adapt. The king is totally wrong for keeping her away from a life she clearly belongs to— like me.

When Giselle parks in front of The Taco Palace, I hop out of the car and am bombarded by a giant hug from Logan, followed by Daisy. I haven't seen my friends since the night I accidentally transformed in front of Giselle on the balcony at the gala. I didn't even tell them goodbye.

I expected them to be a lot angrier, but they surprise me by showing me just as much love as they would've had they known I was leaving.

"Sapphire and Matty went to pick up Chloe," Logan says. He turns to Luna. "This isn't Carter. What'd you do? Get bored and find a new travel companion?"

I playfully slap his arm. "Luna's my new friend. I met her through Carter. He's spending time with his family."

"That's too bad. I thought he could go surfing with us later."

I roll my eyes. "And I thought you'd want to spend the day with me. That hurts, Lo." Fake sarcasm lines my words, but it does sort of annoy me that he would rather spend time surfing with my boyfriend rather than hanging out with me on land.

He chuckles with a shrug.

"Whoa, wait. So, you're not staying long?" Daisy says, pouting. "You just got back after a spontaneous friend-abandonment vacation, if I might add. No invite to join the fun. No video chats or pictures of you. Just lame texts and boring scenic photos." There's the anger I was expecting. The guys have always been more forgiving, but only because it's not like I've spent hours talking on the phone with them to just stop talking to them altogether. And now I have to pretend like it's my choice.

I blink away oncoming tears. "I'm sorry, Daisy. I'll try harder, I swear. But I really can't stay. I promised Carter I'd be his date to this wedding tomorrow." I don't know why I say it, but it's like if I can put the words into the universe, it'll be like my friends could be with me. We've always been together through all the big milestones—I thought we would always be. But mermaid coupling ceremonies weren't exactly on the list.

Before Daisy can respond, Matty yells, "Ava-babe!" from the parking lot. Sapphire hangs on his arm, her tank top sparkling in the sunlight with tiny beads. She tugs him forward, and they hug me together.

Chloe waits her turn before holding me by the shoulders. "You're lucky I don't slap you for abandoning us for the hottie. I can't believe he quit the Ocean Jewel to basically run away with you. You guys are nuts. If I didn't know any better, I'd think he knocked you up, and you don't want to be the talk of the town."

"Logan bet me you eloped," Matty says, smiling. "Tell us who won."

Oh, my God. My friends. Of course they'd come up with this sort of thing. It's bad enough they're basically right about the marriage. I refuse to even think about the other thing.

I glare at Logan. "You think I'd get married and not invite you guys? Where's the fun in that? Plus, my bet's on that Matty and Sapphire head to the altar first."

Logan holds out his hand. "I'll take that bet."

We shake on it and laugh. Things haven't changed one bit even though I haven't been around. It feels so good. I was worried my human life would be in shambles—irreparable—but as it turns out, I have a lot of people who wouldn't give up on me no matter the distance.

Sapphire rolls her eyes. "Great, now my five year plan is going to get messed up because of a bet."

Matty kisses his girlfriend. "You know I love when Logan loses."

Luna steps up next to me, drawing attention to herself. She's been super quiet this whole time, standing next to Giselle, who has been equally quiet—both for the same reason they have no idea they share.

Matty looks between us. "Carter got a lot hotter."

I only laugh to humor him because he thinks he's so funny. "This is Luna." I turn to Luna. "Luna, meet Matty, Sapphire, Logan, Daisy, and Chloe." I point out each of my friends. "Now that everyone has met, can we please go inside? I'm starving. You can't get tacos like this anywhere else."

I hook my arm through Luna's. She stares at the dozen Mexican food posters hung up in the windows of my favorite taco shop. Giselle strolls on my other side, falling into step with me, and we find a big, red leather round booth to sit at in the corner of the shop. Logan and Matty head to the counter to order for us, which will end up being way too much food as always. Too bad tacos won't stay good in the ocean for long.

Sapphire taps my leg with her foot under the table. "Giselle says you've lost your fear of the ocean."

"That's still so strange to me," Luna says.

Chloe leans forward. "She wouldn't go in for like all the time I've known her."

"Why is that, anyway?" Luna asks.

I rub my hands over my cheeks. "I still prefer the land." I don't answer Luna. The last thing I want to do is talk about Bailey and why I'm the one mermaid who hated the ocean before I was forced into it.

"I hate to say it, but Carter's been good for you, Aves," Daisy says, drawing attention away from the fact that I didn't respond to Luna. "I'm a little jealous it was him who helped with your crippling fear and not us. How did he even manage to do that?"

I shrug. "It's hard to explain."

"Do you like the water, Luna?" Sapphire asks, being the good friend and changing the topic I'm clearly uncomfortable talking about.

"I live in it," Luna answers, like it's the most normal thing on the planet.

The others frown. Not because of Luna's answer but because she says it in such a way that would make anyone question whether or not she's being literal. She really is a mermaid out of water.

"Her dad owns one of those vacation resorts where you can rent a room underwater," I say.

Sapphire's face lights up. "That's so cool!"

"It's really exclusive. You basically have to be royalty to even stay there." Which is partially true. You'd also need a tail.

Luna blinks as I create a new life for her—one that is actually pretty fitting for a princess. The boys return to the table with four trays of food just in time to halt any further questions directed at Luna.

I understand what Carter goes through, how he always speaks on my behalf in the colony. I'll be doing that a lot for Luna as well. I feel like I should've better prepared her before dragging her in front of my friends. They'd never in a million years expect we were mermaids—because that's not the first thing someone thinks about—but they might become suspicious if things don't add up. We won't be here long enough to do so, though.

My friends laugh and talk, telling Luna all the same stories they've shared with Carter before. It feels so normal. I can't help wishing that I didn't ever have to go.

Luna and I eat way too many tacos, more than even Matty, and we laugh with each other when Matty nods his approval when we all reach for the last soft taco on the tray.

"Jeez, Ava-babe. When was the last time you two ate?"

"Yesterday," Luna and I say at the same time.

He holds his hands up. "It's all yours."

I tear the taco in half, laughing out of nervousness, because my friends probably think I'm not getting enough to eat on the road though they know my parents are footing the bill for my travels.

"You had better have let them have that last taco," Giselle says. "You owe Ava forever."

No one has to say why—Matty was the one who knocked me overboard on the Ocean Jewel, and I'm absolutely positive Giselle holds it against him. If he hadn't been acting recklessly, I'd have never drowned. Carter and I could've had a normal relationship on land. Things would be a lot less intense. If the situation were different, I might not have even been in love with him yet.

I can't imagine not loving Carter, though. That's a different life altogether.

"Why does he owe you?" Luna whispers between bites of her half of the taco.

"He knocked me overboard while we were all on vacation," I say.

"And if Carter hadn't dove after her, she'd be dead. He saved her life," Giselle says with such certainty, because she knows I did die.

"That's super romantic," Luna says. "I'd love to find my mate that way."

It barely sounds normal enough for my friends not to comment on her word choice. I've grown so used to Carter being referred to as my mate that it takes me a minute to realize what she said might stand out.

"It is now that we know Ava's fine," Giselle says. She pushes her bronze hair from her forehead, meeting my eyes with a look of sadness—the same expression I saw on her when I told her I had to leave after she found out the truth.

The door chimes, drawing my attention away from my friends. My mouth falls open when I see Carter standing in the doorway, his hair dripping water onto his shirt. Luna tenses next to me, and it takes everyone a minute to realize who it is, which is about to blow up my lie in my face.

"Carter? What are you doing here?" I ask, sliding out of the booth. "Is everything all right?" Panic grips my chest. I won't be able to explain to my friends why I need to suddenly leave.

"Carter, man!" Logan says, waving his arms over his head. "You swim here or something?"

"Or something," Carter says with an easy smile.

Before he can come closer, I close the distance, pushing him back out of the taco shop. Luna remains frozen in place, and all my friends watch us through the window. Giselle looks ready to jump up to chase me if she thinks we're about to run.

"I told them you were visiting with your family. They're going to know I lied. What are you even doing here?" I poke him in his hard chest with my finger.

Carter's smile only widens. He looks me up and down, taking in the clothes Giselle gave me. "How was I supposed to know you were planning on hanging out with all of your friends? Where did you even get the dresses—never mind. I know exactly where you got them." Carter raises his hand and waves at Giselle through the window.

She smirks while twitching her fingers. I try to read the lips of my friends as they have an obvious conversation about us. Luna shakes her head a few times and shrugs. Hopefully she's acting as clueless as I was.

"All that doesn't even matter. What are *you* doing here?" He takes my hands in his before I can poke him again.

"I was able to get away from the palace for a bit," he says.

I pull my hands away and place them on my hips. "You're checking up on me."

He sighs. "Well, yeah."

"You didn't have to. It's not like I'm planning to run away with Luna."

"You sure about that?" I know he's joking, but I can't help the grimace that slips onto my face.

"Positive. The only person I'd run away with is you."

Carter closes the distance between us, tugging me to him by my waist. He leans down, brushing his lips against mine, and I sink into him. He softly moans into my lips as he reluctantly pulls away.

"Are you going to send me away?" he asks in nearly a whisper.

I shake my head. "I'm not giving my friends more to talk about. Come on. They've all been asking about you."

17

TRUST

MATTY GIVES CARTER A FIST bump as we stand in front of the taco shop. "You have to reel it in, dude. You're making me and Logan look bad."

Carter chuckles, tipping his head back slightly so the sun sets his brown hair aglow. "Sorry, man. I can give you some pointers if you'd like."

Sapphire laughs from next to her boyfriend. "Hopefully about how not to drive me crazy when we move in together next week."

"Already?" I ask. Summer is flying by faster than I want it to. Soon I'll have to figure out how to tell my parents I'm not coming home or going to college in the fall—that is if I can even manage to find the words. It'll also be when I have to figure out what to tell them about my inability to be around. I'm not sure there's any excuse in the universe that will make this right with them. I can't even fake it like I'm going to college on the other side of the country.

"You guys should come check it out sometime. Add it to your itinerary," Matty says.

Carter nods. "Definitely."

Giselle honks her horn from the parking lot, drawing our attention away from the rest of my friends. Luna sits beside her in the front seat, and I quickly give the others a hug. They're heading to the beach while Giselle is supposed to take us to her new condo—the one that was supposed to be ours.

Carter rests his hand on my lower back, and we stroll through the crowded lot to climb into the back of Giselle's Mustang. The AC blasts through the vents though the top is down, and she plays one of our favorite bands, *Nightmare Madness*, on her stereo.

"I love your friends, Ava," Luna says, twisting in the seat to look at us. "Giselle invited us to stay at her house whenever. She said it's on the beach like yours."

I suck in a long breath through my nose. "That would be great. You know, it was supposed to be my house, too."

"It still can be," Giselle says, wagging her eyebrows.

Luna crinkles her nose. "No, it can't. Ava lives with Carter."

I lightly tap her shoulder, giving her a look that says to watch her mouth. Even though Giselle knows, Luna can't know she knows. She can't slip up either. That'd put Giselle at risk even more.

"We don't live anywhere together yet," Carter says, correcting Luna. "Unless you count hotel rooms."

She covers her mouth for a second, figuring out what she did. "I forgot."

Giselle flicks on her blinker and changes lanes. "I assumed Ava would be moving in with Carter anyway. Can't you see how in love they are? It sucks for me, but I'm happy for my BFF."

"I'm happy for her, too," Luna says, leaning her head on the headrest while looking up at the blue sky.

I smile at my two friends while resting my head on Carter's shoulder. He twines his fingers with mine before bringing my hand to his mouth to kiss the top of it. He smiles, kissing the ring on my finger, and I close my eyes to soak in the sun beaming down while feeling the sea breeze blow through my hair.

When Giselle stops at a stoplight, Carter leans forward in the seat. "Hey, Luna. Can you let me out?"

All three of us look at him. I'm the first one to speak up. "Where are you going?"

"I have some errands to run," he says as Luna rushes to let him out. Carter leans over the side of the car and kisses the top of my head. "You two be careful. I'll come pick you up before sundown." He turns to Giselle. "Sorry I can't hang out longer, Gi. Tomorrow's a big day."

Giselle's eyes widen, remembering what day it is. "Good luck, Carter. I'll catch you around."

With that, Carter jogs from the car and disappears in between two buildings that'll take him to the main stretch of road into the small downtown area of Azure Waters. Luna glances at me from over her shoulder, but she doesn't say anything.

Giselle accelerates through the green light and enters the freeway that'll take us to La Tortuga Point, where the condo is.

Thirty minutes later, Giselle hits the garage opener and pulls her Mustang into the garage attached to a condo at the end of a small complex. We hop out and enter the spacious place. It's a dream—my dream—and my heart hurts seeing all my best friend's stuff.

A new sectional couch rests in the corner of the living room, facing a wall with a flat screen mounted on an entertainment stand. The dark wood floors gleam in the light coming in through the sliding glass door that leads directly to the beach. She has a small folding chair on the concrete slab, but nothing else yet. A collection of surfboards lean on the wall, ready for Giselle to just grab one and go.

She doesn't have a dining room table yet, but two barstools are pushed directly in front of the bar that faces a small white-cupboard and gray granite countertop kitchen. Framed photos, mostly of the two of us, decorate the side table next to the couch, but she hasn't done any more decorating.

"This place is amazing!" I exclaim, spinning around the living room.

And then I start bawling my eyes out. I can't help it. This place was supposed to be mine, too. This was supposed to be my life, living with my best friend in the entire world, having get-togethers with our friends, having the ocean as a backdrop, living life without much to care about except passing classes and making sure I didn't oversleep.

But now, I feel like my life is pointless. I have nothing more to look forward to. And I hate it. How can I love Carter so much but hate everything else around us? This blows.

Giselle sinks onto the floor next to me, cradling me in her arms. She brushes my hair away from my wet cheeks and just comforts me as I sob. Luna takes a quiet seat next to me, touching my knee. Both want to say things, but neither do so.

After a minute, Giselle says, "You know what? I can't pretend anymore." Fire laces her voice, a mixture of fury and protectiveness clinging to her. She's the kind of person to stand up for me even if it puts her in danger. If she had the capability, I'm sure she'd make her way to Pearlestria and give the king a piece of her mind.

I jerk my watery gaze toward her. "Giselle, no." With Luna here, she doesn't really have to. I have no idea what she wants to say next, but it can't be good. It screams danger, and I want nothing more than to hop to my feet, drag Luna away from my best friend, and disappear.

She shifts to look at Luna. "Can I trust you? If I tell you a secret, will you die before sharing it? Because I can die if I tell you."

Luna's brows pucker, considering Giselle's words. She slowly nods her head. "Yes, I can keep your secret."

My heart races, and I feel like I'm about to throw up. Luna

is the king's daughter. Even if she's nice to me now, I've only known her for days. Her life isn't the one hanging in the balance. That would be Giselle's.

I turn to Giselle, considering jumping on her to slap my hand over her mouth. "Giselle. Don't do this."

Giselle huffs a huge breath, ignoring me. "I know, Luna. I know about Ava and Carter...and you. I know you're all merpeople, and that Ava is coupling with Carter tomorrow."

Luna gasps, jumping back in surprise. "What?" She glances at me. "You *told* her?"

I shake my head, my hair hitting my cheeks. "I wasn't so good at controlling the transformation in the beginning. I accidentally did it right in front of her. She's my best friend, though, and I trust her with my life. I hope we can trust you too, Luna. Because if you tell anyone, you know what the consequences are."

"They'll kill her," Luna says quietly, the words more real coming from the princess' mouth.

"It was all an accident, and I've never been more terrified in my life. You have to swear you won't say anything." A dozen threats cross my mind. I never knew I'd be capable of even thinking about hurting someone, but I'd do it to save Giselle. I'd fight and die for her. She's not just my best friend. She's my family.

Luna swallows, wetting her lips. "Of course I won't say anything. You're my friend, Ava, and I don't want you to lose yours. I'd hate for something bad to happen."

Giselle releases a breath. "That makes two of us."

I hug my arms around the both of them, the sudden revelation enough to distract me from breaking down over my ruined life. We're all silent for a long moment as we process the new knowledge we share.

"Is this why you were crying?" Luna asks after another minute.

I shrug. "It's part of it. This was supposed to be my house all before Carter changed me into a mermaid. I was set to go to college and not basically get married. I'm only eighteen." My voice rises through the room. "But I can't back out of it because of your father, Luna. He's made sure that I won't. And at this point, I don't even care. After tomorrow, we're leaving the colony. I can't stay there."

Giselle pets my arm without saying anything. She just embraces me in quiet comfort.

Luna, on the other hand, sits up straighter with a million thoughts crossing her dark blue eyes. "Oh, Ocean! I can't believe my dad. Does Carter know everything?"

I nod. "I just told him. It was his idea to leave. We're going to go to the colony near Australia." If they allow us to.

"Reefaria is beautiful," Luna says. "But I hate that you're leaving."

Giselle clears her throat. "I guess that means I won't be seeing you as often."

More tears prickle my eyes. "We'll manage. Carter can get us back here in a couple days swim."

"My dad's not going to like this," Luna says.

"He doesn't have a say anymore. I'm doing everything he's asked of me."

She rubs the sea stone on her ring. "That's not why. He's going to be upset because I'm coming with you."

The sun hangs low on the horizon, and I've spent the last few hours thinking about what's to come. I know I should try to talk Luna out of leaving Pearlestria—tell her she's being rash—but I don't even know what to say. Maybe it'll take the heat off me and Carter, but it could also make things worse. But who am I to decide what's best for Luna? I already hate that the king thinks he knows what's best for me.

"I want to see you tomorrow, Gi. I'm afraid it might be a while before I get back here, and I need my best friend to give me a pep-talk before everything's official with Carter." I twist the hem of my sundress between my fingers. I've gone all day without thinking of the ocean, and I'm relieved by my control over my transformation.

"I'll wait right here all day," Giselle says. "I just wish I could be there for you."

Luna touches Giselle's shoulder. "I know it's not the same, but I'll be standing in what I guess would be your place if this were to take place on land. I'll make sure everything is perfect for Ava."

Giselle smiles. "Since it can't be me, I'm glad Ava has a princess to watch over her. It's a total fairytale."

One of the old ones with the not so happily ever after endings.

"A what?" Luna asks. Then she smiles. "I'm just kidding. We have stories under the sea, too. Mostly about humans and stuff. I'm sure Ava will be a story everyone tells their merbabes one day."

"Then we better get going, or else it might not have a happy ending," I say.

Giselle frowns with tears in her eyes before she throws her arms around me. This goodbye—with me on my legs—seems ten times worse than the one the other night on the side of the boat. Because now, the temptation to stay is real. We could get in her car and drive to the middle of the continent far away from the ocean and just pray a saltwater bath would suffice come the full moon. *The call of the sea would kill you...*

Pulling away from my best friend, I turn toward the ocean, spotting Carter's head popping up through the waves. Fortunately for us, the beach is empty as most of the condos haven't been bought yet, and the nearest public access is a mile away. It's the only reason I dare to run to the ocean in our sea grass outfits—which are now coming apart from being dry for too long. It doesn't matter though. What matters is I don't have to run completely naked into the sea, since I can't return with Giselle's bikini. Neither can Luna.

Luna dives into the waves before me, sinking under before she disappears into the sun-tinted water. The orange glow makes the ocean look like it's been set ablaze, though the coolness causes my human body to shiver.

Turning around toward the shore, I wave my arms at Giselle before I flip backward into a wave and let it pull me out to sea. I don't even have a chance to get past neck-deep water to transform before warm hands slide around me. Carter hugs me against him, running his fingers along my thighs and down my legs. I kiss his jaw right above his gills, wrapping my legs around his strong tail as he dives us deeper under. I don't even care that my lungs burn from the lack of air. All I care about is letting him hold me in the form I love the most.

He slides his hands up my sides and over my arms until he reaches for my fingers. Gently, he slips my sea stone ring off to trigger the transformation so we won't have to break the surface for me to breathe.

If I were the girl before, I'd panic this deep underwater with no chance to find air, but Carter doesn't let go of me, his intense gaze blurry through the water I haven't adapted to yet. He leans over, kissing me, and cramps seize my legs as I transform. I suck in a deep gulp of seawater, my gills letting me breathe, and I smile against Carter's mouth.

"Luna knows about Giselle," he says into my mind, not really asking, just pointing it out.

"Yeah."

I expect his anger to rush over me, but it doesn't. He just

hugs me instead like he knows I need it.

We don't move for a long moment, just holding each other like we're the only two in the ocean. The seconds after my transformation are always the most intense, like I'm feeling everything again for the first time. The hug of the water around me, the strength of my fin, the warmth as my spark glows in my chest just for Carter. But then reality sinks in and reminds me I'm a mermaid, and this is my life now—a life that just feels like living without a purpose.

"I wish I could be enough for you, Aves," Carter says, thinking into my mind. "But I understand I'm not. And it's okay. I shouldn't be what your life is about."

I didn't realize I was projecting my thoughts out to all who could listen. And I feel absolutely terrible about it. But I was born human—I still think like a human—I can't help it.

"I want it to be enough, too. More than anything. I want to be satisfied to be a mermaid, but I want more from life. More from us. I want to make it count, you know?" I run my fingers along his scruffy jaw line. "I think that's why I was so hesitant to go through with the ceremony in the first place. I'm not just stubborn, I swear."

He laughs out loud, sending a stream of bubbles toward the surface. "I know that, and I love that about you. I wouldn't want you to accept anything less. You're not Ava, Carter Stevens' mate—you're Ava, the fiercely protective and loyal girl, who is smart and kind-hearted. Who might be a little stubborn but only because you know what you want. Not to mention that after everything, you still return my love though I probably don't deserve it. Just because I stole you back from death doesn't mean you owe me anything."

If I could melt, I'd dissolve into the ocean never to be seen again. Carter could rub in the fact that had he not given me this life, I'd be dead. Most people would be grateful—and I am—

but being grateful and my happiness don't always coincide. But he doesn't. He still carries the guilt of not giving me the option. Nothing I say or do will ever change that. It's my actions that have to speak volumes. I have to show him he made the right decision, even if it sometimes doesn't feel that way.

I smile, floating in what feels like a bubble of his love. I was dreading the coupling ceremony—dreading the commitment because I thought I was losing a part of myself. Dreading it because the king didn't give me the choice to wait until I felt like I've done something with my life. I was dreading it because it meant I was accepting I belong to the ocean.

But now, I see it's much more. I'm not losing anything else. Nothing is changing either, because I've already unofficially promised my life to Carter, and by doing so, he's promised his life to me. And together, we're going to do more than live. I know it. We're going to discover whatever else is out there.

I linger an inch away from his face, stopping short of kissing him. Looking into his eyes, I project my thoughts to him. The thoughts I know he deserves. "I don't want you to go into tomorrow thinking I'm unhappy, that I'm only going through with it because I have to. I do want to. I'd do it right now without all the fuss of everything, because I love you. I love you more than the land and the sea. You've been incredible to me. More than I could imagine. And I'm ready to move forward. Right now, even after everything—I'm happy. I'm happy to be alive, to be with you. I'm happy that tomorrow, I'll be your mate for the rest of our lives and even longer."

He closes the distance, kissing me deeply, wrapping me in his warmth against the cool water. He sends me dozens of images, like a slideshow from every moment we've been together. All of his love and memories given to me in a single kiss, one that'll linger with me for a lifetime.

"Ava?" Luna's voice trickles into my mind. I had forgotten

that she was here as she left Carter and me to our private moment. "The king is calling. Want me to keep him busy?"

Pulling away from Carter, I turn toward the princess who
swims far enough away that I wouldn't have seen her if I wasn't
looking. "No, we're ready to go back."

"You sure?" she asks.

I lace my fingers through Carter's, and we swim in her direction. "Absolutely certain. It's our last night in Pearlestria.
Might as well try to enjoy it."

18

OUT OF CONTROL

CARTER'S FAMILY GREETS US AT the palace when we return from Azure Waters. It's customary to have a formal dinner—as formal as you can get in the ocean—before the coupling ceremony.

My stomach rolls at the sight of the dozen fish that are intended to be our meal. They swim around the room without a clue that they're about to become dinner. Carter notices my reaction and gives me an apologetic look. It's a good thing I'm stuffed with enough tacos to last me days. I don't want to seem difficult to the strangers that will now be my merfamily.

"Ava, Carter!" Starla gushes as we enter behind Luna.

Luna swims across the room to the king's side, but no one looks at the two royals. All eyes are on me. Carter's family is a lot larger than I expected. I thought I had already met everyone, but I was wrong. He rarely talks about anyone outside of his parents and Grandmer. I only met his uncle by chance, and it didn't go over so well. I haven't seen him since.

Mateo swims forward and pulls me away from Carter. "Daughter, come say hello to your family. Everyone's so excited to finally meet you."

I force myself to smile though my heart is about to jump from my chest at any moment. Meeting humans has never been a problem for me, but meeting other merpeople—it's tough. It might be because these merpeople are supposed to be my new family. What if they don't like me?

Carter hooks his fingers on my waist even though Mateo grips my hand in his, nearly dragging me to the closest couple. I'm regretting the tacos now, feeling the sudden urge to throw up.

"You're shaking, Aves," Carter whispers into my mind.

I press my lips together, wishing I could look at him. "I'm going to puke."

"You can't puke."

"It sure feels like it."

He swims closer and rests his chin on my shoulder. "They're just my fam—"

"Ava, I want you to meet your Grandmer Oceana and Pops. They're my parents from the Caribbean colony," Mateo says, nearly thrusting me forward.

The woman, slightly more weathered than Carter's other grandma, opens her arms to scoop me into them. She kisses my forehead, petting my blond hair, a contrast to her dark hair with the same blue streaks as Carter's other grandma. Her eyes are the same as Mateo's, so brown they look black. But her tail is the prettiest magenta color I've ever seen.

"My girl," Oceana says into my mind. "I'm so pleased to have a granddaughter, and a worldly one at that. Your Pops and I enjoy the island life occasionally. It's not a wonder that my son and grandson enjoy the land, too."

A smile pulls at my lips. "I'd love to visit sometime."

Pops beams a smile and pulls me to him next. "We'd love that!"

Before the two grandparents can hog me, Mateo guides me forward to meet the rest of the merpeople. Carter stays by my side, proud and protectively, as Mateo introduces me to the rest of his family, who I can only remember the name of his sister, Maka, and then he hands me off to Starla to reintroduce me to her brother, Tobias, and his mate, Sailor, whose parents lived on the land until they passed away, choosing to never return to the water. Carter's the oldest of all his cousins, and I hug the six younger cousins before scooping the tiniest merman I've ever seen into my arms.

He wraps his little fingers in my hair, smiling with half of mouth full of baby teeth, while sending me a dozen random images of fish into my mind instead of the normal verbal thoughts I've grown used to.

I rub my nose against his with a smile, wishing I could just play with the merboy all night instead of answer the dozens of questions I'm sure will head my way.

"This is Reef," Carter says, ruffling the baby's downy hair. "Maka and Flynn's son. He's just over a year."

I swim in a circle with him in my arms. "He's so sweet."

After a moment, Reef wiggles free before swimming back to his mom. Everyone stares at me with smiling eyes, and I can't stop the blush from heating my cheeks.

"A merbabe in your arms suits you, daughter. I can't wait for you and Carter to have a child," Mateo says, wrapping his arms around both our shoulders.

My mouth falls open in surprise. I don't know why I didn't expect that sort of comment—a coupling is equivalent to marriage—but the thought of children never even touched my radar. Just the thought gives me the urge to swim away as fast as I can.

Carter shakes his head with a smile. "You'll be waiting a while, Dad. Ava and I have big plans that involve only us for a while."

"Plans?" For the first time this evening, the king decides to speak up.

Carter stiffens next to me, and I lace my fingers through his, because I'm afraid of where this is heading. "Yes, your majesty. It's a great ocean out there. We'd like to see it all."

Surprisingly, the king smiles. "You won't be disappointed. But Ava, if you choose to travel, you must return here for your ring if you still care for our agreement."

"But that's unfair, my king." I don't know why I say it. I now have my own ring that Luna gave me. It's the sentiment of it all. "What if I choose to spend my few hours somewhere else? You never mentioned I would be limited to here."

The room falls silent, everyone keeping their thoughts to themselves. Starla gives me a don't-you-dare look while Carter pulls me even closer to him.

The king taps his golden staff into the hard rock floor, sending a noise loud enough to make the water quiver around us. "I offered those few hours a month on land to help you maintain your human life enough to keep you satisfied, not to pretend you're the same girl you were before the ocean chose you. It's a privilege, not a right, and if you're unhappy with my decision, then I'm sorry."

"Don't argue, Ava," Carter says to only me. "It's not worth it."

He's right, but I can't stand how much control the king thinks he has over me. I want him to know what it feels like when something happens out of his control. To give him a taste of his own awful medicine.

I close my eyes to get up the nerve to respond without anger in my voice. He can't know how much he got to me, because then leaving here won't be as easy. It'll already be hard enough with—

"Dad, we all get it," Luna says, interrupting not only my response but my thought. "You control everything. The ocean, the merpeople, even Ava's decision to go through with the coupling ceremony. Instead of demonstrating your power, why don't you just let Ava enjoy her night?"

I smile widely at Luna. I can't help it. Everyone else is afraid to stand up to the king but not his daughter. She has nothing to lose. She already doesn't get the choice to live on land. She has never been far from Pearlestria on her own, either, because she's always by the king's side.

The king makes an expression, all brooding eyes and angry lips, but not at Luna. It's directed at me. It's enough to make me swim a few feet backward. "You told Luna about the coupling arrangement," he says only to me. "I warned you."

"You told me I couldn't tell Carter. You didn't mention anyone else, your *majesty*." Anger emanates from me. "How was I supposed to know?"

He fists his hands. He knows I'm right. "That's beside the point. You have a duty to fulfill as a mermaid and as a mate. You put that in jeopardy."

I release Carter's hand to face the king. I don't care that he towers over me or looks like he could send me across the Pacific Ocean with the flick of his tail. I've done nothing wrong...that he knows of. I shouldn't have to feel like my life and wants and needs don't matter. Because they do. "I've put nothing in jeopardy, because I've decided I actually *want* to go through with this and not because you said so. You know, everyone told me what a fair and kind king you are, but they're wrong. You want nothing more than for me to be some compliant little mermaid whose only meaning in life is sitting quietly and doing nothing."

"That is the meaning of your life," the king roars, unable to keep his thoughts directed only to me.

The king's eyes widen as he realizes I got under his skin enough for him to lose his composure. And he's pissed. I swear the water gets hotter around me. He could boil me to death if he wanted to, and there would be nothing anyone could do about it.

Raising his large hand over his head, he aims it at me. The only thing I can do is close my eyes and brace myself for the impact.

Strong hands lock around my waist and yank me back, and I hit the wall behind me with a soft thump. Carter uses his body to shield me, blocking me from the king. Panic grips at my chest, because even Carter can't protect me. The king reaches out and pulls him away, flinging him through the water from me.

Luna steps in next, grabbing onto the king. Towering over me, he shakes her off with the flip of his tail, and she screams for me to swim, but I'm frozen in place. The king hits his staff on the floor again, sending the water churning, making it impossible for anyone to come to my rescue. A whirlpool, strong enough to catch the fish intended for dinner in its current, circles around us like an impenetrable wall.

My gaze flicks to Carter. He presses against the strong current, fear and despair crossing his face. Even Starla looks panicked, something I never thought I'd see in regards to me. I lie helplessly on the rock floor below the king in all his raging glory.

"How dare you disrespect me in front of my merpeople!" The king's sapphire eyes blaze brightly, like they're being lit from behind.

I squirm, the water continuing to warm with his projected anger. It takes everything in me not to start screaming in pain. I'm sure that would please him, hurting me, and I won't give him that kind of sadistic satisfaction. I refuse to break and show Carter just how bad it is. My pain will surely be his undoing. All I can think about is how horrible everyone must feel watching the king lash out at me for something they have no idea about. He'd murder me on the spot if he knew Luna and I went ashore.

"Please," I whisper. My whole body burns. The hot water filling my lungs makes it hard for my gills to work. "You're hurting me."

But he doesn't stop. He aims his staff at the spark in my chest, sending terror to my very soul. "Let me make myself clear, because you can't get it into your mind that you belong to the ocean, and the ocean—it belongs to me."

I nod my head, my vision growing fuzzy. "I understand. I'm sorry."

"I'm not finished." He pokes me once in the chest with his staff, and pain bursts through my body. "I have given you plenty of chances to figure things out on your own. I've been kind enough to give you the opportunity to do something that no human-turned-mer has had the chance to do, and you have the nerve to call me unkind? You're ungratefulness clearly shows me you don't deserve that chance. You don't deserve the gift of life the ocean restored in you."

I close my eyes. I guess he's going to kill me after all and right here in front of Carter—in front of Carter's family and Luna—all because I stood up to him and called him out for what he is.

Maybe I am ungrateful. Maybe I don't deserve this life I've been given.

But that doesn't mean I should die.

Someone brave would stand up and try to fight. Someone brave wouldn't let the king push them around. But right now, I'm terrified. I'm not against groveling.

I latch my fingers around his caudal fin. "Please, your majesty. I get it now, and I'm sorry. I know you're a kind and generous king. I know this life is good for me. I'll do anything."

The water cools as his face softens. "Will you give up your human life?"

I nod even though my heart rips to pieces at the thought.

"Yes," I whisper.

"The safety of the mers is the most important thing to me, and I can't stop thinking you'll jeopardize it all. Your human infatuation will not only get you hurt or worse, but it'll hurt your mate—and with my daughter's growing fascination with you—you might hurt her, too. I can't allow it. This is for the best," he says.

But I know it's not.

Because he doesn't know what's best for me. He'll never know. All he cares about is controlling his kingdom and everything in it. If he cared about me or what was best, he wouldn't have ruined tonight.

The current separating us from the others dissipates, and Carter swims to my side and pulls me from the floor. His blue-green eyes shift wildly as he peers around the room, and I know he's looking for the quickest escape route.

The king bumps his staff on the floor, sending another jolt through the water. "I apologize for losing my temper. Everything was a misunderstanding. Right, Ava?"

I force my head to bob up and down. "Right."

"You all know how important everyone's safety is to me, and I'd hate for something to jeopardize the safety of our colonies. I'm afraid that as a human-born, Ava did not understand the risk. She still has a lot to learn. It's why she's agreed to give up the land and all her human ties, just like it should've been from the start." The king motions to Carter. "And now that your mate has chosen the ocean, you'll no longer need your sea stone ring."

"What?" Carter says, folding his arms over his chest. "I know Ava wouldn't agree to give up the land."

"Just give him the ring, Carter," I whisper.

He turns his gaze to me. "No. He might rule the sea, but we have a choice."

The king holds out his hand. "The ring, Carter."

Carter shakes his head. "It's my right."

"Not if your mate chooses the ocean," the king says, glancing toward me. "Which she has done."

"You manipulated her." Carter's not going to back down. He's going to get himself hurt or worse if I don't say anything.

"Carter, please. Do as he asks. I have chosen the ocean. I want to live here now." The words come out nearly a whisper in my thoughts, but I project them to the entire room, the other merpeople tense with worry.

He swims back. "I'm not giving up my ring. I know you, Ava. I can tell you're lying."

"This is your last chance, Carter. Give me the ring before I take it from you. You heard your mate. She chooses the ocean." The king's voice shakes the ground as it travels through the water and into our thoughts.

"She's not officially my mate," Carter says. "And if this is how it will be, then I'm not going through with the ceremony." Despair crosses his face when he looks at me. "I'm sorry, Ava."

With a quick hand, the king raises his staff at Carter. The world slows, and I watch in horror as a blur of gold cuts through the current and heads straight for the boy who'd die for me.

Darting forward, I swim between Carter and the king, holding my hands out to block Carter from the king's wrath. The staff slows down, like the water has turned to jelly, and I scream out.

"No!" My voice rings out through the water instead of from my mind, and a large pulse erupts from me as I direct my fear and anger toward the king.

He jerks back, like I've physically pushed him. His eyes grow wide, and he stares at me with a startled gaze. Whatever just happened was enough to stop the king in his tracks. And now he's wary of me.

Before we can figure out what has happened, Carter grips me by my arm and pulls me through the nearest tunnel that leads to the grand room. Clinging to his back, I press myself against him, swimming faster than ever before.

"I can't believe you did that," I say to Carter, holding on tightly to his shoulders. "You could've been hurt."

He smiles over his shoulder, the special one that's just for me. "But you saved me."

"So that was me?" I ask. "What was that even?"

"Our last hope."

With those words, we dart into the dark, open sea.

19

TROUBLE

CARTER BANGS ON THE BACK door of Giselle's condo. He's completely naked, dripping wet, and covered in sand. I'm no better, with my sea grass top and my backside showing for the world to see. Thank God it's dark out.

The back patio light flicks on, and Giselle thrusts the blinds open before flicking the lock up to allow us in. She rushes to the bathroom and throws us both towels to cover up with before sliding and locking the door behind us.

"We're in trouble, Gi," I say.

She waves her hands in her face. "Oh, God. What happened? Did they find out about me? Do I need to pack?"

I grip her shoulders. "No, but I did something bad. I stood up to the king, and something happened. I think I can control the sea. It stunned him before he could hurt Carter."

Grandmer mentioned mermaids had gifts, and she thought I might have a connection to animals, but I'm starting to think it's much more. Now that I think about it, this wasn't the first time I've done something to shift the current. I can recall a few times I did it to Starla when she annoyed me. Also, the first day I met the king, I disrupted his black sand pool—something we both noticed. I remember how he looked at me. But it didn't make sense at the time. I didn't know what I did wasn't normal. And then later, I controlled the current with Carter when I thought he was going to make me go back to the palace after the king forced me to agree to the coupling ceremony. I had no idea until this second it was the water reacting to my emotions—that it was allowing me to control it like the king.

Pushing the thought away, I rehash every detail from the moment we arrived for what was supposed to be a celebration dinner that turned into a nightmare fight. I only hope the king doesn't take things out on Carter's family.

I'm a little freaked out about my family on land, but Carter swears the king won't pursue them. They know nothing about me, and it'd only put the king at risk, because I'm sure my parents would fight like crazy. Outside of the sea, he doesn't have the same power. It's not worth it. At least I hope.

Giselle brushes her hair out of her eyes. A moment later, she playfully slaps Carter's arm. "I can't believe you called off your mermaid wedding." Only Giselle would say something like this to lighten the mood.

It's enough to calm my heart. I poke Carter in his bare chest. "Yeah. That's twice now."

He scratches the back of his neck, smiling, though worry lingers in his eyes. "The real one will be worth the wait. Promise."

Giselle makes a strange cooing sound as she glances between us. "Are all mermen like you? Because I might change my mind about the whole thing if you have a cousin."

I kiss Carter's cheek. "He's one of a kind."

Giselle heaves a giant, fake sigh. "Figures. I don't want to live in the ocean anyway. I prefer riding the waves of the shore not swimming beneath them."

I smile at my best friend. The world could be ending, but with her around, things don't seem as dire as I thought they'd be. It's almost like none of tonight happened. Like we're not on the run from the king.

I hug her. "Me, too. This whole thing is crazy. I don't even know what we're going to do. The full moon will force us back into the water tomorrow, and then we'll have nowhere to hide."

"You can't just sit in the bathtub with a gallon of salt?" she asks.

"If only it were that simple," Carter says.

"What if I bought a giant aquarium?" She twists her lips to the side, touching her finger against her chin. The thought of sitting inside a glass tank only makes the fear running through me worse.

"You'd need a swimming pool sized tank," I say. "Carter's nearly eight feet long as a merman."

"Then we'll find a saltwater swimming pool," Giselle says.

I pout my lip. "I wish it were possible, but the sea calls to us like a gravitational pull. You could have the perfect setup, but it doesn't guarantee anything. I'm too new to resist. I'd be in agony."

She places her hands on her hips. "What's a half a day of agony when some evil king merman wants you dead now?"

She has a point.

Carter slides his arms over my shoulders, embracing me from behind. "We'd have a better chance in the sea. The pull of the moon could possibly kill Ava. It's only her third full moon."

I puff air through my lips. "We're screwed. We can't fight against the king, Carter. Death isn't worth the land. Maybe we should just go back and beg for forgiveness."

"And then endure a lifetime of misery?" Carter asks. "The king can't be everywhere at once. We can do this, Ava. Just like we planned before. The king might control the ocean, but he doesn't control us. I'm not going back. I'm not letting you either."

"Then we need to leave. We can't stay here," I say.

Carter rests his head on my shoulder. "I don't trust you to safely fly yet, Ava. Not this close to the full moon. Anything can trigger the transformation early."

"Then we head north," I say.

"Where my parents will surely be looking?"

I shrug away from him to spin and face him. "Then what, Carter? My passport is in my parents' safe at home. Do you even have one? Going south isn't an option unless we swim."

"Then we'll hide. I've swam this area a million times. I know of some caves near the La Tortuga Cliffs. They're like the one you stayed in when you found me in Orange County after the dress fiasco." He's talking about when Giselle accidently took my ring off before the gala. It seems so far away now. A different life altogether.

Giselle claps her hands. "That's it! I can have the car ready and waiting as soon as the moon sets. Your parents won't be able to find you if we're in a car, so we can easily drive through San Francisco. Maybe we can go to Alaska or something. You'd be far enough to swim, right? I could fly."

"We?" She's crazy if she thinks she's going with us anywhere.

"Yes, *we*. Having a human around will make sure the merpeople don't try anything crazy if they find us." Giselle taps her foot on the floor. "I'm already standing on the edge. Might as well dive in."

I open my mouth to argue, but Carter squeezes my arm. "She's right, Ava. As much as I hate the idea of putting her in danger, she can help us. At least until we have a better plan."

"Then it's settled," Giselle says. "I'll start packing."

"Sleep, Ava," Carter whispers into my ear.

I turn in his arms to face him, my nose touching his. His lips brush against mine in the softest of kisses, helping relax the nerves bunching in my back. I've been staring at the sliding glass door for hours in fear of naked people emerging from the sea to take us away.

As unlikely as that is, I can't shake the feeling. I know other merpeople can't find us on land like they can find someone who was their mate, but it isn't entirely impossible to track us. They've done it before. Carter's uncle knows how. And then I have to also worry about Luna. She knows where this place is. What if she gives us away? I know she wanted to come with us, and we had to abandon her.

"I'll sleep later," I say, pulling away. "Right now, I need to think about everything that could possibly go wrong."

"Why not everything that'll go right?" He kisses me again, trailing his lips to my jaw before kissing my neck. "This might not be the way we wanted things to go, but we're together, and we're going to live on the road like we wanted. We could get a boat and travel the world."

Until the king finds us and causes us to shipwreck. I don't say the words out loud, though. Unlike me, Carter carries enough hope for the both of us. He thinks things will go in our favor. He thinks our love can get us through anything. Why do I have to be so cynical? Love only saves the world in fairytales. This is my life. Our love could very well be our end—our undoing.

"I'd love that," I say instead of what's really on my mind. "Who knows? Maybe the king will give up when he realizes I'm not a threat to the mers entire existence."

He chuckles against my lips. "That was overly dramatic, right? The fall of an entire species would not be your fault."

He's right. I'd never put us in that sort of danger. All I want out of life is to live it how I want to, and that doesn't involve revealing myself to the world. That wouldn't accomplish anything except get me stuck in a tank or in some lab—or at least that's what every mermaid I've ever watched on TV was afraid of. I think there are enough good people in the world—

people like my best friend—that would stop that from ever happening. Plus, humans love the ocean. They wouldn't want to risk it turning against them completely.

I suck Carter's bottom lip between mine, needing to take my mind off things outside of us. His hands run over my sides and to my back, and he trails them lower to pull my hips against his. He kisses me deeper, his tongue grazing against mine, tasting like the mint chocolate ice cream we had for dinner since neither of us had an appetite for much else.

Carter makes it easy to lose myself in his kisses, in his arms, in his very essence. As his fingers explore every inch of me, I listen to his deep breathing, something I don't get to hear in the ocean, and to the sound of our beating hearts as they thump-thump, thump-thump in sync.

A quiet knock on the back door causes me to startle in Carter's embrace. His arms tighten around me, like if we lie here quietly, whoever is on the other side of the slider will go away. But another knock sounds out, slightly louder.

Giselle yawns, coming into the room. She doesn't look like she's gotten any sleep either. She saunters past us and to the kitchen where she pulls a kitchen knife from its holder on the counter. I highly doubt it's an intruder—they don't usually knock—but Giselle looks like she's willing to stab anyone who might come to threaten us.

The knocking continues, quick taps that mirror the rapid beating of my heart.

Giselle looks at us frozen on the couch. "I'm going to answer it."

Carter shakes his head. "You shouldn't."

"I'll be fine. You two should go hide. If you have to, pop off my window screen and leave that way." She tiptoes up to her slider with the knife clutched in her hand like whoever is on the other side of the glass will shatter it at any second.

Carter pulls me from the couch bed and guides me down the short hallway to the master suite. I linger outside the door, shrugging him away when he tries to pull me in. I'm not leaving Giselle to answer the door alone. What if it's the king?

"Luna?" Giselle asks out loud. "What are you doing here? Is something wrong? Is Ava okay?" She's a much better actress than I ever could be.

The door lock clicks, and I tense. Giselle shouldn't open the door for anyone. Especially the daughter of King Attilonious.

"I know Ava and Carter are here," Luna says. Her soft voice trickles down the hallway, sending a wave of uneasiness over me. She shouldn't be here. Coming to Giselle's puts everyone at risk. The king could be following her. This is bad.

"I don't know what you're talking about," Giselle says. "It's just me. What happened to Ava?"

"Giselle, please. My father has the entire colony searching the seas for them. They think they're hiding near Azure Waters or San Francisco. No one knows Ava has a ring, but they think Carter would give her his to escape the ocean. Even if they're not here, I know you'd know how to find them. Please, no one knows I'm here. I've come to run with them. What my father did—I just—please, Giselle. I want to help. I know my father and the ocean better than anyone."

Taking a deep breath, I step from the hallway. Luna could very well make a good ally, and she has no reason to lie.

Carter comes up behind me protectively. When I meet Luna's worried gaze, I know immediately she speaks the truth. She's alone and scared, and probably took the one chance she had to leave home, risking the wrath of her father if he were to find out.

Luna rushes forward and wraps her arms around me. "I was so scared, Ava!"

I rub her back. "Your father's crazy."

She hugs me against her. "You've done something no one has ever done before. You put fear into his heart."

"Good," I mutter. I don't know what else to say. I hope the king is shaking in his skin.

"You don't understand," she says. "You've showed an affinity for the ocean. Only my dad has that. It's why he's king."

She confirms my newfound suspicion that I can somehow control the sea. But I don't know how to do that. Creating a current is no match against the merman who can create whirlpools, heat the water to unbearable temperatures, even create the magic stones allowing us to walk on land.

"So, he's going to kill me because I'm suddenly his competition?" I ask. I purse my lips. It wouldn't be the first time someone wanted to eliminate a potential threat to keep a firm hold on power.

"Maybe," she says, sucking in her top lip. "But I don't know. The last mermaid gifted with an affinity for the ocean was my mom. They ruled together until she abandoned us. And the ocean chose you for a reason. No one knows why it does what it does. Only my father could answer a question like that."

I stand frozen, her words sinking in. All merpeople talk about the ocean like it's a living, breathing person, like it's a goddess or something. But the ocean has never felt that way to me. It's always just felt uncontrollable, unforgiving. The ocean and I were never really on good terms. Not even now.

I hug myself. "You're wrong. The ocean didn't pick me. The ocean tried to destroy me. Carter picked me. Carter saved me. Maybe this is why all this is happening. Maybe it's upset it lost me again and again."

Luna's eyes widen, and she covers her hand with her mouth. Shaking her head, she says, "That's not true. Tell her Carter."

"She's right, Ava," he says from behind me. "You wouldn't have been gifted like this if you weren't meant for this."

"Well, I don't want it. I don't want anything to do with this. All I care about is staying far, far away from the ocean."

Carter pulls me away from Luna. "And we will for as long as we can. I'm not putting you in danger of facing the king again."

We all silently stare at each other, and I glance from Carter to Luna and then to Giselle still standing near the door with a knife in her hand.

"So what now?" I ask, not really expecting a plan, but I figure it wouldn't hurt to put out the question to the universe. If only the universe would respond. If only the ocean would. Because as of now, we don't have a choice but to return. And then, I have no idea.

"We sleep," Carter says. "We all need to rest and let our bodies prepare."

"Does this mean I can come with you?" Luna asks.

Carter and I share a long, quiet look. If only I could read his mind while in my human body.

"I'll do whatever I can to help. I just—I can't stay at the palace anymore. Not after tonight. My loyalty lies with you two," she says with a small bow. "I know it's what the ocean wants."

I frown. "Of course you can. I had already promised you."

Carter tilts his head to the side but doesn't say anything. He had no idea of the plans I set with Luna. I never got the chance to tell him.

Luckily, he doesn't care. It never hurts to have a princess on our side.

Giselle clears her throat, drawing attention to herself for the first time since Luna walked in. "Come on, Luna. Let me get you something to wear. You can sleep in my room with me.

And tomorrow, we'll get everything settled. We still have all day to figure things out."

If only it were enough time.

A THREAT

CARTER SLEEPS PEACEFULLY NEXT TO me, his chest rising and falling under my fingers with every deep breath. I have no idea what time it is or how long I've slept, but it couldn't have been more than a few hours since the sun rose.

Streaks of light cut across the wood floor from the blinds of the sliding glass door, and I sneak from the couch bed and tiptoe across the living room to peek outside.

The bluish-green ocean rushes the shore in rolling whitecaps. Puffy clouds float in the endless blue sky like giant cotton balls while the sand is so light, it almost looks white in the sun. La Tortuga Point is as beautiful as Azure Waters, if not more breathtaking.

Tears prickle in the corners of my eyes, thinking about the life I was supposed to have. Waking up here every day with a new take on life was what I wanted. Without the fear of the ocean crippling my life, I could've enjoyed the beauty of it. And whenever I wanted, I could dance among these waves, familiarizing myself with every inch of the beach that was supposed to be my home while I went to college.

But now, I have to stay out of the ocean completely, only following the pull of the full moon as it tries to drag me back into the ocean's depths where my enemies await—the merpeople who'd rather see me suffer than happy.

Anger washes over me, and I glare at the unforgiving sea.

It's enough for me to unlock the door and slide it open. I step into the warm summer air, inhaling a delicious breath of the sea's breeze. It sends chills down my back as I'm repelled by the idea of even an ounce of the ocean getting into my lungs.

Peering around, I step forward into the sand. My foot grazes a smooth rock, and I bend over to pick it up. It's hot from the sun beaming down, but I don't drop it. I want to feel the sensation of it in my palm, because I'm afraid that after tonight, I'll never feel the heat of the sun on my skin again. I have to prepare myself for the worst. I have to prepare for the ocean to lure me in to never release me.

I trudge through the sand and toward the crashing waves, staying just out of their reach. Swinging my arm back before jerking it forward, I chuck the rock as far as I can into the waves.

"I'm not letting you take me," I say out loud, more to myself than anyone. "You've already stolen enough from me. You can't have me again."

I'm not sure if I'm talking to the ocean or to King Attilonious, wherever he may be. Squatting down, I scoop up a handful of sand and throw it at the water, too. It disappears in the wind, and I watch the ocean pull another wave back out to sea.

Seagulls caw from overhead, drawing my attention to the sky. They circle around, looking for their next meal. One lands nearby, squawking as it waddles near. Seagulls here aren't afraid of people, but this bird is especially fearless, because when I wave my hand to shoo it away, it flies up and lands on my arm.

"Get off me, you stupid bird!" Thrashing, I spin around, sending it flying before I fall to the sand.

A shadow stands over me, blocking the sun, and Carter grins down at me.

"Even the birds are out to get me," I say.

Plopping down in the sand, he pulls me into his lap to hold me. "Seagulls are worse than dolphins and seals combined. They'll only befriend you to steal whatever you have that they want."

I rest my head against his firm chest, feeling the rise and fall of it as he breathes. His muscular arms lock around me, holding me to him, even though I want to jump back to my feet to find something else to throw at the water. It's the only thing making me feel slightly better about the situation.

I inhale a long breath and release it. "Do you think we'll be on the run forever?"

Carter leans back, pulling me with him. We lie together in the sand, looking up at the sky. His turquoise eyes glow against his tan skin. Cream-colored sand speckles his dark hair, and I comb my fingers through it to dust it out.

"I hope not, Ava. I want to settle down one day, maybe have a place like this," he says, digging his fingers into the sand.

"And what if we can't?"

Carter kisses my temple. "We will. The king will see you're not a threat. He'll back off."

"That's if we get the chance."

"Aves? Do you think it's a good idea to be lying so close to the ocean? I had a nightmare last night that naked people dragged you under like before." Giselle stands on her patio. The beach around us is empty apart from a man who jogs along the shore in the distance.

I tilt my head back to get an upside down view of my best friend. "We'll be in soon."

She pouts her bottom lip but doesn't say anything as she turns around and goes back inside. I wish I could say something to comfort her, but she should be as prepared as I am for the inevitable if they find us.

"She's going to be okay, you know. Giselle's tough," Carter

says.

I smile. "I know. I just hate I put her through all this."

He bobs his head. "I know what you mean. You don't know how often I go back to the night you went overboard to try to think of another way I could've saved you."

I cup his face in my hand. "It wouldn't have changed anything, Carter. Don't you see? Luna was right. The sea chose me. It's been after me since I was a kid. I think this was fate."

"While I won't argue with the ocean wanting you, I don't believe in fate. We control what we do and how we deal with all this."

"Even though no matter how hard we try, we always end up there?" I point at the blue horizon.

"Even then, Ava. Because as much as the waves pull you in, they always spit you out. We can always swim—even in the roughest water. The ocean, it's no match against you. You always win."

I smile. I never thought about it like that. I guess I have always won. Somehow, I still manage to make it back to shore. And now, it's just another fight to stay above water.

For the first time since last night, I have hope. I have hope, because I know how to swim through the storm.

Giselle hugs me near the edge of the cliff top. The only way to avoid swimming to the caves is to jump, so it's what Carter, Luna, and I are going to do. I'm slightly nervous, but it can't be worse than diving from the balcony of the Grand Le Mer Hotel.

"Everything's ready, and I'll be waiting as soon as the moon sets," Giselle says. "Nothing bad will happen, okay? I'll make sure of it." We took out all the money from both our bank accounts and left it with my car where Giselle's been storing it at a storage facility. She packed as much of her stuff as she could to help us as well. I don't know what I'd do without her.

I force myself to smile. "You better not be planning anything crazy if it does."

She shrugs. "Not at all."

Before I can argue, I feel the pull of the ocean, demanding me to return home. I can't see the moon yet, but I know it's rising in the sky. Neither Carter nor Luna react, but they have better control than I do. The ocean can't pull them away so suddenly. Not like me. If the ocean beckons, I have to go.

My toes tingle, sending prickles up my legs. I push the feeling away the best I can. I'm not ready to say goodbye to my best friend. I don't want to go yet. It isn't fair.

The wind knocks from my chest as I convulse, the moon fighting with the magic of the sea stone ring. It won't be much longer before I lose my legs and gain my tail.

A groan escapes my lips. "It's happening. We need to go."

Falling to my knees, another shudder rolls over me, cramps rushing through my every muscle. My legs are too weak to stand. I couldn't even jump if I wanted to.

"Hurry, Carter," Giselle says. "She's in pain."

Lifting me from the ground, Carter cradles me in his arms. The pull is stronger than ever, ripping through me, causing more pain than I've ever felt during a transformation. I know it's because I'm resisting, but I can't help it.

Tears burst from my eyes, a sob grabbing hold of me. The wind whips around us as Carter stands at the edge of the cliff overlooking the roaring ocean. He holds me tighter the louder I sob, and in one quick motion, he leaps forward, far from the rocks.

My stomach rises into my throat, the world zooming around us, and then suddenly, the ocean embraces us in its cool waters. Carter yanks my bikini bottoms off the second before my legs fuse together into a tail. He pushes me away from him and toward a small cave that hides half under the treacherous waves.

Both Carter and Luna catch up to me before I even make it to the entrance. Carter lifts me up first, followed by Luna, and then he grips the rocks and pulls his tail over the edge. The shallow water causes us to drag ourselves through the cave. A deep pool in the back waits for us as the waves that hit the cave stream in to create a waterfall.

Carter swims in a few quick circles around me, spinning me into his arms. My tail throbs from the crawl, and there are tiny patches of raw skin where my scales rubbed off on the rocks, but other than that, I'm okay.

"This is so strange," Luna says, swimming around the perimeter of the pool. It's just deep enough that we can hover upright, but the space is pretty tight with all three of us. "I never really believed in the call of the ocean until now. It's different when you're in human form."

I blow bubbles through my mouth. "I hate it."

"I kinda do, too," she says.

Carter anxiously circles me again. It's probably because he prefers to swim at ridiculous speeds through the open water when the full moon rises. Here, we're basically trapped in a tank. It sucks, but I'd go through this every month if it means I get to spend the rest of the time as my human self.

"So, what now?" Luna asks, bobbing up and down with the rise and fall of the pool.

Carter stops swimming around me to focus on the princess. "We hope no one finds us."

"And if they do?" she asks.

"We fight."

Our minds fall silent as we think to ourselves. I'm not much of a fighter. I can throw a mean punch if I want to—I took kickboxing for a few summers in high school—but that doesn't do me any good in the water. The force isn't nearly strong enough to outmatch a merperson who's been swimming in the water for years.

"Let's hope it doesn't come to that," I say. "I don't want them to have reason to hurt us."

Carter flares his nostrils for a second. "Then we'll try to flee."

As the night drags on, we spend the time making small talk. Luna tells me about her life as a princess, and for the second time since we've met, she tells me about her mom. King Attilonious doesn't like to talk about his queen, because she always dreamed of the land like Luna. The king wouldn't let his queen make the choice either, and then one day she just disappeared. No one knows how, but the queen died somewhere in the sea. King Attilonious could never find his mate.

I'd think after that, the king would have more pity for me—even for Luna. But maybe he blames the land for the demise of his mate. I'll never know.

"I'm sorry, Luna. That must've been hard," I say, reaching out to hold her hand.

She lifts and drops her shoulders. "I don't even remember her all that well."

"Is that why you stood up for me to your father?" I ask.

She smiles. "Among other things. I never knew a friendship like yours was possible. I always assumed I'd only find one in my mate. The world feels much bigger to me now."

"It's endless, really," I say.

Carter rests his chin on the nape of my neck. Every few minutes he swims around the perimeter of the pool, but he's mostly settled down now that the night is halfway over. "And I can't wait to show you, Aves," Carter whispers into my mind, sending the thought only to me.

I tilt my head back, enjoying the feel of Carter against me. Through the bubbling surface of the pool, a strange light flickers through the cave, sending fear through me. I nudge Carter with my elbow, pointing up, and he flicks his tail, sending us both to the surface.

The hum of the waves rushes my ears, but through the white noise, I can hear the sound of a boat engine nearby. And then the cave is set aglow again by the flickering light.

The light fades away with the sound of the boat.

"They couldn't have gone far. Have you searched the shoreline?" A familiar voice rings through my mind as a merman projects his voice through the sea.

"Starla is cutting through the waves now. I just hope to the ocean we find them first." Grandmer's voice sounds through my mind next.

"Carter, Ava, if you can hear me, please. You have to come back," Grandmer says.

The strange light I saw wasn't random. It was a warning. The boat, while it could've been random, doesn't feel like it. Giselle is somewhere nearby. The merpeople don't know that she can see them in the water because she knows our secret.

And her plan was pretty perfect—reckless—but perfect. No merperson would risk popping their head through the water if a human was nearby. It gives us a better chance of remaining hidden since the cave isn't completely submerged. I just wish she had told me.

Carter pulls me back under and motions me to swim next to Luna. He slinks down next to us, draping his tail across mine like he can protect me from whoever lurks nearby. The voices are clear enough to hear, but it's hard to judge the distance. Hopefully they just pass by.

"Mateo, I've combed the shallows. I say we keep heading south," Starla says. "Maybe we should call for them again?"

"Carter, son? Are you out there? We need to talk. Running away will make things worse. The king believes Princess Luna is with you. He's willing to forgive you if you bring the princess and Ava back to Pearlestria. We can work things out." Mateo's voice sounds out with a sense of urgency. "Please, son. We don't want you getting hurt. We love you and Ava."

Luna clutches my tail. "Tell my father I'm not going back. Tell him I'm my mother's daughter, and I won't stand by him any longer."

The sound of Luna's voice projecting through the sea sends a stream of fear down my back.

Carter rubs his hand down his face but doesn't say anything. Neither of us can stop her from talking.

"Princess Luna, you need to be reasonable. If you refuse to come back, it puts my son and daughter at risk. The king protects you like he does our ocean. Do you want them getting hurt because of you?"

We all look at each other. I shake my head, holding my finger to my lips.

She wrings her hands together next to me. "He's right. This was a mistake. I've made things worse."

I grab her tail. "That's not true, and you don't have to go back. This is what he wants. Your father thinks he can scare us into returning. There is no place for us in Pearlestria. It'll be more of a prison than ever."

Before Luna can respond, two large hands yank her from the spot next to me, pulling her from the pool and into the shallows of the cave. The water muffles her screams as she's taken from us.

The hands reach back down, aiming for me next. I reach up and dig my nails into the merman's forearms, scratching down toward his wrists. Carter thrusts me out of the pool, and I crash into Mateo. He skids across the rocks, hitting his back on the wall with a heavy thud.

"Go, Ava!" Carter yells, sliding up next to me. He doesn't

even give me time to move my arms before he hooks his hands around my waist and yanks me along with him. We tumble out of the cave and into the churning water. The blurry bubbles disorient me, and my shoulder hits against rock. Carter scoops me back up and darts through the waves toward the open water.

But something jerks Carter back, causing me to fly forward without him. My heart pounds in my ears, and I spin around, trying to figure out which way to swim. My gaze falls on the merman I hate most in the ocean. Hovering a few feet away, the king holds his golden staff as it glows in the turbulent ocean.

"Swim, Ava!" Carter yells in my mind.

But I'm surrounded. There's nowhere to go.

Then the glow of the moon shining across the surface catches my attention.

So I swim up.

21

FINISH WHAT THE OCEAN STARTED

"WHEN YOU BREAK THE SURFACE, jump up as high as you can, okay? I'm coming." Carter's voice makes me flick my tail faster through the water.

Stretching my arms over my head, I use every ounce of my strength to breach, sending my entire body from the sea. A hard body crashes against me, but I see the spark in Carter's chest immediately as he grips me to him before diving under.

He bolts across the surface, away from the small ring of merpeople determined to catch us. But what they don't know is their determination is nothing compared to our sheer will to break free.

Carter breaches with me on his back, the moonlight sparkling off our skin. He swims us toward the sandy shore of the beach. At this point, neither of us cares we can't transform yet. If we make it to the beach, at least we might have a chance in the waves.

As fast as Carter swims, he's no match for the older mermen who were gifted with his same affinity. If he weren't carrying my weight, he'd probably make it. But he'd never leave me willingly. I wouldn't want him to either.

A pair of hands wrap around my caudal fin, yanking me hard, sending pain through my tail. I scream out, trying to flick it, but I'm injured. Two bodies crash over the surface, and Carter fights out of the grip of his uncle as he tries to keep him away from me. Using my arms, I freestyle through the water, heading toward the surface again.

A flash of light flicks across the surface, and I head straight for it. The king laughs from behind me, knowing I can't get away. I can barely manage to swim instead of sink. He lets me try though, probably waiting for me to exhaust myself.

But he doesn't know what I'm planning.

The silhouette of a boat blocks the glimmering ripples of the surface in the light of the moon. Grinding my teeth through the pain, I flick my tail as hard as I can before I hook my fingers to the back of the boat, keeping my distance from the motor while letting it propel me forward.

Giselle glances over her shoulder with a smile and steers the boat away from the cliffs and down the shore, heading toward the harbor. My heart slams against my ribcage over and over. The king will now realize my best friend knows of our existence. But Giselle can live her life away from the water. There are ways to make sure she's safe.

"Hang on, Aves!" she yells over the hum of the engine. "We're going to the harbor where the king will be outnumbered by boaters."

"Carter's still back there!" I scream.

"That's the least of our worries," she calls over the hum of the water. "Something is coming up fast behind you!"

I peer over my shoulder, catching sight of a golden tail darting toward me. Using all my strength, I do the only thing I can think to do. I yank myself up and into the boat. My tail flops in the wind as I pull it over, rocking the vessel.

My hands tangle in a small fishing net, and I pick it up and hold it just above the water. The king won't stop now, all his caution thrown to the wind. He'll do anything to catch the both of us.

"Go faster!" I yell.

"I can't! This isn't a speedboat." Giselle turns the wheel to take us closer to the shore. If we can't make it to the harbor, she'll take us straight to the sand. I might not be able to run, but at least she can make it. I'd risk my life to protect her.

"Ava," a familiar voice cuts through my mind. But it isn't Carter's. "You have to tell my son to run. Tell him he has to leave you. It's the only way to save him. The king won't kill you, but he will kill your mate." It's Mateo. His words send tears bursting from my eyes. The last thing I want in this world is for any of the people I love to die on my behalf. And right now, the two people I love most are risking everything.

"Carter?" I send my voice through the water, focusing on his presence that is just out of my grasp. "The king is chasing me. This is your chance to go."

"I'm not leaving you, Aves."

"Your dad said the king will kill you. My life isn't worth your death. You can't expect me to live the rest of my life without you. Please, just go. I'll figure things out."

"Ava, don't do this."

"Please," I beg. "Someone needs to take care of Giselle for me."

"Ava." His voice nearly causes me to break.

"I love you, Carter."

With those words, I bring myself back to the present, readying the net. Giselle growls in frustration as the king comes up under the boat and pushes it up, trying to flip us out. She grips onto the steering wheel, fear in her eyes, and I know if the king gets to us again, he'll be successful.

"Giselle, thanks for being my best friend. Please, tell my parents they were everything I could've asked for. Make sure they know I'm not dead, okay?" I push myself higher to look over the edge at the king ascending toward us.

"Don't talk like that, Aves. This isn't over."

As the words leave her lips, the boat surges above the water. I thrust the net down on the king, tangling him in it, but it's too late for me. I fall overboard into a swell, flailing as pain erupts in my injured tail. Breaking the surface, I spit out water and peer around to get a better idea of where I am. Giselle turns the boat around, heading back toward me.

"Just go!" I scream.

The water swells next to me, the king breaking the surface, cutting through the net with his sharp fingernails. Giselle lifts her flashlight, aiming it for the king's eyes, and he jerks back in the water in surprise. I guess he's not used to battery powered light. Who knows how often he has ever come to the surface.

Giselle rams the boat into the king, knocking him away from me. His voice, much angrier than the thoughts he sends in my direction, cuts through the air. With a flick of his powerful tail, he flips the boat, sending Giselle overboard and into the churning water. He heads straight for her as she gasps for a breath, swimming away.

I fight through the pain to swim to my best friend. If King Attilonious reaches her first, she'll be dead.

Giselle yells out, thrashing through the water, heading in my direction. A flash of gold shimmers beneath her and my screams ring out as she's pulled under by the biggest predator in the ocean.

Diving down, I jet through the water, sticking my hands straight out in front of me. Giselle's panicked eyes meet mine. She fights in the king's grip, digging her thumbs into his face. I stab my nails into his back, but he shifts too quickly for me to injure him.

King Attilonious raises his staff at me, pointing it in my face. Light glows from the diamond on top, and I find myself locked in its magic, unable to move. The water heats around me, bubbles surging toward the surface at the sudden change in temperature.

A figure darts through the water toward my best friend, and I meet Starla's blue eyes. She wraps her arms around Giselle, pulling her back.

"We've won, my king," Starla says. "No need to hurt Ava. I'll take care of the human."

The fire in the king's eyes fades away, and he nods his head at Carter's mom. Giselle's bronze hair floats around her face. She continues to struggle for her life as Starla keeps the air from her. She'll drown in another minute, and there's nothing I can do about it. Once again, this woman rips apart my life all in the name of the ocean and the king.

The king closes the distance between us, hooking his arm around my waist, forcing me to stay by his side. Starla swims away with my best friend, and I watch as one more bubble escapes Giselle's lips as her eyes close.

Then they're gone.

My heart shatters into a million pieces, threatening to stab through my chest to cut out my own spark of life that keeps me a mermaid. King Attilonious drags me deeper into the sea, the world flying by until I can no longer glimpse the full moon slowly setting.

I've never felt so powerless and alone. At least the last time I was taken away from my life on land, I had Carter by my side. I had people who cared about my happiness and wanted me to love the life that was given to me.

But now, under the king's arm, all I can hope for is Carter got away and the king will leave him alone. He's won, and he can live happily knowing he's broken all the hope left in me.

"I've never met someone as brave and determined as you are, Ava," the king says as he descends into the pearlescent glowing colony. "I admire that, you know."

I don't respond to him. Compliments aren't going to

change the fact that he saw to it that my human life, my future, my happiness is all over.

"You have something in you no other mermaid in all the world has," he continues. "Something I haven't seen since I chose Luna's mother as my mate."

I still don't answer him. I don't give a crap about what he sees in me. Because apparently whatever it is, it wasn't good enough to fix things, to save my best friend, to save me.

"And that's why you will be my queen."

What the? Oh, God. This can't be happening. I think I'm going to be sick. The king is like a million years old, mean, and not someone I want to have near me. He's tail-flippin' insane if he thinks I'd ever agree to be his queen. I'm not royalty. I'm not fit to rule. All I want is my freedom. I've already paid the cost for it. I deserve it.

I pound my fists into his shoulder. "No! I won't do it. I'd rather die than be your queen. My heart belongs to Carter. I won't betray him."

The king grabs my hands, locking them in his strong fingers. He leans over, his salt and pepper hair veiling over us, and then he thinks, "You will obey me, Ava. If you want your mate to live to see another day, you will go through with this and vow your loyalty to me. If you don't, I will search both the land and the sea until I find Carter, and then I will break your bond. You'll have no choice but to be my mate."

I cringe at the thought. Being queen is bad enough—but being forced to be the king's mate? That's unthinkable. I didn't even know it was possible. Merpeople choose mates for life. Their bond is eternal. But now, the king threatens to rip that away from me, too.

Then I realize why all this is possible. Carter and I never went through with the coupling ceremony to make things official. While I have Carter's spark in my chest and he transformed me, I never vowed myself to him on the full moon. And now, I'll never be able to.

Voices echo through my mind, pushing away my thoughts, as we're greeted by the entire colony waiting for the arrival of their king. In the small valley, just outside the entrance to the castle, lies a rock platform with four pillars decorated with coral and sea plants. The water sparkles with glowing bubbles, the magic of the moon filtering through Pearlestria.

Without having to ask, I know this is the spot I was supposed to vow my life to Carter. This is where we were supposed to officially couple. And now, this will be the spot where King Attilonious will force me to pledge my loyalty to him as his queen. This is where my life as I know it will end. Because whatever magic stirred in me before—whatever affinity that lies within my body that can control the sea—remains dormant and untouchable as grief consumes me.

The king raises his gold staff into the air. He descends toward the platform, his sharp nails puncturing my side as he tells me to smile. I grind my teeth through the pain. I refuse to act like this is supposed to be the best day of my life. All I want to do is curl up and drown in the despair settling in my soul.

I want to finish what the ocean started all those years ago when it swept Bailey out to sea and rocked my world. If I could go back and change things, I would. Regret holds me by my spark and squeezes my heart. Had I just gone along with things and officially coupled with Carter, had I just sucked it up and dealt with the life I'd been given, if I'd just been the good mermaid and did what I was told, I'd have never been in this mess. But like the sea calls me on the full moon, the earth, the sky, the air—that call is just as strong. And now, King Attilonious will see to it that I'm broken beyond repair.

King Attilonious stops on the platform, still holding me at his side. My hair veils my face, blocking the dozens of onlookers, the ones who came to watch the coupling of me and Carter. Mateo's parents, Grandmer Oceana and Pops, float a few feet from the stage, both frowning when they realize I'm alone.

The rest of Carter's family sends thoughts to me, asking me what's going on. They shoot me a dozen questions, worry and fear in their eyes. I close my eyes. I can't bear to face them with the grief in my heart. I can't bear to face the family that was supposed to be mine.

"Ava," a soft voice says from the crowd. It's Grandmer. She swims up behind her family, her blue-streaked hair pulled back into an intricate braid. "Ava, please hold it together. I'm here for you. I'll help you through this."

But the only one I want to help me through this is the one person who can't.

Mateo slides up beside Grandmer and hooks his arm around her shoulders. My heart swells as I look at Carter's dad with hope in my eyes. Just seeing him, knowing if he's here then that means my mate—my soul mate—must still be out there. As long as Carter is alive and safe, I'll live an eternity of misery for him.

Mateo meets my gaze and nods. "Carter's safe now. You're doing the right thing."

My lip quivers. "Then why does it feel so wrong?"

He turns away with sad eyes without answering my question.

A soft hand touches my shoulder, and the king releases his painful hold on me. Luna pulls me to her, brushing my floating hair from my face. I press my face into the princess' shoulder and let her hug me.

"This isn't over," she whispers into my mind.

But it is.

The king bangs his staff into the rock platform, sending a jolt of energy into the water to quiet the merpeople of

Pearlestria. The muffled thoughts disappear as all eyes fall on us, some in excitement, others in confusion, and the few people who were supposed to be my family stare on in utter melancholy.

King Attilonious pulls me away from his daughter to spin me to face the crowd. "Tonight I have gathered you here to celebrate a great union—one that will empower us all and bring everlasting fortune to our home and to the entire ocean. For tonight, under the full moon, the enchanting Ava Adair, human-born, ocean-chosen mermaid will officially vow her loyalty to me, King Attilonious, as my queen."

The edges of my vision darken with his words. Gasps sound out from the crowd and into my mind, his announcement sinking in.

Then, to my despair, everyone cheers.

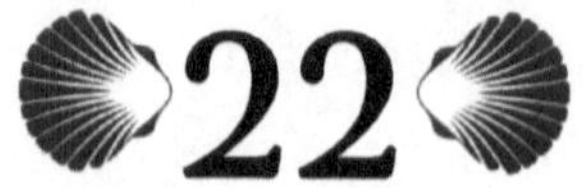

THE VOW

A FEW MERMAIDS PULL ME away to ready me for my sudden coronation as King Attilonious' queen. Luna hovers by my side, holding my hand in hers, as a mermaid strips my bikini top away to replace it with a bejeweled top woven from the softness algae-like material I've ever felt.

It's not until this moment I realize this was supposed to be my outfit for coupling Carter. It sends a shooting pain straight to my heart, and I push the mermaid away. She comes right back toward me to stick her fingers into my hair. Ignoring my cries, she yanks hard enough to ripe my hair free as she braids it into an intricate pattern around my hairline.

Another mermaid swims up behind me and sets a crown of silver on my head. Eerie light reflects from the ruby stones, casting a bloody haze through the water. They adorn my neck with ropes of black and white pearls, and the weight of everything sends my head bowing forward.

I sink to the glittering floor, bringing my fin up to my chest. But the mermaids still don't leave me alone. One scoops some sort of paste from a jar and dabs it across the patches of missing scales on my tail. New scales sprout up as the healer mermaid works some sort of magic on me. Next, she massages my caudal fin, sending pain through me. I flick my tail, knocking her back, but all she does is look at me with curious eyes. It takes another mermaid holding my arms, and Luna whispering for me to calm down in my mind, for the healer to wrap the top of my fin in tight kelp bandages with speckles of rainbow sea glass peeking through to make the bandages look pretty.

I hate to admit it, but it stops the shooting pain up my tail. I despise it though. I should be completely miserable as I face my fate.

When the mermaids leave me with Luna, I finally meet her sapphire eyes for the first time. "Why did you return? You could've escaped."

She pouts her bottom lip. "I promised Carter."

"You spoke to him?" My heart hangs heavy with the light of his spark.

She nods. "I vowed to keep you safe, so I am. It's my fault you've been dragged here. I should've expected they'd use me to get to you. I'm sorry, Ava."

I throw my hands up. "It's not your fault your father is out of his mind. Queen, Luna? I'm going to be his queen. Th—"

"Better than him killing you."

I grimace. "It's worse."

I cover my face with my hands, though the water doesn't let me cry as much as I want it to. Luna rubs her hand over my back, comforting me the best way she can. But she doesn't understand. To her, being queen isn't so bad. Deep down, though her father angers her, she still loves him. She'll forgive him.

"We'll make it through this," she says. "It won't be so bad as long as you stop resisting. You have to get my dad to let his guard down. You have to make him trust you. And when he does, that's when we'll fight to get out of here."

"That could be years," I say. "And Carter—"

"He'll be safe and alive."

But he'll be without me, and I without him. It's like fate wants me to repay him for saving my life, because if I go through with this, I'll be saving his life in return. But what kind of life can we have now? This isn't life. It's just living.

"His majesty is ready, my queen," a mermaid says, sending her thoughts to me. "The moon will be setting soon, and the king will not wait another month, so you better hurry."

I don't move. If the king wants me to appear before him, he'll have to make me.

"Your sadness is killing me, Aves." Carter's voice whispers into my mind.

My heart flutters with hope as I sense him near. "What are you doing, Carter? The king will kill you."

"I'm not letting him take you from me," he says.

"But Carter—"

"Just follow the king's orders."

"He's making me vow to be his queen," I say.

Carter growls in my mind. I can feel his anger in my very bones. "I won't let that happen."

The mermaid, who has come to collect me, swims down and grabs my hand, pulling me toward her, forcing me to move. Luna trails behind us, and we exit the tunnel and into the grand room.

The hum of voices rings loudly in my mind. I push them from my head. No one is going to get to me now.

"Straighten your shoulders. Don't look so defeated," Carter says like he's standing by my side.

A smile crosses my mouth. He whispers his love for me through my mind. The spark in my chest pulls me forward, and I let Carter fill my every thought, forcing away the darkness threatening to consume me.

King Attilonious mistakes my smile for something meant for him, but I don't let him think differently. Luna was right. The best way to fight him is silently, like a good little mermaid who'll answer to his every beck and call.

The king bows deeply and so does the rest of the crowd. I

peer over them, and that's when I see him. In the very back, a small sea of faces away, awaits Carter. He smiles when our eyes meet, and I have to force myself to bow back at the king.

As much as I know how dangerous it is for Carter to be here, I'm relieved he didn't abandon me. If we're going to fight, it's going to be together. Because he's my true mate, and I'd rather see the world end, see the ocean dry up, than give up what my heart desires no matter how selfish that is.

The king offers his hand out to me, and I force myself to let him take my hand. My fingers disappear in his large palm as he pulls me closer to wrap his arms around me. It takes everything in me not to reel backwards and gag.

"You look absolutely stunning, my queen," King Attilonious says, bringing my hand to his mouth to kiss my knuckles. *Stay calm. Keep smiling.*

The crowd coos, breaking through my mind shield for a moment before I push them away. The king stretches tall, towering over me by at least three feet, and he slams his staff into the rock platform, making the water quiver around us.

A moment later, he holds out the end of the staff to me and places my hand on the brilliant diamond.

"I've waited so long to have someone like you by my side as my queen, Ava. And as our kingdom looks upon us under the magic of the full moon, I vow to be your king, your protector. I vow to stand by your side as we rule the ocean together..."

I push his thoughts from my mind. I can't listen to them. He acts like he's been waiting his whole life for me, when he just wants me to fill the void created by the mermaid who had abandoned him.

"Ava," Carter says into my mind. "In front of the witnesses of our colony and under the glow of the full moon, I hereby promise to share the very essence of my being with you, the mermaid who completes me. I vow to always keep you safe and happy, to kiss your pain away, to hold you when you're sad. I vow in the name of the ocean to never stop loving you as my love is greater than the sea, the land, and the sky above. My love for you is unconditional, unending, and eternal. I vow my very soul to you, to be by your side, always and forever."

I turn my gaze away from the king as he continues to drone on, but I don't let his voice reach me. Instead, I project my voice out through the ocean for all to hear.

"Carter, in front of the witnesses of our colony and under the glow of the full moon, I hereby accept your vows as my eternal mate. I promise to share my very essence with you, the merman who promised his life to me to live as part of the great sea. I vow to cherish the gift of life with love, loyalty, respect, and thankfulness."

The king's eyes widen, my words settling in his mind. But I don't stop.

"I vow to stand by your side as your mate through even the roughest storms, for my love for you is greater than the sea, the land, the sky, and every star that shines above us. I promise to protect you with my life, to follow you wherever you lead in the form that you choose to be in. I vow to love you for the rest of my life and beyond. My love for you is unconditional, unending, and eternal. I vow my very soul to you, to be by your side, always and forever." I turn my gaze away from Carter. "And I won't ever let anyone stop me."

The king jerks out his hand to grab me, but I swim back, raising my hands up to protect myself. Carter darts over the crowd in my direction, pulling me to him, before he plants his lips to mine to complete our ceremony.

The king rips Carter away from me with fury blazing in his dark blue eyes. He throws Carter to the rock platform, holding his staff over him, aimed at the spark in his chest.

"No!" I scream out into the water. The ocean vibrates

around me as a shockwave knocks the staff from the king's hand.

Rushing from my place, I link my hands around Carter and tug him back before the king can impale him with his sharp nails. Carter flips through the water, pulling me by my hands, but the king grabs onto my tail, dragging me away from my mate.

King Attilonious glares at me, hovering over me, his chest heaving as he inhales the salty ocean water. His staff floats back to his hand, pushed by the water, and he aims it at me. Death has never felt so close in this moment, but the king isn't aiming to kill me.

"You *will* be my queen!" His voice roars through the water instead of in my mind. Turning away, he throws his staff like a spear, and it cuts through the water heading toward Carter.

There's nothing I can do as the staff smacks Carter in the chest before he even has a chance to move. The water shudders with turbulence, his body flying back and crashing into the sandy floor.

"Carter!" I scream. "No!"

With every ounce of strength in me, I dart forward, cutting through the churning water and throw myself onto my mate. The spark in his chest flickers as he struggles to live. The power of the sea had given him his spark, and it's the sea that can steal it away.

"Carter," I beg, sending my voice into his mind. "Hold on. Please. You can't leave me."

"Ava..." His voice is barely audible in my mind.

"Don't say my name like it's the last thing you'll ever say." I cup his face in my hands, and his eyes close. My chest clenches, our hearts beating out of sync for the first time since I've become a mermaid.

This can't be happening. I can't lose him. Not after everything.

Closing my eyes, I lean forward and kiss him. I kiss him with all the love I have for him. Through our kiss, he sends me a single image. It's a flash of a memory from the first moment he saw me standing on the dock near the Ocean Jewel. My blond hair blows around me as the land sits behind me, the most perfect backdrop. My blue eyes shine in the bright sun, and in that moment, I'm so very human. I'm the girl I've craved to be the last few weeks. The girl I want to be now.

"Carter, I love you," I say into his mind. I send a burst of my own memories to him. I show him how he looked when we first met, his hair shining bronze in the sun, his eyes as clear and as beautiful as the sea that holds his soul. I show him how he looked when he picked me up on our first date and how he closed his eyes when he ate his dessert. Then, I show him as the boy I fell in love with—with his glorious aqua tail. I send him the memory he shared with me weeks ago when he told me I was a mermaid. I send him the image of what his spark looked like in the water, how good it felt when I touched it.

Carter lies still beneath me. I pull away, and my whole world is shaken when I glance down at his chest. The spark we had once shared has faded into darkness. The ocean stole it away.

But the spark still glows from my chest now. And I refuse to carry it without Carter. I can't do this without him.

"I'm not keeping this life. Not without you, Carter." I send the thought into the sea, hoping it reaches every merperson in the world. I want them to know I'm not accepting the gift the sea bestowed on me. I won't do it, not without my mate.

Leaning down, I brush my lips against Carter's, sending the spark he gave me back to him. Because I can't be who I am now without him. I can't let the ocean have me if it won't have him.

"Ava!" the king roars. "Stop!"

It isn't until this moment I realize I've created a whirlpool around us, protecting me and Carter from the entire world. And the king can't touch us. No one can touch us.

I turn back to Carter, his dark hair floating around his head in the current. "Carter," I whisper into his mind. "You once gave me a part of your life so I could live. And now, I'm giving you mine. Please, come back to me. The ocean can't win, remember? No matter how rough it is, we can swim. We'll get through this storm. Because the ocean doesn't control us anymore."

A bright light flashes in my closed eyes through my kiss with Carter. Warm hands wrap around me as Carter accepts my spark into him. It's something I gladly give him and something I'd gladly give up for him.

Leaning back, I smile toward the surface, feeling my life fill Carter's body. He shifts in my arms, and his fin splits apart. He starts transforming into his human form for all the ocean to see.

Flicking my tail, I push us toward the surface.

The sun rises on the horizon somewhere above, stealing the suffocating darkness away. The full moon no longer controls us. Tingles take hold of my body, and I stare in awe as the spark radiates from me, filling Carter whole again, giving him back the merman life that was stolen from him. Our hearts beat in sync in my ears, and then cramps take hold of me.

Giving my spark to Carter triggered my transformation. To give him life, I have to give up my own to the sea. Water burns my lungs as my body transforms back to human. Without air, I'll drown. I am drowning. We're drowning together.

"Ava," Carter whispers into my mind. "You have to let go. Let the sea take you."

And I do. With my last strings of life, I not only vow my life to Carter, I vow my life to the sea.

EPILOGUE

THE LOST COVE

MY EYELIDS SHINE BURGUNDY, THE sun glaring brightly overhead. I don't want to open my eyes. My lungs scream in pain, but at least I'm breathing. The hum of the ocean crashes in the distance, and I can't move even though it calls to me.

A memory flashes into my mind. I drowned in the middle of the ocean above Pearlestria, but somehow, I'm still alive.

"Ava?" Carter asks, his voice wrapping me in familiar warmth. "Ava, can you hear me? Please, open your eyes."

I force my eyes to flutter open and gaze up at my mate. The sun halos him in golden light, shadowing his face. The spark in his chest shines more brightly than ever, and I reach out and brush my fingers against it.

"You're alive," I whisper, my throat burning. My body convulses as I cough, spitting out water from my lungs. "How?"

He smiles once before kissing my lips. A series of images flash through my mind, and I watch our bodies float through the ocean as it carries us from Pearlestria to spit us out on the shore of this island.

"When I died, my spark went to you. It shouldn't have been possible, but you gave it back to me. It was like you were born mermaid, choosing me as your mate like how I chose you.

And the ocean allowed it." He runs his fingers through the wave that creeps over us. "The ocean protected us from the king."

I blink a few times, sitting up. "You're human."

He nods. "For now. I think until the next full moon. It's like I was reborn or something. I can't explain it."

I kick my smooth, unblemished legs. "You sure?"

"I can still feel the ocean's essence. I just can't transform."

It takes me a minute to realize I'm just as human as he is, and I'm without a sea stone ring. I hold my hand out and show him. "What about me? How is this possible?"

"I don't know, Ava. But there has to be a reason."

A million thoughts cross my mind, but I don't want to think about any of it. I just want to revel in the fact I'm on this beach with Carter and we both have legs.

Carter must feel the same way, because he pulls me into his arms and hugs me. I smile against his lips, showering him with desperate kisses. I have no idea what's going on, but it doesn't really matter in this moment, because we're both alive and free from the sea.

"We'll figure this out," Carter says. "But let's just enjoy it for now, okay?"

I nod. I'll enjoy it forever.

As the sun dries my damp skin, the events of last night start to settle into my bones. It's the first time I've had a chance to think, and all I can think about now is how Giselle lost her life for me—Carter, too. I was so close to losing everything.

Tears drip down my cheeks, and I start sobbing. Carter hugs me tighter, kissing my wet face as the tears spill freely. We might have won. We might have survived the storm. But it has left a trail of destruction in its wake.

"Ava, Carter?" A familiar voice sounds out over the waves, taking our attention from each other. "What are you doing here?"

Jerking up my head, I glare at Starla strolling down the beach to me. I fling myself from Carter and rush toward the woman. She wasn't there for the coronation. She was busy murdering my best friend. In this moment, I want her dead.

I ram my shoulder into her chest, and we both tumble to the sand. Screaming, I wrap my hands around her throat. "You killed her!" My yells echo through the air. All I can think about is hurting Starla for taking away my best friend in the entire world, even if it was because of the king.

Hands grab my shoulders, pulling me back, and I thrash to the ground.

"Ava! Ava, I'm alive."

I freeze in my place, bringing my gaze to my best friend.

Giselle thrusts her arms around me. "Starla saved my life. She brought me here."

Carter stands with his mom, and I peer around the secluded beach. "And where is here?"

"Welcome to the Lost Cove," another voice says from behind me.

I turn in the sand, my mouth falling open as my eyes fall on a familiar girl. One I could never forget in my life. Shifting my gaze to Carter, he only offers me a shrug. It takes me a moment to find my strength, but when I do, I run through the sand and embrace the girl with all my might. She might be older, but I'd never forget her face or who she is.

She laughs. "Whoa. What's that for?"

I pull back and look into eyes the same color as mine. "What is this place?"

"A sanctuary for those lucky enough to escape death for discovering the truth about merpeople."

I hug the girl again. "I can't believe it. All this time you've been here."

Her eyes light up, realization taking over her thoughts.

"Ava?" she questions.

"You know her," Carter says, coming to my side.

I smile through my tears. "Yeah." I grab my mate's hand. "Carter, this is Bailey, my sister."

I once thought the ocean had stolen everything from me—my sister, my best friend, my life—but as it turns out, the ocean had been protecting them all along. It's not the deep water that is my enemy. It's the king. The merman who thinks he controls the sea.

And now I know why the ocean has chosen me.

Because like me, it wants to be free.

And I'm going to make it happen.

For everyone I love, including the sea, I will finally beat the storm.

WASHING ASHORE

CAN'T RESIST THE OCEAN

THE UNFORGIVING CURRENT CHURNS AROUND me, tossing my exhausted body back and forth amongst the waves. Every time I break the surface, another swell washes over me, stealing the breath from my lungs and clouding my vision. Utter darkness, one I haven't seen since my mermaid transformation, settles around me. The black ocean cocoons me in its embrace. Soft light emanates from my chest, but it's neither bright enough nor strong enough to push the night ocean away. All it does is blink in quick successions to the racing rhythm of my heartbeat.

"Carter?" I project the words out into the vast void. Fear grips at my chest, tightening my lungs as they beg for me to gulp in the air I so desperately need. But if I breathe now, I'll drown.

The only cramps threatening me are the ones digging at my side from my struggle to stay afloat. It's been weeks since the last full moon and weeks since I've transformed into a mermaid. I refuse to do so without Carter. I'm not risking the seas without my eternal mate and warrior—the boy the ocean fated me to be with. He's the boy who gave his life to save me from a lifetime of misery enslaved to King Attilonious as his new queen, and the boy I refuse to live without. I vowed my life and gave him the spark he had given me—the one I took fully after his death—the spark that brought him back to life and stripped him of his merman form, at least until the next full moon.

Thoughts of Carter push the panic from my mind, and I freeze in the water and peer through the blurry sea. My hair floats around my face, veiling me like it can somehow protect me from what lurks in the ocean I had suddenly awoken in, disoriented, unsure of how I got here.

And it's not the first time either.

"Ava." The soft voice comes from nowhere and everywhere, wrapping its melodic tenor around me, pulling me away from the spot I sway in the current. "Ava, this way."

I find the strength to move, and I swim, stroking out my arms while kicking my legs. I swim until the edges of my vision turn red, and I'm sure I'll open my mouth at any second to breathe in air that isn't there—not without my gills.

I catch myself in another swell, and it lifts me in the water, sending my stomach to my feet. I don't resist it. Instead, I swim with it, ascending in the dark sea for what feels like forever. A haze of light erupts above me, pale beams from the nearly full moon overhead, shining just for me. They beckon me to the surface that still seems so far away.

Too far away.

I can't hold my breath any longer.

Opening my mouth, ocean water fills my throat and nose, sending fear straight to my heart. I thrash about, choking on the sea. It's like it's begging me to transform, forcing me into it to save myself.

I will for the cramps to seize my legs, for the water to fill my heart and embrace me, but still, I can't transform. Something holds me back. A million things, actually. Fear of the king who stole my human world from me. Fear of the unreliable affinity to the ocean bestowed upon me. Fear of everything the ocean has given me suddenly being stolen away. Fear of losing the few good things in my life I've managed to salvage. All these things prevent me from transforming into what I'm supposed to be.

"Ava," the musical voice says, invading my mind. "Ava, you must not fear. You must accept everything you are if you're to make it in this world. Don't let your fear imprison you." It's like the voice read my thoughts. "You have a duty to fulfill."

I blink in and out of consciousness, trying to determine where the voice is coming from, but it's impossible as it echoes only in my mind and only for me to hear.

"Please," I say, my thoughts barely audible in my own head. "I'm trying the best I can."

"I know, my daughter. Give it time. You will figure things out."

I stop fighting the current, defeat clinging to me. "I don't have time. Just tell me the answers. Tell me what I have to do."

A quiet calm settles over me. The voice doesn't respond, leaving me feeling utterly alone and scared. This wouldn't be the first time I've drowned, but this time, Carter isn't here to revive me.

Carter.

A dozen images flash through my mind, all moments of our life together. From the first time I saw him standing on the dock in front of the Ocean Jewel, the luxury yacht where we met, to the moments in Pearlestria where we were forced to accept a life against the one we had planned. His shining, ocean eyes, his dark hair, the curve of his muscles I have memorized with my fingers, the softness of his lips—everything about him fills up my very essence with the love we have for each other, turning these dark moments into nothing but light and hope and assurance.

The icy water turns warm around me, and a flash of light glows on the other side of my closed eyelids, turning my vision red. Hands grip under my arms, my body dragged through the surf, and then suddenly, I'm engulfed in balmy night air.

Something thuds hard against my chest, forcing the water in my lungs to expel. I cough and spit, tears burning my eyes worse than the saltwater clouding my vision. Fluttering my eyes open, I peer up into the brilliant night sky. Stars pepper the world in tiny beads of dazzling light, each one shimmering and blinking like they're shining just for me. Pale moonlight sets the foamy waves aglow in a silver sheen. They crash over my weak legs, pulling the sandy beach out from under me, dragging it back into the surf.

Warm arms pull me farther from the crashing waves until my body rests on powdery soft sand. It clings to every inch of me, from my toes to my blond hair, making me sparkle in the white moonlight.

Water drips onto my face, the droplets pelting my forehead before splashing into my eyes. Carter gazes down at me, a mixture of emotions crossing his face—from uncertainty to fear to love to desire—all of them leaving him speechless.

I take a few more breaths, neither of us saying a word, and Carter holds me until my lungs stop burning. His elbow digs into the sand, and he brushes my tangled hair from my face with his other hand.

He closes the distance between us, kissing me gently at first and then deepening the kiss when my body reacts, craving Carter to kiss me so desperately that I'll forget the panic that immobilized me the second I opened my eyes amid the waves.

Carter tenses as I accidentally send him a dozen memories from the minutes I spent in the water along with everything I had felt in the moments before I thought I was going to die again. I don't mean to, because I want to protect him from experiencing such a thing, but they trickle to him anyway.

Ever so slowly, he pulls away. Tears shine in his blue-green eyes, sending sorrow through my own heart that beats in perfect sync with his. He rests his forehead against mine, taking a moment to compose himself while giving me the chance to find my own bearings.

"If you wanted to go for a late night swim, I'd have joined you," he says, forcing a smile, though his eyes line with worry.

I release a shaking laugh, staring down at the tank top and cotton shorts I had worn to bed, falling asleep in Carter's arms like I've been doing every night since we washed ashore on this island.

"I'll definitely invite you next time," I say, releasing a heaving breath. Neither of us says it, but we both know swimming in the dark ocean was something I'd have never planned. The farthest I go into the water now is not even past my waist in the waves. "If I actually wake up before I jump in."

He frowns at my words. The last few times this has happened, I found myself waking up amid the waves with no recollection of what had happened. I assumed my subconscious had been pissed at me for denying myself the ocean, but tonight felt different. It didn't feel like I just sleepwalked to the beach from our tiny bungalow for a dip. I was far enough out that the water was cooler than in the shallows. I was deep, too. I could sense it.

And the voice.

I think the ocean called me to it and got to me when my guard was down. I've been begging for an explanation—why me? What is so special about me that I've been given the gift to be a human without the enchantment of the sea stone ring created by the king? I want to know why both Carter and I are alive, and what I'm exactly supposed to do with myself. I'm not powerful enough to face King Attilonious like I assume the ocean wants. I can't even manage to keep my head above water.

But for some reason unbeknownst to me, here I am, standing—well, laying—on the sandy shore of the Lost Cove where five humans plus my best friend were brought to live in an attempt to spare them from the dire fate of discovering the mermaid secret. And now, I'm just as lost as they are. I'm not safe in the sea or home with my parents. I can't risk someone discovering that Carter and I didn't perish in what the merpeople of Pearlestria have probably declared a legendary love story. One that breaks my heart and makes me laugh. The silly human who was transformed on a whim, who denied the king her loyalty, giving up her chance to rule all the oceans for a boy who loved the land just as much as she did—that is, if we're even allowed to be mentioned.

King Attilonious was always described as a kind and generous king, one who allowed his people the choice of living on the land among humans or staying in the sea. But he was far from kind to me as he manipulated my life. He was unfair and threatening, using everything I loved as a way to get me to comply. He almost succeeded.

I shiver, pushing the thought away. Carter touches my face, and I realize he's staring at me, waiting for me to respond to the quiet questions he won't ask me. He never does. He's always one to wait until I spill my heart out. I hate and love him for that, but if he'd just ask them, it'd be easier for me to say.

"This isn't the first time this has happened," I admit. I haven't told him about the other times because I didn't want him to worry. He worries about me, and everything else for that matter, enough as it is.

"Ava." The sound of his voice swirling through the air tightens my chest.

I reach up and press my finger against his pouty mouth. "I'm fine. I'm sure it's nothing."

He furrows his brows before pulling me into his lap so I have to face him. My legs wrap around his waist, and I rest my arms around his neck, holding his intense gaze. Looking me deep in the eyes, he studies me, trying to find the answers I'm not quick enough to give him.

"So, I guess those few early morning walks you've claimed to go on weren't actual walks," he says, pointing out the fact that I lied. Well, sort of lied. I did have to walk back to our community from the places I woke up on the beach.

I groan, resting my head on his shoulder. "I'm sorry. I didn't want you to worry."

"I'd have been more prepared if you had just told me. I've never been so scared in my life, waking up alone only to feel your panic wash over me in icy waves. I thought the king had found us and someone had dragged you away all while I was sleeping." His arms tighten around me as he relives his own terror, and I now feel especially guilty. But I had no idea I'd find myself fighting the sea in the middle of the night.

I cup his face between my hands. "Hey, it's okay. I'm fine. We're fine. We're safe here."

He exhales a ragged breath. "I know, it's just—"

I interrupt his worry with another kiss. My lips brush against his, tasting the salt of the sea and feeling tiny grains of sand that cling to the both of us. I kiss him until his shoulders relax, and his breathing turns breathless in a good way.

"I don't want you to lose sleep worrying about me. I know you, Carter. You'd stay up all night just to make sure I'm okay. And that's unfair," I whisper into his lips.

"You're my mate. Of course I will," he says. "You're everything to me, Aves."

I smile. "I love you."

I melt in his arms, basking in the love radiating from him. He means every word he says, and it's because of that, I can't help stress about it. Even though he's so beautifully human in this moment, his heart is still purely merman, and he feels everything much more intensely. His life is mine and mine is his. It's something I can't always grasp no matter how much I feel it inside my soul. A merman's bond is life-long and more. Forever. Something I wasn't expecting to have at eighteen, but I'm lucky for it.

"You're not getting off so easily, Aves," he says, smiling the smile he saves just for me. He does it to lessen my annoyance, because he knows the last thing I like is for him to tell me what I already know even if I try to ignore the fact something is wrong with me.

I run my fingers along his shoulder blades. "You sure about that?" I ask, teasingly, hoping the lightness in my voice pushes away the tenseness of uncertainty we're both feeling. I'm all for irresistible distractions.

Carter scoops me up with him from the sand, spinning me around. "I see what you're trying to do."

"Is it working?" We'd stay here all night, but we're quite a ways away from our tiny beachfront community, and I'd hate for anyone to worry.

"You know it is." He kisses me as he strolls in the direction of our new home. Just like in the ocean, Carter is protective over me, always showing affection either through carrying me or holding me close. He doesn't care who's watching, and I do love his attention.

"Good," I whisper. "'Cause I don't want to think about the ocean anymore tonight. I only want to think about you."

He hums deep in his throat, reacting to my touch, and I nestle my head in the crook of his shoulder. My damp hair sticks to me, though the balmy sea air whisks away some of the sand from my skin.

Glancing at the vast ocean lit by the soft moonlight, I see a blink of light in the water. It disappears as quickly as I see it, and I suppress the urge to jump from Carter's arms and back into the sea.

He freezes in the sand, feeling how I stiffen in his arms.

"What's wrong?"

I blow air through my lips. "Nothing. I think the ocean got to me. I'm seeing things."

Shifting me in his arms, he peers at the ocean with me, but all I see is the dark water that doesn't glow as brightly in my human form, and the waxing moon, reminding me I can't resist the ocean forever.

"I don't see anything," he says.

"It was probably nothing. It's not like we have to worry, though. This cove is safe."

He kisses the tip of my nose. "I know."

But I know it's not the safety of the cove he's worried about. It's me.

And I'm worried, too.

ISLAND LIFE

SUN TRICKLES THROUGH THE CRACKS of our make-shift, palm frond bungalow, which looks like a more sophisticated version of the palm leaf tents I used to make as a child.

Island living—at least secluded island living—is a lot like living in Pearlestria. My new home is bare; there are no electronics or connections to the outside world. Instead of a wall surrounding us, a huge reef extends just past the cove, creating a barrier all the same. It's what keeps us safe along with some other force—the magic of the ocean. Very few merpeople know about the Lost Cove, its secret going back years and years.

According to the longest surviving inhabitant, Sandra, King Attilonious' mate brought a woman here after she canceled her transformation ceremony. Her soon-to-be mate couldn't bear the thought of killing her, asking the king to spare her, but he refused. It was become a mermaid or die. The queen went against the king and used her own magic to create this haven. Sandra said it was why the queen eventually left the king and her daughter, Luna. She doesn't really know the whole truth. The first lost human never confided in anyone, and she died a few years ago when she decided to lose herself to the sea.

Carter's warm hand slides up my side, pulling me from my thoughts of the inhabitants and the former queen. His fingers gently dig into the skin of my stomach, and he curls against me, blowing my blond hair from my neck so he can kiss me in a way that makes it hard to want to get up.

"We missed breakfast," Carter whispers into my ear, sending a shiver over me.

I roll over to face him, the pile of blankets under us shifting with me. It's harder on me to sleep on the sand when I'm not submerged underwater with the buoyancy of the current to lessen my weight. Carter's put down dried leaves to help with the sand, but it still speckles the blankets no matter what we do.

Carter's aqua eyes narrow, intently gazing at me in a way that makes my heart pick up pace. I'm pretty sure he didn't sleep at all, but he'd have had rather let me sleep and miss breakfast than wake me up, especially after last night.

I feel bad that he did, because I can hear his stomach. "You could've woken me up," I say. "I'm getting used to waking with the sun."

"And face the wrath of the beast?" he asks, laughing. "I'd rather starve. Plus, you were saying some interesting stuff in your sleep."

I frown, crinkling my forehead, embarrassment surely turning my cheeks red. "Tell me I gave you some answers and didn't say something mortifying."

"Depends what you'd think would be mortifying."

I glare, pressing my hands against his chest. "Carter."

He leans over and kisses my lips. "Let's call it even for you not telling me about the sleep swimming. I get to keep what you were talking about a secret."

Before I can argue, I catch the sound of a familiar voice growing louder over the rustling of the soft breeze against our makeshift walls. Carter closes his eyes, burying his head into my hair. We both stay absolutely still, just hugging each other. If we're quiet enough, we might get left alone.

"You guys better not be naked when I open your door in three, two—" Giselle shifts a few palm fronds away from the branch-lined entryway into our bungalow, which is the size of a small bedroom. The only furniture we have is a chest where we keep our clothes and a small boulder I perch on when I don't want to sit on the floor.

I smile at my best friend. "Three seconds wouldn't have been enough time to get dressed," I say from my spot on the floor.

She tilts her head back and laughs. "Enough to cover up. You're lucky I didn't come when you guys skipped breakfast."

I groan, sitting up. "Sorry, Gi. I didn't get much sleep last night."

"I caught Ava sleep swimming," Carter adds, remaining on the floor with his hands behind his head.

I cringe and gently knee him in the side. "It's not what it sounds like."

"It's worse," Carter says.

I glower at him.

Giselle's head turns back and forth between us, her gold-flecked eyes wide, nearly bugging from her face. "Whoa, Aves. The last time you sleepwalked was in middle school, and it was only to the guest room because Sapphire opened the window to listen to the waves. But swimming? That's crazy."

"Well, I *am* a mermaid," I say, smirking at the memory she shares with me, one I've forgotten about. Sapphire swore I just stood up all robot-like and left the room the second she had opened the window, but I don't remember doing that. All my friends used to tease me about it until we met Logan in high school, and he once sleepwalked naked across Sapphire's mansion when we all spent the night at her house for her sixteenth birthday.

The memories of my friends pull at my heart. They're probably just as freaked out as our families, wondering what happened to us, and if our missing status is related. I'm happy

Giselle is on this boring island with me, but I'm heartbroken she's here because of me—because she tried to help me escape from the king and revealed she knew my mermaid secret.

If it wasn't for Carter's mom, the king would've killed her. I've never been so thankful for the woman who I held responsible for my life in Pearlestria. It was enough that I have finally forgiven Starla for doing what she thought was the right thing with me even though it clearly wasn't.

"...maybe see if it helps." Giselle's voice tugs at my attention. "What do you think, Ava?"

I blink. "What?"

She sighs. "You really didn't get enough sleep, did you?"

Rubbing my palms into my eyes, I force myself to focus. "Sorry, I was just thinking about..." I don't say our friends' names.

Carter hugs me from behind. "I'm sorry, Aves. I know how much you miss home."

Giselle plops down next to me. "Think of it like this, we were already supposed to be moved out, and you know we wouldn't have visited this soon."

I smile at my BFF's words. She always knows how to make the best of things. To me, we're on a boring, secluded island. To her, we're living in paradise free from the worries of our budding adulthood. Her glass is never half-empty, and if it was, she'd just gulp it down and ask for a refill. She would've made a better mermaid than me. I don't mention it, though.

"I know. It's just—we're probably going to be on this island until we die," I say. Which is true. As long as King Attilonious is in control of the ocean, there's no place for us anywhere else in the world.

"Don't be dramatic. We'll be here for a few years tops," Giselle says.

I groan. "Years?"

"Yeah, because that's all the time I'm giving you to figure this crap out." Giselle offers her hand to me and pulls me to my feet. Flinging her arms around me, she hugs me for a moment. "Now, I want you to forget about this and just enjoy the day with me. I volunteered us for fishing duty and even saved you some breakfast to take along."

I grimace. "Fishing duty?" I'd have preferred to pick fruit or gather firewood or something. We're all responsible for pitching in and helping out in the community, but fishing is my least favorite thing to do. I rarely ever eat what we catch unless it's something I like, which never happens. As a mermaid, I can go long periods of time without eating, which has definitely come to my advantage. I really, really miss tacos.

Giselle shrugs her shoulders. "It's a lot more entertaining than anything else. Plus, you're the best one here at fishing. You don't need a line or net or anything if you'd just transform."

I gawk at her for a moment, thinking she's crazy for even suggesting such a thing. I turn to Carter, who still sits quietly on the floor. "It'd be nice if you'd get your tail back already, you know."

His laughter echoes through the air. "The full moon comes in a couple days, and when it does, I swear you won't have to help fish again." If I couldn't see the mer essence glowing in his chest, I wouldn't be sure he would even transform. But the beacon of light glowing just for me proves it. Neither mentions that I ignored Giselle's transformation suggestion.

Giselle gently pushes me. "Nuh uh. You'll both fish and be loved by all—but especially me."

I sigh. "Whatever you say, Gi."

"You have to be kidding me," I say, crossing my arms. "We can't fish like this."

Giselle beams a bright smile. She holds out a hand-carved

spear to me, but I don't take it. Raising my eyebrows, I look from my best friend to the lapping water she expects us to spear fish in. Looks like no one's eating fish today if they're relying on us to fish like this.

"Sure we can. We have to. Wes lost the last hook yesterday. He and Bailey are fishing on the other side of the bay so don't stress out. One of us is bound to catch something today." She offers me the spear again, and I take it, swinging it out to pelt her in the leg.

She laughs, swinging hers right back at me, and it takes Carter stepping between us to get us to quit fake sword fighting.

"It's not so bad, Ava," he says, gripping his spear and positioning it like he's going to stake a fish from right here on the shore.

"Says the guy who catches fish with his bare hands." I poke him with the blunt edge of my spear.

Jetting out his hand, he grabs the wood and yanks me right into his arms faster than I can brace myself. I fall into his chest, and he catches me before I topple over on the beach and end up with a mouthful of sand.

Cool water sprays over us as Giselle kicks her bare foot through the surf. "Don't even start, you two. We have work to do, and I'm going to prove to Wes and Bailey I can do this so I don't get stuck gathering crap."

If I didn't know any better, I would think Bailey was some other girl and not my sister with the way she's been avoiding me. After spending a few hours with both me and Carter our first day here, she's basically only ever around during meals, and even then, she rarely sits with us.

Discovering my sister was alive, who I had thought drowned years ago, was the last thing I expected. I'd have never believed she was rescued by a mermaid and dropped off here to live for learning the mermaid secret. I can't imagine what she went through all these years without us, yet I'll never know, because she doesn't confide in me. We're basically strangers who share the same DNA and nothing more.

I hope for that to change one day.

"We'd be an embarrassment if we come back empty handed," Carter says, wading his way into the water. "At least you have an excuse, Gi."

I laugh. "You mean you'd be embarrassed, Carter."

Giselle points her spear at me. "I expect double from you."

Rolling my eyes, I follow Carter into the shallow water of the bay. Giselle stays by my side and together we wade up to our waists. A few small fish swim around us since the reef is within swimming distance for even Giselle. We all stand together a few feet apart and just watch the crystal clear water.

Every time a small swell rocks us, the fish dart away, making this task pointless. Carter sinks under and peers around. He stays beneath the surface for an excruciatingly long time, long enough that I think he might've transformed without me. Giselle looks from me to Carter's blurry form, and I shrug.

He pops up empty handed with a look of clear frustration crossing his face as he glares at the water. Shaking his head, he splashes me with sea spray.

"We should swim to the reef," he says, hopping up with a small swell. "I've never speared fish from the shore and might have better luck where there are more fish."

"I'm down with that," Giselle says.

I grimace. "Do I have a choice?"

"Sure, you can either swim with legs or a tail. Your choice," Giselle says.

"Legs it is," I mutter.

The swim to the reef is better than I could imagine. I haven't swam much without my tail, but with how calm the ocean is today and how beautiful our surroundings are, it does feel more like vacation than our new way of living.

The reef teems with life; all sorts of fish swim about or hide in the coral and sea plants. A few good sized gray snappers hunt for their next meal, and Carter already sets his gaze on one. This section around the reef is shallow this time of day, and I can touch the ocean floor without swimming.

I sink under the surface, my vision blurring, but I keep my eyes open anyway. My blond hair floats around my face, veiling the world around me. I extend my hands out in front of me, just swirling them through the water, and a silver fish with a deeply forked tail comes right up to me and swims around my fingers.

A spear cuts right through the water, impaling the fish. I accidentally suck in a gulp of saltwater in surprise. Shooting to the surface, I cough and spit, shoving my wet hair from my face.

"What the hell?" I ask, glaring at Carter, who drops the now dead fish into the bag Giselle holds open. "I can't believe you did that." I shouldn't be surprised. It's not the first time Carter killed a fish right in front of me. I'm just lucky he doesn't start deboning it right in the water to eat in this very spot.

"I know you love all the fish and would rather make all of them your pets, Ava, but we're here for food not to make fishy friends." Like Carter even needs to remind me. I'm more annoyed I didn't get a warning.

"Still not cool," I say, splashing him in the face with water.

He closes the distance between us, wrapping his arms around my waist. His head tilts to the side when I pout my bottom lip out. He kisses it. I don't kiss him back though. Not because I don't want to but because I like to drive him crazy.

"Give the guy a break," Giselle says from her spot a few feet away. "He's trying to feed our poor, starving community."

I roll my eyes. "No one is starving."

"Well, we will be," she quips.

"Forgive me?" Carter asks, a smile on his lips. He knows I've already forgiven him, but he's totally milking the fact that Giselle has picked his side.

"You know I have."

Carter and Giselle take turns trying to catch fish, but the more they move through the water, the more the fish dart away. At this rate, we'll be out here all day with not enough fish to feed everyone dinner.

I blow out a frustrated breath. "Maybe we should relocate."

"All the fish have swam to the other side of the reef," Carter says.

Giselle peers through the crystal clear water, toward the barrier that protects the island. "Then maybe we should, too. It won't hurt if we stay close."

Swimming closer to the barrier, Carter floats above it to look over. "It dips down pretty quickly, but I'm a great diver. I think we can manage to get at least a few more."

I stare between the two of them. "Are you two serious? There's a lot of water within the barrier to relocate to."

"That'll take time," Giselle says. "Don't be scared, Ava. A mermaid isn't going to just materialize and drag us into the abyss. You can see them coming."

She makes a good point, and clearly, they look like they'll cross over whether or not I'll agree. The last thing I want is to watch from the safety of this spot. If anything, I can be the lookout.

I sigh. "Okay, fine. But we're not staying long. If you can't catch another fish in ten minutes, we'll do things my way."

"Deal," both Giselle and Carter say in unison.

Carter swims over the reef first since he's closest, and he treads in the water too deep to touch his feet to the bottom but not deep enough where I can't see it. Giselle crosses over next, a grin lighting her face like we're trespassing somewhere awesome. She swims a few feet away from Carter and dives under.

A small swell pushes me forward a foot, and I kick my legs, swimming to Carter. He wraps his arms around me, his stomach pressing against mine. I kiss him softly and then turn my head to look at Giselle.

Fear shocks me in my heart when I don't spot her right away.

"Where is she?" I ask, spinning in Carter's arms.

A wave of water splashes my face, and Giselle breaks through the surface a dozen feet away. I don't have time to release a breath of relief. From behind her, a swell rises, crashing over all three of us. The last thing I hear is Giselle's scream before we all sink under.

SUBMIT TO THE SEA

A STRONG CURRENT PULLS ME away from Carter, and I let it drag me a few feet into the open water. Through my blurry vision, I spot my mate half a dozen feet away. He's already back to the surface. It's not the first time he's swum in rough waters. He makes staying afloat look effortless, and I can't help just staying underwater in my spot.

He dips back under, spinning to face me. Closing the distance, he locks his fingers on my arm and pulls me back to the surface. I gasp in a deep breath, my mind kicking into action. Something feels strange. It's like I can't keep focus, not with the water encompassing me, inviting me to submerge myself again.

"Ava," Carter says. "I can't see Giselle."

Carter's words blow the fog from my mind, and I swim a few feet away from him to where I last saw Giselle before the wave separated us. A voice echoes through the air, drawing my attention to the open water. Giselle fights a current, trying her best to swim back toward the reef.

Carter swims forward without me, cutting through the water quickly even in his human form. He's not even within twenty feet of her before she sinks back under again. He dives down, now too far for me to keep my eyes on his figure. I can still see the flash of his spark, the one that always allows me to find him, light up the water even with the bright sun overhead.

He resurfaces, taking another breath, and dives back under.

I swim after him, fear pushing me to keep going. We're traveling too far from the reef. If we can't make it back, we'll risk our lives in the open water or risk drowning.

A few bubbles erupt on the surface, and I head in their direction. Neither Carter nor Giselle comes back up, and I dive under and peer around. Bubbles blur the water, and I can't see either of them. I can't believe this is happening. I can't believe I'm about to lose both my mate and my best friend to the ocean that has protected me in the times I've needed it to. The ocean that chose me to be a mermaid.

Tingles crawl up my legs, starting from my toes and working their way to my torso. It's an all too familiar sensation, one I haven't felt since the last full moon where I transformed back into a mermaid to nearly lose everything at the hands of King Attilonious.

Pain washes over me, cramps causing me to arch my back before bending forward. I moan, resisting the change. Nothing—not the constant sound of the sea, the allure of the waves begging me to swim under, nothing—has triggered the transformation, and I thought maybe it wouldn't happen again until Carter transformed under the full moon.

And I'm terrified of what's happening. The king stole my sea stone ring, and I knew I was living on borrowed human time.

Cramps seize through me again in an intense wave unlike anything I've felt before. I bend forward, nearly submerging my head completely under, feeling like my bones are breaking and my skin is tearing away.

"Ava! Help!" Giselle's voice cuts through the air. "Something's out here. It keeps pulling me—"

Water splashes as her words cut off, and she's pulled under again. I resist the change, forcing the pain pulsating through me away and swim forward. My life feels like it's spinning out of control.

Hands lock onto my legs, pulling my head under, and I thrash until I realize it's Carter. He's close enough to see clearly, and I pull us both up to the surface.

"Someone's got Giselle," I say to Carter. "They'll drown her."

Her voice rips through the air again. It's like she's being toyed with, tortured by only being able to stay up long enough to gasp a breath before being pulled under. Tears burn my eyes, blending with the seawater that keeps rising to splash me in the face.

"I can't get to her, Aves. Every time I get within reach, I'm washed back to you," he says, kicking to keep us both afloat.

Another series of cramps jet through me, and I yell out, dipping under. Carter hooks his hands under my arms and pulls me up. Before he has a chance to say anything, a look of panic crosses his face as he realizes what's happening.

All I can think about is I'm changing and my best friend is drowning, and in a few moments, the merperson after her will come after me next, and there won't be anything Carter can do. He's stuck in his human form until the full moon. Though he still wears his sea stone ring, and he'd give it to me, we now have to face what we've been avoiding since we washed ashore on this island. What will we do once the full moon rises and triggers his transformation again? We'll be doomed to split our time away from each other if we want to be on land, or we'd just have to submit to the sea.

Giselle's screams echo through the air again, clenching my heart, and as much as I want to resist and fight the pull of the sea, I can't. I might be our only fighting chance, and there's no way I'm letting someone steal away my best friend again.

Convulsions rip through me again, and Carter helps me strip from my bikini bottoms before my legs fuse together and tear them away. Tears burn in my eyes, a sob taking hold of me. My lungs burn with every gasp of breath, but I don't want to go under. I don't want this to be happening at all.

"Ava, calm down," Carter says. "You have to calm down and dive."

"Not without you," I say, my voice shaking. I'm afraid to face the ocean alone.

Carter tightens his hold on me and dives, dragging me under with him, not giving me a choice in the matter—like I ever had one at all. His fingers cup my cheeks, combing my floating hair from my face. His blue-green eyes sparkle the same turquoise as the ocean, and he squints at me while holding his breath. It's like the first time I transformed into a mermaid all over again. I can almost hear him whisper for me to just breathe.

I inhale the ocean water, letting it push through my gills to ease the ache running through me. It's only when I relax that Carter let's go of me and swims back to the surface for a breath of fresh air.

I don't break the surface though. I swim forward, flicking my tail to force my way through the current that has separated me from my best friend. My vision clears, and I let the ocean fill me, washing away the lingering fear of what lies in the sea's depths. I expect to see an army of the fiercest merpeople warriors or even the king, but no one is in the water apart from Giselle.

She floats a few feet below the surface, her bronze hair covering her face. She doesn't move, and the ocean just suspends her in a haze of sand and bubbles. Swimming as fast as I can, I close the distance between us and hook my arm around her to pull her to the surface.

She automatically gasps in breath and starts flailing. I squeeze her tighter, keeping the both of us above the water.

"Let go of me!" she screams, smacking her hands against me like I'll drag her back under.

"Gi, it's me," I say, using my arm to block her from hitting my face. "Stop. You're okay. I have you."

Pushing the sopping wet hair from her face, I meet her gold-speckled eyes. She releases a long sob, bawling her eyes out as I hold her. I flick my tail, propelling us back toward the reef. Carter meets me with serious eyes, but I don't say anything to him. I can't think about the fact that I'm a mermaid or that my best friend nearly drowned. All I can think about is getting the two most important people in my life back to shore where it's safe, where the ocean or anything in it can't hurt them.

With my free hand, I reach out and lock my fingers with Carter's. I tug him closer, and he swims right next to me. A swell rises in the water, pushing us back over the reef and into the shallow water where both Carter and Giselle can stand.

I still don't let go of either of them.

"We're all okay," Carter muses out loud, like his words will somehow make this whole situation better.

Giselle nods, releasing a shudder as she turns her gaze back to the open ocean. "Remind me to never go over the reef again," she says, her chest still heaving from fear.

"What happened out there anyway?" Carter asks. "Was it a—"

Giselle shakes her head before he can even get his question out. "No. It was just some freaky current."

Carter glances at me. "Did you see anyone?"

"No, but something wasn't right. And now look at me," I say, my voice cracking. "What am I going to do?"

"This is all my fault," Carter says.

"Uh-uh. It's mine, too. We should've listened to you, Aves," Giselle says.

I blink my oncoming tears away. "I—" I snap my mouth

shut, unable to find anything else to say. It is what it is. This is who I am no matter how much I want to deny it. It's Pearlestria all over again, but instead of a mermaid colony, I'm stuck swimming in a bay and around the shallow shores of the island. I might be free of the king, but I'm still imprisoned in the sea.

"Don't panic, Ava," Carter says. "You can have my ring. It's going to be okay."

"It's not. The full moon is coming," I say.

He squeezes my hand. "We'll figure it out."

But I'm not so sure we will. My dreams of us living on the land, even if it's limited to this island, slip through my fingers to get lost on the waves. The king has won. He not only stole my human life from me, but he stole the land, too.

Without saying a word, I swim the three of us through the bay to the shore near our small community. Carter helps Giselle to the beach while I remain in the waves. I'm afraid to face the others in the community.

Bailey comes rushing from the shelters. She waves her hands wildly, pointing in my direction, and I can't stop the sinking feeling in my stomach. I can't hear what she says over the hum of the waves, but it's enough to make Carter run his hand over his head to his neck. He shifts on his feet, and Giselle hugs herself.

The heaviness in my heart threatens to drag me under, and I let it. I know I should wait for Carter to return to me, to bring me his ring, but I just want a moment to myself to think things through, to get used to the idea that'll I'll be staying in the water more than on the land.

Without waiting, I dive down and head to the deepest part of the bay, the part where only the fish can bother me.

I settle in the sand, leaning back on my elbows, and stare up at the glittering surface. Sunlight ripples over the waves, reminding me of all the times I sat on the sea floor in Pearlestria and dreamed of the land.

It's not until this moment, with the peacefulness of the calm bay surrounding me, that I realize I've missed being in the waves. I've missed the freeing feeling of swimming in the water without worry. Sitting here alone allows me to think. Maybe things won't be as bad as I thought. I've dealt before. I can deal again.

Memories from last night trickle into my mind and how I heard a voice through the water. I thought it was my imagination, but what if it was the ocean communicating with me? She said I had to let go of my fear.

And I'm ready to let it go. I can't live my life in constant turmoil. Happiness isn't out of my reach, even if I can't go to shore with Carter. This life is still better than the life the king wanted me to have. At least here, I can have both worlds.

The single thought sends cramps rushing through me. Surprise propels me from the floor, and I rub my hands over my tail as my scales smooth out into skin before it splits, and I gape at my legs. My chest lightens, my gills no longer letting me breathe underwater, but I don't swim up toward the surface.

Instead, I close my eyes and will myself to transform back into a mermaid.

It works, and I didn't even need to breathe air.

Faster than ever, I take on my mermaid form and push water through my gills. Excitement replaces my fear, and in this moment, I realize how much I've missed being a mermaid. It's like it was a part of me I had forgotten about. Without the worry of discovery or the worry of being trapped in the sea, I can actually enjoy what I am.

A shadow overhead blocks the light trickling to me. One of the two small row boats we use to go around the island floats above me. It rocks back and forth on the surface, and then a figure jumps over the side, sending glittering bubbles through the water.

Carter dives down toward me, following the pull he feels from the bond we share as mates. I peer at him for only a second before I push from the sea floor and swim up to meet him. He couldn't possibly make it down to me as a human no matter how hard he tries. But he will try. I know him.

Grimacing, I meet Carter's curious expression underwater. He tilts his head to the side, getting close enough to my face to see me clearly. Bubbles shimmer from his nose as he lets out a tiny breath in front of me, but he doesn't motion for me to head to the surface.

Closing the distance between us completely, he brushes his lips across mine, shifting his hands up to my face to hold himself to me. A dozen images flash through my mind from Carter's, all images that radiate with the love he has for me, and I yearn to hear his voice in my mind. It's been too long.

A sudden wave of emotions crashes over me, coming directly from Carter. He misses being a merman seeing me as I am right now. Unlike me, it's always been a part of him, even if he did claim the land as his home. I'm sure our official coupling shifted something inside him, and it hurts him I'm in a form he cannot take, one he probably feels the most powerful in.

I flick my tail and propel us to the surface. Carter gasps against my mouth, his warm breath making me want to steal it from him with another kiss, which he eagerly accepts. We could survive on our kisses and love if we tried. I'm tempted to do so.

After another long kiss, Carter eases back but doesn't let go of my face. I fan my tail enough to keep us treading water so he doesn't have to. His legs brush against my tail, and it's one of the few times I've felt him as a human against my mermaid form.

"Giselle's going to be fine, you know," he says instead of saying what I know must be on his mind. "And so are you.

Have you...?" His voice trails off.

I don't have to read his thoughts to know he's wondering whether or not I've tried to transform back into my human form.

"I think I want to stay here for a while," I say instead of answering. I'm afraid to admit how alluring the sea is. Not only to him but to myself. I'm afraid because the ocean was more welcoming than I care to admit. I guess losing my old human life in Azure Waters has changed me. I just didn't know how much until now.

Carter presses his lips together into a line. "Okay, if that's what you want. I can wait on the shore."

It's tempting to let him go so I can sink back to the bottom of the bay. But the sadness in his eyes pulls at my heart. "Stay with me?" I ask. Just because Carter can't transform, doesn't mean he can't still be with me.

He smiles. "I'd like that." Reaching down, he caresses the small ridge on my back and pulls me closer by the backside of my tail. "I've missed this, you know. Just you and me in the water."

"Is that so?" I ask, peppering him with salty kisses.

"More than you know."

"Then let's swim."

NO ESCAPE

CARTER SITS ON A ROCK AMID the waves. White foam bubbles around me, and I sway back and forth in the current, holding onto his legs. We're down the shore from the bay, far enough away from our little community not to be bothered.

In this section, the reef rests closer to shore, but the distance is far enough from home that no one really comes here unless they plan on walking the shore for a few hours. In my mermaid form, I could swim around the island in that time, and Carter could do it even faster.

I dip under the water and let the wave suck me a few feet from Carter before it pushes me back toward him. The sun hangs low in the sky, turning the blue color yellow. The expansive ocean disappears into the horizon, and I imagine swimming freely like we used to do in Azure Waters.

Carter's gaze never wavers away from me, and I arch to dive backward, sending a wave of ocean water over him. Smiling, I pop back to the surface to see water dripping from Carter's grinning face. He shakes his head, sending water droplets cascading through the air, and then he holds open his arms for me.

I swim forward, and he pulls me up onto the rock next to him, adjusting me so my tail rests on his legs and slaps against the rising tide. His fingers send tingles over me, his touch exploring my smooth scales shimmering like diamonds in the setting sun.

Carter twines his fingers with mine, sliding them back and forth against the webbing that stops just below my knuckles. Unsaid words hang between us, threatening to ruin what feels like a perfect moment after a scary and strange day.

We haven't talked about what happened earlier, and I almost don't want to go back to our community so I don't have to think about it. But Giselle would be furious if I abandoned her overnight without a word. She'd assume the worst, and I couldn't put her through that.

"Why do I have the feeling you don't want to go back?" Carter asks, finally speaking what's weighing on his mind.

I shrug. "Because you know me so well." Resting my head on his shoulder, I watch the foamy waves curl and splash toward the beach. "I just—I'm afraid."

He sucks in his bottom lip, looking so kissable. "Me too."

Those weren't the words I was expecting him to say, and I shift to look him straight in the eyes. "You are?"

A sad smile crosses his face, and he pulls me closer against him. "You know, I never imagined my life would turn out this way."

Transforming into a mermaid definitely wasn't a part of my five year plan, but I don't have to tell Carter that. Instead, I ask, "And what did you imagine?"

It's something I've never asked him, and the fact that I have to tightens my chest with guilt. I fail more often than not when it comes to thinking about something besides my own ruined life. But Carter's life has been ruined, too.

"Before or after I met you?" he asks, reaching down to cup water in his hand to sprinkle across my tail.

"Before."

He doesn't respond right away, almost as if he doesn't really want to answer my question. It takes him a minute of looking at the sun fading completely into the horizon for him to answer.

"I was working on the Ocean Jewel to save up to start a water-sports store. I had imagined living on a beach somewhere, maybe in a small apartment above my shop and then I'd offer lessons or whatever, but then I met you."

"And I had to go and mess up everything," I say.

He wags his head and then leans over and kisses my temple. "You made it better."

"Yeah, right."

Chuckling, he kisses the bridge of my nose. "Seriously, Ava. Meeting you was an unexpected good surprise. You know I don't like to believe in fate, but I do believe it was more than a coincidence that I met you. It's like your soul called to me." He turns his face away. "This sounds so lame now that I'm saying it out loud."

I grin, because he's right. It sounds cheesy as hell, but it doesn't change that I love every single second of his admission. And in his admission, that's where I can see our differences. Carter doesn't like the idea of having some force mess with his life. It's why he fought to have me continue my human life as it was. I don't blame him for thinking that way, either. I hate the idea that things happen for a reason without giving us a choice in the matter, but just because I hate it, doesn't mean I don't believe it.

Out of all the humans in the world, I just happened to meet one who was born a merman in the ocean I had once feared. And Carter isn't just some ordinary merman. He's been gifted with speed, strength, courage, and an unending devotion to me I can't even grasp. He's a born protector of our people, one who would serve the king well, but instead, he's here with me. He's my warrior. The ocean picked me for him when I fell off the yacht.

It was more than an accident. It was destiny. I know that now. But why? It's something I've yet to find out.

"So, why are you afraid," I ask, redirecting the subject away from all the what-if possibilities that were never meant to happen, of the life we were never meant to have no matter how much we wanted it.

"Why are you?" he asks.

I fake glare at him. "Not fair."

"Ava," he says.

"Carter." I pout my bottom lip for a second. He brushes the pad of his thumb across it to hold my chin so I don't look away, but he doesn't let me in on what he's thinking. I pull his hand away and grasp both of his between mine. "You can be incredibly frustrating. I feel like the worst mate because you're always worrying about me and how I'm doing. But you know what? I'm worried about you. I want to know what you're afraid of for once without you being concerned about my fears."

He tilts his head up and meets my gaze, a strange look crossing his face. His expression is a mixture of curiosity, surprise, and even joy. His mouth is gaping but also half smiling, and his eyes blink a few times. I've caught him off guard, and he's not sure what to make of me.

"So spill," I say, nudging him with my shoulder. A wave collides into the rock beneath us, soaking us in tropical water.

He sucks in his top lip in consideration. "Okay, fine, but let me tell you something first. I sometimes feel like it's me who is the worst mate. Like I'm undeserving of your love, which you give so much of to me. I feel like it's my fault we're in this mess and that I've failed you."

"You didn't fail me. Carter. Never think that," I say. "You gave up your life and family for me to make sure I didn't end up with a monster. You could've just left me and moved on, living the way you wanted on the land."

"I'd have never—"

I hold my hand up. "And that means the world to me. It

means everything. I might not be living with Giselle in some beachfront condo about to go to college, but that doesn't even matter to me anymore. What matters is we're both alive and away from King Attilonious and we're figuring all this out together. And you know what else? I thank the unpredictable ocean every day you were the one who saved me."

"God, I love you, Ava," he says. "No matter what form you're in, I love you."

I gently kiss him. "Is this what you're afraid of?" I ask, waving my hand over my tail. "That I'm going to stay like this?"

"It sounds bad when it comes from you," he says. "But that's not all of it. I'm afraid the sea got to you. I'm afraid even though we're not in Pearlestria that you don't have a choice, that we never had one to begin with."

I think over his fears. They're the same ones I thought about earlier when my transformation was triggered, but I'm not afraid now. I know I can. Because the ocean was right. Fear has been imprisoning me, stopping me from accepting that I am who I am, and there's nothing to be done to change it—not that I want to now.

"I think you're wrong. We do have a choice, but we just weren't seeing the options." I release Carter's hands and jump back into the waves, ducking my head under. Closing my eyes, I will my transformation to take hold of me and turn back into the human I was born as. It happens so suddenly, I accidentally try to breathe underwater. Kicking to the surface, I cough and spit, and Carter reaches down and pulls me up by my wrists, taking in my half-naked human form.

Weeks ago, I'd have blushed. I'd have panicked about the possibility of being seen by someone. But no one is here. Only the brave would swim out to this rock during the high tide in a churning sea.

"And the ocean didn't get to me, Carter," I add, sitting on

his lap. "It's had me all along."

Breaking the surface, I spit out a mouthful of water like a fountain over Carter's head. He laughs, pulling my bikini bottoms from the pocket of his board shorts and tosses them to me. The weight of the world seems less heavy now that Carter and I have spoken our fears to each other.

I slip into my bottoms, using Carter to keep me from being sucked back into the wave. When I'm dressed, I hop into his arms and he charges through the waves all the way to the dry sand. He sets me on the beach, flopping down next to me and cradles me against his sandy body, just holding me like we haven't spent most of the day alone together in the water.

"I thought you guys got washed out to sea," Giselle says, getting up from her spot leaning against a palm tree. It's dark enough I didn't even notice her there, and I wonder how long she's been waiting for us.

"Sorry, Gi. I didn't think we'd be gone this long," I say, getting off Carter's lap and back to my feet.

She stands in front of me. "I was worried you wouldn't be able to come back to shore."

I wrap my arms around her. "I'd have figured out a way. I wouldn't abandon you."

"Good, because if you haven't heard—"

Carter clears his throat, cutting her off. "I haven't told her yet."

My forehead crinkles. "Told me what? Is this about the conversation you had with my sister?"

Giselle lifts her chin, straightening her shoulders. "Yes and no."

I study her for a moment and then glance at Carter. Someone better start talking soon. "One of you spill."

"There's a reason no one goes on the other side of the reef,"

Carter says, finally speaking up.

"Obviously," I say.

"The island doesn't only protect us from the king, Aves. It also stops humans from leaving. There's no way I'll ever make it off this island alive. This is it for me." For the first time since our arrival, Giselle sounds hopeless.

Her words lace around me, squeezing me tight enough to leave me breathless. It's like I'm suddenly floating amid the dark ocean with no sense of direction to the surface. Every ounce of hope for a future back in the human world swirls down an imaginary drain. All three of us have been treating this place like a pit stop, not our final destination, but now that I know the reality of it, I can't stop the ache clenching my heart.

"No," I whisper.

Giselle shrugs. "Look at it this way. At least it's better than the alternative. I'd much rather be living in boring, blissful paradise than to not live at all."

"Doesn't make it suck any less. We don't belong here."

"Technically, it's only you and Carter who don't belong here. This is my life sentence. Not yours. You can leave at anytime." She doesn't say it in a mean way but just a way that states the facts. "The king isn't the only thing protecting the mermaid secret. The ocean does a great job at doing that, too. But at least here, we're given a chance to live."

I'm stunned speechless. I had no idea the inhabitants of the Lost Cove never left the island because they couldn't. I had assumed they were too scared to risk their lives in the human world. Even being land locked couldn't protect them if the king was determined enough. The full moon only keeps merpeople in the water for a short time out of a whole month if they choose to remain on land.

My gaze flicks from Giselle to Carter. "No wonder I feel like some people are uncomfortable with us here." No one has ever downright said it, but I can tell a few of the inhabitants distrust me and Carter. They avoid us unless forced to be pleasant otherwise. Even Bailey. I hate to think it, but she clearly holds something against me. And now I know it's probably because I'm not a prisoner here. I stay by my own freewill. Well, I stay because I'm not ready to face what lurks in the deep water.

Carter wraps his arms around me from behind, resting his head on my shoulder. "Don't stress over it, Ava. We have enough to worry about as it is. A few people's opinions don't change the fact that we're in just as much, if not even more, danger than they are."

He's right about it, but it's like my mind just expands to let in all the extra worry freely. I hate that I'm as different on this island as I was in Pearlestria. I miss Azure Waters more than ever. It is the only place I feel I belong.

I slump my shoulders. "I guess you're right. But it still doesn't mean I want to endure any more community time than I have to, especially since I know what's up. Why don't we make things a little easier and pack a dinner and head down the beach to have a bonfire, just the three of us?"

Giselle claps her hands in her regular excited fashion, the heaviness of the conversation now tossed to the sea with everything else we can't change in the moment. "God, yes. I'll pass on awkward community dinner every day of the week if I could."

"Totally," I say.

"Now, if only the ocean would send a hot guy my way, I'd be set." She laughs at her own thought, tilting her head back.

I beam her a smile, my heart already feeling lighter. "I'll put in a good word."

"You can do that?"

Carter laughs. "You never know."

WASHING ASHORE

OH, NO.

Not again.

Opening my eyes, I stare into vast, utter darkness. The churning ocean sends me adrift in a current so strong I can't even manage to swim out of it. My heart pounds in my ears, the only sound I hear through the muted sea that steals all my senses away.

I kick my legs, trying to swim to the surface to gasp for air, but when I get close enough to see the nearly full moon, I'm dragged down farther.

"Why am I here?" I ask, sending the thought out to whoever is willing to hear it but afraid of who might respond. Panic threatens to consume me. With every passing second, my lungs burn more and more.

I will myself to transform into my mermaid form, imagining submitting to the ocean that clearly wants my attention, so much so it risks drowning me. But nothing happens. My body agrees with what my heart wants, which is to make my way to the surface to swim back to shore, wherever that may be.

"Please," I say, "answer me. Tell me what you want."

Exhaustion washes over me, and I give up trying to swim to the surface just out of my reach. Silence wraps around me, squeezing me as tightly as the darkness of the water, and I almost feel as if I don't exist at all. I would believe it if it weren't for the excruciating pain I fight against to stop myself from swallowing a mouthful of the ocean.

"Please," I beg again.

The temperature of the ocean shifts from cool to warm, and a swell pushes me up through the water. "You must not give up, my daughter. You still cling to your fears. You still resist."

"I'm not resisting," I whisper. "I accept who I am."

"You don't."

I fade in and out of consciousness, the foreign thoughts, swirling through my mind, almost mocking me. Another strong current pushes me, and I tumble through the wave, letting it take me with it.

Like the flip of a switch, the world suddenly turns on as my head breaks through the surface. I automatically gasp, filling my lungs with balmy night air. A sudden bright light cuts through the darkness, igniting the night, and my knees hit the soft yet solid ground. Another wave tosses me right back to shore, the ocean rejecting me.

I roll over and push to my hands and knees, coughing and spitting the sea foam coating my face. My whole body hurts like I've spent hours at the gym, and I fall forward and rest my cheek on the sand.

Glowing light turns my eyelids red, and warm hands dig under my arms and pull me farther from the waves crashing over me. Through my bleary eyes, I gaze at a figure shadowed in the firelight coming from the torch staked right into the beach.

"Ava, what are you doing?" a familiar voice asks.

I blink the salty water from my eyes and meet Bailey's questioning gaze. I half expected for her to be Carter, but he's nowhere to be found. Instead, I face my sister who carries an empty bag on her shoulder.

I groan, sitting up. "Swimming." More like drowning.

That's all I remember. Waking up in the sea before it spit me out instead of sinking me to its depths.

"In your pajamas?" she asks, kneeling next to me in the sand. "And you're hurt." She leans down and inspects my legs. Now that she's mentioned it, they do sting. Blood trickles from the scrapes on my legs and into the sand. They're nothing to worry about, because I heal much faster than a human, but I'm still surprised by them.

"I'll be fine. What are you doing out here anyway?" I peer around. We're probably a good mile from our community. I've ended up near this exact spot before—one of the few things I do remember from the other times. "This isn't exactly close to home."

Stars shine brightly overhead like silver glitter tossed onto midnight fabric, and the moon sets the beach aglow in soft light. My sister's sky blue eyes shine in the firelight from her torch, and it looks like she might consider getting up and walking away instead of talking to me. Clearly, eight years away from each other has turned us into awkward strangers. She never wants anything to do with me though the ocean reunited us after it tore us apart.

She shifts and stands up, towering over me. "There was supposed to be a drop-off of supplies, but it didn't make it ashore."

"Oh." I had no idea someone dropped off supplies. I had assumed everything we had here was stuff that usually washed ashore. All the clothes and basic necessities we have came from Carter's mom, and she's not to come back. The less merpeople who visit, the safer it is.

"I'm not too worried about it. It's not the first time. I was just really looking forward to replenishing the supplies. As you know, we've lost our last fishing hook," she says. "Food might get a little light around here without them."

Offering out her hand, Bailey helps me to my feet. My knees shake for a moment, and it takes me walking a few feet to find it in me not to limp the whole way back to our community. Bailey yanks the torch from the ground, and I stroll along next to her, keeping my eyes trained on the foamy waves that seem a lot less threatening from my spot on the beach.

"I can catch fish," I say after a quiet moment.

I had resisted transforming into a mermaid until it was triggered today because I was afraid to do it without Carter, afraid to face that we might have to share a ring to go ashore, but now that I know something's changed in me after denying the king my eternity, I'll transform to help out the best I can. Even with how much I despise fishing. If it came down to people eating or starving, I'll catch the damn fish. It might make things a little less uncomfortable for me in the community anyway.

She doesn't respond right away, just keeps strolling along, keeping all her thoughts to herself. Without her leading the conversation, finding anything to talk about with Bailey feels like I'm reaching into a deep hole and unable to grab things from the bottom. It's frustrating.

"I don't mind transforming into a mermaid if it helps," I add so she knows I don't mean I'll be on the shore to spearfish like today.

She glances at me in her peripheral vision, swinging the bag from her hand in one arm while keeping the torch steady in the other. "That'll be extremely helpful. Thank you."

The polite small talk is killing me. It's tempting to jump back into the water and just swim the rest of the way. She's my sister for crying out loud. It shouldn't be this hard.

"Is this how it's always going to be between us?" I ask instead of responding with more excruciating pleasantries. "I've spent the last eight years of my life missing you every day. I've dreamed of what it would've been like had we chosen to stay in the sand that day and how our lives would be. I was so happy to find out you were alive, even if we're both stuck on this crappy island."

"I'm the one who is stuck here, not you, Ava," Bailey says. I guess my suspicions were right all along.

I blink the surprise from my eyes. "Do you have any idea what I've been through?"

"Do you have any idea what *I've* been through? What it was like for me?" she questions.

I throw my hands up. "If you'd just talk to me like we're sisters and not like we're strangers then maybe I would."

She waves the torch in front of her. "Don't you get it? We're not sisters anymore."

"What's that supposed to mean?"

"We're not even the same species."

Her words burrow deep into my soul, hurting me in a way I never thought she'd ever hurt me. I'm beyond hurt. I'm devastated.

The ocean might not have killed us, but it ruined us. The sister I looked up to as a child lost herself among the waves like I lost my human self. I hate to admit it, but whatever hope I had for us as a family has been snuffed out like the torch she holds hitting the waves.

Tears well in my eyes, my heart aching, and I don't bother arguing with her. Whatever grudge she holds against me runs far deeper than even the ocean. She made up her mind about me the moment she realized I wasn't a human. That I wasn't brought to shore over the same secret that brought her here. For her, washing ashore was a curse. For me, it was a blessing.

Dashing away, I leave her behind. I can't stand to be around her for another second because now I can see the reason for her shutting me out. I can feel it flowing through my veins.

I run along the shore out of the reach of the waves. Bailey doesn't call out to me or try to stop me. She just lets me go.

Sea spray coats my face, cooling my skin in the breeze, and I don't stop running until I see the faint glow of the fire burning from the clusters of palm frond shelters. A figure sits in the sand, and I head straight for him. Carter faces the ocean, staring off into the distance. He's so focused he doesn't hear me coming over the hum of the waves.

He startles when I fall next to him and embrace him, burying my face in the damp cotton of his black shirt.

"You were too far. I couldn't reach you," he says, breathing into the nook of my neck. "I didn't mean to doze off. I hate this, Aves."

I sniffle, feeling his emotions wash over me. "I'm fine, Carter. I don't think the ocean wants me to drown. It's trying to tell me something."

"You know, I never looked forward to a full moon before," he says. "At least if I can transform, I can protect you like I should."

"Don't blame yourself. It's been a long day for the both of us." I kiss him, holding onto him in the sand. "I just want to go back to our little house and forget about everything."

He shifts back to look at me, noticing the tear stains cutting through the sand sticking to my face. His eyes travel from mine to the blood dried on my knees. "What happened?"

I shrug, not wanting to talk about it, so I kiss him again and show him the memory instead—from the moment I remember in the ocean to my sister pulling me from the sea.

"She hates me," I whisper.

He pushes my sandy hair from my face. "I'm sorry, Ava. We'll get this figured out, okay?"

I nod without saying anything.

I'm not so sure that we can.

You still cling to your fears. You still resist.

The words haunt me, though I can't remember what they sounded like in my mind. The harder I try to think about last night, the foggier things become. I barely remember seeing Bailey on the shore or the conversation we had. All I know is whatever familial bond we had was severed the moment she realized I was a mermaid. Seems cruel of the ocean to reunite me with Bailey only to make sure I know I'm no longer the person I once was. I thought I accepted that. I thought I accepted this is my life now—whatever home I left in Azure Waters is gone.

But I guess I haven't accepted this at all. Maybe the ocean is right. I'm still resisting. But why shouldn't I? This is my life. I have to fight for it like I've been fighting all along.

Tears sting my eyes, thinking about my parents and the grief I'm putting them through. Even if I manage to safely get away from this island. I can't go home, and especially not without Giselle and Bailey. But I doubt Bailey would even consider coming with me. She doesn't trust me at all.

"Ava?" a masculine voice asks from behind me.

I shift in the sand, turning away from the lapping waves. "What's up?"

Wes stands ten feet away without a shirt, his long hair, which he usually wears down, twisted into a knot on the back of his head. Sand clings to his legs like it clings to everything else, and he crosses his arms over his broad chest, staring at me for a second before closing the distance between us.

He shocks me by sitting down. "I'm surprised to see you away from Carter."

I hold my expression calm, even though I want to frown. I haven't talked to the others much, and definitely not to Wes except to offer him a friendly hello when we gather for meal times. Giselle usually does all the talking. She's basically inserted herself in the community like she belongs here—which she technically does. And now that I know what my sister truly thinks, I'll be pulling away even more. I'm basically isolated with Carter just like in Pearlestria. At least this time, Giselle hangs out with me, too.

"I'm surprised to see you away from my si—Bailey," I say. I've never actually seen Wes and Bailey kiss, or even hold hands for that matter, but they're always together. They even share a place.

He holds a serious expression, matching mine, and digs his bare feet into the sand until they're completely covered. "She wanted me to see if you were still willing to—um, go fishing."

I turn away. She couldn't even face me herself to ask. "Why wouldn't I be?"

"She thought after last—"

I hold up my hand, cutting him off. "I'm not going to punish this community because my sister—or anyone else for that matter—hates me."

"She doesn't hate you, she just—"

I release a frustrated growl, and he snaps his mouth closed. "If she wants to explain herself, she can, but I—"

It's his turn to cut me off. "Hey, don't kill the messenger. And if it makes you feel any better, if you were my sister and just washed ashore, I'd be so happy you were here. Hell, I am happy you're here. Carter and Giselle, too. The more the merrier in my book. Maybe one day we can turn this place into a civilized world or something."

His words surprise me, fizzling out my anger. "I'm sorry. I just had a rough night. A rough few months, really."

"I can relate. I've been on this island going on eleven years."

"So, you were here when my sister arrived," I ask.

"With a welcome packet and everything. You know she

thought you drowned? She hated it was her who was rescued. She does love you, even if she's having a hard time right now," he says.

I kind of doubt it. I don't mention it, though. With his words, her weirdness toward me makes better sense. She thought I died, but then she discovered I hadn't and have been living the life we were both supposed to and still managed to mess it up and end up here, as a mermaid no less. I think I'd be pissed off at me, too. But I'd never disown Bailey and say she wasn't my sister.

"You mean she doesn't always act like this?" I ask.

He tilts his head back and releases a loud laugh. "Definitely not. She's the most caring of the bunch. Selfless. She's risked her life countless times for us over the years, even crossed the reef once to rescue Reyna when she tried to leave in one of our boats after her arrival. She'd do it for any one of us." I search my mind for knowledge on Reyna and remember Giselle telling me her sad story. She didn't happen upon a mermaid. Her own brother, who chose the merman life, decided he wanted his sister to join and tried to set her up with a friend from the Caribbean colony, who flashed his fins, expecting her to just join them. Her brother was gone for over five years, and Reyna married during that time, so of course she wasn't going to willingly leave her husband. To escape death by the hands of the jerk she rejected, she wound up here after her brother's mate saved her from that fate.

"Not for me," I say, pushing Reyna's heartbreaking story away.

"Well, you *can* change into a mermaid."

A laugh bubbles in my throat, the sound surprising me when it comes out. I'm kind of annoyed by it. I shouldn't be laughing. I came on this beach to sulk and feel sorry for myself.

"So, what do you say? Do that mermaid thing of yours and

catch us some lunch and dinner?" he asks like I was ever going to say no.

I nod. "I'll go find Carter now."

Wes helps me to my feet and dusts the sand off his shorts. "Everyone will appreciate it, Ava." Turning away from me, he strolls in the direction of our bungalows.

"Hey, Wes?" I ask.

He looks over his shoulder.

"Will you do me a favor and tell Bailey I'm sorry."

"Sure thing. I'll tell her to chill out, too. We're lucky to have you here, and I mean it," he says.

For the first time in weeks, someone's finally made me feel like I belong here.

Maybe I do.

POWER

GISELLE'S LAUGHTER ECHOES THROUGH THE air, a sound so musical and carefree, it brings a huge smile to my face. She clings onto my back, holding on for dear life as I cut through the water fast enough to make her scream.

"Get ready to hold your breath," I say. The moment I hear Giselle's inhale, I flick my tail, sending us into the air before I dive underwater. I swim past a school of tiny silver fish too small to eat and travel along the reef outside the bay.

Sunlight sparkles across the surface like a glittering mirror, and I speed toward it and breach, flipping backward, taking Giselle with me. She releases my shoulders the moment we hit the water and swims up to take a breath of air. She treads in place, floating with a swell, and I watch as she lets it take her toward the shore. I don't let her get far. Popping up next to her, I spit water over her head and laugh.

She splashes water into my face. "That was way more fun than my trip here with Carter's mom."

"Probably because you thought you were going to die," I say, trying not to frown at the memory.

"And to think I used to be so jealous that Sapphire got to swim with the dolphins in Hawaii. My best friend is a mermaid! A mermaid!" She says it like she's just letting the information sink in. It probably helps we're enjoying ourselves during somewhat lighter circumstances. No one's trying to kill us, and

I'm not being imprisoned by the ocean.

I flick water at her. "Shhh, you're giving away my secret."

She laughs, rolling her eyes, and then swims closer and locks her fingers onto my shoulders. "Imagine how I felt when I couldn't say that out loud?"

"It probably wasn't as hard on you as it was me." I swim forward, making her squeal, and cut through the current straight to shore.

The waves drag us both forward, and we skid to a stop in water shallow enough that I can't dip my head under unless I flatten myself against the sand. Giselle gets to her feet and stares down at me as I lie in the sand, feeling the warm sun on my scales. It's a lot more comfortable than perching on the rocks off shore.

"I thought you decided to abandon me for a girl's day," Carter says. He stands in front of me with dry sand sticking to his muscular legs. Giselle insisted I drop him off here first so she wouldn't have to wait alone.

Using my upper body strength, I drag myself closer and struggle to flip over so I can sit up and face the waves. I don't know why I do it, why I remain in my mermaid form when it'd be easier to transform back, but there's something freeing about sitting on the beach as a mermaid without having to worry about who sees me.

"We almost did," Giselle says. "You can't hog all of Ava's mermaid time, you know."

Carter sits in the sand next to me, stroking his fingers along my tail like he can't resist touching me. Who knows? Maybe he can't. "I can see that now. Just don't give the whole island ideas, okay? We don't need Darren asking for a ride up the shore all the time."

Giselle tilts her head back and laughs. Darren is the oldest inhabitant in our community and claims to have been here for twenty years, which is crazy to think about, considering he hasn't even been here the longest.

"Definitely not happening," I say, smacking my tail on the lapping waves. "You should've seen him earlier when I brought the fish. He kept making jokes that I'd be the best fishing buddy he's ever had and even told Carter he should take the day off so he could help me instead."

Giselle cracks up even harder. "He didn't!"

"I told him you were just as talented," I say, flicking water at Giselle.

"Ava!"

After I had brought back enough fish for lunch and dinner, I was completely surprised how excited and welcoming everyone was to me. Sure, I might have sort of bought their friendliness in the form of fish, but the atmosphere had definitely changed. I suspect Wes might've had something to do with it as well.

"What? He's a nice man, and he did technically wash ashore," I say with a laugh.

She drops a handful of wet sand on my head. "Like fifty million years ago."

Her response gets a chuckle out of Carter. She scoops a handful of sand up and drops it on his head, too. Before Carter can do anything to retaliate, Giselle dashes away, heading farther down the beach.

"Come on, Ava," she calls. "Lose the tail so we can have some human fun."

I dig my hands into the sand, attempting to pull myself forward, but I'm too far away from the buoyancy of the water to swim back into the wave. Giselle releases a loud laugh toward the sky, and I fall back in the sand, splaying out. Warmth flourishes in my cheeks as embarrassment clings to me.

Staring at my tail, I will it to transform into legs so I don't have to ask for help getting back in the water. Nothing happens.

An ounce of fear trickles through me, and I continue to glare at my caudal fin slapping against the lazy surf barely caressing the tip of my tail.

"Are you kidding me?" I ask, poking my finger into my scales. "I can't change."

Carter chuckles next to me. "Let me help you back into the water."

I wave my hand at him. "I can do this."

"Don't be stubborn, Aves," Giselle calls, kicking sand up as she walks closer. "Let the guy help your beached ass."

Maybe I want to be stubborn. Carter would do everything for me if I allowed him to, and it's something I don't want. I don't want to be coddled. I like doing things for myself. It makes me feel better, like I can do this on my own.

Carter ignores my protests and reaches down to pull me into his arms. It annoys me more than it should, and I flick my tail, throwing him off balance. We both fall to the sand. Giselle laughs again, and I burn her a heated look, my eyes narrowed and my lips pursed. It wouldn't be so funny if she was in my position.

A small wave rolls over my tail, sparkling in the sunlight. I swing out my arm and slap my hand against it. The sudden movement causes a swell to rise up where the ocean drags the wave back, and it crashes forward. Water cascades over my head, lifting me from the sand. I flip to my stomach, riding the wave back until I'm no longer stuck.

Water fills my lungs, and I swim deeper, my tail no longer hitting the bottom. I spin in a quick circle. If I could hug the ocean, I would. It's the first time its bent to my will since the last full moon, and the rush of power fills me with something light, something magical. It's like I've cracked the wall of my imaginary tank to set myself free.

I don't stay under for long. I let the cramps seize my tail

and wait a moment for my lungs to start burning before I kick to the surface. I spit out seawater and spin to face the shore. Surprise peaks my brows when I see the change in the surf. Large swells pulverize the beach. Giselle stands near the tree line, her hair dripping wet, and a startled expression widening her eyes.

Carter swims through the rising swells in my direction, diving under before the waves can collide into him and send him back to shore. I meet him halfway, letting him wrap his arms around me. We float up and down, lifted with every wave, and it takes a look into his blue-green eyes to realize this isn't some natural occurrence. It's reminiscent of the king's power.

"What's happening?" I ask.

"Relax, Ava. It's okay," he says.

The rough waters threaten to rip us apart, but Carter's strong grip keeps me against him. Lifting his hand, he presses his fingers against my chest over the spark flickering in sync with his. It's enough to suppress my oncoming panic, and I exhale a long breath. The waves settle, leaving us standing waist deep in the now tranquil ocean.

Scrunching my brows together, I look around again. "Was that—?"

"Yeah," he says. "That was all you."

Carter embraces me as I hold myself, letting it all sink in. I knew I was connected to the ocean on a deeper level, that somewhere, buried within me was an ability that could protect me when I needed it to, but I wasn't expecting it could also attempt to wreck things on my behalf. All I wanted was to return to the ocean on my own. I didn't want to nearly wipe Giselle and Carter out with a swell.

"Whoa," is all I can say.

Carter hands me my bikini bottoms, letting me brace myself against him to get dressed, and together we head to shore to meet Giselle. She hesitates a moment, turning her eyes on the now lapping waves like they'll somehow surprise her and drag her out to sea. I pout my bottom lip, breaking away from Carter to run to my best friend.

"I'm so sorry, Gi," I say. "I could've hurt you."

She pulls back and holds me in her gaze. "Hey, you don't need to apologize. That was actually pretty awesome. If only I had my surfboard."

I smile at her glass-always-half-full mentality. "Only you would think that."

"I'm being serious," she says. "My best friend rocks."

I don't feel like I rock. I feel like if something so small could set off threatening waves that I'm a disaster waiting to happen. One look at Carter tells me he's thinking the same thing I am.

I grimace. "No one would agree with you, Gi. Can you imagine how Bailey would act if she knew?"

"She'll be ecstatic," Giselle says.

"Where have you been? You know she holds a grudge against me because I'm a mermaid," I say.

"But that's because she doesn't know how amazing you are." Giselle reaches up and shakes my shoulders. "You can control the ocean. Do you know what that means?"

I suck in my bottom lip and don't answer. I can't see where she's going with this.

"I don't think it's going to be that simple," Carter says, interrupting.

"Of course it's that simple," Giselle says. "If she can control the waves here on shore, she can control the ones on the other side of the reef."

Everything sinks in. Giselle thinks because I got the waves to rise to shore to help me get back into the water I somehow possess the ability to stop whatever magical force traps her on this island. She thinks I'll be able to get her off.

"Giselle," I say, cutting off her thoughts. I can't give her hope if I don't have it. "Carter's right. This was a rare occurrence. I can't just tell the ocean to quit trapping everyone here. It doesn't work like that."

She pushes strands of drying hair from her face. "Maybe with practice."

"And then what? We all just go home and pretend none of this ever happened?" I ask. "Because I think you're forgetting the reason we're here in the first place."

"I'm not afraid of the king, Aves. He might rule the ocean and tries to rule the merpeople, but he can't rule us," she says.

But he can. He does.

Sadness washes over me. Giselle will never understand. She wasn't there to face the king. She's not a mermaid and doesn't have to deal with the fear that comes with our secret. She might be my best friend, but maybe my sister was right last night. We're not the same species. It does make a difference in the grand scheme of things.

Carter comes up behind me and rests his chin on my shoulder, hugging me from behind without a word. My emotions run hot, flowing from me to him, and without having to tell me, he senses the despair washing over me, putting a wedge between the humanity I cherish so dearly and who I've become.

"You're right, Gi," I say even though I don't believe in the words. "Just don't expect things to happen overnight."

She nods her head. "Of course I don't."

I force myself to smile. "Good, because I don't want to disappoint you."

"You could never," she says.

"She's right," Carter adds. "But I still don't think you should tell anyone. Ava's under enough pressure as it is."

Giselle leans forward and wraps her arms around both me

and Carter, squishing me between them. "Totally understand. I'll do whatever I can to help, okay?"

"Okay," I say.

"Now, come on. Let's stop thinking about the ocean and enjoy the land," she says.

But I'm not sure I can enjoy it in this moment, not when I can't stop thinking about the sea or how I could very well ruin everything here. For the first time since I've arrived, I'm not scared of what hides in the ocean.

I'm afraid of me.

DISASTER WAITING TO HAPPEN

"DON'T STRESS, AVES," GISELLE SAYS. She points at our small community. "Everything looks fine."

From my place holding Giselle in the bay, I can see everyone gathered around the fire as they prepare dinner. The sun hangs low in the sky, and I know I should just hurry and pick up Carter from where I left him on the beach to return back and enjoy a quiet dinner, but the more I look at the others, the less I want to return to shore.

Flicking my fin, I propel us until we're close enough that she can swim to shore on her own. She pushes away from my back and swims in front of me to tread water. My gaze flicks away from her and to the beach where I catch sight of Bailey coming out of her shelter with Wes behind her. Our gazes lock for a quick second before she turns away to say something to Darren, who slices some fruit at a table made from a cut down tree.

"Don't be mad at me, okay," I say to Giselle instead of responding to her comment. "But I think I'm going to stay in the water for a while longer."

She frowns. "But why?"

I shrug. "I don't know. It helps me think."

"You need to stop thinking," she argues.

I roll my eyes. "I'm not abandoning you, if that's what's on your mind."

"What about Carter? You know it'll bother him if you decide not to come back to shore with him," she says.

I lift an eyebrow. She says it like I don't understand my mate and what he's going through. Of course I know what he's going through. I can feel his emotions through our bond. He used to hide them from me, but ever since our coupling, I have complete access to them. And now, the last thing I need is for Giselle to use Carter to make me reconsider my need for space.

"Don't worry about us, okay? I don't want you to wait up, either," I say.

Before Giselle can argue, I sink under the water and remain there until she gives up on waiting for me to break the surface again. She spins and swims in the direction of the shore. I only pop back up to ensure she makes it to the sand. Without another glance, I dive and swim out of the bay and along the shore a few miles from our community. I let my bond pull me directly to Carter.

Our gazes lock the second I surface. He stands amid the waves, letting them flow around him. The sun fades behind me, the water darkening enough to set my nighttime vision aglow. Carter looks even sexier with the way the shadows define his tight abs and the hard muscles of his chest and arms.

He wades in, dipping down until the water reaches his neck. I close the distance between us, locking my hands around his and pull him deeper until my tail no longer sweeps against the soft sand. We hold each other amid the rocking sea, letting it drift us farther away from shore.

"I'd give anything to transform and go for a real swim with you," Carter says. He leans forward and brushes his lips against mine, breathing his warm breath against me.

"Soon." It'll only be a few days before the full moon rises and forces Carter to transform again into the merman he was born as. "We'll be back to normal soon."

His longing encompasses me. "I can't wait."

We just hold each other for a while, kissing, feeling our bodies against each other—me as a mermaid and Carter as a human. He doesn't ask me why I'm not quick to hurry back, and I think he already knows the answer. If only we could sink to the bottom of the bay together and feel like it's just the two of us in the world, things might not feel so heavy. I miss the days before I was dragged to Pearlestria, when we could explore the ocean on our own terms without having to be confined.

Dipping under, I transform into my human self and pop back up to clear my lungs of seawater. Carter doesn't wait to pull me in the direction of the shore. I put on my bottoms and emerge from the water with him, and together we lie in the sand and watch twilight fade into night. Stars sparkle overhead, shining brighter than I've seen them since we lie in the dark without the glow of a fire.

"You were amazing today," Carter says, drawing away from his inner thoughts. "I know you're worried about what all this means, but what you did—it was incredible."

"More like terrifying. I'm out of control all over again. But instead of accidentally revealing myself to Giselle, I might send the whole island underwater." I sigh, rubbing my fingers against my temples.

Carter leans on his elbow. The rising moon gives us enough light that I can see his eyes shining. "You just need practice. Things won't be overwhelming once you hone your skills. I'll help you the best I can."

"I'm afraid to even try," I argue.

He brushes strands of hair from my face. "Don't be afraid of what you're capable of, Ava. It'll just make it harder to figure things out."

His words resonate with me, stirring the memory of the voice I heard when I awoke in the ocean—the one telling me I was still afraid and resisting. Maybe it wasn't referencing my transformation at all. Maybe it was referencing me.

I close the distance and kiss Carter, sliding my hands over his taut shoulders to caress the muscles on his back. He slides his tongue into my mouth, kissing me deeply, like kissing me will ease the anxiety threatening to wash me out to sea. And it does. When I can concentrate on just Carter and the feelings we share, I don't think about what else is happening. I don't need to be in the ocean to feel as if it's just the two of us in the world after all. Because lying on this beach under the pale moonlight in the powdery sand away from the community gives me exactly that. A life where I don't have to worry about anything except the feeling of his skin against mine, the way his sweet lips taste, how he makes me feel like I'm not a disaster waiting to happen.

"Can we stay here tonight?" I ask, whispering into his mouth.

He hugs me tighter. "If that's what you want."

I nod. "More than anything."

"Ava," a voice whispers.

Snapping my eyes open, I glance around the dark beach. The hum of the ocean echoes in my ears, suddenly loud on this quiet night. Carter sleeps soundlessly next to me in the sand, and I maneuver his arm off me to sit up. We both fell asleep right on the beach where we've spent nearly half the night talking and sharing memories with each other through our kisses.

"Ava, your fear will keep you lost forever. You must let it go." The voice comes from everywhere and nowhere, drifting into my mind.

I don't respond. Instead, I push to my feet. Sand sprinkles from my tangled hair, and I dust myself off and stroll straight to the edge of the water where the surf pushes and pulls against the sand. The foamy waves glow in the light, and the white moon above creates a glittering trail I can imagine walking on, letting it take me into the black horizon.

Water rolls around my ankles, cooler than the balmy air, and I crouch down to run my fingers across the frothy surface. I scoop up a handful of water, holding it in my palm, and watch the pale light of the moon bounce off it. It looks magical in this moment, unmoving in my hand, like the glass surface of a mirror.

Flicking my fingers, I toss the water back into the waves. The surface explodes in a large splash like I threw a boulder into it. The sudden sound startles me, and I jump back and fall into the sand. A swell rises, spilling onto my legs. I don't even have a chance to move as it hits me in the chest, knocking me flat on my back. It steals my breath away like it steals the sand right out from under me, dragging me from shore.

I thrash for a moment, trying to break free of the strong current, but it's useless. I'm being swept away, and there's nothing I can do about it.

Ocean water burns my eyes. I try to focus on which direction leads to the surface. Sand clouds everything around me, and unless I can transform into a mermaid, there is no way for my vision to adjust to the fullest ability. The water isn't completely dark, an inner light still manages to glow within every tiny bubble, but it's not clear enough to see.

I roll through the wave, concentrating on pinpointing the light of the moon. If I can spot it, I'll know exactly which direction to head. But it's like the night sky swallowed it whole. After another few seconds, my lungs burn, begging to take a breath that'll only cause me to drown if I don't transform.

Calming my nerves, I concentrate on changing, but in the moment I need to, it doesn't happen. I groan, hearing my muted voice hum through the water to my ears. I didn't have any problems transforming all day, but now something stops me.

It's like the ocean wants me to be weak while I'm held in its clutches.

"Please, let me go. I can't transform." I send the thought into the water like it'll somehow make a difference.

I'm greeted with silence.

"Why did you draw me to you if you won't let me transform? Why are you punishing me?" Fear trickles through my mind when I'm greeted by more silence.

I'm sure I heard the voice on the shore. But now, as I hover in the dark abyss, I'm starting to think that maybe I've been imagining it all along. That it's all in my head.

My chest heaves, my body reacting to the lack of oxygen. I inhale salty water, unable to keep my mouth closed any longer. Panic seizes me, and I kick my legs, thrashing against the current that wants me to drown.

Exhaustion rolls over me. Shadows crowd the edges of my already dark and blurry vision as I drift in and out of consciousness.

"Ava, let go of the fear," the quiet voice whispers in my mind.

I don't respond to the nagging voice. I can't. All I can do is wait until I lose myself completely.

I close my eyes, my body too tired to fight any longer, and the ocean settles around me. Light breaks through from the surface, and I realize I'm hovering only a few feet below it. I rise with another wave, bubbles clinging to me, and without even having to move, I float up and cut through to fresh air.

Water spews from my nose and mouth, my lungs expelling it not unlike when I transform from a mermaid to a human, but this time it's more forceful and out of my control. I cough and spit, splashing until I'm upright.

I heave a few deep breaths, just letting the air in and out of my lungs. Water drips from my hair onto my forehead, and I wipe it away with the back of my hand. Spinning around, I gaze at the vast ocean and then turn toward the moonlit shores.

"Ava!" Carter's voice echoes through the silent night.

I follow the sound of his voice and spot his spark through the water as he swims in my direction. My legs and arms ache with fatigue, but I manage to stay afloat until Carter pulls me into his arms and does the rest of the work for me.

He carries me to shore, pelting me with cool water drops from his dark hair. Within his usual bright eyes lies a sorrow comparable to the hours after he admitted to me I had drowned in the ocean, and he saved my life by transforming me into a mermaid.

Strolling all the way to the tree line that leads inland, Carter sits as far away from the ocean as he can get without actually going into the tropical forest. He cradles me in his arms, brushing his lips across my forehead a dozen times without a word. I laugh when he showers my cheeks with a handful more and then kisses my lips, sending a dozen images into my mind—but they're not the usual ones I expect from him. He shares with me the fear he had from the moment a wave woke him up to the moment he tried to get into the water only to be stopped by another wave that refused to allow him into the surf. His fear's enough to send tears spilling onto my cheeks.

"I'm sorry," I whisper. "I heard a voice, and things got out of control."

"You didn't sleepwalk?" he asks.

"I—" I don't really know. "I don't think I did, but now it's all blurry in my mind. Do you think I caused the waves?" I've never manifested power in my human form, but I know the waves that dragged me from shore were not a natural occurrence. "What if it wasn't me? What if it was someone else?"

He kisses my hair, thinking over my questions. "I know what you are capable of, and that was definitely you, Aves."

I release a shuddering breath. "I'm scared, Carter. I don't want this."

Gently pinching my chin in his fingers, he forces me to look at him. "It's because it's new. The full moon rising is increasing your instability, but don't let that freak you out. We'll practice more. You'll get it under control." He runs his finger along my cheek. "And when you do, who knows? Maybe Giselle is right. Maybe this island living doesn't have to be forever. We can protect each other. Maybe make a new haven elsewhere."

"But the king," I say.

"Screw Attilonious, Ava. He doesn't scare me, but you know what? I think you scare him. He was so scared of you that he went against his own laws. He tried to force you into coupling with him. A merperson never finds a new mate if something happens to theirs. It's unheard of, yet he tried to do it."

I shiver at the thought. "That's why he won't waste time if he ever realizes I'm alive. He'll murder me."

"I'd never let that happen, understand?" he says, holding me close. "I'd die for you."

A pit settles in my stomach. Carter did die for me, and I never—and I mean never—want to go through that ever again. Just thinking about it sends my heart racing, my palms sweating, and my breath quaking.

"Never again, Carter," I say quietly. "I'd rather stay lost on this island forever than risk losing you."

"You won't lose me. You know how I know?" he asks.

I just snuggle my face against his damp chest without answering.

"Because you're the most powerful, beautiful mermaid I know." He runs his fingers over the spark in my chest. "I can feel it right here." Moving his hand, he places it over his own heart. "And here."

"You really think this is only temporary?" I ask.

He nods. "I know so. Attilonious might try to rule the sea, but he can't rule us."

Deep down, I know he's right.

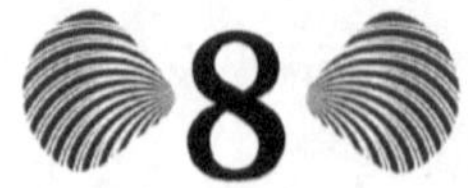

8

CHOOSING THE OCEAN

"AVES! THANK GOD YOU'RE BACK," Giselle yells from her place in the sand just outside the palm frond shelters. She hops to her feet and sprints toward me, nearly knocking me over with a huge hug. "I thought I might've lost you to the waves forever."

I push her back a little so I can look into her golden amber eyes. "I promised I'd never do that, but Carter and I have been talking and—"

"Don't you dare say what I think you're going to say," she says, wagging her head back and forth hard enough that strands of her bronze hair hit me in the face.

"Hear me out." After last night, all I can think about is the risk I'll cause everyone. It was like the ocean entranced me and bent to my will by accident. Like with the rocky waves yesterday, things could get worse and worse. "I accidentally caused some rough water last night while I was in my human form. I feel out of control enough as it is, but it's like the ocean is messing with my head when I'm most vulnerable. I don't want to put anyone at risk. We'll just sleep elsewhere, okay? Maybe even in the water when Carter can transform."

She scrunches her face, her lips puckering up to her nose and her eyebrows lowering on her forehead. Her expression speaks volumes. "Why does it feel like you're choosing the ocean over the land now?"

I huff a breath. "I'm not. I promise. I just don't want anything to happen. What would you do if you were me and could possibly wipe out our island?"

Her gaze drops to the sand. "Do what I can to make sure it doesn't happen. But it doesn't make me less sad."

I hug her again. "Same. But you know what? You can have me all day today, okay?"

"What about Carter?"

I peer over my shoulder at him as he talks to Wes, giving me the space he knew I needed to talk to Giselle. He offers me a smile, though his eyes don't crinkle in the corners with the happiness I wish he could carry around all the time.

"Carter will be fine. He'll be busy getting things ready for us," I say.

She beams a smile, shaking my shoulders. "Can we go for a swim? I mean, can you take me for a swim?"

I laugh. "Whatever you want."

"Okay, all powerful mermaid, show me what you got," Giselle says, standing in waist deep water next to me while I float on my back.

"You didn't just seriously ask me to try to control the sea, did you?" I stare up at the crystalline sky instead of Giselle.

Smacking her hand on the water, she creates a small wave that splashes me in the face. "I'm not asking you to create a tidal wave. Just show me something cool. You gotta practice, Aves. I wasn't kidding about using you as my ticket out of here."

I roll my eyes. "I will practice. Just not with you."

Her eyes narrow, and she slaps the water again. "I'm your best friend. Carter isn't the only one who can help you. Please, just try something small."

"No, Gi," I say. "Maybe after I get better control."

"Don't let the ocean scare you," she argues. "Eight years

was enough time."

"I'm not afraid of the ocean." Not in the sense she's implying. I'm afraid of what the ocean can do under my control, considering I don't have much of it.

"Liar," she says.

Annoyance washes over me. I know she wants to be helpful. She wants to be here for me. But that's my problem. I don't want to mess things up because she's here with me.

"Why does everyone keep saying I'm afraid?" I ask.

"Because you are."

"I am not!" I lift and smack my tail against the water, sending a current over the surface. The water quivers, rolling away from me and toward the shore. Giselle claps her hands when the surf rolls all the way up the sand like the high tide, before dragging itself in our direction, pulling us along with it until we're in water deep enough that I can float upright without hitting my tail on the sea floor.

Another wave swells, lifting us higher, and Giselle screams out in both excitement and fear. I lock my fingers onto her, stopping her from getting caught in the current I created, and I flick my tail a few times to take us closer to the shore.

A scream rips through the air, drawing my attention away from Giselle. It came from the bay. Fear rushes through me, and I meet Giselle's now wide eyes for a moment. Without a word, she locks her fingers to my shoulders and inhales a deep breath before I dive under and swim in the direction of the scream.

With Giselle, swimming takes a few minutes longer because I have to surface every thirty seconds for her to breathe unlike with Carter who can hold his breath for minutes. I swim us along the reef, scaring fish out of the way, and rise up at the edge of the bay to get a good look around.

The waves rock us back and forth in the water, unusually

rough in the bay, and I know I'm the reason for this. Another scream rips through the air, and I focus my attention on the rowboat across the bay in the spot my sister and Wes favor fishing.

The boat floats on the water in the direction of the reef leading to the open sea. Two figures struggle to paddle to get the boat under control, but it's like the ocean is determined to drag them beyond the border that means certain death.

"Oh, my God," Giselle says. "It's Bailey and Wes."

"This is why I didn't want to mess with my affinity, Gi," I say, panic welling in my chest.

"I'm sorry. Last time the waves didn't reach here. I thought we were far enough away."

Even if I swim my fastest, I'll never reach the boat in time. I clench my teeth, willing the current to stop, to calm down so they don't cross the barrier, but nothing works. If anything, the waves grow higher, pushing their boat even harder.

A few voices yell from the shore, but no one rushes out to try to help. Bailey jumps from the boat first, sinking under the wave, and soon Wes follows. The boat drifts out to sea without them, but the rough waves make it hard for them to swim.

Without thinking, I dart forward, cutting through the bay as fast as I can. Giselle squeezes against me, pressing her cheek into my back, and I make her wait an extra twenty seconds to break through the surface to get air.

My heart seizes the closer I get. Both Bailey and Wes struggle to stay afloat and fight against the sea to remain in the bay. The current sucks Wes under, and he smashes against the reef. Bailey screams as a swell lifts her up and over it, forcing her into the ocean that will kill her even for an accidental escape. Blood stains the clear sea red, sending my heart into my stomach. Wes is tossed around since he's been knocked unconscious. I've lost sight of Bailey altogether.

"Swim a bit from the reef and leave me," Giselle says into my ear. "I'm a great swimmer. I'll make it back to shore."

The last thing I want to do is to leave Giselle to fend for herself, but I know it'll be hard to help three people. Two will be pushing it. Giselle loosens her grip like if I don't swim her away from the reef she'll let go of me right here. It's enough to make me switch course.

"You can do this, Aves," Giselle says. "Remember you're the one in control." Giselle releases me, dipping under, but she pops back up and strokes her arms while kicking to swim to the shore. My nerves calm knowing, she'll be fine. My emotions shifting from fear to relief triggers something in the water, and the rocky waves settle until the bay turns as calm as an untouched lake.

Another scream rips through the air, and I catch sight of Bailey trying to reach the reef to hold onto it. She can't swim over it on her own as a swell pushes and pulls against it. I narrow my gaze on her, looking past the tiny bubbles settling within the sea, and spot Wes' body on the other side of the reef from Bailey. He floats face down, unmoving. Bailey yells, trying everything she can to cross back over to reach him, but the ocean stops her.

I dive down, navigating the bottom to the shallow water near the reef. I reach Wes first and flip him over and hold him upright. Blood drips down a gash on his forehead, staining the front of my pale pink bikini top.

"Ava!" Bailey screams.

Water sprays through the air as my sister sinks under. Without Wes being conscious to hold onto me, it makes it harder to swim to my sister. He'll die if I leave him, but my sister will die if I don't. She'll also kill me if I choose her over Wes.

"What do I do?" I ask out loud, like someone will give me

the answer. *Control the water. You can control it. Make it listen.*

With one hand on Wes' chest and my other reaching out toward my sister, I imagine the sea coming to me. I concentrate with my entire being, pulling the sea, forcing it to create my own personal current.

The water churns around me, stirring up sand and catching tiny reef fish in my small whirlpool that travels around me. Wes coughs from my arms, throwing up water, and then he gasps for breath. I not only summoned the sea around me, I managed to pull it right from his lungs, allowing him to breathe.

I listen for my sister but can only hear the ragged breath of Wes inhaling and exhaling. His eyes remain closed, though. Swimming forward, I grab at the water with my hands, pulling more and more to me, dragging a new current from the open sea.

I manage to bring the rowboat back over the reef, and I lift Wes over my head and push him into it, letting the boat drift into the bay. Diving down, I jet through a tunnel in the reef to the other side of the barrier and glance around the clear water.

Bailey flails about, spinning and flipping just under the surface. Every time she gets close to breaking through, she sinks deeper and deeper.

"Release her," I say, sending my thoughts into the sea. My voice resonates in my mind, and a trickle of fear swells in my chest. If there are any merpeople nearby, it's possible they've heard my command. But I can't think about that now. I need to get to my sister and get us back to where it's safe.

Bailey floats toward the surface, kicking her legs. The ocean no longer holds her under, and I watch the surface explode in glittering bubbles when she breaks through. Closing the distance, I swim under her and pop up a foot away from her. She screams out, slapping me in the face, and I use my arm to shield myself.

"It's me!" I yell. "It's okay. I'm here. You're safe."

For the first time since our one and only hug moments after I arrived here, Bailey embraces me. Her arms lock around my neck, and she sobs in my shoulder, burying her face against my neck as I tread us in place.

I swim us from the spot without going under and let her cling onto me all the way to the rowboat. Wes is still unconscious and bleeding, but his chest rises and falls as he breathes. I just hope he can recover. If something more happens to him—if something more happens to anyone—I don't know how I'll live with myself. The guilt and grief would be enough to send me into the sea and away from humans forever, even if it means my own life would be at risk.

Bailey climbs into the boat and pulls her wet shirt over her head. She presses the fabric against the gash on Wes' forehead while whispering something in his ear I can't hear.

I'd give anything to have been gifted with a healing ability like Carter's mom and grandma. I'd trade my ability to walk on land for it. But my thoughts are pointless, because the ocean might be powerful, but it seems I've already used my one miracle on Carter. There's nothing I can do for Wes except hope for the best.

"Get Sandra!" Bailey yells from the boat when we're within reach of the shore.

I dip underwater and will my transformation to take place. Cramps wash over me but disappear within seconds. I break through the surface and expel the ocean from my lungs in time to touch my feet to the sandy floor.

Darren and Giselle rush into the water and pull the boat into the sand. I stumble onto the shore and help the two of them get Wes out. More blood drips onto me, and I look like I've just survived a shark attack.

Sandra rushes from the palm tree shelters with Reyna behind her, and the two of them help Darren with Wes as Giselle helps Bailey from the boat, supporting her while they follow the others.

"Ava!" Carter's voice echoes through the air, and I catch sight of him running from down the shore where he was working on setting up a new shelter for us away from everything. He probably felt my fear and ran the whole way back here.

Instead of running to him, I just fall back in the sand and stare up at the bright sun through the tall palm trees. The blood in the sand spreads out with every wave, staining the shore around me in its crimson color. I'm too exhausted to do anything about it. All I want to do is close my eyes and fall asleep. Maybe if I do, all of this will have been a dream. Wes wouldn't be hurt. I wouldn't be drowning in my own guilt. And Bailey wouldn't have another reason to hate me.

"Oh, God, you're hurt," Carter says, falling to his knees next to me.

He brushes his fingers over my skin, using a handful of seawater to clean off my chest. He searches for wounds that aren't there, and I reach out and lock my hand around his wrist and just hold his hand between mine over my heart while I compose myself enough to talk.

"I'm fine," I finally manage to whisper. "This isn't my blood."

"What happened? Who's hurt? Is it Giselle?" His wide eyes search my face for answers when I'm not quick enough to tell him no.

I shake my head. "It's Wes." My voice trembles as the words escape. "This is all my fault."

Carter pulls me into his lap. He wraps his arms around me and kisses my hair. A wave washes over us, rinsing the blood away, and drags it into the bay where it disappears in the water. I sniffle through each breath, my heart aching as much as the rest of me. If Carter wasn't holding me, if he wasn't whispering in my ear that everything will be okay, I'd surely fall apart.

My heart clenches when I hear my sister sobbing from within her bungalow. "I need to see Bailey," I whisper. I'd much prefer to run away and never look back, but I have to face what I've done head on.

Carter only nods and lifts me up without setting me on my feet. "Don't tell her, Aves. It'll make things worse for everyone. This wasn't really your fault."

"She deserves to know," I say.

He shakes his head. "Not right now. She has enough to worry about. We'll reassess things later."

I bury my face in his shoulder, knowing he's right. If I told Bailey I was responsible for this, she might try to murder me. I'd probably try to murder me.

Taking a deep breath, I say, "Okay. You're right."

Carter takes me to the entrance of Bailey's bungalow, and we peek in and see her kneeling on one side of Wes with Sandra on the other. Reyna, Darren, and Giselle sit out of the way and just watch Sandra stitch up the gash on Wes' forehead with a pretty pathetic first aid kit.

"Anything we can do?" Carter asks without ducking down to take us inside the already crowded shelter.

Bailey looks up at me with watery eyes but doesn't say anything. Sandra finishes her last suture and pours fresh water over her work before drying it and taping gauze to Wes' forehead.

She meets our gazes. "If he doesn't wake up soon, he's not going to make it. We don't have the medical equipment to take care of him."

I suck in a breath. "Oh, God." The words only come out as a whisper.

What have I done?

9

LOST FOREVER

THE GLOW OF FIRELIGHT CASTS the shadows of the palm trees behind me across the sand. They stretch out to the foamy waves, making bar-like patterns—a reminder of how the island holds everyone apart from me as its prisoner.

"Walk me back?" Giselle asks, plopping down next to me by the fire.

She's been here since this afternoon after she told me there wasn't any change with Wes. If there's no sign of improvement by tomorrow, then all hope for his recovery will be washed out to sea. I shiver at the thought.

"Mind if Carter walks you?" I glance at Carter, who stands quietly by a large palm, his back pressed against it.

He's been reserved most of the day. I can't tell if it's because the full moon rises tomorrow or if it's because I've shut him out. I don't want to hear him tell me one more time that everything's going to be okay when it's not.

Giselle squeezes my shoulder. "You sure? Maybe I can just stay the night here."

I thrash my hair back and forth, the blond strands slapping my cheeks. "No way are you staying here."

"Then come with me. Bailey asked about you," she says.

"I can't face her, Gi. I can't even look any of them in the eyes. No wonder they don't like me. I'm a monster." I push to my feet and spin to turn away. Sorrow washes over me in waves strong enough to drag me out to sea where I belong.

"Aves, you're not a monster," Giselle argues. "Monsters don't feel guilt."

"But they do hurt others. Now please, just let Carter walk you back. I'll see you in the morning, okay?"

Carter shifts from his spot, lighting a torch in the fire. His gaze locks onto mine. His sad eyes shine in the firelight, and he clenches his jaw like he's holding back from saying something.

I don't give either of them a chance to argue with me. I strip off my shirt and shorts and drop them in the sand. Leaving my bikini bottoms close by them, I rush into the waves. Giselle's voice cuts off the moment I dive under, kicking far enough out that I can transform without getting stuck in the shallow water.

I know abandoning Carter and Giselle hurts them—it hurts me—but I just need to swim and not think about anything. I need to face the fact that maybe the ocean isn't my friend after all. It might've saved me from King Attilonious' clutches, but it's no better than him, forcing me here to wait for Carter to transform, forcing me to see all the possible damage I can cause humans by accident. It's like it gave me the ability to be a human, but also wants me to see that just because I can be one doesn't mean I am one.

Swimming in a few quick circles through the glowing waves, I flick my tail and pop back up high enough to see the beach without expelling water from my lungs. Carter holds the torch, meandering next to Giselle. They're deep in conversation, probably planning some mermaid intervention. It takes Carter looking in my direction to make me dip back under. Our bond allows him to find me anywhere, but with him in human form and me as a mermaid, I can go places he can't follow.

And I do just that.

I swim in the opposite direction to where the island jets from the ocean to create cliffs, and I maneuver through the black rocks to the base of the cliffs where the whitecaps smack against the rocks. This spot is only accessible by sea without rappelling from the cliff tops, and I haven't been here before, but I knew it was here from a swim with Carter. We just got close enough to check them out.

Pulling myself up onto a rock, I sit with my tail pulled to my chest, my whole body out of the water. The glowing ocean expands for miles like the sun shines from underneath the surface instead of from above it where the nearly full moon casts a beam of shimmering light in a moonlit pathway leading out to sea.

The balmy air dries my hair and skin, and I listen to the sound of the waves around me. Out here, nothing seems suffocating. I can breathe in and out without my chest aching, without the spark in my heart flickering a million beats a minute. But out here, I feel so utterly alone in the world, and I already feel lonely enough even with the others around. I might have been an outsider within my group of friends back in Azure Waters, but I was never treated like one. What I wouldn't give to swim away from here—even if only for a day—to go back home where I've always felt I belonged, even now if I don't.

"Your fear will keep you lost forever, my daughter," a soft voice says into my mind.

I jerk my head up and peer at the sea. "I'm getting really sick of you. Just leave me alone!" I yell, my voice cutting over the sound of the waves.

The voice doesn't respond.

Searching the sea, I look for signs of life, of a mermaid who could be taking pleasure in making me look crazy—or maybe I am crazy. Maybe the sea has really gotten to me, crawled not only into my heart but into my head.

I might have the ability to control the water, but the ocean clearly still controls me. How King Attilonious does it, I have no idea. It's not like I can swim up to him and ask why these things are happening and what I'm supposed to do about it.

Just because I can control the ocean doesn't mean I should. I'm not trying to protect a kingdom. I'm not even trying to protect the lost ones. I have no true purpose. I can't face the king and get my life back. I can't even help Wes. All I'm good at is causing one disaster after another. The ocean claims my fear will keep me lost forever but maybe it's what I deserve.

I slap my tail against the surf, and a swell curves high above me, knocking me hard against the rocks before dragging me across them and into the sea. I grind my teeth as pain cuts across my back and tail, and if I could see, I'd probably glimpse blood tinting the water.

Another wave crashes into me, forcing me to cling onto one of the rocks so I'm not thrown into the side of the cliff. Regret washes over me. I shouldn't have come here. Now, I might end up injured like Wes in a place no one can help me—though I doubt anyone would try apart from Carter.

The moment his name enters my mind, I unleash a wave of panic thinking about what I'm putting him through this second. What if he tries to swim out here? I wouldn't put it past him.

Sucking water into my lungs, I push it out through my gills to relax. I stop fighting the current and allow it to drag me from the rocks far enough into the sea that I manage to swim through the narrow channels and back into the deep water.

I swallow my fear, and the water stops pushing me around as if it's intertwined with my every feeling. Drifting on a current of my own making, I let it take me back to the shore. A flash of light glows in the darkness, a single torch on the beach, but the light of the fire can't compete with the light shining from

Carter's chest.

He drops the torch in the waves, pulls off his shirt to discard it on shore, and runs deeper into the water. He swims in long, even strokes, surfacing only once for air until he reaches me. His strong arms pull me to him, and he presses his lips to mine, sending a dozen memories to me—the ones he always sends that remind me of our happiest moments together.

"Are you okay?" he whispers in between kisses. He can't see me through the darkness like he could if he were a merman. If he could, he'd probably freak out over the cuts and bruises from the rocks.

I shake my head. "No."

He kisses me again, holding me to him. His legs brush against the sore scales on my tail, and I keep my face buried in his neck so he doesn't see me grimace.

"The ocean spoke to me again," I say, knowing full well that it sounds crazy coming from my mouth.

Carter cups my face. "You've been under a lot of stress, Aves."

I pull away. "I'm serious, Carter. We don't belong here. I think it's why things are getting worse and worse with the full moon nearing."

"Of course we belong here," he says. "And even if we didn't, I can't leave until the full moon."

"That's tomorrow."

"So, you want to leave? What about Giselle?" he asks.

I lift and drop my shoulders. "I don't know. All I know is we can't stay here forever. I'm afraid if we do someone else will—" The words stick to my tongue. Wes is not dead yet. Not if I can help it.

With the thought, hope lights within me like a spark in the water—like the spark that gave me life, that bound me to Carter. Wes doesn't need the human world after all. He needs a mermaid, one who can heal him.

And I know where to find one.

I bring my gaze up to Carter's. "Actually, I know exactly where we're going to go."

He stares at me intently, already knowing what I'm thinking before the words slip from my mouth. "Ava, that's too dangerous."

"We don't have a choice. Your mom is one of the only merpeople who knows about this place. She can help Wes."

"You sure about all this?" he asks, pressing his forehead against mine.

I kiss him. "Never more sure of anything."

A FLAME AMID THE DARKNESS

"I CAN'T DO THIS," I say, yanking away from Carter to head back in the direction of our new shelter a good two miles away from the bay.

I thought I could face Bailey, face Wes, but I don't have it in me. What if I can't come through with bringing Carter's mom back? Or what if she can't heal him? I'm afraid to get my sister's hopes up just to have them fizzle out. I don't even want to get my own hopes up.

"Yes, you can," Carter says, grabbing me by the shoulder to spin me back around. "I'll be here for you the whole time."

"Can't you tell them for me?" I know if I bat my eyelashes hard enough and pout my lip, he won't be able to resist my pleas.

"Ava." Uh-oh. He's using his please-don't-use-my-affection-to-get-what-you-want voice.

I pout my lip farther out. "Please."

He closes his eyes for a second, still holding onto my arm. "No."

I sigh, scrunching my nose.

He releases a chuckle and kisses the frown off my face. "You make resisting you incredibly hard, but I do think this is something you need to do."

I sigh again. "Fine."

Carter leads the way, nearly dragging me down the beach. I

kick up sand with every step. The closer we get to the community, the more anxiety grips at my chest. It's the same feeling I used to get looking at the ocean. But now, I feel like death is lurking on the other side of the palm frond walls. But not my death.

I suck in a few quick breaths, my hands shaking enough that Carter pulls me to a stop to wrap his arms around me. I think he's about to change his mind about making me confront my sister, because I'm sure he can feel what I'm feeling, but a murmur of voices cut through my heavy breathing and then someone calls my name.

"Ava, you're here," Giselle says, rushing from the spot where she was hanging wet clothes to dry.

I half hug myself. "Any change?"

Her smile falters, and she shakes her head. "No."

Tears well in my eyes, and I turn to Carter. "Maybe I should go alone now instead of waiting for you."

His tense jaw and furrowed brows shoot the idea down before he can even open his mouth. "It'll take a day of me swimming to get to San Francisco, and you don't know how to navigate the ocean. You'll get lost or worse."

He's right. I can barely navigate the shallows near Azure Waters. I have no idea where we are, only that we're in the Pacific Ocean because that's where Pearlestria was and we only drifted on the sea for a few hours. At least if Carter stayed here, I'd know how to come back...I think.

"What if we wait too long?" I ask.

"Too long for what?" The voice comes from behind me, and I turn to catch sight of Bailey hovering in front of her shelter. I'm sure she's heard the entire conversation and only asks to find out exactly what I'm planning to do.

I straighten my shoulders. "I don't want to get your hopes up, Bailey," I say, because I'm afraid of hurting her more than I already have. "But I've decided to leave the island to get help from a healer—Carter's mom to be more specific."

Her eyes widen. "You'll do that for Wes?"

I nod. "I'd do it for anyone here." Her eyes soften, and I remember Wes' words about how selfless he thought Bailey was and how he thought she'd risk her life for anyone here. Maybe Bailey and I are more alike than I thought. "I just can't stand around and do nothing when I can leave."

Bailey closes the distance between us, stepping in front of a suddenly quiet Giselle and Carter, and wraps me in a hug. It feels more than a thank you hug, like Bailey is finally starting to think I'm not a monster after all, even if I don't necessarily agree with her. Wes wouldn't be in this position if it wasn't for me.

"You have no idea what this means to me, Avie," she says, surprising me by using my childhood nickname, the one only my parents and Giselle's mom use now. "Wes is—" She sucks in a deep, shuddering breath. "Wes is everything to me."

Carter clears his throat, drawing both our attention to him. "We'll leave first thing when the moon sets."

I twist my lips to the side. "We can leave when the moon rises."

"It's too dangerous. We need to be able to leave the sea if we have to," he argues. "You know how the full moon affects us. Everyone will be out swimming away from the colonies."

I open my mouth to respond, but Bailey nods her head.

"He's right," she says. "And I'm sure Wes wouldn't want you to risk unnecessary danger when he's stable. Who knows? He could wake up at any second, and then you wouldn't have to go."

I guess I'm outnumbered. It doesn't make me feel any better, though. We could already be in San Francisco come morning and back here tomorrow night. But that's not even what

I'm most concerned about. I'm afraid to stay here for the moon's pull. I'm afraid of what it'll do to me. What it will do to this island.

"We can only hope," Giselle says, speaking up.

But that's the problem. I'm feeling all sorts of hopeless.

"You have to keep practicing," Carter says, running his arms up mine as he holds me amid the waves. "We're putting ourselves at risk, and we need to do everything we can to protect ourselves, including having you grasp how to use even an ounce of your power."

"You don't think I know this?" I ask. We're as far away as I can possibly be from the others on the island. Carter insisted we spend our day doing something productive to us, and I couldn't exactly tell that gorgeous face of his no.

"Then stop resisting. You're fighting your instincts. I can feel it," he says.

I huff and try to summon water up to splash him, but my water affinity is still a hit or miss no matter how hard I try to keep it in control. Negative emotions leave it volatile while my positive emotions barely keep water from seeping through my fingers.

Spending nearly all day wading among the waves—sometimes in quiet contemplation and other times kicking and screaming in frustration—hasn't helped much. And Carter's as lost as I am, standing behind me like he can get the ocean to obey me if he intimidates it enough.

"I'm trying not to, but I have a lot on my mind," I say.

"Just take a breath," he says.

I do as he says, inhaling a long breath of the briny air. It settles in my chest, helping ease some of the tension roiling through my body. And then there's the sudden distracting pull of the soon-to-be rising full moon that'll finally unite Carter with me as a merman.

The longer I stand amid the waves, the more I start to feel the pull of the sea. It'll be too strong for me to resist soon, even if I'm able to remain on land without the sea stone ring.

"Can we stop?" I tilt my head toward the sky. "I can't concentrate on the water anymore, not when I can't stop thinking about—" I spin around and press my body against Carter's, brushing my lips to his to send him a dozen images of us together in our true forms.

Warm arms wrap around me, and Carter kisses me more deeply. He lifts me into his arms, and I hook my legs around his waist. My kiss makes him antsy, and he releases a low moan that vibrates over my lips, sending tingles down my spine.

"It's almost time," Carter says, breaking away from me. "I haven't felt the pull so strongly before."

"It's because it's like you're a new merman." Before I saved Carter's life, he could hold off for a couple of hours before going into the water. The pull was there, but it didn't make him sick like it did me. The pull always made me feel like I would die if I didn't succumb to it because I was new. It's weird that the roles have been reversed.

"Why am I so nervous?" he asks, mostly to himself. He rests his head in the crook of my neck.

I respond anyway. "Because this time is different. The circumstances are different." I hold him tighter, my lips lingering near his ear. "I'll hold your hand if you want."

He chuckles and hums against my damp skin. "You know I always want that."

I release a laugh. "Good."

We stand together and watch the sun dip into the horizon, leaving a golden sky in its wake. Oranges and reds bounce off the fluffy clouds, and I soak in the mesmerizing warmth of the twilight. The moon will rise from behind us, and I can already sense the pull that makes me take an automatic step forward. Tonight, I'm not resisting it.

Carter's eyes trail from my face to my cerulean bikini, one that matches my soon-to-be fin, as he stands me on my feet. Strolling together hand in hand, we head deeper into the waves. A million thoughts flash through my mind. I can't believe that come morning, instead of heading back to shore we'll be leaving straight out to sea and to San Francisco.

The thought weighs heavy in my mind, because just going to Carter's parents' apartment puts us at risk. Starla, Carter's mom, told us she couldn't tell Mateo about us. He has no idea about the island, and I don't know what kind of damage this sort of secret would have on their relationship. The bond between mates is eternal, but I never really considered what happens when something threatens it—like with what happened between the queen and king. She gave up her bond—though I have no idea how real it was to begin with. Maybe he used her like he tried to use me.

"What's wrong, Aves?" Carter asks, bobbing in the waves next to me.

I blink the tears from my eyes before they can fall. "I'm fine. I was just thinking."

"About tomorrow?"

I shrug. "About everything."

Leaning forward, he kisses my head. "Let me take your mind off of things for now."

His lips travel from my forehead to brush against my cheek and then to my lips. His arms, so strong and muscular, hold me against him, gently traveling down my back and to my hips where he plays with the strings of my bottoms.

The waves roll higher around us as Carter gently guides me deeper and away from shore. He sends image after image of us together through his mind before showering me with a wave of pure desire and need, one that leaves me breathless.

Carter strips from his board shorts and tucks them into the bag slung across his broad back while I cling onto him. My bottoms go next, but all we do is continue to kiss, strolling into the water until we're no longer able to touch, just treading together in the sea.

The current drifts around us, swirling my long hair out behind me. I refuse to let go of Carter, and he dives under the water, taking me with him and swims until we're a dozen feet below the surface as night grabs hold and the sea calls to us.

His hands release my waist to clasp my hand, and then his fingers tighten their grip. Closing my eyes, I will my transformation to take hold, allowing the cramps to rush from my toes to my spine. My dorsal fin pushes against the strap of my bikini, and my pectoral fins on my arms glitter through the water, catching on the light of the spark in Carter's chest.

My vision adjusts, lightening the dark water even more, and I take in a deep breath of the ocean to fill my lungs with what it needs to breathe. Bubbles and sand swirl through the ocean with the current, turning the world into a brilliant, magical place I've never been so happy to share with Carter.

His eyes remain closed, tiny bubbles clinging to his face, and he slowly starts to transform. Before, his transformation used to take seconds, but now, it's taking the same amount of time it took me to go through my first transformation.

Blue-green scales sprout on his legs, crawling from his ankles to his thighs, and he arches as his dorsal fin protrudes from his back. I swim closer, bringing up my free hand to his face and graze my fingers along his strong jaw.

"You're almost done," I say, projecting my thoughts into his mind.

His eyes flutter open, their jewel-like color dazzling me like the first time I saw him as a merman. A smile lights his face, and then a second later his legs fuse completely, and he opens his mouth and sucks in the ocean water.

He pulls me close enough that our noses touch, and then he kisses me like the dozens of times before, holding me in a way I can feel his entire body against mine, where it feels like we're almost one.

"I forgot how much I missed your voice in my head," he says, sending his thoughts to me. Flicking his tail, he tugs me with him, swimming a few dozen feet in a matter of seconds. "And swimming like this. Feeling how perfect you fit against me."

I smile as he basks in everything he loved about the ocean. In this moment, nothing else really matters. It reminds me of all the times we swam alone without a care, focusing on us and losing ourselves together in the sea.

I trail my fingers down his sides, running them over the ridge between his torso and tail. He sucks in his bottom lip, letting me explore his merman form, memorizing every glittering scale, creating a map of his body for me to hold in my mind like I've done with his human form a dozen times.

When he can't take it anymore, he swims quick laps around me, twirling me in a current of his making before pulling me back into his arms to kiss me. I can tell he's anxious to swim, to feel how powerful he is in this form among the waves. I ease away and spin him around to lock my arms to his chest to press myself to his back.

"Know what I missed?" I ask, kissing the nook of his neck. "Swimming with you like this."

He flicks his tail, propelling us forward so the world blurs around us. Carter darts along the shallows, dipping low to run his fingers over the sea grass, stirring up sand. We can't go as deep here as we did in Azure Waters, since the reef traps us, but it's better than nothing.

Once we make it around the island, Carter slows down and dips to the bottom of the bay just outside our community. Manta rays congregate above us, gliding through the water like gentle underwater butterflies. It's an enchanting sight to see since I've never seen one in the day around here. Swimming up and away from Carter, I float along with the majestic animal, smiling when its mouth widens like it's grinning at me.

"It's so cute," I say to Carter.

His hands lock around the base of my tail and he gently tugs me down. A frown puckers his eyebrows, causing me to grimace.

I reach out and touch his face. "What is it?"

"I forgot how seeing animals up close like this makes you so happy, and I can't even show you all there is out there on our own terms without having to constantly worry." His voice is barely a whisper in my mind as he motions toward the reef, but I know he's referring to the ocean beyond it.

His sudden sadness ignites anger in me, not at him, but at all the circumstances that have led to this moment. I knew being here would wear on him, but it's happening more quickly than I anticipated. It's such a cruel fate that we're supposed to spend our lives here. I refuse to accept it. I won't. I just hope tomorrow goes smoothly. If Carter can see it's a big ocean and that we're not as trapped as we think, maybe things can start to change.

"I hate this," I say, slicing my hand through the water. A strong current erupts in the bay, sending the manta rays swimming away from us, unhappy with the sudden swell in the calm water. "It's Pearlestria all over again. The king shouldn't have this kind of control over us anymore."

The churning current rocks us back and forth, and Carter swims forward to grab onto my hands to keep us from separating. But I can't calm down. I can't do anything except imagine pummeling the king with the waves, treating him the way he treated me, hurting him the way he hurt me, stealing what he loves the way he stole from me.

"Ava, calm down before you wipe out the community," Carter says, pulling me against him. His arms wrap around me, encasing me in his love. Our chests glow, warmth traveling from his heart to mine until the water mellows and he doesn't have to fight to keep us from washing away on the swells.

Fanning my tail, I propel him up to the surface so I can take a few calming breaths of sea air. He hovers in front of me, still holding me, and I tilt my head back and stare at the glittering sky to get my racing heart to slow and to clear my head.

"I'm sorry." My voice echoes through the quiet air. "Tonight wasn't supposed to be like this. I should enjoy being with you instead of getting mad at things I can't change."

"This is my fault." Carter brushes wet strands of hair from my face. "I pushed you too hard today."

"But it's not. It's my fault. We'd have never been in this position if it weren't for my recklessness and my stubbornness."

He kisses the words from my lips like he can't stand to hear me say them out loud. "Stop, Ava," Carter says into my mind instead of speaking. "There's nothing we can do tonight."

"You mustn't fear, my daughter." The familiar, haunting voice sneaks into my mind, pushing Carter's voice away.

I yank back and stare around with startled eyes. "Did you hear that?" I ask Carter.

His brows scrunch. "Hear what?"

"The voice."

He turns to peer around the water, but it looks the same as it did a moment ago. "I don't hear anything," he finally says.

"I'm not dreaming, right?" I ask, pinching myself for good measure.

"No, I—"

"You mustn't fear and remain lost. It's time to prepare. It's time to get ready for what lies ahead," the voice says into my mind again, forcing Carter's voice away once more.

"I'm not afraid!" I call out through the air.

"You are," it says. "Your fear imprisons you. Come to me, my daughter."

"Where are you?" I ask. A wave rises and curls before crashing to the now rocky surface of the bay.

I pull away, breaking free from Carter. His voice echoes through the balmy air, and I can't focus on what he's saying. I think it's my name, but all I want to do is find where the voice is coming from. I want to confront whoever it is.

"Push the fear away. Be the brave girl I've chosen," the voice says.

Anger washes through me in hot waves, and I swear the water heats around us, sending steaming bubbles to the surface. I smack the water again, sending a swell crashing toward the shore. I can't help it. The voice is more haunting than ever, and all I want is it to either be straight with me or leave me alone.

"Tell me where you are!" I scream. "Stop playing these games."

I swim a few dozen feet toward the reef, daring the being behind the voice to reveal herself. The full moon hangs overhead, lighting a path for me. One I can't resist following even though I have no idea where it'll take me. I can't see beyond the horizon. Staying here in the bay, on this island, isn't giving me the answers I need.

"Ava, stop." Carter's voice erupts in my mind, and I flinch at the sudden fear in his voice. "Ava, please."

"Don't be afraid, Carter," I say, projecting my voice into his mind.

Swimming faster, I head right for the tunnel in the reef that'll take me to the open sea. I've been beyond it twice now, and if I can just go out again, maybe I'll get the answers, because whoever speaks to me isn't within the protection of the reef.

Hands lock around my waist, stopping me in place, and I thrash in the water. "Ava, please. Talk to me. Tell me what's going on."

The ocean churns around us, and I suddenly feel suffocated and claustrophobic. The bay feels ten times smaller now that I have the open sea in sight.

"I can't stay here," I manage to say, calming myself enough so I don't send us crashing into the reef.

"It's dangerous out there right now, Aves," Carter says. "Morning will be here soon enough."

I close my eyes and let water push through my gills. "I don't care. I need to go."

His forehead presses against mine. "You know the risks we'll face. If King Attilonious discovers us—"

"I'm willing to risk it," I say. "Please, just trust me. You don't hear what I do. I need answers."

"What do you mean?" he asks.

"I won't find them here," I say, ignoring his question. I'm afraid if we don't hurry that whoever wants me to find them will leave, and I'll stay lost. "But don't worry. I'll protect you."

"Hey, I'm supposed to be the one protecting you." His thought is lighter, more like him than the sudden uncertainty that was gripping his emotions moments ago. "And if you feel we must leave the reef now, then okay. I trust you."

"Just outside. We won't go far."

Carter turns his back on me, letting me cling to his shoulders. He swims us to the reef and toward the tunnel too narrow for us to fit through together. I flick my tail, cutting ahead of him to go through first.

Tiny tropical fish scatter, swimming out of my way, and I

follow the soft light of the moon shining on the other side of the narrow tunnel.

The moment I'm through, a strange wave of joy swirls through my heart, and I bolt away without even waiting for Carter. I can't help it. It's like moving from a bath tub into an Olympic-sized swimming pool, and I want to test myself to see how far I can go.

"I'm here," I call out through the sea. "Please, show yourself."

No one responds, so I keep swimming. The ocean wraps me in comfort instead of fear, and even outside of the protective barrier, I feel safe. I feel like I can do anything.

The water sparkles in front of me, glittering above the drop-off that'll take me deeper into the ocean to unknown waters I've never had the chance to explore. Without hesitating, I dive down, loving that the bottom doesn't sneak up on me like it does in the bay. A swordfish darts through the water, its full length as long as I am, and I swim next to it, matching its pace.

A shadow falls over me, and I flip in the water, swimming with my face toward the surface and catch sight of Carter swimming right along with me but with caution unlike my new carefree attitude. He doesn't dip down to hold onto me as always, letting me lead the way.

I break away from the swordfish and race up toward Carter, latching my hands around him until he follows me toward the surface. Together, we breach out of the water, cool air circling around us, the moonlight shimmering off our pearlescent skin. My hands break back through the surface, and I dive down again a few feet.

And then I see it.

A glowing light flickers below me, freezing me in place. Carter swims circles around me, and I push him back before he can lock his hands on me to pull me away with him.

The light intensifies, growing brighter and brighter, rising from the deep, and I push my fear away. I want so much to swim as fast as I can back to the safety of the island, but something stops me.

"What is it, Ava?" Carter asks.

I extend my arm out and point to the light, like a flame burning underwater, as it floats in our direction. It's not unlike Carter's spark, the one he gave to me to bring me back to life as a mermaid after I drowned.

"Do you see it?" I ask.

Carter pulls me to him, wrapping his arms around me. "I don't see anything." His fear creeps into me, but I resist letting him pull me away.

I rip free of him and swim forward. Carter's voice echoes in my mind, and his fingers lock around my caudal fin, but I wave my hand, sending a swell directly at him, breaking him free of me.

Jetting forward, I descend deeper, following the light. Neither fear nor worry grips at me, just the strong urge to see what it is, to touch it. It's like I'm stuck in a gravitational pull and can't get myself away.

"Do not fear, my daughter," the familiar, feminine voice says.

The spark radiates with a light that reminds me of the sun shining from the surface. It's as small as the palm of my hand, just floating in front of me, and I reach out and touch it. Heat travels through my fingers and into my arm, coursing through my entire body, setting me aglow with the light.

"Ava!" Carter's voice cuts through my mind, but I can't see him past the light.

My heart quickens, the light becoming all consuming, shining so brightly I can't see anything else. It's like all I am is light, a flame amid the darkness.

Suddenly, the light disappears, and I'm left floating in the churning sea.

ANOTHER LIFE

MY MIND FOGS WITH HUNDREDS of memories that don't belong to me.

Small pieces of a mermaid's life scatter across my vision like a puzzle to be assembled without a guide. I glimpse rainbow light, like the sun shining into a crystal prism, the light coming from silver scales so breathtaking they look ethereal.

Tendrils of midnight hair curtain my face, hiding me from a world I'm excited yet afraid to enter, though I know it's not me. I see a diamond the size of my palm, weighing heavily in my hand. It reminds me of the one in King Attilonious' staff, the same staff he channels his ocean magic through. But this one is different. It doesn't belong to him but to the mermaid filling up my mind. All these tiny pieces of someone else's life shift and move through me not unlike when Carter revealed his whole life to me through his kisses.

But the life flashing before my eyes isn't just any ordinary person's—it's the life belonging to Celestiana, the missing queen who abandoned her kingdom for the land. The queen thought dead by the king after he could no longer find her essence through their eternal bond. A bond she broke to create the island of the lost to protect the humans fated to death by a mighty king who would destroy the land to keep the merpeople hidden.

More memories flood my mind. An old human man and

older mermaid with a merbaby girl swimming in the waves—grandparents with their granddaughter. It's a moment from the queen's childhood. Her love of the land sparking from her grandmer, who loved a human without bonding with him. I see a young mermaid playing in the water just offshore, younger than me. She waves at the land, and I bask in the love radiating from her. It's different. Deeper. It's not just love. The mermaid is in love. Another image swirls through my mind. Pearlestria and all the merpeople. Sparkling bubbles. A merman. The king. Enchantment and respect replacing the love within me.

"Ava," a soft voice calls, pulling me from the memories. "Ava, come back to me."

Slowly opening my eyes, I peek through my lashes at the bright sun overhead. Salty air expands my lungs with every deep breath I take, and the soft sand beneath me begs for me to close my eyes again to fall asleep.

I stretch my arms over my head, yawning, trying to fight the exhaustion consuming my body, which happens after a night of swimming. A soft thud sounds near my ear, and colorful light blinds me as I stare at the multi-faceted surface of a huge diamond on a chain—the gem shaped like half a heart, the same one from the foreign memory in my head.

Jolting upright, I glance in front of me at the cerulean sky merging with the crystalline ocean in the horizon. Puffs of white clouds litter the atmosphere and reflect onto the water. A sudden peace blankets the panic rising in my chest, and a warm hand squeezes my fingers, drawing my attention away from the sea filled with unraveling secrets.

"Ava," Carter says. "Thank God."

"What happened?" I ask, flicking wet sand from my tail.

Carter leans back on his arms, stretching his tail out so the next wave can roll over him. "You tell me. I couldn't swim through the current you created until you fell unconscious. I spent most of the night holding you until the moon set."

"I'm sorry," I say quietly. "Something came over me."

Carter shifts, wrapping an arm around me to pull me closer. I lean into him, meeting his lips to mine, and show him the memories flooding through my mind. I can't stop them as they pour from me to him in a confusing wave that makes him jerk away from me to stare at me with startled eyes.

He flicks his gaze to the sand and scoops up the diamond in his hand like he's seeing it for the first time. "Not something. Someone. Ava, this belonged to the queen."

Searching through the memories that were bestowed upon me, I know he's right. An image flashes through my mind, the queen floating in front of a mirror with the stone weighing over the spark in her heart. Another image shimmers into my mind, one of her and King Attilonious, hand in hand, hovering on a platform like the one he had set up for my coupling ceremony to Carter, which he turned into a nightmare coronation to swear my loyalty to him. The king looks younger, black hair like the queen, but her eyes mirror the sea while his eyes mirror the night.

They kiss each other, the fascination the queen has for him rolling over me. The sparks from their chests travel up to each half of their diamond, lighting the sea in a glow like the full moon before returning back to their chests, bonding them with magic. It's something that didn't happen at my failed coronation the king tried to force upon me. And I'm glad for it, because in this moment, holding the queen's half of the stone, I realize that he wouldn't have shared his magic with me like he did with Celestiana. He'd have taken mine altogether. But I don't have to worry about that now. I have the queen's heart, her essence, her everything in this diamond the ocean gave me.

It'll protect me.

But just because I have the essence of the ocean embodied

in my hand, doesn't mean I'm strong enough or powerful enough to face the king yet. I will be, though. And when I am, I'll get my life back. I'll give Carter his life back and all the others on this island.

Carter gently digs his fingers into my side, and I turn and catch him watching me as I try to pull myself from my thoughts. He's giving me time to process without badgering me, something he's always been good at.

I dangle the chain with the diamond. "This belongs to me now. Help me put it on?"

Carter takes it from me, and I lift my long hair so he can clasp it around my neck. It thuds against my chest, sending beams of light sparkling across the surf and both our glittering tails like specks of a rainbow.

"This is all so surreal," he says, breathing on my neck. "That stone is for royalty, Ava. It's half of a matching set. You don't think it means you're meant—"

"I'm meant for you, Carter. Don't you even think for a second I'm supposed to be with King Attilonious."

He smirks. "That's not what I was going to say. I definitely know you're my soul mate. I promised you forever. What I was going to say is that maybe this is some sort of sign."

"I'm tired of signs. I'm tired of trying to figure things out on our own. I'm tired of thinking about all of this, really. I just want to go to San Francisco, get your mom, and then figure this out later. Who knows, maybe she'll have some answers."

"Okay," he says.

Carter shimmies from his spot on the sand until a wave lifts him so he can propel us both back into the water from the shore. He reaches up and hooks his arm around my waist, pulling me into the sea with him and diving down.

I inhale a long breath of water into my lungs and push it out through my gills. The gemstone around my neck glitters in the water, each facet projecting white light through the sea. Carter hovers in front of me, stroking his fingers on the surface of the diamond like it'll somehow give us a plan.

He darts us along the reef until we reach the calm bay in front of our community. We pop to the surface, and I catch sight of Giselle sitting on the sand alone near the water. I lift my hand up and wave, and she blows me a kiss, waiting for us to dive under.

"So, you're absolutely certain about this?" Carter asks, staring at the open sea before us.

"I'm not afraid anymore, Carter." I reach up and run my fingers over the diamond around my neck. The spark in my chest sends beams of light scattering across his chest and through the water around us. "This will keep us safe."

It's not until this moment I finally understand what my dreams have been telling me all along. I don't know if it was the queen or the ocean speaking to me, telling me not to fear, to accept who I am, and to prepare or else I'd be lost forever, but whoever it was had answered my question all along.

It wasn't my fear of transforming I had to overcome. It was the fear of the open sea, of the world that lies hidden among the waves. It wasn't my mermaid form I had to accept. I had to accept I was given these abilities, given this life, for a reason. With these things, I can now prepare myself for what is to come. Because I'm not supposed to hide here in the Lost Cove. If I do, I'll be lost forever. Giselle and the others will be lost forever, too.

Carter studies the stone for a moment longer before he motions for me to hold onto his back so he can lead the way. With a flick of his tail, we surge forward. He breaches out of the water and over the huge reef in an elegant arc that puts us in the open sea.

I expect a dozen negative emotions to grip at my chest, to

squeeze my heart and warn me what I'm doing is dangerous, but all I feel is hope. I now feel like I'm finally making my way home.

12

RETURN TO SHORE

"CARTER, YOU'RE GOING TO WEAR yourself down," I say into his mind, resting my chin on his shoulder.

I've been swimming off and on since we left the Lost Cove, but the light now fades from above, and the only signs of life come from the shadow of a vessel on the surface. I'm afraid if he continues at this pace, he'll do more damage than good.

"I don't want to stop until we get there," he says, his voice sounding as tired as I'm sure he feels.

"Then let me swim us. I know I'm not as fast, but I can handle it."

He slows, relenting to my suggestion. We switch places with him wrapping his arms around my ribs instead of on my shoulders like I usually position myself. I twine my fingers with his, letting him hold me, and then flick my tail, jolting us forward.

It's a lot more awkward than I expected it to be. Carter makes it look so effortless with me on his back. But his body is more rigid compared to mine, heavier even in the water, and it takes me a good mile before I get used to pulling him along.

I'm half as fast, but Carter doesn't complain. All he does is rest against me, his heart beating on my back. I close my eyes, letting my body take over so my mind can wander to the task at hand. Carter's parents live close enough to the beach that we can walk to their apartment.

I refuse to even think about Carter's dad and what will surely be a surprised reaction, discovering we didn't drown in the sea together after I returned the spark to Carter when the king stole his life away.

Carter brushes his lips on my neck, drawing my attention out of my mind and to him. I'm glad for it. I hate thinking about that night—the night that changed everything.

I open my eyes, glancing at the wide ocean in front of us. A school of Pacific bluefin tuna swim around us, darting out of the way before I can get too close. Some of the fish are as long as we are, and swimming among them freaks me out just a little.

"I never thought I'd say this, but the ocean is feeling kind of crowded," I say, thinking my words to Carter.

Bubbles erupt at my ear, tickling the side of my face. It's rare for him to laugh out loud underwater, but I'm glad he does, because it makes my heavy heart feel a little lighter. As much as I try to push the doubt away, it still clings to me with every breath of ocean I take. I'm afraid Starla can't or won't help us. I'm afraid Wes' condition will change while we're gone. But at least I'm not afraid of the water. It's comforting as it surrounds us, reminding me I'm where I should be—at least in this moment.

With a strong flick of his tail, Carter propels us faster and then leans his weight heavy on my shoulders, pushing me down to dive. He navigates our way out of the school from below and then shoots us toward the surface when we're in front of it. I expect him to stop swimming and let me take over, but he just continues to hold me to him, our fingers still intertwined, and pushes us forward at his usual fast pace.

"Carter," I complain. "What did I tell you?"

"I'm good, Aves. I got the break I needed. It's only two more hours until we reach the San Francisco Bay."

I scrunch my nose even though he can't see it. "You're

coddling me."

"And?" Carter's laughter fills my mind. I shift, spinning in his arms and lock my fingers around the back of his neck so I can face him. His fingers press into my sides, stirring tingles through me. I lean up and suck his bottom lip into my mouth. We kiss while he navigates the sea like he's made the trip a million times, his body taking over while his mind stays with me, imagining all the things we love about each other.

"Continue to kiss me like this, and we might never make it back to the water once we leave the bay," Carter says, letting me go to swim a few quick circles around me. He catches me as his current spins me and locks me in his arms again, pressing his chest to mine.

I kiss him once more. "You're making it incredibly hard to focus on what we need to do."

He turns his face away before I kiss him again. "We can't have that now, can we?"

"Are you trying to resist me?" I ask.

He grins. "Now, you're the one making it hard to focus."

Carter swims me forward through the shallows to the beach closest to his parents' apartment. We hover for a few minutes in the waves, like neither of us is ready to leave the sea to face what we need to do. We're both aware of the danger that comes with revealing ourselves, but we have to trust that Mateo is as loyal to Carter and me as he is to the king. I know he doesn't want to see his son hurt, but he's the one who convinced me to give in to the king. He stood by and did nothing during my coronation except look at me with pity. All along, I had a distrust of Carter's mom, but the more I think about Mateo, the more I worry.

"You're having doubts," Carter says, waiting for me to transform first.

"It's just—your dad," I say. "Your mom wasn't going to

tell him about us for a reason."

Carter brushes his fingers through my floating hair. "Don't worry about him, Aves. He will understand."

"And what if he wants me to return to Pearlestria so you can get your life back? What if he blames me for the position we're in?"

Carter shrugs. "He'd never ask me to give up my mate. He considers you his daughter."

I can only hope that's still the case.

Kissing Carter once more, I take a moment to transform back into my human self. Carter hands me my bikini bottoms and helps me put them on. I hold my breath and remain in place in his arms, waiting for him to transform next. He closes his eyes, leans forward to press his forehead to mine.

Nothing happens. He doesn't transform.

And I can't wait much longer. Without his voice in my head, I can't hear his thoughts. He just shakes his head and points to the surface. Propelling up, we break through together, and I gasp a breath of cool air into my lungs. It's been a while since I've felt a crisp night with how humid the Lost Cove is with its never-changing weather.

I shiver in Carter's arms, adjusting to what feels like freezing waters, and he rubs his hands up and down my arms.

"I guess I'm not used to changing back," he says, letting me steal as much of his body heat as I can.

"It's okay. I'll wait here."

Sinking back under, Carter swims a few circles around me. I watch the flicker of his spark light up the tiny whirlpool around me. The bay's dark enough that no one will spot me here, and I can't see any activity on the shore where we're supposed to emerge.

Another minute later, Carter pops back to the surface and spits out water next to me. I blink, staring at the fins still shimmering on his arms. Fear nudges my mind as I take in Carter still in his merman form.

"Something's wrong," I say.

Carter presses his lips into a thin line. "I can't transform."

My forehead scrunches, and I pull his hand from the water and look at his sea stone ring. "Try again."

He releases a small sigh. "Ava, it's not that I'm not trying. I can't. Look at my ring again."

I study the stone in the dark night and realize something's different about it. The sea that used to swirl through the tiny gem has disappeared. It's now just a colorless stone on a piece of silver. The magic that allowed Carter to transform from a merman to a human before is now gone.

"This can't be," I say. "How is it possible?"

He holds me tight. "I don't know."

Pulling back, I glance between him and the nearby beach. "I'll go to shore alone."

"Ava," he argues.

"Carter, we didn't come all this way for nothing. Your mom might know something we don't. I'll be okay."

His eyes line with a sadness I haven't seen in them before. This is the first time I'm going to land without him being able to follow, and it reminds me of all the times he used to go to land without me. I wish with everything in me he didn't feel like I did in those moments. I know what it's like to be bound to the sea, and it's a terrible, heartbreaking feeling not being able to follow your mate.

I run my fingers through the short tendrils of wet hair hanging on his head. "I'll be back as fast as I can, okay? Just wait here."

He nods because he doesn't have a choice. I'm going to shore. Not only does Wes need our help, but now so does Carter.

Carter leans forward, pressing his lips to mine, and sends a dozen images into my head. He reminds me how to get to his parents' apartment, taking me down the least busy streets through his mind.

Without a towel to dry off, this will be one of the most uncomfortable night walks of my life, especially since I now have to do it alone. I don't even have shoes. The only thing I have going for me is that Mateo and Starla live near the beach. Otherwise, I'd draw attention to myself, strolling through the city covered in sand and drying seawater.

"Be careful," Carter says. "I don't know what I'd do if something happened to you, Aves."

I kiss him once more. "Nothing will happen. I know how to protect myself if it came down to it."

Carter nods without a word and swims me as far as he can to the beach. I search the shore for a moment, finding it deserted and dark, and then swim away from Carter and let a small swell carry me to the sand.

I remain on my hands and knees, adjusting to how solid the ground feels compared to the open ocean. The sound of the waves hums in my ears, and I consider lying in the sand, but a siren in the distance makes me push to my feet. I slide into wet shorts from the bag Carter brought and head toward the path that'll take me to the nearest street.

With my hands dangling at my sides, I strut down the sidewalk ignoring an unwanted catcall from a passing car. Luckily, I can shake off the few curious gazes and not let them get to me. If I wasn't a mermaid on a mission, I'd feel all sorts of self-conscious. But now? I just need to hurry.

Starla and Mateo's apartment complex looks exactly how I remember it. A sprawling lawn with flowerbeds decorates the outside of the small complex, and the three-story, U-shaped building surrounds a gated-in swimming pool. Each door faces the courtyard with Carter's parents' ground floor apartment in the center.

I stroll around the pool to their apartment. Unlike the last time, the window and door is closed, the lights all off. Taking a deep breath, I raise my hand and knock on the screen door a few times, hoping they're sleeping and not gone.

After my third set of knocks, I step back and cross my arms. No one answers, which means they're definitely not home.

"The Stevens' left yesterday and haven't been back yet. They usually take a trip to see family once a month," a voice says from overhead.

Cigarette smoke trickles to me, and I crinkle my nose before I look up. Starla's neighbor, an old man who I remember Carter calling Mr. Mooney, stands outside his apartment door, blowing the smoke from a cigarette into the night. He must've come out of his apartment seconds ago because I didn't see him on my walk around the pool.

Straightening my shoulders, I force myself to smile. "Hey, Mr. Mooney. I don't know if you remember me, but I'm—"

"Mateo's daughter-in-law. I remember you," the old man says, offering me a warm smile. His eyes flick over my tangled, now dry hair to my bare feet. "Your father-in-law never shuts up about you. How's Carter? He hasn't been around in a while."

I release a small breath in relief. This could've gone terribly wrong if Mateo had told Mr. Mooney that Carter had died. His father, everyone apart from Starla, thinks we drowned in the ocean after I transformed Carter into a human again to save his life.

"Carter's great. Spending a lot of time on the ocean with me," I say. Technically, he's *in* the ocean, but Mr. Mooney doesn't need to know that. "We've actually just docked in the bay. Starla and Mateo said they'd be back, but I guess they're running late. We don't get the best cell reception on the yacht." The lie comes so easily I wish it was true.

Mr. Mooney studies me for a second. "I have a spare key in case of emergencies. I'm sure your in-laws would give me hell if I didn't give it to you to wait inside."

"That would be great," I say. Carter might start to worry if I stay here long, but I can't just leave if his parents might come back.

"Let me get my keys." The old man snuffs out his cigarette and tosses the butt in a small coffee can by his door.

Mr. Mooney heads inside. The screen closes with a bang, and I listen as keys clank against each other. He returns in under a minute and drops the apartment key to me with a smile on his face.

"Tell Carter to come by sometime to say hello, will ya?" he asks.

I force my head to nod. "Of course." Holding up the key, I wave it back and forth. "And thanks for this."

Leaving Mr. Mooney, I enter Carter's parents' apartment. I peer around at the white and blue décor, the hints of the ocean woven throughout the paintings and knick-knacks lying around.

I flick on a light before shutting and locking the door behind me, feeling odd standing in the quaint living room alone, but its familiarity wraps me in a comforting blanket. The familiarity comes from the memories Carter shared with me and not my own, but it doesn't make a difference to me.

My footsteps mute on the soft carpet, and I head toward the kitchen first. It's been weeks since I've eaten anything that wasn't caught or grown on the island, and I can't stop myself from flinging open the fridge to peer inside.

My heart slides into my stomach. It has been completely

cleared out and turned off. The cupboard isn't any better. The only things that remain in the pantry are some spices, a few jars of jam and peanut butter, and a box of spaghetti noodles.

I swipe the jar of peanut butter and pull a plastic spoon from the cabinet with disposable plates and cutlery—things that have never even been opened. Something is utterly wrong. Who cleans out their fridge and pantry if they don't plan on being away a while? But where would they go? Mr. Mooney expects them to be back, but after looking around, I'm not so sure. At least not anytime soon.

While scooping spoonfuls of peanut butter in my mouth, I stroll down the dark hallway that leads to two bedrooms and a single bathroom. This is the first time I'll ever see things for myself apart from Carter's memories, and I can't help how excited I am entering the room Carter grew up in—the room that hasn't changed even though he moved away a year ago to work on the Ocean Jewel luxury yacht.

The scent of sunscreen and the sea clings to the entire room, and I can't stop myself from flopping onto his double bed. The sheets smell like fresh laundry, like Starla might've washed them before she left, and I bury my face in his pillow. I could fall asleep if I allowed myself to, because it's been so long since I've laid in an actual bed.

I breathe in and out a few times and finally drag myself away. Looking in Carter's closet, I spot a waterproof bag and pull it out. I also grab one of his shirts and slide into it. It's long enough to be a dress so I tie a knot in the back to cinch it. I can't help myself, and Carter won't mind.

Moving to his parents' bedroom next, I peer at Starla's half of the closet. I feel weird going through her things, but I want some sandals or flip flops to take back with me. I pick out a few sundresses while I'm at it and shove them in the bag, and then I load it with a few necessities, including a hairbrush and a towel, things that are sorely lacking on the island.

I crinkle my nose, looking around for anything else I can take. I catch sight of Starla's purse hanging on a hook by the door, and I dig through it and find a twenty dollar bill in her wallet. Using a pen I found next to it, I write a quick note on the back of a receipt and apologize for taking what I did. I doubt Starla would care, but it makes me feel better.

When I'm through, I head to the front door. I sniff the air to see if Mr. Mooney is back outside. The air smells clean, so I jog around the pool and out the entrance without returning the key to the apartment.

I pass by a twenty-four hour grocery store on my way back to the beach, and I can't stop myself from going inside. If I have to go back to the Lost Cove without Starla, the last thing I'm going to do is return empty handed. I grab a first aid kit, a travel-sized bottle of sunscreen, and some over-the-counter medicine. I wish I had more money and there was a way to load up and swim with a suitcase, but it's not really possible. The Lost Cove is too far from here.

Up ahead, just a block from where I'll turn to enter the beach, a crowd of people hang out on a gated off patio of a bar. Music hums through the air, a few girls laugh, clutching glasses of clear liquid, and a few bar-goers stare in my direction. I hadn't come down this street on the way to the apartment, but my detour at the store had me going a different way back.

"Looks like someone was kicked out," a guy says to me as I pass by. He stands near a table with another man and two girls, and they all share a laugh at my expense.

I roll my eyes and continue walking toward the path that'll drop me directly into the sand. The Golden Gate Bridge glows in the distance and city lights pepper the dark night like tiny stars brought to earth.

Laughter sounds out from the stairs above me, and I grimace, seeing the group of people that were at the bar.

"Hey," the same guy calls out. "You plan on sleeping on the beach or something?"

I don't respond but instead stare at the dark waves, looking for Carter's spark. I see it just past the night swells as he waits for me to return.

"Too good to answer me?" the guy asks, forcing me to stop in my tracks. I'm afraid he'll continue to follow me, which will prevent me from returning to the sea.

He jogs down the stairs, leaving his group of friends at the top, and they just laugh when I glare up at them.

"I'm sorry, but I'm busy," I say as the guy approaches. I don't wait to let him close the distance though. Instead, I kick sand up and head toward the roaring surf.

"You don't look busy. You look like you have nowhere to go."

"And why does that concern you?" I ask, spinning around to face him.

His eyes flick from mine to the bag on my shoulder before stopping at the diamond on my neck. It would pass as costume jewelry from the sheer size of it, not to mention I don't exactly scream wealth at the moment.

"It doesn't, but my girlfriend likes your necklace, and I have cash. You look like you need some. You wouldn't have to sleep on the beach then." Without hesitating, he reaches into his back pocket and pulls out his wallet. He wavers on his feet, clearly drunk.

I purse my lips at the three twenty dollar bills he holds out to me. "Thanks for your concern and all, but I'm not sleeping on the beach, and I don't need your money." Without waiting for him to respond, I turn away and stroll into the water, hop-ing it'll get him to leave me alone since he's wearing dress pants and shoes.

A bony hand locks onto my shoulder and tugs me back. I stumble and fall into the sand with the guy looming over me. Anger splashes over me in a waterfall of heat, and I glare, scooping up a handful of sand. I throw it in his eyes without hesitating.

He yells out, and voices sound from the stairs. His three companions rush toward us on the beach, and panic squeezes my chest, stealing my breath away. The guy takes their arrival in stride, acting as if they'll back him up, and he reaches down and locks his hand around my ankle to pull me toward him.

"Come on, Donnie. Leave her alone. I don't want the necklace that bad," one of the girl's, a pretty redhead in a tight black dress, says. "I only wanted you to make an offer."

The guy, Donnie, shakes his head, refusing to let my ankle go.

I scream, my voice ripping through the air, and I throw more sand. It doesn't stop him from bending down and locking his fingers around the diamond on my neck. The second his fingers touch it, a wave swells next to us, causing his companions to yell out. I reach out and dig my nails into the skin of his wrist, stopping him from breaking the chain from my neck. The wave crashes over us, knocking the guy away and off his feet.

I sit in my spot, now soaking wet, and watch the sea drag him underwater. Carter's spark glows through the surf nearby, circling the man, and for the first time ever, I imagine Carter doing something unthinkable on my behalf.

The redhead, who I assume is Donnie's girlfriend, runs into the waves. His voice echoes out as he pops to the surface long enough to be pulled back under—not by a wave or the current but by Carter.

Another wave swells, slamming into the girl before she can get in past her knees, sending her to the shore. The others start screaming for help, and I know if they continue, they'll bring attention to us if they haven't already.

Pushing to my feet, I run through the waves and make my way to where I see Carter circling, pulling the guy under every time he pops back up for air. I wish I could scream his name, tell him to stop, but I can't. Instead, I slap my hand on the water, sending a current strong enough to push Carter away.

His rage and fear floods through me, and I know he's doing this because he's feeling the despair that comes with his inability to leave the water to protect me. As merpeople, we're fiercely protective, putting each other first. I just know Carter will regret his actions once his mind clears.

The voices of the panicking humans disappear when I dive under and swim in the direction of Donnie. It'd be easier to transform, but then I'm pretty sure we'd have to take four people back with us to the Lost Cove, and that's the last thing I want to do. All I want is to get out of here and figure out what to do next.

Before I can get within reach of the now drowning drunk, Carter locks his strong hands around my waist and pulls me under. My eyes blur in the saltwater, and I can't tell him to let me go, so I press my hands into his chest and push him until he releases me.

I swim underwater to where Donnie floats amid the sea and grab him by the back of his button-up and yank him to the surface. He spits and coughs, his wild eyes meeting mine, but he doesn't fight me. He tries his best to swim with me as I help him back to shore until our feet touch the sandy ground.

He falls to his knees, and his friends rush to him to pull him out of the waves. The redhead rushes over to me, trying to see if I'm okay. I walk backwards to keep space between us because I want her nowhere near me.

"Stay away," I say. "Your boyfriend is a psycho."

She ignores my words and says, "I'm sorry. He gets a little carried away when he drinks."

I grimace. That was far from getting carried away. "He's lucky, you know. I could've let him die out there."

"Let me help you. My apartment is just around the corner. You can take a shower and warm up there. I won't let Donnie come either," she says, surprising me. "We'll order some take-out. Whatever you want." I can't tell if she's being nice because she wants to be or because she's worried I'll get the police involved.

I shake my head, my wet hair slapping against my cheeks. "Thanks but no. I'm on my way home."

Reaching down, I pick up my discarded belongings and swing the waterproof bag over my shoulder. I might regret doing this, but I'm so over the land in this moment that all I can think about is jumping back into the sea.

And that's what I do.

I stroll a few feet away from her and head straight into the water, not caring that she calls out her protests. She doesn't follow me in, though. I gaze over my shoulder once, smiling at the four people staring at me, and then I duck under the waves and swim a few feet until Carter drags me away from the surface completely, probably leaving the group with confusion that'll last them the rest of their lives.

The second my lungs burn, I tug off my bikini bottoms and transform, leaving on the T-shirt I stole from Carter's room. His lips meet mine, his thoughts rushing at me faster than I can comprehend, and all I do is hug him, pressing my body against his, and wait for him to calm down.

"Carter," I say, finally getting a word in. "What you did back there..." My voice trails off.

"I was so close to coming to shore to reveal myself," he says.

"You could've killed that guy."

"I wanted to."

I frown, pressing my forehead to his. "And that scares me. I know you want to protect me, that you'll do whatever you can to protect me, but I don't ever want you doing that. It's not you. We're not those people. That's something the king would do."

"Ava." His voice is a small whisper in my mind. "I'm sorry. You were so scared, and I just couldn't handle it. I can't handle it."

"But you have to trust that I can," I say.

He closes his eyes, pushing water through his gills. I hate seeing Carter like this—lost and uncertain. I hate seeing him feel like he's no longer good enough for me because he can't go on land.

"And we have bigger problems to worry about than some stupid drunk wanting my necklace," I add, holding his face between my hands.

He stiffens in my arms. "My parents weren't home?"

I shake my head, my hair veiling my face in the water. "No, and it looks like they're not going to be home anytime soon. I think the king—" I don't want to even project the words to Carter.

"You think he's the reason my ring's not working?"

I squeeze my eyes shut. "I think he called everyone back into the sea."

13

PROTECTED

"NO," CARTER SAYS. "THERE'S NO way we're going back there."

We sit on some large rocks offshore just outside of the San Francisco Bay. A lighthouse shines in the distance, but no one will see us this time of night from our position facing away from the shore.

"But, Carter. Wes needs help. And what do you expect to do? Just stay in our protective little bay all the time? That's like putting you in a tank."

"Going to Pearlestria is suicide, Ava. I don't care if you think that necklace will keep us safe. I don't want to risk it—not for someone we barely know." He rubs his hands up his face and into his hair, pushing the strands out of his eyes. He sounds more exhausted than anything, and I'm sure the journey has worn him out. It's why we sit here sharing the rest of the jar of peanut butter I stole from Starla's.

"He's like that because of me," I say. "I can't go back there without help, Carter. I can't face my sister."

"Then we'll risk it out here and stay far away from any of the colonies," he says.

I huff. Anger rushes through me hot and fast, and it's sudden enough that Carter snaps his head in my direction. This is the second time tonight I've been mad at him, and I don't know if it's the sea or his inability to transform that's getting between us, but I don't like feeling like this. I don't like that he's the reason I feel this way.

Without saying a word, Carter jumps back into the water and swims a few small circles not far from where I remain. The cloudy current he creates collides into the rock, knocking me back, and I flip over the edge and land in the water. Another wave catches me and pushes me into the rock where I hit my shoulder, sending pain through me.

I don't even have a chance to cry. Carter pulls me into his arms and away from the current of his creation and swims us back a dozen feet.

"Ava, I'm sorry. I didn't mean—God." His guilt pours over me in cold streams. His eyes glass over under the light of the moon, and he runs his fingers along the red mark forming on my arm that will surely bruise.

"It was an accident," I say. "I'll live."

"I'm failing you." Carter's words surprise me.

I purse my lips and cup his face to look into his jewel-like eyes. His brows hang low, and a crease pinches his forehead. His emotions are all over the place, batting me with grief, worry, guilt, sadness, and his ever-present love. All of his feelings are because of me. I'm the one doing this to him.

"Why would you say that?" I ask.

"Because I'm a coward. I should be on your side. I should want to help you no matter what. I should be able to protect you no matter what. But I—" He sighs and stops talking, just hangs his head while ocean water mists his face.

"You're the bravest person I know," I say. "You've done nothing but fight for me and protect me. You saved me not only from death but from the king."

"You think I'm brave? You're the brave one, Ava. You fell into my arms in stride, fighting the fear of the ocean, and then the fear of losing your human life. You've held strong to what you've wanted instead of just accepting this was how things were going to be. You stood up to the king, fought the king, and even after everything he's put us through, you're still willing to go back and risk facing him again. And for what? A human. I do what I do for you, Ava. But you, you do things for anyone." He rests his head on my forehead, our lips hovering close enough to kiss.

I smile, hearing his thoughts of me put into words. Thoughts I never considered to be true about me. I've always considered myself selfish and Carter as selfless, but in the end, we've been doing the best we can in the uncontrollable circumstances of our lives together.

"I don't even know how to respond to that," I say. "I think you have me confused with someone else. Maybe the sea is getting to your head. I'm pretty sure I want to do this for me."

He laughs, tilting forward even more until his voice hums against my lips. "If it was for you, then you'd listen to me and go back to the Lost Cove. We'd have never left in the first place."

"So, you know I'm not going to listen to you," I say.

"You might be the bravest person I know, but you're also stubborn as hell, Aves." His lips disappear as he presses them together. "And I want you to know I'm still not on board bu—"

I frown. "Carter, I don't want to fight."

"Just hear me out."

I snap my mouth closed.

"I'm willing to make a compromise," he says. "We'll go back to Pearlestria, but we're not going past the wall. If my mom is there, she'll come to us. If she's not, then I'm sorry. There's nothing else we can do for Wes. I'm not getting anyone else tangled in our life."

Hope swells in my chest, and I lean forward and kiss him like he's told me he figured out a way for us all to go home. He holds me tightly as we tread in the water. A dozen warm, inviting emotions swirl between us, and for the first time in days I have hope.

Carter pulls me down with him, and we sink under the waves crashing against the rocks. The moon shimmers across the water above us, and Carter swims us into a dense kelp forest. It's closer to Pearlestria than it is to the Lost Cove, but they're both west of us now.

"I need to rest a while longer, Ava," Carter says into my mind. "I'm not taking us into dangerous waters when I'm not in the best condition."

I relent to his needs and curl against him on the sand amid the kelp forest that'll protect us. He slaps his tail along the bottom a few times, and I listen to his muted heartbeat as he drifts off.

I can't sleep, though. I'm too wound up. I shift in Carter's arms, digging my chin into his chest.

A leopard shark swims nearby, and I suck a breath of water into my mouth to push it out through my gills. The shark jets by close enough to touch, but all I do is watch it weave through the kelp until it disappears. I just stare at the ocean life, the fish and crustaceans, navigating through the glowing forest. At least I don't have to worry about any of them bothering us.

I shift again in Carter's arms, and this time he opens his eyes to look at me. Running his fingers through my floating hair, he pushes it out of my face so he can peer into my eyes. The sea gently swirls around us, making the kelp sway, but Carter's heavy enough that neither of us moves.

"What's wrong, Ava?" Carter asks into my mind.

I turn away from his eyes and press my cheek against his chest. "I can't sleep. I'm too nervous."

"Would it make you feel better if I stayed awake until you do?" he asks.

It would, but I don't want to ask that of him. He shouldn't have to suffer through exhaustion because I'm worried about a million things despite knowing the diamond hanging over my chest protects me.

"No," I say.

He pouts his bottom lip out, shifts up, and pulls me onto his lap, cradling me. I laugh as he rocks me back and forth, and he plants his lips to mine, kissing me deeply like his kiss can somehow push away all the dark feelings competing with the dark water.

Trailing my fingers over his shoulders, I trace the curve of his taut muscles down his back. He moans into my lips, the vibrations cutting through the water. It stirs desire in me, and I press against him, pushing him back in the sand. I lie on top of him, resting my body against his. Running his fingers down the fin on my back to my tail, he locks them onto the ridge that separates my tail from my torso. His lips travel along my jaw, and he releases tiny bubbles from his mouth as he makes his way to my neck.

In a quick motion, he flips me off him and onto my back. Sand swirls around us, glittering in the pale moonlight shining down from the surface. Carter sends a dozen memories to me, reminding me of his favorite moments of us together, including some that ignite a fire in my stomach in a good way.

His spark blinks rapidly in his chest, bouncing light off my necklace and through the water. He rests his elbows on both sides of my head, kissing me deep enough that I smack my tail on the ocean floor sending a ripple through the water, making the sea life scatter.

The shadow of an early morning vessel about to fish the kelp forest draws my attention away from Carter, and I freeze mid-kiss. While our sparks protect us from being discovered, I still get nervous seeing humans above us. Carter presses me into the sea floor, resting his cheek against mine like I somehow need to be shielded from the rest of the world in my moment of nervousness.

"You okay?" Carter asks into my mind after a moment.

"I'm just a little on edge is all," I say. "It's weird being out in the open like this. The boat overhead doesn't help."

"How about I keep a lookout, and you try to get some sleep? You'll feel better after you get some rest." He rolls off me and sits in the sand next to me. Pulling me halfway onto him, he brushes his fingers through my floating hair, letting me use him as a pillow.

"I don't think I can. Why don't you try to distract me again?" I ask, reaching up to touch his face.

He runs his fingers along my hairline. "It's kind of hard when I can feel your nerves."

I blush, my face warming. "I—"

He brushes his lips across mine. "It's fine. Just try to sleep, okay?"

Relenting to his suggestion, I curl up in the sand, resting my head on his lap so he can play with my hair while I hug against his strong tail. I close my eyes, trying my best to push away all the thoughts from the last day from my mind. Carter hums softly into my mind, a familiar song I can't put my finger on, but I realize I'm too tired to care.

I drift in and out of sleep, startling every time a current tries to shift us in the water. Through my closed lids, I can see the light of my necklace growing brighter and brighter, and it becomes so intense I snap my eyes open to suddenly black waters. The light disappears, leaving me blind.

But that's not the worst of it. My legs cramp, a sudden transformation taking hold of me. A strong current knocks into me, pulling me away from Carter, who I can no longer hear in my mind. I thrash in the sea, tangling myself in the long strands of kelp and try to scream, but my lungs are still full of the ocean since I haven't surfaced for a breath of fresh air.

"You might not fear, but you have not accepted who you are," a familiar feminine voice says.

"But I have," I think, sending the voice into the sea.

"If you remain lost, you will be found," the voice responds. "Heed my warning."

The voice disappears, leaving me in cold darkness in a kelp forest threatening to strangle me. I pull against the ropes, snapping them with my hands, and finally manage to break free to swim to the surface.

The glow of the moon reflects on the water, and I see my reflection staring back at me in the mirror-like surface. Instead of breaking through to air, I stare into my blue eyes, shining silver in the light. Tiny bubbles cling to my face like orbs, and my human body reminds me just how weak I am in this state.

But I can't transform. As much as I will for it to take hold, nothing happens. I remain in the form I'm most familiar with, my lungs burning, threatening to drown me.

Kicking once more, I break through the surface, spitting out water to gulp in fresh air. I don't stay up long. Hands lock around me, yanking me back under, and I scream out through the ocean.

"Ava, calm down. It's me," Carter says, his eyes wide and wild.

I blink the confusion away and realize I'm not in my human form after all. I'm still a mermaid. "Carter, something's wrong," I say.

"We're fine. Everything's fine," he says.

I shake my head, my hair veiling between us. "We have to go."

"It was just a dream, Aves. You created a current in your sleep, and I couldn't hold onto you. I'm sorry I wasn't quick to catch you before you surfaced." Everything he says sinks in, but it doesn't lessen the fear gripping me, begging me to swim away as fast as I can.

"Car—"

A flash of light blinks in the water, cutting off my words. I'd recognize the light anywhere. It looks like the one sparkling from my chest—from Carter's, too. I shouldn't be able to see another merperson's spark, but I'm also not supposed to be able to transform without a ring either. Something in my essence is different. I feel different ever since the ocean dragged us away from a terrible fate at the hands of an unfair and unkind king.

Carter tenses next to me, following my line of vision. Through the glowing water, a shadow cuts through the kelp forest in our direction. It doesn't belong to a large fish or shark. It's definitely another merperson.

I don't even have to tell Carter we need to leave. He hooks his arm around my waist and swims in the opposite direction of the approaching merman. My tail smacks along the long ropes of kelp, and I wave my hand through the water, sending a current strong enough to entangle them so it's nearly impossible to follow us without cutting a way through.

"They're a long way from Pearlestria," I say into Carter's mind, because saying nothing at all squeezes my chest as I fight away the rolling panic. If it weren't for the warning in my dream, they would've stumbled upon us. Pearlestria was small enough that we would've been recognized. The whole ocean could probably recognize us with how merpeople can pass on detailed information—clear images—with their minds.

"It's not uncommon to leave," Carter says. "Look how often we did. It's a big world. We might live in colonies, but we do like to explore."

When we're a few miles away from the kelp forest, Carter loosens his hold on me, allowing me to position myself on his back instead of being pulled along like a doll. Our in-sync hearts slow, and our nerves settle, and after another mile of swimming, Carter finally stops and relaxes.

"That was too close, Ava. I should've listened to you," he says.

I cup his face in my hands. "It's not your fault. Neither of us could've known." I never expected the diamond on my neck would protect us with words of warning. I had no idea what to expect from it, but deep down, I knew it would keep us safe, and it did.

"This is why I'm nervous," he says. "We might not be so lucky near Pearlestria. I don't know what the king will do to us if he discovers we're alive."

I lean my forehead against his. "Nothing," I say. "I won't allow it."

"Ava," Carter whispers into my mind.

"Just trust me," I say.

But I can see it's not me he doesn't trust. It's the rest of the ocean.

I don't blame him. I don't trust it, either.

14

POWER ATTRACTS POWER

"JUST ANOTHER MILE," CARTER SAYS into my mind.

His voice startles me awake, and I blink my eyes a few times. I didn't even realize how tired I was until Carter started swimming after he slept for a measly hour, one in which I stayed awake from fear. If he wasn't holding my arms in his, I'd have floated away in the sea.

Nerves tie a dozen knots in my stomach. "Can we reach out to her from here?" I ask.

Carter dives deeper, and I spot the sleepy colony behind the shimmering wall that looks like the inside of a shiny sea-shell. An intense fear burns in my spark just looking at the place that imprisoned me for weeks. The only thing we have going for us is that all the merpeople hide away in their rock houses, sleeping.

Even the castle lacks activity from the center of the colony, looking more foreboding than beautiful like it used to. Because behind its gem-encrusted walls lies a king who would break my bond with Carter to steal the magic flowing through my veins.

Warmth erupts in my chest, and a bright glow flashes from the diamond necklace over my heart. The sudden light startles me, and I let go of Carter to hide it between the palms of my hands afraid the beacon of light will draw the whole colony right to us.

Carter spins, not letting me get far. "Is someone coming?"

"My necklace," I say, slowly unlacing my fingers. "It's glowing."

Carter's brows furrow, his head tilting to the side. "I can't see it."

Carter would have to be blind not to see how brightly it shines, sending colorful light through the sea around us. It's enough that I consider taking it off to shove in the bag slung across Carter's shoulder.

With a reach of his hand, Carter grabs my wrists and stops me from yanking the chain free. "Don't take it off. I think only you can see it."

"But why is it glowing?"

A sudden current wraps around us, yanking us back. Through the shift in the water, I spot a lone figure swimming straight for the surface from outside the main channel in Pearlestria. I'd recognize the glittering gold tail anywhere. Luna, King Attilonious' daughter, swims toward the surface to break through. It's something we've done together before when we became fast friends. She tried to run away with me and Carter to go ashore, because she always wanted to experience life on the land, not unlike her mother, the queen. But King Attilonious never allowed it. She still goes to the surface now to dream.

"Luna," I whisper, holding the warm diamond between my fingers. The words stay locked between me and Carter. No one else can hear us unless we want them to.

Carter pulls me close. "Careful, Ava. Luna might be your friend, but she's the king's daughter. She doesn't see the world like we do. Her loyalty will be to her dad."

I frown. I wouldn't blame her, but I'd hope she would stand up to him if it came down to it. It's always nice to have someone on your side.

"I know," I whisper. "I just—I wish she didn't think we

died."

His lip pouts. "I wish a lot of people didn't think that."

"I'm sorry." My voice is barely a whisper between us. "I know you miss your dad. I miss mine, too." I miss a bunch of people.

"It won't always be this way. Now, come on. We have to hurry. I want to get out of here before dawn."

Carter swims forward, down to where the wall obscures our arrival. We stop outside the barrier, closest to the spot where Carter and I had shared a small rock house together on the outskirts of the community. If Starla and Mateo are back in Pearlestria, then that would be the place they would stay since they don't have their own home here. Well, it'd be their home now without me and Carter around.

Carter's gaze falls on mine as we share a silent conversation to see who will call for his mom first.

"Starla?" I ask, beating him to it. His hesitation might keep us here well past the sunrise. "Starla, are you here?"

"Ava?" a familiar voice questions. "Oh, no. What are you doing here? Is Carter..." Her voice trails off before she can relay her concerns to me.

"I'm fine, Mom," Carter says, taking over. "We're together."

"You shouldn't be here," she says, her voice whispering through our minds like if she projects it too loudly, the whole colony might hear.

"You shouldn't be here either," Carter says. "We went to San Francisco looking for you, but you weren't there."

She doesn't respond right away. It takes a few minutes of silence before I say, "Starla, are you still there? We know about the sea stone rings, but that's not why we're here. We need your help."

"Oh, Ava. I was hoping the island would protect you," she

says. "But I don't know what it is I can help you with. Everyone's been called back to the colonies by King Attilonious."

I close my eyes, twisting my lips to the side at her words. I knew the king removed magic from Carter's sea stone ring, but I didn't realize he called everyone back to the sea on the full moon. And I can't help but think this is all my fault. I caused so much trouble for the king that he probably doesn't want to risk another human standing up to him again if they were chosen as a mate.

"He's scared," Carter says, thinking my next thought for me.

"He should be," I mutter to him, allowing Starla to hear through the water.

"Ava, Carter," Starla says, "you shouldn't talk like that, especially this close to the colony. The king has power that extends through the whole ocean. We don't know what his limitations are. What if he senses you? You two need to leave. Go back to the island. Live life the best you can in those waters."

"The king can't touch us, Starla." At least I hope. "And we're not leaving without you. We need you. One of the lost ones is hurt."

"I'm sorry to hear that," she says. "But I can't return to land."

"Then I'll bring him to the sea. Please, come with us."

"But Mateo. It's hard enough holding this secret," she says.

My hope for Starla's help dwindles the longer our telepathic conversation continues. She's not involved with the people of the island. She doesn't have to live with the consequences of accidentally hurting someone with power. She's a healer. It's all she does. She fixes things while I, like an unstoppable storm, leave everything a wreck in my path.

"Please, Starla. Just this once. I can't go back to the island otherwise."

"Oh, Ava."

Without thinking, I pull from Carter and swim up and over the wall. If she can see my face, look into my eyes, she might agree. I can't go back without trying everything short of forcing her to come with me. Carter swims above me, locking his hands on my waist. I expect him to pull me back over the wall and away from the colony, but he only swims me faster until we're through the door of our old rock house.

Things have changed. It's no longer bare like I used to keep it. Starla brought in more stones for seating and has draped woven sea grass over them. A large chest sits in the corner of our old living room with a few decorative vases she either brought from shore or found somewhere along the way. Within them are stands of kelp that float to the ceiling, and even more fish have moved into the reef lining the perimeter of the room.

The sea glass mural climbing the wall is exactly the same as we left it, the scene reminiscent of the sun setting on water. Though that's the same, Starla's spent time covering the cutouts with seaweed curtains, so people can no longer peer inside without her permission, something we never bothered with because no one ever visited.

"Starla," I whisper telepathically. "We're in the living room."

The current shifts, a stream coming from the bedroom she had claimed while we lived together. It's smaller than mine and Carter's, and I'm surprised they didn't move into that room. Starla pulls the curtain back, and grimaces at the both of us.

She swims closer, pulling Carter into her arms first. "You never could listen," she says, smiling sadly, a mixture of love and worry marring her soft features. Her eyes, the same blue-green as Carter's, shift to my face before they drop to the diamond hanging around my neck over the T-shirt of Carter's I'm still wearing. "Ava, where did you get that?"

I guess no warm hug for me. Reaching up, I lock my fingers around the glittering stone. "It was a gift."

"That belonged to the queen," she says.

I nod. "I know. The island—it's been doing things to me."

I can't decipher the next look that crosses her face. Surprise? Fear? Confusion? Her perfectly arched brows lower on her smooth forehead, and she cups her hand over mine while I hold the stone.

"Ava's been sleep-swimming and seeing things I can't," Carter adds. "Her water affinity is all over the place. She's the reason we need your help, Mom. She hurt someone by accident while practicing. I don't even know how much longer we can stay on the island. Ava already wants to leave. The others will find out about her, and it's bad enough as it is. Her own sister looks at her with distrust."

Starla pouts her bottom lip and pulls me into a hug. "I'm so sorry for how everything is turning out for you both. I never imagined Carter would have such a life. You both were supposed to be free to live wherever you chose, make the kind of life you're happy to live. You were supposed to have so much joy, just being together. It's all I ever wanted. What your dad wanted, too. Even after your accidental bonding, I still had hope for that life. If I could face the king myself, I would. I'd do anything to make your lives the best they can be."

"But you can't face the king," Carter says.

"But I can help you." She touches my necklace once more. "I always expected my son would choose a special mate, Ava, but I had never imagined this."

I frown. We've always had tension between us—right up to the moment I realized Starla spared Giselle's life. But hearing her admit all this makes me feel like an utter disappointment. I'm nothing like the daughter she had ever imagined gaining. I've done nothing but ruin everything for her, including her life on land.

"I'm sorry, Starla," I whisper.

She pushes my floating blond hair from my face. "I didn't mean that in a bad way. I just never imagined the queen would pass her essence to you. Power attracts power, and you must've showed her something."

"You knew the queen?" I ask.

"We were childhood friends and grew up together. We had both dreamed of moving from the sea to the land. Your grandmer, Carter, she raised me between here and the land. Celestiana used to visit, and she met someone—a human. But when her affinity started showing, the king took great interest in her. He swept her on the waves, promised her the ocean, everything she could ever imagine in a mate. And she felt herself pull away from the human she loved. She enjoyed the king's company, and he taught her how to harness her magic, but soon after the coupling ceremony, he wanted her to stop returning to the land. And she had agreed for many years." She stops speaking, her blue eyes blinking a few times as she pushes whatever memory away.

"But she wanted to return?"

Starla nods. "Can you blame her? Once you love the human world, you never stop loving it. She took interest in every new human transformed into merperson and would travel the world to offer her support through the transition."

"Is that why she created the Lost Cove?" I ask. I know the rumors. I know it is said that the queen created the sanctuary for a woman who refused to transform after discovering the mer-secret.

"It is. And she kept it from the king, but it turned too difficult to protect the island and remain in Pearlestria, especially with the bond she shared with the king."

"So, she left." It's not a question. I know it's true. "I can't believe she left Luna behind like that."

"It wasn't her intention. She had planned to give up her magic and renounce her reign over the sea, but in doing so, it'd have gone to King Attilonious. They shared a bond and their magic."

My heart hangs heavy in my chest. "She died to protect that island and to keep the king from getting her magic."

Starla nods. "She gave her essence back to the sea. The sea gave her a human life in exchange and it stopped her from returning to Luna. It broke the bond she had for the king. But without her mermaid essence and the weight of the broken bond—it was too much."

I blink surprise from my face. "You mean...I can give up this life completely? I can renounce my essence." I turn to Carter. "Why didn't you tell me?"

Starla touches my arm. "Carter knows nothing of this. It's an impossible situation. If any merperson could do it, we wouldn't need rings to go to land. The moon would never call to us. The queen had the ocean's magic in her heart like you, but it doesn't go without consequence. You've bonded with Carter through the essence. Renouncing it will break it like it did between the king and queen. The king survives because they both share magic. Carter doesn't. It could very well kill him."

My lips form an O-shape. As much as the idea of returning to the human world as completely human stirs something within me, I could never do it. I could never break Carter's heart like that. I could never risk his life.

"I'd never," I whisper. "I promised you forever."

Carter's mouth pulls up into a half-smile, and then he leans over and kisses my cheek. "I know, Aves."

"Starla?" a masculine voice sounds through all our minds. "Where are you?"

Carter hooks his arm around my waist and pulls us

through the door before Mateo swims into the living room to find us. My heartbeat pounds in my ears, and I panic at the idea that I've spent too much time learning about the queen, and now I might've missed my opportunity to take Starla back to the Lost Cove.

"My love, you caught me," Starla says, letting us hear her conversation with Mateo. "I was about to sneak out. I wanted to surprise you with a few things."

"How about I close my eyes and pretend I didn't see you?" Mateo asks.

I raise my eyebrows, glancing at Carter who shakes his head.

"Perfect," Starla says. "Now, enjoy your day. I'll be back by sunset."

Carter swims me up and over the wall before Mateo can watch Starla leave. My necklace suddenly sparks brightly on my neck, sending a flash of panic to my heart, but it's only Starla who swims over the wall above us.

"We must be quick," she says, looking down at us.

I blow a bubble through my mouth, letting it trickle to the surface. My necklace still glows brightly, sending rainbow sparkles through the water. No one but me sees it, and I tuck it under my shirt. It might be going off because the sun has already risen overhead and the colony will awaken soon.

Carter responds to his mom with a nod. I climb on his back, and he takes off. I take one last look behind us, fear sneaking into my heart. Making her way down from the surface is Luna, and her eyes meet mine from over my shoulder.

But she doesn't move from her spot.

All she does is watch us leave.

15

REMAIN LOST

"AVA, YOU CAN STILL TRANSFORM?" Starla asks, floating in the middle of the bay next to me and Carter. Her brown hair is tied in a tight bun on the nape of her neck, and she wears a decorative sea grass wrap around her chest, a popular look in the colony, though some mermaids do go topless. It's something I never got used to, even though merpeople don't judge bodies the same as humans.

I pull myself from my thoughts and nod. Tugging my hand from Carter, I hold out my fingers so Starla can see I'm not wearing a sea stone ring. She didn't stay long the last time I saw her, and I was so caught up with Giselle and Bailey I didn't even mention my lack of one before she left.

"I don't even need a ring," I say.

Closing my eyes, I let the transformation take hold of me. After a quick rush of cramps, I change back into my human self, and Carter propels us to the surface to break through. Starla remains underwater, and Carter helps me get my bottoms on and then hands me the bag with the supplies I picked up in San Francisco.

Starla swims behind us, never breaking the surface, and waits with Carter just past the waves where they won't have to hunch to stay underwater. It's my job to get Wes to them so Starla can see what she can do.

My legs give out the moment I reach the shore of the bay,

and I stay on my hands and knees for a good few minutes just inhaling and exhaling the briny air. My sopping hair sticks to my face and sand covers me from head to toe, peppering the shirt of Carter's I still wear even though swimming without it would be a million times easier.

"Ava?" Giselle's familiar voice rings through the air. "Bailey! Ava's back!"

Everyone from our little community rushes onto the beach to gape at me getting back to my feet. I wring the seawater from my shirt and force myself to smile. Giselle rushes to me, throwing her arms around me, holding me as tight as she possibly can.

I laugh, pushing her back just enough so I can breathe. "How's Wes?" I ask, turning my gaze to Bailey.

Her lip quivers and she doesn't even have to say anything for me to know he's either gotten worse or nothing has changed. "He's dehydrated." Her brows pinch together. "Where's Carter? Is everything okay?"

I swallow the lump in my throat. "He's with his mom in the bay. We need to get Wes to her."

Giselle turns to the water. "Why don't they come on land?"

Tears prickle in my eyes, and I blink them away. "It's a long story, but we don't have much time. If you all can help me carry Wes to the water, I can swim him myself."

"I'm coming with you," Bailey says.

I nod. There's no way I'm going to tell her it's better if she remains on land where it's safe, because who knows what'll happen with me around. Instead, Darren, Sandra, and Reyna lead the way to Bailey's bungalow. We all take a section of the blanket Wes rests on and carry him all the way into the waves.

Carter surfaces the moment the others leave me and Bailey, and he takes Wes from us. In Carter's arms, Wes looks years younger and smaller. Water splashes his face, gaining no reaction, and I wonder if the damage done to him can be fixed. He hit his head and stopped breathing before I pulled the water from his lungs—there's a lot that can be wrong. Even if I could get him to a hospital, there might not be anything we can do.

I push the thought away. I refuse to think it. If there was one thing I learned from being a mermaid, it's that magic is real and the ocean doesn't only steal life away. It creates it, too.

We reach the center of the bay, and Starla breaks the surface for the first time. Carter flicks his tail, keeping Wes above the water. I tread water next to Bailey, remaining in my human form though transforming would be so much easier. I remain human not only for Bailey's sake, but because I'm slightly afraid.

What if Starla can't heal Wes, and I lose control of my emotions? I'm much stronger as a mermaid. I can't let anything happen. Not anymore.

"I need to submerge him," Starla says, running her fingers along Wes' forehead.

"He's not like you," Bailey argues. "You'll drown him."

Starla swims back, putting space between her and Bailey. "Then I can't help you. I'm sorry. I need the water to heal him."

Bailey's eyes glass over, her lip quivering. She's torn between her hatred of our kind and her love of Wes. Merpeople are responsible for both of them being on this island. I don't blame her for not trusting us.

Blowing strands of damp hair from my face, I reach out and grab Bailey's hand in the water. "This is Wes' only chance," I say. "Getting him to a hospital might be nearly impossible. And if I do take him to one, I won't be going back for him. You won't ever see him again. But if you'd rather put your faith in a human, I understand. Just do what you think Wes would want."

Bailey rubs water from her face with her free hand. "He'd let you try," she whispers.

I nod. "I promise we'll do everything we can."

Dipping under, I transform into a mermaid, kicking a current around us that jostles Bailey. She swims closer, locking her hands on my shoulders. I don't argue that she should stay above the water, because she's having a hard enough time trusting us as it is.

"You have to have him back up for air when I need it," Bailey says.

Starla nods. "I'll be as quick as I can."

Carter covers Wes' mouth and nose with his hand, and when Starla's ready, we all sink under together, swimming deeper into the bay. Bailey grips my neck, resting her chin on my shoulder, and I watch Starla prod her fingers around Wes' head.

She brushes her fingers along the fresh stitches and uses her sharp nail to cut right through them. Blood trickles into the water in a small pink-tinted cloud, and Bailey squeezes my shoulders so hard I flinch and grab her hands.

The seconds tick by as Starla massages her fingers in Wes' wound, making my stomach roll. Carter remains silent, still preventing Wes from automatically sucking in water. Bailey pinches me, pointing to the surface, but Starla shakes her head at her. She needs more time.

"I need at least a minute more. If I stop now, there won't be anything else I can do," Starla says.

"But he'll suffocate," I say.

"He's already dying, Ava," Starla says softly. "It's a chance we must risk."

Wes' body jerks in Carter's arms, startling me, and Bailey locks her fingers into my hair, ripping at the strands. She attempts to swim forward, but I yank her back so she can't get in between Starla and Wes.

Bubbles erupt from my sister's mouth, ridding her lungs of the oxygen she needs to survive. She struggles to hold onto me, but if she does any longer, she'll open her mouth and let water into her lungs.

I don't give her the chance.

With the flick of my tail, I shoot us both up to the surface, but I don't break through. I wave my hand through the water, sending her in a current that takes her right to the air. Tilting my head down, I peer down at the others. Carter grips Wes in his arms as he continues to thrash, and Starla holds his forehead between her hands, her eyes closed.

For the first time ever, I see the glow of her spark in her chest. It's like her healing ability calls to me. It lights up the water surrounding them, the glow catching off the facets of my necklace, sending rainbow light through the water.

Bubbles erupt around me as Bailey dives back under, but she won't be able to reach Wes quick enough at her pace. Holding my hand out, I imagine calming the water. I want so badly to stop time to give Starla what she needs to heal Wes.

Carter's head jerks up to look at me, and it's not until our eyes meet that I realize all the bubbles surrounding us lie frozen in the water, suspended in the still bay. I run my hand through the water, gathering up the biggest pools of oxygen created by Bailey's thrashing. It's like I've somehow created a veil between her at the surface and us amid the sea. She continues to fight while the rest of us remain calm.

Diving down, I close the distance between me and Carter, still carrying the balloon sized pocket of air with me. Light shimmers around it, casting it in an iridescent glow, and I maneuver it in front of Wes' face until his mouth and nose break through the barrier.

Carter and Starla freeze, the intensity of their eyes hot

enough to ignite something deep in my soul. Carter shifts his hands, Wes gasps a huge breath, and then the water erupts back to life, the bubbles scattering and catching on invisible streams that take them to the surface.

Wes falls limp in Carter's arms, tiny bubbles still clinging to his face and Carter's strong hands.

Starla's spark in her chest increases in intensity nearly blinding me, and a second later, she says, "I've done all I can. His injuries are healed, but now it's up to Wes to decide."

I don't follow Carter up to the surface where he takes Wes and instead remain at Starla's side. When our gazes meet, I fling my arms out and embrace her like I've never hugged her before. She rubs her fingers over my back, pushing my hair away from my skin.

"Ava, what you did…" Her voice trails off. The last time anyone beside Carter and Giselle witnessed my water affinity was when I used it against the king at my failed coronation. Starla wasn't there.

"Do I scare you?" I ask, feeling self-conscious as she studies me.

She shakes her head. "No, but I am afraid for you. If the king were to ever realize you were alive, he'd do everything he could to find you. He'd assure your bond to Carter was broken, and he would force you to bow before him. He won't be kind like he was with Celestiana. He won't try to win you. He'll take what he thinks is rightfully his."

"But I'm not his," I say.

She purses her lips. "He won't see things as you do."

"I won't let him take Carter from me," I say. "I won't bow down to him, either."

She nods, hugging me again. "I hope it never comes to that. I don't want to lose my son—I don't want to lose you."

"You won't," I say. "We'll be safe."

"Please, just take my advice and never come to Pearlestria again. Don't leave these protected waters. I'd much rather never see you again and know you're safe than lose you completely."

I frown. "But Starla."

She shakes her head. "Please, just promise me."

But I can't. I refuse to trap Carter here like he's in some tank, especially since he can't transform back into a human.

I open my mouth to respond, but my necklace flashes brightly, sending fear straight to my very core. "Starla, my necklace. It's telling me danger lurks by. Do you think someone followed us?"

She draws her eyes to the reef. "Even if they did, they can't come in."

That doesn't make me feel better. "You have to go. You have to get back to the colony before Mateo gets anxious."

She hugs me. "Please, remember what I asked."

"I—okay," I say without arguing. A terrible feeling sinks into me, and my first thought travels to Luna. I'm almost a hundred percent certain she saw us, but I don't want to believe she told her dad. And if she did? *Stop. Luna was your friend.*

"Ava?" Luna's soft voice hums through the current and into my mind. "Where are you?"

I freeze, half expecting her to come through the reef at any moment. "Starla, you have to go to her. You have to make sure she returns to Pearlestria with you."

The water shifts around us as Carter swims below us and toward the reef. His hot emotions rush through me, causing me to wave my hand out. I shift the water, creating a current that stops him from exiting the reef into the open sea.

He still tries to fight the current.

"Carter, stop! What do you think you're doing?" I ask.

He spins to face me from fifty feet away. "I heard the princess, Ava. She can't be here. She'll lead the king right to us."

"So, what do you think you're going to do? She was my friend."

"She's the king's daughter."

"That doesn't make her our enemy. If you even think about doing something crazy, even if you think it's because you want to protect us, I'll transform right now and go back to the beach and stay. Is she worth that to you? Because I don't like what's gotten into you, and I won't stand for it."

The shock that crosses his face strikes me right in the heart, but I don't know what else to say to bring him back to his senses. This feels like it did in San Francisco. It's like he's changed with his merman transformation, and I'm seeing a side of him I didn't know—one I don't like. Being protective is one thing, but wanting to face Luna head on like a threat is different.

I close the distance between us and wrap my arms around him. His hard face softens under my touch. "Let me handle this. I don't want you doing something you'll later regret."

"I'll never regret keeping you safe."

I want to put space between me and Carter for the first time ever. I want to swim away from him and be alone. And it's in this moment I know why. He reminds me of the king in his reasoning. It's unsettling.

Still holding onto Carter, I shift and gaze at Starla from over my shoulder. "Please, you have to go. You have to make sure she goes back with you. Tell her enough to satisfy her, but don't tell her about the humans here, okay?"

"You want my mom to tell her about us? But, Ava—"

I give Carter a stern look, cutting off his thoughts. "The human's secret is more important. This island is theirs, not ours. I won't jeopardize them."

Starla nods, concern lining her brows, but she doesn't argue with him. She swims by, touching Carter's arm once, and then jets through the water without a goodbye and breaches over the reef to the open sea.

"Ava, I don't like this. Our secret is out," Carter says.

I hold his face between my hands. "That's the least of my worries. I can't think about the rest of the world until everything is fixed here. I need to check on Wes."

"Let the others worry about him. You've done enough."

"But I haven't."

"Ava..."

"Please, I need to go to land." I don't say it, but I need the fresh air to clear the water from my lungs. I need to think about everything that's happening. I need to figure out what happens next.

If only the ocean would just give me the answers.

16

ONCOMING STORM

I THOUGHT FACING MY SISTER before was scary, but now, after what I did in the bay while Wes was underwater, how I forced her to surface so I could keep him under long enough for Starla to finish healing him, has me beyond panicking to face her. But I have to. Carter can't access the land like I can. He can't even intervene if things get heated.

Carter sits in the sand, slapping his fin against a wave, because he didn't want to remain in the water alone. I'd give anything to have him stand with me right now, but his attitude isn't helping the stress I'm feeling. His anger keeps trickling into me, confusing me in a moment where I'm trying to stay composed.

I kneel in the sand next to him and grab his hands. "Please, you have to chill out. You're making things worse."

He releases a breath. "I'm sorry, Aves. It's just—"

"I know this isn't ideal, but I have other things I need to worry about now. I can't be stressing about you while I need to face Bailey," I say, cutting him off. "And we'll talk about the rest of it later. But I have to check on Wes. Maybe you should go for a swim. It might be good for you."

"I'm not leaving you," he says.

I sigh. "Then please, just keep yourself in control for five minutes."

Standing up, I catch sight of Giselle hovering on the outskirts of the shelters. I wave her over, and she jogs my way, kicking up sand. We meet in the middle of the beach between the community and shore.

"Is he?" I ask, talking about Wes.

"I don't know. Sandra and Bailey are with him. Bailey looked like she wanted to murder someone, so we're staying out of the way," she says.

Great. I knew I had upset her, and now I'm going to have to face her wrath. If Wes dies, she'll surely try to kill me herself. But how could I blame her?

I wring my hands together. "Think you can hang out with Carter? He could use a friendly face."

Giselle grimaces. "I don't know. I can feel his tension from here, and it's ridiculously uncomfortable."

"Please," I beg.

She droops her shoulders. "Fine, but you owe me."

"You can have the jar of jam I brought," I offer.

She purses her lips, narrowing her eyes in a fake glare. "What? No peanut butter?"

I laugh. "Sorry, I got hungry."

With a dramatic sigh, Giselle strolls away from me and heads toward Carter. She plants herself in the space next to him and stretches her legs out in front of her, allowing the waves to wash the sand off her feet.

I wait a minute longer, watching the two of them to make sure everything's okay before I head toward my sister's shelter. Quiet murmurs sound from the other side of the palm fronds, and I stand and eavesdrop for a moment.

I don't catch much of the conversation before Sandra shifts the leaves to let herself out. She offers me a sad smile, pats my shoulder, and then heads toward the tree line that'll take her inland toward the orchard of fruit trees and beyond them, a fresh water creek.

I straighten my shoulders, tempted to turn around and run back to the sea, but before I can, Bailey clears her throat. She watches me stand outside her bungalow, her intense gaze hot enough to ignite me from the inside. I suck in a small breath, steeling myself, and then I hunch down to enter her shelter.

Wes sleeps on a blanket, his clothes damp from the sea water. His head is no longer cut, but he's still not awake. It's enough to send my heart sliding to my feet to splatter onto the floor. I had wished with everything in me that I'd enter her bungalow to see him sitting up and smiling, chatting like nothing had happened, but he's exactly as he was before.

"Bailey." My sister's name nearly sticks in my throat. "I'm sorry."

Her hands curl into fists. "What you did out there, Ava. You could've—"

"Ava..."

I crinkle my nose, hearing the soft whisper of my name.

Bailey hops to her feet, rushing to Wes' side, and I gape at him with my mouth hanging open. He doesn't sit up or move but just blinks his eyes, staring at the palm leaf roof of the bungalow he and Bailey have shared for who knows how long. Neither of them has ever told me.

"Wes, God. You're awake. I've been so scared," Bailey says, tears dripping down her cheeks to roll off her chin to pelt Wes in the face.

He reaches up and wipes his fingers across her tears, smearing them away. "What happened?"

"Our boat was dragged beyond the reef, and we jumped, but you hit your head pretty hard. You've been unconscious for days." The words spill out of Bailey's mouth faster than her tears do from her eyes. "But all that doesn't matter now. You're okay. Ava saved you."

I back away from the two of them, wanting nothing more

than to leave them to their private moment, but the second Bailey says my name, they both glance in my direction.

I freeze and force myself to smile. "No, Starla saved him. I was just the errand girl."

Wes' eyes study me for an uncomfortable moment before he asks, "You left the cove for me?"

"I couldn't let you die," I say.

He nods his head but doesn't look surprised. "Thank you," he says. "I owe you my life."

My hair smacks my cheeks as I shake my head. "It's fine, really."

"Ava," he says.

"It's fine," I repeat.

I can't stand the look of gratitude and awe crossing his face, so I do the only thing I can think of. I back out of the bungalow, telling him it's fine once more, and then leave Wes and Bailey alone.

His voice echoes through the air, drawing everyone's attention to Bailey's shelter, and I run. Something feels so strange about everything. I can't get far away fast enough. I even ignore Carter and Giselle as they call my name.

I run along the shore and don't stop running until the hum of voices disappears, the bay can no longer be seen over my shoulder, and I'm greeted by comforting waves that invite me to swim among them.

I strut into the water, pushing through the waves until I have to swim. I don't transform and keep swimming in the surf, heading out to the rocks not far from the reef. I pull myself onto them, facing the ocean, and for the first time in a long time, I sob.

My chest heaves, my eyes burning from tears, my whole body shaking with each shuddering breath. I muffle my wail with the palm of my hand, just letting things sink in. I've been bottling up everything, trying to keep myself strong, but the events of the last few days sneak up on me.

From the moment I realized Carter couldn't return to his human form to the drunk guy who frightened me on the beach—almost being spotted by mermen, our trip to Pearlestria, Starla healing Wes, Luna showing up, and Wes telling me he owes me his life even though I was responsible for his injuries. Each moment plays over and over in my mind, and the longer I think about everything, the harder I cry. I cry so many tears I'm sure the sea has risen. The salty water washes over my bare legs like it's attempting to hug me, but I flick my hand, sending the wave in the opposite direction.

A dark head of hair pops from the water, and Carter swims closer through the current I created. Without a word, he pulls himself onto the rock next to me and wraps his muscular arms around me.

"Ava, I'm sorry," Carter whispers. "I wish I could pull every bad thing you feel out of you and take it into me."

I sniffle, wiping my face with my palms. "I feel so lost," I whisper. "What is the point to all this?"

He holds me tighter. "I wish I had the answers. All I know is you're strong and brave and the most powerful person I've ever met. We're going to get through this. We're going to figure out how to make this all work so we can have the happiness I've been trying so hard to give you."

"It's not all about me," I say.

He kisses my temple. "I know, Ava. And we'll figure it out. Let's just take a moment to breathe, okay? You've been through a lot."

I hold his hand in mine. "So have you."

"Then we'll process this all together. If there's one thing I know about us, it's that we can get through anything."

His words bring a smile to my face.

Gently pinching my chin, he turns my head so I have to look at him. His beautiful smile, the one he saves just for me, lights his face brighter than the spark in either of our chests. It shines brighter than the low-hanging sun. Probably the rest of the universe, too.

"You always know what to say to make me feel better," I say, leaning my forehead against his. "Did you know I happen to have the best mate in the entire ocean? The entire world even."

He chuckles. "I don't know...I think *I* might."

I grin wider and shift my legs over Carter's tail. We sit in silence, just holding each other. For the first time in a while, it feels like as long as Carter's holding me we'll be okay. That the world will be okay.

I can only hope.

A flash of lightning sparkles on the horizon, drawing my gaze away from Carter. It's the first storm I've ever seen out here, and it looks massive, coming this way. I don't know why I thought this island was protected from more than merpeople, but I guess magic has its limitations and a storm is one of them.

Wind whips through my salty blond hair, blowing it off my damp neck, causing me to shiver. Carter holds me close to him in the sand, because I wasn't ready to return to the water. Something has me on edge, and I feel like the shore is safer than the water. Most merpeople usually wouldn't leave the ocean, but now they can't. No one can follow me.

"If you want to sleep on land..." Carter says, his voice trailing off.

I raise my eyebrows. "The only way I'm sleeping on land is if you do it too and with the way that storm looks, sleeping in this spot doesn't seem like an option."

Leaning over, he plants his lips to my cheek. "The surface

will be rough, but if we go to the deepest part of the bay, it won't be so bad. I wish I had time to build you a house like back in Pearlestria. I know how much sleeping in the open bothers you."

"We'll work on it in the morning, okay?" I say.

"Hey, Aves," Giselle calls from behind me. She strolls through the sand, flicking her gaze from me to the ocean. "Sandra wants us to pack up to head inland. You sure you two will be okay out here?"

I grimace. "We have to be. Carter can't spend the whole night out of the water."

"I guess we'll have to invest in a saltwater swimming pool when we get off this island," she muses, smiling brightly at her idea.

I don't have the heart to tell her if we ever make it off this island that Carter and I won't be making a permanent residence anywhere, and he definitely won't be living in some pool all so I can have a human life.

"You have some big dreams, Gi," Carter says with a smirk.

"Hey, I know people. I can make it happen."

"I'm sure Sapphire will be dying to know why you're suddenly interested in enormous aquariums. You really want to let her in on our secret, too?" I ask.

Giselle frowns for a split second before rolling her eyes. "Matty would complain that Carter has definitely set the bar too high considering how obsessed we were with mermaids...before, you know."

Talking about Giselle's cousin and our friends back in Azure Waters both pains me and lifts my spirits. I miss everyone immensely and can't stop wondering what they're up to. Sapphire and Matty are surely living it up in LA. Their penthouse apartment probably does have a saltwater swimming pool...of course it's probably on the roof of the high rise they live in.

More lightning strikes in the clouds, startling me. Giselle hugs herself, and I'm sure she wishes I'd come to shore to stay with her. The storm rolling in looks nothing like anything we had in Azure Waters. Thunder and lightning were as rare as a downpour.

"You two stay safe, okay?" Giselle says, stepping farther from a wave that sneaks up on me, smashing into Carter's tail and up and over it to splash me in the face.

"You, too." I climb to my feet so I can hug my best friend for a moment.

The others gather near the shelters, packing things up to take inland to wherever it is they're going.

Carter pulls himself into the surf first, watching me from the swells, and I wave once before waltzing into the whitecaps.

"Ava!" a masculine voice calls out. I turn to glance at Wes over my shoulder. "Ava, wait! Where are you going?"

"Underwater," I say.

"No, you're not. You're coming with us."

Wes' eyes shine with a wildness I've never seen before, and he rushes toward me. He reaches out to me, trying to lock his fingers on my arm, and I stumble away, doing the only thing I can think of. I push him back and run into the water.

"Ava!" he screams again.

"Get back, Wes," I warn.

He doesn't.

In a blink of my eyes, Carter's between us. Fear washes over me at his anger, and I hold my breath as he wraps his arms around Wes in the surf.

I turn my gaze away. I can't look.

This time, Bailey's the one to scream.

BAD FEELING

"WES!" MY SISTER'S VOICE CUTS through the wind whistling around us.

Carter doesn't let Wes go, but he doesn't hurt him either. All he does is restrain him so he can't get any closer to me.

I hate that I automatically assumed the worse, but after San Francisco and the way he reacted hearing Luna's voice, I wasn't sure what to expect. Without being able to transform, something's changed in him. He's more protective of me than ever.

"I just need to talk to her!" Wes hollers, thrashing in Carter's arms, trying to fight my mate amid the waves. "Why won't you let me go?"

I wish I had transformed back into a mermaid so Carter and I could leave, but I'm afraid Wes would now try to follow.

"Ava!" Wes yells again. "Ava, please, you have to tell him to let me go."

My heart rams against my ribcage at the desperation in Wes' voice. But my own desperation prevents me from wanting Carter to give Wes a moment to talk to me. Something in him has snapped, freaking me out, and I have no idea what's wrong. Ever since he woke up with my name on his lips, I felt something was off.

"Wes, come on. We have to go," Bailey says from her place on the sand.

He ignores her.

The others stand back on the beach, almost like they're afraid of the ocean...or maybe they're afraid of me. I have no idea. All I know is it takes everything in me to close the distance between me and Wes as he continues to fight against Carter's strong hold.

"Wes?" My soft voice barely whispers over the wind. I need to get his attention before he ends up hurt by accident. "What's the matter?"

The moment he hears my voice, he stops struggling against Carter. His wide green eyes look almost brown in the night, and he's wearing only a pair of shorts. His long hair falls from his knotted bun, and the way he gapes at me frightens me even more.

He doesn't respond to me for an uncomfortable minute.

"Wes? Are you okay?" I ask, hoping he'll say something.

"I—" Wes opens and shuts his mouth, confusion crossing his thick brows. "I'm not sure. Something feels wrong. You can't go."

Lightning strikes, startling me, and I fall into a wave and sink under. Hands grab onto me, pulling me up, and then another pair of hands yank me away. Carter holds me against him instead of onto Wes. He slaps the waves with his strong tail, forcing Wes to stay back while keeping us afloat. I cough and spit out the water I inhaled, gasping as another wave attempts to rip me from Carter.

Wes raises his arms up in surrender and doesn't move forward. Another wave rolls into us, pushing him toward shore, but he fights to stay in the surf. His intense stare bores into me, crawling under my skin. I wish he'd say what he was thinking so I could understand the weirdness he's forcing upon me.

"You should come to shore with me, Ava," Wes says, offering his hand out.

Carter swims us farther away. "I think you need to go back.

You're still recovering." The tenseness bunching Carter's muscles has me on edge.

"He's right, Wes," I say. "You need to rest, and I can't leave the water. Things have changed since the full moon, and I won't abandon my mate."

"Please, Ava," he says, his voice getting lost on the intense wind. "Ever since I woke up, I've had a horrible feeling that something was coming. I didn't realize what it was about until I saw you enter the waves. The feeling was about you. I don't know how to explain it. You saved my life, and I can't live with myself knowing that something will happen to you."

He says it with such certainty that it leaves me on the brink of panicking. I have no idea what's gotten into him and why he has this sudden need to protect me. I'm not even the one who saved him. All I did was get Starla to come here. But it's like the water got to his head—maybe it did.

Or maybe it was my magic. I did use it to pull the sea from his lungs. I also used it to give him the air he needed to remain under long enough for Starla to heal him. Did it somehow get to him? Maybe it's lingering in the shadows of his mind and that's why he's acting so strange.

I shake my head. "Wes, you're probably nervous because of the storm, but I'm a mermaid. I'll be okay." Shifting in Carter's arms, I give my mate a look. Carter releases me, letting me stand in the chest high water on my own. "Come on, let me walk you to shore."

As the words escape my mouth, another wave knocks into Wes, dragging him under. A yell echoes from the shore, and my attention draws to Bailey as she rushes toward us, not even caring that huge waves collide against the sand, threatening to rise all the way to the shelters to wash them away.

Before Bailey can enter the surf, Wes pops out of the wave. I close the distance between us and stop him from getting sucked back under. His green eyes meet mine, and he locks me in his stare.

"Okay," he says. "I guess you're right."

"I promise I'll be fine." I help Wes closer to the shore with Carter right behind us.

Another flash of lightning lights up the night, and I nearly jump from my skin. When we're close enough to the shore, I let go of Wes' arm as Bailey closes the distance. She reaches out for him, but a strange look crosses his face, all wild eyes. He shuffles around Bailey and charges me. I don't even have time to react. His sinewy arms wrap around me, and he drags me from the water, throwing me onto his shoulder.

Carter yells out, swimming onto the shore and out of the waves, but without being able to transform, he can't get to me. Wes holds his hand out to the others who try to close in on us. I scratch my nails into his back and then thrash, doing everything I can to get him to let me go. His strength overpowers me, and he walks backward away from everyone.

"Wes, don't do this," I say. "Please, you're scaring me."

"I have to, Ava," he says. "You need to stay on land."

"Please, I'll be fine," I say.

"You can't know that."

Tears prickle in my eyes. I can't believe this is happening. If I wasn't worried about hurting him, I'd bring the whole sea upon us to wash me away, but he's not acting like himself, and I'm afraid I'm responsible.

"But I do. Now, please. Just put me down."

"I'm sorry. I can't. You're coming with me."

Wes didn't stop running until we were far from shore and deep within the island. I couldn't see where we were heading in the dark, but I could hear the trickling creek until the skies opened up to release a waterfall of rain on us.

And now, I press my back into the hard rock of a cave, wishing with everything in me that I wasn't here. I'd rather brave the open ocean than be here.

A flash of lightning streaks through sky, lighting up the cave. I jump, hugging myself tighter. Carter's out there in the storm, facing waves comparable to the ones I create, and I can't stop the fear from slicing through me. Luckily, no crazy emotions come from him—just a whole lot of annoyance. It makes even me annoyed.

"You going to stare at me all night?" My voice echoes over the pelting rain. "It's creepy."

Wes' forehead crinkles at my words. "I'm sorry. I didn't realize I was."

I raise my eyebrows. "What has gotten into you? You know you're jeopardizing my relationship with my mate, right? And my sister." Because I know I'm going to have to stand between Carter and Wes even though a part of me wants to toss Wes to the waves. And Bailey? I'm sure she's thinking I'm getting in the middle of her and Wes. God, why did this have to happen?

Wes' mouth hangs open like he had no idea his actions were going to impact things. "You never have a bad feeling before?"

"My whole life is one big bad feeling. But that doesn't mean I should run and hide all the time. I shouldn't be in this cave, Wes. I don't want you getting hurt again because of me."

"Because of you?" he questions, his voice only a murmur.

I nod. "The accident. I had no idea I'd create such rough water."

He's silent for a moment, letting my confession sink in. I expect him to start yelling, to throw all his hatred at me. I expect him to tell me to leave. But he doesn't do any of that. All he does is rub his cheeks while gazing at me.

After an almost painful minute, he says, "Accidents happen."

"This one shouldn't have. I shouldn't be here," I repeat.

"So, you think I'm feeling this way because of you? Bailey said you saved me when I hit my head."

I purse my lips, remembering back. Remembering the choice I thought I had to make between saving my sister or saving Wes and then pulling the water from his lungs while attempting to bring Bailey back over the reef. I didn't think about it until this very moment, but one thought fills up my mind. It's so intense I can't think of anything else until I say it out loud.

"You drowned," I whisper.

"What do you mean I drowned? I thought I just hit my head."

"My water affinity saved you. I pulled the ocean from your lungs and gave you your breath again." Confusion and fear prickle through me. Obviously, I didn't give Wes my essence. Carter was my one unexpected transformation after the king ended Carter's life—something I shouldn't have been able to do as a human-born mermaid—and I would have known. It's why I can feel Carter more than ever. Why my love for him feels ten times more powerful. But what if saving Wes the way I did messed with him? He might not be in love with me, but his sudden need to protect me is totally unwarranted.

"Don't humans who get brought back to life turn into merpeople? Isn't that what happened to you? Giselle said—"

"You're not a merman, Wes. The full moon passed and you didn't transform. But I think I did something else to you. I don't know." I push off the ground and get to my feet. "But I need to find out, and the answers don't lie in this cave."

"You can't be serious. This can wait until morning," he argues.

I shake my head. "No, I need to go. I don't belong here."

"Ava, I'm not letting you leave."

I raise my hand out, keeping it aimed at him as he gets to his own feet. "I'm not letting you stop me."

"Then I'm coming with you," he says.

"No, you can't. Stay here."

He rushes me, but I'm prepared this time. I dodge around him, clocking him in the shoulder hard enough with my fist that he falls back into the cave wall with a thud. I run from the cave and into the dense forest. It's nearly pitch-black apart from the lightning storm above.

I glance once over my shoulder, half expecting Wes to be on my heels, chasing me, but he's nowhere to be found. I just hope he realized how crazy he was acting, especially knowing about what I did to him, that he won't risk his life in this seemingly unrelenting storm.

Through the dark trees, I carefully hike through the forest, following the pull in my heart. It's the only way I know which direction to go, because without the sun or the moon, I'm basically traveling blindly. And even in the day, I'm not sure I'd have any idea of where I'm going because I've never traveled far up the creek. Wes has been on this island for years. He probably knows the terrain by heart.

My bare feet sink into the muddy water, pooling all around from the heavy rains. The wind whistles in my ears, cutting off the noise of everything else. If I didn't shield my eyes from the rain falling on my head, I'd have a hard time seeing.

"Ava," a voice whispers. It takes me a moment to realize it's in my mind. "You must return to the sea. The answers you seek lie beyond the barrier. Your fear will keep you lost forever. Now, come to me."

Thrashing my head, I shake the voice away. I take another step forward through the dark trees. The sparkle from my necklace lights up like rainbow beams. It glows brighter and brighter, so brightly that the world around me can be seen clear as day even though morning won't come for hours. It's then I realize I'm walking on the edge of a ravine, halfway filled with running rainwater. I automatically step back, but the soggy ground beneath my bare feet gives way, and I slide into the few feet of rushing water.

The world slips past me as I'm caught in the rainwater river. I flail, looking for anything to grab onto, but none of the roots hold. My screams echo through the air, catching on the wind, and my stomach flies into my throat when I hit a sudden drop that propels me toward the edge of a cliff—the same cliffs with rocks that can only be accessed by the ocean.

Huge swells crash into the cliff, sending white waves through the air, lit up by the lightning sporadically striking within the clouds. Horror and fear rush through my mind. All I can think about is how I'm going to die at any second. There are too many rocks below. I'm bound to splatter against one of them.

Squeezing my eyes shut, I wave my hands out, calling on a miracle from the ocean, praying that I haven't used all my miracles up. My feet break through a swell rising over the rocks. It cushions my fall, and I sink under and let the current drag me away.

The ocean glows around me, my body thrashing in the rough waves too enormous to swim in. There's no way I can even make my way to the surface for a breath, one I desperately need.

"You must trust yourself," a voice says into my mind. "Let it all go."

I do exactly that. I inhale a long, burning breath of the ocean, filling up my very essence with the sea I've become so connected to.

A dozen images flash through my mind, none of which are

my own. My body screams in pain, my head feeling like it'll suddenly explode. And then I feel nothing at all.

I black out.

18

CELESTIANA

"MY DAUGHTER, YOU'VE MADE IT to me," a feminine voice says, the melodious sound so soothing and heartwarming that I want to wrap it around me like a blanket after facing a frozen sea.

"Like I had a choice. This storm—"

"Is the consequence of remaining hidden, my daughter. You can't stay lost forever."

Celestiana hovers before me in crystalline waters undisturbed by ocean life, currents, or even the gentle wave of her silver tail. A tail so sparkling, it almost looks as if rainbows project from it. Her black hair floats in a thick braid, and a silver and diamond crown glitters on her head. She looks exactly like her memories, but this isn't a memory.

"I'm not your daughter," I say, projecting my thoughts into her mind. "I'm not even a daughter of the ocean. I was human-born."

She smirks, like what I've said was funny. "But you were chosen."

"By Carter," I say before she can tell me the ocean picked me.

"A suitable warrior for a suitable queen," she says, closing the distance. Raising her hand, she brushes her fingers over my cheek and pushes the veil of blond hair from my face. "I always knew Starla and Mateo would raise a fine man with a love of the land who would choose a mate worthy of the sea."

Confusion knits my brows. "I don't understand. I was afraid of the ocean. I didn't want to be a mermaid. All I wanted—want—is to go home to my family."

"Which is why you've been chosen. Your desires can never be under Attilonious' rule. By his need to protect the colonies, he's grown too distant from the land. He's isolated the kingdom. His distrust of humans will hurt us all in the end."

"Why are you telling me this? You can't expect me to face the king and demand him to renounce his crown. He'll kill me," I say. "And if he doesn't, then what? I'm not some queen to look after the sea. This is all crazy." With a flick of my hand, I yank off the necklace and hold it out to her. "I don't think I want this after all."

She doesn't respond, just looks at me with the same smirk she had when I told her I wasn't her daughter or a daughter of the ocean.

I hold up the necklace again, dangling it in the water between us, but she doesn't grab it. "Take it, please. I already hate how everything is. I don't want any more madness in my life. I've already almost killed one human, and now he's acting strange toward me. Keeping this necklace puts everyone around me at risk."

She still doesn't take it. Instead, she strokes my cheek with her knuckles. "You're pure of heart and that makes you exceptional."

"Do you not care about the humans you gave up your magic for on that island?" I ask.

"I care immensely. There's a man there who kept a part of my heart before I was enchanted by Attilonious' magic."

"Darren?"

Her smile is enough to tell me it is him. He's one of the few who never told me how he ended up there, but he wasn't the first to arrive.

"He tied me to the land. He gave up everything for me willingly, but we were never bonded. I couldn't ask that of him. It was more than him that I loved. It was his humanity. The king thought I was fleeing for him, but I was fleeing for me. I was selfish."

That makes two of us. "If you care about Darren, you wouldn't ask me to keep this. You'd tell me how to fix Wes and tell me where I can go with Carter that's away from here. You'd tell me what to do about Luna knowing we're alive, too. You remember your real daughter, right?"

For the first time since I opened my eyes, the queen frowns. "Luna will make a good ally. She knows the seas better than anyone. And as for Wes, you've given him a gift he'll repay with his loyalty. It never hurts to have ties to the land and the sea."

"His behavior will get him killed," I say. "He kidnapped me over a bad feeling."

"He knows the time is coming. He knows the dangers that lie within the deep."

I blow a bubble through my lips. "Dangers you want *me* to face."

"My daughter, please. You can't see past your fear. The king does not care for those who are not under his rule. Your empathy and connection to the world outside the sea will help the colonies flourish."

"How? No one can leave the sea."

"It's not only the king's magic that can unite the sea with the land." She moves her hand to the spark in my chest. "The answer lies here."

"You mean *I* can create sea stone rings?" If I wasn't floating underwater, I'd be crying. Relief and joy washes through me at just the thought. If I can infuse Carter's ring with magic, I can give him the life on land he deserves. We can still have a life outside the ocean.

She nods without a word. I expect her to give me the answer, to give me something more to work with, but the light in the crystal clear water dims, leaving us in darkness. The sea shifts, a current swirling around us, stirring up sand from the sea floor, and the queen drops her hand from me and lets me go.

A huge swell sweeps me away from the queen, and I tumble through the current of the unforgiving ocean. The only light comes from the spark in my chest, but it's not enough to see where I'm going.

My lungs erupt in pain, a burning sensation so intense it makes my eyes widen. I swallow water, and panic rushes through me when I realize I'm no longer a mermaid. A flash of light draws my attention above me, and I kick my way toward the surface lit by the massive storm.

Before I break through, fingers lock on my hips and spin me around. I meet Carter's jewel-like eyes only inches away. With a flick of his tail, he ascends to the surface, taking me with him. I expel the water from my lungs, coughing and spitting, gasping breath after breath.

"Ava, you have to transform," Carter says.

I squeeze my eyes shut, willing the transformation to happen, but my mind wanders elsewhere and nothing I do triggers the cramps to come. Carter struggles to hold me above water in the raging waves, and I fall under a swell. It rips me from Carter, thrashing me about.

My head spins, and I can't focus on anything but the lack of oxygen, how my lungs scream, and how no matter how hard I fight, I get nowhere.

I just want it all to stop.

I project my thoughts into the sea, and the ocean complies.

The waves die down around me, the water turning utterly still. The ripple of the now unmoving current shines around me in thousands of tiny bubbles, and I slowly gather them the same way I did for Wes, collecting them into a huge sphere that I can breathe.

I inhale the bubble of air, filling my lungs to the brim, and kick my way to the surface. Lightning flickers above, and rain cascades down like a waterfall, but the ocean remains as calm as it is on the most tranquil days.

"Ava," Carter's voice sounds out through the air. "We have to go back."

It's in this moment I realize we're in the open water and away from the island. I can't even see it from our spot. Fear grips at my heart, threatening to send it bursting from my chest.

"I can't transform. Can you swim me?" I ask.

Carter nods and pulls me closer so I can hold onto his neck. He swims us forward, staying above the surface instead of going under. He probably would if I wasn't gasping, but I can't help it. Everything is too much. Now that I'm not drowning, I can't stop thinking about the queen and the dream—if it was even a dream.

I hug tightly to Carter, just feeling the smooth muscles of his back. His fingers lock with mine, their strength cutting off my circulation. I'm sure he's afraid if he's not gripping me I'll somehow wash away even if the ocean is placid despite the storm pelting us.

A sudden blink of light erupts in my vision, my diamond glowing brighter and brighter. It's a warning, something I can't ignore knowing we're quite a distance from the protection only the Lost Cove brings. If I'd just listened to Wes and stayed put, I wouldn't be out here. I wouldn't be putting Carter at risk, because he followed the pull of my spark. And now, someone is close by.

"You have to dive. Someone's nearby," I say.

Carter stiffens. "I hear them."

"What are they saying?"

"They're talking about Luna." Carter nearly spits the words. "There's hostility between her and the king."

"It was fate for Luna to see us. She is our best ally, Carter. She knows the ocean probably as good as her father," I say. "She can help us."

"Help us to do what?"

"Get away from here. We can find somewhere to go on land," I say.

"Ava, I can't."

"You can. I just need to figure out how to help you. The queen, she—"

"This is why you were out here?"

"I think her magic forced me away from the island. She doesn't want us to remain lost."

"I don't under—" Carter suddenly dives, dragging me down with him. His voice is lost to me since I can't hear him.

His fear washes over me, and I peer through my blurry vision. It's hard to make them out, but up ahead I spot two dark figures in the water. One of them hovers upright, combing their fingers through the unmoving bubbles, creating swirls that glitter every time lightning strikes.

I do the only thing I can think of, I thrust my hand forward, anger and fear rushing from me, and jumpstart the ocean, turning the calm waters violent. I'm not fast enough, though, because I meet the glowing amber eyes of a mermaid seconds before she's caught on a current and swept away along with her mate.

Carter remains swimming in the rough waters though he'd be faster if he'd dive with me. At least here, we're less likely to be followed. Because I'm sure our secret is out. It won't be long until the whole ocean hears of our sudden appearance.

Cramps rush through me, my transformation suddenly taking hold, and I inhale a long breath of water, letting it sink deep into me to push away all my thoughts. I can't help feeling betrayed by the ocean that gave me this life. It's like it was the queen's plan all along.

I don't care who she thinks I am or what she thinks I should do, I'm so over having my life messed with. I'm over fearing all the time.

I'm so over this supposed fate.

"Ava," Carter whispers in my mind. "Do you hear them?"

I close my eyes and concentrate. Faint voices echo through my mind, and a chill runs up my spine. They're calling for their queen. But it's not Celestiana's name they're saying. It's mine.

Shivering, I force the voices away and swim faster.

"This is bad, Aves," Carter thinks to me.

I hold him tighter. This is the queen's fault. It's the ocean's fault. They're forcing me away from the island, and once again I'm losing control over my life. But this is different. I'm not supposed to sit back and hope for the best. I need to fight.

"We'll be okay," I whisper. I'm afraid to tell him what's on my mind. I'm afraid to tell him I have a feeling that everything is about to get worse.

<h1 style="text-align:center">19</h1>

SOMETHING WORTH FIGHTING FOR

"OH, NO," I WHISPER, PUSHING to my feet in the sand. "Everything is gone." The ocean did this. It's trying to force me to leave, first by revealing me to the merpeople and now this. The storm passed an hour ago, but I've been too nervous to resurface. I ran away from Wes during the worst of it. If he followed, he could very well be dead, and once again, I'd be to blame for another bad thing happening.

"They'll rebuild," Carter says from his spot in the sand. "I'm sure it's not the first hurricane to roll through."

I kick my bare foot against some debris. "This is my fault. The ocean doesn't want me here anymore. It's a warning just like Celestiana said."

There's nothing left of the shelters on the beach. The storm wiped them all away, leaving behind remnants in the form of broken wood, palm fronds, and what's left of the pieces of furniture that either washed ashore, was made, or brought by one of the few merpeople that would do deliveries before the king stole their ability to come on land.

"Hurricanes happen all the time, Aves. Celestiana—she was just a dream."

"It was very much real, Carter," I say. I bend down and collect a few ratty blankets that were left behind and then push an old trunk out of the water, dragging it up to the tree line. "Why else would all this be happening? You saw what I saw.

How can you deny it?"

"Because what she wants is a death sentence." I shared my vision of Celestiana through a kiss, revealing everything she told me about King Attilonious, about him dooming the colonies by cutting them off from the human world, about my supposed purpose. I can't blame him for being skeptical. I think the queen's crazy, but I know only more trouble will befall on the island if we stay.

"There's still no denying the truth, no matter how much you want to."

"Then what do you expect us to do?"

Voices murmur from somewhere beyond the trees, cutting off our conversation. It's the others making their way back.

"Wes, you have to calm down. I'm sure Ava is fine. What you did was insane, you know." It's Bailey.

I puff a breath of relief through my lips, realizing that Wes is fine, and he managed to find the others again.

"You don't know that," Wes says. "I looked everywhere for her. She doesn't know the island like we do. What if she's lost?" I cringe at the abnormal shrillness in his usually deep voice.

"What has gotten into you? Why do you even care?" Bailey asks.

I grimace. I can't help it. The coldness in my sister's voice freezes my heart. I'd hoped maybe she'd be a little bit concerned about me, but I guess I should get used to the idea that she will never be.

"Ava and I think it's because she brought me back to life after she lost control," Wes says, repeating our conversation from last night. He's so casual about it, that it sounds like what I've done is totally normal.

"What?" Bailey's voice erupts through the air.

I scramble backward, putting space between me and the tree line as I spot the group making their way to where they'll discover the mess the storm left behind. I turn to run back to Carter, but then a familiar voice calls my name, cutting Bailey and Wes off.

"You're safe!" Giselle says, rushing past them to me. She slings her arms around me and pushes me back toward the water. "Oh, my God, Aves. Last night was nuts. Wes showed up like a lunatic in a panic because you ran away from him. He hasn't shut up since. Bailey is freaking out. It's drama-land. Like, if the ocean didn't try to drown us, I'm pretty sure the rest of us would make an escape just so we don't have to hear Wes and Bailey argue over you anymore."

"I shouldn't be here then," I say.

"Of course you should be here." Wes' voice draws my attention away from Giselle.

I ignore him and stroll toward Carter.

"No, actually, she shouldn't," Bailey says. "She's messing with your head, Wes."

I cringe, refusing to look at Bailey.

"Hey! Ava's not doing anything," Giselle says.

"Are you kidding?" Bailey throws her hands up. "All she's done is mess things up around here. This place wasn't meant for her kind."

"It was created by her *kind*." The heat in Giselle's voice makes my eyes widen. I've always known she was protective of me, but she's never been one to blatantly put herself out there.

"She's right," Wes says.

Bailey points her finger at Wes. "Stay out of it, Wes. You can't see it because she got into your head."

"It was an accident," Giselle says. "It was my fault, not Ava's. I was pressuring her."

"To do what?" Bailey asks.

"Gi, stop," I say.

"No, Ava. Bailey has some stupid problem that no one else

has. I think she's just jealous."

"The last person I'd be jealous of is her," Bailey snaps.

"Come on, Aves," Carter says.

Wes steps away from Bailey. "Stay, Ava."

There's too much going on. My mind whirls with everyone's voices as they try to speak all at once. All I want to do is run back to the water and dive.

A huge wave swells up next to me, crashing into the shore. It surprises everyone, knocking us onto the beach. I shake sand from my hair and get to my feet while the others slowly get back to theirs.

"I'm sorry." I can't help apologizing. This whole conversation has me on edge. Celestiana did say that Wes would continue to show loyalty no matter how much I don't want it. "I didn't mean to do that."

"What do you mean by that?" Bailey asks, glaring. All the others fall silent.

I sigh. What's the point in hiding it? "I can control the sea," I finally say.

Giselle strolls closer to me, putting herself in the path between Bailey and me. "And she's awesome. She's going to help us get off this island, now cool it."

Bailey ignores Giselle. "So, it was you that day? You're the reason we had to jump from the boat." She doesn't wait for my response, because I'm sure it's clearly written on my face. "I should've known."

I wring my hands together. "Bailey, I'm sorry."

She swings her arm out to point at Wes. "Look what you did to him."

"It was an accident," Wes says, standing up for me.

Bailey huffs. "One she's responsible for."

Wes scowls. "Bailey."

"No, I don't think so. You will *not* stand up for her. She

did this. She probably caused the storm, too!" She turns her attention to me, pointing her finger. "I want you out of here."

"Hey, you can't do that," Giselle says.

"Go!" Bailey screams.

She charges me, fury lining her blue eyes. Carter grabs me by the ankle, yanking me off my feet to pull me into the water before Bailey can get close enough to touch me. I'm pretty sure she'd have attacked me if she could have. But now, Wes grips her shoulders.

She struggles against him. "Let me go."

"No, you need to calm down," he says. "Ava isn't our enemy. You can't blame her for this."

"He's right." For the first time since seeing the others come through the trees do I notice Darren. He stands back, lingering next to Sandra and Reyna, who look like they want nothing to do with any of this. "This is the doing of King Attilonious. None of us would be here if it weren't for him."

Bailey turns her gaze to Darren. "That doesn't make a difference. He's not here. She is."

"You should be happy about that," Giselle says, speaking up. "That guy is a monster."

"Ava," Carter says, drawing my attention to him. "Someone's calling for us."

All the others fall silent at the sound of Carter's words.

"We have to go," he says.

Fear stirs in my heart. I knew we were spotted last night, but I was hoping we'd still have time. The last thing I need is to have the whole ocean calling for us. A thousand thoughts spin through my head, making me dizzy. I can think of a million terrible things the king could do to lure us out, but neither Carter nor I even want to think about them. His family would be the first to face the king's wrath.

I release a small breath and turn my gaze to Bailey. "You'll be happy to know I was spotted last night, and the king knows I'm alive." I half hug myself. "You'll get your wish, because I can't put you all in any more danger."

"What?" Giselle and Wes ask in unison.

I squeeze my eyes shut. "I'm not abandoning you, Gi, but Bailey is right. I can't stay on this island. But I'll figure out how to get you off. I promise."

"Aves, please. We can figure this out," Giselle says.

"Come on, Ava," Carter says.

Tears line Giselle's eyes. "You can't go."

"I have to. I have to figure out what happens next."

"But—"

"But nothing. I can't hide forever. The ocean has made it quite clear."

"Aves, please."

"Trust that I'll fix this."

"How?"

"It's time to face what I've been running from."

"Ava, no!"

I sink under the waves before Giselle can talk me out of leaving. Carter pulls me deeper into the bay and away from my last connection to the land, one I'll have to fight for if I'm ever going to keep it.

The queen was right. I'll never get everything I want under the king's rule, and now that he knows I'm alive, it won't be long until our magic collides. I just hope I can survive in the end. For everyone's sakes.

Sucking in water to fill my lungs, I push away all my fear as my transformation takes hold. Fear will leave me lost forever.

I'm done being afraid. I'm done hiding.

For the first time in a long time, I feel brave. I feel like I have a fighting chance. Because even if I can't do anything about the king, even if I can't get my old life back, I can at least say that I tried. Not only for myself, but for everyone else. With others at risk, I finally have something worth fighting for.

NEVER BE FREE

"AVA, CARTER." THE FAMILIAR, FEMININE voice sounds through my mind. "I know you're around here some-where. Please, you have to talk to me. My dad knows you're alive." When Carter said someone was calling us, I had expected his mom. I wasn't expecting Luna.

Carter holds me beneath him, his chest pressing into my back and his strong arms locked just below my ribcage. I'd usu-ally hold onto his back, but I think he's afraid I'll let go and leave him behind, so he's not taking any chances. It's almost ridiculous, because I'd never out swim him.

"Luna, you shouldn't have come," I say, projecting my thoughts back to her. "What if your dad followed you?"

"He didn't," she says.

"And how do you know?" Carter asks, speaking up.

Up ahead, a figure comes into view. It takes us swimming a good few dozen feet past the reef to see the open ocean clearly. Luna's hair floats around her like a black veil, and the sun from above glints off her golden tail.

"Because my dad left Pearlestria before I did," she says.

"So, why did you come here? Didn't Starla tell you we were protected?" I ask.

Carter closes the distance between us and Luna. Her dark sapphire eyes glow in the water, and she surprises the both of us by flinging her arms around us the moment Carter swims us upright to meet her face-to-face.

"My family," Carter says, fear lining his thoughts, projecting into me. "Are they—?" I hate to admit the thought crossed my mind, too.

"It was your mother who sent me. The colonies are under lockdown. No one that isn't a king's guard can leave. They're now searching all the seas for you. I could only leave because I stole this." Luna holds up a small bracelet with an onyx stone on it. "It's a guard's key."

Carter holds his hand out, and Luna drops the bracelet into his palm. He studies it for a long moment. "Can you steal more?"

She shakes her head. "If I could, I would. But it wouldn't make a difference. Your mom and grandmer have been locked away in the castle."

"And my dad?" Carter asks.

"With the king," she says.

Carter grimaces.

"Why would he be with the king?" I ask.

"Leverage," Carter says. "I can't think of any other reason."

I could see that. King Attilonious isn't stupid. He knows the importance of family and bonds. If he were to find us, one way to get us to comply would be to threaten someone Carter cares about.

"Oh, God," I say.

"Carter," Luna says. "Mateo offered his services to the king. He wants nothing more than to have you back. I saw his face when the king made the announcement. He didn't know you were alive, did he?"

I shake my head. "Only Starla."

"We have to go to Pearlestria then," Carter says. "We have to get my mom and grandmer."

Before Carter can swim forward, Luna raises her hand.

"That's not why I'm here."

Fear squeezes my heart at her words. Realization settles into my bones with the sad look Luna gives me. She doesn't even have to utter the words for me to know what the king is planning to do. He threatened my entire human life once to get me to comply.

"My family." My thought is barely a whisper in my mind.

Luna nods. "I'm so sorry, Ava. I came here as fast as I could."

"We have to go to Azure Waters, Carter," I say.

"What if it's too late?" he asks. "We'll risk our lives for nothing."

"I don't care," I say. "I'm going whether or not you follow me."

He squeezes my hand. "Ava, I'll follow you anywhere. You know that."

I turn to Luna. "Go back to Pearlestria. Help Starla."

Before she can nod, Carter releases me and bolts forward, locking his hand around Luna's wrist. "No, Ava. We need her."

"What do you mean?" I ask into his mind. "You're crazy if you think I'm going to let you hurt—"

"The king doesn't know that," he says only to me. "But you can't tell her. It has to look real."

I swallow the lump forming in my throat and glance at Luna. "I'm sorry, Luna. I guess you're coming with us."

"Please, Ava. You don't have to do this. You know I'll help you," Luna says.

Carter grips her in his arms while I hold onto his shoulders. She doesn't fight or resist, but she's been begging me for miles to just let her help. The desperation in her voice almost causes me to tell her the truth—that there's no way we'd ever hurt her, but Carter's right. Luna is the one mermaid in the ocean that would make the king stop in his tracks if her life were in danger. She'll be the key to surviving this.

"He's your father, Luna," I say. "If it comes down to his life or mine, you'll choose his. I'm not stupid."

"You don't know him like I do. This won't work," she says.

"Well, I have to try."

A sudden swell jerks Carter off course, and I tumble through the water away from him. The ocean sways back and forth the closer we get to Azure Waters, and I suppress my fear as much as I can. Fish get trapped in strong currents, making it nearly impossible for them to swim. They cruise with the waves, just going with the flow.

I fight my way back to Carter, creating our own current to fight against the unnatural one that tries to stop us in our path. A shadow falls over us, and I glance up at the rocking boat on the surface above. The vessel rises and falls in the water, stirring up waves that glimmer in the sunlight. The humans aboard are probably freaking out over the strange waters that shouldn't be this rough on a beautiful day.

"Carter, swim faster," I say. We're both exhausted from our night without sleep, and I'm surviving on adrenaline to get us through this.

"You have to do something, Ava," he says into my mind. "The water is too rough. It doesn't even change the deeper I go."

Closing my eyes, I concentrate on the relentless current. Bubbles fizzle around us, stinging against my skin in a blast of heat. This isn't like controlling the bay back at the Lost Cove. This is different. The ocean here buzzes with magic that isn't mine. It's foreign and intrusive and threatens to suppress every attempt I make to bend the sea to my will.

The diamond around my neck sparks, sending rainbow light around us, shimmering off all the tiny bubbles, and then suddenly the waves stop around us. Carter jolts forward, cutting through the placid waves faster than ever. It's like he's flying through the water. I manage to keep the water still in our own calm current that slices through the rolling ocean still hell-bent on destroying everything.

A familiar kelp forest comes into view up ahead, the kelp vines thrashing in the waves that threaten to uproot them. Another vessel, one much smaller than the one before, rocks on the surface. My heart nearly seizes in my chest at the sight of a body tangled amid the kelp. It's not only the shores of Azure Waters I need to worry about; it's the fishermen and boaters, too.

I release Carter and swim right for the body. Carter yells out my name, but I don't stop. I summon a current strong enough to sweep me from Carter so quickly he doesn't have a chance to grab onto my tail.

The spark in my heart flashes in quick successions, racing with my heart thudding against my ribs. Without even stopping to check out the body, I latch my fingers to the back of the fisherman's shirt and hoist him to the surface where his boat rocks on the rolling waves.

A scream rips through the air, startling me, and I nearly sink back under. A girl with golden hair, a shade darker than mine, holds onto her seat in the boat, trying to stop herself from falling overboard.

Everything in me yells to dive. Instead, I ignore my inner voice and hold the guy in my arms with one hand while hooking my other arm over the side of the boat.

"Grab him," I say, trying my best to push the fisherman back into the boat.

The girl hesitates for only a second before sliding over to help me. With a flick of my wrist, I pull the ocean from his lungs, and he gasps and spits. A mix between a moan and a yell erupts from his mouth, and he snaps his eyes open. Saltwater sprinkles over his face. The man's brown eyes meet mine for a second, and he reaches up and runs his rough fingers over my cheeks.

"Ava!" Carter yells, surfacing from behind me. "What are you doing?"

I graze my fingers across the sloshing waves, coaxing them to settle down under my touch. It's enough to get the boat to stop rocking. "What do you think? I'm saving them."

"They know our secret," Carter says.

"Well, I'm not letting them die, and I'm not taking them back to the Lost Cove. No one will believe them," I say.

The man sits up higher, and they gape at me for a long moment. Carter propels closer, Luna still locked in one of his arms. She doesn't say a word as he grabs my hand and pulls me away, taking us underwater.

"That was incredibly stupid, Ava," Carter says, dragging me with him.

"Then maybe that's what I am," I snap. "I'm sorry I'm not like you. I'm sorry if I care about—"

He stops swimming and surprisingly releases Luna to draw me into his arms. I want to yell at him, to push him away with a current. Because hovering here is slowing us down. We don't have time for this.

"I'm sorry, Ava," Carter says.

"We have to go," I say.

He shakes his head. "Not until you know I didn't mean what I said. I love you, and I love that you care so much about others. We're about to face the king and there's no way I'm going to have us go in there with you thinking I don't care about anything apart from you. Because I do. If I didn't, I wouldn't be here. I wouldn't want to stand against a tyrant who wants nothing more than to destroy us for not complying. If that means we give away the secret of our people, then so be it."

I slowly nod my head and lean in for a kiss. "That's one way of taking power from the king," I say with a smirk. But that's the last thing I want. Not everyone is like Giselle, or Wes and Darren even. I can't fault the king for keeping the secret from humans. I just don't agree with how he goes about it. I don't agree with murdering people or forcing anyone into the merpeople life. "But we need to find another way."

I turn to glance at Luna. I had expected her to swim away as fast as she could, but she remains exactly where Carter released her. Looking into her sapphire eyes, I study her face for a long moment.

"Luna, you can leave. I can't go through with using you as leverage to get the king to comply. It's not who I am. You're my friend, and I don't want you to accidentally get hurt," I say.

Carter frowns but doesn't argue. He knows I'd like nothing more than to see the two of them leave me altogether so I don't have to worry.

"Ava," Luna says, her voice nearly a whisper. "Listen."

I calm my roaring thoughts and do as she says. A murmur of voices drifts into my mind, cooling my blood. Carter stiffens next to me. He pulls me closer to him like he can stop me from falling apart and disappearing into the waves.

"Please, they could be anywhere in the world, my king. This isn't necessary," Mateo says, his voice projecting through the water.

"It must be done." The king's voice strikes me right in the heart, edging my vision in shadows. "There are consequences for rising against me."

"I'm asking you as a father to show some mercy. Had I known Starla was hiding them, I'd have told you sooner. My mate, she cares immensely about our children. You know she's always had a love of the land not unlike the quee—"

The water shudders, cutting off Mateo's words.

"She should've been the one to tell me."

"They're just children," Mateo says. "They don't understand."

Another shudder cuts through the water, startling me.

"This must be done. It's too much of a risk. Ava is too connected to the land," the king says.

"But she's a daughter of the sea."

"Her mindset is dangerous. I can't risk all the colonies."

"Please, my king. Give me a day. I'll find them myself. I'll bring them to you."

"No. It still must be done. All her ties to the land must be severed. She must have nothing left."

The next shudder in the water is enough to break me and Carter apart. Luna gets washed away from us on a current. The whole ocean bends to the will of the king. The sea around us presses into me, slowly growing higher and higher, lifting me toward the surface.

"No!" I scream, my voice projecting through the water.

"Ava, it's too late. We have to get out of here," Carter says, locking his fingers to my wrist.

"I'm not leaving!" I yell.

Squeezing my eyes shut, I force the ocean to freeze. A sudden calm falls over the sea, and the only thing I can hear is the sound of my heart thudding in my ears.

"King Attilonious!" I yell. "If you want me, you have to stop."

"Ava, no," Carter says only to me.

Our gazes lock for a long moment. "Don't let him catch you, okay?"

"What are you doing?" he asks.

"I'm saving Azure Waters."

"But, Ava," he argues.

I shake my head. "Trust me." I kiss him gently on the lips.

The water bubbles around us, quivering again under the king's power. Without another word, I pull away from Carter. Luna grabs his arm, stopping him from following me. I just hope this works. Because if it doesn't, I'll never be free.

21

A WARRIOR FOR A QUEEN

THE DIAMOND AROUND MY NECK glows so brightly I have to squint to see through the turbulent water. My whole body shakes with nerves, but I don't let it stop me from swimming along the familiar shore. A weird sensation crawls over me, and it's like I'm suddenly being pulled toward a force that leaves everything in me screaming in the most horrible way. My stomach knots, my fingers clench into fists, my body reacting to the dread stealing all the freedom and strength I usually feel with every flick of my tail.

I suck in a gulp of water through my mouth and push it out through my gills. The usually cold water off the coast of Azure Waters turns warmer and warmer the closer I head toward the harbor. The heat slows me down, making it hard to stay focused.

I jerk in the current as another jolt cuts through me, and a swell yanks me toward the surface. King Attilonious wills the ocean to rise, and it takes me fighting free of the current to stop myself from being pulled into the harbor where dozens of boats dock. I can't see them from here, but I'm sure they're helpless against the power of the king.

"Stop!" I project my voice toward the figures in front of me, lurking below the surface. It takes everything in me to keep swimming even though I'd rather turn around and flee back to the safest spot in all the ocean—not the Lost Cove—but

Carter's arms. Because with him, I don't feel like a weak, insignificant mermaid with a death wish. His strength reflects into me and steels me against everything I'm afraid of. With Carter, the world doesn't feel out of control. Because he's my world and has been my world for weeks. But Azure Waters? The rest of the ocean? That's our universe.

King Attilonious, in all his terrifying, god-like glory, points his golden staff directly at me. The diamond at the end, the other half to the one blazing on my neck, lights up like a beacon, but not a beacon of hope. It's like a sign that destruction isn't far away. That even if I can control the waters, even if I have magic in my essence, that maybe I'm still not powerful enough to face the king who has been reigning over the seas for more than a century.

I imagine Carter locking his hands around me to pull me forward with his strength, channeling my warrior mate into myself. Even though I made him stay behind, his presence lingers in my essence. He's always with me regardless. It's enough to push me forward.

The water quakes around me. Instead of knocking me back, it drags me forward in a nearly boiling current hot enough to redden my skin. I cry out, my voice erupting in the water with a dozen bubbles. I wave my hand, drawing water from the outside of this hot current leading to the king and wrap myself in a stream of icy water cool enough to fight against the king's rage. But it's not enough to slow me down or protect me.

A small army of merpeople surrounds the king, blocking him like he somehow needs their protection. Mateo is among them, his dark hair longer than the last time I saw him, and when our gazes lock, a strange look crosses his face—one I don't want to find myself caught it. It's not the usual love and adoration he's previously had for me. This one is dark and crawls under my skin, leaving me wanting to curl up in a ball and cry.

Beside him is a muscular mermaid with white hair despite the youthfulness of her gorgeous face. She narrows her saucer-wide, honey eyes, tightening her lips into a glower. She hates me without even knowing me, all because of the king. On her other side is another merman, one as brawny as Mateo but a good foot shorter. He wears no emotions on his face. I can't read him at all.

The hot current dissipates when I'm ten feet away from the king, and I flick my tail, propelling myself another five feet back. The king looms over his small army, his salt and pepper hair flowing behind him in a current he creates on his own. His sapphire eyes, as dark as the night without a moon, bore into mine for a second before his gaze flicks down and stops at the diamond around my neck.

I cover it with my hand, gripping it in my fingers like it'd somehow stop him from focusing on it. He tries to intimidate me with his sheer size, a good few feet longer than I am. His thick brows lower, nearly covering his eyes, and he bares his teeth in a smile that awakens the fear I've been suppressing.

"Where is your mate?" King Attilonious asks, peering around the ocean like Carter will try to sneak up on him.

"You need to stop this," I say instead of answering his question. "These people are innocent. They don't deserve your wrath." Waving my hand, I motion to the shore. My remodeled Victorian house is nestled right on the beach two miles away. Maybe the distance will keep them out of this mess.

"You can only blame yourself. I had offered you a great life and a powerful kingdom, and how did you repay me?" the king asks. King Attilonious is as delusional as I remember. A great life? No. A powerful kingdom? It wouldn't have been mine.

My nose crinkles. A million responses fly through my mind even though I know he's not expecting me to answer his question. I consider yelling that a life being imprisoned to the sea is not a great life at all. Having Carter ripped from me is not a life I'd ever want to live. Being by the king's side as his queen is equivalent to hell in my mind. But all my thoughts remain locked away. Anything I say will set him off. I'm not here to start a war. I'm here to save the place I grew up. I'm here to save my family and friends. Everything I've ever known.

"Please," I say, desperation squeezing my chest. If there was one thing I learned from the few moments of being around King Attilonious is that standing up to him only leaves him needing to prove how mighty he is. "I'm begging you. I'll do whatever you want. Just leave Azure Waters alone."

He holds his staff out to me, a smug smile on his face. My heart races, causing my hands to shake. If I were breathing air, I'd be panting. His drawn out pause threatens to send me into full blown panic.

King Attilonious straightens his shoulders. "No. You'll do what I say regardless."

With a wave of his hand, he shifts the ocean above us, sending an enormous tidal wave toward the shore, one big enough to pulverize anything in its path. For the first time since seeing Mateo again do I see something flash in his eyes— sadness? Pity? I can't tell.

It's enough to set me off. With a flick of my tail, I propel forward and straight for the king. The current around me thrusts me at the king, moving me faster than I could ever possibly swim. I beg the ocean to bend to my will.

The diamond around my neck flashes, and I thrust my hand out, sending the small army of merpeople out of the way. Something flickers in King Attilonious' eyes, but I don't even get within a few feet of him when he raises his staff, sending a pulse through the water directly at me.

It hits me in the chest, knocking me back, making it hard to gasp water. The edges of my vision darken, the sky shimmering through the surface turning dark. The ocean continues to rise, but there's nothing I can do. The last thing I see is the glow of the queen's diamond as it lights up my vision.

But even with the magic of the queen's heart, I know I've failed.

Bright sunlight shines overhead, bouncing off my cerulean scales. I dig my hands into the powdery sand, only to sink deeper into the unfamiliar shore around me. The last thing I remember was the king at the harbor of Azure Waters ready to wipe my beloved town off the map.

But now, I'm somewhere I've never been.

Fear pulls at my heart when I concentrate on Carter but can't feel him at all. If King Attilonious hurt him, I don't know what I'd do. I can't stand the thought of losing him again. He was supposed to stay away. He was supposed to trust me to take care of things. *But you failed.*

"It's not the end of the world, my daughter," a familiar voice says.

I exhale a long breath, loosening the nerves tightening my chest, making it hard to breathe. "What happened? Where am I? Am I dead?" A million questions try to escape my lips all at once. There is no other explanation as to why I'm here and why I can't feel Carter anymore other than the king ended my life before destroying the rest of my human world forever.

A cool hand rests on my tail, and I draw my gaze to the glittering sharp nails of the queen. "You mustn't be afraid," she says without answering any of my questions. "You'll figure this all out."

"I don't think I can," I say. "What's even the point anymore? I should've never left the Lost Cove."

Celestiana frowns. "And I thought you were a suitable queen."

I should be offended. But I'm tired. Exhausted. A hopelessness comparable to the moment Starla took my sea stone ring away from me burrows deep into my soul, my essence, threatening to shred me into tiny pieces to scatter along the shore like the glittering sea glass that sparkles in the warm sunlight above.

I bend forward, pulling my tail up to my chest and then wrap my arms around it to hold me in place. "I told you I don't want to be a queen. I don't want magic. All I want is my life back. I want to go home, but I don't even think I have a home anymore."

"So, you want to renounce your mermaid essence?"

"I—" I pause. Could I just go back to being a human? I could move somewhere land-locked and forget that the ocean exists. Carter and I, we could...we couldn't do any of that. If I gave up my mermaid essence, I'd have to give up Carter. The permanent change would sever our bond like it did between the king and queen.

"Something holds you back," she says.

A tear drips onto my cheek. "Carter."

"The perfect warrior for the perfect queen," she says.

It's not the first time she has said this, but it doesn't make me feel better. Carter's lived most of his life on land. It wasn't until me that he lived in the water. He might have been gifted the ability to be a warrior, but he doesn't have the training the king's guards do. Mateo was right. In this moment, I feel like a child. I feel like I know nothing.

"I don't want him fighting for me," I say.

"He will fight with you. He'll protect you. Your magic reflects your emotions. Together, you will set things right," she says. "The colonies weren't always about living a simple life. Life isn't about just existing. The ocean didn't instill its magic into us only to have a king lock us away and cut us off from the human world many used to freely go into."

"And what about our secret?"

"Do you know why you triggered your transformation in front of your human companion and revealed the secret to her?" the queen asks.

I shift to meet her soft smile. "Because I lacked control."

She shakes her head. "Because you could trust her. The ocean has spent forever, for as long as anyone can remember, protecting us. Only the ones worthy of our secret discover it."

"That's why you created the Lost Cove. It wasn't only to save those humans because they discovered our secret," I say.

She beams me a smile. "I created the island to protect those the ocean saw as worthy allies. A way to keep us connected."

My sister flashes through my mind. She's not exactly my ally. "But Bailey, she—"

"She will see."

"I don't know," I say.

"Then you will show her."

An ominous storm materializes in the distance, turning the crystalline sky dark with thunderous clouds. Lightning strikes, startling me, and before I have a chance to say another word to Celestiana, a huge swell crashes over us, sweeping me away.

Dark waters encompass me, dragging me deeper into the sea until I can no longer see the surface above. I flail in the current, trying my best to swim. But it's too strong, and I'm too exhausted.

"Ava," a voice whispers into my mind. "Ava, my daughter. It's okay. You're okay."

I snap my eyes open and jerk my arms out, sending a forceful current in front of me. It crashes into a pearlescent wall before bouncing back to send me flying into someone else's warm arms.

"Let me go!" I scream, struggling to break free.

"Shhh. You must calm down before you hurt one of us," Starla says.

I freeze at the sound of her voice and spin to face her. The moment I meet her blue-green eyes, ones the same color as Carter's, I sink against her, letting her hold me in a hug tight enough to force away the nervous shakes that grip me.

"Starla," I whisper, projecting my thoughts only to her. "My home. My parents. The king." Panic, grief, anguish, despair—so many heart-wrenching emotions wash over me, threatening to send me to the sea floor where I want to curl in on myself and disappear.

Everything feels so heavy—my thoughts, the sea, the shimmering room around us—closes in on me, trying to smother me. I can't breathe. I can't get my gills to work. To pull oxygen from the water.

I need to escape. I can't be here.

I need to find Carter.

Despite Starla hugging me and whispering to me that everything will be okay, I feel like I'm dying, like the ocean is rejecting me. My skin tingles, my heart thrashing in quick, painful beats, and I start to panic, thinking I'm about to transform into a human at any second.

"Just breathe." The two little words drift into my mind, settling deep in my essence. Carter's voice flows into me along with his emotions, pushing all of the horrible thoughts away. His calmness blankets my panic and the intensity of his love burns away all the doubt and despair from my very being. *The perfect warrior for the perfect queen...*

For the first time, Celestiana's words ring true. And it's in this moment I realize I've been wrong. I thought in Celestiana's mind that Carter was supposed to protect me, fight for me, die for me—do everything in his power to see to it that I'm safe and alive and free.

But that's not what being my warrior or mate means. He's not here to serve me. I'm no queen. I'm his other half, and we're in this together. Together, we're whole. Carter isn't my warrior in the sense that he must do everything for me, but he can help me do everything myself. He can make it possible for me to be strong, to be powerful, to stay in control. Through our bond, we share a connection unlike anything in the world. He's my mate, my love, my everything. He brings out the good in me. He'll get me through it all. Together. Always together.

I suck in a deep breath of the ocean, letting it fill me to the brim. The water soothes the fissures in my soul that threaten to break me apart and leave me useless. With every breath, every beat of my heart, the weight of my situation lifts, freeing me.

"Carter," I whisper to only him. "You shouldn't be here. If the king discovers you..." I can't bear to put my thoughts into words.

"Don't worry, I'm safe. Luna says the king doesn't know she took a guard's key so he'll never expect me to be here," he says. "You're getting out tonight."

"But your family," I say.

"Ava." Starla touches my shoulder, drawing my attention away from the wall. I turn and meet her gaze and then realize we're not alone. Grandmer, Starla's mom, hovers just behind her daughter with a sad smile on her face. "You need to listen to Carter."

I frown. "You know?"

"I'm the one who called to him when Mateo brought you here. The king wanted you in his chambers, but Mateo convinced Attilonious to let you be with us for now."

I grind my teeth, just the thought of waking up in King Attilonious' chambers freaking me out. Does he expect that since he ruined my life I'll submit to him and be the perfect little queen? Ew. I'll never resort to that.

"How are you so calm about Mateo, Starla?" I ask.

She pouts her bottom lip. "He's doing what he thinks is right for our family."

"He wants me by the king's side," I say.

"He wants you alive, Ava. He wants Carter alive. He's not aiding the king because he's against you. Someone must be there for you if things don't go as planned," Grandmer says, speaking up.

"They already haven't," I say.

"Calm down, Ava," Carter says into my mind. "You won't have to worry for much longer." But he can't make any guarantees. I'm locked in a room in the castle with no escape.

A sudden rumble causes the water to quiver, and the boulder blocking the only entrance and exit moves out of the way. Light streams in through the cutout, brightening the darkness of the room lit only by my spark.

"My queen," a masculine voice says.

"Carter," I say only to him. "I'm being moved."

"Your king requests your presence," the merman says, poking his head in. I don't recognize him.

I hug myself. "No. I don't want to see him."

"Please, my queen. I don't want to restrain you," the merman says. He swims into the small room, forcing Starla and Grandmer to move to the outskirts of the room.

I hold up my hand, willing a current to push him away. But it's not strong enough. He locks his fingers around my arm and tugs me with him.

"Stop!" I yell. "Let me go!"

But he doesn't, and no one tries to help me. Another mermaid grabs my other arm, allowing the merman to block the exit to the room again, cutting me off from Starla, who tells me to be strong.

"Don't resist, Ava," Carter whispers into my mind. "Don't

give the king a reason to hurt you."

"I'm scared," I whisper.

"I'm here," Carter says. "I know you can do this."

But I'm not so sure I can.

Because I really don't want to.

REBEL

I WAVE MY HAND THROUGH the water, sending a current into the closest mermaid, who holds up a sea grass woven top. Her dark auburn hair veils her face as she flies across the open room, hitting her back on the pearlescent wall.

"Queen Ava," another mermaid says. "Please, we're trying to help you." The mermaid swims closer, cringing when I hold my hand up, but I don't use any of my magic. Her steel gray eyes line with sadness when I sink to the floor and curl in on myself.

A small hand touches my shoulder and then shifts to push my hair from my face. I roll over and stare up at the young mermaid. She motions for the other two to leave the room, and they listen without arguing.

"I know this is hard," the girl says, shifting in the sand so her forest green tail doesn't brush mine. "But the king asked that we make you presentable."

"I don't want to see him," I mutter.

She cups my hand. "I know. It pains me to see you like this."

I sit up, surprise widening my eyes. "Why? You don't even know me."

"I was here during your coronation. What the king did..." Her voice trails off in my head. She tightens her hand around mine. "Thinking about it makes my heart hurt. You promised yourself to someone else. It doesn't make sense for the king to have done this."

I consider telling her the reason he has. I consider spilling my heart to her, so she can see what pain I'm in. So she can make sense of all this. But I can't. The words stay locked deep in my mind.

"Thank you for sharing your thoughts," I say instead of what's on my mind. "And I'm sorry for not complying. I'm glad you understand."

She nods, moving away so I can compose myself. "I'm not going to make you change for the king. I'll keep the others away as well."

I tilt my head. "No, it's fine. I don't want you to face his fury. Not on my behalf. Let's just get this over with." As much as I want to be stubborn, to send everyone away and let no one near me, I wouldn't put it past King Attilonious to punish those who comply with my will instead of his. Carter was right. I need to do what I'm told so the king doesn't hurt me.

I swallow the rising lump in my throat.

"Relax, Aves," Carter says. "I'm still here with you."

"I love you," I whisper.

"Don't say it like that."

"Would you like me to help you with your top, Queen Ava," the mermaid says, pulling my thoughts away from Carter.

I shake my head and unhook my bikini top myself, using my arm to hide my bare chest even though the mermaid doesn't gape at me. She tucks my bikini top into a small bag and hands me the grass woven top with tiny pieces of blue sea glass strung through it.

I struggle for a moment, trying to tie the top around back. Without asking, the mermaid swims behind me and does it herself before quickly running her fingers through my hair, untangling the knots as she goes. She twists my blond locks into a braid that stops just past the strap of my new top.

The mermaid moves around to sit in front of me and holds out a dainty silver crown, one studded with sparkling diamonds and pearls, and sets it on top of my head despite my protests. She holds up a mirror so I can see myself. I frown.

I hate it. I hate everything about it. I don't want to look the part of a queen, which the king expects me to play. I don't want to find myself beautiful as I stare at my reflection—my sad cerulean eyes the same shade as my tail, how my skin shimmers in a pearlescent sheen, giving me a glow I could never manage as a human. How perfect my hair looks even underwater, and how the queen's heart around my neck projects enchanting rainbow beams, even though I'm sure only I can see them.

But what I hate most is Carter isn't here to see me. I'm not dressed up for him to appreciate. I've been dolled up like a pretty little mermaid queen to please the one merman I want nothing to do with. One who will probably kill me if I fight too hard. The thought makes me sick to my stomach. I don't want to be pretty for him. I don't want the king to look at me like some jewel he can hide away in his treasure chest. I want to be repulsive.

"What's the matter?" the mermaid asks.

I cover my face with my hands, sobbing silently. My tears blend with the salty sea, my chest heaving. If I could get sick, I would, but I can't even remember the last time I've eaten. San Francisco? That feels like an eternity ago.

"Please, don't cry," Carter whispers into my mind. "I can't bear it."

"You should be here. You should get to see me right now. Not him." The words escape so sharply the sand stirs from the floor without me even moving. Fear pokes me in the mind, but the mermaid doesn't react. I didn't accidentally send the words out for the entire ocean to hear. "I don't want him to see me like this."

"Queen Ava?" the mermaid asks.

"It's going to be okay, Aves," Carter assures, talking over the mermaid.

"Everything is so screwed up," I say, projecting my voice for everyone to hear. "I hate this."

"Would you like to try another top?" the mermaid asks.

I thrash my head back and forth. "It's not that. It's all of it."

The mermaid floats in front of me, a grimace marring her delicate features. "You look lovely, Queen Ava."

"That's the point. I don't want to," I say.

I cover my face with my hands again, but this time, I don't cry. Instead, I drag the sharp nail of my index finger down my cheek. A small pool of blood tints the sea pink in front of me, causing the mermaid to gasp. The thin cut only hurts a little, and it'll heal by nightfall, but in this moment, it's a glaring mark on my once flawless skin. It's my way of protesting. Rebelling. The king can try to have power over me all he wants, but he can never truly control me.

"I need a healer!" the mermaid calls.

I reach out and grab her arm. "No. I'm through here. Take me to the king."

"But you've injured yourself," the mermaid says, trying to reach up to touch the cut.

I turn away. "I'm fine. I'm perfect. Take me to the king."

"But—"

"I *said* take me to the king."

The mermaid nods, her lips tilted downward, and swims across the room to the cutout where the muscular guard with short dark gray hair waits for me. The moment his eyes fall on the cut on my cheek, I know King Attilonious will be displeased. It gives me the courage to straighten my shoulders and let him take me by the arm.

"Now's a good time to give me all your strength, my warrior mate," I whisper to Carter in my mind. My heart tugs as I try to pinpoint where he is, and I know if I just follow the pull, it'll take me into his arms.

"You're the bravest being in the universe," he whispers into my mind. "You're strong and smart and everything I could've ever dreamed of. The king doesn't stand a chance against you, my mate—my queen."

A smile crosses my lips, hearing him whisper through my mind. It's the first time he's ever called me his queen, and while it sounds cheesy, it feels honest and so full of love that I already feel a thousand times stronger. I feel like I can face whatever the king has to throw at me. Because he can't break me. He can't make me bow.

"Against us," I whisper back, sending my thoughts only to him.

The guard guides me through a tunnel and into the grand room of the castle filled with remnants of sunken ships. Before, I thought everything here was collected from accidental shipwrecks. But now? I know the pieces are trophies collected by the king from ships he probably destroyed without reason, just because he could.

Voices murmur through my mind, drawing my attention from the glittering room to those who hover around me. Dozens of smiling faces greet me, some reaching out to touch my arm or my tail, totally invading my space. As much as I want to jerk away and lash out, I don't. The merpeople are merely excited about my arrival, lost in their own naivety which I can't blame them for.

Forcing myself to smile, I gently touch the cheeks of those close enough for me to reach. I hum to myself, trying my best to push out the harmonious voices overtaking my thoughts, making it hard to think. The melody stirs sadness in my heart for a split second when I realize I'm humming a song my mom used to sing to me long ago. I can almost hear her voice now.

The guard motions for the others to back away and swims me up to the balcony that overlooks the grand room. It'll lead to the throne room and then the king's chambers, the last place I want to be. I'd rather stay where everyone can see.

Suddenly, the room falls silent and merpeople start bowing around me. A shadow falls over me, and I steel myself to face King Attilonious as he hovers on the balcony. The guard tries to force me to bow next to him, but I hold my head high and bring my eyes to meet the king's.

Something indecipherable flickers on his face, so quickly I nearly miss it, before he offers me a brilliant smile, one that would've once dazzled me. But he can't charm me now. I will not allow him to have any sort of power over me.

"Welcome home, Ava," King Attilonious says, bending low to bow before me. "You're as beautiful as ever."

I grin. I can't help it. Not because I'm flattered by his compliment, but because I now know what the look I saw was. Dissatisfaction. But he can't react. Something like a cut or blemish would never get in the way of the bond between mates. But I'm not bonded with the king. I'll never be.

I don't respond to his compliment or bow. All I do is cross my arms and continue to grin. I catch sight of the guard next to me, and he gives me a funny look, mouth hanging open with squinty eyes—one that almost looks fearful, probably because I don't do anything.

Even the king looks uncomfortable.

The king closes the distance between us, grabbing both my hands in his, and then he brings them up to kiss my knuckles. I clench my jaw to keep from grimacing. But I can't stop the falter of my smile when he leans over and tries to kiss me on the lips.

I turn my head, and his lips brush against my cheek. "Try that again, and I'll make a scene." I direct the thought only to the king.

With narrowed eyes, King Attilonious leans away from me but doesn't let me go. He nearly drags me from the crowd and through the throne room to his chambers, leaving the crowd cheering like what they witnessed was the most magical thing ever.

"You will not disrespect me!" King Attilonious bellows, swinging his staff toward me.

A current knocks me across the room, and I skid over his black sand pool. Heat rushes around me, threatening to boil me. I twist on the floor, my once neat hair now loose from the braid. I grip the diamond on my neck and inhale a breath of the hot water. It courses through me, igniting my spark even brighter, and I thrust my arm out, sending the hot current right back to the king.

He sways in the current, but the strength from his tail combats the shift in the water. "I am your king, and you will accept your place by my side. The ocean picked you for me and gifted you with an affinity found only in those meant to be roy-alty."

"The ocean did not pick me, Carter did. For him. Not you." Celestiana was right about him being so closed off from the world. He's not some king trying to protect his kingdom. He's protecting what he thinks is rightfully his. Me included. He sees no reason and his power has gotten to his head. "I will never accept a place by your side."

In a bout of rage, he hits his staff on the ground again, except this time, I'm prepared. I deflect his current and remain in my spot on the sand. I'm only ten feet away from the balcony that leads to the open water of the colony, and if I can make it there, it'll be harder to stop me.

King Attilonious holds his staff up but doesn't hit me with his magic. "Oh, but you will. It won't be long before I find your mate. He won't be able to stay away from you. And when he comes, I won't attempt to sever your bond."

I hold my face expressionless. I refuse to give him a reaction.

"He'll feel whatever you feel. You might be able to withstand my power, but can he? Can you watch your mate suffer?"

My lip quivers, giving him the reaction he was looking for. "I won't allow it."

"Allow it? Do you honestly think you're a match against me?"

"I don't get it. Why not just kill me? Why go through this trouble?" I don't know why I feel the need to ask, but if my existence is so horrible to him, why bother?

His mouth twitches, and I'm sure he's thought about it. "My kingdom is important, and the colonies have already accepted your place."

I remember now that there's never been an uprising because the merpeople adored him. Hurting me wouldn't risk the colonies. It'd risk him.

"It doesn't have to be this way, though. I want my queen to be happy. I want you to want to be by my side. You've been gifted, and I can help you," he says, closing the distance. Lowering himself to the floor, he reaches out and brushes strands of my hair away from my face. "If you swear your loyalty to me, I'll stop the hunt for Carter. I'll release his family. I might even grant you freedom to leave Pearlestria with a guard. I need our kingdom united, and you've put a rift among our people. That's something I can't allow to continue."

"Me? You did that yourself. You couldn't just leave me alone," I say.

"To give away our secret? To put everyone at risk because you're a stubborn, spoiled mermaid?" Nothing he says will faze me. "I cannot allow it. I'm giving you an opportunity most yearn for. Sometimes we have to do things we don't like because it's the right thing to do. It's time you learn that. It's time to learn your place in the ocean."

"And if I resist? If I don't comply?" I ask.

"That's not an option. I'll make you see."

The water warms around us, and I realize it's not by the king's doing. It's me. Rage rushes over me, and I swim up from my spot, putting space between us. The king is quick to propel toward me, but he doesn't have a chance to touch me before a figure darts between us.

"Dad, stop!" Luna yells, projecting her voice out.

King Attilonious freezes, staff aimed and ready to strike me, but Luna blocks his way. She holds her hands up, trying to fill the space in front of me so that King Attilonious can't get a shot.

"Move, Luna," he says, trying to knock her away with a wave, but I grab her hand and swim with her.

"You will not stand against me, my daughter." The viciousness in the king's voice makes me pull Luna back.

"You can't hurt her," she says. "I won't let you."

"You don't understand, Luna. She'll destroy us all. She doesn't understand our traditions and ways. Without me, her power runs wild. It must be given to me. Do you even know what she wears around her neck?"

Luna peers over her shoulder at me, glancing at the necklace. She doesn't respond to her father.

"That was your mother's. It was a wedding gift from me. It was lost with her," he says. "Ava should not have it."

Luna turns from the king to meet my gaze. "Is that true? You mean?"

This is not the conversation I want to have right now only feet from my escape. But how can I deny Luna the answers she seeks? If my mother disappeared when I was a merbabe, I'd want to know the truth.

"She renounced her mermaid essence," I say quietly. "The queen's heart was a gift to me."

"But why would she do that? I knew she loved the land, but I don't understand," she says.

"Please, Luna. I'll explain everything. But not here. We have to go," I say, sending my thought to her alone.

Luna gives me a tiny nod and turns to face her father. Neither of us has time to react when he swings his staff out and knocks Luna away. She flies through the water and clatters to the floor. Her black hair veils her face, and she lies there unmoving.

"Swear your loyalty, Ava," the king says, closing the distance.

"No," I say.

"Do it now!" he roars, grabbing me by the hair and shaking me once. I swing my arm out and smack his shoulder, using the force of the current to knock him away from me. With a flick of my tail, I propel toward my only exit, praying I can somehow get through the protective barrier of Pearlestria the king set to imprison us all.

I don't make it far.

Strong hands latch around the base of my tale and yank me back. Bubbles erupt from my mouth as I scream out in the water. The king pins me down, one hand digging into my shoulder and the other one locked around the chain on my neck.

The diamond burns brightly, setting the entire room aglow. The king brushes his fingers on the diamond, and the stone floor quakes beneath us. It shocks the king, stopping him from stealing the stone from my neck. He swims up, putting space between us and then aligns his staff with my heart.

I squeeze my eyes shut, bracing for the impact, for what could possibly be the end of my life but nothing happens. Peeking through my eyelashes, I stare at King Attilonious through the fastest current I've ever seen. It blocks me from the king, moving so quickly his staff can't touch me.

He snarls, swimming back. My chest heaves as I inhale and exhale cool water, trying to calm down my racing heart.

"This isn't over," he says, the new calmness in his voice making me shiver. "You will swear your loyalty to me and our kingdom."

I don't respond. I can't.

Without another word, King Attilonious leaves both me and Luna in his chambers. Two guards enter the room, one blocking each exit.

My chance of escaping seems impossible now. I don't even know how we'll get through the barrier imprisoning all merpeople here.

"Ava, say something to me," Carter says in my mind. "Your emotions are all over the place."

"Carter, you have to get as far away as possible. The king is depending on you showing up," I say. "I can't let him get to you."

"I'm not leaving without you," he says.

"Please," I beg.

"Ava, don't ask me again."

So, I don't. Instead, I look around the king's chambers. The king was right. This isn't over. It's just begun.

23

BETRAYAL

"I COMMAND YOU TO LET me go," Luna says, jabbing her finger into the guard's rock-hard chest.

Moments after the king left, three healers came into the chambers to fix the damage caused to the both of us, including my self-inflicted cut on my face. It took two of them and the guard to hold me down, and also Carter talking me out of blasting them all into a wall, to allow them to mend the scrapes on my still tender tail.

"I'm sorry, princess. We're under strict orders," the guard says, keeping his eyes trained above Luna's head.

"Then I want to talk to my dad," she argues.

A bubble of panic rises in my chest at the thought of King Attilonious returning. "It's not worth it, Luna."

She turns to glance at me, her lips barely a visible line as she presses them together. My thoughts must be written all over my face because she immediately backs away from the guard but not before kicking up an arc of black sand from the pool into his face with a flick of her tail.

He closes his eyes, the tiny grains pelting him, but he remains firm in his position in front of the exit.

With a wave of my hand, I send a cool current at him, making him waver in the water. He brings his attention to me for the first time since his arrival. His firm mouth hides under facial hair, but it doesn't conceal how he clenches his jaw under my scrutiny. He's obviously uncomfortable, and I use that to my advantage. Too bad the king's messenger, Tide, isn't here. I could probably scare him away easily enough.

I wiggle my index finger at the guard and wink, and he flushes. One thing I remember from my weeks within the walls of this colony is that it's unheard of for a coupled mermaid to show attention to anyone apart from their mate.

Giselle would laugh hysterically if she were here. She'd attempt to make the guard even more uncomfortable for the sheer fun of it. All I want is for him to turn around and stand guard outside the door.

"Carter?" I whisper through the water with my mind. "I'm trying to get the guard to take post outside of the chambers. What can I say that'll make him leave?"

"Compliment his tail," Carter says. A small chuckle sounds through my mind, making my heart soar.

Heat crawls up my neck for no other reason than this feels super awkward. I force myself from my spot on the floor and swim closer to the guard. Luna tilts her head to the side, studying me. I smirk at her before hiding my smile with my hand.

"What's this guy's name?" I ask only to her.

"Why?"

"I'm going to compliment his tail."

Her mouth falls open. "That's something you say to a potential mate," she whispers only to me.

I suck in my bottom lip to stop myself from laughing into the water. "Just tell me his name."

"He goes by Blue," she says.

Inhaling a deep breath of the ocean, I rise in the water so I can meet Blue's eyes, though he trains them on the ceiling above my head. I float in place for an excruciating moment, taking in his hard features, from the sharpness of his nose to his dark brown eyes. Nothing about him is blue.

"Where's a good place to rest my hand, Carter?" I ask only to him. My heart constantly aches because I can't follow the pull that wants to lead me to him.

"Should I be worried?" he asks.

"You should bask in my brilliance," I say.

"You know I bask in your everything."

His words bring a huge smile to my lips, and Blue visibly stiffens. I might not even have to say anything at all to him before he swims out of here to escape the awkwardness I'm about to thrust upon him.

"And to answer your question, grasp him on the crook of his neck and shoulder, and tap right below his gills."

"So, Blue," I say, projecting my thoughts through the water.

Luna watches me in fascination while the guard refuses to look at me at all. I wonder if any of my fake advances will even work. He could be immune to my charm, and then I'll just embarrass myself.

"Have you ever been to shore before?" I ask.

He doesn't respond.

I tighten my jaw and flick my gaze to Luna. "I'm starting to feel unwelcome in my own kingdom."

Blue fidgets in place and says, "I'm sorry, my queen. The king didn't mention if I'm allowed to speak to you."

"Why wouldn't you be?" I ask. "He's not my mate, you know."

"Yes, your highness. But you are my queen."

It's starting to get awkward on my part as I lose my bravado. "Which means you should at least be courteous enough to respond when I'm speaking to you."

"My apologies, your highness. I've never been to the shore before. I'm not familiar with human customs," he says.

"But I'm not human." I float a few inches closer, and his

caudal fin brushes against mine. He doesn't move away but tenses.

"I'm sorry, my queen. I just know—"

I reach up and grasp his shoulder, sliding my hand up his tight muscles to the spot Carter mentioned. "You don't have to apologize to me, Blue. I'm happy to have you in my presence." I gently tap my finger to his neck. "Your tail is the—" Prettiest? Strongest? Oh, God, this is so uncomfortable.

"Pardon me, my queen. I'm being summoned," Blue says, nearly barreling through the cutout that leads to the grand room.

I meet Luna's wide eyes and offer her my most dazzling smile. I swim the few feet between us and nestle myself next to her, flopping my tail down in front of me, stirring up the black sand of the pool.

"What? I was tired of him watching our every move," I say.

"We're still not going to be able to leave," she says.

"I have a plan for that, too."

"What is it?"

I can only smile. Being stuck in a room with nothing to do but think and talk to Carter has given me the chance to plan my escape. It's going to be a long shot, but I'm going to risk it. I just need to create a distraction. One that sends not only the king from Pearlestria but his guards, too.

"Carter's going to rescue me," I say. "Because there's no way he's going to allow the king to try to steal my power. The ocean gave me a warrior for this reason. The king might be mighty, but he doesn't stand a chance against my mate."

"Ava, tone it down," Carter says in my mind.

Luna reaches out and touches my hand. "This is a terrible idea. You don't know what my dad is capable of."

"Oh, I know," I say, gripping the necklace. "Celestiana, your mom, she told me he'll be the cause of our destruction." I let my thoughts project through the water for all to hear. "She wants nothing more than to make sure things return as they should be."

Luna frowns. "You talked to my mom? I don't understand."

I nearly regret telling her. Her brows hang low on her head, and she pouts her bottom lip. It's in this moment I realize how unfair all of this really is for both me and Luna. I shouldn't be in this position, and Luna, she should be the one to hold her mother's essence, the essence that blinks in the diamond around my neck. But Luna only knows the sea while I know the land.

"It's hard to explain. Can I show you?" I ask.

"Ava, we're running out of time," Carter says in my mind.

"I have to do something first," I tell him.

Luna nods, drawing my attention back to her. Leaning forward, I do the only thing I know how to do to allow her to glimpse my memories. I press my lips against hers, sending the thousands of images the queen bestowed on me into Luna's mind. One after another flickers through, showing Luna her mother's life from her time on land, visiting her human grandfather to her falling in love with Darren to how the king swept her into the world of royalty, even to the moment she gazed upon a young Luna knowing she might never see her daughter again.

Luna jerks back and covers her mouth with her hand. "Oh, Ava," she says. "It was really her."

I nod. "I wish it was you who could talk to her."

"But you've given me something I never thought I'd ever get. I don't know how to thank you," she says.

"I might have something in mind."

"Anything."

"I need you to betray me," I say.

24

SINK OR SWIM

"ARE YOU INSANE?" LUNA ASKS, her voice projecting through the water. She stands near the cutout where Blue waits outside. He's eased closer since I tried telling anyone nearby what the queen had told me. "I'm not going to let you risk your life like that. I know you don't want to be here, but my dad is so powerful. You know what he's capable of."

"Luna, keep your voice down," I say. "This is supposed to be between you and me."

Luna swims in a quick circle. Her black hair veils her face, and she sinks to the stone floor and brings her tail up to her chest to rest her chin on it. "Someone could get hurt. You might not care about everyone here, but I do. You should just tell him to leave. If he were my mate, I'd want to protect him. You're selfish, you know."

My nose crinkles at her words. I tell myself I'm selfish all the time, but it sounds weird coming from someone else, even if she doesn't truly believe it.

"Please, Luna. You have no idea what it's like. I'd rather fight and die together than remain here for the rest of my life." Dramatic? Definitely. True? Absolutely. But I don't plan on dying any time soon.

A pout crosses her face, and she brings her eyes to mine. "I thought we were friends. I might not be your mate, but I thought you cared about me. I stood up for you to my dad."

"I know. And I appreciate it. But this—" I motion around the room. "This isn't what I want."

"I'm sorry, Ava," Luna says, her voice nearly a whisper.

A moment of panic blossoms in my chest, pulling at my spark so hard my hands fly up to hug myself. Blue enters the room, and then another guard flies in from outside. They both close in on me like I'll suddenly do something to escape. And I'm about to.

"What have you done, Luna?" I ask, throwing my hand out.

"I'm sorry," she whispers again.

"Carter, you have to run! They know you're here!" I scream, letting my voice project through the water.

"Be brave, Ava," he says only to me.

I spin around in a circle, thrusting a current at the guards as they try to close in on me. They fly back a few feet, barely fazed by my attempt to keep them away.

"Queen Ava, you must calm down. We have strict orders from the king. He says if you try to fight us that he won't bring back your mate alive," Blue says. "He's already been spotted on the outskirts of the kingdom."

It takes everything in me not to blast the two guards away. "I swear if any of you hurt him, I'll—"

"My queen, that's the last thing any of us want. I grew up with your mate's father," the other guard, who I have no idea what his name is, says. "I don't want anything to happen to his son."

"Then why are you helping Attilonious?" I ask. His admission throws me off. Most of the merpeople have been kind and compassionate, but it's like all they can do is feel bad. Only Luna's been brave enough to stand up with me.

"He is our king," the guard says.

"He's not my king," I say.

"But he is," Blue says.

Luna swims closer and takes my hand. "Ava, it's going to be okay."

Closing my eyes, I summon the courage I can feel coursing from Carter as he evades the king and his guards. I hold on tightly to his love, his loyalty, all his strength. Because I'm going to need it to do what I'm about to do next.

I can't escape Pearlestria as a mermaid, but the king's imprisoning magic can't hold me here if I change forms. He didn't account for the fact that I can still transform into a human. He doesn't have a clue.

"I know it will be," I say. "Because I'm counting on you to not let me die."

She nods once, still gripping my hand, and I will my human transformation to take hold. Cramps seize my muscles, sending me bowing, but they disappear a second later before my lungs scream in pain. Silence veils over me. The only sound I can hear is my racing heart beating in sync with Carter's as he lures the king away.

And he's not just luring him anywhere. He's taking him to the one place he's never supposed to go. Because the Lost Cove is where we have the advantage. It's where Celestiana's magic resonates in every molecule of the water, water I'm familiar with.

Opening my eyes, I stare through the dark room, nearly blinded. Without my mermaid vision and with the sun already set, I have to rely on my other senses to get me out of here. But in my human form, I can't make it alone.

Luna pulls me to her and away from the two guards. My necklace erupts in magical light silhouetting them long enough that I wave my arm in their direction and send a current their way.

The water quivers from the force in which they strike the

wall, and Luna yanks me toward the cutout leading to the open sea of Pearlestria. Shadows edge my vision from the lack of oxygen, and I fight to stay awake.

Something hits me hard in the side, and a muffled scream sounds through the water. I'm ripped away from Luna, a pair of strong arms locking around me. I thrash, fighting as hard as I can, but with every passing second, I become weaker and weaker. And as a human, no one can hear my thoughts. But I refuse to transform back. I'm not even sure I can in this moment.

A flash of gold erupts in my vision, the sparkle of Luna's tail cutting through the water in my direction. Bubbles fizzle around me, and I manage to elbow my captor right in the gills, forcing him to release me. I thrust out both hands and send a cold current right at the guard, knocking him away. His spark blinks as he lands in the channel between the houses where all the unsuspecting merpeople hide away. I don't know why I can see it, but I can.

Kicking my legs, I swim a few feet in the direction I think is the surface. It's hard to tell in this state. I sink lower despite my kicking, and my hope dwindles to the ocean floor. Luna was supposed to swim me to the surface, but she's nowhere to be found. She was supposed to help me cross the barrier. The guards were supposed to let her because they shouldn't have wanted to see me drown. How can they let their queen die?

But maybe I'm not really their queen. The king can call me that all he wants. Everyone can pretend I'm royalty. But when it all comes down to it, I'm a human-born mermaid, who's coupled with a boy who loves the land more than the sea. In the end, I'm not the queen of the ocean. I'm not as powerful as the king.

I'm no one.

Celestiana was wrong. The ocean was wrong. Carter isn't the perfect warrior for the perfect queen. I'm an accidental mermaid, and he's my hero.

"Ava," a voice says. It's not in my mind, but I can hear it through the hum of the ocean around me. "Ava-girl, stay with me."

Strong hands encircle my waist and drag me from the spot I float above all the rock houses of Pearlestria. The ocean zooms around me, and I close my eyes, taking comfort in the heat of the sturdy body that sends the icy chill away from my bones.

My ears ring with every heartbeat, and the water grows warmer and warmer. Moonlight trickles into the now crystal clear ocean, and Mateo concentrates on swimming me to the air I need to breathe.

In one thrust, Mateo sends me to the surface. I spit, expelling the ocean from my lungs. Pale moonlight sets me aglow in the middle of the endless sea, and relief rushes over me with every gasp of breath.

A swell rises next to me, and Mateo breaks the surface. "Ava, what are you thinking? You could've died."

I bob under, struggling to stay afloat. "I don't belong here, Mateo."

"You have to transform back. If King Attilonious discovers you've figured out a way to leave, he'll kill my son the moment he catches him."

"He won't catch him," I say.

"How are you so sure?"

"Trust me."

"The only thing I can trust is that you've gotten in over your head. I know you didn't choose this life and my son made a grave mistake, but please, you have to reconsider what you're doing. You might have bonded with Carter, but you obviously don't share the same feelings mates usually feel. If you care about Carter even a little, you'll transform and return to the castle," he says.

Anger sneaks up on me. "No wonder Starla didn't tell you we survived. You have so little faith in me and Carter. And if *you* love Carter like you claim to, you'd help me swim across the barrier. You'll take me where I need to go since I'm obviously not transforming so you can drag me back to the castle. Carter's counting on me to be there for him. And so you know, I love Carter more than the sea, more than land, and more than even myself. So don't you dare doubt my love for your son."

He doesn't move from his spot, so I start swimming away the best I can, following the pull of my heart that'll lead me directly to Carter. Every few feet I sink under from utter exhaustion that I know I'll have to transform. But I'm no match for Mateo's speed. He's as fast as his son.

I stifle a frustrated sob, stroking my arms out while kicking my legs. The motion awakens a small current to help move me forward, but it's still not fast enough. My hope dwindles, sinking every time I do.

"Ava," Mateo says, swimming up next to me. "I'm sorry. I can't take you to where you need to go, but I will help you cross the barrier, and I won't stop you. I just—I can't risk my mate's life for disobeying the king. I hope you understand."

Relief floods over me in a warm wave, and I nod my head. Locking my fingers to Mateo's broad shoulders, I hold on while he swims me forward, remaining above water so I don't have to hold my breath. The water shimmers with tiny bubbles the farther away we get from the castle, and then Mateo stops where there's a visible line of bubbles—magic—before us.

I release him and tread in place. "Thank you, Mateo. You have no idea how much this means to me."

"Just take care of Carter, Ava," he says.

"Take care of yourself, too."

I hug him in the water, and he embraces me, pressing his warm lips to my cool forehead in the same way my dad used to kiss me. The gesture stirs sadness within me that I push away, because in this moment, I can't think about all the things I miss. All the ways I've been wronged. I must remember and hold onto all the good in my life. All the love. All the strength. All the people I still have that rely on me and who I rely on.

Because I'm going to need it.

I'm never going back to Pearlestria as the king's queen if I ever go back again.

Mateo releases me and throws me up and into the air. I land feet first in the water and transform the moment my head dips under. When I spin in place, Mateo's already swimming back to the colony, leaving me alone.

In this spot, I'm too far to hear the voices of the merpeople of Pearlestria and too far from the Lost Cove to hear Carter. The ocean feels lonely despite its vastness.

With a flick of my tail, I propel myself forward, cutting through the water as quickly as the magical current I've created can take me. I just hope I'm not too late. Because once the king discovers the Lost Cove, he'll do everything he can to break the magic, leaving the inhabitants defenseless.

If the king gets through the protective barrier, he'll send the island to the ocean floor.

But I won't let that happen.

I might not be the queen everyone wants me to be, but I'll fight for the land.

I'll fight to protect the humans.

One way or another, King Attilonious' reign will end.

I just hope I don't end with it.

25

LAST CHANCE

I COAST THE SURFACE SO I can get a clear view of anyone who tries to sneak up on me from below. I doubt they'll be able to, not without me knowing since the diamond on my neck will warn me.

I've never swam this far alone, and it's less pleasant than I thought it would be. I don't know if it's because I'm bored—on land, I've always traveled with music or something—or if it's because I'm freaking out a bit. Who knows? But I can't wait to hit familiar waters. I want nothing more than to return to shore.

Up ahead, a frenzy of blue sharks crowd the sea for what looks like forever. I push away my human fears, because the biggest predator in the ocean to me is King Attilonious, and swim right into the fray of things. A few sharks bump into me, making it hard to swim. I'll get pretty bruised up if I continue, but it's safer to stay in the frenzy since merpeople would usually dive down to swim around it.

Most of the sharks are shorter in length than I am, considering I'm longer as a mermaid than in my human form, but the sheer amount of them swimming around me, feeding on a school of mackerel, makes me keep my arms clenched against my chest.

A smaller shark brushes against me, its skin feeling almost like sandpaper compared to my slippery scales. I nudge it away and finally give up after another shark bumps into my tail. Diving down, I swim out of the frenzy and into the open sea.

The silhouettes of the sharks above me send goosebumps over my skin. But they don't leave me as on edge as the bottomless ocean below me. I can only see so far and every blurry figure of an ocean animal makes my heart pound and my stomach clench in knots.

Pushing myself harder, I swim as fast as I can. The ocean floor rises below me, the pull in my chest stronger than ever. I haven't swam much outside the reef barrier of the Lost Cove, but I'd recognize these familiar waters. Part of it feels like home—like as long as I'm here, things will turn out okay.

Heat crawls from my chest to my neck, and bright light erupts, sending a stream of dazzling, colorful beams through the water. Without seeing the king or his guards, I can sense them near. I dart down, staying along the bottom of the shallows, navigating around the tropical fish surrounding me in such a way it feels like they're protecting me.

"Follow the barrier. See if there is any weakness in the magic. All I need is a small crack, and I can blast it wide open." King Attilonious' voice sneaks into my mind as he projects it out for his small army of merpeople to hear.

"Carter?" I whisper, afraid that if I push my voice too hard the others will hear it. "I'm here."

"Thank God, Ava. I was getting worried." I blow a bubble through my lips, hearing the sound of Carter's voice in my head.

"It's all okay. I'm okay. But I don't know how to get to you. The king has his guards circling the reef. I'm afraid of coming any closer," I say.

"Don't worry, Aves. I'll come for you. Just stay there," he says.

My heart clenches at the thought of Carter leaving the protection of the cove. He shouldn't have to risk his life to get me.

The king doesn't even know I'm here.

"No, Carter. I don't want you to come out here. It isn't safe for you," I say.

He doesn't respond for a moment, and I wring my hands together, afraid he's already on his way, that he'll ignore my pleas and get us both caught.

"I have an idea," he finally says. "But you might not like it."

I crinkle my nose. "What is it?"

"I'm going to need you to transform."

I hide among the kelp growing right before the shallows dip into the open sea. Flicking my gaze from the surface to the area around me, I anxiously await for the shadow of the boat to cross over the reef.

King Attilonious disappeared minutes ago to swim around the reef himself, and a lonely guard hovers in the sea, peering at the reef like it'll somehow open up and let him in. The magic only allows the merpeople loyal to the inhabitants of the Lost Cove in, and since none of the guards or the king knows of their existence, they won't be able to get through unless King Attilonious can break the protective barrier.

My heart soars in my throat the second the shadow of the small boat crosses the reef. I bob back and forth in the suddenly choppy water, and I realize what's happening the second I see a paddle break the surface.

"Carter?" I ask. "Who's in the boat? I thought you were going to push it over."

"The guard would be curious if he knew it was empty. This was the only way to get him to back off," Carter says.

And he's right. The moment the guard spots the boat, the merman swims away from his spot looking at the reef. The ocean essence protects us from being seen from boats, but it still doesn't stop the unease that comes with seeing humans on the surface. I should know.

A huge swell rises, lifting and dropping the boat in attempt to keep its passenger from floating to the open sea. No human can leave the island just like no ordinary merperson can cross the reef. Swimming forward, I close the distance between me and the boat.

"My king, there are humans on the other side of the reef," a voice says, cutting through my mind.

"Humans?" King Attilonious asks.

"A boat just crossed over."

Panic slips through me, and I close my eyes, concentrating on transforming into my human self. I kick to the surface, spitting out water, and strong hands lift me from the choppy water and drag me into the boat.

It won't be long until King Attilonious comes to investigate, and I wouldn't put it past him to flip the boat over. If he does, he'll realize I've escaped Pearlestria.

"Here, Ava. Put this on," Wes says, drawing my attention from the rocking waves. He hands me a dress without looking at me.

I slide it on over my head and take one of the paddles. "You're crazy for coming out here. The king will get to us at any second. We need to paddle."

Wes nods, dipping his paddle into the rough water, and we both struggle to bring the boat back over the reef. The ocean wants to send Wes under, but there's no way I'm going to let him fall overboard, especially not with the king around.

"Come on," I say more to myself, slicing my paddle through the water.

Something knocks into the boat, sending my heart to my feet. It definitely wasn't just another swell trying to knock the boat over. The force was intentional, hard enough to knock the paddle right from Wes' hand. It drifts away, leaving us with one.

With a wave of my hand, I create a current strong enough to propel us toward the reef. I didn't want to use my magic, but I was left with no choice. And it's still not strong enough. A huge wave cascades over us, filling the boat with a foot of water. Hands reach from the sea and lock onto the edge of the boat. My voice rings through the air as surprise grabs hold of me.

I meet King Attilonious' dark, heated gaze.

Without hesitating, I grab onto Wes' hand and pull him with me. We dive over the edge of the boat and away from the king. Blindly, I flick out my hand, shooting a wave of water behind us. Strong hands grab me by the waist, and I scream through the water, thrashing and kicking, refusing to let go of Wes.

"Ava, it's me," Carter says, pulling me from the king who raises his staff in our direction.

Thrusting out my freehand, I blast King Attilonious with an icy current, knocking his staff sideways. The motion is enough to propel us back, and Carter breaches from the water, taking both me and Wes over the barrier and back into the bay of the Lost Cove.

A huge wave swells from the other side of the reef, rising high into the air. The king sends the ocean directly at us from his spot, even though he can't cross over. It's in this moment I realize that even though King Attilonious can't reach us, the ocean—the water he controls—can, and it won't be long until he tries to sweep us all away.

"Ava!" King Attilonious' voice stabs me in my mind. The force of his words nearly leaves me breathless as another wave steals my oxygen away. "I'm giving you one opportunity to return to my side. If you do, I'll leave this place alone. I'll let that little human who is helping you live. But if you don't, you can consider yourself an enemy, and I will not rest until I take back what is mine."

I don't respond to him. The shock of being able to hear the king, even in my human form, frightens me. We shouldn't be so connected. I can't even hear Carter in this state.

"Come on, Ava. You need to transform," Carter says. He's holding onto both me and Wes in the unrelenting waves created by King Attilonious.

"Take him to shore," I say, motioning to Wes.

"What are you going to do?" Carter asks.

"I'm going to try to stop the king from wiping us out," I say.

Carter presses his lips to mine for a quick second, just long enough that I can feel his strength and courage wash through me. "I'll be right back."

I nod instead of arguing. Sinking under, I transform into a mermaid. A thousand bubbles prickle against my skin. The water shudders around me, scaring the ocean life away. Fish scatter, swimming in all different directions, and the water grows hazy as sand swirls through the current with every new wave.

Holding my hands out, I push back at the water, imagining it bending to my will. My cold current hits King Attilonious' hot one, forcing it back toward the reef. I swim forward with it, doing my best to calm the water around me.

"This is your last chance, Ava," the king says again. "I will punish Carter's family on your behalf. Their lives will be on you. Are you really going to let that happen? All because you're too stubborn to see how the world works."

I still refuse to respond to the king.

Carter swims up next to me, taking my hand in his, and we both stare at the dangerous sea before us.

"Carter, he's threatening your family," I say.

He holds me tighter. "He's bluffing."

"And if he isn't?" I ask.

"I'm not letting you go out there. I won't let him win," he says.

Closing my eyes, I focus on the love radiating from Carter—the love that pushes away the panic threatening to be my undoing. "I think he might've already won."

"If he had won, he wouldn't be trying so hard, Aves. You've got him scared. He thinks you're a threat to him. It's why he's doing this."

"He's not afraid of me," I say.

"He's shaking."

Carter's words ease the fear clenching my chest, and I suck in water to push it out through my gills. We hold tightly to each other as another wave cascades over the reef, high enough to reach the shore. I push it back with a flick of my hand, and the sudden movement drags us forward. This push and pull of magic leaves me dizzy, and it takes everything in me to constantly fight the king's attempts to make me comply.

"Carter, I don't know how much of this I can take," I say. "There has to be something more we can do."

We meet each other's gazes in the water. Carter's bright bluish-green eyes look like two jewels, sparkling at me. I know he'd attempt to fight the king if I asked him. He'd be by my side, keeping me safe, while I try to get the king to back off. But even now, even in the Lost Cove, I still don't feel as powerful as I need to be to get King Attilonious to leave us alone, to revert things back to how they were. It'll all come down to who wants it more, and I'm not sure that's me.

"He'll give up, Ava," Carter says. "When he does, we'll think things through. We'll beat him on our terms. We'll use our strengths against him."

I blink a few times as his words sink into my bones. Carter's right about one thing. I need to turn this power struggle around to where it's on my terms. The king holds strong because he knows how to control his power. He knows the ocean doesn't have a choice. He's all powerful in the water. But there is one place he isn't.

"The land, Carter. I thought I could defend us because I knew the water here, because Celestiana's essence is the strongest here, but I was wrong. The only place I'll be able to stop King Attilonious is on land. We have to get him to shore," I say.

"But I can't go there," Carter says. "And the others. What about them?"

I reach out and cup his face in my hands. It might be a long shot, but it's the only way any of us will have a fighting chance. I can't stay here, fighting the waves forever. I can't hope and pray the king will give up so we can rest. Because that'll give the king a chance to get stronger.

All this has to end now.

It has to end on my terms.

I'm fighting for the land and the sea, and that's why I have to use them together.

"The others will be fine, but I need you in the water, okay? I need you to keep the guards away," I say. "Do you think you can do that?"

He hesitates, not because he doesn't think he's capable of keeping the guards away, but because he's unsure if he's capable of leaving me. But he has to be.

"We can do this, Carter," I say. "We *have* to do this. We haven't been through so much just to stop now. I'm not going to risk being apart from you anymore. I'm not going to let the king threaten your family or our lives just because he can't get what he wants. The ocean needs us. The land needs us. Do you remember why you chose me, Carter?" I ask.

"Because all I could see was our future. How much I felt

connected to you because you loved the land as much as me," he says.

"And I can see that future now," I say. "I can finally see what you saw in me."

He smiles, pushing away the fear in his eyes. It's the same smile I saw on him the first time our eyes met on the dock. It's the smile that is only for me. "You're the perfect mate for me, you know."

"Forever," I say.

I lean over and kiss him. Not like it's the last kiss we'll ever share, but like the first real one we shared on the night of my transformation when my life was changed forever. This is the kiss that'll linger with me to remind me what I'm fighting for. The kiss that'll make sure I do everything I can to see that I win. Because I'm tired of not getting to make the choices in my life. I'm tired of feeling like fate controls me.

"Ready?" Carter asks, pulling me forward in the rolling bay.

I straighten my shoulders, channeling Carter's bravery into my heart where his essence entangles with mine. "Yeah. Let's get our lives back."

<h1 style="text-align:center">26</h1>

DON'T DESERVE OCEAN MAGIC

REACHING MY HANDS OUT AND pulling them to me, I summon a wave from the other side of the reef. At the same time it crashes over me, Carter jumps from the water and over the protective barrier leading to the open ocean where the king's guards wait.

A heavy body collides with mine, sending me tumbling through the bay. A cloud of sand engulfs me, turning the clear water hazy. I don't have a chance to move before the king jabs his staff into my chest, sending a shuddering pulse over me.

Shadows edge the corners of my vision. Locking my fingers around the staff, I use it to pull myself from the ground when the king jerks his arm back. I cling on to his staff, refusing to let it go. King Attilonious grabs me by the hair and forces me away from him. I land on my back in the sand at the bottom of the bay.

I'm up in seconds, swimming backward in the current while sending a stream of cool water in his direction. It slows him down just enough that I can flip to swim toward the shore and to the spot I need him to be.

Heat courses over me as the temperature shifts from warm to hot to match the king's rage. I flick my tail hard, propelling forward. I don't glance behind me. I don't have to. I can feel the tingling sensation of King Attilonious' magic sliding over me, threatening to send me back to the bay floor.

A shockwave erupts from the queen's diamond on my neck, and King Attilonious yells through my mind in surprise. It's like the stone does everything it can to protect me, to make sure I end up where I need to be.

"You can't escape me, Ava. I will have your power, even if you don't willingly give it to me. I'll take it," the king says.

"You won't," I say. "It's not yours to take."

"You could've made this so easy on yourself. All you had to do was pledge your loyalty to me. It didn't have to come down to this." Nails dig into the base of my tail, and King Attilonious jerks me toward him, forcing me to stop. "You could've had the whole ocean at your fingertips."

Swinging out my hand, I hit him with a current that snaps his head to the side. "I don't want the ocean!"

"And that's why you don't deserve what it bestowed upon you, you ungrateful girl." King Attilonious' eyes burn bright through the water. Power radiates from him, shimmering around us in a million tiny bubbles zinging over my skin, engulfing me in a tingling sensation that creeps into my very essence with every breath of water I suck into my lungs.

It stings me from the inside out, threatening to consume me and rip my own mermaid essence from my heart. I struggle in the king's grip as he holds me before him in the water. His eyes bore into mine. My heart races, lighting up the water around us in quick successions. It feels like it'll leap from my chest and land against the king where he can snuff out my spark of life.

"It's over, Ava," he says.

But I refuse to believe it.

The surface lightens overhead, the morning pushing away the darkness of night. The ripples shine purple, and I wish with everything in me that I could kick to the surface to watch the sunrise one last time.

"Don't give up, Ava," Carter whispers into my mind. "I'm coming for you."

"But the guards," I whisper.

"They're gone," he says. "Just hold on."

But I don't think I can.

The shadow of a boat crosses overhead, and I pout my bottom lip out. The humans of the Lost Cove don't stand a chance the moment I'm gone. It breaks my heart.

Tears drip from my eyes and disappear into the sea. King Attilonious draws me closer, and I can't find the will to resist when he presses his lips against mine. A thousand images crash into my mind, and my whole body burns as he slowly steals my life essence and magic away.

"Ava!" Carter's voice erupts in my mind.

The king stiffens and pulls away. He raises his staff at my mate, ready to blast him with the ocean's magic. A splash shifts the water from overhead, drawing the king's attention away for a split second. My mouth drops open the moment I see both Wes and Giselle enter the water, each holding a spear in their hands like they stand a chance against the most powerful being in all the seas.

King Attilonious jerks his staff toward my friends, aiming it away from Carter, and a pulse cuts through the water, sending a hot current their way.

My heart stalls, the blink of light in my chest freezing. It glows so brightly I'm sure the king sees it. A look of shock crosses his face, and we fly through the water on a wave that blasts from me, sending us both toward the shore.

The ocean moves with my instincts instead of bending to my will, and it catches me in a now placid surf while the king still flies through the current until he hits the sand, sending a cloud into the water. But he's not down for long, and I'm too slow. He slaps his mighty tail, shooting him forward. The weight of his body knocks me back, pulling me deeper into the water.

The world spins as another figure smashes into the king, ripping me from him. Carter grabs King Attilonious from behind, hooking his muscular arm around the king's neck. The king tries to elbow him in the face, but Carter is quick to move, scratching his sharp nails over King Attilonious' throat. The ocean rises, turning the shallows of the shore a few feet deeper, and it pushes Carter and the king forward fast enough that Carter loses his grip.

In one swift motion, the king grabs my mate and launches him through the water in front of him. He raises his staff, splitting the waves so Carter drops to the sandy floor. Water expels from Carter's lungs, forcing him to breathe in the dome of air. It surprises him, slowing him down. He only has time to roll into the wave to get out of the way, but King Attilonious smashes down his staff into Carter's tail, spearing him.

Carter yells out through the water and through my mind, sending me flying toward the king. Pain washes through my tail, the raw emotion coming from Carter. I don't let it slow me down. It merely pushes me faster.

I ram my shoulder into King Attilonious' back. He turns his attention away from Carter and back to me. With a thrust of my hands, I slam into the king's chest while kicking my tail, and I push us so close to the shore that when he tries to flick his tail, it smacks on the sand and forces both our heads above water.

Surprise widens the king's eyes before rage narrows them. He locks his fingers around my arms and flips me over his shoulder. I hit my back on the sand, and a wave washes over my face, causing me to choke.

King Attilonious rises above me, lifted higher on a wave, and he holds his staff up to me. The surf slides over me, heavier than I've ever felt it. It locks me in place, and all I can do is watch as King Attilonious prepares to try to steal my magic.

"Ava," Carter whispers into my mind. "You have to transform. Do it now."

As King Attilonious swings his staff at me through the water, aiming for the spark in my chest, I close my eyes and let the transformation take hold of me. Cramps seize me for a second, causing me to jerk up, and the staff whips my shoulder. A scream rips from my mouth, and my whole body shudders with a pain so intense that I fall back to the sand. A wave rips me away from the king, dragging me toward land, and he zooms after me. His long fingers wrap around my ankle, but I don't let him grab hold of me. I transform back into a mermaid and slap him in the face with my cerulean tail.

Pulling my hands toward my chest, I summon the water around the king, and it propels him closer to me. The massive wave sends us to the shore so far that I plow into a young palm tree. It cracks, falling forward, and lands on the king's tail. He hollers and picks it up to throw it off of him. It lands in the receding waves and rolls into the surf.

King Attilonious narrows his gaze on me and rides a small wave in my direction. Closing my eyes, I will myself to transform into a human. I expel the water from my lungs and scramble to my feet.

A hot whitecap crashes into me, knocking me sideways, and I flail as I'm dragged closer to King Attilonious. He locks his hand around my neck, squeezing my airway. Shadows edge my vision, trying to steal my consciousness.

Lying under his power, I've never felt so utterly wrong. Because even out of the sea he controls, he's still powerful. He's twice as strong and heavy without the water cushioning us. His weight presses me into the sand, and I know at any second, I'll break.

I open and close my mouth, trying to force air out so I can talk. "Ple—" I can't do it. He's not even going to let me say final words.

This is it.

A shadow falls over me, blocking the halo of sun around the king's salt and pepper hair. He huffs, bending closer, and loses his balance. His hand slides from my throat and into the sand, but the weight of his tail still crushes my legs.

King Attilonious growls, grinding his teeth, and a palm-sized rock lands in the sand next to us. Then another and another. The inhabitants of the Lost Cove throw everything they can find at the king, giving me the precious moment I need. With a flick of my hand, I call the ocean to me, pulling a wave from the bay. It crashes onto us, lifting the king from me, and I scramble away.

Hands lock onto my waist, pulling me deeper, and I meet Carter's blue-green eyes. We share a look, one that speaks volumes without even being able to communicate with me in my human form, and he propels us forward where the six people we've been sharing this island with attack the king with whatever they can get their hands on. They won't last long though, because the ocean swells around us, and as soon as King Attilonious gives his command, it'll wipe everyone away.

Holding my hands out while Carter swims us forward, I steal the ocean back, forcing it out to sea instead of land. Carter pushes me onto the beach, and I get to my feet, still holding off the waves King Attilonious struggles to control. My torn dress clings to my wet skin, and I clutch the stone around my neck.

"Attilonious!" I yell, my voice echoing through the air. "You've lost! The ocean here belongs to us."

He shifts in the sand, the sun glittering off his golden tail. He raises his staff, trying to break the hold I have on the water, but I refuse to give it up. He can try all he wants, but these sands are mine. The land, the shores—they're mine.

All the king does is laugh, mocking me as I try to stand tall before him. "Is that what you think, Ava? That just because you wear the queen's heart—part of *my* heart—that you can steal from me? You will give back to me what is rightfully mine. Don't think I won't sink this entire island. Celestiana was just as foolish as you for even thinking she could ever save these humans."

I glance from the ocean behind me, seeing Carter's spark through the sand-clouded wave to the tree line where I spot Giselle holding onto one of the palm trees, preparing herself along with the others if I can't stop Attilonious.

"I won't let you," I say.

"You don't have a choice." King Attilonious brings his staff down hard on the unmoving water, breaking my hold on it, and the wave cascades over us, blocking the morning sun from my vision.

I will my mermaid transformation to take hold and suck in water the moment it slams into me, leaving me trapped on the sea floor.

"Carter!" I scream in my mind. "Save the others!"

"But the king," he says.

"Save them," I say again.

King Attilonious wraps me in a hot whirlpool, cutting us off from the rest of the world. Even if Carter wanted to save me, he could never get to me. I'd rather him save the ones I care about. The ones who were never supposed to be in this mess to begin with.

"Tell me, Ava. Was this worth it?" The king's voice echoes through my mind.

I cringe, feeling his thoughts overpower mine. He hovers over me in the water, his staff gripped in his hand. The diamond on the end glows as brightly as the one on my neck, and I blink a few times to try to see through the shimmering haze of bubbles.

I don't answer his question and instead say, "You'll doom everyone. You know the land and the sea should be united. You know it wasn't always this way. Even your own daughter has the land in her blood, just like Celestiana. Like me."

"And that's why you'll never be as powerful as I am. You don't deserve the magic of the ocean." King Attilonious aims his staff at my spark. This time, there's no one here to stop him.

"And neither do you," I spit out.

He slams his staff against my chest, hitting me in my heart. I arch my back, the force of his power shuddering through me. It leaves me immobilized as he leans over me, pressing his lips against mine to take my mermaid essence away.

Cramps roll over me, seizing my tail and tingling up my back to where my dorsal fin presses against my ripped dress. Fire courses through my veins, and I thrash and claw at the king as I feel my very essence slip away.

I transform into a human, the spark in my chest slowing down and fading. The king isn't just killing me, he's taking away everything Carter had given me. He's severing our bond and forcing me to renounce the ocean against my will.

My lungs scream, aching to breathe in air that'll never come. Because the king isn't letting me survive this. He's not going to just let me live with the dark hole that ices my chest as the remaining fire of my spark smolders out.

The king pulls away, his dark eyes glowing through the blurry water. The spark in his chest shines brighter than ever— or maybe it's because my vision grows dark the longer he keeps me from breathing the air.

My lungs can't hold off any longer, and I take an automatic breath of the ocean. It burns down my throat, filling my lungs in pain and bitterness. When I close my eyes, all I envision is Carter. I'd give anything to see him one more time. To kiss him one more time. But none of that is possible. The last face I'll ever see is that of the king. He truly wanted me to die knowing that I could've never beaten him, that all the fighting I did was for nothing in the end.

"Ava," a voice whispers to me. "Don't let go." It's Carter.

But I can't hold on anymore.

With the remaining strength in my body, I lock my fingers around the queen's heart. King Attilonious aims his staff at me once more. He slams down his staff, striking the diamond I clutch to my chest, sending a jolt of power around us.

It cuts through his hot whirlpool, breaking the king's hold. Rainbow light shimmers around me, and in this moment I realize that both of our diamonds have shattered. The magic within them leaks into the sea.

But none of that matters now.

Because no matter how hard I tried, the king still stole everything from me.

"Ava, my daughter," a familiar voice whispers. "Do not fear. If you fear, you'll be lost forever."

I close my eyes and let the voice take me away. The ocean wraps me in its comforting embrace, pulling me from the king.

Two bright, blue-green eyes glow in the waves in front of me and a love unlike any other washes through me.

It's the last thing I feel before the world disappears.

TIME FOR CHANGE

"I'VE FAILED." I SIT IN the sand in my human form, stretching out my legs in front of me.

"You didn't fail, my daughter. You broke the king's hold on the ocean," Celestiana says from next to me. Her silver tail slaps against the waves on our tropical paradise island with glittering sands and crystalline water that goes on forever in front of us.

"But he stole the ocean away from me. I felt it. I felt it leave me. And now…" It's hard to spit the words out. "And now I'm here with you. Wherever this is."

Her dainty hand reaches out and touches mine. "Oh, Ava. Just because you're here doesn't mean you're dead. We're linked and always will be. Attilonious underestimated you and your connection to the sea. Even he doesn't have the kind of power to take away what has been given to you by the ocean."

"You mean I'm alive?"

"Very much so. All you have to do is open your eyes," she says.

I tense. I'm not so sure I'm ready to face the destruction caused by the king. "But the king."

"Isn't the king anymore. He can't harm you ever again. The ocean made sure of it," she says.

I close my eyes, just letting it all sink in. The warm sun pushes away the coldness clinging to my bones, and I suck in a few deep breaths of balmy air. "What happens now?" I ask, holding onto the serenity of the moment and the paradise created for me and Celestiana.

"The ocean has given you everything you need, including your warrior who can follow you anywhere. You'll make a beautiful queen."

"I don't want to be queen. I want to go home with Carter and figure my life out," I say.

"You'll make it work. This is nothing you can't handle. You don't have to choose between the land or the sea anymore."

I snap open my eyes to look at her, but she's gone. Warm arms cradle me, and I shift and meet Carter's gaze. Sparkling tears glitter on his cheeks, and he showers me with a dozen kisses, making me laugh.

"I wasn't sure you'd ever wake up," he whispers.

"It's only been a few minutes," I say, brushing sand from his face.

"No, it's been hours."

I frown, but Carter kisses the expression from my lips. He kisses me so passionately, so deeply, it's like his very essence travels from his heart to his lips to fill me up and leave me gasping for more of his love.

We break apart, and he just cradles me some more like he'll never let me go again. He holds me against him, resting his chin on the crook of my neck without saying a word. And he doesn't have to. We could spend the rest of our lives without speaking and be okay, because all that matters is that we're alive and free from the king's reign.

"Ava," a soft voice says from behind me.

As much as I don't want to move, don't want to pull myself away from Carter, I force myself to my feet. It's only then that I realize Carter sits in the sand just as human as I am. He has a small gash on his shin from where Attilonious speared him with his staff, but it's already healing.

Whatever I did, whatever happened after I allowed the ocean into me, has done something to break the king's hold on Carter's merman essence. *The queen said the ocean gave you everything you need to figure it out...including a warrior to follow you anywhere, meaning between the land and the sea.*

Carter stands with me, holding a tattered blanket to cover himself. Giselle closes the distance between us, and I wrap my arms around my best friend. We cry together, all snotty and heaving chests, full on sobs that even Carter can't rub away.

"I knew my BFF was awesome, but damn," Giselle says, laughing through her tears. "Does this mean it's finally over?"

I pull away and turn to look at Carter before turning back to Giselle. "Yeah, it's over. We can go ho—" I snap my mouth shut at the thought. I'm not even sure Azure Waters is still there after what the ki—what Attilonious did.

Giselle stifles a gasp. "What aren't you telling me?"

Carter puts his arms around the both of us. "We'll figure it all out."

Someone clears their throat from behind us, and we all turn to meet the gazes of Bailey, Wes, Reyna, Darren, and Sandra. My heart slams against my ribcage seeing the unmoving body of Attilonious at their feet, in all his naked, human glory. His salt and pepper hair hangs limply over his face as he lies on his stomach with his cheek pressed into the sand. Seeing him like this fills me with pity, and a tiny bit of sadness—not for him but for Luna. He was her dad after all.

"He's still breathing," Wes says, nudging Attilonious with his bare foot.

Carter tenses next to me. "Not for long."

I lock my fingers through his, stopping him in his tracks. His brows hang low over his oceanic eyes, and he studies me for a minute as I gather my thoughts.

I should be the first person to want Attilonious dead. I should send him into the waves and drown him myself for everything he's done. But something holds me back. I'm not a murderer, especially of someone who can't even get to his feet—feet that are brand new, in a body that is brand new, even in a life that is all new to him. What the ocean gave to him was taken back, and now he'll live out the rest of his life as the species he refused to unite with.

"He's no longer a threat to us," I say, turning away from Carter to the others. "Killing him goes against everything in me. He will not be harmed. Do you all understand?"

"How are you so sure? He's the reason we're all here." Bailey crosses her arms over her chest. "And there's no way I'm living on this island with him."

I rub my lips together, tasting the ever-present saltwater that clings to me. "You don't have to. You can all come with me. We'll work things out. We can have our lives back. I figured I could use this island to help the colonies adjust, so they can enter the human world if they want to. What better way to protect the ocean than from on the surface and below?"

Darren and Sandra look at each other for a moment, then Darren says, "My life is here. There's no place for me in the human world anymore."

"I'm afraid that goes for me, too. This is my home. It might not be much, but I don't think I want to leave," Sandra says.

Sadness rises in my heart. I can't imagine going through what they're going through. The world isn't the same place it was when they left. A lot has changed in twenty plus years.

Brushing my hand through my tangled hair, I stare at them. I try to think of a million reasons to convince them to leave the island, but nothing sounds as good as their reason to want to stay.

"What about the rest of you?" I ask.

Wes slings his arm around Bailey's shoulder. "Whatever she decides. We're both here for you, Ava. Whatever we can do to help you, we will." I'm not sure if it's really him talking or the fact that I saved his life—either way, I guess it doesn't matter now. We're all in this together.

"I have a husband to get back to," Reyna says, cutting in when Bailey doesn't speak right away. "I haven't been here as long as any of the others."

Bailey looks at Reyna and then to the sand like she'll find the answer written on the beach before her. "I don't know what I want. It's been so long. Mom and Dad, they—"

"We'll work it out. I'm your sister, Bailey. If you want to leave, I won't abandon you. Even if you choose to stay, I still won't abandon you. But Attilonious. He can't leave. The ocean won't allow him to." I don't have to test my theory to know. Attilonious is truly one of the lost now.

Bailey nods. "I want to leave then, even if going home isn't an option for me."

It might not be an option for any of us, but I'm afraid to say it. Carter hugs me from behind, leaning down to rest his chin on my shoulder. He's thinking what I'm thinking, but the only way we'll know for sure is if we see things for ourselves.

Before I can make a plan, Attilonious moans from the ground. He spits sand from his mouth and pushes himself up to steady his upper body on his hands without getting to his feet. Everyone takes a few steps back, putting distance between them and the fallen king, but I stand my ground with Carter by my side.

"Attilonious, your reign of the sea has ended. If you attempt to fight or hurt any of us, the ocean will end your life," I say.

He falls back to the ground and just lays there without a

word. I'm not in the mood to coddle him or tell him it'll be okay, because I don't care. He got what he deserved. As long as he knows his new place in this bright new world, I'm satisfied with never looking in his eyes, never hearing his voice in my mind again.

"Carter? Ava?" a familiar voice asks from the water. "Oh, thank God!"

Carter tugs me from my spot in front of Attilonious and into the lapping surf. We meet Starla and Mateo in chest high water, and they nearly tackle the both of us. Mateo spins me around, creating a current with his tail. Starla hugs Carter for so long that he laughs and pulls himself away.

"The guards returned to Pearlestria. They said something had gotten into the king. Something you did changed things for them, Ava. They refused to stand by the king against you," Mateo says.

It wasn't me who got to them. It was the very ocean surrounding us. It was the queen's essence lingering in these waves and in my heart, even without the diamond that bound us.

"And then the magical barrier disappeared, and we came as soon as we could. Is Attilonious?" Starla asks.

A small wave splashes me, and another head pops up to the surface. Black hair veils Luna's face, and she meets my gaze with serious eyes.

"Where is he?" Luna asks.

"Luna," I say. "It's okay. Everything's going to be okay. Attilonious, he—"

She pouts, grief crinkling her eyes in the corners. "He's gone, right?" she asks, interrupting like she can't bear to hear me say the words out loud. "I knew he'd push you, and I knew this would be a possibility. I was just hoping you could work it out. But I felt something shift in the water. I know I shouldn't have followed Starla, but I couldn't stay in Pearlestria and wait.

Can you take me to him? Or did the sea... Oh, my Ocean—"
Tears spring from her eyes, and she thrusts her arms around me.

I shake her for a moment as she breaks down without even letting me get in a word. "Luna, listen to me. Attilonious is alive."

"But—"

"I broke his hold on the ocean by shattering the diamond that held his magic, and then I stole it from him completely. The ocean took his merman essence after. He's human now," I say.

"Oh, Ocean," Luna says, her eyes widening. "I must go to him."

"He's on the shore," I say.

Luna dives underwater without another word, leaving me and Carter with his parents.

"You know what this makes you, Ava-girl, right?" Mateo asks. "The ocean has chosen her true queen. The colonies, they'll be—"

I crinkle my nose, raising my hand to stop him. "About that—"

"My beautiful, brave, powerful queen," Carter says, smiling so wide I softly punch him in the shoulder. "She's about to make some big changes."

Starla nods. "Good. I think change is exactly what everyone needs."

"We won't be long. A day or two tops," I say, wrapping my arms around Giselle. "Luna and Mateo are going to stay here the entire time."

My best friend squeezes me tighter. "The first thing we're going to do when we get home is going to eat at the Taco Palace. I'm dying for tacos."

I laugh. "I'll bring some back with me."

"Enough for everyone," Wes says, grinning from his spot in the sand next to Bailey in front of the fire.

A few feet away, sitting in the lapping waves, remains Attilonious with both Luna and Mateo. It'll be a hard adjustment for Attilonious, but he'll get through it for his daughter's sake. It helps how much she loves the land. It shines so brightly in her eyes that it'll shine a new light on her father.

"Of course," I say to Wes, drawing my eyes from Attilonious. "We'll see you all soon."

Carter slides his hands around my waist and pulls me with him into the water where Starla waits for us in the waves. Our first stop will be to Azure Waters, and then we'll head to San Francisco where we can get what we need since Starla had hoped to return to land one day.

We swim to the middle of the bay in our human forms, and Carter locks his fingers through mine, staring deeply into my eyes. The sky shines purple with twilight, and I lean forward to kiss him once more.

"Don't be afraid to transform," I say, knowing Carter's hesitating. "As my mate, you don't need the sea stone anymore. Celestiana told me so."

"What about the others?" he asks.

"I can't restore the magic of the sea stone rings until the full moon," I say. "We can use the time until then to get things ready. I want to use this island to help anyone who wants to visit the land adjust. With the way Attilonious ruled, it was nearly impossible to go to land. Your parents were lucky they had your grandparents."

Carter once told me everyone had a choice. They could live on the land or in the sea. But knowing what I do now, his lifestyle was an exception. Merpeople can't just emerge from the water to join the human world. They need help. And I'll be able to give it to them. All of those on this island now can help me.

"And the colonies are lucky they have you," he says, running his fingers along my cheek to push my hair behind my ear.

"Us, you mean."

With a deep breath, Carter pulls me under the water with him. His hands never leave me as we transform together. Starla swims up next to us, hovering amid the placid bay. I swirl my finger through the water, creating a small whirlpool. The magic of the ocean resides in me more powerful than ever. I no longer have to struggle with the water. I no longer have to fight Attilonious' control. The magic is just there now—in every bubble, in every current, in every creature. It's not a gift bestowed upon me. It is me.

"You okay?" Carter asks, sending his thoughts into my mind.

I bob my head, leaning forward to kiss him. "I'm better than okay. I feel free."

He smiles into my lips. "We are free."

"I want you to show me everything," I say. "I want to go everywhere with you."

"I like the sound of that, Aves. You and me and the ocean."

"And the land."

"Always the land."

THE AFTERMATH

THE SHALLOWS OF AZURE WATERS don't look any different from the last time I was here. The faint memory of Attilonious' rage warms the water around me, but it's not real. The water is still cool like usual, and soon to be colder when I transform back into my human self to face the aftermath.

"Want me to look first?" Carter asks, his voice wrapping around me in a comforting familiarity that eases the nerves bunching the muscles on my back.

"Or I can," Starla says, holding one of my hands.

I shake my head as much as I want him to. "No, I have to do this myself."

"Then whenever you're ready."

I consider popping to the surface without transforming, but I'm afraid if I don't, then I might take one look and dive back into the deep. I need to return to shore and see things for myself. The only way to get my life back is to summon my courage and face what I've left behind, no matter what it is or how hard it is to face.

Closing my eyes, I borrow the strength and courage resonating from Carter and hold it in my heart as I transform. We hover together for only a second and rise to the surface to expel the sea from our lungs, leaving Starla behind.

Bright stars shine overhead, and the beach in front of us is speckled with soft, man-made light. It sends relief through me, and I swim forward, breaking away from Carter. I head directly to the empty beach in front of my house. I never thought I'd ever see it again, but there it is, looming in front of me with a light shining from upstairs.

"Ava," Carter calls from behind me.

I sink to my knees in the sand just outside the surf and cry into my hands. Even though the small fence that surrounds my back patio is broken, even though wooden boards cover all of the downstairs windows and most of the windows of my neighbors for as far as I can see in the dark, everything is still standing. Azure Waters is still here.

And I'm home.

"Ava, you have to stop," Carter says.

He races to me and wraps his arms around me before I can run to my back door. Because I don't care if I'm dripping wet and half naked. I don't care if there will be a million questions. I can't wait any longer.

"I need to see them, Carter," I say.

"Please, you have to think this through. No one knows what people think or how much the police are involved. Your parents thought we were traveling together when you stopped calling them. It's been over a month. What if they assume the worst about me? I know you want them to know you're okay, but we need to know what we'd be returning to. We'll call when we get to San Francisco."

Tears burst from my eyes at his rational thinking, and I hate that he's right. I can't just knock on the door and tell my parents that I've just washed ashore.

I can't pretend my phone died or I went somewhere without reception. Giselle was amazing at faking my presence, and since she couldn't do so after she was taken to the Lost Cove, who knows what's going on.

All I know is it could be anything. Starla and Mateo were

never contacted, but it could've been because they were hard to find. I'll have a lot of explaining to do, and it'll take too much time to do so tonight. The others of the Lost Cove depend on me now. Giselle and Bailey depend on me. The merpeople colonies depend on me.

Carter pulls me back into the surf, petting my hair and holding me as we go. I stare at the light on the second story of my house until he lowers me under where he transforms into a merman before me. I take an extra minute, just listening to the silence of the sea, and then gulp in a breath of water as I transform.

Starla treads in the exact spot we left her, and she hugs me close, glimpsing the sad look crossing my face.

"Things are better than we expected," Carter says for me. "I promised Ava she could call her parents when we get to San Francisco."

"Ava," Starla says. "You sure about that? I know you said you wanted to return to the land, but it might not be safe for you to do that here. I thought maybe you and the others could join me and Mateo in San Francisco. There's still a lot you need to learn, things I can help you with."

I used to fight so hard against Starla and her mermaid traditions, but she might be right. It doesn't change the fact that I'm going to call my parents. Celestiana said only those worthy of the mermaid secret find out. If the ocean lets me tell them, then I know I can trust them. There's not even a doubt in my mind about it.

"I know," I say. "But I can't just let them think something happened to me. And my sister, I want to at least try for her."

Starla nods. "It seems you've made up your mind then."

"I have."

"And I stand by her decision," Carter says, speaking up.

Starla reaches out her hand to me and takes mine in hers.

"Then so do I. I just want you to prepare yourself if things can't work out."

"Thank you, Starla. I mean for everything. I don't think I could do this without you."

"I'd do anything for you. You're my daughter," she says.

I smile. "And I'm so glad for that."

Sunshine glitters off the murky water of the marina not far from Starla's apartment. It's not until this moment that I realize how little I know about Carter's parents. Sure, I basically grew up with them through Carter's memories, but some things never really stayed with me.

Like the fact that the store Starla and Mateo own not only has everything ocean-related any beach-goer could ever need, but they also have a number of boats that they do day and evening cruises with, including one for personal use. It's how Carter got his job on the *Ocean Jewel* before we met when he wanted to leave home and make a life for himself. While he wasn't raised in the water, he was raised on the water. It's just so strange seeing things through my own eyes instead of through his memory.

"She's all set," a woman with dark hair pulled into a ponytail says, stepping onto the wooden dock where Carter's parents are slip owners, even with a live-aboard permit for their own small yacht, well, small in comparison to the *Ocean Jewel*, the only other yacht I've been aboard. This one can be manned by Carter alone, and he's done it numerous times.

"Thanks for coming down here on such short notice, Nicole," Carter says. "I'll have her back in a day or two. Just taking a short trip with my m—fiancée."

If my heart could escape my chest and splash into the water, it would. Hearing Carter call me his fiancée to a stranger—stranger to me—is something I didn't expect. The smile he gives me when he glances at me nearly makes me melt into a puddle. I think the manager of his parents' shop is about to do the same.

"Of course. I was thrilled when your mom called and told me you were in town," Nicole says. "It's been too long."

Carter hugs her. "I know. Been busy. But my mom asked me to watch over things while she and my dad are gone."

"I bet they're having a blast in Hawaii. If I didn't know any better, I'd think they weren't coming back," she says.

Carter laughs and his uneasiness washes over me. "They changed their minds when I told them we were considering moving here."

She only laughs and hugs Carter once more. We stay on the dock until Nicole disappears and then Carter helps me aboard the Sultry Mermaid. I couldn't stop laughing at the name. Carter said Mateo named it after Starla, which warmed my heart.

The sleek slate gray and white yacht looks nearly new. I run my finger along the tan vinyl seating of the wraparound lounge area that includes a fridge and wetbar right by the cockpit. All whites and tans, the rest of the craft is more spacious than I realized, and it's basically like an RV on the water with a master stateroom.

A cushioned headboard sits behind the queen-sized bed, and gleaming storage cabinets line the perimeter, which could fit everything needed for a long ocean excursion. A privacy curtain blocks off the stateroom from the galley and the saloon with white seating and six portholes that give us a view of the marina around us. It's amazing. I'm slightly sad this isn't some romantic getaway but a rescue mission.

"All set?" Carter asks.

"As soon as I call my parents," I say.

"You still sure about it?"

I nod. "Give me a minute?"

Carter leaves me sitting in the saloon, clutching the prepaid phone we picked up on the way here from Starla's apartment. I figured if I do it the second before we head back to the Lost Cove, it might make things easier on me, and I won't want to dive into the ocean and swim back to Azure Waters alone.

My breathing blows static into the receiver when the phone rings three times. It clicks on the fourth, and I nearly hang up. My mom's voice sounds through the line, causing my voice to stick. I blink away my tears, wipe my nose on the sleeve of my shirt, and then release a long breath.

"Hey, Mom. It's me."

I'm greeted with utter silence for a few seconds, and then my mom says, "Ava? Oh, my God. Where are you? Are you okay?"

"I'm fine," I say, my voice only quivering a little. "I'm in San Francisco. I'm sorry I didn't call you sooner. Things have been crazy."

"It's been over a month!"

I cringe as my mom's worry turns into anger. "I know, and I swear I'll explain everything to you, but I can't right now. I just wanted to let you know I'm okay. I'm still with Carter. And Giselle, she—"

"What trouble have you gotten yourselves into? You've been lying to me. If Sapphire didn't tell us you'd come to town without telling us and had lunch with them, I'd thought you were dead. You know, I thought you could tell us anything. If you needed help, you should've called. Then you had to drag Giselle into whatever the hell you've done."

"I'm sorry. I didn't mean to worry you. I swear I have a good reason. But I need to know if I can come home," I say.

"Of course you can. Why wouldn't you be able to?" she asks.

"Well, if the whole world thinks I went missing...or if you called the police."

She sighs. "What have you done?"

"Mom, please."

"I'm not stupid, Avie. We saw you withdrew all the money from your bank account and lied about traveling. When Giselle didn't call Anaya back after a few days, she went to the condo and saw Giselle cleared out her clothes. Then Anaya found the emails on Giselle's laptop...you were never in Washington. I knew we should've put more thought into your sudden attitude change and your need to travel after meeting Carter. God, I hate to ask, but what has he gotten you into that made you need to leave and stop all contact with us? I'm scared for you. We have great lawyers. Whatever it is, you can trust us. I thought you knew that."

She doesn't mention Giselle's rental boat, and I wonder if Attilonious had sunk it completely. I thought for sure that they'd have called in search parties. I thought they knew us better than thinking we'd run off without word.

I'm sure if it had been any longer, things would've been different. But now, we're just inconsiderate kids avoiding the law.

"We're not in trouble," I say.

"So, what? You just ran off?"

"I swear I'll explain."

"I don't like this, Avie. We raised you better than this. Carter's changed you," she says.

I sigh. "You're right. It's just not in the way you'd expect."

"Then just tell me."

"Tomorrow, okay? And only you and dad. Please, don't tell anyone we're coming home."

"I have to tell Anaya. She's been worried sick about Giselle."

I huff into the phone. "Please, Mom. Wait until after you talk to me."

"Ava."

"I mean it," I say, closing my eyes. "If you tell her, I can't promise we'll even stay."

"What do you mean?"

"I have to go, Mom. I love you. Tell Dad I love him, too. You can tell Anaya Giselle's safe, but I mean it. No one can know I'm coming home."

With my words, I hang up. I can't listen to my mom beg and plead with me any longer. I need to do what we've been planning to do.

Walking back up to the cockpit, I slide into the warm seat next to Carter, who sits waiting for me at the helm of the yacht. I rub my hands over my face, smoothing out the worry wrinkles creasing my forehead.

"Everything okay?" he asks.

I meet his eyes. "I think so. My mom's pissed, but we got pretty lucky. They think we're criminals on the run or something."

Carter laughs. "Why does everyone always assume I'm some bad guy?"

"Oh, I don't know. The life changing secrets, maybe?"

He smothers his laugh by biting his lip. "If all else fails and we have to pretend to be criminals, we still have a shiny new castle in Pearlestria, my queen."

I playfully slap his arm. "Don't even start."

"But it's fun."

I roll my eyes, though it feels so good to have Carter be able to tease me about that now. It's almost like the last few weeks never happened. Almost. "Come on, my warrior. Let's get going. We have people to save."

"And then we can enjoy the yacht," he says with a smile.

I lean back and grin. "I'd enjoy even a rowboat as long as it's with you."

HOME

CARTER DROPS THE ANCHOR JUST outside of the reef that surrounds the Lost Cove. If it weren't for Starla guiding our way, we'd have had a hard time finding it. The magic remains quite powerful here, and it'll keep those who remain on the island or who choose to spend time in the bay safe from the outside world. It is very much still a trusted merpeople-access only place, which makes it perfect to help transition those who want to explore the land.

Holding his hand out to me, Carter helps me over the fold-down sun bed to the short swimming platform. We lock our fingers together and jump from the yacht to swim the rest of the way to the shore.

"Gi!" I yell, hopping into my bikini bottoms to meet her on shore. "We can go home! We're in probably a hell of a lot of trouble with our parents, but we can go home."

She jumps up and down in the sand, clapping her hands. "Seriously?"

I nod. "It's happening. It's really happening."

We both squeal and hug each other for a long moment while the others gather around us. Starla hugs Mateo in the surf and I spy Luna and Attilonious keeping to themselves a good distance away.

"And us?" Bailey asks, stepping forward.

I take a deep breath. "You're coming home, too. Both you

and Wes."

"You mean you're going to share your secret?" she asks.

"Yeah. How else am I supposed to explain that I found you on a random island that no one knows about? Or you know, how I'm going to be unreachable every full moon or longer. But I trust Mom and Dad. They might have a hard time believing us, but I guess we'll find out."

Bailey rocks on her heels. "I guess so. Hey, if it doesn't work out, there's always this island you can drop them off on."

She makes a good point, even if she's joking, but I hope to never have to bring someone here against their will again. I need to trust that Celestiana was right, that only the worthy discover the truth. And I know deep in my heart that my parents are worthy. They wouldn't want me to have to abandon them for the sea. I might be a mermaid, but I'm still Ava Adair.

"It'll work out," I say.

"If you believe that, then so do I."

Maybe the relationship I've wanted to have with Bailey is still possible after all. Fate might've ripped us apart and put a huge wall between us, but we're strong enough to tear it down. We're strong enough to get back what we've lost.

"I do."

"Then let's get off this godforsaken island already."

We grin at each other before we hug. Carter helps Wes with the small rowboat, and Giselle, Bailey, and Reyna get into it. I transform back into a mermaid and swim alongside Carter as he pushes the boat over the reef. It only shakes for a minute before Carter ties it to the yacht.

Carter transforms back into a human and helps the others load the rowboat with the supplies Darren and Sandra, and even Attilonious, will need since they have to start over again. Carter and I leave the others on the yacht to make one last trip to shore.

Darren helps Carter with the supplies, and I remain in my mermaid form to meet Mateo, Starla, and Luna, who has left her dad sitting, staring at the ocean.

"As soon as I get everyone home and everything settled on land, I guess I'll return to Pearlestria," I say. "At least for a bit." Thinking about returning to Pearlestria leaves a bitter taste in my mouth. I know Attilonious is no longer there, but I don't even know what to expect. The merpeople are expecting some mighty queen to guide them, not some uncertain mermaid who just wants to eat tacos with her best friend.

"Don't be nervous, Ava. The colonies already love you," Starla says.

"Thanks," I say. "I'll try my best."

"And I'll be here for you too, Ava," Luna says.

I hug her. "We can teach each other."

"Definitely."

Hands encircle my waist, and Carter presses against me in the water. "We're all set to go. You ready?"

I spin and kiss him. "More than you know."

We leave the yacht anchored just off the coast of Azure Waters and swim to shore. It's been a long boat ride, taking Reyna back to her home in Orange County and staying only for a moment to make sure she was safe.

Carter swims with Giselle and Bailey in each of his arms while Wes holds onto my shoulders until we make it close enough for them to swim on their own.

The private beach behind my house is quiet due to the time of night, but I didn't feel right about docking in the harbor and finding a ride home. I need to be able to leave if I have to without getting trapped.

Who even knows how my parents will react after my phone call yesterday. I just hope they don't have police waiting to question us.

We all lie in the sand for a moment, chests heaving. Carter helps me to my feet before he helps the others, and we stand near my back patio just looking at the boarded up window on the door. *This is what you've wanted all along. Just knock.*

Taking a breath of salty air, I curl my fingers into a fist and knock on the door. Carter drapes his arms over my shoulders, pressing against my back. My knees tremble, and I consider sitting down right on the concrete since the patio furniture is no longer there.

Just when I think I'll have to go around to the front to let us all in through the guest house above the garage, the door cracks before opening completely. Both of my parents hover in the now empty entertainment room in their pajamas. I expect them to drag me inside to yell at me, but my mom surprises me with a hug, and then my dad wraps his arms around the both of us.

"You have no idea what you've put us through, Ava," Dad says, pulling away. "Where did you all even come from? Looks like you swam here."

I release a nervous laugh. "We did. We have a yacht off shore."

"Ava," Mom says. "I don't understand. You've been living at sea? What have you gotten yourself into?"

My chest tightens as I summon the courage to give my parents the explanation I owe them. "Sort of. It's all going to sound so crazy," I say. "You see, it all started on vacation."

My dad turns his narrowed eyes to Carter. "So, this is all your fault."

"Dad," I say. "Let me explain."

"Well, let's first get you all some towels and take this into the kitchen," Mom says. "I have a feeling I'm going to need to sit down. And cake. I'm going to need cake."

A few minutes later, we all sit around the kitchen table; our kitchen untouched by the water damage the entertainment room acquired, with cake in front of us. I start with our vacation on the yacht, how I met Carter, and just let the truth spill out. Everyone sits in utter silence, and Carter squeezes my hand on top of the table, his plate of cake just as untouched as mine is.

"It's all true," Giselle says, speaking up. "I've seen it all myself."

"I don't even know what to say," Mom says. She turns her eyes to Wes and Bailey. "How do you two fit into all this? Are you mer—I can't even say it."

Bailey straightens in her seat. I skipped over revealing she's my sister and their daughter. Revealing I'm a mermaid was hard enough. I didn't even tell them about how serious my relationship with Carter is or how I'm kind of mermaid royalty.

"We met Ava and Carter when they washed ashore the island we were stranded on. They helped me and Bailey escape. We're just lost humans, really. It's been ten years since I've seen civilization and eight for Bailey."

My parents have been so concerned with me that they haven't paid anyone else much attention, but now that my mom looks at her lost daughter, her eyes light up with recognition. "Bailey?" Mom repeats my sister's name. A strange look crosses her face, and she gapes at my dad before turning to me.

"Bailey didn't drown, Mom," I finally say. "It's all really complicated, and I want to explain everything, but you have to understand—"

"Oh, God. Bailey," Mom says, cutting me off. She jumps from her seat and hovers in front of my sister. "I was so distracted with—" She takes a breath. She can't even repeat anything I've told her yet. Can't really blame her. "I don't know why I didn't see it before."

My dad follows her lead and hugs Bailey. I remain in my seat next to Carter. Tears blur my eyes, and I just soak in the happiness radiating from my family. My parents don't even care I revealed I'm a mermaid. They don't even care things are going to be different. They're just so happy we're all here in this moment together, exactly how it should've always been.

"So, is it okay if we stay here for a while?" Bailey asks. "I know it's been so long—"

"Of course you can. You can all stay. I want you to all stay," Mom says.

"Mom," I whisper. "I want to stay here. I do. But I have things I have to take care of."

My parents stare at me for a long moment in silence, almost like what I revealed was something they could just ignore because I'm home, in my human form, and I brought our family back together.

"You're leaving already? You just got home."

"I know," I say. "But it's all going to be okay. Things have changed for me in a good way. It's safe for me to come home whenever I want, and I'm still going to start college in the fall. But right now, I have to go for a bit."

"You're going with her?" Dad asks Carter.

He nods. "Yes, sir. I've made a vow to your daughter. I'll always keep her safe."

Both my parents hug me and Carter, and then I turn and wrap my arms around Giselle. Bailey and Wes hug me last, and I've never felt more at home even if I'm not going to stay. Because these people are my home, and knowing they're on the land will always bring me back to Azure Waters.

Carter leads me back out to the beach, and the others follow behind us but remain on the back patio. The moon shines above us, creating a path on the ocean, and I smile over my shoulder and wave once before wading in.

I never thought I'd ever get the chance to live my life how I wanted to since the moment I transformed into a mermaid. I always thought I'd spend my life on the run, constantly hiding my secret, and then I thought I'd never get to see the land again. I've struggled between wanting to love the ocean and blame it for everything wrong in my life, but after everything, the ocean was never my enemy. It brought so much love and happiness into my life, something the girl on the dock, standing in front of the Ocean Jewel, would've never imagined or thought possible.

"You know, we don't have to return to Pearlestria tonight," Carter says the moment we both transform.

I smile in the water, pulling him so close that our lips meet. "I wasn't planning on it."

He presses his tail against mine. "Good. I was serious about enjoying the yacht."

"And I was serious about enjoying you."

With a smile, Carter dives us deeper and into the ocean that once again feels like our own private world.

 EPILOGUE

UNITED

THE FULL MOON HANGS LOW on the horizon as the night disappears into day. Hundreds of merpeople from all over the world gather in the bay of the Lost Cove. I've spent the last three weeks traveling to all seven colonies, trying my best to remember the names of every merperson in the kingdom.

Together, there are nearly a thousand merpeople, only four of which were human-born like me. The whole, plenty of fish analogy is totally wrong when it comes to merpeople, and Luna was right about thinking she'd never find a mate, because I'm pretty sure she was destined to find one on land.

Carter swims next to me as I'm basically passed around and hugged and kissed by everyone. I'm actually starting to get used to merpeople affection, and it no longer feels like they're invading my space but welcoming me into their own.

Tonight is the night everyone's been waiting for. Under the full moon, I'll officially accept my place as a liaison between the land and ocean. I'm not accepting my place as a ruler but as a guide. I want the colonies to flourish the way Attilonious wouldn't allow. He was too concerned about protecting us from humans instead of entrusting those who can work together with us to help protect not only the ocean but all that is in it. To make life better for everyone.

Carter swims us to the deepest part of the bay where the moon's rays sparkle on the glittering sea floor. I open the small chest of rings brought by Luna and hold my hands over them, feeling the magic of the ocean and the pull of the moon between my fingers.

A thousand sparks blink through the bay like dazzling stars as I turn my attention to the merpeople of the ocean, sparks I feel connected to now more than ever. Sparks that remind me of the gift bestowed on me, how my life is connected to everything good about the sea.

"As the moon sets and the sun brings a new day, it'll also bring a new life to our colonies. It's time to bring our knowledge of the sea to the land and bring a piece of the land into the sea. It's time to reunite with the humans worthy of our secret and work together to find balance between our two worlds. So tonight, under the light of the full moon that binds us to the ocean, I'm restoring the ocean magic into the sea stone rings. I hope you'll all agree to take one even if you choose not to go to land, but I want to encourage you to try. I want to encourage you to explore the world I grew up in and love. I want to encourage you to do what makes you the most happy."

With a twirl of my hands, I summon a small current between my palms, and it picks up the light of the moon and sets the chest of rings aglow.

Carter smiles at me when I meet his gaze, and the whole bay hums with excited voices. Because for some, this will be the first time they'll make it to land, even if it's only the Lost Cove, which I've renamed Celestiana Cove, to honor the queen who made this all possible.

Pale morning light trickles through the bay, and I spin in the water and transform into a human in front of everyone. Carter follows me a moment later, and we both kick to the surface together and gasp in the balmy sea air.

"Aves!" Giselle's voice rings out over the bay, and I wave my hand at the group of people waiting for us on the shore.

A few more people pop to the surface next to me, and I smile at Carter's—my—family. Luna surfaces next with the guard, Blue, and even Tide, Attilonious' old messenger, a merman I met during my first stay at Pearlestria, joins us.

We swim to the shore, and I exit the surf first and take a towel from Giselle. Darren and Sandra help the others from the water, providing them what they need to be on land, and everyone smiles and laughs. It feels so normal.

"Ava-babe! Carter," Matty says. "This is insane. It's the first time me and Logan both lost a bet. We were thinking marriage not mermaids."

Carter fist bumps Matty. It took a lot of consideration whether or not to tell my friends the truth about everything, but they deserved to know. We always shared everything between each other. And just like Celestiana said, only those worthy of my secret would know.

"So when are you going to find us mates?" Chloe says, standing next to Giselle.

I laugh, shaking my head. "Why don't you go introduce yourselves around?"

Giselle grins at me. "Don't mind if we do."

"Ava?" My parents stand together just outside the group of people. It's taken them some time, but they've finally accepted I'm not the same girl I was before I stepped aboard the Ocean Jewel. They've finally realized I'm so much more. And they love me for it. "This place is incredible."

I smile and hug them both. "It's a lot better now. I'm so glad you agreed to come."

"Of course we would."

"There are a few people I want you to meet."

I motion for Carter to bring his parents over to meet mine. It's something that hasn't happened in so long—blending a family of those from land and sea—and I'm so happy we can finally do it.

"Mom, Dad, this is Starla and Mateo Stevens, Carter's parents," I say. "Starla, meet my parents, Beatrice and Allen Adair."

Mateo ignores my dad's handshake and offers him a huge bear hug, making us all laugh. "Ava is the best thing to have come into our lives," he says. "I'm so happy to have her as a daughter."

My cheeks burn when my parents give me a strange look. "Merpeople relationships are a tad different," I say, answering their silent question.

Mom raises her eyebrows but instead of commenting, says, "We're just so relieved Ava has someone like your son watching out for her, and we're happy you've taken her under your care. We appreciate you looking after Ava."

"That's what family is for," Starla says. "And now we're all family. We look forward to getting to know you all and would love to visit Azure Waters. You are always welcome in San Francisco, too."

Our parents hit it off right away, and I turn to slide my arms around Carter's neck. He holds me against him, and I bask in the love and adoration radiating from his very essence.

"You're amazing," he whispers into my ear. "I never thought I'd ever see a day like this."

"It's great, isn't it?" I ask. "I don't think I've ever been so happy."

"I'll never get over that feeling washing through me. It's all I've ever wanted for us, you know. To be happy together no matter if we're on the land or in the sea." Carter slides his hand into his pocket and pulls out a set of rings, ones we no longer need to transform. He slides one onto my finger anyway.

I stare at the sea stone swirling with the magic of the ocean, and then I take his ring from him and slide it on his finger. "As long as we're together. I love you, Carter. More than the sea or the sand. More than anything. Forever."

"I like the sound of that." He pulls me into a kiss, sending me a dozen images showing me exactly how much he loves me, and I send even more right back to him.

I couldn't have asked for a more perfect merman to be my mate. I might be an accidental mermaid, and he might've given me his spark on a whim, but there's no doubt in my mind that this is how things were always supposed to be.

I've spent weeks fighting between my love of the land and the sea that lingers in my heart. Now, I get both. They share me equally. I get a future even better than one of my wildest dreams. I have the whole world in front of me. With it, I can do anything. I can face anything, especially with Carter by my side.

I finally get to live my life exactly how I want to on land and in the sea with the boy chosen just for me. Together, we'll always find happiness. Together, we'll change our world for the better. Because no matter how rough the water is or where life takes us, we'll always be able to swim. We'll always have our sparks to light our way.

~The End~

Loved Ava and Carter's story? Check out *A Very Mer-Merry Holiday*. Out now!

THANK YOU!

THANK YOU SO MUCH FOR following Ava and Carter's adventure to get the future together they desired. I do hope you enjoyed diving into the Spark of Life world as much as I did. As an independent author, I rely heavily on word of mouth to get my books out into the world. If you could please take a moment, I'd love for you to post a review online from the retailer you picked up your copy from. I'd appreciate it with my whole heart. Thanks again for taking a chance on me! I know it's a big book world out there.

To keep up-to-date with what comes next, please make sure to subscribe to my newsletter online at www.GinnaMoran.com. You can also follow me online on Facebook, Twitter, Instagram, and Snapchat.

ACKNOWLEDGEMENTS

THIS SERIES WAS SUCH A blast to write. It wouldn't have been possible without the invaluable help from some incredible people. As always, many thanks to the team who has provided me with amazing help—from plotting to blurb destroying, editing, proofreading, and even a listening ear—Sarah Collier, Katie Harder-Schauer, Jan Moran, Nikki Godwin, Jamie Hall, and Amy Holliday; you are all the best!

Thanks to the professional merpeople on Instagram—especially the Hawaiian Merman and Project Mermaids—who have given me such magical inspiration through sharing your journeys. I'm in awe of your passion and connection to the sea.

Lastly, many thanks to my family and friends, who have been so incredibly supportive of my writing journey. Much love!

ABOUT GINNA MORAN

GINNA MORAN IS A WRITER from sunny Southern California. She started writing poetry as a teenager in a spiral notebook that she still has tucked away on her desk today. Her love of writing grew after she graduated high school, and she completed her first unpublished manuscript at age eighteen.

When she realized her love of writing was her life's passion, she studied literature at Mira Costa College in Northern San Diego. Besides writing novels, she was senior editor, content manager, and image coordinator for Crescent House Publishing Inc. for four years.

Aside from Ginna's professional life, she enjoys binge watching television shows, playing pretend with her daughter, and cuddling with her dogs. Some of her favorite things include chocolate, anything that glitters, cheesy jokes, and organizing her bookshelf.

Ginna Moran loves to hear from her readers so visit her online at www.GinnaMoran.com. You can also find her on Facebook, Twitter, Instagram, and Snapchat(@GinnaMoran). To stay up-to-date on new releases, sign up to her newsletter. You'll not only get a FREE story, but you'll be able to participate in monthly giveaways!

Ginna Moran is currently hard at work on her next novel.